EMILY OF :
EMILY CLIMBS
& EMILY'S QUEST

BY

L. M. MONTGOMERY

Author of
"Anne of Green Gables,"
"Anne of Avonlea,"
"Kilmeny of the Orchard," etc.

Emily of New Moon first published 1923
Emily Climbs first published 1925
Emily's Quest first Published 1927

This edition published by Read Books Ltd.
Copyright © 2017 Read Books Ltd.
This book is copyright and may not be
reproduced or copied in any way without
the express permission of the publisher in writing

British Library Cataloguing-in-Publication Data
A catalogue record for this book is available
from the British Library

CONTENTS

LUCY MAUD MONTGOMERY

Lucy Maud Montgomery was born on 30th November 1874, on Prince Edward Island, Canada. Her mother, Clara Woolner (Macneil), died before Lucy reached the age of two and so she was raised by her maternal grandparents in a family of wealthy Scottish immigrants. The Family were deeply rooted in the development of the island, having arrived there in the 1770's, and both Lucy's grandfather and great grandfather had been figures in the province's governance.

As a young girl, Montgomery had a very privileged upbringing. Due to the families wealth, she had access to a greater number of books than was usual in this era. These resources, coupled with the family's Scottish traditions of oral storytelling, gave her a taste for literature.

Montgomery took a teacher's degree at Charlottetown's Prince of Wales College before beginning work at a rural school to raise funds for and additional year at Dalhousie University. She continued to teach for a couple of years until her income from writing enabled her to become a full-time author. She then moved back home to live with her grandmother. In 1908, Montgomery produced her first full-length novel, titled *Anne of Green Gables*. It was an instant success and, following it up with several sequels, Montgomery became a regular on the best-seller list and an international household name.

In 1911 she married Ewan Macdonald, a Presbyterian minister, following the death of her grandmother. They had two sons together but the marriage was fraught with difficulties. Ewan had a severe mental disorder that frequently left him incapacitated, seriously hampering his career and eventually forcing him to resign from the ministry in 1935. The couple retired to Toronto and resided there together until Montgomery's death on 24th April 1942.

EMILY OF NEW MOON

THE HOUSE IN THE HOLLOW

The house in the hollow was "a mile from anywhere"—so Maywood people said. It was situated in a grassy little dale, looking as if it had never been built like other houses but had grown up there like a big, brown mushroom. It was reached by a long, green lane and almost hidden from view by an encircling growth of young birches. No other house could be seen from it although the village was just over the hill. Ellen Greene said it was the lonesomest place in the world and vowed that she wouldn't stay there a day if it wasn't that she pitied the child.

Emily didn't know she was being pitied and didn't know what lonesomeness meant. She had plenty of company. There was Father—and Mike—and Saucy Sal. The Wind Woman was always around; and there were the trees—Adam-and-Eve, and the Rooster Pine, and all the friendly lady-birches.

And there was "the flash," too. She never knew when it might come, and the possibility of it kept her a-thrill and expectant.

Emily had slipped away in the chilly twilight for a walk. She remembered that walk very vividly all her life—perhaps because of a certain eerie beauty that was in it—perhaps because "the flash" came for the first time in weeks—more likely because of what happened after she came back from it.

It had been a dull, cold day in early May, threatening to rain but never raining. Father had lain on the sitting-room lounge all day. He had coughed a good deal and he had not talked much to Emily, which was a very unusual thing for him. Most of the time he lay with his hands clasped under his head and his large, sunken, dark-blue eyes

7

fixed dreamily and unseeingly on the cloudy sky that was visible between the boughs of the two big spruces in the front yard—Adam-and-Eve, they always called those spruces, because of a whimsical resemblance Emily had traced between their position, with reference to a small apple-tree between them, and that of Adam and Eve and the Tree of Knowledge in an old-fashioned picture in one of Ellen Greene's books. The Tree of Knowledge looked exactly like the squat little apple-tree, and Adam and Eve stood up on either side as stiffly and rigidly as did the spruces.

Emily wondered what Father was thinking of, but she never bothered him with questions when his cough was bad. She only wished she had somebody to talk to. Ellen Greene wouldn't talk that day either. She did nothing but grunt, and grunts meant that Ellen was disturbed about something. She had grunted last night after the doctor had whispered to her in the kitchen, and she had grunted when she gave Emily a bedtime snack of bread and molasses. Emily did not like bread and molasses, but she ate it because she did not want to hurt Ellen's feelings. It was not often that Ellen allowed her anything to eat before going to bed, and when she did it meant that for some reason or other she wanted to confer a special favour.

Emily expected the grunting attack would wear off over night, as it generally did; but it had not, so no company was to be found in Ellen. Not that there was a great deal to be found at any time. Douglas Starr had once, in a fit of exasperation, told Emily that "Ellen Greene was a fat, lazy old thing of no importance," and Emily, whenever she looked at Ellen after that, thought the description fitted her to a hair. So Emily had curled herself up in the ragged, comfortable old wing-chair and read *The Pilgrim's Progress* all the afternoon. Emily loved *The Pilgrim's Progress*. Many a time had she walked the straight and narrow path with *Christian* and *Christiana*—although she never liked *Christiana's* adventures half as well as *Christian's*. For one thing, there was always such a crowd with *Christiana*. She had not half the fascination of that solitary, intrepid figure who faced all alone the shadows of the Dark Valley and the encounter with Apollyon. Darkness and hobgoblins were nothing when you had plenty of company. But to be *alone*—ah, Emily shivered with the delicious horror of it!

When Ellen announced that supper was ready Douglas Starr told

Emily to go out to it.

"I don't want anything to-night. I'll just lie here and rest. And when you come in again we'll have a real talk, Elfkin."

He smiled up at her his old, beautiful smile, with the love behind it, that Emily always found so sweet. She ate her supper quite happily—though it wasn't a good supper. The bread was soggy and her egg was underdone, but for a wonder she was allowed to have both Saucy Sal and Mike sitting, one on each side of her, and Ellen only grunted when Emily fed them wee bits of bread and butter.

Mike had such a cute way of sitting up on his haunches and catching the bits in his paws, and Saucy Sal had *her* trick of touching Emily's ankle with an almost human touch when her turn was too long in coming. Emily loved them both, but Mike was her favourite. He was a handsome, dark-grey cat with huge owl-like eyes, and he was so soft and fat and fluffy. Sal was always thin; no amount of feeding put any flesh on her bones. Emily liked her, but never cared to cuddle or stroke her because of her thinness. Yet there was a sort of weird beauty about her that appealed to Emily. She was grey-and-white—very white and very sleek, with a long, pointed face, very long ears and very green eyes. She was a redoubtable fighter, and strange cats were vanquished in one round. The fearless little spitfire would even attack dogs and rout them utterly.

Emily loved her pussies. She had brought them up herself, as she proudly said. They had been given to her when they were kittens by her Sunday-school teacher.

"A *living* present is so nice," she told Ellen, "because it keeps on getting nicer all the time."

But she worried considerably because Saucy Sal didn't have kittens.

"I don't know why she doesn't," she complained to Ellen Greene. "Most cats seem to have more kittens than they know what to do with."

After supper Emily went in and found that her father had fallen asleep. She was very glad of this; she knew he had not slept much for two nights; but she was a little disappointed that they were not going to have that "real talk." "Real" talks with Father were always such delightful things. But next best would be a walk—a lovely all-by-your-lonesome walk through the grey evening of the young spring. It was so long since she had had a walk.

"You put on your hood and mind you scoot back if it starts to rain," warned Ellen. "*You* can't monkey with colds the way some kids can."

"Why can't I?" Emily asked rather indignantly. Why must *she* be debarred from "monkeying with colds" if other children could? It wasn't fair.

But Ellen only grunted. Emily muttered under her breath for her own satisfaction, "You are a fat old thing of no importance!" and slipped upstairs to get her hood—rather reluctantly, for she loved to run bareheaded. She put the faded blue hood on over her long, heavy braid of glossy, jet-black hair, and smiled chummily at her reflection in the little greenish glass. The smile began at the corners of her lips and spread over her face in a slow, subtle, very wonderful way, as Douglas Starr often thought. It was her dead mother's smile—the thing that had caught and held him long ago when he had first seen Juliet Murray. It seemed to be Emily's only physical inheritance from her mother. In all else, he thought, she was like the Starrs—in her large, purplish-grey eyes with their very long lashes and black brows, in her high, white forehead—too high for beauty—in the delicate modelling of her pale oval face and sensitive mouth, in the little ears that were pointed just a wee bit to show that she was kin to tribes of elfland.

"I'm going for a walk with the Wind Woman, dear," said Emily. "I wish I could take you, too. Do you *ever* get out of that room, I wonder. The Wind Woman is going to be out in the fields to-night. She is tall and misty, with thin, grey, silky clothes blowing all about her—and wings like a bat's—only you can see through them—and shining eyes like stars looking through her long, loose hair. She can fly—but to-night she will walk with me all over the fields. She's a *great* friend of mine—the Wind Woman is. I've known her ever since I was six. We're *old, old* friends—but not quite so old as you and I, little Emily-in-the-glass. We've been friends *always*, haven't we?"

With a blown kiss to little Emily-in-the-glass, Emily-out-of-the-glass was off.

The Wind Woman was waiting for her outside—ruffling the little spears of striped grass that were sticking up stiffly in the bed under the sitting-room window—tossing the big boughs of Adam-and-Eve—whispering among the misty green branches of the birches—teasing the "Rooster Pine" behind the house—it really did look like

10

an enormous, ridiculous rooster, with a huge, bunchy tail and a head thrown back to crow.

It was so long since Emily had been out for a walk that she was half crazy with the joy of it. The winter had been so stormy and the snow so deep that she was never allowed out; April had been a month of rain and wind; so on this May evening she felt like a released prisoner. Where should she go? Down the brook—or over the fields to the spruce barrens? Emily chose the latter.

She loved the spruce barrens, away at the further end of the long, sloping pasture. That was a place where magic was made. She came more fully into her fairy birthright there than in any other place. Nobody who saw Emily skimming over the bare field would have envied her. She was little and pale and poorly clad; sometimes she shivered in her thin jacket; yet a queen might have gladly given a crown for her visions—her dreams of wonder. The brown, frosted grasses under her feet were velvet piles. The old mossy, gnarled half-dead spruce-tree, under which she paused for a moment to look up into the sky, was a marble column in a palace of the gods; the far dusky hills were the ramparts of a city of wonder. And for companions she had all the fairies of the country-side—for she could believe in them here—the fairies of the white clover and satin catkins, the little green folk of the grass, the elves of the young fir-trees, sprites of wind and wild fern and thistledown. Anything might happen there—everything might come true.

And the barrens were such a splendid place in which to play hide and seek with the Wind Woman. She was so very *real* there; if you could just spring quickly enough around a little cluster of spruces— only you never could—you would *see* her as well as feel her and hear her. There she was—that *was* the sweep of her grey cloak—no, she was laughing up in the very top of the taller trees—and the chase was on again—till, all at once, it seemed as if the Wind Woman were gone— and the evening was bathed in a wonderful silence—and there was a sudden rift in the curdled clouds westward, and a lovely, pale, pinky-green lake of sky with a new moon in it.

Emily stood and looked at it with clasped hands and her little black head upturned. She must go home and write down a description of it in the yellow account-book, where the last thing written had been, "Mike's Biography." It would hurt her with its beauty until she wrote it down. Then she would read it to Father. She must not forget how the tips of the trees on the hill came out like fine black lace across the edge of the pinky-green sky.

And then, for one glorious, supreme moment, came "the flash."

Emily called it that, although she felt that the name didn't exactly describe it. It couldn't be described—not even to Father, who always seemed a little puzzled by it. Emily never spoke of it to any one else.

It had always seemed to Emily, ever since she could remember, that she was very, very near to a world of wonderful beauty. Between it and herself hung only a thin curtain; she could never draw the curtain aside—but sometimes, just for a moment, a wind fluttered it and then it was as if she caught a glimpse of the enchanting realm beyond—only a glimpse—and heard a note of unearthly music.

This moment came rarely—went swiftly, leaving her breathless with the inexpressible delight of it. She could never recall it—never summon it—never pretend it; but the wonder of it stayed with her for days. It never came twice with the same thing. To-night the dark boughs against that far-off sky had given it. It had come with a high, wild note of wind in the night, with a shadow wave over a ripe field, with a greybird lighting on her window-sill in a storm, with the singing of "Holy, holy, holy" in church, with a glimpse of the kitchen fire when she had come home on a dark autumn night, with the spirit-like blue of ice palms on a twilit pane, with a felicitous new word when she was writing down a "description" of something. And always when the flash came to her Emily felt that life was a wonderful, mysterious thing of persistent beauty.

She scuttled back to the house in the hollow, through the gathering twilight, all agog to get home and write down her "description" before the memory picture of what she had seen grew a little blurred. She knew just how she would begin it—the sentence seemed to shape itself in her mind: "The hill called to me and something in me called back to it."

She found Ellen Greene waiting for her on the sunken front-doorstep. Emily was so full of happiness that she loved everything at that moment, even fat things of no importance. She flung her arms around Ellen's knees and hugged them. Ellen looked down gloomily into the rapt little face, where excitement had kindled a faint wild-rose flush, and said, with a ponderous sigh:

"Do you know that your pa has only a week or two more to live?"

A WATCH IN THE NIGHT

Emily stood quite still and looked up at Ellen's broad, red face—as still as if she had been suddenly turned to stone. She felt as if she had. She was as stunned as if Ellen had struck her a physical blow. The colour faded out of her little face and her pupils dilated until they swallowed up the irises and turned her eyes into pools of blackness. The effect was so startling that even Ellen Greene felt uncomfortable.

"I'm telling you this because I think it's high time you was told," she said. "I've been at your pa for months to tell you, but he's kept putting it off and off. I says to him, says I, 'You know how hard she takes things, and if you drop off suddent some day it'll most kill her if she hasn't been prepared. It's your duty to prepare her,' and he says, says he, 'There's time enough yet, Ellen.' But he's never said a word, and when the doctor told me last night that the end might come any time now, I just made up my mind that *I'd* do what was right and drop a hint to prepare you. Laws-a-massy, child, don't look like that! You'll be looked after. Your ma's people will see to that—on account of the Murray pride, if for no other reason. They won't let one of their own blood starve or go to strangers—even if they have always hated your pa like p'isen. You'll have a good home—better'n you've ever had here. You needn't worry a mite. As for your pa, you ought to be thankful to see him at rest. He's been dying by inches for the last five years. He's kept it from you, but he's been a great sufferer. Folks say his heart broke when your ma died—it came on him so suddent-like—she was only sick three days. That's why I want you to know what's coming, so's you won't be all upset when it happens. For mercy's sake, Emily Byrd Starr, don't stand there staring like that! You give me the creeps! You ain't the first child that's been left an orphan and you won't be the last. Try and be sensible. And don't go pestering your pa about what I've told you, mind that. Come you in now, out of the damp, and I'll give you a cooky 'fore you go to bed."

Ellen stepped 'down as if to take the child's hand. The power of motion returned to Emily—she must scream if Ellen even touched her *now*. With one sudden, sharp, bitter little cry she avoided Ellen's hand, darted through the door and fled up the dark staircase.

Ellen shook her head and waddled back to her kitchen. "Anyhow, I've done *my* duty," she reflected. "He'd have just kept saying 'time enough' and put it off till he was dead and then there'd have been no managing her. She'll have time now to get used to it, and she'll brace up in a day or two. I will say for her she's got spunk—which is lucky, from all I've heard of the Murrays. They won't find it easy to overcrow *her*. She's got a streak of their pride, too, and that'll help her through. I wish I dared send some of the Murrays word that he's dying, but I don't dast go that far. There's no telling what *he'd* do. Well, I've stuck on here to the last and I ain't sorry. Not many women would 'a' done it, living as they do here. It's a shame the way that child's been brought up—never even sent to school. Well, I've told him often enough what I've thought of it—it ain't on *my* conscience, that's one comfort. Here, you Sal-thing, you git out! Where's Mike, too?"

Ellen could not find Mike for the very good reason that he was upstairs with Emily, held tightly in her arms, as she sat in the darkness on her little cot-bed. Amid her agony and desolation there was a certain comfort in the feel of his soft fur and round velvety head.

Emily was not crying; she stared straight into the darkness, trying to face the awful thing Ellen had told her. She did not doubt it—something told her it was true. Why couldn't she die, too? She couldn't go on living without Father.

"If I was God I wouldn't let things like this happen," she said.

She felt it was very wicked of her to say such a thing—Ellen had told her once that it was the wickest thing any one could do to find fault with God. But she didn't care. Perhaps if she were wicked enough God would strike her dead and then she and Father could keep on being together.

But nothing happened—only Mike got tired of being held so tightly and squirmed away. She was all alone now, with this terrible burning pain that seemed all over her and yet was not of the body. She could never get rid of it. She couldn't help it by writing about it in the old

14

yellow account-book. She had written there about her Sunday-school teacher going away, and of being hungry when she went to bed, and Ellen telling her she must be half-crazy to talk of Wind Women and flashes; and after she had written down all about them these things hadn't hurt her any more. But this couldn't be written about. She could not even go to Father for comfort, as she had gone when she burned her hand so badly, picking up the red-hot poker by mistake. Father had held her in his arms all that night and told her stories and helped her to bear the pain. But Father, so Ellen had said, was going to die in a week or two. Emily felt as if Ellen had told her this years and years ago. It surely couldn't be less than an hour since she had been playing with the Wind Woman in the barrens and looking at the new moon in the pinky-green sky.

"The flash will never come again—it can't," she thought.

But Emily had inherited certain things from her fine old ancestors—the power to fight—to suffer,—to pity—to love very deeply—to rejoice—to endure. These things were all in her and looked out at you through her purplish-grey eyes. Her heritage of endurance came to her aid now and bore her up. She must not let Father know what Ellen had told her—it might hurt him. She must keep it all to herself and *love* Father, oh, so much, in the little while she could yet have him. She heard him cough in the room below: she must be in bed when he came up; she undressed as swiftly as her cold fingers permitted and crept into the little cot-bed which stood across the open window. The voices of the gentle spring night called to her all unheeded—unheard the Wind Woman whistled by the eaves. For the fairies dwell only in the kingdom of Happiness; having no souls they cannot enter the kingdom of Sorrow.

She lay there cold and tearless and motionless when her father came into the room. How very slowly he walked—how very slowly he took off his clothes. How was it she had never noticed these things before? But he was not coughing at all. Oh, what if Ellen were mistaken?—what if—a wild hope shot through her aching heart. She gave a little gasp.

Douglas Starr came over to her bed. She felt his dear nearness as he sat down on the chair beside her, in his old red dressing-gown. Oh, how she loved him! There was no other Father like him in all the world—there never could have been—so tender, so understanding, so wonderful! They had always been such chums—they had loved each other so much—it couldn't be that they were to be separated.

"Winkums, are you asleep?"

"No," whispered Emily.

"Are you sleepy, small dear?"

"No—no—not sleepy."

Douglas Starr took her hand and held it tightly.

"Then we'll have our talk, honey. I can't sleep either. I want to tell you something."

"Oh—I know it—I know it!" burst out Emily. "Oh, Father, I know it! Ellen told me."

Douglas Starr was silent for a moment. Then he said under his breath, "The old fool—the *fat* old fool!"—as if Ellen's fatness was an added aggravation of her folly. Again, for the last time, Emily hoped. Perhaps it was all a dreadful mistake—just some more of Ellen's fat foolishness.

"It—it isn't true, is it, Father?" she whispered.

"Emily, child," said her father, "I can't lift you up—I haven't the strength—but climb up and sit on my knee—in the old way."

Emily slipped out of bed and got on her father's knee. He wrapped the old dressing-gown about her and held her close with his face against hers.

"Dear little child—little beloved Emilykin, it is quite true," he said. "I meant to tell you myself to-night. And now the old absurdity of an Ellen has told you—brutally I suppose—and hurt you dreadfully. She has the brain of a hen and the sensibility of a cow. May jackals sit on her grandmother's grave! *I* wouldn't have hurt you, dear."

Emily fought something down that wanted to choke her.

"Father, I can't—I can't bear it."

"Yes, you can and will. You will live because there is something for you to do, I think. You have my gift—along with something I never had. You will succeed where I failed, Emily. I haven't been able to do much for you, sweetheart, but I've done what I could. I've taught you something, I think—in spite of Ellen Greene. Emily, do you remember your mother?"

"Just a little—here and there—like lovely bits of dreams."

"You were only four when she died. I've never talked much to you about her—I couldn't. But I'm going to tell you all about her to-night. It

16

doesn't hurt me to talk of her now—I'll see her so soon again. You don't look like her, Emily—only when you smile. For the rest, you're like your namesake, my mother. When you were born I wanted to call you Juliet, too. But your mother wouldn't. She said if we called you Juliet then I'd soon take to calling her 'Mother' to distinguish between you, and she couldn't endure *that*. She said her Aunt Nancy had once said to her, 'The first time your husband calls you "Mother" the romance of life is over.' So we called you after my mother—*her* maiden name was Emily Byrd. Your mother thought Emily the prettiest name in the world—it was quaint and arch and delightful, she said. Emily, your mother was the sweetest woman ever made."

His voice trembled and Emily snuggled close.

"I met her twelve years ago, when I was sub-editor of the *Enterprise* up in Charlottetown and she was in her last year at Queen's. She was tall and fair and blue-eyed. She looked a little like your Aunt Laura, but Laura was never so pretty. Their eyes were very much alike—and their voices. She was one of the Murrays from Blair Water. I've never told you much about your mother's people, Emily. They live up on the old north shore at Blair Water on New Moon Farm—always have lived there since the first Murray came out from the Old Country in 1790. The ship he came on was called the *New Moon* and he named his farm after her."

"It's a nice name—the new moon is such a pretty thing," said Emily, interested for a moment.

"There's been a Murray ever since at New Moon Farm. They're a proud family—the Murray pride is a byword along the north shore, Emily. Well, they had some things to be proud of, that cannot be denied—but they carried it too far. Folks call them 'the chosen people' up there.

"They increased and multiplied and scattered all over, but the old stock at New Moon Farm is pretty well run out. Only your aunts, Elizabeth and Laura, live there now, and their cousin, Jimmy Murray. They never married—could not find any one good enough for a Murray, so it used to be said. Your Uncle Oliver and your Uncle Wallace live in Summerside, your Aunt Ruth in Shrewsbury, and your Great-Aunt Nancy at Priest Pond."

"Priest Pond—that's an *interesting* name—not a pretty name like New Moon and Blair Water—but interesting," said Emily. Feeling

Father's arm around her the horror had momentarily shrunk away. For just a little while she ceased to believe it.

Douglas Starr tucked the dressing-gown a little more closely around her, kissed her black head, and went on.

"Elizabeth and Laura and Wallace and Oliver and Ruth were old Archibald Murray's children. His first wife was their mother. When he was sixty he married again—a young slip of a girl—who died when your mother was born. Juliet was twenty years younger than her half-family, as she used to call them. She was very pretty and charming and they all loved and petted her and were very proud of her. When she fell in love with me, a poor young journalist, with nothing in the world but his pen and his ambition, there was a family earthquake. The Murray pride couldn't tolerate the thing at all. I won't rake it all up—but things were said I could never forget or forgive. Your mother married me, Emily—and the New Moon people would have nothing more to do with her. Can you believe that, in spite of it, she was never sorry for marrying me?"

Emily put up her hand and patted her father's hollow cheek.

"Of *course* she wouldn't be sorry. Of *course* she'd rather have you than all the Murrays of any kind of a moon."

Father laughed a little—and there was just a note of triumph in his laugh.

"Yes, she seemed to feel that way about it. And we were so happy—oh, Emilykin, there never were two happier people in the world. You were the child of that happiness. I remember the night you were born in the little house in Charlottetown. It was in May and a west wind was blowing silvery clouds over the moon. There was a star or two here and there. In our tiny garden—everything we had was small except our love and our happiness—it was dark and blossomy. I walked up and down the path between the beds of violets your mother had planted—and prayed. The pale east was just beginning to glow like a rosy pearl when someone came and told me I had a little daughter. I went in—and your mother, white and weak, smiled just that dear, slow, wonderful smile I loved, and said, 'We've—got—the—only—baby—of any importance—in—the—world, dear. Just—think—of that!'"

"I wish people could remember from the very moment they're born," said Emily. "It would be so very interesting."

18

"I dare say we'd have a lot of uncomfortable memories," said her father, laughing a little. "It can't be very pleasant getting used to living—no pleasanter than getting used to stopping it. But you didn't seem to find it hard, for you were a good wee kidlet, Emily. We had four more happy years, and then—do you remember the time your mother died, Emily?"

"I remember the funeral, Father—I remember it *distinctly*. You were standing in the middle of a room, holding me in your arms, and Mother was lying just before us in a long, black box. And you were crying—and I couldn't think why—and I wondered why Mother looked so white and wouldn't open her eyes. And I leaned down and touched her cheek—and oh, it was so cold. It made me shiver. And somebody in the room said, 'Poor little thing!' and I was frightened and put my face down on your shoulder."

"Yes, I recall that. Your mother died very suddenly. I don't think we'll talk about it. The Murrays all came to her funeral. The Murrays have certain traditions and they live up to them very strictly. One of them is that nothing but candles shall be burned for light at New Moon—and another is that no quarrel must be carried past the grave. They came when she was dead—they would have come when she was ill if they had known, I will say that much for them. And they behaved very well—oh, very well indeed. They were not the Murrays of New Moon for nothing. Your Aunt Elizabeth wore her best black satin dress to the funeral. For any funeral but a Murray's the second best one would have done; and they made no serious objection when I said your mother would be buried in the Starr plot in Charlottetown cemetery. They would have liked to take her back to the old Murray burying-ground in Blair Water—they had their own private burying-ground, you know—no indiscriminate graveyard for *them*. But your Uncle Wallace handsomely admitted that a woman should belong to her husband's family in death as in life. And then they offered to take you and bring you up—to 'give you your mother's place.' I refused to let them have you—then. Did I do right, Emily?"

"Yes—yes—yes!" whispered Emily, with a hug at every "yes."

"I told Oliver Murray—it was he who spoke to me about you—that as long as I lived I would not be parted from my child. He said, 'If you ever change your mind, let us know.' But I did not change my mind—not even three years later when my doctor told me I must give up work.

'If you don't, I give you a year,' he said, 'if you do, and live out-of-doors all you can, I give you three—or possibly four.' He was a good prophet. I came out here and we've had four lovely years together, haven't we, small dear one?"

"Yes—oh, yes!"

"Those years and what I've taught you in them are the only legacy I can leave you, Emily. We've been living on a tiny income I have from a life interest that was left me in an old uncle's estate—an uncle who died before I was married. The estate goes to a charity now, and this little house is only a rented one. From a worldly point of view I've certainly been a failure. But your mother's people will care for you—I know that. The Murray pride will guarantee so much, if nothing else. And they can't help loving you. Perhaps I should have sent for them before— perhaps I ought to do it yet. But I have pride of a kind, too—the Starrs are not entirely traditionless—and the Murrays said some very bitter things to me when I married your mother. Will I send to New Moon and ask them to come, Emily?"

"No!" said Emily, almost fiercely.

She did not want any one to come between her and Father for the few precious days left. The thought was horrible to her. It would be bad enough if they had to come—afterwards. But she would not mind anything much—then.

"We'll stay together to the very end, then, little Emily-child. We won't be parted for a minute. And I want you to be brave. You mustn't be afraid of *anything*, Emily. Death isn't terrible. The universe is full of love—and spring comes everywhere—and in death you open and shut a door. There are beautiful things on the other side of the door. I'll find your mother there—I've doubted many things, but I've never doubted *that*. Sometimes I've been afraid that she would get so far ahead of me in the ways of eternity that I'd never catch up. But I feel *now* that she's waiting for me. And we'll wait for you—we won't hurry—we'll loiter and linger till you catch up with us."

"I wish you—could take me right through the door with you," whispered Emily.

"After a little while you won't wish that. You have yet to learn how kind time is. And life has something for you—I feel it. Go forward to meet it fearlessly, dear. I know you don't feel like that just now—but

20

you will remember my words by and by."

"I feel just now," said Emily, who couldn't bear to hide anything from Father, "that I don't like God any more."

Douglas Starr laughed—the laugh Emily liked best. It was such a dear laugh—she caught her breath over the dearness of it. She felt his arms tightening round her.

"Yes, you do, honey. You can't help liking God. He is Love itself, you know. You mustn't mix Him up with Ellen Greene's God, of course."

Emily didn't know exactly what Father meant. But all at once she found that she wasn't afraid any longer—and the bitterness had gone out of her sorrow, and the unbearable pain out of her heart. She felt as if love was all about her and around her, breathed out from some great, invisible, hovering Tenderness. One couldn't be afraid or bitter where love was—and love was everywhere. Father was going through the door—no, he was going to lift a curtain—she liked *that* thought better, because a curtain wasn't as hard and fast as a door—and he would slip into that world of which the flash had given her glimpses. He would be there in its beauty—never very far away from her. She could bear anything if she could only feel that Father wasn't very far away from her—just beyond that wavering curtain.

Douglas Starr held her until she fell asleep; and then in spite of his weakness he managed to lay her down in her little bed.

"She will love deeply—she will suffer terribly—she will have glorious moments to compensate—as I have had. As her mother's people deal with her, so may God deal with them," he murmured brokenly.

A HOP OUT OF KIN

Douglas Starr lived two weeks more. In after years when the pain had gone out of their recollection, Emily thought they were the most precious of her memories. They were beautiful weeks—beautiful and not sad. And one night, when he was lying on the couch in the sitting-room, with Emily beside him in the old wing-chair, he went past the curtain—went so quietly and easily that Emily did not know he was

21

gone until she suddenly felt the strange *stillness* of the room—there was no breathing in it but her own.

"Father—Father!" she cried. Then she screamed for Ellen.

Ellen Greene told the Murrays when they came that Emily had behaved real well, when you took everything into account. To be sure, she had cried all night and hadn't slept a wink; none of the Maywood people who came flocking kindly in to help could comfort her; but when morning came her tears were all shed. She was pale and quiet and docile.

"That's right, now," said Ellen, "that's what comes of being properly prepared. Your pa was so mad at me for warning you that he wasn't rightly civil to me since—and him a dying man. But I don't hold any grudge against him. *I* did my duty. Mrs Hubbard's fixing up a black dress for you, and it'll be ready by supper-time. Your ma's people will be here to-night, so they've telegraphed, and I'm bound they'll find you looking respectable. They're well off and they'll provide for you. Your pa hasn't left a cent but there ain't any debts, I'll say *that* for him. Have you been in to see the body?"

"Don't call him *that*," cried Emily, wincing. It was horrible to hear Father called *that*.

"Why not? If you ain't the queerest child! He makes a better-looking corpse than I thought he would, what with being so wasted and all. He was always a pretty man, though too thin."

"Ellen Greene," said Emily, suddenly, "if you say any more of—those things—about Father, I will put the black curse on you!"

Ellen Greene stared.

"I don't know what on earth you mean. But that's no way to talk to me, after all I've done for you. You'd better not let the Murrays' hear you talking like that or they won't want much to do with you. The black curse indeed! Well, here's gratitude!"

Emily's eyes smarted. She was just a lonely, solitary little creature and she felt very friendless. But she was not at all remorseful for what she had said to Ellen and she was not going to pretend she was.

"Come you here and help me wash these dishes," ordered Ellen. "It'll do you good to have something to take up your mind and then you won't be after putting curses on people who have worked their fingers to the bone for you."

Emily, with an eloquent glance at Ellen's hands, went and got a dish-towel.

"Your hands are fat and pudgy," she said. "The bones don't show at all."

"Never mind sassing back! It's awful, with your poor pa dead in there. But if your Aunt Ruth takes you she'll soon cure you of that."

"Is Aunt Ruth going to take me?"

"I don't know, but she ought to. She's a widow with no chick or child, and well-to-do."

"I don't think I want Aunt Ruth to take me," said Emily, deliberately, after a moment's reflection.

"Well, *you* won't have the choosing likely. You ought to be thankful to get a home anywhere. Remember you're not of much importance."

"I am important to myself," cried Emily proudly.

"It'll be some chore to bring *you* up," muttered Ellen. "Your Aunt Ruth is the one to do it, in my opinion. *She* won't stand no nonsense. A fine woman she is and the neatest housekeeper on P. E. Island. You could eat off her floor."

"I don't want to eat off her floor. I don't care if a floor is dirty as long as the tablecloth is clean."

"Well, her tablecloths are clean too, I reckon. She's got an elegant house in Shrewsbury with bow windows and wooden lace all round the roof. It's very stylish. It would be a fine home for you. She'd learn you some sense and do you a world of good."

"I don't want to learn sense and be done a world of good to," cried Emily with a quivering lip. "I—I want somebody to love me."

"Well, you've got to behave yourself if you want people to like you. You're not to blame so much—your pa has spoiled you. I told him so often enough, but he just laughed. I hope he ain't sorry for it now. The fact is, Emily Starr, you're queer, and folks don't care for queer children."

"How am I queer?" demanded Emily.

"You talk queer—and you act queer—and at times you look queer. And you're too old for your age—though that ain't *your* fault. It comes of never mixing with other children. I've always threaped at your father to send you to school—learning at home ain't the same thing—but he wouldn't listen to me, of course. I don't say but what you are as far along in book learning as you need to be, but what you want is to learn how to be like other children. In one way it would be a good thing if your Uncle Oliver would take you, for he's got a big family. But he's not as well off as the rest, so it ain't likely he will. Your Uncle Wallace might, seeing as he reckons himself the head of the family. He's only got a grown-up daughter. But his wife's delicate—or fancies she is."

"I wish Aunt Laura would take me," said Emily. She remembered that Father had said Aunt Laura was something like her mother.

"Aunt Laura! *She* won't have no say in it—Elizabeth's boss at New Moon. Jimmy Murray runs the farm, but he ain't quite all there, I'm told—"

"What part of him isn't there?" asked Emily curiously.

"Laws, it's something about his mind, child. He's a bit simple—some accident or other when he was a youngster, I've heard. It addled his head, kind of. Elizabeth was mixed up in it some way—I've never heard the rights of it. I don't reckon the New Moon people will want to be bothered with you. They're awful set in their ways. You take my advice and try to please your Aunt Ruth. Be polite—and well-behaved—mebbe she'll take a fancy to you. There, that's all the dishes. You'd better go upstairs and be out of the way."

"Can I take Mike and Saucy Sal?" asked Emily.

"No, you can't."

"They'd be company for me," pleaded Emily.

"Company or no company, you can't have them. They're outside and they'll stay outside. I ain't going to have them tracking all over the house. The floor's been scrubbed."

"Why didn't you scrub the floor when Father was alive?" asked Emily. "He liked things to be clean. You hardly ever scrubbed it then. Why do you do it now?"

"Listen to her! Was I to be always scrubbing floors with my rheumatiz? Get off upstairs and you'd better lie down awhile."

"I'm going upstairs, but I'm not going to lie down," said Emily. "I've got a lot of thinking to do."

"There's one thing I'd advise you to do," said Ellen, determined to lose no chance of doing her duty, "and that is to kneel down and pray to God to make you a good and respectful and grateful child."

Emily paused at the foot of the stairs and looked back.

"Father said I wasn't to have anything to do with your God," she said gravely.

Ellen gasped foolishly, but could not think of any reply to this heathenish statement. She appealed to the universe.

"Did any one ever hear the like!"

"I know what *your* God is like," said Emily. "I saw His picture in that Adam-and-Eve book of yours. He has whiskers and wears a nightgown. I don't like Him. But I like Father's God."

"And what is your father's God like, if I may ask?" demanded Ellen sarcastically.

Emily hadn't any idea what Father's God was like, but she was determined not to be posed by Ellen.

"He is clear as the moon, fair as the sun, and terrible as an army with banners," she said triumphantly.

"Well, you're bound to have the last word, but the Murrays will teach you what's what," said Ellen, giving up the argument. "They're strict Presbyterians and won't hold by any of your father's awful notions. Get off upstairs."

Emily went up to the south room, feeling very desolate.

"There isn't anybody in the world who loves me now," she said, as she curled up on her bed by the window. But she was determined she would not cry. The Murrays, who had hated her father, should not see her crying. She felt that she detested them all—except perhaps Aunt Laura. How very big and empty the world had suddenly become. Nothing was interesting any more. It did not matter that the little squat apple-tree between Adam-and-Eve had become a thing of rose-and-snow beauty—that the hills beyond the hollow were of green silk, purple-misted—that the daffodils were out in the garden—that the birches were hung all over with golden tassels—that the Wind Woman was blowing white young clouds across the sky. None of these things had any charm or consolation for her now. In her inexperience she believed they never would have again.

"But I promised Father I'd be brave," she whispered, clenching her little fists, "and I will. And I *won't* let the Murrays see I'm afraid of them—I won't *be* afraid of them!"

When the far-off whistle of the afternoon train blew beyond the hills, Emily's heart began to beat. She clasped her hands and lifted her face.

"Please help me, Father's God—*not* Ellen's God," she said. "Help me

25

to be brave and not cry before the Murrays."

Soon after there was the sound of wheels below—and voices—loud, decided voices. Then Ellen came puffing up the stairs with the black dress—a sleazy thing of cheap merino.

"Mrs Hubbard just got it done in time, thanks be. I wouldn't 'a' had the Murrays see you not in black for the world. They can't say I haven't done my duty. They're all here—the New Moon people and Oliver and his wife, your Aunt Addie, and Wallace and his wife, your Aunt Eva, and Aunt Ruth—Mrs Dutton, *her* name is. There, you're ready now. Come along."

"Can't I put my Venetian beads on?" asked Emily.

"Did ever any mortal! Venetian beads with a mourning dress! Shame on you! Is this a time to be thinking of vanity?"

"It isn't vanity!" cried Emily. "Father gave me those beads last Christmas—and I want to show the Murrays that I've got *something*!"

"No more of your nonsense! Come along, I say! Mind your manners—there's a good deal depends on the impression you make on them."

Emily walked rigidly downstairs before Ellen and into the parlour. Eight people were sitting around it—and she instantly felt the critical gaze of sixteen stranger eyes. She looked very pale and plain in her black dress; the purple shadows left by weeping made her large eyes look too large and hollow. She was desperately afraid, and she knew it—but she would not let the Murrays see it. She held up her head and faced the ordeal before her gallantly.

"This," said Ellen, turning her around by the shoulder, "is your Uncle Wallace."

Emily shuddered and put out a cold hand. She did not like Uncle Wallace—she knew that at once—he was black and grim and ugly, with frowning, bristly brows and a stern, unpitying mouth. He had big pouches under his eyes, and carefully-trimmed black side-whiskers. Emily decided then and there that she did not admire side-whiskers.

"How do you do, Emily?" he said coldly—and just as coldly he bent forward and kissed her cheek.

A sudden wave of indignation swept over Emily's soul. How *dared* he kiss her—he had hated her father and disowned her mother! She would have none of his kisses! Flash-quick, she snatched her handkerchief from her pocket and wiped her outraged cheek.

"Well—*well!*" exclaimed a disagreeable voice from the other side of the room.

Uncle Wallace looked as if he would like to say a great many things but couldn't think of them. Ellen, with a grunt of despair, propelled Emily to the next sitter.

"Your Aunt Eva," she said.

Aunt Eva was sitting huddled up in a shawl. She had the fretful face of the imaginary invalid. She shook hands with Emily and said nothing. Neither did Emily.

"Your Uncle Oliver," announced Ellen.

Emily rather liked Uncle Oliver's appearance. He was big and fat and rosy and jolly-looking. She thought she would not mind so much if *he* kissed her, in spite of his bristly white moustache. But Uncle Oliver had learned Uncle Wallace's lesson.

"I'll give you a quarter for a kiss," he whispered genially. A joke was Uncle Oliver's idea of being kind and sympathetic, but Emily did not know this, and resented it.

"I don't *sell* my kisses," she said, lifting her head as haughtily as any Murray of them all could do.

Uncle Oliver chuckled and seemed infinitely amused and not a bit offended. But Emily heard a sniff across the room.

Aunt Addie was next. She was as fat and rosy and jolly-looking as her husband and she gave Emily's cold hand a nice, gentle squeeze.

"How are you, dear?" she said.

That "dear" touched Emily and thawed her a trifle. But the next in turn froze her up instantly again. It was Aunt Ruth—Emily knew it was Aunt Ruth before Ellen said so, and she knew it was Aunt Ruth who had "well—welled" and sniffed. She knew the cold, grey eyes, the prim, dull brown hair, the short, stout figure, the thin, pinched, merciless mouth.

Aunt Ruth held out the tips of her fingers, but Emily did not take them.

"Shake hands with your Aunt," said Ellen in an angry whisper.

"She does not want to shake hands with me," said Emily, distinctly, "and so I am not going to do it."

Aunt Ruth folded her scorned hands back on her black silk lap.

"You are a very ill-bred child," she said; "but of course it was only what was to be expected."

Emily felt a sudden compunction. Had she cast a reflection on her father by her behaviour? Perhaps after all she should have shaken hands with Aunt Ruth. But it was too late now—Ellen had already jerked her on.

"This is your Cousin, Mr James Murray," said Ellen, in the disgusted tone of one who gives up something as a bad job and is only anxious to be done with it.

"Cousin Jimmy—Cousin Jimmy," said that individual. Emily looked steadily at him, and liked him at once without any reservations.

He had a little, rosy, elfish face with a forked grey beard; his hair curled over his head in a most un-Murray-like mop of glossy brown; and his large, brown eyes were as kind and frank as a child's. He gave Emily a hearty handshake, though he looked askance at the lady across from him while doing it.

"Hello, pussy!" he said.

Emily began to smile at him, but her smile was, as always, so slow in developing that Ellen had whisked her on before it was in full flower, and it was Aunt Laura who got the benefit of it. Aunt Laura started and paled.

"Juliet's smile!" she said, half under her breath. And again Aunt Ruth sniffed.

Aunt Laura did not look like anyone else in the room. She was almost pretty, with her delicate features and the heavy coils of pale, sleek, fair hair, faintly greyed, pinned closely all around her head. But it was her eyes that won Emily. They were such round blue, *blue* eyes. One never quite got over the shock of their blueness. And when she spoke it was in a beautiful, soft voice.

"You poor, dear, little child," she said, and put her arm around Emily for a gentle hug.

Emily returned the hug and had a narrow escape then from letting the Murrays see her cry. All that saved her was the fact that Ellen suddenly pushed her on into the corner by the window.

"And this is your Aunt Elizabeth."

Yes, this was Aunt Elizabeth. No doubt about that—and she had on a stiff, black satin dress, so stiff and rich that Emily felt sure it must be her very best. This pleased Emily. Whatever Aunt Elizabeth thought of her father, at least she had paid him the respect of her best dress. And Aunt Elizabeth was quite fine looking in a tall, thin, austere style, with clear-cut features and a massive coronet of iron-grey hair under her black lace cap. But her eyes, though steel-blue, were as cold as Aunt Ruth's, and her long, thin mouth was compressed severely. Under her cool, appraising glance Emily retreated into herself and shut the door of her soul. She would have liked to please Aunt Elizabeth—who was "boss" at New Moon—but she felt she could not do it.

Aunt Elizabeth shook hands and said nothing—the truth being that she did not know exactly what to say. Elizabeth Murray would not have felt "put about" before King or Governor-General. The Murray pride would have carried her through there; but she did feel disturbed in the presence of this alien, level-gazing child who had already shown that she was anything but meek and humble. Though Elizabeth Murray would never have admitted it, she did not want to be snubbed as Wallace and Ruth had been.

"Go and sit on the sofa," ordered Ellen.

Emily sat on the sofa with her eyes cast down, a slight, black, indomitable little figure. She folded her hands on her lap and crossed her ankles. They should see she had manners.

Ellen had retreated to the kitchen, thanking her stars that *that* was over. Emily did not like Ellen but she felt deserted when Ellen had gone. She was alone now before the bar of Murray opinion. She would have given anything to be out of the room. Yet in the back of her mind a design was forming of writing all about it in the old account-book. It would be interesting. She could describe them all—she knew she could. She had the very word for Aunt Ruth's eyes—"stone-grey." They were just like stones—as hard and cold and relentless. Then a pang tore through her heart. Father could never again read what she wrote in the account-book.

Still—she felt that she would rather like to write it all out. How could she best describe Aunt Laura's eyes? They were such beautiful eyes—just to call them "blue" meant nothing—hundreds of people had blue eyes—oh, she had it—"wells of blue"—that was the very thing.

And then the flash came!

It was the first time since the dreadful night when Ellen had met her on the doorstep. She had thought it could never come again—and now in this most unlikely place and time it *had* come—she had seen, with other eyes than those of sense, the wonderful world behind the veil. Courage and hope flooded her cold little soul like a wave of rosy light. She lifted her head and looked about her undauntedly—"brazenly" Aunt Ruth afterwards declared.

"Yes, she *would* write them all out in the account-book—describe every last one of them—sweet Aunt Laura, nice Cousin Jimmy, grim old Uncle Wallace, and moon-faced Uncle Oliver, stately Aunt Elizabeth and detestable Aunt Ruth.

"She's a delicate-looking child," said Aunt Eva, suddenly, in her fretful, colourless voice.

"Well, what else could you expect?" said Aunt Addie, with a sigh that seemed to Emily to hold some dire significance. "She's too pale—if she had a little colour she wouldn't be bad-looking."

"I don't know who she looks like," said Uncle Oliver, staring at Emily.

"She is not a Murray, that is plain to be seen," said Aunt Elizabeth, decidedly and disapprovingly.

"They are talking about me just as if I wasn't here," thought Emily, her heart swelling with indignation over the indecency of it.

"I wouldn't call her a Starr either," said Uncle Oliver. "Seems to me she's more like the Byrds—she's got her grandmother's hair and eyes."

"She's got old George Byrd's nose," said Aunt Ruth, in a tone that left no doubt as to her opinion of George's nose.

"She's got her father's forehead," said Aunt Eva, also disapprovingly.

"She has her mother's smile," said Aunt Laura, but in such a low tone that nobody heard her.

"And Juliet's long lashes—hadn't Juliet very long lashes?" said Aunt Addie.

Emily had reached the limit of her endurance.

"You make me feel as if I was made up of scraps and patches!" she burst out indignantly.

The Murrays stared at her. Perhaps they felt some compunction—for, after all, none of them were ogres and all were human, more or less. Apparently nobody could think of anything to say, but the shocked silence was broken by a chuckle from Cousin Jimmy—a low chuckle, full of mirth and free from malice.

"That's right, puss," he said. "Stand up to them—take your own part."

"Jimmy!" said Aunt Ruth.

Jimmy subsided.

Aunt Ruth looked at Emily.

"When I was a little girl," she said, "I never spoke until I was spoken to."

"But if nobody ever spoke until they were spoken to there would be no conversation," said Emily argumentatively.

"I never answered back," Aunt Ruth went on severely. "In those days little girls were trained properly. We were polite and respectful to our elders. We were taught our place and we kept it."

"I don't believe you ever had much fun," said Emily—and then gasped in horror. She hadn't meant to say that out loud—she had only meant to *think* it. But she had such an old habit of thinking aloud to Father.

"Fun!" said Aunt Ruth, in a shocked tone. "I did not think of fun when I was a little girl."

"No, I know," said Emily gravely. Her voice and manner were perfectly respectful, for she was anxious to atone for her involuntary lapse. Yet Aunt Ruth looked as if she would like to box her ears. This child was *pitying* her—insulting her by being sorry for *her*—because of her prim, impeccable childhood. It was unendurable—especially in a Starr. And that abominable Jimmy was chuckling again! Elizabeth should suppress him!

Fortunately Ellen Greene appeared at this juncture and announced supper.

"You've got to wait," she whispered to Emily. "There ain't room for you at the table."

Emily was glad. She knew she could not eat a bite under the Murray eyes. Her aunts and uncles filed out stiffly without looking at her—all except Aunt Laura, who turned at the door and blew her a tiny, furtive kiss. Before Emily could respond Ellen Greene had shut the door.

Emily was left all alone in the room that was filling with twilight shadows. The pride that had sustained her in the presence of the Murrays suddenly failed her and she knew that tears were coming. She went straight to the closed door at the end of the parlour, opened it, and went in. Her father's coffin stood in the centre of the small room which had been a bedroom. It was heaped with flowers—the Murrays

31

had done the proper thing in that as in all else. The great anchor of white roses Uncle Wallace had brought stood up aggressively on the small table at the head. Emily could not see her father's face for Aunt Ruth's heavily-fragrant pillow of white hyacinths lying on the glass, and she dared not move it. But she curled herself up on the floor and laid her cheek against the polished side of the casket. They found her there asleep when they came in after supper. Aunt Laura lifted her up and said,

"I'm going to take the poor child up to bed—she's worn right out."

Emily opened her eyes and looked drowsily about her.

"Can I have Mike?" she said.

"Who is Mike?"

"My cat—my big grey cat."

"A cat!" exclaimed Aunt Elizabeth in a shocked tone. "You must not have a cat in your bedroom!"

"Why not—for once?" pleaded Laura.

"Certainly not!" said Aunt Elizabeth. "A cat is a most unwholesome thing in a sleeping compartment. I'm surprised at you, Laura! Take the child up to bed and see that there are plenty of bedclothes. It's a cold night—but let me hear no more talk of sleeping with cats."

"Mike is a clean cat," said Emily. "He washes himself—every day."

"Take her up to bed, Laura!" said Aunt Elizabeth, ignoring Emily.

Aunt Laura yielded meekly. She carried Emily upstairs, helped her undress, and tucked her into bed. Emily was very sleepy. But before she was wholly asleep she felt something, soft and warm and purry and companionable, snuggling down by her shoulder. Aunt Laura had sneaked down, found Mike and brought him up to her. Aunt Elizabeth never knew and Ellen Greene dared not say a word in protest—for was not Laura a Murray of New Moon?

A FAMILY CONCLAVE

Emily wakened at daylight the next morning. Through her low, uncurtained window the splendour of the sunrise was coming in, and one faint, white star was still lingering in the crystal-green sky over the Rooster Pine. A fresh sweet wind of lawn was blowing around the eaves. Ellen Greene was sleeping in the big bed and snoring soundly. Except for that the little house was very still. It was the chance for which Emily had waited.

Very carefully she slipped from her bed, tiptoed across the room and opened the door. Mike uncoiled himself from the mat on the middle of the floor and followed her, rubbing his warm sides against her chilly little ankles. Almost guiltily she crept down the bare, dark staircase. How the steps creaked—surely it would waken everybody! But nobody appeared and Emily got down and slipped into the parlour, drawing a long breath of relief as she closed the door. She almost ran across the room to the other door.

Aunt Ruth's floral pillow still covered the glass of the casket. Emily, with a tightening of the lips that gave her face an odd resemblance to Aunt Elizabeth, lifted up the pillow and set it on the floor.

"Oh, Father—Father!" she whispered, putting her hand to her throat to keep something down. She stood there, a little shivering, white-clad figure, and looked at her father. This was to be her good-bye; she must say it when they were alone together—she would not say it before the Murrays.

Father looked so beautiful. All the lines of pain had vanished—his face looked almost like a boy's except for the silver hair above it. And he was smiling—such a nice, whimsical, wise little smile, as if he had suddenly discovered something lovely and unexpected and surprising. She had seen many nice smiles on his face in life but never one just like this.

"Father, I didn't cry before them," she whispered. "I'm sure I didn't disgrace the Starrs. Not shaking hands with Aunt Ruth wasn't disgracing the Starrs, was it? Because she didn't really want me to—oh, Father, I don't think any of them like me, unless perhaps Aunt Laura does a little. And I'm going to cry a little bit now, Father, because I can't keep it back *all* the time."

She laid her face on the cold glass and sobbed bitterly but briefly. She must say good-bye before any one found her. Raising her head she looked long and earnestly at the beloved face.

"Good-bye, dearest darling," she whispered chokingly.

Dashing away her blinding tears she replaced Aunt Ruth's pillow, hiding her father's face from her for ever. Then she slipped out, intent on speedily regaining her room. At the door she almost fell over Cousin Jimmy, who was sitting on a chair before it, swathed in a huge, checked dressing-gown, and nursing Mike.

"S-s-h!" he whispered, patting her on the shoulder. "I heard you coming down and followed you. *I* knew what you wanted. I've been sitting here to keep them out if any of them came after you. Here, take this and hurry back to your bed, small pussy."

"This" was a roll of peppermint lozenges. Emily clutched it and fled, overcome with shame at being seen by Cousin Jimmy in her nightgown. She hated peppermints and never ate them, but the fact of Cousin Jimmy Murray's kindness in giving them to her sent a thrill of delight to her heart. And he called her "small pussy," too—she liked that. She had thought nobody would ever call her nice pet names again. Father had had so many of them for her—"sweetheart" and "darling" and "Emily-child" and "dear wee kidlet" and "honey" and "elfkin." He had a pet name for every mood and she had loved them all. As for Cousin Jimmy, he was nice. Whatever part of him was missing it wasn't his heart. She felt so grateful to him that after she was safely in her bed again she forced herself to eat one of the lozenges, though it took all her grit to worry it down.

The funeral was held that forenoon. For once the lonesome little house in the hollow was filled. The coffin was taken into the parlour and the Murrays as mourners sat stiffly and decorously all round it, Emily among them, pale and prim in her black dress. She sat between Aunt Elizabeth and Uncle Wallace and dared not move a muscle. No other Starr was present. Her father had no near living relatives. The Maywood people came and looked at his dead face with a freedom and insolent curiosity they would never have presumed on in life. Emily hated to have them looking at her father like that. They had no right—they hadn't been friendly to him while he was alive—they had said harsh things of him—Ellen Greene had sometimes repeated them. Every glance that fell on him hurt Emily; but she sat still and gave no outward sign. Aunt Ruth said afterwards that she had never seen a child so absolutely devoid of all natural feeling.

When the service was over the Murrays rose and marched around the coffin for a dutiful look of farewell. Aunt Elizabeth took Emily's hand and tried to draw her along with them, but Emily pulled it back and shook her head. She had said her good-bye already. Aunt Elizabeth seemed for a moment to be on the point of insisting; then she grimly swept onward, alone, looking every inch a Murray. No scene must be made at a funeral.

Douglas Starr was to be taken to Charlottetown for burial beside his wife. The Murrays were all going but Emily was not to go. She watched the funeral procession as it wound up the long, grassy hill, through the light grey rain that was beginning to fall. Emily was glad it was raining; many a time she had heard Ellen Greene say that happy was the corpse the rain fell on; and it was easier to see Father go away in that soft, kind, grey mist than through sparkling, laughing sunshine.

"Well, I must say the funeral went off fine," said Ellen Greene at her shoulder. "Everything's been done regardless. If your father was looking down from heaven at it, Emily, I'm sure he'd be pleased."

"He isn't in heaven," said Emily.

"Good gracious! Of all the children!" Ellen could say no more.

"He isn't there *yet*. He's only on the way. He said he'd wait around and go slow until I died, too, so that I could catch up with him. I hope I'll die soon."

"That's a wicked, wicked thing to wish," rebuked Ellen.

When the last buggy had disappeared Emily went back to the sitting-room, got a book out of the bookcase, and buried herself in the wing-chair. The women who were tidying up were glad she was quiet and out of the way.

"It's well she can read," said Mrs Hubbard gloomily. "Some little girls couldn't be so composed—Jennie Hood just screamed and shrieked after they carried her mother out—the Hoods are all such a *feeling* people."

Emily was not reading. She was thinking. She knew the Murrays would be back in the afternoon; and she knew her fate would probably be settled then. "We'll talk the matter over when we come back," she had heard Uncle Wallace saying that morning after breakfast. Some instinct told her just what "the matter" was; and she would have given one of her pointed ears to hear the discussion with the other. But she knew very well she would be sent out of the way. So she was not surprised when Ellen came to her in the twilight and said:

"You'd better go upstairs, Emily. Your aunts and uncles are coming in here to talk over the business."

"Can't I help to get supper?" asked Emily, who thought that if she were going and coming around the kitchen she might catch a word or two.

"No. You'd be more bother than help. March, now."

Ellen waddled out to the kitchen, without waiting to see if Emily marched. Emily got up reluctantly. How could she sleep to-night if she did not know what was going to happen to her? And she felt quite sure she would not be told till morning, if then.

Her eyes fell on the oblong table in the centre of the room. Its cloth was of generous proportions, falling in heavy folds to the floor. There was a flash of black stockings across the rug, a sudden disturbance of drapery, and then—silence. Emily, on the floor under the table, arranged her legs comfortably and sat triumphant. She would hear what was decided and nobody would be any the wiser.

She had never been told that it was not considered strictly honourable to eavesdrop, no occasion for such instruction ever having arisen in her life with her father; and she considered that it was a bit of pure luck that she had thought of hiding under the table. She could even see dimly through the cloth. Her heart beat so loudly in her excitement that she was afraid they would hear it; there was no other sound save the soft, faraway singing of frogs through the rain, that sounded through the open window.

In they came; down they sat around the room; Emily held her breath; for a few minutes nobody spoke, though Aunt Eva sighed long and heavily. Then Uncle Wallace cleared his throat and said,

"Well, what is to be done with the child?"

Nobody was in a hurry to answer. Emily thought they would *never* speak. Finally Aunt Eva said with a whine,

"She's such a difficult child—so odd. *I* can't understand her at all."

"I think," said Aunt Laura timidly, "that she has what one might call an artistic temperament."

"She's a spoiled child," said Aunt Ruth very decidedly. "There's work ahead to straighten out *her* manners, if you ask me."

(The little listener under the table turned her head and shot a scornful glance at Aunt Ruth through the tablecloth. "*I* think that your own manners have a slight curve." Emily did not dare even to murmur the words under her breath, but she shaped them with her mouth; this was a great relief and satisfaction.)

"I agree with you," said Aunt Eva, "and I for one do not feel equal to the task."

(Emily understood that this meant Uncle Wallace didn't mean to take her and she rejoiced thereat.)

"The truth is," said Uncle Wallace, "Aunt Nancy ought to take her. She has more of this world's goods than any of us."

"Aunt Nancy would never dream of taking her and you know it well enough!" said Uncle Oliver. "Besides, she's entirely too old to have the bringing up of a child—her and that old witch Caroline. Upon my soul, I don't believe either of them is human. I would like to take Emily—but I feel that I can hardly do it. I've a large family to provide for."

"She'll not likely live long to bother anyone," said Aunt Elizabeth crisply. "She'll probably die of consumption same as her father did."

("I won't—I won't!" exclaimed Emily—at least she *thought* it with such vim that it almost seemed that she exclaimed it. She forgot that she had wanted to die soon, so that she could overtake Father. She wanted to live now, just to put the Murrays in the wrong. "I haven't *any* intention of dying. I'm going to live—for ages—and be a famous *authoress*—you'll just see if I don't, Aunt Elizabeth Murray!")

"She *is* a weedy-looking child," acknowledged Uncle Wallace.

(Emily relieved her outraged feelings by making a face at Uncle Wallace through the tablecloth. "If I ever possess a pig I am going to name it after *you*," she thought—and then felt quite satisfied with her revenge.)

"Somebody has to look after her as long as she's alive though, you know," said Uncle Oliver.

("It would serve you all right if I did *die* and you suffered terrible remorse for it all the rest of your lives," Emily thought. Then in the pause that happened to follow, she dramatically pictured out her funeral, selected her pall-bearers, and tried to choose the hymn verse that she wanted engraved on her tombstone. But before she could settle this Uncle Wallace began again.)

"Well, we are not getting anywhere. We have to look after the child—"

("I *wish* you wouldn't call me '*the child*,'" thought Emily bitterly.)

"—and some of us must give her a home. Juliet's daughter must not be left to the mercy of strangers. Personally, I feel that Eva's health is not equal to the care and training of a child—"

"Of *such* a child," said Aunt Eva.

(Emily stuck out her tongue at Aunt Eva.)

"Poor little soul," said Aunt Laura gently.

(Something frozen in Emily's heart melted at that moment. She was pitifully pleased over being called "poor little soul" so tenderly.)

"I do not think you need pity her overmuch, Laura," said Uncle Wallace decidedly. "It is evident that she has very little feeling. I have not seen her shed a tear since we came here."

"Did you notice that she would not even take a last look at her father?" said Aunt Elizabeth.

Cousin Jimmy suddenly whistled at the ceiling.

"She feels so much that she has to hide it," said Aunt Laura.

Uncle Wallace snorted.

"Don't you think *we* might take her, Elizabeth?" Laura went on timidly.

Aunt Elizabeth stirred restlessly.

"I don't suppose she'd be contented at New Moon, with three old people like us."

("I would—I would!" thought Emily.)

"Ruth, what about you?" said Uncle Wallace. "You're all alone in that big house. It would be a good thing for you to have some company."

"I don't like her," said Aunt Ruth sharply. "She is as sly as a snake."

("I'm *not*!" thought Emily.)

"With wise and careful training many of her faults may be cured," said Uncle Wallace, pompously.

("I don't *want* them cured!" Emily was getting angrier and angrier all the time under the table. "I like *my* faults better than I do *your—your—*" she fumbled mentally for a word—then triumphantly recalled a phrase of her father's—"your *abominable* virtues!")

"I doubt it," said Aunt Ruth, in a biting tone. "What's bred in the bone comes out in the flesh. As for Douglas Starr, I think that it was perfectly disgraceful for him to die and leave that child without a cent."

"Did he do it on purpose?" asked Cousin Jimmy blandly. It was the first time he had spoken.

"He was a miserable failure," snapped Aunt Ruth.

"He wasn't—he wasn't!" screamed Emily, suddenly sticking her head out under the tablecloth, between the end legs of the table.

For a moment the Murrays sat silent and motionless as if her outburst had turned them to stone. Then Aunt Ruth rose, stalked to the table, and lifted the cloth, behind which Emily had retired in dismay, realizing what she had done.

"Get up and come out of that, Em'ly Starr!" said Aunt Ruth.

"Em'ly Starr" got up and came out. She was not specially frightened—she was too angry to be that. Her eyes had gone black and her cheeks crimson.

"What a little beauty—what a regular little beauty!" said Cousin Jimmy. But nobody heard him. Aunt Ruth had the floor.

"You shameless little eavesdropper!" she said. "There's the Starr blood coming out—a Murray would never have done such a thing. You ought to be whipped!"

"Father wasn't a failure!" cried Emily, choking with anger. "You had no right to call him a failure. Nobody who was loved as much as he was could be a failure. I don't believe anybody *ever* loved you. So it's *you,* that's a failure. And I'm *not* going to die of consumption."

"Do you realize what a shameful thing you have been guilty of?" demanded Aunt Ruth, cold with anger.

"I wanted to hear what was going to become of me," cried Emily. "I didn't know it was such a dreadful thing to do—I didn't know you were going to say such horrid things about me."

"Listeners never hear any good of themselves," said Aunt Elizabeth impressively. "Your mother would *never* have done that, Emily."

The bravado all went out of poor Emily. She felt guilty and miserable—oh, so miserable. She hadn't known—but it seemed she had committed a terrible sin.

"Go upstairs," said Aunt Ruth.

Emily went, without a protest. But before going she looked around the room.

"While I was under the table," she said, "I made a face at Uncle Wallace and stuck my tongue out at Aunt Eva."

She said it sorrowfully, desiring to make a clean breast of her transgressions; but so easily do we misunderstand each other that the Murrays actually thought that she was indulging in a piece of gratuitous impertinence. When the door had closed behind her they all—except Aunt Laura and Cousin Jimmy—shook their heads and groaned.

Emily went upstairs in a state of bitter humiliation. She felt that she had done something that gave the Murrays the right to despise her, and they thought it was the Starr coming out in her—and she had not even found out what her fate was to be.

She looked dismally at little Emily-in-the-glass.

"I didn't know—I didn't know," she whispered. "But I'll know after this," she added with sudden vim, "and I'll never, *never* do it again."

For a moment she thought she would throw herself on her bed and cry. She *couldn't* bear all the pain and shame that was burning in her heart. Then her eyes fell on the old yellow account-book on her little table. A minute later Emily was curled up on her bed, Turk-fashion, writing eagerly in the old book with her little stubby lead-pencil. As her fingers flew over the faded lines her cheeks flushed and her eyes shone. She forgot the Murrays although she was writing about them— she forgot her humiliation—although she was describing what had happened; for an hour she wrote steadily by the wretched light of her smoky little lamp, never pausing, save now and then, to gaze out of the window into the dim beauty of the misty night, while she hunted through her consciousness for a certain word she wanted; when she found it she gave a happy sigh and fell to again.

When she heard the Murrays coming upstairs she put her book away. She had finished; she had written a description of the whole occurrence and of that conclave ring of Murrays, and she had wound up by a pathetic description of her own deathbed, with the Murrays standing around imploring her forgiveness. At first she depicted Aunt Ruth as doing it on her knees in an agony of remorseful sobs. Then she suspended her pencil—"Aunt Ruth couldn't *ever* feel as bad as *that* over anything," she thought—and drew her pencil through the line.

In the writing, pain and humiliation had passed away. She only felt tired and rather happy. It *had* been fun, finding words to fit Uncle Wallace; and what exquisite satisfaction it had been to describe Aunt Ruth as "a dumpy little woman."

"I wonder what my uncles and aunts would say if they knew what I *really* think of them," she murmured as she got into bed.

DIAMOND CUT DIAMOND

Emily, who had been pointedly ignored by the Murrays at breakfast, was called into the parlour when the meal was over.

They were all there—the whole phalanx of them—and it occurred to Emily as she looked at Uncle Wallace, sitting in the spring sunshine, that she had not just found the exact word after all to express his peculiar quality of grimness.

Aunt Elizabeth stood unsmilingly by the table with slips of paper in her hand.

"Emily," she said, "last night we could not decide who should take you. I may say that none of us feel very much like doing so, for you have behaved very badly in many respects—"

"Oh, Elizabeth—" protested Laura. "She—she is our sister's child."

Elizabeth lifted a hand regally.

"*I* am doing this, Laura. Have the goodness not to interrupt me. As I was saying, Emily, we could not decide as to who should have the care of you. So we have agreed to Cousin Jimmy's suggestion that we settle the matter by lot. I have our names here, written on these slips of paper. You will draw one and the one whose name is on it will give you a home."

Aunt Elizabeth held out the slips of paper. Emily trembled so violently that at first she could not draw one. This was terrible—it seemed as if she must blindly settle her own fate.

"Draw," said Aunt Elizabeth.

41

Emily set her teeth, threw back her head with the air of one who challenges destiny, and drew. Aunt Elizabeth took the slip from the little shaking hand and held it up. On it was her own name—"Elizabeth Murray." Laura Murray suddenly put her handkerchief to her eyes.

"Well, that's settled," said Uncle Wallace, getting up with an air of relief. "And if I'm going to catch that train I've got to hurry. Of course, as far as the matter of expense goes, Elizabeth, I'll do my share."

"We are not paupers at New Moon," said Aunt Elizabeth rather coldly. "Since it has fallen to me to take her, I shall do all that is necessary, Wallace. I do not shirk my duty."

"*I* am her duty," thought Emily. "Father said nobody ever liked a duty. So Aunt Elizabeth will never like me."

"You've got more of the Murray pride than all the rest of us put together, Elizabeth," laughed Uncle Wallace.

They all followed him out—all except Aunt Laura. She came up to Emily, standing alone in the middle of the room, and drew her into her arms.

"I'm so glad, Emily—I'm so glad," she whispered. "Don't fret, dear child. I love you already—and New Moon is a nice place, Emily."

"It has—a pretty name," said Emily, struggling for self-control. "I've—always hoped—I could go with you, Aunt Laura. I think I am going to cry—but it's not because I'm sorry I'm going there. My manners are *not* as bad as you may think, Aunt Laura—and I wouldn't have listened last night if I'd known it was wrong."

"Of course you wouldn't," said Aunt Laura.

"But I'm not a Murray, you know."

Then Aunt Laura said a queer thing—for a Murray.

"Thank heaven for that!" said Aunt Laura.

Cousin Jimmy followed Emily out and overtook her in the little hall. Looking carefully around to ensure privacy, he whispered.

"Your Aunt Laura is a great hand at making an apple turnover, pussy."

Emily thought apple turnover sounded nice, though she did not know what it was. She whispered back a question which she would never have dared ask Aunt Elizabeth or even Aunt Laura.

"Cousin Jimmy, when they make a cake at New Moon, will they let me scrape out the mixing-bowl and eat the scrapings?"

"Laura will—Elizabeth won't," whispered Cousin Jimmy solemnly.

"And put my feet in the oven when they get cold? And have a cooky before I go to bed?"

"Answer same as before," said Cousin Jimmy. "*I'll* recite my poetry to you. It's very few people I do that for. I've composed a thousand poems. They're not written down—I carry them here." Cousin Jimmy tapped his forehead.

"Is it very hard to write poetry?" asked Emily, looking with new respect at Cousin Jimmy.

"Easy as rolling off a log if you can find enough rhymes," said Cousin Jimmy.

They all went away that morning except the New Moon people. Aunt Elizabeth announced that they would stay until the next day to pack up and take Emily with them.

"Most of the furniture belongs to the house," she said, "so it won't take us long to get ready. There are only Douglas Starr's books and his few personal belongings to pack."

"How shall I carry my cats?" asked Emily anxiously.

Aunt Elizabeth stared.

"Cats! You'll take no cats, miss."

"Oh, I must take Mike and Saucy Sal!" cried Emily wildly. "I can't leave them behind. I can't live without a cat."

"Nonsense! There are barn cats at New Moon, but they are never allowed in the house."

"Don't you like cats?" asked Emily wonderingly.

"No, I do *not*."

"Don't you like the *feel* of a nice, soft, fat cat?" persisted Emily.

"No; I would as soon touch a snake."

"There's a lovely old wax doll of your mother's up there," said Aunt Laura. "I'll dress it up for you."

"I don't like dolls—they can't talk," exclaimed Emily.

"Neither can cats."

"Oh, can't they! Mike and Saucy Sal can. Oh, I *must* take them. Oh, please, Aunt Elizabeth. I *love* those cats. And they're the only things left in the world that love me. Please!"

"What's a cat more or less on two hundred acres?" said Cousin Jimmy, pulling his forked beard. "Take 'em along, Elizabeth."

Aunt Elizabeth considered for a moment. She couldn't understand

43

why anybody should want a cat. Aunt Elizabeth was one of those people who never do understand anything unless it is told them in plain language and hammered into their heads. And *then* they understand it only with their brains and not with their hearts.

"You may take *one* of your cats," she said at last, with the air of a person making a great concession. "One—and no more. No, don't argue. You may as well learn first as last, Emily, that when *I* say a thing I mean it. That's enough, Jimmy."

Cousin Jimmy bit off something he had tried to say, stuck his hands in his pockets, and whistled at the ceiling.

"When she won't, she won't—Murray-like. We're all born with that kink in us, small pussy, and you'll have to put up with it—more by token that you're full of it yourself, you know. Talk about your not being Murray! The Starr is only skin deep with you."

"It isn't—I'm *all* Starr—I *want* to be," cried Emily. "And, oh, how can I choose between Mike and Saucy Sal?"

This was indeed a problem. Emily wrestled with it all day, her heart bursting. She liked Mike best—there was no doubt of that; but she *couldn't* leave Saucy Sal to Ellen's tender mercies. Ellen had always hated Sal; but she rather liked Mike and she would be good to him. Ellen was going back to her own little house in Maywood village and she wanted a cat. At last in the evening, Emily made her bitter decision. She would take Saucy Sal.

"Better take the Tom," said Cousin Jimmy. "Not so much bother with kittens you know, Emily."

"Jimmy!" said Aunt Elizabeth sternly. Emily wondered over the sternness. Why weren't kittens to be spoken of? But she didn't like to hear Mike called "the Tom." It sounded insulting, someway.

And she didn't like the bustle and commotion of packing up. She longed for the old quiet and the sweet, remembered talks with her father. She felt as if he had been thrust far away from her by this influx of Murrays.

"What's this?" said Aunt Elizabeth suddenly, pausing for a moment in her packing. Emily looked up and saw with dismay that Aunt Elizabeth had in her hands the old account-book—that she was opening it—that she was *reading* in it. Emily sprang across the floor and snatched the book.

"You mustn't read that, Aunt Elizabeth," she cried indignantly, "that's mine—my own *private property*."

"Hoity-toity, Miss Starr," said Aunt Elizabeth, staring at her, "let me tell you that I have a right to read your books. I am responsible for you now. I am not going to have anything hidden or underhanded, understand that. You have evidently something there that you are ashamed to have seen and I mean to see it. Give me that book."

"I'm *not* ashamed of it," cried Emily, backing away, hugging her precious book to her breast. "But I won't let you—or *anybody*—see it."

Aunt Elizabeth followed.

"Emily Starr, do you hear what I say? Give me that book—at *once*."

"No—no!" Emily turned and ran. She would *never* let Aunt Elizabeth see that book. She fled to the kitchen stove—she whisked off a cover—she crammed the book into the glowing fire. It caught and blazed merrily. Emily watched it in agony. It seemed as if part of herself were burning there. But Aunt Elizabeth should never see it— see all the little things she had written and read to Father—all her fancies about the Wind Woman—and Emily-in-the-glass—all her little cat dialogues—all the things she had said in it last night about the Murrays. She watched the leaves shrivel and shudder, as if they were sentient things, and then turn black. A line of white writing came out vividly on one. "Aunt Elizabeth is very cold and *hawty*." What if Aunt Elizabeth had seen *that*? What if she were seeing it now! Emily glanced apprehensively over her shoulder. No, Aunt Elizabeth had gone back to the room and shut the door with what, in anybody but a Murray, would have been called a bang. The account-book was a little heap of white film on the glowing coals. Emily sat down by the stove and cried. She felt as if she had lost something incalculably precious. It was terrible to think that all those dear things were gone. She could never write them again—not just the same; and if she could she wouldn't dare— she would never dare to write *anything* again, if Aunt Elizabeth must see everything. Father never insisted on seeing them. She liked to read them to *him*—but if she hadn't wanted to do it he would never have made her. Suddenly Emily, with tears glistening on her cheeks, wrote a line in an imaginary account-book.

"Aunt Elizabeth is cold and hawty; and she is *not fair*."

Next morning, while Cousin Jimmy was tying the boxes at the back of the double-seated buggy, and Aunt Elizabeth was giving Ellen her final instructions, Emily said good-bye to everything—to the Rooster Pine and Adam-and-Eve—"they'll miss me so when I'm gone; there won't be any one here to love them," she said wistfully—to the spider crack in the kitchen window—to the old wing-chair—to the bed of striped grass—to the silver birch-ladies. Then she went upstairs to the window of her own old room. That little window had always seemed to Emily to open on a world of wonder. In the burned account-book there had been one piece of which she was especially proud. "A deskripshun of the vew from my Window." She had sat there and dreamed; at night she used to kneel there and say her little prayers. Sometimes the stars shone through it—sometimes the rain beat against it—sometimes the little greybirds and swallows visited it—sometimes airy fragrances floated in from apple and lilac blossom—sometimes the Wind Woman laughed and sighed and sang and whistled round it—Emily had heard her there in the dark nights and in wild, white winter storms. She did not say good-bye to the Wind Woman, for she knew the Wind Woman would be at New Moon, too; but she said good-bye to the little window and the green hill she had loved, and to her fairy-haunted barrens and to little Emily-in-the-glass. There might be another Emily-in-the-glass at New Moon, but she wouldn't be the same one. And she unpinned from the wall and stowed away in her pocket the picture of the ball dress she had cut from a fashion sheet. It was such a wonderful dress—all white lace and wreaths of rosebuds, with a long, long train of lace flounces that must reach clear across a room. Emily had pictured herself a thousand times wearing that dress, sweeping, a queen of beauty, across a ballroom door.

Downstairs they were waiting for her. Emily said good-bye to Ellen Greene rather indifferently—she had never liked Ellen Greene at any time, and since the night Ellen had told her her father was going to die she had hated and feared her.

Ellen amazed Emily by bursting into tears and hugging her—begging her not to forget her—asking her to write to her—calling her "my blessed child."

"I am not your blessed child," said Emily, "but I will write to you. And will you be very good to Mike?"

"I b'lieve you feel worse over leaving that cat than you do over leaving me," sniffed Ellen.

"Why, of course I do," said Emily, amazed that there could be any question about it.

It took all her resolution not to cry when she bade farewell to Mike, who was curled up on the sun-warm grass at the back door.

"Maybe I'll see you again sometime," she whispered as she hugged him. "I'm sure *good* pussy cats go to heaven."

Then they were off in the double-seated buggy with its fringed canopy, always affected by the Murrays of New Moon. Emily had never driven in anything so splendid before. She had never had many drives. Once or twice her father had borrowed Mr Hubbard's old buckboard and grey pony and driven to Charlottetown. The buckboard was rattly and the pony slow, but Father had talked to her all the way and made the road a wonder.

Cousin Jimmy and Aunt Elizabeth sat in front, the latter very imposing in black lace bonnet and mantle. Aunt Laura and Emily occupied the seat behind, with Saucy Sal between them in a basket, shrieking piteously.

Emily glanced back as they drove up the grassy lane, and thought the little, old, brown house in the hollow had a brokenhearted look. She longed to run back and comfort it. In spite of her resolution, the tears came into her eyes; but Aunt Laura put a kid-gloved hand across Sal's basket and caught Emily's in a close, understanding squeeze.

"Oh, I just love you, Aunt Laura," whispered Emily.

And Aunt Laura's eyes were very, very blue and deep and kind.

NEW MOON

Emily found the drive through the blossomy June world pleasant. Nobody talked much; even Saucy Sal had subsided into the silence of despair; now and then Cousin Jimmy made a remark, more to himself, as it seemed, than to anybody else. Sometimes Aunt Elizabeth answered it, sometimes not. She always spoke crisply and used no unnecessary words.

They stopped in Charlottetown and had dinner. Emily, who had

had no appetite since her father's death, could not eat the roast beef which the boarding-house waitress put before her. Whereupon Aunt Elizabeth whispered mysteriously to the waitress who went away and presently returned with a plateful of delicate cold chicken—fine white slices, beautifully trimmed with lettuce frills.

"Can you eat *that*?" said Aunt Elizabeth sternly, as to a culprit at the bar.

"I'll—try," whispered Emily.

She was too frightened just then to say more, but by the time she had forced down some of the chicken she had made up her small mind that a certain matter must be put right.

"Aunt Elizabeth," she said.

"Hey, what?" said Aunt Elizabeth, directing her steel-blue eyes straight at her niece's troubled ones.

"I would like you to understand," said Emily, speaking very primly and precisely so that she would be sure to get things right, "that it was not because I did not like the roast beef I did not eat it. I was not hungry at all; and I just et some of the chicken to oblige you, not because I liked it any better."

"Children should eat what is put before them and never turn up their noses at good, wholesome food," said Aunt Elizabeth severely. So Emily felt that Aunt Elizabeth had not understood after all and she was unhappy about it.

After dinner Aunt Elizabeth announced to Aunt Laura that they would do some shopping.

"We must get some things for the child," she said.

"Oh, please don't call me 'the child,'" exclaimed Emily. "It makes me feel as if I didn't belong anywhere. Don't you like my name, Aunt Elizabeth? Mother thought it so pretty. And I don't need any 'things.' I have two whole sets of underclothes—only one is patched—"

"S-s-sh!" said Cousin Jimmy, gently kicking Emily's shins under the table.

Cousin Jimmy only meant that it would be better if she let Aunt Elizabeth buy "things" for her when she was in the humour for it; but Emily thought he was rebuking her for mentioning such matters as underclothes and subsided in scarlet confusion. Aunt Elizabeth went on talking to Laura as if she had not heard.

"She must not wear that cheap black dress in Blair Water. You could sift oatmeal through it. It is nonsense expecting a child of ten to wear black at all. I shall get her a nice white dress with a black sash for good, and some black-and-white-check gingham for school. Jimmy, we'll leave the child with you. Look after her."

Cousin Jimmy's method of looking after her was to take her to a restaurant down street and fill her up with ice-cream. Emily had never had many chances at ice-cream and she needed no urging, even with lack of appetite, to eat two saucerfuls. Cousin Jimmy eyed her with satisfaction.

"No use my getting anything for you that Elizabeth could see," he said. "But she can't see what is inside of you. Make the most of your chance, for goodness alone knows when you'll get any more."

"Do you never have ice-cream at New Moon?"

Cousin Jimmy shook his head.

"Your Aunt Elizabeth doesn't like new-fangled things. In the house, we belong to fifty years ago, but on the farm she has to give way. In the house—candles; in the dairy, her grandmother's big pans to set the milk in. But, pussy, New Moon is a pretty good place after all. You'll like it some day."

"Are there any fairies there?" asked Emily, wistfully.

"The woods are full of 'em," said Cousin Jimmy. "And so are the columbines in the old orchard. We grow columbines there on purpose for the fairies."

Emily sighed. Since she was eight she had known there were no fairies anywhere nowadays; yet she hadn't quite given up the hope that one or two might linger in old-fashioned, out-of-the-way spots. And where so likely as at New Moon?"

"Really-truly fairies?" she questioned.

"Why, you know, if a fairy was really-truly it wouldn't *be* a fairy," said Cousin Jimmy seriously. "Could it, now?"

Before Emily could think this out the aunts returned and soon they were all on the road again. It was sunset when they came to Blair Water—a rosy sunset that flooded the long, sandy sea-coast with colour and brought red road and fir-darkened hill out in fleeting clearness of outline. Emily looked about her on her new environment and found it good. She saw a big house peering whitely through a veil of tall old trees—no mushroom growth of yesterday's birches but trees that had loved and been loved by three generations—a glimpse of silver water glistening through the dark spruces—that was the Blair Water itself, she knew—and a tall, golden-white church spire shooting up above the maple woods in the valley below. But it was none of these that brought her the flash—*that* came with the sudden glimpse of the dear, friendly, little dormer window peeping through vines on the roof—and right over it, in the opalescent sky, a real new moon, golden and slender. Emily was tingling all over with it as Cousin Jimmy lifted her from the buggy and carried her into the kitchen.

She sat on a long wooden bench that was satin-smooth with age and scrubbing, and watched Aunt Elizabeth lighting candles here and there, in great, shining, brass candlesticks—on the shelf between the windows, on the high dresser where the row of blue and white plates began to wink her a friendly welcome, on the long table in the corner. And as she lighted them, elvish "rabbits' candles" flashed up amid the trees outside the windows.

Emily had never seen a kitchen like this before. It had dark wooden walls and low ceiling, with black rafters crossing it, from which hung hams and sides of bacon and bunches of herbs and new socks and mittens, and many other things, the names and uses of which Emily could not imagine. The sanded floor was spotlessly white, but the boards had been scrubbed away through the years until the knots in them stuck up all over in funny little bosses, and in front of the stove they had sagged, making a queer, shallow little hollow. In one corner of the ceiling was a large square hole which looked black and spookish in the candlelight, and made her feel creepy. *Something* might pop down out of a hole like that if one hadn't behaved just right, you know. And candles cast such queer wavering shadows. Emily didn't know whether she liked the New Moon kitchen or not. It was an interesting place— and she rather thought she would like to describe it in the old account-book, if it hadn't been burned—but Emily suddenly found herself trembling on the verge of tears.

"Cold?" said Aunt Laura kindly. "These June evenings are chilly yet. Come into the sitting-room—Jimmy has kindled a fire in the stove there."

Emily, fighting desperately for self-control, went into the sitting-room. It was much more cheerful than the kitchen. The floor was covered with gay-striped homespun, the table had a bright crimson cloth, the walls were hung with pretty, diamond-patterned paper, the curtains were of wonderful pale-red damask with a design of white ferns scattered all over them. They looked very rich and imposing and Murray-like. Emily had never seen such curtains before. But best of all were the friendly gleams and flickers from the jolly hardwood fire in the open stove that mellowed the ghostly candlelight with something warm and rosy-golden. Emily toasted her toes before it and felt reviving interest in her surroundings. What lovely little leaded glass doors closed the china closets on either side of the high, black, polished mantel! What a funny, delightful shadow the carved ornament on the sideboard cast on the wall behind it—just like a negro's side-face, Emily decided. What mysteries might lurk behind the chintz-lined glass doors of the bookcase! Books were Emily's friends wherever she found them. She flew over to the bookcase and opened the door. But before she could see more than the backs of rather ponderous volumes, Aunt Elizabeth came in, with a mug of milk and a plate whereon lay two little oatmeal cakes.

"Emily," said Aunt Elizabeth sternly, "shut that door. Remember that after this you are not to meddle with things that don't belong to you."

"I thought books belonged to everybody," said Emily.

"Ours don't," said Aunt Elizabeth, contriving to convey the impression that New Moon books were in a class by themselves. "Here is your supper, Emily. We are all so tired that we are just having a lunch. Eat it and then we will go to bed."

Emily drank the milk and worried down the oatcakes, still gazing about her. How pretty the wallpaper was, with the garland of roses inside the gilt diamond! Emily wondered if she could "see it in the air." She tried—yes, she could—there it hung, a yard from her eyes, a little fairy pattern, suspended in mid-air like a screen. Emily had discovered that she possessed this odd knack when she was six. By a certain movement of the muscles of her eyes, which she could never describe, she could produce a tiny replica of the wallpaper in the air before her— could hold it there and look at it as long as she liked—could shift it back and forth, to any distance she chose, making it larger or smaller as it went farther away or came nearer. It was one of her secret joys when she went into a new room anywhere to "see the paper in the air." And

51

this New Moon paper made the prettiest fairy paper she had ever seen.

"What are you staring at nothing in that queer way for?" demanded Aunt Elizabeth, suddenly returning.

Emily shrank into herself. She couldn't explain to Aunt Elizabeth— Aunt Elizabeth would be like Ellen Greene and say she was "crazy."

"I—I wasn't staring at anything."

"Don't contradict. I say you were," retorted Aunt Elizabeth. "Don't do it again. It gives your face an unnatural expression. Come now—we will go upstairs. You are to sleep with me."

Emily gave a gasp of dismay. She had hoped it might be with Aunt Laura. Sleeping with Aunt Elizabeth seemed a very formidable thing. But she dared not protest. They went up to Aunt Elizabeth's big, sombre bedroom where there was dark, grim wallpaper that could never be transformed into a fairy curtain, a high black bureau, topped with a tiny swing-mirror, so far above her that there could be no Emily-in-the-glass, tightly closed windows with dark-green curtains, a high bedstead with a dark-green canopy, and a huge, fat, smothering feather-bed, with high, hard pillows.

Emily stood still, gazing about her.

"Why don't you get undressed?" asked Aunt Elizabeth.

"I—I don't like to undress before you," faltered Emily.

Aunt Elizabeth looked at Emily through her cold, spectacled eyes.

"Take off your clothes, *at once*," she said.

Emily obeyed, tingling with anger and shame. It was abominable— taking off her clothes while Aunt Elizabeth stood and watched her. The outrage of it was unspeakable. It was even harder to say her prayers before Aunt Elizabeth. Emily felt that it was not much good to pray under such circumstances. Father's God seemed very far away and she suspected that Aunt Elizabeth's was too much like Ellen Greene's.

"Get into bed," said Aunt Elizabeth, turning down the clothes.

Emily glanced at the shrouded window.

"Aren't you going to open the window, Aunt Elizabeth?"

Aunt Elizabeth looked at Emily as if the latter had suggested removing the roof.

"Open the window—and let in the night air!" she exclaimed. "Certainly not!"

"Father and I always had our window open," cried Emily.

"No wonder he died of consumption," said Aunt Elizabeth. "Night air is poison."

"What air is there at night but night air?" asked Emily.

"Emily," said Aunt Elizabeth icily, "get—into—bed."

Emily got in.

But it was utterly impossible to sleep, lying there in that engulfing bed that seemed to swallow her up, with that cloud of blackness above her and not a gleam of light anywhere—and Aunt Elizabeth lying beside her, long and stiff and bony.

"I feel as if I was in bed with a griffin," thought Emily. "Oh—oh—oh—I'm going to cry—I know I am."

Desperately and vainly she strove to keep the tears back—they *would* come. She felt utterly alone and lonely—there in that darkness, with an alien, hostile world all around her—for it seemed hostile now. And there was such a strange, mysterious, mournful sound in the air—far away, yet clear. It was the murmur of the sea, but Emily did not know that and it frightened her. Oh, for her little bed at home—oh, for Father's soft breathing in the room—oh, for the dancing friendliness of well-known stars shining down through her open window! She *must* go back—she couldn't stay here—she would never be happy here! But there wasn't any "back" to go to—no home—no father—. A great sob burst from her—another followed and then another. It was no use to clench her hands and set her teeth—and chew the inside of her cheeks—nature conquered pride and determination and had her way.

"What are you crying for?" asked Aunt Elizabeth.

To tell the truth Aunt Elizabeth felt quite as uncomfortable and disjointed as Emily did. She was not used to a bedfellow; she didn't want to sleep with Emily any more than Emily wanted to sleep with her. But she considered it quite impossible that the child should be put off by herself in one of the big, lonely New Moon rooms; and Laura was a poor sleeper, easily disturbed; children always kicked, Elizabeth Murray had heard. So there was nothing to do but take Emily in with her; and when she had sacrificed comfort and inclination to do her unwelcome duty this ungrateful and unsatisfactory child was not contented.

"I asked you what you were crying for, Emily?" she repeated.

"I'm—homesick, I guess," sobbed Emily.

Aunt Elizabeth was annoyed.

"A nice home you had to be homesick for," she said sharply.

"It—it wasn't as elegant—as New Moon," sobbed Emily, "but—
Father was there. I guess I'm Fathersick, Aunt Elizabeth. Didn't you
feel awfully lonely when *your* father died?"

Elizabeth Murray involuntarily remembered the ashamed,
smothered feeling of relief when old Archibald Murray had died—the
handsome, intolerant, autocratic old man who had ruled his family
with a rod of iron all his life and had made existence at New Moon
miserable with the petulant tyranny of the five years of invalidism that
had closed his career. The surviving Murrays had behaved impeccably,
and wept decorously, and printed a long and flattering obituary. But
had one genuine feeling of regret followed Archibald Murray to his
tomb? Elizabeth did not like the memory and was angry with Emily
for evoking it.

"I was resigned to the will of Providence," she said coldly. "Emily,
you must understand right now that you are to be grateful and obedient
and show your appreciation of what is being done for you. I won't have
tears and repining. What would you have done if you had no friends to
take you in? Answer me that."

"I suppose I would have starved to death," admitted Emily—
instantly beholding a dramatic vision of herself lying dead, looking
exactly like the pictures she had seen in one of Ellen Greene's
missionary magazines depicting the victims of an Indian famine.

"Not exactly—but you would have been sent to some orphanage
where you would have been half-starved, probably. You little know
what you have escaped. You have come to a good home where you will
be cared for and educated properly."

Emily did not altogether like the sound of being "educated properly."
But she said humbly,

"I know it was very good of you to bring me to New Moon, Aunt
Elizabeth. And I won't bother you long, you know. I'll soon be grown-
up and able to earn my own living. What do you think is the earliest
age a person can be called grown-up, Aunt Elizabeth?"

"You needn't think about that," said Aunt Elizabeth shortly. "The
Murray women have never been under any necessity for earning their
own living. All we require of you is to be a good and contented child
and to conduct yourself with becoming prudence and modesty."

This sounded terribly hard.

"I *will* be," said Emily, suddenly determining to be heroic, like the girl in the stories she had read. "Perhaps it won't be so very hard after all, Aunt Elizabeth,"—Emily happened at this point to recall a speech she had heard her father use once, and thought this a good opportunity to work it in—"because, you know, God is good and the devil might be worse."

Poor Aunt Elizabeth! To have a speech like that fired at her in the darkness of the night from that unwelcome little interloper into her orderly life and peaceful bed! Was it any wonder that for a moment or so she was too paralysed to reply! Then she exclaimed in tones of horror, "Emily, *never* say that again!"

"All right," said Emily meekly. "But," she added defiantly under her breath, "I'll go on thinking it."

"And now," said Aunt Elizabeth, "I want to say that I am not in the habit of talking all night if you are. I tell you to go to sleep, and I *expect* you to obey me. Good night."

The tone of Aunt Elizabeth's good night would have spoiled the best night in the world. But Emily lay very still and sobbed no more, though the noiseless tears trickled down her cheeks in the darkness for some time. She lay so still that Aunt Elizabeth imagined she was asleep and went to sleep herself.

"I wonder if anybody in the world is awake but me," thought Emily, feeling a sickening loneliness. "If I only had Saucy Sal here! She isn't so cuddly as Mike but she'd be better than nothing. I wonder where she is. I wonder if they gave her any supper."

Aunt Elizabeth had handed Sal's basket to Cousin Jimmy with an impatient, "Here—look to this cat," and Jimmy had carried it off. Where had he put it? Perhaps Saucy Sal would get out and go home— Emily had heard cats always went back home. She wished *she* could get out and go home—she pictured herself and her cat running eagerly along the dark, starlit roads to the little house in the hollow—back to the birches and Adam-and-Eve and Mike, and the old wing-chair and her dear little cot and the open window where the Wind Woman sang to her and at dawn one could see the blue of the mist on the homeland hills.

"Will it ever be morning?" thought Emily. "Perhaps things won't be so bad in the morning."

And then—she heard the Wind Woman at the window—she heard the little, low, whispering murmur of the June night breeze—cooing, friendly, lovesome.

"Oh, you're out there, are you, dearest one?" she whispered, stretching out her arms. "Oh, I'm so glad to hear you. You're such company, Wind Woman. I'm not lonesome any more. And the flash came, too! I was afraid it might never come at New Moon."

Her soul suddenly escaped from the bondage of Aunt Elizabeth's stuffy feather-bed and gloomy canopy and sealed windows. She was out in the open with the Wind Woman and the other gipsies of the night—the fireflies, the moths, the brooks, the clouds. Far and wide she wandered in enchanted reverie until she coasted the shore of dreams and fell soundly asleep on the fat, hard pillow, while the Wind Woman sang softly and luringly in the vines that clustered over New Moon.

THE BOOK OF YESTERDAY

That first Saturday and Sunday at New Moon always stood out in Emily's memory as a very wonderful time, so crowded was it with new and generally delightful impressions. If it be true that we "count time by heart throbs" Emily lived two years in it instead of two days. Everything was fascinating from the moment she came down the long, polished staircase into the square hall that was filled with a soft, rosy light coming through the red glass panes of the front door. Emily gazed through the panes delightedly. What a strange, fascinating, red world she beheld, with a weird red sky that looked, she thought, as if it belonged to the Day of Judgment.

There was a certain charm about the old house which Emily felt keenly and responded to, although she was too young to understand it. It was a house which aforetime had had vivid brides and mothers and wives, and the atmosphere of their loves and lives still hung around it, not yet banished by the old-maidishness of the regime of Elizabeth and Laura.

"Why—I'm going to *love* New Moon," thought Emily, quite amazed at the idea.

Aunt Laura was setting the breakfast table in the kitchen, which seemed quite bright and jolly in the glow of morning sunshine. Even the black hole in the ceiling had ceased to be spookish and become only a commonplace entrance to the kitchen loft. And on the red-sandstone doorstep Saucy Sal was sitting, preening her fur as contentedly as if she had lived at New Moon all her life. Emily did not know it, but Sal had already drunk deep the delight of battle with her peers that morning and taught the barn cats their place once and for all. Cousin Jimmy's big yellow Tom had got a fearful drubbing, and was minus several bits of his anatomy, while a stuck-up, black lady-cat, who fancied herself considerably, had made up her mind that if that grey-and-white, narrow-faced interloper from goodness knew where was going to stay at New Moon, *she* was not.

Emily gathered Sal up in her arms and kissed her joyously, to the horror of Aunt Elizabeth, who was coming across the platform from the cook-house with a plate of sizzling bacon in her hands.

"Don't ever let me see you kissing a cat again," she ordered.

"Oh, all right," agreed Emily cheerfully, "I'll only kiss her when you don't see me after this."

"I don't want any of your pertness, miss. You are not to kiss cats at all."

"But Aunt Elizabeth, I didn't kiss her on her mouth, *of course*. I just kissed her between her ears. It's nice—won't you just try it for once and see for yourself?"

"That will do, Emily. You have said quite enough." And Aunt Elizabeth sailed on into the kitchen majestically, leaving Emily momentarily wretched. She felt that she had offended Aunt Elizabeth, and she hadn't the least notion why or how.

But the scene before her was too interesting to worry long about Aunt Elizabeth. Delicious smells were coming from the cook-house—a little, slant-roofed building at the corner where the big cooking-stove was placed in summer. It was thickly overgrown with hop vines, as most of the New Moon buildings were. To the right was the "new" orchard, very wonderful now in blossom, but a rather commonplace spot after all, since Cousin Jimmy cultivated it in most up-to-date fashion and had grain growing in the wide spaces between the straight rows of trees that looked all alike. But on the other side of the barn lane, just behind the well, was the "old orchard," where Cousin Jimmy said the columbines grew and which seemed to be a delightful place where trees had come up at their own sweet will, and grown into individual shapes and sizes, where blue-eyed ivy twined about their roots and wild-briar roses rioted over the grey paling fence. Straight ahead, closing the vista between the orchards, was a little slope covered with huge white birches, among which were the big New Moon barns, and beyond the new orchard a little, lovable red road looped lightly up and up, over a hill, until it seemed to touch the vivid blue of the sky.

Cousin Jimmy came down from the barns, carrying brimming pails of milk, and Emily ran with him to the dairy behind the cook-house. Such a delightful spot she had never seen or imagined. It was a snow-white little building in a clump of tall balm-of-gileads. Its grey roof was dotted over with cushions of moss like fat green-velvet mice. You went down six sand-stone steps with ferns crowding about them, and opened a white door with a glass panel in it, and went down three more steps. And then you were in a clean, earthy-smelling, damp, cool place with an earthen floor and windows screened by the delicate emerald of young hop vines, and broad wooden shelves all around, whereon stood wide, shallow pans of glossy brown ware, full of milk coated over with cream so rich that it was positively yellow.

Aunt Laura was waiting for them and she strained the milk into empty pans and then skimmed some of the full ones. Emily thought skimming was a lovely occupation and longed to try her hand at it. She also longed to sit right down and write a description of that dear dairy; but alas, there was no account-book; still, she could write it in her head. She squatted down on a little three-legged stool in a dim corner and proceeded to do it, sitting so still that Jimmy and Laura forgot her and went away and later had to hunt for her a quarter of an hour. This delayed breakfast and made Aunt Elizabeth very cross. But Emily had found just the right sentence to define the clear yet dim green light that filled the dairy and was so happy over it that she didn't mind Aunt Elizabeth's black looks a bit.

After breakfast Aunt Elizabeth informed Emily that henceforth it would be one of her duties to drive the cows to pasture every morning.

"Jimmy has no hired man just now and it will save him a few

minutes."

"And don't be afraid," added Aunt Laura, "the cows know the way so well they'll go of themselves. You have only to follow and shut the gates."

"I'm not afraid," said Emily.

But she was. She knew nothing about cows; still, she was determined that the Murrays should not suspect a Starr was scared. So, her heart beating like a trip-hammer, she sallied valiantly forth and found that what Aunt Laura had said was true and cows were not such ferocious animals after all. They went gravely on ahead and she had only to follow, through the old orchard and then through the scrub maple growth beyond, along a twisted ferny path where the Wind Woman was purring and peeping around the maple clumps.

Emily loitered by the pasture gate until her eager eyes had taken in all the geography of the landscape. The old pasture ran before her in a succession of little green bosoms right down to the famous Blair Water—an almost perfectly round pond, with grassy, sloping, treeless margins. Beyond it was the Blair Water valley, filled with homesteads, and further out the great sweep of the white-capped gulf. It seemed to Emily's eyes a charming land of green shadows, and blue waters. Down in one corner of the pasture, walled off by an old stone dyke, was the little private graveyard where the dead-and-gone Murrays were buried. Emily wanted to go and explore it, but was afraid to trust herself in the pasture.

"I'll go as soon as I get better acquainted with the cows," she resolved.

Off to the right, on the crest of a steep little hill, covered with young birches and firs, was a house that puzzled and intrigued Emily. It was grey and weather-worn, but it didn't look old. It had never been finished; the roof was shingled but the sides were not, and the windows were boarded over. Why had it never been finished? And it was meant to be such a pretty little house—a house you could love—a house where there would be nice chairs and cosy fires and bookcases and lovely, fat, purry cats and unexpected corners; then and there she named it the Disappointed House, and many an hour thereafter did she spend finishing that house, furnishing it as it should be furnished, and inventing the proper people and animals to live in it.

To the left of the pasture-field was another house of a quite different type—a big, old house, tangled over with vines, flat-roofed, with mansard windows, and a general air of indifference and neglect about it. A large, untidy lawn, overgrown with unpruned shrubs and trees, straggled right down to the pond, where enormous willows drooped over the water. Emily decided that she would ask Cousin Jimmy about these houses when she got a good chance.

She felt that, before she went back, she must slip along the pasture fence and explore a certain path which she saw entering the grove of spruce and maple further down. She did—and found that it led straight into Fairyland—along the bank of a wide, lovely brook—a wild, dear, little path with lady-ferns beckoning and blowing along it, the shyest of elfin June-bells under the firs, and little whims of loveliness at every curve. She breathed in the tang of fir-balsam and saw the shimmer of gossamers high up in the boughs, and everywhere the frolic of elfin lights and shadows. Here and there the young maple branches interlaced as if to make a screen for dryad faces—Emily knew all about dryads, thanks to her father—and the great sheets of moss under the trees were meet for Titania's couch.

"This is one of the places where dreams grow," said Emily happily.

She wished the path might go on forever, but presently it veered away from the brook, and when she had scrambled over a mossy, old board fence she found herself in the "front garden" of New Moon, where Cousin Jimmy was pruning some spirea bushes.

"Oh, Cousin Jimmy, I've found the dearest little road," said Emily breathlessly.

"Coming up through Lofty John's bush?"

"Isn't it our bush?" asked Emily, rather disappointed.

"No, but it ought to be. Fifty years ago Uncle Archibald sold that jog of land to Lofty John's father—old Mike Sullivan. He built a little house down near the pond and lived there till he quarrelled with Uncle Archibald—which wasn't long, of course. Then he moved his house across the road—and Lofty John lives there now. Elizabeth has tried to buy the land back from him—she's offered him far more than it's worth—but Lofty John won't sell—just for spite, seeing that he has a good farm of his own and this piece isn't much good to him. He only pastures a few young cattle on it through the summer, and what was cleared is all growing up with scrub maple. It's a thorn in Elizabeth's side and likely to be as long as Lofty John nurses his spite."

"Why is he called Lofty John?"

"Because he's a high and lofty fellow. But never mind him. I want to show you round my garden, Emily. It's mine. Elizabeth bosses the farm; but she lets me run the garden—to make up for pushing me into the well."

"*Did* she do that?"

"Yes. She didn't mean to, of course. We were just children—I was here on a visit—and the men were putting a new hood on the well and cleaning it. It was open—and we were playing tag around it. I made Elizabeth mad—forget what I said—'twasn't hard to make her mad you understand—and she made to give me a bang on the head. I saw it coming—and stepped back to get out of the way—and down I went, head first. Don't remember anything more about it. There was nothing but mud at the bottom—but my head struck the stones at the side. I was took up for dead—my head all cut up. Poor Elizabeth was—" Cousin Jimmy shook his head, as if to intimate that it was impossible to describe how or what poor Elizabeth was. "I got about after a while, though—pretty near as good as new. Folks say I've never been quite right since—but they only say that because I'm a poet, and because nothing ever worries me. Poets are so scarce in Blair Water folks don't understand them, and most people worry so much, they think you're not right if you don't worry."

"Won't you recite some of your poetry to me, Cousin Jimmy?" asked Emily eagerly.

"When the spirit moves me I will. It's no use to ask me when the spirit don't move me."

"But how am I to know when the spirit moves you, Cousin Jimmy?"

"I'll begin of my own accord to recite my compositions. But I'll tell you this—the spirit generally moves me when I'm boiling the pigs' potatoes in the fall. Remember that and be around."

"Why don't you write your poetry down?"

"Paper's too scarce at New Moon. Elizabeth has some pet economies and writing-paper of any kind is one of them.

"But haven't you any money of your own, Cousin Jimmy?"

"Oh, Elizabeth pays me good wages. But she puts all my money in the bank and just doles out a few dollars to me once in a while. She says I'm not fit to be trusted with money. When I came here to work for her she paid me my wages at the end of the month and I started for Shrewsbury to put it in the bank. Met a tramp on the road—a poor, forlorn creature without a cent. I gave *him* the money. Why not? *I* had a good home and a steady job and clothes enough to do me for years. I s'pose it was the foolishest thing I ever did—and the nicest. But Elizabeth never got over it. *She's* managed my money ever since. But come you now, and I'll show you my garden before I have to go and sow turnips."

The garden was a beautiful place, well worthy Cousin Jimmy's pride. It seemed like a garden where no frost could wither or rough wind blow—a garden remembering a hundred vanished summers. There was a high hedge of clipped spruce all around it, spaced at intervals by tall Lombardies. The north side was closed in by a thick grove of spruce against which a long row of peonies grew, their great red blossoms splendid against its darkness. One big spruce grew in the centre of the garden and underneath it was a stone bench, made of flat shore stones worn smooth by long polish of wind and wave. In the south-east corner was an enormous clump of lilacs, trimmed into the semblance of one large drooping-boughed tree, gloried over with purple. An old summer-house, covered with vines, filled the south-west corner. And in the north-west corner there was a sundial of grey stone, placed just where the broad red walk that was bordered with striped grass, and picked out with pink conchs, ran off into Lofty John's bush. Emily had never seen a sundial before and hung over it enraptured.

"Your great-great-grandfather, Hugh Murray, had that brought out from the Old Country," said Cousin Jimmy. "There isn't as fine a one in the Maritime Provinces. And Uncle George Murray brought those conchs from the Indies. He was a sea-captain."

Emily looked about her with delight. The garden was lovely and the house quite splendid to her childish eyes. It had a big front porch with Grecian columns. These were thought very elegant in Blair Water, and went far to justify the Murray pride. A schoolmaster had said they gave the house a classical air. To be sure, the classical effect was just now rather smothered in hop-vines that rioted over the whole porch and hung in pale-green festoons above the rows of potted scarlet geraniums that flanked the steps.

Emily's heart swelled with pride.

"It's a noble house," she said.

"And what about my garden?" demanded Cousin Jimmy jealously.

"It's fit for a queen," said Emily, gravely and sincerely.

Cousin Jimmy nodded, well pleased, and then a strange sound crept into his voice and an odd look into his eyes.

"There is a spell woven round this garden. The blight shall spare it and the green worm pass it by. Drought dares not invade it and the rain comes here gently."

Emily took an involuntary step backward—she almost felt like running away. But now Cousin Jimmy was himself again.

"Isn't this grass about the sundial like green velvet? I've taken some pains with it, I can tell you. You make yourself at home in this garden." Cousin Jimmy made a splendid gesture. "I confer the freedom of it upon you. Good-luck to you, and may you find the Lost Diamond."

"The Lost Diamond?" said Emily wonderingly. What fascinating thing was this?

"Never hear the story? I'll tell it to-morrow—Sunday's lazy day at New Moon. I must get off to my turnips now or I'll have Elizabeth out looking at me. She won't say anything—she'll just *look*. Ever seen the real Murray look?"

"I guess I saw it when Aunt Ruth pulled me out from under the table," said Emily ruefully.

"No—no. That was the Ruth Dutton look—spite and malice and all uncharitableness. I hate Ruth Dutton. She laughs at my poetry— not that she ever hears any of it. The spirit never moves when Ruth is around. Dunno where they got her. Elizabeth is a crank but she's sound as a nut, and Laura's a saint. But Ruth's worm-eaten. As for the Murray look, you'll know it when you see it. It's as well known as the Murray pride. We're a darn queer lot—but we're the finest people ever happened. I'll tell you all about us to-morrow."

Cousin Jimmy kept his promise while the aunts were away at church. It had been decided in family conclave that Emily was not to go to church that day.

"She has nothing suitable to wear," said Aunt Elizabeth. "By next Sunday we will have her white dress ready."

Emily was disappointed that she was not to go to church. She had always found church very interesting on the rare occasions when she got there. It had been too far at Maywood for her father to walk but sometimes Ellen Greene's brother had taken her and Ellen.

"Do you think, Aunt Elizabeth," she said wistfully, "that God would be much offended if I wore my black dress to church? Of course it's cheap—I think Ellen Greene paid for it herself—but it covers me all up."

"Little girls who do not understand things should hold their tongues," said Aunt Elizabeth. "I do not choose that Blair Water people should see my niece in such a dress as that wretched black merino. And if Ellen Greene paid for it we must repay her. You should have told us that before we came away from Maywood. No, you are not going to church to-day. You can wear the black dress to school to-morrow. We can cover it up with an apron."

Emily resigned herself with a sigh of disappointment to staying home; but it was very pleasant after all. Cousin Jimmy took her for a walk to the pond, showed her the graveyard and opened the book of yesterday for her.

"Why are all the Murrays buried here?" asked Emily. "Is it really because they are too good to be buried with common people?"

"No—no, pussy. We don't carry our pride as far as *that*. When old Hugh Murray settled at New Moon there was nothing much but woods for miles and no graveyards nearer than Charlottetown. That's why the old Murrays were buried here—and later on we kept it up because we wanted to lie with our own, here on the green, green banks of the old Blair Water."

"That sounds like a line out of a poem, Cousin Jimmy," said Emily.

"So it is—out of one of my poems."

"I kind of like the idea of a 'sclusive burying-ground like this," said Emily decidedly, looking around her approvingly at the velvet grass sloping down to the fairy-blue pond, the neat walks, the well-kept graves.

Cousin Jimmy chuckled.

"And yet they say you ain't a Murray," he said. "Murray and Byrd and Starr—and a dash of Shipley to boot, or Cousin Jimmy Murray is much mistaken."

"Shipley?"

"Yes—Hugh Murray's wife—your great-great-grandmother—was a Shipley—an Englishwoman. Ever hear of how the Murrays came to

New Moon?"

"No."

"They were bound for Quebec—hadn't any notion of coming to P. E. I. They had a long rough voyage and water got scarce, so the captain of the *New Moon* put in here to get some. Mary Murray had nearly died of seasickness coming but—never seemed to get her sea-legs—so the captain, being sorry for her, told her she could go ashore with the men and feel solid ground under her for an hour or so. Very gladly she went and when she got to shore she said, 'Here I stay.' And stay she did; nothing could budge her; old Hugh—he was young Hugh then, of course, coaxed and stormed and raged and argued—and even cried, I've been told—but Mary wouldn't be moved. In the end he gave in and had his belongings landed and stayed, too. So that is how the Murrays came to P. E. Island."

"I'm glad it happened like that," said Emily.

"So was old Hugh in the long run. And yet it rankled, Emily—it rankled. He never forgave his wife with a whole heart. Her grave is over there in the corner—that one with the flat red stone. Go you and look at what he had put on it."

Emily ran curiously over. The big flat stone was inscribed with one of the long, discursive epitaphs of an older day. But beneath the epitaph was no scriptural verse or pious psalm. Clear and distinct, in spite of age and lichen, ran the line, "Here I stay."

"*That's* how he got even with her," said Cousin Jimmy. "He was a good husband to her—and she was a good wife and bore him a fine family—and he never was the same after her death. But that rankled in him until it had to come out."

Emily gave a little shiver. Somehow, the idea of that grim old ancestor with his undying grudge against his nearest and dearest was rather terrifying.

"I'm glad I'm only *half* Murray," she said to herself. Aloud—"Father told me it was a Murray tradition not to carry spite past the grave."

"So 'tis now—but it took its rise from this very thing. His family were so horrified at it, you see. It made considerable of a scandal. Some folks twisted it round to mean that Old Hugh didn't believe in the resurrection, and there was talk of the session taking it up, but after a while the talk died away."

Emily skipped over to another lichen-grown stone.

"Elizabeth Burnley—who was she, Cousin Jimmy?"

"Old William Murray's wife. He was Hugh's brother, and came out here five years after Hugh did. His wife was a great beauty and had been a belle in the Old Country. She didn't like the P. E. Island woods. She was homesick, Emily—scandalous homesick. For weeks after she came here she wouldn't take off her bonnet—just walked the floor in it, demanding to be taken back home."

"Didn't she take it off when she went to bed?" asked Emily.

"Dunno if she did go to bed. Anyway, William wouldn't take her back home so in time she took off her bonnet and resigned herself. Her daughter married Hugh's son, so Elizabeth was your great-great-grandmother."

Emily looked down at the sunken green grave and wondered if any homesick dreams haunted Elizabeth Burnley's slumber of a hundred years.

"It's dreadful to be homesick—*I* know," she thought sympathetically.

"Little Stephen Murray is buried over there," said Cousin Jimmy. "His was the first marble stone in the burying-ground. He was your grandfather's brother—died when he was twelve. He has," said Cousin Jimmy solemnly, "became a Murray tradition."

"Why?"

"He was so beautiful and clever and good. He hadn't a fault—so of course he couldn't live. They say there never was such a handsome child in the connection. And lovable—everybody loved him. He has been dead for ninety years—not a Murray living to-day ever saw him—and yet we talk about him at family gatherings—he's more real than lots of living people. So you see, Emily, he must have been an extraordinary child—but it ended in that—" Cousin Jimmy waved his hand towards the grassy grave and the white, prim headstone.

"I wonder," thought Emily, "if anyone will remember *me* ninety years after I'm dead."

"This old yard is nearly full," reflected Cousin Jimmy. "There's just room in yonder corner for Elizabeth and Laura—and me. None for you, Emily."

"I don't want to be buried here," flashed Emily. "I think it's splendid to have a graveyard like this in the family—but *I* am going to be buried in Charlottetown graveyard with Father and Mother. But there's one thing worries me Cousin Jimmy, do *you* think I'm likely to die of consumption?"

Cousin Jimmy looked judicially down into her eyes.

"No," he said, "no, Miss Puss. You've got enough life in *you* to carry you far. You aren't meant for death."

"I feel that, too," said Emily, nodding. "And now, Cousin Jimmy, *why* is that house over there disappointed?"

"Which one?—oh, Fred Clifford's house. Fred Clifford began to build that house thirty years ago. He was to be married and his lady picked out the plan. And when the house was just as far along as you see she jilted him, Emily—right in the face of day she jilted him. Never another nail was driven in the house. Fred went out to British Columbia. He's living there yet—married and happy. But he won't sell that lot to anyone—so I reckon he feels the sting yet."

"I'm so sorry for that house. I *wish* it had been finished. It *wants* to be—even yet it *wants* to be."

"Well, I reckon it never will. Fred had a bit of Shipley in him, too, you see. One of old Hugh's girls was his grandmother. And Doctor Burnley up there in the big grey house has more than a bit."

"Is he a relation of ours, too, Cousin Jimmy?"

"Forty-second cousin. Way back he had a cousin of Mary Shipley's for a great-something. That was in the Old Country—his forebears came out here after we did. He's a good doctor but an odd stick—odder by far than I am, Emily, and yet nobody ever says he's not all there. Can you account for that? *He* doesn't believe in God—and *I* am not such a fool as that."

"Not in *any* God?"

"Not in any God. He's an infidel, Emily. And he's bringing his little girl up the same way, which *I* think is a shame, Emily," said Cousin Jimmy confidentially.

"Doesn't her mother teach her things?"

"Her mother is—dead," answered Cousin Jimmy, with a little odd hesitation. "Dead these ten years," he added in a firmer tone. "Ilse Burnley is a great girl—hair like daffodils and eyes like yellow diamonds."

"Oh, Cousin Jimmy, you promised you'd tell me about the Lost Diamond," cried Emily eagerly.

"To be sure—to be sure. Well, it's there—somewhere in or about the old summer-house, Emily. Fifty years ago Edward Murray and his wife came here from Kingsport for a visit. A great lady she was, and wearing silks and diamonds like a queen, though no beauty. She had a ring on with a stone in it that cost two hundred pounds, Emily. That was a big lot of money to be wearing on one wee woman-finger, wasn't it? It sparkled on her white hand as she held her dress going up the steps of the summer-house; but when she came down the steps it was gone."

"And was it *never* found?" asked Emily breathlessly.

"Never—and for no lack of searching. Edward Murray wanted to have the house pulled down—but Uncle Archibald wouldn't hear of it—because he had built it for his bride. The two brothers quarrelled over it and were never good friends again. Everybody in the connection has taken a spell hunting for the diamond. Most folks think it fell out of the summer-house among the flowers or shrubs. But I know better, Emily. I know Miriam Murray's diamond is somewhere about that old house yet. On moonlit nights, Emily, I've seen it glinting—glinting and beckoning. But never in the same place—and when you go to it—it's gone, and you see it laughing at you from somewhere else."

Again there was that eerie, indefinable something in Cousin Jimmy's voice or look that gave Emily a sudden crinkly feeling in her spine. But she loved the way he talked to her, as if she were grown-up; and she loved the beautiful land around her; and, in spite of the ache for her father and the house in the hollow which persisted all the time and hurt her so much at night that her pillow was wet with secret tears, she was beginning to be a little glad again in sunset and bird song and early white stars, in moonlit nights and singing winds. She knew life was going to be wonderful here—wonderful and interesting, what with out-door cook-houses and cream-girdled dairies and pond paths and sundials, and Lost Diamonds, and Disappointed Houses and men who didn't believe in *any* God—not even Ellen Greene's God. Emily hoped she would soon see Dr Burnley. She was very curious to see what an infidel looked like. And she had already quite made up her mind that she would find the Lost Diamond.

TRIAL BY FIRE

Aunt Elizabeth drove Emily to school the next morning. Aunt Laura had thought that, since there was only a month before vacation, it was not worth while for Emily to "start school." But Aunt Elizabeth did not yet feel comfortable with a small niece skipping around New Moon, poking into everything insatiably, and was resolved that Emily must go to school to get her out of the way. Emily herself, always avid for new experiences, was quite keen to go, but for all that she was seething with rebellion as they drove along. Aunt Elizabeth had produced a terrible gingham apron and an equally terrible gingham sunbonnet from somewhere in the New Moon garret, and made Emily put them on. The apron was a long sack-like garment, high in the neck, with *sleeves*. Those sleeves were the crowning indignity. Emily had never seen any little girl wearing an apron with sleeves. She rebelled to the point of tears over wearing it, but Aunt Elizabeth was not going to have any nonsense. Emily saw the Murray look then; and when she saw it she buttoned her rebellious feeling tightly up in her soul and let Aunt Elizabeth put the apron on her.

"It was one of your mother's aprons when she was a little girl, Emily," said Aunt Laura comfortingly, and rather sentimentally.

"Then," said Emily, uncomforted and unsentimental, "I don't wonder she ran away with Father when she grew up."

Aunt Elizabeth finished buttoning the apron and gave Emily a none too gentle push away from her.

"Put on your sunbonnet," she ordered.

"Oh, please, Aunt Elizabeth, don't make me wear that horrid thing."

Aunt Elizabeth, wasting no further words, picked up the bonnet and tied it on Emily's head. Emily had to yield. But from the depths of the sunbonnet issued a voice, defiant though tremulous.

"Anyway, Aunt Elizabeth, you can't boss God," it said.

Aunt Elizabeth was too cross to speak all the way to the schoolhouse. She introduced Emily to Miss Brownell, and drove away. School was already "in," so Emily hung her sunbonnet on the porch nail and went to the desk Miss Brownell assigned her. She had already made up her mind that she did not like Miss Brownell and never would like her.

Miss Brownell had the reputation in Blair Water of being a fine teacher—due mainly to the fact that she was a strict disciplinarian and kept excellent "order." She was a thin, middle-aged person with a colourless face, prominent teeth, most of which she showed when she laughed, and cold, watchful grey eyes—colder even than Aunt Ruth's. Emily felt as if those merciless agate eyes saw clean through her to the core of her sensitive little soul. Emily could be fearless enough on occasion; but in the presence of a nature which she instinctively felt to be hostile to hers she shrank away in something that was more repulsion than fear.

She was a target for curious glances all the morning. The Blair Water school was large and there were at least twenty little girls of about her own age. Emily looked back curiously at them all and thought the way they whispered to each other behind hands and books when they looked at her very ill-mannered. She felt suddenly unhappy and homesick and lonesome—she wanted her father and her old home and the dear things she loved.

"The New Moon girl is crying," whispered a black-eyed girl across the aisle. And then came a cruel little giggle.

"What is the matter with you, Emily?" said Miss Brownell suddenly and accusingly.

Emily was silent. She could not tell Miss Brownell what was the matter with her—especially when Miss Brownell used such a tone.

"When I ask one of my pupils a question, Emily, I am accustomed to having an answer. Why are you crying?"

There was another giggle from across the aisle. Emily lifted miserable eyes and in her extremity fell back on a phrase of her father's.

"It is a matter that concerns only myself," she said.

A red spot suddenly appeared in Miss Brownell's sallow cheek. Her eyes gleamed with cold fire.

"You will remain in during recess as a punishment for your impertinence," she said—but she left Emily alone the rest of the day.

Emily did not in the least mind staying in at recess, for, acutely sensitive to her environment as she was, she realized that, for some reason she could not fathom, the atmosphere of the school was antagonistic. The glances cast at her were not only curious but ill-natured. She did not want to go out to the playground with those girls. She did not want to go to school in Blair Water. But she would not cry any more. She sat erect and kept her eyes on her book. Suddenly a soft, malignant hiss came across the aisle.

"Miss Pridey—Miss Pridey!"

Emily looked across at the girl. Large, steady, purplish-grey eyes gazed into beady, twinkling, black ones—gazed unquailingly—with something in them that cowed and compelled. The black eyes wavered and fell, their owner covering her retreat with another giggle and toss of her short braid of hair.

"I can master *her*," thought Emily, with a thrill of triumph.

But there is strength in numbers and at noon hour Emily found herself standing alone on the playground facing a crowd of unfriendly faces. Children can be the most cruel creatures alive. They have the herd instinct of prejudice against any outsider, and they are merciless in its indulgence. Emily was a stranger and one of the proud Murrays—two counts against her. And there was about her, small and ginghamed and sunbonneted as she was, a certain reserve and dignity and fineness that they resented. And they resented the level way she looked at them, with that disdainful face under cloudy black hair, instead of being shy and drooping as became an interloper on probation.

"You are a proud one," said Black-eyes. "Oh, my, you may have buttoned boots, but you are living on charity."

Emily had not wanted to put on the buttoned boots. She wanted to go barefoot as she had always done in summer. But Aunt Elizabeth had told her that no child from New Moon had ever gone barefoot to school.

"Oh, just look at the baby apron," laughed another girl, with a head of chestnut curls.

Now Emily flushed. This was indeed the vulnerable point in her armour. Delighted at her success in drawing blood the curled one tried again.

"Is that your grandmother's sunbonnet?"

There was a chorus of giggles.

"Oh, she wears a sunbonnet to save her complexion," said a bigger girl. "That's the Murray pride. The Murrays are rotten with pride, my mother says."

"You're awful ugly," said a fat, squat little miss, nearly as broad as she was long. "Your ears look like a cat's."

"You needn't be so proud," said Black-eyes. "Your kitchen ceiling isn't plastered even."

"And your Cousin Jimmy is an idiot," said Chestnut-curls.

"He isn't!" cried Emily. "He has more sense than any of you. You can say what you like about me but you are not going to *insult my family*. If you say one more word about them I'll look you over with the evil eye."

Nobody understood what this threat meant, but that made it all the more effective. It produced a brief silence. Then the baiting began again in a different form.

"Can you sing?" asked a thin, freckled girl, who yet contrived to be very pretty in spite of thinness and freckles.

"No," said Emily.

"Can you dance?"

"No."

"Can you sew?"

"No."

"Can you cook?"

"No."

"Can you knit lace?"

"No."

"Can you crochet?"

"No."

"Then what *can* you do?" said the Freckled-one in a contemptuous tone.

"I can write poetry," said Emily, without in the least meaning to say it. But at that instant she knew she *could* write poetry. And with this queer unreasonable conviction came—the flash! Right there, surrounded by hostility and suspicion, fighting alone for her standing, without backing or advantage, came the wonderful moment when soul seemed to cast aside the bonds of flesh and spring upward to the stars. The rapture and delight on Emily's face amazed and enraged her foes. They thought it a manifestation of Murray pride in an uncommon accomplishment.

"You lie," said Black-eyes bluntly.

"A Starr does not lie," retorted Emily. The flash was gone, but its uplift remained. She looked them all over with a cool detachment that quelled them temporarily.

"Why don't you like me?" she asked directly.

There was no reply. Emily looked straight at Chestnut-curls and repeated her question. Chestnut-curls felt herself compelled to answer it.

"Because you ain't a bit like us," she muttered.

"I wouldn't want to be," said Emily scornfully.

"Oh, my, you are one of the Chosen People," mocked Black-eyes.

"Of course I am," retorted Emily.

She walked away to the schoolhouse, conqueror in that battle.

But the forces against her were not so easily cowed. There was much whispering and plotting after she had gone in, a conference with some of the boys, and a handing over of bedizened pencils and chews of gum for value received.

An agreeable sense of victory and the afterglow of the flash carried Emily through the afternoon in spite of the fact that Miss Brownell ridiculed her for her mistakes in spelling. Miss Brownell was very fond of ridiculing her pupils. All the girls in the class giggled except one who had not been there in the morning and was consequently at the tail. Emily had been wondering who she was. She was as unlike the rest of the girls as Emily herself, but in a totally different style. She was tall, oddly dressed in an overlong dress of faded, striped print, and barefooted. Her thick hair, cut short, fluffed out all around her head in a bushy wave that seemed to be of brilliant spun gold; and her glowing eyes were of a brown so light and translucent as to be almost amber. Her mouth was large, and she had a saucy, pronounced chin. Pretty she might not be called, but her face was so vivid and mobile that Emily could not drag her fascinated eyes from it. And she was the only girl in class who did not, sometime through the lesson, get a barb of sarcasm from Miss Brownell, though she made as many mistakes as the rest of them.

At recess one of the girls came up to Emily with a box in her hand. Emily knew that she was Rhoda Stuart and thought her very pretty and sweet. Rhoda had been in the crowd around her at the noon hour but she had not said anything. She was dressed in crispy pink gingham; she had smooth, lustrous braids of sugar-brown hair, big blue eyes, a rose-bud mouth, doll-like features and a sweet voice. If Miss Brownell could be said to have a favourite it was Rhoda Stuart, and she seemed generally popular in her own set and much petted by the older girls.

"Here is a present for you," she said sweetly.

Emily took the box unsuspectingly. Rhoda's smile would have disarmed any suspicion. For a moment Emily was happily anticipant as she removed the cover. Then with a shriek she flung the box from her, and stood pale and trembling from head to foot. There was a snake in the box—whether dead or alive she did not know and did not care. For any snake Emily had a horror and repulsion she could not overcome. The very sight of one almost paralysed her.

A chorus of giggles ran around the porch. "Who'd be so scared of an old dead snake?" scoffed Black-eyes.

"Can you write poetry about *that*?" giggled Chestnut-curls.

"I *hate* you—I hate you!" cried Emily. "You are mean, hateful girls!"

"Calling names isn't ladylike," said the Freckled-one. "I thought a Murray would be too grand for that."

"If you come to school to-morrow, *Miss* Starr," said Black-eyes deliberately, "we are going to take that snake and put it around your neck."

"Let me see you do it!" cried a clear, ringing voice. Into their midst with a bound came the girl with amber eyes and short hair. "Just let me *see* you do it, Jennie Strang!"

"This isn't any of your business, Ilse Burnley," muttered Jennie, sullenly.

"Oh, isn't it? Don't you sass me, Piggy-eyes." Ilse walked up to the retreating Jennie and shook a sunburned fist in her face. "If I catch you teasing Emily Starr to-morrow with that snake again I'll take *it* by the tail and *you* by *your* tail, and slash you across the face with it. Mind that, Piggy-eyes. Now you go and pick up that precious snake of yours and throw it down on the ash pile."

Jennie actually went and did it. Ilse faced the others.

"Clear out, all of you, and leave the New Moon girl alone after this," she said. "If I hear of any more meddling and sneaking I'll slit your throats, and rip out your hearts and tear your eyes out. Yes, and I'll cut off your ears and wear them pinned on my dress!"

Cowed by these ferocious threats, or by something in Ilse's

personality, Emily's persecutors drifted away. Ilse turned to Emily.

"Don't mind them," she said contemptuously. "They're jealous of you, that's all—jealous because you live at New Moon and ride in a fringed-top buggy and wear buttoned boots. You smack their mugs if they give you any more of their jaw."

Ilse vaulted the fence and tore off into the maple bush without another glance at Emily. Only Rhoda Stuart remained.

"Emily, I'm awful sorry," she said, rolling her big blue eyes appealingly. "I didn't know there was a snake in that box, cross my heart I didn't. The girls just told me it was a present for you. You're not mad at me, are you? Because I like you."

Emily had been "mad" and hurt and outraged. But this little bit of friendliness melted her instantly. In a moment she and Rhoda had their arms around each other, parading across the playground.

"I'm going to ask Miss Brownell to let you sit with me," said Rhoda. "I used to sit with Annie Gregg but she's moved away. You'd like to sit with me, wouldn't you?"

"I'd love it," said Emily warmly. She was as happy as she had been miserable. Here was the friend of her dreams. Already she worshipped Rhoda.

"We *ought* to sit together," said Rhoda importantly. "We belong to the two best families in Blair Water. Do you know that if my father had his rights he would be on the throne of England?"

"England!" said Emily, too amazed to be anything but an echo.

"Yes. We are descended from the kings of Scotland," said Rhoda. "So of course we don't 'sociate with everybody. My father keeps store and I'm taking music lessons. Is your Aunt Elizabeth going to give you music lessons?"

"I don't know."

"She ought to. She is very rich, isn't she?"

"I don't know," said Emily again. She wished Rhoda would not ask such questions. Emily thought it was hardly good manners. But surely a descendant of the Stuart kings ought to know the rules of breeding, if anybody did.

"She's got an awful temper, hasn't she?" asked Rhoda.

"No, she hasn't!" cried Emily.

"Well, she nearly killed your Cousin Jimmy in one of her rages," said Rhoda. "That's true—Mother told me. Why doesn't your Aunt

Laura get married? Has she got a beau? What wages does your Aunt Elizabeth pay your Cousin Jimmy?"

"I don't know."

"Well," said Rhoda, rather disappointedly. "I suppose you haven't been at New Moon long enough to find things out. But it must be very different from what you've been used to, I guess. Your father was as poor as a church mouse, wasn't he?"

"My father was a very, *very* rich man," said Emily deliberately.

Rhoda stared.

"I thought he hadn't a cent."

"Neither he had. But people can be rich without money."

"I don't see how. But anyhow, *you'll* be rich some day—your Aunt Elizabeth will likely leave you all her money, Mother says. So I don't care if you *are* living on charity—I love you and I'm going to stick up for you. Have you got a beau, Emily?"

"No," cried Emily, blushing violently and quite scandalized at the idea. "Why, I'm only eleven."

"Oh, everybody in our class has a beau. Mine is Teddy Kent. I shook hands with him after I'd counted nine stars for nine nights without missing a night. If you do that the first boy you shake hands with afterwards is to be your beau. But it's awful hard to do. It took me all winter. Teddy wasn't in school to-day—he's been sick all June. He's the best-looking boy in Blair Water. You'll have to have a beau, too, Emily."

"I won't," declared Emily angrily. "I don't know a thing about beaux and I won't have one."

Rhoda tossed her head.

"Oh, I s'pose you think there's nobody good enough for you, living at New Moon. Well, you won't be able to play Clap-in-and-clap-out if you haven't a beau."

Emily knew nothing of the mysteries of Clap-in-and-clap-out, and didn't care. Anyway, she wasn't going to have a beau and she repeated this in such decided tones that Rhoda deemed it wise to drop the subject.

Emily was rather glad when the bell rang. Miss Brownell granted Rhoda's request quite graciously and Emily transferred her goods and chattels to Rhoda's seat. Rhoda whispered a good deal during the last hour and Emily got scolded for it but did not mind.

"I'm going to have a birthday party the first week in July, and I'm going to invite you, if your aunts will let you come. I'm not going to have Ilse Burnley though."

"Don't you like her?"

"No. She's an awful tomboy. And then her father is an infidel. And so's she. She always spells 'God' with a little 'g' in her dictation. Miss Brownell scolds her for it, but she does it right along. Miss Brownell won't whip *her* because she's setting her cap for Dr Burnley. But Ma says she won't get him because he hates women. *I* don't think it's proper to 'sociate with such people. Ilse is an awful wild queer girl and has an awful temper. So has her father. She doesn't chum with anybody. Isn't it ridic'lus the way she wears her hair? *You* ought to have a bang, Emily. They're all the rage and you'd look well with one because you've such a high forehead. It would make a real beauty of you. My, but you have lovely hair, and your hands are just lovely. All the Murrays have pretty hands. And you have the *sweetest* eyes, Emily."

Emily had never received so many compliments in her life. Rhoda laid flattery on with a trowel. Her head was quite turned and she went home from school determined to ask Aunt Elizabeth to cut her hair in a bang. If it would make a beauty of her it must be compassed somehow. And she would also ask Aunt Elizabeth if she might wear her Venetian beads to school next day.

"The other girls may *respect* me more then," she thought.

She was alone from the crossroads, where she had parted company with Rhoda, and she reviewed the events of the day with a feeling that, after all, she had kept the Starr flag flying, except for a temporary reverse in the matter of the snake. School was very different from what she had expected it to be, but that was the way in life, she had heard Ellen Greene say, and you just had to make the best of it. Rhoda was a darling; and there was something about Ilse Burnley that one liked; and as for the rest of the girls Emily got square with them by pretending she saw them all being hanged in a row for frightening her to death with a snake, and felt no more resentment towards them, although some of the things that had been said to her rankled bitterly in her heart for many a day. She had no father to tell them to, and no account-book to write them out in, so she could not exorcise them.

She had no speedy chance to ask for a bang, for there was company at New Moon and her aunts were busy getting ready an elaborate supper. But when the preserves were brought on Emily snatched the opportunity of a lull in the older conversation.

"Aunt Elizabeth," she said, "can I have a bang?"

Aunt Elizabeth looked her disdain.

"No," she said, "I do not approve of bangs. Of all the silly fashions that have come in nowadays, bangs are the silliest."

"Oh, Aunt Elizabeth, *do* let me have a bang. It would make a beauty of me—Rhoda says so."

"It would take a good deal more than a bang to do that, Emily. We will not have bangs at New Moon—except on the Molly cows. *They* are the only creatures that should wear bangs."

Aunt Elizabeth smiled triumphantly around the table—Aunt Elizabeth *did* smile sometimes when she thought she had silenced some small person by exquisite ridicule. Emily understood that it was no use to hope for bangs. Loveliness did not lie that way for her. It was mean of Aunt Elizabeth—mean. She heaved a sigh of disappointment and dismissed the idea for the present. There was something else she wanted to know.

"Why doesn't Ilse Burnley's father believe in God?" she asked.

"'Cause of the trick her mother played him," said Mr Slade, with a chuckle. Mr Slade was a fat, jolly-looking old man with bushy hair and whiskers. He had already said some things Emily could not understand and which had seemed greatly to embarrass his very lady-like wife.

"What trick did Ilse's mother play?" asked Emily, all agog with interest.

Now Aunt Laura looked at Aunt Elizabeth and Aunt Elizabeth looked at Aunt Laura. Then the latter said: "Run out and feed the chickens, Emily."

Emily rose with dignity.

"You might just as well tell me that Ilse's mother isn't to be talked about and I will obey you. I understand *perfectly* what you mean," she said as she left the table.

A SPECIAL PROVIDENCE

Emily was sure on that first day at school that she would never like it. She must go, she knew, in order to get an education and be ready to earn her own living; but it would always be what Ellen Greene solemnly called "a cross." Consequently Emily felt quite astonished when, after going to school a few days, it dawned upon her that she was liking it. To be sure, Miss Brownell did not improve on acquaintance; but the other girls no longer tormented her—indeed, to her amazement, they seemed suddenly to forget all that had happened and hailed her as one of themselves. She was admitted to the fellowship of the pack and, although in some occasional tiff she got a dig about baby aprons and Murray pride, there was no more hostility, veiled or open. Besides, Emily was quite able to give "digs" herself, as she learned more about the girls and their weak points, and she could give them with such merciless lucidity and irony that the others soon learned not to provoke them. Chestnut-curls, whose name was Grace Wells, and the Freckled-one, whose name was Carrie King, and Jennie Strang became quite chummy with her, and Jennie sent chews of gum and tissue thumb-papers across the aisle instead of giggles. Emily allowed them all to enter the outer court of her temple of friendship but only Rhoda was admitted to the inner shrine. As for Ilse Burnley, she did not appear after that first day. Ilse, so Rhoda said, came to school or not, just as she liked. Her father never bothered about her. Emily always felt a certain hankering to know more of Ilse, but it did not seem likely to be gratified.

Emily was insensibly becoming happy again. Already she felt as if she belonged to this old cradle of her family. She thought a great deal about the old Murrays; she liked to picture them revisiting the glimpses of New Moon—Great-grandmother rubbing up her candlesticks and making cheeses; Great-aunt Miriam stealing about looking for her lost treasure; homesick Great-great-aunt Elizabeth stalking about in her bonnet; Captain George, the dashing, bronzed sea-captain, coming home with the spotted shells of the Indies; Stephen, the beloved of all, smiling from its windows; her own mother dreaming of Father—they all seemed as real to her as if she had known them in life.

She still had terrible hours when she was overwhelmed by grief for her father and when all the splendours of New Moon could not stifle the longing for the shabby little house in the hollow where they had loved each other so. Then Emily fled to some secret corner and cried her heart out, emerging with red eyes that always seemed to annoy Aunt Elizabeth. Aunt Elizabeth had become used to having Emily at New Moon but she had not drawn any nearer to the child. This hurt Emily always; but Aunt Laura and Cousin Jimmy loved her and she had Saucy Sal and Rhoda, fields creamy with clover, soft dark trees against amber skies, and the madcap music the Wind Woman made in the firs behind the barns when she blew straight up from the gulf; her days became vivid and interesting, full of little pleasures and delights, like tiny, opening, golden buds on the tree of life. If she could only have had her old yellow account-book, or some equivalent, she could have been fully content. She missed it next to her father, and its enforced burning was something for which she held Aunt Elizabeth responsible and for which she felt she could never wholly forgive her. It did not seem possible to get any substitute. As Cousin Jimmy had said, writing-paper of any kind was scarce at New Moon. Letters were seldom written, and when they were a sheet of note-paper sufficed. Emily dared not ask Aunt Elizabeth for any. There were times when she felt she would burst if she couldn't write out some of the things that came to her. She found a certain safety valve in writing on her slate in school; but these scribblings had to be rubbed off sooner or later—which left Emily with a sense of loss—and there was always the danger that Miss Brownell would see them. That, Emily felt, would be unendurable. No stranger eyes must behold these sacred productions. Sometimes she let Rhoda read them, though Rhoda rasped her by giggling over her finest flights. Emily thought Rhoda as near perfection as a human being could be, but giggling was her fault.

But there is a destiny which shapes the ends of young misses who are born with the itch for writing tingling in their baby fingertips, and in the fullness of time this destiny gave to Emily the desire of her heart—gave it to her, too, on the very day when she most needed it.

That was the day, the ill-starred day, when Miss Brownell elected to show the fifth class, by example as well as precept, how the *Bugle Song* should be read.

Standing on the platform Miss Brownell, who was not devoid of a superficial, elocutionary knack, read those three wonderful verses. Emily, who should have been doing a sum in long division, dropped her pencil and listened entranced. She had never heard the *Bugle Song* before—but now she heard it—and *saw* it—the rose-red splendour falling on those storied, snowy summits and ruined castles—the lights that never were on land or sea streaming over the lakes—she heard the wild echoes flying through the purple valleys and the misty passes—the mere sound of the words seemed to make an exquisite echo in her soul—and when Miss Brownell came to "Horns of elf-land faintly blowing" Emily trembled with delight. She was snatched out of herself. She forgot everything but the magic of that unequalled line— she sprang from her seat, knocking her slate to the floor with a clatter, she rushed up the aisle, she caught Miss Brownell's arm.

"Oh, teacher," she cried with passionate earnestness, "read that line over again—oh, read that line over again!"

Miss Brownell, thus suddenly halted in her elocutionary display, looked down into a rapt, uplifted face where great purplish-grey eyes were shining with the radiance of a divine vision—and Miss Brownell was angry. Angry with this breach of her strict discipline—angry with this unseemly display of interest in a third-class atom whose attention should have been focused on long division. Miss Brownell shut her book and shut her lips and gave Emily a resounding slap on her face.

"Go right back to your seat and mind your own business, Emily Starr," said Miss Brownell, her cold eyes malignant with her fury.

Emily, thus dashed to earth, moved back to her seat in a daze. Her smitten cheek was crimson, but the wound was in her heart. One moment ago in the seventh heaven—and now *this*—pain, humiliation, misunderstanding! She could not bear it. What had she done to deserve it? She had never been slapped in her life before. The degradation and the injustice ate into her soul. She could not cry—this was "a grief too deep for tears"—she went home from school in a suppressed anguish of bitterness and shame and resentment—an anguish that had no outlet, for she dared not tell her story at New Moon. Aunt Elizabeth, she felt sure, would say that Miss Brownell had done quite right, and even

Aunt Laura, kind and sweet as she was, would not understand. She would be grieved because Emily had misbehaved in school and had had to be punished.

"Oh, if I could only tell Father all about it!" thought Emily.

She could not eat any supper—she did not think she would ever be able to eat again. And oh, how she hated that unjust, horrid Miss Brownell! She could never forgive her—never! If there were only some way in which she could get square with Miss Brownell! Emily, sitting small and pale and quiet at the New Moon supper-table, was a seething volcano of wounded feeling and misery and pride—ay, pride! Worse even than the injustice was the sting of humiliation over this thing that had happened. She, Emily Byrd Starr, on whom no hand had ever before been ungently laid, had been slapped like a naughty baby before the whole school. Who could endure this and live?

Then destiny stepped in and drew Aunt Laura to the sitting-room bookcase to look in its lower compartment for a certain letter she wanted to see. She took Emily with her to show her a curious old snuff-box that had belonged to Hugh Murray, and in rummaging for it lifted out a big, flat bundle of dusty paper—paper of a deep pink colour in oddly long and narrow sheets.

"It's time these old letter-bills were burned," she said. "What a pile of them! They've been here gathering dust for years and they are no earthly good. Father once kept the post-office here at New Moon, you know, Emily. The mail came only three times a week then, and each day there was one of these long red 'letter-bills,' as they were called. Mother always kept them, though when once used they were of no further use. But I'm going to burn them right away."

"Oh, Aunt Laura," gasped Emily, so torn between desire and fear that she could hardly speak. "Oh, don't do that—give them to me— *please* give them to me."

"Why, child, what ever do you want of them?"

"Oh, Aunty, they have such lovely blank backs for writing on. Please, Aunt Laura, it would be a *sin* to burn those letter-bills."

"You can have them, dear. Only you'd better not let Elizabeth see them."

"I won't—I won't," breathed Emily.

She gathered her precious booty into her arms and fairly ran upstairs—and then upstairs again into the garret, where she already had her "favourite haunt," in which her uncomfortable habit of thinking of things thousands of miles away could not vex Aunt Elizabeth. This was the quiet corner of the dormer-window, where shadows always moved about, softly and swingingly, and beautiful mosaics patterned the bare floor. From it one could see over the tree-tops right down to the Blair Water. The walls were hung around with great bundles of soft fluffy rolls, all ready for spinning, and hanks of untwisted yarn. Sometimes Aunt Laura spun on the great wheel at the other end of the garret and Emily loved the whir of it.

In the recess of the dormer-window she crouched—breathlessly she selected a letter-bill and extracted a lead-pencil from her pocket. An old sheet of cardboard served as a desk; she began to write feverishly.

"Dear Father"—and then she poured out her tale of the day—of her rapture and her pain—writing heedlessly and intently until the sunset faded into dim, starlitten twilight. The chickens went unfed—Cousin Jimmy had to go himself for the cows—Saucy Sal got no new milk—Aunt Laura had to wash the dishes—what mattered it? Emily, in the delightful throes of literary composition, was lost to all worldly things.

When she had covered the backs of four letter-bills she could see to write no more. But she had emptied out her soul and it was once more free from evil passions. She even felt curiously indifferent to Miss Brownell. Emily folded up her letter-bills and wrote clearly across the packet.

Mr Douglas Starr,

On the Road to Heaven.

Then she stepped softly across to an old, worn-out sofa in a far corner and knelt down, stowing away her letter and her "letter-bills" snugly on a little shelf formed by a board nailed across it underneath. Emily had discovered this one day when playing in the garret and had noted it as a lovely hiding-place for secret documents. Nobody would ever come across them there. She had writing-paper enough to last for months—there must be hundreds of those jolly old letter-bills.

"Oh," cried Emily, dancing down the garret stairs, "I feel as if I was made out of star-dust."

Thereafter few evenings passed on which Emily did not steal up to the garret and write a letter, long or short, to her father. The bitterness died out of her grief. Writing to him seemed to bring him so near; and she told him everything, with a certain honesty of confession that was characteristic of her—her triumphs, her failures, her joys, her sorrows, everything went down on the letter-bills of a Government which had not been so economical of paper as it afterwards became. There was fully half a yard of paper in each bill and Emily wrote a small hand and made the most of every inch.

"I like New Moon. It's so *stately* and *splendid* here," she told her father. "And it seems as if we must be very aristokratik when we have a sun dyal. I can't help feeling proud of it all. I am afraid I have too much pride and so I ask God every night to take *most* of it away but not quite all. It is very easy to get a repputation for pride in Blair Water school. If you walk straight and hold your head up you are a proud one. Rhoda is proud, too, because her father ought to be King of England. I wonder how Queen Victoria would feel if she knew that. It's very wonderful to have a friend who would be a princess if every one had their rites. I love Rhoda with all my heart. She is so sweet and kind. But I don't like her giggles. And when I told her I could see the school wallpaper small in the air she said You lie. It hurt me awfully to have my dearest friend say that to me. And it hurt me worse when I woke up in the night and thought about it. I had to stay awake ever so long, too, because I was tired lying on one side and I was afraid to turn over because Aunt Elizabeth would think I was figitting.

"I didn't dare tell Rhoda about the Wind Woman because I suppose that really is a kind of lie, though she seems so real to me. I hear her now singing up on the roof around the big chimneys. I have no Emily-in-the-glass here. The looking-glasses are all too high up in the rooms I've been in. I've never been in the look-out. It is always locked. It was Mother's room and Cousin Jimmy says her father locked it up after she ran away with you and Aunt Elizabeth keeps it locked still out of respect to his memory, though Cousin Jimmy says Aunt Elizabeth used to fight with her father something scandalus when he was alive though no outsider knew of it because of the Murray pride. I feel that way myself. When Rhoda asked me if Aunt Elizabeth burned candles because she was old-fashioned I answered hawtily no, it was a Murray tradishun. Cousin Jimmy has told me all the tradishuns of the Murrays. Saucy Sal is very well and bosses the barns but still she will not have kittens and I can't understand it. I asked Aunt Elizabeth about it and she said nice little girls didn't talk about such things but I cannot see why kittens are improper. When Aunt Elizabeth is away Aunt Laura and I smuggle Sal into the house but when Aunt Elizabeth comes back I always feel gilty and wish I hadn't. *But the next time I do it again.* I think that very strange. I never hear about dear Mike. I wrote Ellen Greene and asked about him and she replyed and never mentioned Mike but told me all about her roomatism. As if I cared about her roomatism.

"Rhoda is going to have a birthday party and she is going to invite me. I am so excited. You know I never was to a party before. I think about it a great deal and picture it out. Rhoda is not going to invite all the girls but only a favered few. I hope Aunt Elizabeth will let me ware my white dress and good hat. Oh, Father, I pinned that lovely picture of the lace ball dress up on the wall of Aunt Elizabeth's room, just like I had it at home and Aunt Elizabeth took it down and burned it and skolded me for making pin marks in the paper. I said Aunt Elizabeth you should not have burned that picture. I wanted to have it when I grow up to have a dress made like it for balls. And Aunt Elizabeth said Do you expect to attend many balls if I may ask and I said Yes when I am rich and famus and Aunt Elizabeth said Yes when the moon is made of green cheese.

"I saw Dr Burnley yesterday when he came over to buy some eggs from Aunt Elizabeth. I was disappointed because he looks just like other people. I thought a man who didn't believe in God would look queer in some way. He did not sware either and I was sorry for I have never heard any one sware and I am very angshus to. He has big yellow eyes like Ilse and a loud voice and Rhoda says when he gets mad you can hear him yelling all over Blair Water. There is some mystery about Ilse's mother which I cannot fathom. Dr Burnley and Ilse live alone. Rhoda says Dr Burnley says he will have no devils of women in that house. That speech is wikked but striking. Old Mrs Simms goes over and cooks dinner and supper for them and then vamooses and they get their own breakfast. The doctor sweeps out the house now and then and Ilse never does anything but run wild. The doctor never smiles so Rhoda says. He must be like King Henry the Second.

"I would like to get akwanted with Ilse. She isn't as sweet as Rhoda but I like her looks, too. But she doesn't come to school much and Rhoda says I mustn't have any chum but her or she will cry her eyes out. Rhoda loves me as much as I love her. We are both going to pray that we may live together all our lives and die the same day.

"Aunt Elizabeth always puts up my school dinner for me. She won't give me anything but plain bread and butter but she cuts good thick slices and the butter is thick too and never has the horrid taste Ellen Greene's butter used to have. And Aunt Laura slips in a cooky or an apple turnover when Aunt Elizabeth's back is turned. Aunt Elizabeth says apple turnovers are not helthy for me. Why is it that the nicest things never are helthy, Father? Ellen Greene used to say that too.

"My teacher's name is Miss Brownell. I don't like the cut of her jib. (That is a naughtical frays that Cousin Jimmy uses. I know frays is not spelled right but there is no dixonary at New Moon but that is the sound of it.) She is too sarkastik and she likes to make you rediklus. Then she laughs at you in a disagreeable, snorting way. But I forgave her for slapping me and I took a bouquet to her to school next day to make up. She receeved it very coldly and let it fade on her desk. In a story she would have wepped on my neck. I don't know whether it is any use forgiving people or not. Yes, it is, it makes you feel more comfortable yourself. You never had to ware baby aprons and sunbonnets because you were a boy so you can't understand how I feel about it. And the aprons are made of such good stuff that they will never ware out and it will be years before I grow out of them. But I have a white dress for church with a black silk sash and a white leghorn hat with black bows and black kid slippers, and I feel very elegant in them. I wish I could have a bang but Aunt Elizabeth will not hear of it. Rhoda told me I had beautiful eyes. I wish she hadn't. I have always suspekted my eyes were beautiful but I was not sure. Now that I know they are I'm afraid I'll always be wondering if people notis it. I have to go to bed at half past eight and I don't like it but I sit up in bed and look out of the window till it gets dark, so I get square with Aunt Elizabeth that way, and I listen to the sound the sea makes. I like it now though it always makes me feel sorrowful, but it's a kind of a nice sorrow. I have to sleep with Aunt Elizabeth and I don't like that either because if I move ever so little she says I figit but she admits that I don't kick. And

86

she won't let me put the window up. She doesn't like fresh air or light in the house. The parlour is dark as a toomb. I went in one day and rolled up all the blinds and Aunt Elizabeth was horrified and called me a little hussy and gave me the Murray look. You would suppose I had committed a crime. I felt so insulted that I came up to the garret and wrote a deskription of myself being drowned on a letter-bill and then I felt better. Aunt Elizabeth said I was never to go into the parlour again without permission but I don't want to. I am afraid of the parlour. All the walls are hung over with pictures of our ancestors and there is not one good-looking person among them except Grand-father Murray who looks handsome but very cross. The spare-room is upstairs and is just as gloomy as the parlour. Aunt Elizabeth only lets distingwished people sleep there. I like the kitchen in daytime, and the garret and the cook-house and the sitting-room and the hall because of the lovely red front door and I love the dairy, but I don't like the other New Moon rooms. Oh, I forgot the cellar cubbord. I love to go down there and look at the beautiful rows of jam and jelly pots. Cousin Jimmy says it is a New Moon tradishun that the jam pots must never be empty. What a lot of tradishuns New Moon has. It is a very spashus house, and the trees are lovely. I have named the three lombardys at the garden gate the Three Princesses and I have named the old summer house Emily's Bower, and the big apple-tree by the old orchard gate the Praying Tree because it holds up its long boughs exactly as Mr Dare holds up his arms in church when he prays.

"Aunt Elizabeth has given me the little right hand top burow drawer to keep my things in.

"Oh, Father dear, I have made a great diskoverry. I wish I had made it when you were alive for I think you'd have liked to know. *I can write poetry*. Perhaps I could have written it long ago if I'd tried. But after that first day in school I felt I was bound in honnour to try and it is so easy. There is a little curly black-covered book in Aunt Elizabeth's bookcase called Thompson's Seasons and I decided I would write a poem on a season and the first three lines are,

Now Autumn comes ripe with the peech and pear,

The sportsman's horn is heard throughout the land,

And the poor partridge fluttering falls dead.

"Of course there are no peeches in P. E. Island and I never heard a sportsman's horn here either, but you don't have to stick too close to facts in poetry. I filled a whole letter-bill with it and then I ran and read it to Aunt Laura. I thought she would be overjoyed to find she had a niece who could write poetry but she took it very coolly and said it didn't sound much like poetry. It's blank verse I cryed. *Very* blank said Aunt Elizabeth sarcastically though I hadn't asked *her* opinion. But I think I will write ryming poetry after this so that there will be no mistake about it and I intend to be a poetess when I grow up and become famus. I hope also that I will be silph-like. A poetess should be silph-like. Cousin Jimmy makes poetry too. He has made over 1000 pieces but he never writes any down but carries them in his head. I offered to give him some of my letter-bills—for he is very kind to me—but he said he was too old to learn new habits. I haven't heard any of his poetry yet because the spirit hasn't moved him but I am very angshus to and I am sorry they don't fatten the pigs till the fall. I like Cousin Jimmy more and more all the time, except when he takes his queer spells of looking and talking. Then he fritens me but they never last long. I have read a good many of the books in the New Moon bookcase. A history of the reformation in France, very relijus and sad. A little fat book deskribing the months in England and the afoursaid Thompson's Seasons. I like to read them because they have so many pretty words in them, but I don't like the feel of them. The paper is so rough and thick it makes me creepy. Travels in Spain, very fassinating, with lovely smooth shiny paper, a missionary book on the Pacific Islands, pictures very interesting because of the way the heathen chiefs arrange their hair. After they became Christians they cut it off which I think was a pity. Mrs Hemans Poems. I am passhunately fond of poetry, also of stories about desert islands. Rob Roy, a novel, but I only read a little of it when Aunt Elizabeth said I must stop because I must not read novels. Aunt Laura says to read it on the sly. I don't see why it wouldn't be all right to obey Aunt Laura but I have a queer feeling about it and I haven't yet. A lovely Tiger-book, full of pictures and stories of tigers that make me feel so nice and shivery. The Royal Road, also relijus but some fun in it so very good for Sundays. Reuben and Grace, a story but not a novel, because Reuben and Grace are brother and sister and there is no getting married. Little Katy and Jolly Jim, same as above but not so exciting and traggic. Nature's Mighty Wonders which is good and improving. Alice in Wonderland, which is perfectly lovely, and the Memoirs of Anzonetta B. Peters who was converted at seven and died at twelve. When anybody asked for a question she answered with a hym verse. That is after she was converted. Before that she spoke English. Aunt Elizabeth told me I ought to try to be like Anzonetta. I think I might be an Alice under more faverable circumstances but I am sure I can never be as good as Anzonetta was and I don't believe I want to be because she never had any fun. She got sick as soon as she was converted and suffered aggonies for years. Besides I am sure that if I talked hyms to people it would exite ridicule. I tried it once. Aunt Laura asked me the other day if I would like blue stripes better than red in my next winter's stockings and I answered just as Anzonetta did when asked a similar question, only different, about a sack,

Jesus Thy blood and rightchusness

My beauty are, my glorious dress.

And Aunt Laura said was I crazy and Aunt Elizabeth said I was irreverent. So I know it wouldn't work. Besides, Anzonetta couldn't eat anything for years having ulsers in her stomach and I am pretty fond of good eating.

"Old Mr Wales on the Derry Pond Road is dying of canser. Jennie Strang says his wife has her morning all ready.

"I wrote a biograffy of Saucy Sal to-day and a deskripshun of the road in Lofty John's bush. I will pin them to this letter so you can read them too. Good night my beloved Father.

"Yours most obedient humble servant,

"*Emily B. Starr.*

"P. S. I think Aunt Laura loves me. I like to be loved, Father dear.

"*E. B. S.*"

GROWING PAINS

There was a great deal of suppressed excitement in school during the last week in June, the cause thereof being Rhoda Stuart's birthday party, which was to take place early in July. The amount of heart-burning was incredible. Who was to be invited? That was the great question. There were some who knew they wouldn't and some who knew they would; but there were more who were in truly horrible suspense. Everybody paid court to Emily because she was Rhoda's dearest friend and might conceivably have some voice in the selection of guests. Jennie Strang even went as far as bluntly to offer Emily a beautiful white box with a gorgeous picture of Queen Victoria on the cover, to keep her pencils in, if she would procure her an invitation. Emily refused the bribe and said grandly that she could not interfere in such a delicate matter. Emily really did put on some airs about it. *She* was sure of her invitation. Rhoda had told her about the party weeks before and had talked it all over with her. It was to be a very grand affair—a birthday cake covered with pink icing and adorned with ten tall pink candles—ice-cream and oranges—and written invitations on pink, gilt-edged note-paper *sent through the post-office*—this last being an added touch of exclusiveness. Emily dreamed about that party day and night and had her present all ready for Rhoda—a pretty hair-ribbon which Aunt Laura had brought from Shrewsbury.

On the first Sunday in July Emily found herself sitting beside Jennie Strang in Sunday-school for the opening exercises. Generally she and Rhoda sat together, but now Rhoda was sitting three seats ahead with a strange little girl—a very gay and gorgeous little girl, dressed in blue silk, with a large, flower-wreathed leghorn hat on her elaborately curled hair, white lace-work stockings on her pudgy legs and a bang that came clean down to her eyes. Not all her fine feathers could make a really fine bird of her, however; she was not in the least pretty and her expression was cross and contemptuous.

"Who is the girl sitting with Rhoda?" whispered Emily.

"Oh, she's Muriel Porter," answered Jennie. "She's a towny, you know. She's come out to spend her vacation with her aunt, Jane Beatty. I hate her. If I was her I'd never *dream* of wearing blue with a skin as dark as hers. But the Porters are rich and Muriel thinks she's a wonder. They say Rhoda and her have been *awful thick* since she came out— Rhoda's always chasing after anybody she thinks is up in the world."

Emily stiffened up. She was not going to listen to disparaging remarks about her friends. Jennie felt the stiffening and changed her note.

"Anway, I'm *glad* I'm not invited to Rhoda's old party. I wouldn't *want* to go when Muriel Porter will be there, putting on her airs."

"How do you know you are not invited?" wondered Emily.

"Why, the invitations went out yesterday. Didn't you get yours?"

"No—o—o."

"Did you get your mail?"

"Yes—Cousin Jimmy got it."

"Well, maybe Mrs Beecher forgot to give it to him. Likely you'll get it to-morrow."

Emily agreed that it was likely. But a queer cold sensation of dismay had invaded her being, which was not removed by the fact that after Sunday-school Rhoda strutted away with Muriel Porter without a glance at any one else. On Monday Emily herself went to the post-office, but there was no pink envelope for her. She cried herself to sleep that night, but did not quite give up hope until Tuesday had passed. Then she faced the terrible truth—that she—she, Emily Byrd Starr, of New Moon—had not been invited to Rhoda's party. The thing was incredible. There *must* be a mistake somewhere. Had Cousin Jimmy lost the invitation on the road home? Had Rhoda's grown-up sister who wrote the invitations overlooked her name? Had—Emily's unhappy doubts were for ever resolved into bitter certainty by Jennie, who joined her as she left the post-office. There was a malicious light in Jennie's beady eyes. Jennie liked Emily quite well by now, in spite of their passage-at-arms on the day of their first meeting, but she liked to see her pride humbled for all that.

"So you're not invited to Rhoda's party after all."

"No," admitted Emily.

It was a very bitter moment for her. The Murray pride was sorely wrung—and, beneath the Murray pride, something else had been grievously wounded but was not yet quite dead.

"Well, I call it dirt mean," said Jennie, quite honestly sympathetic in spite of her secret satisfaction. "After all the fuss she's made over you, too! But that's Rhoda Stuart all over. Deceitful is no name for *her.*"

"I don't think she's deceitful," said Emily, loyal to the last ditch. "I believe there's some mistake about my not being invited."

Jennie stared.

"Then you don't know the reason? Why, Beth Beatty told me the whole story. Muriel Porter hates you and she just up and told Rhoda that she would not go to her party if you were invited. And Rhoda was so crazy to have a town girl there that she promised she wouldn't invite you."

"Muriel Porter doesn't know me," gasped Emily. "How can she hate me?"

Jennie grinned impishly.

"*I* can tell you. She's *dead struck* on Fred Stuart and Fred knows it and he teased her by praising *you* up to her—told her you were the sweetest girl in Blair Water and he meant to have you for *his girl* when you were a little older. And Muriel was so mad and jealous she made Rhoda leave you out. *I* wouldn't care if I was you. A Murray of New Moon is away above such trash. As for Rhoda not being deceitful, I can tell you she *is.* Why, she told you that she didn't know that snake was in the box, when it was her thought of doing it in the first place."

Emily was too crushed to reply. She was glad that Jennie had to switch off down her own lane and leave her alone. She hurried home, afraid that she could not keep the tears back until she got there. Disappointment about the party—humiliation over the insult— all were swallowed up in the anguish of a faith betrayed and a trust outraged. Her love of Rhoda was quite dead now and Emily smarted to the core of her soul with the pain of the blow that had killed it. It was a child's tragedy—and all the more bitter for that, since there was no one to understand. Aunt Elizabeth told her that birthday parties were all nonsense and that the Stuarts were not a family that the Murrays had ever associated with. And even Aunt Laura, though she petted and comforted, did not realize how deep and grievous the hurt had been— so deep and grievous that Emily could not even write about it to her father, and had no outlet for the violence of emotion that racked her being.

The next Sunday Rhoda was alone in Sunday-school, Muriel Porter having been suddenly summoned back to town by her father's illness; and Rhoda looked sweetly towards Emily. But Emily sailed past her with a head held very high and scorn on every lineament. She would *never* have anything to do with Rhoda Stuart again—she couldn't. She despised Rhoda more than ever for trying to get back with her, now that the town girl for whom she had sacrificed her was gone. It was not for Rhoda she mourned—it was for the friendship that had been so dear to her. Rhoda *had* been dear and sweet on the surface at least, and Emily had found intense happiness in their companionship. Now it was gone and she could never, *never* love or trust anybody again. *There* lay the sting.

It poisoned everything. Emily was of a nature which even as a child, did not readily recover from or forget such a blow. She moped about New Moon, lost her appetite and grew thin. She hated to go to Sunday-school because she thought the other girls exulted in her humiliation and her estrangement from Rhoda. Some slight feeling of the kind there was, perhaps, but Emily morbidly exaggerated it. If two girls whispered or giggled together she thought she was being discussed and laughed at. If one of them walked home with her she thought it was out of condescending pity because she was friendless. For a month Emily was the most unhappy little being in Blair Water.

"I think I must have been put under a curse at birth," she reflected disconsolately.

Aunt Elizabeth had a more prosaic idea to account for Emily's langour and lack of appetite. She had come to the conclusion that Emily's heavy masses of hair "took from her strength" and that she would be much stronger and better if it were cut off. With Aunt Elizabeth to decide was to act. One morning she coolly informed Emily that her hair was to be "shingled."

Emily could not believe her ears.

"You don't mean that you are going to cut off my hair, Aunt Elizabeth," she exclaimed.

"Yes, I mean exactly that," said Aunt Elizabeth firmly. "You have entirely too much hair especially for hot weather. I feel sure that is why you have been so miserable lately. Now, I don't want any crying."

But Emily could not keep the tears back.

"Don't cut it *all* off," she pleaded. "Just cut a good big bang. Lots of the girls have their hair banged clean from the crown of their heads. That would take half my hair off and the rest won't take too much strength."

"There will be no bangs here," said Aunt Elizabeth. "I've told you so often enough. I'm going to shingle your hair close all over your head for the hot weather. You'll be thankful to me some day for it."

Emily felt anything but thankful just then.

"It's my one beauty," she sobbed, "it and my lashes. I suppose you want to cut off my lashes too."

Aunt Elizabeth *did* distrust those long, upcurled fringes of Emily's, which were an inheritance from the girlish stepmother, and too un-Murray-like to be approved; but she had no designs against them. The hair must go, however, and she curtly bade Emily wait there, without any fuss, until she got the scissors.

Emily waited—quite hopelessly. She must lose her lovely hair—the hair her father had been so proud of. It might grow again in time—if Aunt Elizabeth let it—but that would take years, and meanwhile what a fright she would be! Aunt Laura and Cousin Jimmy were out; she had no one to back her up; this horrible thing must happen.

Aunt Elizabeth returned with the scissors; they clicked suggestively as she opened them; that click, as if by magic, seemed to loosen something—some strange formidable power in Emily's soul. She turned deliberately around and faced her aunt. She felt her brows drawing together in an unaccustomed way—she felt an uprush as from unknown depths of some irresistible surge of energy.

"Aunt Elizabeth," she said, looking straight at the lady with the scissors, *"my hair is not going to be cut off.* Let me hear no more of this."

An amazing thing happened to Aunt Elizabeth. She turned pale—she laid the scissors down—she looked aghast for one moment at the transformed or possessed child before her—and then for the first time in her life Elizabeth Murray turned tail and fled—literally fled—to the kitchen.

"What is the matter, Elizabeth?" cried Laura, coming in from the cook-house.

"I saw—Father—looking from her face," gasped Elizabeth,

trembling. "And she said, 'Let me hear no more of this'—just as *he* always said it—his very words."

Emily overheard her and ran to the sideboard mirror. She had had, while she was speaking, an uncanny feeling of wearing somebody else's face instead of her own. It was vanishing now—but Emily caught a glimpse of it as it left—the Murray look, she supposed. No wonder it had frightened Aunt Elizabeth—it frightened herself—she was glad that it had gone. She shivered—she fled to her garret retreat and cried; but somehow, she knew that her hair would not be cut.

Nor was it; Aunt Elizabeth never referred to the matter again. But several days passed before she meddled much with Emily.

It was a rather curious fact that from that day Emily ceased to grieve over her lost friend. The matter had suddenly become of small importance. It was as if it had happened so long ago that nothing, save the mere emotionless memory of it, remained. Emily speedily regained appetite and animation, resumed her letters to her father and found that life tasted good again, marred only by a mysterious prescience that Aunt Elizabeth had it in for her in regard to her defeat in the matter of her hair and would get even sooner or later.

Aunt Elizabeth "got even" within the week. Emily was to go on an errand to the shop. It was a broiling day and she had been allowed to go barefooted at home; but now she must put on boots and stockings. Emily rebelled—it was too hot—it was too dusty—she couldn't walk that long half-mile in buttoned boots. Aunt Elizabeth was inexorable. No Murray must be seen barefooted away from home—and on they went. But the minute Emily was outside the New Moon gate she deliberately sat down, took them off, stowed them in a hole in the dyke, and pranced away barefooted.

She did her errand and returned with an untroubled conscience. How beautiful the world was—how softly blue was the great, round Blair Water—how glorious that miracle of buttercups in the wet field below Lofty John's bush! At sight of it Emily stood stock still and composed a verse of poetry.

Buttercup, flower of the yellow dye,

I see thy cheerful face

Greeting and nodding everywhere

Careless of time and place.

In boggy field or public road

Or cultured garden's pale

You sport your petals satin-soft,

And down within the vale.

So far, so good. But Emily wanted another verse to round the poem off properly and the divine afflatus seemed gone. She walked dreamily home, and by the time she reached New Moon she had got her verse and was reciting it to herself with an agreeable sense of completion.

You cast your loveliness around

Where'er you chance to be,

And you shall always, buttercup,

Be a flower dear to me.

Emily felt very proud. This was her third poem and undoubtedly her best. Nobody could say *it* was very blank. She must hurry up to the garret and write it on a letter-bill. But Aunt Elizabeth was confronting her on the steps.

"Emily, where are your boots and stockings?"

Emily came back from cloudland with a disagreeable jolt. She had forgotten all about boots and stockings.

"In the hole by the gate," she said flatly.

"You went to the store barefooted?"

"Yes."

"After I had told you not to?"

This seemed to Emily a superfluous question and she did not answer it. But Aunt Elizabeth's turn had come.

Ilse

Emily was locked in the spare-room and told that she must stay there until bedtime. She had pleaded against such a punishment in vain. She had tried to give the Murray look but it seemed that—in her case at any rate—it did not come at will.

"Oh, don't shut me up alone there, Aunt Elizabeth," she implored. "I know I was naughty—but don't put me in the spare-room."

Aunt Elizabeth was inexorable. She knew that it was a cruel thing to shut an over-sensitive child like Emily in that gloomy room. But she thought she was doing her duty. She did not realize and would not have for a moment believed that she was really wreaking her own smothered resentment with Emily for her defeat and fright on the day of the threatened hair-cutting. Aunt Elizabeth believed she had been stampeded on that occasion by a chance family resemblance coming out under stress, and she was ashamed of it. The Murray pride had smarted under that humbling, and the smart ceased to annoy her only when she turned the key of the spare-room on the white-faced culprit.

Emily, looking very small and lost and lonely, her eyes full of such fear as should have no place in a child's eyes, shrank close against the door of the spare-room. It was better that way. She could not imagine things behind her then. And the room was so big and dim that a dreadful number of things could be imagined in it. Its bigness and dimness filled her with a terror against which she could not strive. Ever since she could remember she had had a horror of being shut up alone in semi-darkness. She was not frightened of twilight out-of-doors, but this shadowy, walled gloom made of the spare-room a place of dread.

The window was hung with heavy, dark-green material, reinforced by drawn slat blinds. The big canopied bed, jutting out from the wall into the middle of the floor, was high and rigid and curtained also with dark draperies. *Anything* might jump at her out of such a bed. What if some great black hand should suddenly reach out of it—reach right across the floor—and pluck at her? The walls, like those of the parlour, were adorned with pictures of departed relatives. There *was* such a large connection of dead Murrays. The glasses of their frames gave out weird reflections of the spectral threads of light struggling through the slat blinds. Worst of all, right across the room from her, high up on the top of the black wardrobe, was a huge, stuffed white Arctic owl, staring at her with uncanny eyes. Emily shrieked aloud when she saw it, and then cowered down in her corner aghast at the sound she had made in the great, silent, echoing room. She wished that something *would* jump out of the bed and put an end to her.

"I wonder what Aunt Elizabeth would feel like if I was found here *dead*," she thought, vindictively.

In spite of her fright she began to dramatize it and felt Aunt Elizabeth's remorse so keenly that she decided only to be unconscious and come back to life when everybody was sufficiently scared and penitent. But people *had* died in this room—dozens of them. According to Cousin Jimmy it was a New Moon tradition that when any member of the family was near death he or she was promptly removed to the spare-room, to die amid surroundings of proper grandeur. Emily could *see* them dying, in that terrible bed. She felt that she was going to scream again, but she fought the impulse down. A Starr must not be a coward. Oh, that owl! Suppose, when she looked away from it and then looked back she would find that it had silently hopped down from the wardrobe and was coming towards her. Emily dared not look at it for fear that was just what had happened. *Didn't* the bed curtains stir and waver! She felt beads of cold perspiration on her forehead.

Then something did happen. A beam of sunlight struck through a small break in one of the slats of the blind and fell directly athwart the picture of Grandfather Murray hanging over the mantelpiece. It was a crayon "enlargement" copied from an old daguerreotype in the parlour below. In that gleam of light his face seemed veritably to leap out of the gloom at Emily with its grim frown strangely exaggerated. Emily's nerve gave way completely. In an ungovernable spasm of panic she rushed madly across the room to the window, dashed the curtains aside, and caught up the slat blind. A blessed flood of sunshine burst in. Outside was a wholesome, friendly, human world. And, of all wonders, there, leaning right against the window-sill was a ladder! For a moment Emily almost believed that a miracle had been worked for her escape.

Cousin Jimmy had tripped that morning over the ladder, lying lost among the burdocks under the balm-of-gileads behind the dairy. It was very rotten and he decided it was time it was disposed of. He had shouldered it up against the house so that he would be sure to see it on his return from the hayfield.

In less time than it takes to write of it Emily had got the window up, climbed out on the sill, and backed down the ladder. She was too intent on escaping from that horrible room to be conscious of the shakiness of the rotten rungs. When she reached the ground she bolted through the balm-of-gileads and over the fence into Lofty John's bush, nor did she stop running till she reached the path by the brook.

Then she paused for breath, exultant. She was full of a fearful joy with an elfin delight running through it. Sweet was the wind of freedom that was blowing over the ferns. She had escaped from the spare-room and its ghosts—she had got the better of mean old Aunt Elizabeth.

"I feel as if I was a little bird that had just got out of a cage," she told herself; and then she danced with joy of it all along her fairy path to the very end, where she found Ilse Burnley huddled up on the top of a fence panel, her pale-gold head making a spot of brilliance against the dark young firs that crowded around her. Emily had not seen her since that first day of school and again she thought she had never seen or pretended anybody just like Ilse.

"Well, Emily of New Moon," said Ilse, "where are you running to?"

"I'm running away," said Emily, frankly. "I was bad—at least, I was a little bad—and Aunt Elizabeth locked me in the spare-room. I hadn't been bad enough for *that*—it wasn't fair—so I got out of the window and down the ladder."

"You little cuss! I didn't think you'd gimp enough for that," said Ilse.

Emily gasped. It seemed very dreadful to be called a little cuss. But Ilse had said it quite admiringly.

"I don't think it was gimp," said Emily, too honest to take a compliment she didn't deserve. "I was too scared to stay in that room."

"Well, where are you going now?" asked Ilse. "You'll have to go somewhere—you can't stay out-doors. There's a thunderstorm coming up."

So there was. Emily did not like thunderstorms. And her conscience smote her.

"Oh," she said, "do you suppose God is bringing up that storm to punish me because I've run away?"

"No," said Ilse scornfully. "If there is any God He wouldn't make such a fuss over nothing."

"Oh, Ilse, don't you believe there is a God?"

"I don't know. Father says there isn't. But in that case how did things happen? Some days I believe there's a God and some days I don't. You'd better come home with me. There's nobody there. I was so dod-gastedly lonesome I took to the bush."

Ilse sprang down and held out her sunburned paw to Emily. Emily took it and they ran together over Lofty John's pasture to the old Burnley house which looked like a huge grey cat basking in the warm late sunshine, that had not yet been swallowed up by the menacing thunder-heads. Inside, it was full of furniture that must have been quite splendid once; but the disorder was dreadful and the dust lay thickly over everything. Nothing was in the right place apparently, and Aunt Laura would certainly have fainted with horror if she had seen the kitchen. But it was a good place to play. You didn't have to be careful not to mess things up. Ilse and Emily had a glorious game of hide and seek all over the house until the thunder got so heavy and the lightning so bright that Emily felt she must huddle on the sofa and nurse her courage.

"Aren't you ever afraid of thunder?" she asked Ilse.

"No, I ain't afraid of anything except the devil," said Ilse.

"I thought you didn't believe in the devil either—Rhoda said you didn't."

"Oh, there's a devil all right, Father says. It's only God he doesn't believe in. And if there *is* a devil and no God to keep him in order, is it any wonder I'm scared of him? Look here, Emily Byrd Starr, I like you—heaps. I've always liked you. I knew you'd soon be good and sick of that little, white-livered lying sneak of a Rhoda Stuart. *I* never tell lies. Father told me once he'd kill me if he ever caught me telling a lie. I want you for *my* chum. I'd go to school regular if I could sit with you."

"All right," said Emily off-handedly. No more sentimental Rhodian vows of eternal devotion for her. *That* phase was over.

"And you'll tell me things—nobody ever tells me things. And let *me* tell *you* things—I haven't anybody to tell things to," said Ilse. "And you won't be ashamed of me because my clothes are always queer and because I don't believe in God?"

"No. But if you knew Father's God you'd believe in *Him*."

"I wouldn't. Besides, there's only one God if there is any at all."

"I don't know," said Emily perplexedly. "No, it can't be like that. Ellen Greene's God isn't a bit like Father's, and neither is Aunt Elizabeth's. I don't think I'd *like* Aunt Elizabeth's, but He is a *dignified* God at least, and Ellen's isn't. And I'm sure Aunt Laura's is another one still—nice and kind but not wonderful like Father's."

"Well never mind—I don't like talking about God," said Ilse uncomfortably.

"*I* do," said Emily. "I think God is a very interesting subject, and I'm going to pray for you, Ilse, that you can believe in Father's God."

"Don't you dast!" shouted Ilse, who for some mysterious reason did not like the idea. "I won't be prayed for!"

"Don't you ever pray yourself, Ilse?"

"Oh, now and then—when I feel lonesome at night—or when I'm in a scrape. But I don't want any one else to pray for me. If I catch you doing it, Emily Starr, I'll tear your eyes out. And don't you go sneaking and praying for me behind my back either."

"All right, I won't," said Emily sharply, mortified at the failure of her well-meant offer. "I'll pray for every single soul I know, but I'll leave you out."

For a moment Ilse looked as if she didn't like this either. Then she laughed and gave Emily a volcanic hug.

"Well, anyway, please like me. Nobody likes me, you know."

"Your father *must* like you, Ilse."

"He doesn't," said Ilse positively. "Father doesn't care a hoot about me. I think there's times when he hates the sight of me. I wish he *did* like me because he can be awful nice when he likes any one. Do you know what I'm going to be when I grow up? I'm going to be an elo-cu-tion-ist."

"What's that?"

"A woman who recites at concerts. I can do it dandy. What are you going to be?"

"A poetess."

"Golly!" said Ilse, apparently overcome. "I don't believe *you* can write poetry," she added.

"I can so, true," cried Emily. "I've written three pieces—'Autumn' and 'Lines to Rhoda'—only I burned *that*—and 'An Address to a Buttercup.' I composed it to-day and it is my—my masterpiece."

"Let's hear it," ordered Ilse.

Nothing loath, Emily proudly repeated her lines. Somehow she did not mind letting Ilse hear them.

"Emily Byrd Starr, you *didn't* make that out of your own head?"

"I did."

"Cross your heart?"

"Cross my heart."

"Well"—Ilse drew a long breath—"I guess you *are* a poetess all right."

It was a very proud moment for Emily—one of the great moments of life, in fact. Her world had conceded her standing. But now other things had to be thought of. The storm was over and the sun had set. It was twilight—it would soon be dark. She must get home and back into the spare-room before her absence was discovered. It was dreadful to think of going back but she must do it lest a worse thing come upon her at Aunt Elizabeth's hands. Just now, under the inspiration of Ilse's personality, she was full of Dutch courage. Besides, it would soon be her bedtime and she would be let out. She trotted home through Lofty John's bush, that was full of the wandering, mysterious lamps of the fireflies, dodged cautiously through the balm-of-gileads—and stopped short in dismay. The ladder was gone!

Emily went around to the kitchen door, feeling that she was going straight to her doom. But for once the way of the transgressor was made sinfully easy. Aunt Laura was alone in the kitchen.

"Emily dear, where on earth did you come from?" she exclaimed. "I was just going up to let you out. Elizabeth said I might—she's gone to prayer-meeting."

Aunt Laura did not say that she had tiptoed several times to the spare-room door and had been racked with anxiety over the silence behind it. Was the child unconscious from fright? Not even while the thunderstorm was going on would relentless Elizabeth allow that door to be opened. And here was Miss Emily walking unconcernedly in out of the twilight after all this agony. For a moment even Aunt Laura was annoyed. But when she heard Emily's tale her only feeling was thankfulness that Juliet's child had not broken her neck on that rotten ladder.

Emily felt that she had got off better than she deserved. She knew

Aunt Laura would keep the secret; and Aunt Laura let her give Saucy Sal a whole cupful of strippings, and gave her a big plummy cooky and put her to bed with kisses.

"You oughtn't to be so good to me because I *was* bad to-day," Emily said, between delicious mouthfuls. "I suppose I disgraced the Murrays going barefoot."

"If I were you I'd hide my boots every time I went out of the gate," said Aunt Laura. "But I wouldn't forget to put them on before I came back. What Elizabeth doesn't know will never hurt her."

Emily reflected over this until she had finished her cooky. Then she said,

"That would be nice, but I don't mean to do it any more. I guess I must obey Aunt Elizabeth because she's the head of the family."

"Where do you get such notions?" said Aunt Laura.

"Out of my head. Aunt Laura, Ilse Burnley and I are going to be chums. I like her—I've always felt I'd like her if I had the chance. I don't believe I can ever *love* any girl again, but I *like* her."

"Poor Ilse!" said Aunt Laura, sighing.

"Yes, her father doesn't like her. Isn't it dreadful?" said Emily. "Why doesn't he?"

"He does—really. He only thinks he doesn't."

"But *why* does he think it?"

"You are too young to understand, Emily."

Emily hated to be told she was too young to understand. She felt that she could understand perfectly well if only people would take the trouble to explain things to her and not be so mysterious.

"I wish I could pray for her. It wouldn't be fair, though, when I know how she feels about it. But I've always asked God to bless all my friends so she'll be in *that* and maybe some good will come of it. Is 'golly' a proper word to say, Aunt Laura?"

"No—no!"

"I'm sorry for that," said Emily, seriously, "because it's very striking."

THE TANSY PATCH

Emily and Ilse had a splendid fortnight of fun before their first fight. It was really quite a terrible fight, arising out of a simple argument as to whether they would or would not have a parlour in the playhouse they were building in Lofty John's bush. Emily wanted a parlour and Ilse didn't. Ilse lost her temper at once, and went into a true Burnley tantrum. She was very fluent in her rages and the volley of abusive "dictionary words" which she hurled at Emily would have staggered most of the Blair Water girls. But Emily was too much at home with words to be floored so easily; she grew angry too, but in the cool, dignified, Murray way which was more exasperating than violence. When Ilse had to pause for breath in her diatribes, Emily, sitting on a big stone with her knees crossed, her eyes black and her cheeks crimson, interjected little sarcastic retorts that infuriated Ilse still further. Ilse was crimson, too, and her eyes were pools of scintillating, tawny fire. They were both so pretty in their fury that it was almost a pity they couldn't have been angry all the time.

"You needn't suppose, you little puling, snivelling chit, that you are going to boss *me,* just because you live at New Moon," shrieked Ilse, as an ultimatum, stamping her foot.

"I'm not going to boss you—I'm not going to associate with you ever again," retorted Emily, disdainfully.

"I'm glad to be rid of you—you proud, stuck-up, conceited, top-lofty *biped,*" cried Ilse. "Never you speak to me again. And don't you go about Blair Water saying things about me, either."

This was unbearable to a girl who *never* "said things" about her friends or once-friends.

"I'm not going to *say* things about you," said Emily deliberately. "I'm just going to *think* them."

This was far more aggravating than speech and Emily knew it. Ilse was driven quite frantic by it. Who knew what unearthly things Emily might be thinking about her any time she took the notion to? Ilse had already discovered what a fertile imagination Emily had.

"Do you suppose I care what you think, you insignificant serpent? Why, you haven't *any* sense."

"I've got something then that's far better," said Emily, with a maddening superior smile. "Something that *you* can *never* have, Ilse Burnley."

Ilse doubled her fists as if she would like to demolish Emily by physical force.

"If I couldn't write better poetry than you, I'd hang myself," she derided.

"I'll lend you a dime to buy a rope," said Emily.

Ilse glared at her, vanquished.

"You can go to the devil!" she said.

Emily got up and went, not to the devil, but back to New Moon. Ilse relieved *her* feelings by knocking the boards of their china closet down, and kicking their "moss gardens" to pieces, and departed also.

Emily felt exceedingly badly. Here was another friendship destroyed—a friendship, too, that had been very delightful and satisfying. Ilse *had* been a splendid chum—there was no doubt about that. After Emily had cooled down she went to the dormer-window and cried.

"Wretched, wretched me!" she sobbed, dramatically, but very sincerely.

Yet the bitterness of her break with Rhoda was not present. *This* quarrel was fair and open and above-board. She had not been stabbed in the back. But of course she and Ilse would never be chums again. You couldn't be chums with a person who called you a chit and a biped, and a serpent, and told you to go to the devil. The thing was impossible. And besides, Ilse could *never* forgive *her*—for Emily was honest enough to admit to herself that she had been very aggravating, too.

Yet, when Emily went to the playhouse next morning, bent on retrieving her share of broken dishes and boards, there was Ilse, skipping around, hard at work, with all the shelves back in place, the moss garden re-made, and a beautiful parlour laid out and connected with the living-room by a spruce arch.

"Hello, you. Here's your parlour and I hope you'll be satisfied now," she said gaily. "What's kept you so long? I thought you were never coming."

This rather posed Emily after her tragic night, wherein she had buried her second friendship and wept over its grave. She was not prepared for so speedy a resurrection. As far as Ilse was concerned it seemed as if no quarrel had ever taken place.

"Why, that was *yesterday*," she said in amazement, when Emily, rather distantly, referred to it. Yesterday and to-day were two entirely different things in Ilse's philosophy. Emily accepted it—she found she had to. Ilse, it transpired, could no more help flying into tantrums now and then than she could help being jolly and affectionate between them. What amazed Emily, in whom things were bound to rankle for a time, was the way in which Ilse appeared to forget a quarrel the moment it was over. To be called a serpent and a crocodile one minute and hugged and darling-ed the next was somewhat disconcerting until time and experience took the edge off it.

"Aren't I nice enough between times to make up for it?" demanded Ilse. "Dot Payne never flies into tempers, but would you like *her* for a chum?"

"No, she's too stupid," admitted Emily.

"And Rhoda Stuart is never out of temper, but you got enough of *her*. Do you think I'd ever treat you as she did?"

No, Emily had no doubt on this point. Whatever Ilse was or was not, she was loyal and true.

And certainly Rhoda Stuart and Dot Payne compared to Ilse were "as moonlight unto sunlight and as water unto wine"—or would have been if Emily had as yet known anything more of her Tennyson than the *Bugle Song*.

"You can't have everything," said Ilse. "I've got Dad's temper and that's all there is to it. Wait till you see *him* in one of his rages."

Emily had not seen this so far. She had often been down in the Burnley's house but on the few occasions when Dr Burnley had been home he had ignored her save for a curt nod. He was a busy man, for, whatever his shortcomings were, his skill was unquestioned and the bounds of his practice extended far. By the sick-bed he was as gentle and sympathetic as he was brusque and sarcastic away from it. As long as you were ill there was nothing Dr Burnley would not do for you; once you were well he had apparently no further use for you. He had been absorbed all through July trying to save Teddy Kent's life up at the Tansy Patch. Teddy was out of danger now and able to be up, but his improvement was not speedy enough to satisfy Dr Burnley. One day he held up Emily and Ilse, who were heading through the lawn to the pond, with fishing-hooks and a can of fat, abominable worms—the latter manipulated solely by Ilse—and ordered them to betake themselves up to the Tansy Patch and play with Teddy Kent.

"He's lonesome and moping. Go and cheer him up," said the doctor.

Ilse was rather loath to go. She liked Teddy, but it seemed she did not like his mother. Emily was secretly not averse. She had seen Teddy Kent but once, at Sunday-school the day before he was taken seriously ill, and she had liked his looks. It had seemed that he liked hers, too, for she caught him staring shyly at her over the intervening pews several times. He was very handsome, Emily decided. She liked his thick, dark-brown hair and his black-browed blue eyes, and for the first time it occurred to her that it might be rather nice to have a boy playmate, too. Not a "beau" of course. Emily hated the school jargon that called a boy your "beau" if he happened to give you a pencil or an apple and picked you out frequently for his partner in the games.

"Teddy's nice but his mother is queer," Ilse told her on their way to the Tansy Patch. "She never goes out anywhere—not even to church—but I guess it's because of the scar on her face. They're not Blair Water people—they've only been living at the Tansy Patch since last fall. They're poor and proud and not many people visit them. But Teddy is awfully nice, so if his mother gives us some black looks we needn't mind."

Mrs Kent gave them no black looks, though her reception was rather distant. Perhaps she, too, had received some orders from the doctor. She was a tiny creature, with enormous masses of dull, soft, silky, fawn hair, dark, mournful eyes, and a broad scar running slantwise across her pale face. Without the scar she must have been pretty, and she had a voice as soft and uncertain as the wind in the tansy. Emily, with her instinctive faculty of sizing up people she met, felt that Mrs Kent was not a happy woman.

The Tansy Patch was east of the Disappointed House, between the Blair Water and the sand-dunes. Most people considered it a bare, lonely, neglected place, but Emily thought it was fascinating. The little clap-boarded house topped a small hill, over which tansy grew in a hard, flaunting, aromatic luxuriance, rising steeply and abruptly from a main road. A straggling rail fence, almost smothered in wild rosebushes, bounded the domain, and a sagging, ill-used little gate gave ingress from the road. Stones were let into the side of the hill for steps up to the front door. Behind the house was a tumbledown little barn, and a field of flowering buckwheat, creamy green, sloping down to the Blair Water. In front was a crazy veranda around which a brilliant band of red poppies held up their enchanted cups.

Teddy was unfeignedly glad to see them, and they had a happy afternoon together. There was some colour in Teddy's clear olive skin when it ended and his dark-blue eyes were brighter. Mrs Kent took in these signs greedily and asked the girls to come back, with an eagerness that was yet not cordiality. But they had found the Tansy Patch a charming place and were glad to go again. For the rest of the vacation there was hardly a day when they did not go up to it—preferably in the long, smoky, delicious August evenings when the white moths sailed over the tansy plantation and the golden twilight faded into dusk and purple over the green slopes beyond and fireflies lighted their goblin torches by the pond. Sometimes they played games in the tansy patch, when Teddy and Emily somehow generally found themselves on the same side and then no more than a match for agile, quick-witted Ilse; sometimes Teddy took them to the barn loft and showed them his little collection of drawings. Both girls thought them very wonderful without knowing in the least how wonderful they really were. It seemed like magic to see Teddy take a pencil and bit of paper and with a few quick strokes of his slim brown fingers bring out a sketch of Ilse or Emily or Smoke or Buttercup, that looked ready to speak—or meow.

Smoke and Buttercup were the Tansy Patch cats. Buttercup was a chubby, yellow, delightful creature hardly out of kitten-hood. Smoke was a big Maltese and an aristocrat from the tip of his nose to the tip of his tail. There was no doubt whatever that he belonged to the cat caste of Vere de Vere. He had emerald eyes and a coat of plush. The only white thing about him was an adorable dicky.

Emily thought of all the pleasant hours spent at the Tansy Patch the pleasantest were those, when, tired with play, they all three sat on the crazy veranda steps in the mystery and enchantment of the borderland 'tween light and dark when the little clump of spruce behind the barn looked like beautiful, dark, phantom trees. The clouds of the west faded into grey and a great round yellow moon rose over the fields to be reflected brokenly in the pond, where the Wind Woman was making wonderful, woven lights and shadows.

Mrs Kent never joined them, though Emily had a creepy conviction that she was watching them stealthily from behind the kitchen blind. Teddy and Ilse sang school ditties, and Ilse recited, and Emily told stories; or they sat in happy silence, each anchored in some secret port of dreams, while the cats chased each other madly over the hill and through the tansy, tearing round and round the house like possessed creatures. They would spring up at the children with sudden pounces and spring as suddenly away. Their eyes gleamed like jewels, their tails swayed like plumes. They were palpitating with nervous, stealthy life.

"Oh, isn't it good to be alive—like this?" Emily said once. "Wouldn't it be dreadful if one had never lived?"

Still, existence was not wholly unclouded—Aunt Elizabeth took care of that. Aunt Elizabeth only permitted the visits to the Tansy Patch under protest, and because Dr Burnley had ordered them.

"Aunt Elizabeth does not approve of Teddy," Emily wrote in one of her letters to her father—which epistles were steadily multiplying on the old garret sofa shelf. "The first time I asked her if I might go and play with Teddy she looked at me *severely* and said, Who is this Teddy person. We do not know anything about these Kents. Remember, Emily, the Murrays do not associate with every one. I said I am a Starr—I am not a Murray, you said so yourself. Dear Father I did not mean to be impertent but Aunt Elizabeth said I was and would not speak to me the rest of the day. She seemed to think that was a very bad punishment but I did not mind it much only it is rather unpleasant to have your own family preserve a disdaneful silence towards you. But since then she lets me go to the Tansy Patch because Dr Burnley came and told her to. Dr Burnley has a *strange inflewence* over Aunt Elizabeth. I do not understand it. Rhoda said once that Aunt Elizabeth hoped Dr Burnley and Aunt Laura would make a match of it—which, you know means get married—but that is not so. Mrs Thomas Anderson was here one afternoon to tea. (Mrs Thomas Anderson is a big fat woman and her grandmother was a Murray and there is nothing else to say about *her*.) She asked Aunt Elizabeth if she thought Dr Burnley would marry again and Aunt Elizabeth said no, he would not and she did not think it right for people to marry a second time. Mrs Anderson said Sometimes I have thought he would take Laura. Aunt Elizabeth just swept her a hawty glance. There is no use in denying it, there are times when I am very proud of Aunt Elizabeth, even if I do not like her.

"Teddy is a very nice boy, Father. I think you would aprove of him. Should there be two p's in aprove? He can make splendid pictures and he is going to be a famus artist some day, and then he is going to paint my portrate. He keeps his pictures in the barn loft because his mother doesn't like to see them. He can whistle just like a bird. The Tansy Patch is a *very quante* place—espesially at night. I love the twilight there. We always have such fun in the twilight. The Wind Woman makes herself small in the tansy just like a tiny, tiny fairy and the cats are so queer and creepy and delightful then. They belong to Mrs Kent and Teddy is afraid to pet them much for fear she will drown them. She drowned a kitten once because she thought he liked it better than her. But he didn't because Teddy is *very much attatched* to his mother. He washes the dishes for her and helps her in all the house work. Ilse says the boys in school call him sissy for that but I think it is noble and manley of him. Teddy wishes she would let him have a dog but she wont. I have thought Aunt Elizabeth was tirannical but Mrs Kent is far worse in some ways. But then she loves Teddy and Aunt Elizabeth does not love me.

"But Mrs Kent doesn't like Ilse or me. She never says so but we feel it. She *never* asks us to stay to tea—and we've always been so polite to her. I believe she is jellus of us because Teddy likes us. Teddy gave me the sweetest picture of the Blair Water he had painted on a big white cowhawk shell but he said I mustn't let his mother know about it because she would cry. Mrs Kent is a very misterious person, very like some people you read of in books. I like misterious people but not too close. Her eyes always look hungry though she has plenty to eat. She never goes anywhere because she has a scar on her face where she was burned with a lamp exploding. It made my blood run cold, dear Father. How thankful I am that Aunt Elizabeth only burns candles. Some of the Murray tradishuns are very sensible. Mrs Kent is very relijus— what she calls relijus. She prays even in the middle of the day. Teddy says that before he was born into this world he lived in another one where there were two suns, one red and one blue. The days were red and the nights blue. I don't know where he got the idea but it sounds attractive to me. And he says the brooks run honey instead of water. But what did you do when you were thirsty, I said. Oh, we were never thirsty there. But I think I would *like* to be thirsty because then cold water tastes so good. *I* would like to live in the moon. It must be such a nice silvery place.

"Ilse says Teddy ought to like her best because there is more fun in her than in me but that is not true. There is just as much fun in me when my conshence doesn't bother me. I guess Ilse wants Teddy to like her best but she is not a jellus girl.

"I am glad to say that Aunt Elizabeth and Aunt Laura both aprove of my friendship with Ilse. It is so seldom they aprove of the same thing. I am getting used to fighting with Ilse now and don't mind it much. Besides I can fight pretty well myself when my blood is up. We fight about once a week but we make up right away and Ilse says things would be dull if there was never a row. I would like it better without rows but you can never tell what will make Ilse mad. She never gets mad twice over the same thing. She calls me dreadful names. Yesterday she called me a lousy lizard and a toothless viper. But somehow I didn't mind it much because I knew I wasn't lousy or toothless and she knew it too. I don't call her names because that is unladylike but I smile and that makes Ilse far madder than if I skowled and stamped as she does, and that is why I do it. Aunt Laura says I must be careful not to pick up the words Ilse uses and try to set her a good example because the poor child has no one to look after her propperly. I wish I could use some of her words because they are so striking. She gets them from her father. I think my aunts are too perticular. One night when the Rev. Mr Dare was here to tea I used the word bull in my conversashun. I said Ilse and I were afraid to go through Mr James Lee's pasture where the old well was because he had a cross bull there. After Mr Dare had gone Aunt Elizabeth gave me an awful skolding and told me I was never to use *that word* again. But she had been talking of tigers at tea—in connexshun with missionaries—and I can't understand why it is more disgraceful to talk about bulls than tigers. Of course bulls are feroshus animals but so are tigers. But Aunt Elizabeth says I am always disgracing them when they have company. When Mrs Lockwood was here from Shrewsbury last week they were talking about Mrs Foster Beck, who is a bride, and I said Dr Burnley thought she was devilishly pretty. Aunt Elizabeth said EMILY in an awful tone. She was pale with rath. Dr Burnley said it, I cryed, I am only kwoting. And Dr Burnley did say it the day I stayed to dinner with Ilse and Dr Jameson was there from Shrewsbury. I saw Dr Burnley in one of his rages that afternoon over something Mrs Simms had done in his office. It was a groosome sight. His big yellow eyes blazed and he tore about and kicked over a chair and threw a mat at the wall and fired a vase out of the window and said *terrible things.* I sat on the sofa and stared at him like one fassinated. It was so interesting I was sorry when he cooled down which he soon did because he is like Ilse and never stays mad long. He never gets mad at Ilse though. Ilse says she wishes he would—it would be better than being taken no notis of. She is as much of an orfan as I am, poor child. Last Sunday she went to church with her old faded blue dress on. There was a tare right in front of it. Aunt Laura wepped when she came home and then spoke to Mrs Simms about it because she did not dare speak to Dr Burnley. Mrs Simms was cross and said it was not her place to look after Ilses close but she said she had got Dr Burnley to get Ilse a nice sprigged muslin dress and Ilse had got egg stane on it, and when Mrs Simms skolded her for being so careless Ilse flew into a rage and went upstairs and tore the muslin dress to pieces, and Mrs Simms said she wasn't going to bother her head again about a child like that and there was nothing for her to ware but her old blue but Mrs Simms didn't know it was tore. So I sneaked Ilses dress over to New Moon and Aunt Laura mended it neetly and hid the tare with a pocket. Ilse said she tore up her muslin dress one of the days she didn't believe in God and didn't care what she did. Ilse found a mouse in her bed one night and she just shook it out and jumped in. Oh, how brave. I could never be as brave as that. It is not true that Dr Burnley never smiles. I have seen him do it but not often. He just smiles with his lips but not his eyes and it makes me feel uncomfortable. Mostly he laughs in a horrid sarcastic way like *Jolly Jim's* uncle.

"We had barley soup for dinner that day—very watery.

"Aunt Laura is giving me five cents a week for washing the dishes. I can only spend one cent of it and the other four have to be put in the toad bank in the sitting-room on the mantel. The toad is made of brass and sits on top of the bank and you put the cents in his mouth one at a time. He swallows them and they drop into the bank. It's very fassinating (I should not write fassinating again because you told me I must not use the same word too often but I cant think of any other that deskribes my feelings so well). The toad bank is Aunt Laura's but she said I could use it. I just hugged her. Of course I never hug Aunt Elizabeth. She is too rijid and bony. She does not aprove of Aunt Laura paying me for washing dishes. I tremble to think what she would say if she knew Cousin Jimmy gave me a whole dollar on the sly last week.

"I wish he had not given me so much. It worrys me. It is an awful responsibility. It will be so diffikult to spend it wisely also without Aunt Elizabeth finding out about it. I hope I shall never have a million dollars. I am sure it would crush me utterly. I keep my dollar hid on the shelf with my letters and I put it in an old envelope and wrote on it Cousin Jimmy Murray gave me this so that if I died suddenly and Aunt Elizabeth found it she would know I came by it honestly.

"Now that the days are getting cool Aunt Elizabeth makes me wear my thick flannel petticoat. I hate it. It makes me so bunchy. But Aunt Elizabeth says I must wear it because you died of consumption. I wish close could be both graceful and helthy. I read the story of Red Riding Hood to-day. I think the wolf was the most intresting caracter in it. Red Riding Hood was a stupid little thing so easily fooled.

"I wrote two poems yesterday. One was short and entitelled Lines Addressed to a blue-eyed-grass flower gathered in the Old Orchard. Here it is,

Sweet little flower thy modest face

Is ever lifted tords the sky

And a reflexshun of its face

Is caught within thine own blue eye.

The meadow queens are tall and fair

The columbines are lovely too.

But the poor talent I possess

Shall laurel thee my flower of blue.

"The other poem was long and I wrote it on a letterbill. It is called The Monark of the Forest. The Monark is the big birch in Lofty John's bush. I love that bush so much it hurts. Do you understand that kind of hurting. Ilse likes it too and we play there most of the time when we are not at the Tansy Patch. We have three paths in it. We call them the To-day Road, the Yesterday Road and the To-morrow Road. The To-day Road is by the brook and we call it that because it is lovely now. The Yesterday Road is out in the stumps where Lofty John cut some trees down and we call it that because it used to be lovely. The To-morrow Road is just a tiny path in the maple clearing and we call it that because it is going to be lovely some day, when the maples grow bigger. But oh Father dear I haven't forgotten the dear old trees down home. I always think of them after I go to bed. But I am happy here. It isn't wrong to be happy, is it Father. Aunt Elizabeth says I got over being homesick very quick but I am often homesick *inside*. I have got akwanted with Lofty John. Ilse is a great friend of his and often goes there to watch him working in his carpenter shop. He says he has made enough ladders to get to heaven without the priest but that is just his joke. He is really a very devowt Catholic and goes to the chapel at White Cross every Sunday. I go with Ilse though perhaps I ought not to when he is an enemy of my family. He is of stately baring and refined manners—very sivil to me but I don't always like him. When I ask him a serius question he always winks over my head when he ansers. That is insulting. Of course I never ask any questions on relijus subjects but Ilse does. She likes him but she says he would burn us all at the stake if he had the power. She asked him right out if he wouldn't and he winked at me and said Oh, we wouldn't burn nice pretty little Protestants like you. We would only burn the old ugly ones. That was a frivellus reply. Mrs Lofty John is a nice woman and not at all proud. She looks just like a little rosy rinkled apple.

"On rainy days we play at Ilses. We can slide down the bannisters and do what we like. Nobody cares only when the doctor is home we have to be quiet because he cant bear any noise in the house except what he makes himself. The roof is flat and we can get out on it through a door in the garret ceiling. It is very exciting to be up on the roof of a house. We had a yelling contest there the other night to see which could yell the loudest. To my surprise I found I could. You never can tell what you can do till you try. But too many people heard us and Aunt Elizabeth was very angry. She asked me what made me do such a thing. That is an okward question because often I cant tell what makes me do things. Sometimes I do them just to find out what I feel like doing them. And sometimes I do them because I want to have some exciting things to tell my grandchildren. Is it impropper to talk about haveing grandchildren. I have discovered that it is impropper to talk about haveing children. One evening when people were here Aunt Laura said to me quite kindly What are you thinking so ernestly about, Emily, and I said I am picking names for my children. I mean to have ten. And after the company had gone Aunt Elizabeth said to Aunt Laura *icilly* I think it will be better in the future Laura if you do *not* ask that child what she is thinking of. If Aunt Laura doesn't I shall be sorry because when I have an intresting thought I like to tell it.

"School begins again next week. Ilse is going to ask Miss Brownell if I can sit with her. I intend to act as if Rhoda was not there at all. Teddy is going too. Dr Burnley says he is well enough to go though his mother doesnt like the idea. Teddy says she never likes to have him go to school but she is glad that he hates Miss Brownell. Aunt Laura says the right way to end a letter to a dear friend is yours affeckshunately.

"So I am yours very affeckshunately.

"*Emily Byrd Starr.*

"P. S. Because *you* are my *very dearest friend still,* Father. Ilse says she loves me best of anything in the world and her red leather boots that Mrs Simms gave her next."

A DAUGHTER OF EVE

New moon was noted for its apples and on that first autumn of Emily's life there both the "old" and the "new" orchards bore a bumper crop. In the new were the titled and pedigreed apples; and in the old the seedlings, unknown to catalogues, that yet had a flavour wildly sweet and all their own. There was no taboo on any apple and Emily was free to eat all she wanted of each and every kind—the only prohibition being that she must not take any to bed with her. Aunt Elizabeth, very properly, did not want her bed messed up with apple seeds; and Aunt Laura had a horror of anyone eating apples in the dark lest they might eat an apple worm into the bargain. Emily, therefore, should have been able fully to satisfy her appetite for apples at home; but there is a certain odd kink in human nature by reason of which the flavour of the apples belonging to somebody else is always vastly superior to our own—as the crafty serpent of Eden very well knew. Emily, like most people, possessed this kink, and consequently thought that nowhere were there such delicious apples as those belonging to Lofty John. He was in the habit of keeping a long row of apples on one of the beams in his workshop and it was understood that she and Ilse might help themselves freely whenever they visited that charming, dusty, shaving-carpeted spot. Three varieties of Lofty John's apples were their especial favourites—the "scabby apples," that looked as if they had leprosy but were of unsurpassed deliciousness under their queerly blotched skins; the "little red apples," scarcely bigger than a crab, deep crimson all over and glossy as satin, that had such a sweet, nutty flavour; and the big green "sweet apples" that children usually thought the best of all. Emily considered that day wasted whose low descending sun had not beheld her munching one of Lofty John's big green sweets.

In the back of her mind Emily knew quite well that she should not be going to Lofty John's at all. To be sure, she had never been forbidden to go—simply because it had never occurred to her aunts that an inmate of New Moon could so forget the beloved old family feud between the houses of Murray and Sullivan belonging to two generations back. It was an inheritance that any proper Murray would live up to as a matter of course. But when Emily was off with that wild little Ishmaelite of an Ilse, traditions lost their power under the allurement of Lofty John's "reds" and "scabs."

She wandered rather lonesomely into his workshop one September evening at twilight. She had been alone since she came from school; her aunts and Cousin Jimmy had gone to Shrewsbury, promising to be back by sunset. Ilse was away also, her father, prodded thereto by Mrs Simms, having taken her to Charlottetown to get her a winter coat. Emily liked being alone very well at first. She felt quite important over being in charge of New Moon. She ate the supper Aunt Laura had left on the cook-house dresser for her and she went into the dairy and skimmed six lovely big pans of milk. She had no business at all to do this but she had always hankered to do it and this was too good a chance to be missed. She did it beautifully and nobody ever knew—each aunt supposing the other had done it—and so she was never scolded for it. This does not point any particular moral, of course; in a proper yarn Emily should either have been found out and punished for disobedience or been driven by an uneasy conscience to confess; but I am sorry—or ought to be—to have to state that Emily's conscience never worried her about the matter at all. Still, she was doomed to suffer enough that night from an entirely different cause, to balance all her little peccadillos.

By the time the cream was skimmed and poured into the big stone crock and well stirred—Emily didn't forget *that,* either—it was after sunset and still nobody had come home. Emily didn't like the idea of going alone into the big, dusky, echoing house; so she hied her to Lofty John's shop, which she found unoccupied, though the plane halted midway on a board indicated that Lofty John had been working there quite recently and would probably return. Emily sat down on a round section of a huge log and looked around to see what she could get to eat. There was a row of "reds" and "scabs" clean across the side of the shop but no "sweet" among them; and Emily felt that what she needed just then was a "sweet" and nothing else.

Then she spied one—a huge one—the biggest "sweet" Emily had ever seen, all by itself on one of the steps of the stair leading up to the loft. She climbed up, possessed herself of it and ate it out of hand. She was gnawing happily at the core when Lofty John came in. He nodded to her with a seemingly careless glance around.

"Just been in to get my supper," he said. "The wife's away so I had to get it myself."

He fell to planing in silence. Emily sat on the stairs, counting the seeds of the big "sweet"—you told your fortunes by the seeds—listening to the Wind Woman whistling elfishly through a knot hole in the loft, and composing a "Deskripshun of Lofty John's Carpenter

Shop By Lantern Light," to be written later on a letter-bill. She was lost in a mental hunt for an accurate phrase to picture the absurd elongated shadow of Lofty John's nose on the opposite wall when Lofty John whirled about, so suddenly that the shadow of his nose shot upward like a huge spear to the ceiling, and demanded in a startled voice,

"What's become av that big sweet apple that was on that stair?"

"Why—I—I et it," stammered Emily.

Lofty John dropped his plane, threw up his hands and looked at Emily with a horrified face.

"The saints preserve us, child. Ye never et that apple—don't tell me ye've gone and et *that* apple!"

"Yes, I did," said Emily uncomfortably. "I didn't think it was any harm—I—"

"Harm! Listen to her, will you? That apple was poisoned for the rats! They've been plaguing me life out here and I had me mind made up to finish their fun. And now you've et the apple—it would kill a dozen av ye in a brace of shakes."

Lofty John saw a white face and a gingham apron flash through the workshop and out into the dark. Emily's first wild impulse was to get home at once—before she dropped dead. She tore across the field through the bush and the garden and dashed into the house. It was still silent and dark—nobody was home yet. Emily gave a bitter little shriek of despair—when they came they would find her stiff and cold, black in the face likely, everything in this dear world ended for her for ever, all because she had eaten an apple which she thought she was perfectly welcome to eat. It wasn't fair—she didn't want to die.

But she must. She only hoped desperately that some one would come before she was dead. It would be so terrible to die there all alone in that great, big, empty New Moon. She dared not try to go anywhere for help. It was too dark now and she would likely drop dead on the way. To die out there—alone—in the dark—oh, that would be too dreadful. It did not occur to her that anything could be done for her; she thought if you once swallowed poison that was the end of you.

With hands shaking in panic she got a candle lighted. It wasn't quite so bad then—you *could* face things in the light. And Emily, pale, terrified, alone, was already deciding that this must be faced bravely. She must not shame the Starrs and the Murrays. She clenched her cold hands and tried to stop trembling. How long would it be before she died, she wondered. Lofty John had said the apple would kill her in a "brace of shakes." What did that mean? How long was a brace of shakes? Would it hurt her to die? She had a vague idea that poison did hurt you awfully. Oh; and just a little while ago she had been so happy! She had thought she was going to live for years and write great poems and be famous like Mrs Hemans. She had had a fight with Ilse the night before and hadn't made it up yet—never could make it up now. And Ilse would feel so terribly. She must write her a note and forgive her. Was there time for that much? Oh, how cold her hands were! Perhaps that meant she was dying already. She had heard or read that your hands turned cold when you were dying. She wondered if her face was turning black. She grasped her candle and hurried up the stairs to the spare-room. There was a looking-glass there—the only one in the house hung low enough for her to see her reflection if she tipped the bottom of it back. Ordinarily Emily would have been frightened to death at the mere thought of going into that spare-room by dim, flickering candlelight. But the one great terror had swallowed up all lesser ones. She looked at her reflection, amid the sleek, black flow of her hair, in the upward-striking light on the dark background of the shadowy room. Oh, she was pale as the dead already. Yes, that was a dying face—there could be no doubt of it.

Something rose up in Emily and took possession of her—some inheritance from the good old stock behind her. She ceased to tremble—she accepted her fate—with bitter regret, but calmly.

"I don't want to die but since I have to I'll die as becomes a Murray," she said. She had read a similar sentence in a book and it came pat to the moment. And now she must hurry. That letter to Ilse must be written. Emily went to Aunt Elizabeth's room first, to assure herself that her right-hand top bureau drawer was quite tidy; then she flitted up the garret stairs to her dormer corner. The great place was full of lurking, pouncing shadows that crowded about the little island of faint candlelight, but they had no terrors for Emily now.

"And to think I was feeling so bad to-day because my petticoat was bunchy," she thought, as she got one of her dear letter-bills—the last she would ever write on. There was no need to write to Father—she would see him soon—but Ilse must have her letter—dear, loving, jolly, hot-tempered Ilse, who, just the day before had shrieked insulting epithets after her and who would be haunted by remorse all her life for it.

"Dearest Ilse," wrote Emily, her hand shaking a little but her lips firmly set. "I am going to die. I have been poisoned by an apple Lofty John had put for rats. I will never see you again, but I am writing this to tell you I love you and you are not to feel bad because you called me a skunk and a bloodthirsty mink yesterday. I forgive you, so do not worry over it. And I am sorry I told you that you were beneath contemt because I didn't mean a word of it. I leave you all my share of the broken dishes in our playhouse and please tell Teddy good-bye for me. He will never be able to teach me how to put worms on a fish-hook now. I promised him I would learn because I did not want him to think I was a coward but I am glad I did not for I know what the worm feels like now. I do not feel sick yet but I don't know what the simptoms of poisoning are and Lofty John said there was enough to kill a dozen of me so I cant have long to live. If Aunt Elizabeth is willing you can have my necklace of Venetian beads. It is the only valuable possession I have. Don't let anybody do anything to Lofty John because he did not mean to poison me and it was all my own fault for being so greedy. Perhaps people will think he did it on purpose because I am a Protestant but I feel sure he did not and please tell him not to be hawnted by remorse. I think I feel a pain in my stomach now so I guess that the end draws ni. Fare well and remember her who died so young.

"Your own devoted,

"*Emily.*"

As Emily folded up her letter-bill she heard the sound of wheels in the yard below. A moment later Elizabeth and Laura Murray were confronted in the kitchen by a tragic-faced little creature, grasping a guttering candle in one hand and a red letter-bill in the other.

"Emily, what is the matter?" cried Aunt Laura.

"I'm dying," said Emily solemnly. "I et an apple Lofty John had poisoned for rats. I have only a few minutes to live, Aunt Laura."

Laura Murray dropped down on the black bench with her hand at her heart. Elizabeth turned as pale as Emily herself.

"Emily, is this some play-acting of yours?" she demanded sternly.

"No," cried Emily, quite indignantly. "It's the truth. Do you suppose a dying person would be play-acting? And oh, Aunt Elizabeth, please will you give this letter to Ilse—and please forgive me for being naughty—though I wasn't always naughty when you thought I was—and don't let any one see after I'm dead if I turn black—especially Rhoda Stuart."

By this time Aunt Elizabeth was herself again.

"How long ago is it since you ate that apple, Emily?"

"About an hour."

"If you'd eaten a poisoned apple an hour ago you'd be dead or sick by now—"

"Oh," cried Emily transformed in a second. A wild, sweet hope sprang up in her heart—was there a chance for her after all? Then she added despairingly, "But I felt another pain in my stomach just as I came downstairs."

"Laura," said Aunt Elizabeth, "take this child out to the cook-house and give her a good dose of mustard and water at once. It will do no harm and *may* do some good, if there's anything in this yarn of hers. I'm going down to the doctor's—he may be back—but I'll see Lofty John on the way."

Aunt Elizabeth went out—-and Aunt Elizabeth went out very quickly—if it had been any one else it might have been said she ran. As for Emily—well, Aunt Laura gave her that emetic in short order and two minutes later Emily had no doubt at all that she was dying then and there—and the sooner the better. When Aunt Elizabeth returned Emily was lying on the sofa in the kitchen, as white as the pillow under her head, and as limp as a faded lily.

"Wasn't the doctor home?" cried Aunt Laura desperately.

"I don't know—there's no need of the doctor. I didn't think there was from the first. It was just one of Lofty John's jokes. He thought he'd give Emily a fright—just for fun—*his* idea of fun. March you off to bed, Miss Emily. You deserve all you've got for going over there to Lofty John's at all and I don't pity you a particle. I haven't had such a turn for years."

"I *did* have a pain in my stomach," wailed Emily, in whom fright and mustard-and-water combined had temporarily extinguished all spirit.

"Any one who eats apples from dawn to dark must expect a few pains in her stomach. You won't have any more tonight, I reckon—the mustard will remedy that. Take your candle and go."

"Well," said Emily, getting unsteadily to her feet. "I *hate* that dod-gasted Lofty John."

121

"Emily!" said both aunts together.

"He *deserves* it," said Emily vindictively.

"Oh, Emily—that dreadful word you used!" Aunt Laura seemed curiously upset about something.

"Why, what's the matter with dod-gasted?" said Emily, quite mystified. "Cousin Jimmy uses it often, when things vex him. He used it to-day—he said that dod-gasted heifer had broken out of the graveyard pasture again."

"Emily," said Aunt Elizabeth, with the air of one impaling herself on the easiest horn of a dilemma, "your Cousin Jimmy is a man—and men sometimes use expressions, in the heat of anger, that are not proper for little girls."

"But what *is* the matter with dod-gasted?" persisted Emily. "It isn't a swear word, is it? And if it isn't, why can't I use it?"

"It isn't a—a ladylike word," said Aunt Laura.

"Well, then, I won't use it any more," said Emily resignedly, "but Lofty John *is* dod-gasted."

Aunt Laura laughed so much after Emily had gone upstairs that Aunt Elizabeth told her a woman of her age should have more sense.

"Elizabeth, you *know* it was funny," protested Laura.

Emily being safely out of sight, Elizabeth permitted herself a somewhat grim smile.

"I told Lofty John a few plain truths—he'll not go telling children they're poisoned again in a hurry. I left him fairly dancing with rage."

Worn out, Emily fell asleep as soon as she was in bed; but an hour later she awakened. Aunt Elizabeth had not yet come to bed so the blind was still up and Emily saw a dear, friendly star winking down at her. Far away the sea moaned alluringly. Oh, it was nice just to be alone and to be alive. Life tasted good to her again—"tasted like more," as Cousin Jimmy said. She could have a chance to write more letter-bills, and poetry—Emily already saw a yard of verses entitled "Thoughts of One Doomed to Sudden Death"—and play with Ilse and Teddy—scour the barns with Saucy Sal, watch Aunt Laura skim cream in the dairy and help Cousin Jimmy garden—read books in Emily's Bower and trot along the To-day Road—but *not* visit Lofty John's workshop. She determined that she would never have anything to do with Lofty John again after his diabolical cruelty. She felt so indignant with him for frightening her—after they had been such good friends, too—that she could not go to sleep until she had composed an account of her death by poison, of Lofty John being tried for her murder and condemned to death, and of his being hanged on a gibbet as lofty as himself, Emily being present at the dreadful scene, in spite of the fact that she was dead by his act. When she had finally cut him down and buried him with obloquy—the tears streaming down her face out of sympathy for Mrs Lofty John—she forgave him. Very likely he was not dod-gasted after all.

She wrote it all down on a letter-bill in the garret the next day.

FANCY FED

In October Cousin Jimmy began to boil the pigs' potatoes—unromantic name for a most romantic occupation—or so it appeared to Emily, whose love of the beautiful and picturesque was satisfied as it had never yet been on those long, cool, starry twilights of the waning year at New Moon.

There was a clump of spruce-trees in a corner of the old orchard, and under them an immense iron pot was hung over a circle of large stones—a pot so big that an ox could have been comfortably stewed in it. Emily thought it must have come down from the days of fairy tales and been some giant's porridge pot; but Cousin Jimmy told her that it was only a hundred years old and old Hugh Murray had had it sent out from England.

"We've used it ever since to boil the potatoes for the New Moon pigs," he said. "Blair Water folks think it old-fashioned; they've all got boiler-houses now, with built-in boilers; but as long as Elizabeth's boss at New Moon we'll use this."

Emily was sure no built-in boiler could have the charm of the big pot. She helped Cousin Jimmy fill it full of potatoes, after she came from school; then, when supper was over, Cousin Jimmy lighted the fire under it and pottered about it all the evening. Sometimes he poked the fire—Emily loved that part of the performance—sending glorious streams of rosy sparks upward into the darkness; sometimes he stirred the potatoes with a long pole, looking, with his queer, forked grey beard and belted "jumper," just like some old gnome or troll of northland story mixing the contents of a magical cauldron; and sometimes he sat beside Emily on the grey granite boulder near the pot and recited his poetry for her. Emily liked this best of all, for Cousin Jimmy's poetry was surprisingly good—at least in spots—and Cousin Jimmy had "fit audience though few" in this slender little maiden with her pale eager face and rapt eyes.

They were an odd couple and they were perfectly happy together. Blair Water people thought Cousin Jimmy a failure and a mental weakling. But he dwelt in an ideal world of which none of them knew anything. He had recited his poems a hundred times thus, as he boiled the pigs' potatoes; the ghosts of a score of autumns haunted the clump of spruces for him. He was an odd, ridiculous figure enough, bent and wrinkled and unkempt, gesticulating awkwardly as he recited. But it was his hour; he was no longer "simple Jimmy Murray" but a prince in his own realm. For a little while he was strong and young and splendid and beautiful, accredited master of song to a listening, enraptured world. None of his prosperous, sensible Blair Water neighbours ever lived through such an hour. He would not have exchanged places with one of them. Emily, listening to him, felt vaguely that if it had not been for that unlucky push into the New Moon well, this queer little man beside her might have stood in the presence of kings.

But Elizabeth *had* pushed him into the New Moon well and as a consequence he boiled pigs' potatoes and recited poetry to Emily— Emily, who wrote poetry too, and loved these evenings so much that she could not sleep after she went to bed until she had composed a minute description of them. The flash came almost every evening over something or other. The Wind Woman swooped or purred in the tossing boughs above them—Emily had never been so near to seeing her; the sharp air was full of the pleasant tang of the burning spruce cones Cousin Jimmy shovelled under the pot; Emily's furry kitten, Mike II, frisked and scampered about like a small, charming demon of the night; the fire glowed with beautiful redness and allure through the gloom; there were nice whispery sounds everywhere; the "great big dark" lay spread around them full of mysteries that daylight never revealed; and over all a purple sky powdered with stars.

Ilse and Teddy came, too, on some evenings. Emily always knew when Teddy was coming, for when he reached the old orchard he whistled his "call"—the one he used just for her—a funny, dear little call, like three clear bird notes, the first just medium pitch, the second higher, the third dropping away into lowness and sweetness long-drawn out—like the echoes in the *Bugle Song* that went clearer and further in their dying. That call always had an odd effect on Emily; it seemed to her that it fairly drew the heart out of her body—and she *had* to follow it. She thought Teddy could have whistled her clear across the world with those three magic notes. Whenever she heard it she ran quickly through the orchard and told Teddy whether Cousin Jimmy wanted him or not, because it was only on certain nights that Cousin Jimmy wanted anybody but her. He would never recite his poetry to Ilse or Teddy; but he told them fairy stories, and tales about the old dead-and-gone Murrays in the pond graveyard that were as queer, sometimes, as the fairy stories; and Ilse would recite too, doing better there than she ever did anywhere else; and sometimes Teddy lay sprawled out on the ground beside the big pot and drew pictures by the light of the fire—pictures of Cousin Jimmy stirring the potatoes—pictures of Ilse and Emily dancing hand in hand around it like two small witches, pictures of Mike's cunning, little, whiskered face peering around the old boulder, pictures of weird, vague faces crowding in the darkness outside their enchanted circle. They had very wonderful evenings there, those four children.

"Oh, don't you like the world at night, Ilse?" Emily once said rapturously.

Ilse glanced happily around her—poor little neglected Ilse, who found in Emily's companionship what she had hungered for all her short life and who was, even now, being led by love into something of her rightful heritage.

"Yes," she said. "And I always believe there *is* a God when I'm here like this."

Then the potatoes were done—and Cousin Jimmy gave each of them one before he mixed in the bran; they broke them in pieces on plates of birch-bark, sprinkled them with salt which Emily had cached in a small box under the roots of the biggest spruce, and ate them with gusto. No banquet of gods was ever as delicious as those potatoes. Then finally came Aunt Laura's kind, silvery voice calling through the frosty dark; Ilse and Teddy scampered homewards; and Emily captured Mike II and shut him up safely for the night in the New Moon dog-house which had held no dog for years, but was still carefully preserved and whitewashed every spring. Emily's heart would have broken if anything had happened to Mike II.

"Old Kelly," the tin pedlar, had given him to her. Old Kelly had come round through Blair Water every fortnight from May to November for thirty years, perched on the seat of a bright red pedlar's waggon and behind a dusty, ambling, red pony of that peculiar gait and appearance pertaining to the ponies of country pedlars—a certain placid, unhasting leanness as of a nag that has encountered troubles of his own and has lived them down by sheer patience and staying power. From the bright red waggon proceeded a certain metallic rumbling and clinking as it bowled along, and two huge nests of tin pans on its flat, rope-encircled roof, flashed back the sunlight so dazzlingly that Old Kelly seemed the beaming sun of a little planetary system all his own. A new broom, sticking up aggressively at each of the four corners gave the waggon a resemblance to a triumphal chariot. Emily hankered secretly for a ride in Old Kelly's waggon. She thought it must be very delightful.

Old Kelly and she were great friends. She liked his red, clean-shaven face under his plug hat, his nice, twinkly, blue eyes, his brush of upstanding, sandy hair, and his comical pursed-up mouth, the shape of which was partly due to nature and partly to much whistling. He always had a little three-cornered paper bag of "lemon drops" for her, or a candy stick of many colours, which he smuggled into her pocket when Aunt Elizabeth wasn't looking. And he never forgot to tell her that he supposed she'd soon be thinking of getting married—for Old Kelly thought that the surest way to please a female creature of any age was to tease her about getting married.

One day, instead of candy, he produced a plump grey kitten from the back drawer of his waggon and told her it was for her. Emily received the gift rapturously, but after Old Kelly had rattled and clattered away Aunt Elizabeth told her they did not want any more cats at New Moon.

"Oh, please let me keep it, Aunt Elizabeth," Emily begged. "It won't be a bit of bother to you. *I* have had experience in bringing up cats. And

I'm so lonesome for a kitten. Saucy Sal is getting so wild running with the barn cats that I can't 'sociate with her like I used to do—and she never was nice to cuddle. *Please,* Aunt Elizabeth."

Aunt Elizabeth would not and did not please. She was in a very bad humour that day, anyhow—nobody knew just why. In such a mood she was entirely unreasonable. She would not listen to anybody—Laura and Cousin Jimmy had to hold their tongues, and Cousin Jimmy was bidden to take the grey kitten down to the Blair Water and drown it. Emily burst into tears over this cruel command, and this aggravated Aunt Elizabeth still further. She was so cross that Cousin Jimmy dared not smuggle the kitten up to the barn as he had at first planned to do.

"Take that beast down to the pond and throw it in and come back and tell me you've done it," said Elizabeth angrily. "I mean to be obeyed—New Moon is not going to be made a dumping-ground for Old Jock Kelly's superfluous cats."

Cousin Jimmy did as he was told and Emily would not eat any dinner. After dinner she stole mournfully away through the old orchard down the pasture to the pond. Just why she went she could not have told, but she felt that go she must. When she reached the bank of the little creek where Lofty John's brook ran into Blair Water, she heard piteous shrieks; and there, marooned on a tiny islet of sere marsh grass in the creek, was an unhappy, little beast, its soaking fur plastered against, its sides, shivering and trembling in the wind of the sharp autumnal day. The old oat-bag in which Cousin Jimmy had imprisoned it was floating out into the pond.

Emily did not stop to think, or look for a board, or count the consequences. She plunged in the creek up to her knees, she waded out to the clump of grass and caught the kitten up. She was so hot with indignation that she did not feel the cold of the water or the chill of the wind as she ran back to New Moon. A suffering or tortured animal always filled her with such a surge of sympathy that it lifted her clean out of herself. She burst into the cook-house where Aunt Elizabeth was frying doughnuts.

"Aunt Elizabeth," she cried, "the kitten wasn't drowned after all—and I *am* going to keep it."

"You're not," said Aunt Elizabeth.

Emily looked her aunt in the face. Again she felt that odd sensation that had come when Aunt Elizabeth brought the scissors to cut her hair.

"Aunt Elizabeth, this poor little kitten is cold and starving, and oh, so miserable. It has been suffering for hours. It shall *not* be drowned again."

Archibald Murray's look was on her face and Archibald Murray's tone was in her voice. This happened only when the deeps of her being were stirred by some peculiarly poignant emotion. Just now she was in an agony of pity and anger.

When Elizabeth Murray saw her father looking at her out of Emily's little white face, she surrendered without a struggle, rage at herself as she might afterwards for her weakness. It was her one vulnerable point. The thing might not have been so uncanny if Emily had resembled the Murrays. But to see the Murray look suddenly superimposed like a mask over alien features, was such a shock to her nerves that she could not stand up against it. A ghost from the grave could not have cowed her more speedily.

She turned her back on Emily in silence but Emily knew that she had won her second victory. The grey kitten stayed at New Moon and waxed fat and lovable, and Aunt Elizabeth never took the slightest notice of its existence, save to sweep it out of the house when Emily was not about. But it was weeks before Emily was really forgiven and she felt uncomfortable enough over it. Aunt Elizabeth could be a not ungenerous conqueror but she was very disagreeable in defeat. It was really just as well that Emily could not summon the Murray look at will.

VARIOUS TRAGEDIES

Emily, obedient to Aunt Elizabeth's command, had eliminated the word "bull" from her vocabulary. But to ignore the existence of bulls was not to do away with them—and specifically with Mr James Lee's English bull, who inhabited the big windy pasture west of Blair Water and who bore a dreadful reputation. He was certainly an awesome looking creature and Emily sometimes had fearful dreams of being chased by him and being unable to move. And one sharp November day these dreams came true.

There was a certain well at the far end of the pasture concerning which Emily felt a curiosity, because Cousin Jimmy had told her a dreadful tale about it. The well had been dug sixty years ago by two brothers who lived in a little house which was built down near the shore. It was a very deep well, which was considered a curious thing in that low-lying land near pond and sea; the brothers had gone ninety feet before they found a spring. Then the sides of the well had been stoned up—but the work never went farther. Thomas and Silas Lee had quarrelled over some trivial difference of opinion as to what kind of a hood should be put over it; and in the heat of his anger Silas had struck Thomas on the head with his hammer and killed him.

The well-house was never built. Silas Lee was sent to prison for manslaughter and died there. The farm passed to another brother— Mr James Lee's father—who moved the house to the other end of it and planked the well over. Cousin Jimmy added that Tom Lee's ghost was supposed to haunt the scene of his tragic death but he couldn't vouch for that, though he had written a poem on it. A very eerie poem it was, too, and made Emily's blood run cold with a fearful joy when he recited it to her one misty night by the big potato pot. Ever since she had wanted to see the old well.

Her chance came one Saturday when she was prowling alone in the old graveyard. Beyond it lay the Lee pasture and there was apparently not a sign of a bull in or about it. Emily decided to pay a visit to the old well and went skimming down the field against the sweep of the north wind racing across the gulf. The Wind Woman was a giantess that day and a mighty swirl she was stirring up along the shore; but as Emily drew near the big sand-dunes they made a little harbour of calmness around the old well.

Emily coolly lifted up one of the planks, knelt on the others and peered down. Fortunately the planks were strong and comparatively new—otherwise the small maiden of New Moon might have explored the well more thoroughly than she desired to do. As it was, she could see little of it; huge ferns grew thickly out of the crevices among the stones of its sides and reached across it, shutting out the view of its gloomy depths. Rather disappointed, Emily replaced the plank and started homeward. She had not gone ten steps before she stopped. Mr James Lee's bull was coming straight towards her and was less than twenty yards away.

The shore fence was not far behind Emily, and she might possibly have reached it in time had she run. But she was incapable of running; as she wrote that night in her letter to her father she was "parralised" with terror and could no more move than she could in her dreams of this very occurrence. It is quite conceivable that a dreadful thing might have happened then and there had not a certain boy been sitting on the shore fence. He had been sitting there unnoticed all the time Emily had been peering into the well, now he sprang down.

Emily saw, or sensed, a sturdy body dashing past her. The owner thereof ran to within ten feet of the bull, hurled a stone squarely into the monster's hairy face, then sped off at right angles towards the side fence. The bull, thus insulted, turned with a menacing rumble and lumbered off after this intruder.

"Run now!" screamed the boy over his shoulder to Emily.

Emily did not run. Terrified as she was, there was something in her that would not let her run until she saw whether her gallant rescuer made good his escape. He reached his fence in the nick of time. Then and not till then Emily ran too, and scrambled over the shore fence just as the bull started back across the pasture, evidently determined to catch somebody. Trembling, she made her way through the spiky grass of the sand-hills and met the boy at the corner. They stood and looked at each other for a moment.

The boy was a stranger to Emily. He had a cheery, impudent, clean-cut face, with keen, grey eyes and plenty of tawny curls. He wore as few clothes as decency permitted and had only the pretence of a hat. Emily liked him; there was nothing of Teddy's subtle charm in him but he had a certain forceful attraction of his own and he had just saved her from a terrible death.

"Thank you," said Emily shyly, looking up at him with great grey eyes that looked blue under her long lashes. It was a very effective look which lost nothing of effectiveness from being wholly unconscious. Nobody had as yet told Emily how very winsome that shy, sudden, up-glance of hers was.

"Isn't he a rip-snorter?" said the boy easily. He thrust his hands into his ragged pockets and stared at Emily so fixedly that she dropped her eyes in confusion—thereby doing further damage with those demure lids and silken fringes.

"He's dreadful," she said with a shudder. "And I was so scared."

"Were you now? And me thinking you were full of grit to be standing there like that looking at him cool as a cucumber. What's it like to be afraid?"

"Weren't *you* ever afraid?" asked Emily.

"No—don't know what it's like," said the boy carelessly, and a bit boastfully. "What's your name?"

"Emily Byrd Starr."

"Live round here?"

"I live at New Moon."

"Where Simple Jimmy Murray lives?"

"He *isn't* simple," cried Emily indignantly.

"Oh, all right. I don't know him. But I'm going to. I'm going to hire with him for chore boy for the winter."

"I didn't know," said Emily, surprised. "Are you really?"

"Yep. I didn't know it myself till just this minute. He was asking Aunt Tom about me last week but I didn't mean to hire out then. Now I guess I will. Want to know my name?"

"Of course."

"Perry Miller. I live with my old beast of an Aunt Tom down at Stovepipe Town. Dad was a sea captain and I uster sail with him when he was alive—sailed everywhere. Go to school?"

"Yes."

"I don't—never did. Aunt Tom lives so far away. Anyhow, I didn't think I'd like it. Guess I'll go now, though."

"Can't you read?" asked Emily wonderingly.

"Yes—some—and figger. Dad learned me some when he was alive. I hain't bothered with it since—I'd ruther be down round the harbour. Great fun there. But if I make up my mind to go to school I'll learn like thunder. I s'pose you're awful clever."

"No—not very. Father said I was a genius, but Aunt Elizabeth says I'm just queer."

"What's a genius?"

"I'm not sure. Sometimes it's a person who writes poetry. *I* write poetry."

Perry stared at her.

"Golly. I'll write poetry too, then."

"I don't believe *you* could write poetry," said Emily—a little disdainfully, it must be admitted. "Teddy can't—and he's *very* clever."

"Who's Teddy?"

"A friend of mine." There was just a trace of stiffness in Emily's voice.

"Then," said Perry, folding his arms across his breast and scowling, "I'm going to punch this friend of yours' head for him."

"You're not," cried Emily. She was very indignant and quite forgot for the moment that Perry had rescued her from the bull. She tossed her own head and started homeward. Perry turned too.

"May as well go up and see Jimmy Murray about hiring 'fore I go home," he said. "Don't be mad, now. If you don't want anybody's head punched I won't punch it. Only you've gotter like me, too."

"Why, of course I'll like you," said Emily, as if there could be no question about it. She smiled her slow, blossoming smile at Perry and thereby reduced him to hopeless bondage.

Two days later Perry Miller was installed as chore boy at New Moon and in a fortnight's time Emily felt as if he must have been there always.

"Aunt Elizabeth didn't want Cousin Jimmy to hire him," she wrote to her father, "because he was one of the boys who did a dreadful thing one night last fall. They changed all the horses that were tied to the fence one Sunday night when preaching was going on and when folks came out the confushun was awful. Aunt Elizabeth said it wouldn't be safe to have him round the place. But Cousin Jimmy said it was awful hard to get a chore boy and that we ode Perry something for saving my life from the bull. So Aunt Elizabeth gave in and lets him sit at the table with us but he has to stay in the kitchen in the evenings. The rest of us are in the sitting-room, but I am allowed to go out and help Perry with his lessons. He can only have one candle and the light is very dim. It keeps us snuffing it all the time. It is great fun to snuff candles. Perry is head of his class in school already. He is only in the third book allthough he is nearly twelve. Miss Brownell said something sarkastik to him the first day in school and he just threw back his head and laughed loud and long. Miss Brownell gave him a whipping for it but she has never been sarkastik to him again. She does not like to be laughed at I can see. Perry isn't afraid of anything. I thought he might not go to school any more when she whipped him but he says a little thing like that isn't going to keep him from getting an educashun since he has made up his mind to it. He is very determined.

"Aunt Elizabeth is determined too. But she says Perry is stubborn. I am teaching Perry grammar. He says he wants to learn to speak properly. I told him he should not call his Aunt Tom an old beast but he said he had to because she wasn't a young beast. He says the place he lives in is called Stovepipe Town because the houses have no chimneys, only pipes sticking out of the roof, but he would live in a manshun some day. Aunt Elizabeth says I ought not to be so friendly with a hired boy. But he is a nice boy though his manners are crood. Aunt Laura says they are crood. I don't know what it means but I guess it means he always says what he thinks right out and eats beans with his knife. I like Perry but in a different way from Teddy. Isn't it funny, dear Father, how many kinds of ways of liking there are? I don't think Ilse likes him. She makes fun of his ignerance and turns up her nose at him because his close are patched though her own close are queer enough. Teddy doesn't like him much and he drew such a funny picture of Perry hanging by his heels from a gallos. The face looked like Perrys and still it didn't. Cousin Jimmy said it was a carrycachure and laughed at it but I dared not show it to Perry for fear he would punch Teddys head. I showed it to Ilse and she got mad and tore it in two. I cant imagine why.

"Perry says he can recite as well as Ilse and could draw pictures too if he put his mind to it. I can see he doesnt like to think anybody can do anything he cant. But he cant see the wallpaper in the air like I can though he tries until I fear he will strane his eyes. He can make better speeches than any of us. He says he used to mean to be a sailer like his father but now he thinks he will be a lawyer when he grows up and go to parlament. Teddy is going to be an artist if his mother will let him, and Ilse is going to be a concert reciter—there is another name but I don't know how it is spelled—and I am going to be a poetess. I think we are a tallented crowd. Perhaps that is a vane thing to say, dear Father.

"A very terrible thing happened the day before yesterday. On Saturday morning we were at family prayers, all kneeling quite solemn around the kitchen. I just looked at Perry once and he made such a funny face at me that I laughed right out loud before I could help it. (*That* was not the terrible thing.) Aunt Elizabeth was *very* angry. I would not tell that it was Perry made me laugh because I was afraid he might be sent away if I did. So Aunt Elizabeth said I was to be punished and I was not let go to Jennie Strangs party in the afternoon. (It was a dreadful disappointment but *it* was not the terrible thing either.) Perry was away with Cousin Jimmy all day and when he came home at night he said to me, very feerce, Who has been making you cry. I said I had been crying—a little but not much—because I was not let go to the party because I had laughed at prayers. And Perry marched right up to Aunt Elizabeth and told her it was all his fault that I laughed. Aunt Elizabeth said I should not have laughed anyhow, but Aunt Laura was *greevously* upset and said my punishment had been far too severe; and she said that she would let me ware her pearl ring to school Monday to make up for it. I was enraptured for it is a lovely ring and no other girl has one. As soon as roll call was over Monday morning I put up my hand to ask Miss Brownell a question but really to show off my ring. That was wikked pride and I was punished. At recess Cora Lee, one of the big girls in the sixth class came and asked me to let her ware the ring for a while. I didnt want to but she said if I didnt she would get all the girls in my class to send me to Coventry (which is a dreadful thing, dear Father, and makes you feel like an outcast). So I let her and she kept it on till the afternoon recess and then she came and told me she had lost it in the brook. (This was the terrible thing.) Oh, Father dear, I was nearly wild. I dared not go home and face Aunt Laura. I had promised her I would be so careful with the ring. I thought I might earn money to get her another ring but when I figgered it out on my slate I knew I would have to wash dishes for twenty years to do it. I wepped in my despare. Perry saw me and after school he marched up to Cora Lee and said You fork over that ring or I'll tell Miss Brownell about it. And Cora Lee forked it over, very meek and said I was going to give it to her anyhow. I was just playing a joke and Perry said, Dont you play any more jokes on Emily or I'll joke you. It is very comforting to have such a champeen! I tremble to think what it would have been like if I had had to go home and tell Aunt Laura I had lost her ring. But it was crewel of Cora Lee to tell me she had lost it when she had not and harrow up my mind so. I could not be so crewel to an orfan girl.

"When I got home I looked in the glass to see if my hair had turned white. I am told that sometimes happens. But it hadnt.

"Perry knows more geograffy than any of us because he has been nearly everywhere in the world with his father. He tells me such fassinating stories after his lessons are done. He talks till the candle is burned to the last inch and then he uses that to go to bed with up the black hole into the kitchen loft because Aunt Elizabeth will not let him have more than one candle a night.

"Ilse and I had a fight yesterday about which we'd rather be Joan of Arc or Frances Willard. We didn't begin it as a fight but just as an argewment but it ended that way. *I* would rather be Frances Willard because she is alive.

"We had the first snow yesterday. I made a poem on it. This is it.

Along the snow the sunbeams glide,

Earth is a peerless, gleaming bride,

Dripping with diamonds, clad in traling white,

No bride was ever half so fair and bright.

"I read it to Perry and he said he could make poetry just as good and he said right off,

Mike has made a long row

of tracks across the snow.

Now isnt that as good as yours. I didnt think it was because you could say it just as well in prose. But when you talk of peerless gleaming brides in prose it sounds funny. Mike *did* make a row of little tracks right across the barn field and they looked so pretty, but not so pretty as the mice tracks in some flour Cousin Jimmy spilled on the granary floor. They are the dearest little things. They *look* like poetry.

"I am sorry winter has come because Ilse and I cant play in our house in Lofty Johns bush any more till spring or outside at the Tansy Patch. Sometimes we play indoors at the Tansy Patch but Mrs Kent makes us feel queer. She sits and watches us all the time. So we dont go only when Teddy coaxes very hard. And the pigs have been killed, poor things, so Cousin Jimmy doesnt boil for them any more. But there is one consolashun I do not have to ware a sunbonnet to school now. Aunt Laura made me such a pretty red hood with ribbons on it at which Aunt Elizabeth looked skornfully saying it was extravagant. I like school here better every day but I cant like Miss Brownell. She isnt fair. She told us she would give the one who wrote the best conposishun a pink ribbon to wear from Friday night to Monday. I wrote The Brooks Story about the brook in Lofty John's bush—all its advenshures and thoughts—and Miss Brownell said I must have copyed it and Rhoda Stuart got the ribbon. Aunt Elizabeth said You waste enough time writing trash I think you might have won that ribbon. She was mortifyed (I think) because I had disgraced New Moon by not getting it but I did not tell her what had happened. Teddy says a *good sport* never whines over losing. I want to be a good sport. Rhoda is so hateful to me now. She says she is surprised that a New Moon girl should have a hired boy for a bow. That is very silly because Perry is not my bow. Perry told her she had more gab than sense. That was not polite but it is true. One day in class Rhoda said the moon was situated east of Canada. Perry laughed right out and Miss Brownell made him stay in at recess but she never said anything to Rhoda for saying such a ridiklus thing. But the meanest thing Rhoda said was that she had forgiven me for the way I had used her. That made my blood boil when I hadnt done anything to be forgiven for. The idea.

"We have begun to eat the big beef ham that hung in the south-west corner of the kitchen.

"The other Wednesday night Perry and I helped Cousin Jimmy pick a road through the turnips in the first cellar. We have to go through it to the second cellar because the outside hatch is banked up now. It was great fun. We had a candle stuck up in a hole in the wall and it made such lovely shadows and we coud eat all the apples we wanted from the big barrel in the corner and the spirit moved Cousin Jimmy to recite some of his poetry as he threw the turnips.

"I am reading The Alhambra. It belongs to our book case. Aunt Elizabeth does not like to say it isnt fit for me to read because it was one of her fathers books, but I dont believe she aproves because she knits very furiously and looks black at me over her glasses. Teddy lent me Hans Andersons stories. I love them—only I always think of a different end for the Ice Maiden and save Rudy.

"They say Mrs John Killegrew has swallowed her wedding-ring. I wonder what she did that for.

"Cousin Jimmy says there is to be an eklips of the sun in December. I hope it wont interfear with Chrismas.

"My hands are chapped. Aunt Laura rubs mutton tallow on them every night when I go to bed. It is hard to write poetry with chapped hands. I wonder if Mrs Hemans ever had chapped hands. It does not mention anything like that in her biograffy.

"Jimmy Ball has to be a minister when he grows up. His mother told Aunt Laura that she consekrated him to it in his cradle. I wonder how she did it.

"We have brekfast by candlelight now and I like it.

"Ilse was up here Sunday afternoon and we went up in the garret and talked about God, because that is propper on Sundays. We have to be very careful what we do on Sundays. It is a traddishun of New Moon to keep Sundays very holy. Grandfather Murray was very strikt. Cousin Jimmy told me a story about him. They always cut the wood for Sunday on Saturday night, but one time they forgot and there was no wood on Sunday to cook the dinner, so Grandfather Murray said you must not cut wood on Sundays, boys, but just break a little with the back of the axe. Ilse is very curious about God although she doesnt believe in Him most of the time and doesnt like to talk about Him but still wants to find out about Him. She says she thinks she might like Him if she knew Him. She spells his name with a Capital G now because it is best to be on the safe side. *I* think God is just like my flash, only *it* lasts only a second and He lasts always. We talked so long we got hungry and I went down to the sitting-room cubbord and got two donuts. I forgot Aunt Elizabeth had told me I could not have donuts between meals. It was not stealing it was just forgetting. But Ilse got mad at the last and said I was a she jakobite (whatever that is) and a thief and that no Christian would steal donuts from her poor old aunt. So I went and confessed to Aunt Elizabeth and she said I was not to have a donut at supper. It was hard to see the others eating them. I thought Perry et his very quick but after supper he bekoned me out doors and gave me half his donut which he had kept for me. He had rapped it in his hangkerchief which was not very clean but I et it because I did not want to hurt his feelings.

137

"Aunt Laura says Ilse has a nice smile. I wonder if I have a nice smile. I looked at the glass in Ilse's room and smiled but it did not seem to me very nice.

"Now the nights have got cold Aunt Elizabeth always puts a gin jar full of hot water in the bed. I like to put my toes against it. That is all we use the gin jar for nowadays. But Grandfather Murray used to keep real gin in it.

"Now that the snow has come Cousin Jimmy cant work in his garden any more and he is very lonesome. I think the garden is just as pretty in winter as in summer. There are such pretty dimples and baby hills where the snow has covered up the flower beds. And in the evenings it is all pink and rosy at sunset and by moonlight it is like dreamland. I like to look out of the sitting-room window at it and watch the rabbits candles floting in the air above it and wonder what all the little roots and seeds are thinking of down under the snow. And it gives me a lovely creepy feeling to look at it through the red glass in the front door.

"There is a beautiful fringe of isikles along the cook-house roof. But there will be much more beautiful things in heaven. I was reading about Anzonetta to-day and it made me feel relijus. Good night, my dearest of fathers.

"*Emily.*

"P. S. That doesnt mean that I have any other Father. It is just a way of saying *very very* dear.

"*E. B. S.*"

CHECK FOR MISS BROWNELL

Emily and Ilse were sitting out on the side bench of Blair Water school writing poetry on their slates—at least, Emily was writing poetry and Ilse was reading it as she wrote and occasionally suggesting a rhyme when Emily was momentarily stuck for one. It may as well be admitted here and now that they had no business whatever to be doing this. They should have been "doing sums," as Miss Brownell supposed they were. But Emily never did sums when she took it into her black head to write poetry, and Ilse hated arithmetic on general principles. Miss Brownell was hearing the geography class at the other side of the room, the pleasant sunshine was showering in over them through the big window, and everything seemed propitious for a flight with the muses. Emily began to write a poem about the view from the school window.

It was quite a long time since she had been allowed to sit out on the side bench. This was a boon reserved for those pupils who had found favour in Miss Brownell's cold eyes—and Emily had never been one of those. But this afternoon Ilse had asked for both herself and Emily, and Miss Brownell had let both go, not being able to think of any valid reason for permitting Ilse and refusing Emily—as she would have liked to do, for she had one of those petty natures which never forget or forgive any offence. Emily, on her first day of school, had, so Miss Brownell believed, been guilty of impertinence and defiance— and successful defiance at that. This rankled in Miss Brownell's mind still and Emily felt its venom in a score of subtle ways. She never received any commendation—she was a target for Miss Brownell's sarcasm continually—and the small favours that other girls received never came her way. So this opportunity to sit on the side bench was a pleasing novelty.

There were points about sitting on the side bench. You could see all over the school without turning your head—and Miss Brownell could not sneak up behind you and look over your shoulder to see what you were up to; but in Emily's eyes the finest thing about it was that you could look right down into the "school bush," and watch the old spruces where the Wind Woman played, the long, grey-green trails of moss hanging from the branches, like banners of Elfland, the little red squirrels running along the fence, and the wonderful white aisles of snow where splashes of sunlight fell like pools of golden wine; and there was one little opening in the trees through which you could see right over the Blair Water valley to the sand-hills and the gulf beyond. To-day the sand-hills were softly rounded and gleaming white under the snow, but beyond them the gulf was darkly, deeply blue with dazzling white masses of ice like baby icebergs, floating about in it. Just to look at it thrilled Emily with a delight that was unutterable but which she yet must try to utter. She began her poem. Fractions were utterly forgotten—what had numerators and denominators to do with those curving bosoms of white snow—that heavenly blue—those crossed dark fir tips against the pearly skies—those ethereal woodland aisles of pearl and gold? Emily was lost to her world—so lost that she did not know the geography class had scattered to their respective seats and that Miss Brownell, catching sight of Emily's entranced gaze skywards as she searched for a rhyme, was stepping softly towards her. Ilse was drawing a picture on her slate and did not see her or she would have warned Emily. The latter suddenly felt her slate drawn out of her hand and heard Miss Brownell saying:

"I suppose you have finished those sums, Emily?"

Emily had not finished even one sum—she had only covered her slate with verses—verses that Miss Brownell must not see—*must not see!* Emily sprang to her feet and clutched wildly after her slate. But Miss Brownell, with a smile of malicious enjoyment on her thin lips, held it beyond her reach.

"What is this? It does not look—exactly—like fractions. 'Lines on the View—v-e-w—from the Window of Blair Water School.' Really, children, we seem to have a budding poet among us."

The words were harmless enough, but—oh, the hateful sneer that ran through the tone—the contempt, the mockery that was in it! It seared Emily's soul like a whip-lash. Nothing was more terrible to her than the thought of having her beloved "poems" read by stranger eyes—cold, unsympathetic, derisive, stranger eyes.

"Please—please, Miss Brownell," she stammered miserably, "don't read it—I'll rub it off—I'll do my sums right away. Only please don't read it. It—it isn't anything."

Miss Brownell laughed cruelly.

"You are too modest, Emily. It is a whole slateful of—*poetry*—think of that, children—*poetry*. We have a pupil in this school who can write—*poetry*. And she does not want us to read this—*poetry*. I am afraid Emily is selfish. I am sure we should all enjoy this—*poetry*."

Emily cringed every time Miss Brownell said *"poetry"* with that jeering emphasis and that hateful pause before it. Many of the children giggled, partly because they enjoyed seeing a "Murray of New Moon" grilled, partly because they realized that Miss Brownell expected them to giggle. Rhoda Stuart giggled louder than any one else; but Jennie

Strang, who had tormented Emily on her first day at school, refused to giggle and scowled blackly at Miss Brownell instead.

Miss Brownell held up the slate and read Emily's poem aloud, in a sing-song nasal voice, with absurd intonations and gestures that made it seem a very ridiculous thing. The lines Emily had thought the finest seemed the most ridiculous. The other pupils laughed more than ever and Emily felt that the bitterness of the moment could never go out of her heart. The little fancies that had been so beautiful when they came to her as she wrote were shattered and bruised now, like torn and mangled butterflies—"vistas in some fairy dream," chanted Miss Brownell, shutting her eyes and wagging her head from side to side. The giggles became shouts of laughter.

"Oh," thought Emily, clenching her hands, "I wish—I wish the bears that ate the naughty children in the Bible would come and eat *you*."

There were no nice, retributive bears in the school bush, however, and Miss Brownell read the whole "poem" through. She was enjoying herself hugely. To ridicule a pupil always gave her pleasure and when that pupil was Emily of New Moon, in whose heart and soul she had always sensed something fundamentally different from her own, the pleasure was exquisite.

When she reached the end she handed the slate back to the crimson-cheeked Emily.

"Take your—*poetry*, Emily," she said.

Emily snatched the slate. No slate "rag" was handy but Emily gave the palm of her hand a fierce lick and one side of the slate was wiped off. Another lick—and the rest of the poem went. It had been disgraced—degraded—it must be blotted out of existence. To the end of her life Emily never forgot the pain and humiliation of that experience.

Miss Brownell laughed again.

"What a pity to obliterate such—*poetry*, Emily," she said. "Suppose you do those sums now. They are not—*poetry*, but I am in this school to teach arithmetic and I am not here to teach the art of writing—*poetry*. Go to your own seat. Yes, Rhoda?"

For Rhoda Stuart was holding up her hand and snapping her fingers.

"Please, Miss Brownell," she said, with distinct triumph in her tones, "Emily Starr has a whole bunch of poetry in her desk. She was reading it to Ilse Burnley this morning while you thought they were learning history."

Perry Miller turned around and a delightful missile, compounded of chewed paper and known as a "spit pill," flew across the room and struck Rhoda squarely in the face. But Miss Brownell was already at Emily's desk, having reached it one jump before Emily herself.

"Don't touch them—you have no *right*!" gasped Emily frantically.

But Miss Brownell had the "bunch of poetry" in her hands. She turned and walked up to the platform. Emily followed. Those poems were very dear to her. She had composed them during the various stormy recesses when it had been impossible to play out of doors and written them down on disreputable scraps of paper borrowed from her mates. She had meant to take them home that very evening and copy them on letter-bills. And now this horrible woman was going to read them to the whole jeering, giggling school.

But Miss Brownell realized that the time was too short for that. She had to content herself with reading over the titles, with some appropriate comments.

Meanwhile Perry Miller was relieving his feelings by bombarding Rhoda Stuart with spit pills, so craftily timed that Rhoda had no idea from what quarter of the room they were coming and so could not "tell" on any one. They greatly interfered with her enjoyment of Emily's scrape, however. As for Teddy Kent, who did not wage war with spit pills but preferred subtler methods of revenge, he was busy drawing something on a sheet of paper. Rhoda found the sheet on her desk the next morning; on it was depicted a small, scrawny monkey, hanging by its tail from a branch; and the face of the monkey was as the face of Rhoda Stuart. Whereat Rhoda Stuart waxed wrath, but for the sake of her own vanity tore the sketch to tatters and kept silence regarding it. She did not know that Teddy had made a similar sketch, with Miss Brownell figuring as a vampirish-looking bat, and thrust it into Emily's hand as they left school.

"'The Lost Dimond—a Romantic Tale,'" read Miss Brownell. "'Lines on a Birch Tree'—looks to me more like lines on a very dirty piece of paper, Emily—'Lines Written on a Sundial in our Garden'—ditto—'Lines to my Favourite Cat"—another romantic *tail*, I presume—'Ode to Ilse'—'Thy neck is of a wondrous pearly sheen'—hardly that, I should say. Ilse's neck is very sunburned—'A Deskripshun of Our Parlour,' 'The Violets Spell'—I hope the violet *spells* better than you do,

142

Emily—'The Disappointed House'—

"Lilies lifted up white cups

For the bees to *dr—r—i—i—nk*."

"I didn't write it that way!" cried tortured Emily.

"'Lines to a Piece of Brokade in Aunt Laura's Burow Drawer,' 'Farewell on Leaving Home,' 'Lines to a Spruce Tree'—'It keeps off heat and sun and glare, Tis a goodly tree I ween'—are you quite sure that you know what 'ween' means, Emily?—'Poem on Mr Tom Bennet's Field'— 'Poem on the Vew from Aunt Elizabeth's Window'—you are strong on 'v-e-w-s,' Emily—'Epitaff on a Drowned Kitten,' 'Meditashuns at the tomb of my great great grandmother'—poor lady—'To my Northern Birds'—'Lines composed on the bank of Blair Water gazing at the stars'—h'm—h'm—

"Crusted with uncounted gems,

Those stars so distant, cold and true,

Don't try to pass those lines off as your own, Emily. You couldn't have written them."

"I did—I did!" Emily was white with sense of outrage. "And I've written lots far better."

Miss Brownell suddenly crumpled the ragged little papers up in her hand.

"We have wasted enough time over this trash," she said. "Go to your seat, Emily."

She moved towards the stove. For a moment Emily did not realize her purpose. Then, as Miss Brownell opened the stove door, Emily understood and bounded forward. She caught at the papers and tore them from Miss Brownell's hand before the latter could tighten her grasp.

"You *shall not* burn them—you shall not have them," gasped Emily. She crammed the poems into the pocket of her "baby apron" and faced Miss Brownell in a kind of calm rage. The Murray look was on her face—and although Miss Brownell was not so violently affected by it as Aunt Elizabeth had been, it nevertheless gave her an unpleasant sensation, as of having roused forces with which she dared not tamper further. This tormented child looked quite capable of flying at her, tooth and claw.

"Give me those papers, Emily,"—but she said it rather uncertainly.

"I will not," said Emily stormily. "They are mine. You have no right to them. I wrote them at recesses—I didn't break any rules. You"—Emily looked defiantly into Miss Brownell's cold eyes—"You are an unjust, tyrannical *person.*"

Miss Brownell turned to her desk.

"I am coming up to New Moon to-night to tell your Aunt Elizabeth of this," she said.

Emily was at first too much excited over saving her precious poetry to pay much heed to this threat. But as her excitement ebbed cold dread flowed in. She knew she had an unpleasant time ahead of her. But at all events they should not get her poems—not one of them, no matter what they did to *her.* As soon as she got home from school she flew to the garret and secreted them on the shelf of the old sofa.

She wanted terribly to cry but she would not. Miss Brownell was coming and Miss Brownell should *not* see her with red eyes. But her heart burned within her. Some sacred temple of her being had been desecrated and shamed. And more was yet to come, she felt wretchedly sure. Aunt Elizabeth was certain to side with Miss Brownell. Emily shrank from the impending ordeal with all the dread of a sensitive, fine strung nature facing humiliation. She would not have been afraid of justice; but she knew at the bar of Aunt Elizabeth and Miss Brownell she would not have justice.

"And I can't write Father about it," she thought, her little breast heaving. The shame of it all was too deep and intimate to be written out, and so she could find no relief for her pain.

They did not have supper at New Moon in winter time until Cousin Jimmy had finished his chores and was ready to stay in for the night. So Emily was left undisturbed in the garret.

From the dormer-window she looked down on a dreamland scene that would ordinarily have delighted her. There was a red sunset behind the white, distant hills, shining through the dark trees like a great fire; there was a delicate blue tracery of bare branch shadows all over the crusted garden; there was a pale, ethereal alpen-glow all over the south-eastern sky; and presently there was a little, lovely new moon in the silvery arch over Lofty John's bush. But Emily found no pleasure in any of them.

Presently she saw Miss Brownell coming up the lane, under the white arms of the birches, with her mannish stride.

"If my father was alive," said Emily, looking down at her, "you would go away from this place with a flea in your ear."

The minutes passed, each seeming very long to Emily. At last Aunt Laura came up.

"Your Aunt Elizabeth wants you to come down to the kitchen, Emily."

Aunt Laura's voice was kind and sad. Emily fought down a sob. She hated to have Aunt Laura think she had been naughty, but she could not trust herself to explain. Aunt Laura would sympathize and sympathy would break her down. She went silently down the two long flights of stairs before Aunt Laura and out to the kitchen.

The supper-table was set and the candles were lighted. The big black-raftered kitchen looked spookish and weird, as it always did by candlelight. Aunt Elizabeth sat rigidly by the table and her face was very hard. Miss Brownell sat in the rocking-chair, her pale eyes glittering with triumphant malice. There seemed something baleful and poisonous in her very glance. Also her nose was very red—which did not add to her charm.

Cousin Jimmy, in his grey jumper, was perched on the edge of the wood-box, whistling at the ceiling, and looking more gnome-like than ever. Perry was nowhere to be seen. Emily was sorry for this. The presence of Perry, who was on her side, would have been a great moral support.

"I am sorry to say, Emily, that I have been hearing some very bad things about your behaviour in school to-day," said Aunt Elizabeth.

"No, I don't think you are sorry," said Emily, gravely.

Now that the crisis had come she found herself able to confront it coolly—nay, more, to take a curious interest in it under all her secret fear and shame, as if some part of her had detached itself from the rest and was interestedly absorbing impressions and analysing motives and describing settings. She felt that when she wrote about this scene later on she must not forget to describe the odd shadows the candle

145

under Aunt Elizabeth's nose cast upward on her face, producing a rather skeletonic effect. As for Miss Brownell, could *she* ever have been a baby—a dimpled, fat, laughing baby? The thing was unbelievable.

"Don't speak impertinently to *me*," said Aunt Elizabeth.

"You see," said Miss Brownell, significantly.

"I don't mean to be impertinent, but you are *not* sorry," persisted Emily. "You are angry because you think I have disgraced New Moon, but you are a little glad that you have got someone to agree with you that I'm bad."

"What a *grateful* child," said Miss Brownell—flashing her eyes up at the ceiling—where they encountered a surprising sight. Perry Miller's head—and no more of him—was stuck down out of the "black hole" and on Perry Miller's upside-down face was a most disrespectful and impish grimace. Face and head disappeared in a flash, leaving Miss Brownell staring foolishly at the ceiling.

"You have been behaving disgracefully in school," said Aunt Elizabeth, who had not seen this by-play. "I am ashamed of you."

"It was not as bad as that, Aunt Elizabeth," said Emily steadily. "You see it was this way—"

"I don't want to hear anything more about it," said Aunt Elizabeth.

"But you must," cried Emily. "It isn't fair to listen only to *her* side. I was a little bad—but not so bad as she says—"

"Not another word! I have heard the whole story," said Aunt Elizabeth grimly.

"You heard a pack of lies," said Perry, suddenly sticking his head down through the black hole again.

Everybody jumped—even Aunt Elizabeth, who at once became angrier than ever because she *had* jumped.

"Perry Miller, come down out of that loft instantly!" she commanded.

"Can't," said Perry laconically.

"At once, I say!"

"Can't," repeated Perry, winking audaciously at Miss Brownell.

"Perry Miller, come down! I *will* be obeyed. I am mistress here *yet*."

"Oh, all right," said Perry cheerfully. "If I must."

He swung himself down until his toes touched the ladder. Aunt Laura gave a little shriek. Everybody also seemed to be stricken dumb.

"I've just got my wet duds off," Perry was saying cheerfully, waving his legs about to get a foothold on the ladder while he hung to the sides of the black hole with his elbows. "Fell into the brook when I was watering the cows. Was going to put on dry ones—but just as you say—"

"Jimmy," implored poor Elizabeth Murray, surrendering at discretion. *She* could not cope with the situation.

"Perry, get back into that loft and get your clothes on this minute!" ordered Cousin Jimmy.

The bare legs shot up and disappeared. There was a chuckle as mirthful and malicious as an owl's beyond the black hole. Aunt Elizabeth gave a convulsive gasp of relief and turned to Emily. She was determined to regain ascendancy and Emily must be thoroughly humbled.

"Emily, kneel down here before Miss Brownell and ask her pardon for your conduct to-day," she said.

Into Emily's pale cheek came a scarlet protest. She could not do this—she would ask pardon of Miss Brownell but not on her knees. To kneel to this cruel woman who had hurt her so—she could not—would not do it. Her whole nature rose up in protest against such a humiliation.

"Kneel down," repeated Aunt Elizabeth.

Miss Brownell looked pleased and expectant. It would be very satisfying to see this child who had defied her kneeling before her as a penitent. Never again, Miss Brownell felt, would Emily be able to look levelly at her with those dauntless eyes that bespoke a soul untamable and free, no matter what punishment might be inflicted upon body or mind. The memory of this moment would always be with Emily—she could never forget that she had knelt in abasement. Emily felt this as clearly as Miss Brownell did and remained stubbornly on her feet.

"Aunt Elizabeth, *please* let me tell my side of the story," she pleaded.

"I have heard all I wish to hear of the matter. You will do as I say, Emily, or you will be outcast in this house until you do. No one will talk to you—play with you—eat with you—have anything to do with you until you have obeyed me."

Emily shuddered. *That* was a punishment she could not face. To be cut off from her world—she knew it would bring her to terms before long. She might as well yield at once—but, ah, the bitterness, the shame of it!

"A human being should not kneel to any one but God," said Cousin Jimmy, unexpectedly, still staring at the ceiling.

A sudden strange change came over Elizabeth Murray's proud, angry face. She stood very still, looking at Cousin Jimmy—stood so long that Miss Brownell made a motion of petulant impatience.

"Emily," said Aunt Elizabeth in a different tone. "I was wrong—I shall not ask you to kneel. But you must apologize to your teacher—and I shall punish you later on."

Emily put her hands behind her and looked straight into Miss Brownell's eyes again.

"I am sorry for anything I did to-day that was wrong," she said, "and I ask your pardon for it."

Miss Brownell got on her feet. She felt herself cheated of a legitimate triumph. Whatever Emily's punishment would be she would not have the satisfaction of seeing it. She could have shaken "Simple Jimmy Murray" with a right good will. But it would hardly do to show all she felt. Elizabeth Murray was not a trustee but she was the heaviest ratepayer in New Moon and had great influence with the School Board.

"I shall excuse your conduct if you behave yourself in future, Emily," she said coldly. "I feel that I have only done my duty in putting the matter before your Aunt. No, thank you, Miss Murray, I cannot stay to supper—I want to get home before it is too dark."

"God speed all travellers," said Perry cheerfully, climbing down his ladder—this time with his clothes on.

Aunt Elizabeth ignored him—she was not going to have a scene with a hired boy before Miss Brownell. The latter switched herself out and Aunt Elizabeth looked at Emily.

"You will eat your supper alone to-night, Emily, in the pantry—you will have bread and milk only. And you will not speak one word to any one until to-morrow morning."

"But you won't forbid me to think?" said Emily anxiously.

Aunt Elizabeth made no reply but sat haughtily down at the supper-table. Emily went into the pantry and ate her bread and milk, with the odour of delicious sausages the others were eating for savour. Emily liked sausages, and New Moon sausages were the last word in sausages. Elizabeth Burnley had brought the recipe out from the Old Country and its secret was carefully guarded. And Emily was hungry. But she had escaped the unbearable, and things might be worse. It suddenly occurred to her that she would write an epic poem in imitation of *The Lay of the Last Minstrel.* Cousin Jimmy had read *The Lay* to her last Saturday. She would begin the first canto right off. When Laura Murray came into the pantry, Emily, her bread and milk only half eaten, was leaning her elbows on the dresser, gazing into space, with faintly moving lips and the light that never was on land or sea in her young eyes. Even the aroma of sausages was forgotten—was she not drinking from a fount of Castaly?

"Emily," said Aunt Laura, shutting the door, and looking very lovingly upon Emily out of her kind blue eyes, "you can talk to *me* all you want to. I don't like Miss Brownell and I don't think you were altogether in the wrong—although of course you shouldn't be writing poetry when you have sums to do. And there are some ginger cookies in that box."

"I don't want to talk to any one, dear Aunt Laura—I'm too happy," said Emily dreamily. "I'm composing an epic—it is to be called *The White Lady,* and I've got twenty lines of it made already—and two of them are thrilling. The heroine wants to go into a convent and her father warns her that if she does she will never be able to

Come back to the life you gave

With all its pleasures to the grave.

Oh, Aunt Laura, when I composed those lines the flash came to me. And ginger cookies are nothing to me any more."

Aunt Laura smiled again.

"Not just now perhaps, dear. But when the moment of inspiration has passed it will do no harm to remember that the cookies in the box have not been counted and that they are as much mine as Elizabeth's."

Living Epistles

"DEAR FATHER:

"Oh, I have such an exiting thing to tell you. I have been the heroin of an adventure. One day last week Ilse asked me if I would go and stay all night with her because her father was away and wouldn't be home till very late and Ilse said she wasn't fritened but very lonesome. So I asked Aunt Elizabeth if I could. I hardly dared hope, dear Father, that

EMILY OF NEW MOON

she would let me, for she doesn't aprove of little girls being away from home at night but to my surprise she said I could go very kindly. And then I heard her say in the pantry to Aunt Laura It is a shame the way the doctor leaves that poor child so much alone at nights. It is *wikked* of him. And Aunt Laura said The poor man is warped. You know he was not a bit like that before his wife—and then just as it was getting intresting Aunt Elizabeth gave Aunt Laura a nudge and said s-s-s-h, little pitchers have big ears. I knew she meant me though my ears are not big, only pointed. I do wish I could find out what Ilse's mother did. It worrys me after I go to bed. I lie awake for ever so long thinking about it. Ilse has no idea. Once she asked her father and he told her (in a *voice of thunder*) never to mention *that woman* to him again. And there is something else that worrys me too. I keep thinking of Silas Lee who killed his brother at the old well. How dreadful the poor man must have felt. And what is it to be warped.

"I went over to Ilses and we played in the garret. I like playing there because we dont have to be careful and tidy like we do in our garret. Ilses garret is very untidy and cant have been dusted for years. The rag room is worse than the rest. It is boarded off at one end of the garret and it is full of old close and bags of rags and broken furniture. I dont like the smell of it. The kitchen chimney goes up through it and things hang round it (or did). For all this is in the past now, dear Father.

"When we got tired playing we sat down on an old chest and talked. This is splendid in daytime I said but it must be awful queer at night. Mice, said Ilse—and spiders and gosts. I dont believe in gosts I said skornfully. There isnt any such thing. (But maybe there is for all that, dear Father.) I believe this garret is hawnted, said Ilse. They say garrets always are. Nonsense I said. You know dear Father it would not do for a New Moon person to believe in gosts. But I felt very queer. Its easy to talk said Ilse beginning to be mad (though I wasnt trying to run down her garret) but you wouldnt stay here alone at night. I wouldnt mind it a bit I said. Then I dare you to do it said Ilse. I dare you to come up here at bedtime and sleep here all night. Then I saw I was in an awful skrape Father dear. It is a foolish thing to bost. I knew not what to do. It was dreadful to think of sleeping alone in that garret but if I didn't Ilse would always cast it up to me whenever we fought and worse than that she would tell Teddy and he would think me a coward. So I said

150

proudly Ill do it Ilse Burnley and Im not afraid either. (But oh I was—inside.) The mice will run over you said Ilse. O I wouldnt be you for the world. It was mean of Ilse to make things worse than they were. But I could feel she admired me too and that helped me a great deal. We dragged an old feather bed out of the rag room and Ilse gave me a pillow and half her close. It was dark by this time and Ilse wouldnt go up into the garret again. So I said my prayers very carefully and then I took a lamp and started up. I am so used to candles now that the lamp made me nervus. Ilse said I looked scared to death. My knees shook dear Father but for the honnor of the Starrs (and the Murrays too) I went on. I had undressed in Ilses room, so I got right into bed and blew out the lamp. But I couldnt go to sleep for a long time. The moonlight made the garret look weerd. I don't know exactly what weerd means but I feel the garret was it. The bags and old close hanging from the beams looked like creatures. I thought I need not be fritened. The angels are here. But then I felt as if I would be as much fritened of angels as of anything else. And I could hear rats and mice scrambling over things. I thought What if a rat was to run over me, and then I thought that next day I would write out a descripshon of the garret by moonlight and my feelings. At last I heard the doctor driving in and then I heard him knocking round in the kitchen and I felt better and before very long I went to sleep and dreamed a dreadful dream. I dreamed the door of the rag room opened and a big newspaper came out and chased me all around the garret. And then it went on fire and I could smell the smoke plain as plain and it was just on me when I skreamed and woke up. I was sitting right up in bed and the newspaper was gone but I could smell smoke still. I looked at the rag room door and smoke was coming out under it and I saw firelight through the cracks of the boards. I just yelled at the top of my voice and tore down to Ilses room and she rushed across the hall and woke her father. He said dam but he got right up and then all three of us kept running up and down the garret stairs with pails of water and we made an awful mess but we got the fire out. It was just the bags of wool that had been hanging close to the chimney that had caught fire. When all was over the doctor wiped the persperation from his manly brow and said That was a close call. A few minutes later would have been too late. I put on a fire when I came in to make a cup of tea and I suppose those bags must have caught fire from a spark. I see theres a hole here where the plaster has tumbled out. I must have this whole place cleaned out. How in the world did you come to diskover the fire, Emily. I was sleeping in the garret I said. Sleeping in the garret said the doctor, what in—what the—*what* were you doing there. Ilse dared me I said. She said Id be too scared to stay there and I said I wouldnt. I fell asleep and woke up and smelled smoke. You little devil, said the doctor. I suppose it was a dreadful thing to be called a devil but the doctor looked at me so admiringly that I felt as if he was paying me a compelment. He has queer ways of talking. Ilse says the only time he ever said a kind thing to her was once when she had a sore throat he called her "a poor little animal" and looked as if he was sorry for her. I feel sure Ilse feels dreadfully bad because her father doesnt like her though she pretends she doesnt care. But oh dear Father there is more to tell. Yesterday the Shrewsbury *Weekly Times* came and in the Blair Notes it told all about the fire at the doctors and said it had been fortunately diskovered in time by Miss Emily Starr. I cant tell you what I felt like when I saw my name in the paper. I felt *famus*. And I never was called Miss in ernest before.

"Last Saturday Aunt Elizabeth and Aunt Laura went to Shrewsbury for the day and left Cousin Jimmy and me to keep house. We had such fun and Cousin Jimmy let me skim all the milk pans. But after dinner unexpekted company came and there was no cake in the house. That was a dreadful thing. It never happened before in the annels of New Moon. Aunt Elizabeth had toothache all day yesterday and Aunt Laura was away at Priest Pond visiting Great Aunt Nancy, so no cake was made. I prayed about it and then I went to work and made a cake by Aunt Laura's receet and it turned out all right. Cousin Jimmy helped me set the table and get supper, and I poured the tea and never slopped any over in the saucers. You would have been proud of me Father. Mrs Lewis took a second piece of cake and said I would know Elizabeth Murray's cake if I found it in central Africa. I said not a word for the honour of the family. But I felt very proud. I had saved the Murrays from disgrace. When Aunt Elizabeth came home and heard the tale she looked grim and tasted a piece that was left and then she said Well, you have got *some* Murray in you anyway. That is the first time Aunt Elizabeth has ever praised me. She had three teeth out so they will not ache any more. I am glad for her sake. Before I went to bed I got the cook-book and picked out all the things Id like to make. Queen

Pudding, Sea-foam Sauce, Blackeyed Susans, Pigs In Blankets. They sound just lovely.

"I can see such beautiful fluffy white clouds over Lofty Johns bush. I wish I could sore up and drop right into them. I cant believe they would be wet and messy like Teddy says. Teddy cut my initials and his together on the Monark of The Forest but somebody has cut them out. I don't know whether it was Perry or Ilse.

"Miss Brownell hardly ever gives me good deportment marks now and Aunt Elizabeth is much displeased on Friday nights but Aunt Laura understands. I wrote an account of the afternoon when Miss Brownell made fun of my poems and put it in an old envelope and wrote Aunt Elizabeths name on it and put it among my papers. If I die of consumption Aunt Elizabeth will find it and know the rites of it and mourn that she was so unjust to me. But I dont think I will die because Im getting much fatter and Ilse told me she heard her father tell Aunt Laura I would be handsome if I had more color. Is it wrong to want to be handsome, dearest Father. Aunt Elizabeth says it is and when I said to her Wouldnt *you* like to be handsome, Aunt Elizabeth, she seemed anoyed about something.

"Miss Brownell has had a spite at Perry ever since that evening and treats him very mean but he is meek and says he wont kick up any fuss in school because he wants to learn and get ahead. He keeps saying his rymes are as good as mine and I know they are not and it exassperates me. If I do not pay attention all the time in school Miss Brownell says I suppose you are composing—poetry Emily and then everybody laughs. No not everybody. I must not exagerate. Teddy and Perry and Ilse and Jennie never laugh. It is funny that I like Jennie so well now and I hated her so that first day in school. Her eyes are not piggy after all. They are small but they are jolly and twinkly. She is quite poplar in school. I do hate Frank Barker. He took my new reader and wrote in a big sprawly way all over the front page

Steal not this book for fear of shame

For on it is the owners name

And when you die the Lord will say

Where is the book you stole away

And when you say you do not know

The Lord will say go down below.

"That is not a refined poem and besides it is not the rite way to speak about God. I tore out the leaf and burned it and Aunt Elizabeth was angry and even when I explained why her rath was not apeased. Ilse says she is going to call God Alla after this. I think it is a nicer name myself. It is so soft and doesn't sound so stern. But I fear its not relijus enough.

MAY 20.

"Yesterday was my birthday dear Father. It will soon be a year since I came to New Moon. I feel as if I had always lived here. I have grown two inches. Cousin Jimmy measured me by a mark on the dairy door. My birthday was very nice. Aunt Laura made a lovely cake and gave me a beautiful new white pettycoat with an embroidered flounce. She had run a blue ribbon through it but Aunt Elizabeth made her pull it out. Aunt Laura also gave me that piece of pink satin brokade in her burow drawer. I have longed for it ever since I saw it but never hoped to possess it. Ilse asked me what I meant to do with it but I dont mean to do anything with it. Only keep it up here in the garret with my treasures and look at it because it is beautiful. Aunt Elizabeth gave me a dixonary. That was a useful present. I feel I ought to like it. You will soon notice an improovement in my spelling, I hope. The only trouble is when I am writing something interesting I get so exited it is just awful to have to stop and hunt up a word to see how it is spelled. I looked up ween in it and Miss Brownell was right. I did not know what it really meant. It rymed so well with sheen and I thought it meant to behold or see but it means to think. Cousin Jimmy gave me a big thick blank book. I am so proud of it. It will be so nice to write pieces in. But I will still use the letter-bills to write to you, dear Father, because I can fold each one up by itself and adress it like a real letter. Teddy gave me a picture of myself. He painted it in water colors and called it The Smiling Girl. I look as if I was listening to something that made me very happy. Ilse says it flatters me. It does make me better looking than

154

I am but not any better than I would be if I could have a bang. Teddy says he is going to paint a real big picture of me when he grows up. Perry walked all the way to Shrewsbury to get me a necklace of pearl beads and lost it. He had no more money so he went home to Stovepipe Town and got a young hen from his Aunt Tom and gave me that. He is a very persistent boy. I am to have all the eggs the hen lays to sell the pedler for myself. Ilse gave me a box of candy. I am only going to eat one piece a day to make it last a long time. I wanted Ilse to eat some but she said she wouldnt because it would be mean to help eat a present you had given and I insisted and then we fought over it and Ilse said I was a caterwawling quadruped (which was ridiklus) and didn't know enough to come in when it rained. And I said I knew enough to have some manners at least. Ilse got so mad she went home but she cooled off soon and came back for supper.

"It is raining to-night and it sounds like fairies feet dancing over the garret roof. If it had not rained Teddy was going to come down and help me look for the Lost Dimond. Wouldnt it be splendid if we could find it.

"Cousin Jimmy is fixing up the garden. He lets me help him and I have a little flower bed of my own. I always run out first thing every morning to see how much the things have grown since yesterday. Spring is such a happyfying time isnt it, Father. The little Blue People are all out round the summer-house. That is what Cousin Jimmy calls the violets and I think it is lovely. He has names like that for all the flowers. The roses are the Queens and the June lilies are the Snow Ladies and the tulips are the Gay Folk and the daffodils are the Golden Ones and the China Asters are My Pink Friends.

"Mike II is here with me, sitting on the window-sill. Mike is a smee cat. Smee is not in the dictionary. It is a word I invented myself. I could not think of any English word which just describes Mike II so I made this up. It means sleek and glossy and soft and fluffy all in one and something else besides that I cant express.

"Aunt Laura is teaching me to sew. She says I must learn to make a hem on muslin that cant be seen (tradishun). I hope she will teach me how to make point lace some day. All the Murrays of New Moon have been noted for making point lace (I mean all the women Murrays). None of the girls in school can make point lace. Aunt Laura says she will make me a point lace hangkerchief when I get married. All the

New Moon brides had point lace hangkerchiefs except my mother who ran away. But you didnt mind her not having one did you Father. Aunt Laura talks a good bit about my mother to me but not when Aunt Elizabeth is around. Aunt Elizabeth never mentions her name. Aunt Laura wants to show me Mothers room but she has never been able to find the key yet because Aunt Elizabeth keeps it hid. Aunt Laura says Aunt Elizabeth loved my mother very much. You would think she would love her daughter some wouldnt you. But she doesnt. She is just bringing me up as a duty.

"JUNE 1.

"DEAR FATHER:

"This has been a very important day. I wrote my first letter. I mean the first letter that was really to go in the mail. It was to Great-Aunt Nancy who lives at Priest Pond and is very old. She wrote Aunt Elizabeth and said I might write now and then to a poor old woman. My heart was touched and I wanted to. Aunt Elizabeth said We might as well let her. And she said to me You must be careful to write a nice letter and I will read it over when it is written. If you make a good impression on Aunt Nancy she may do something for you. I wrote the letter very carefully but it didnt sound a bit like me when it was finished. I couldn't write a good letter when I knew Aunt Elizabeth was going to read it. I felt paralized.

"JUNE 7.

"Dear Father, my letter did not make a good impression on Great-Aunt Nancy. She did not answer it but she wrote Aunt Elizabeth that I must be a very stupid child to write such a stupid letter. I feel insulted because I am not stupid. Perry says he feels like going to Priest Pond and knocking the daylights out of Great-Aunt Nancy. I told him he must not talk like that about my family, and anyhow I dont see how knocking the daylights out of Great-Aunt Nancy would make her change her opinion about me being stupid. (I wonder what daylights are and how you knock them out of people.)

"I have three cantos of *The White Lady* finished. I have the heroin imured in a convent and I don't know how to get her out because I am not a Catholic. I suppose it would have been better if I had a Protestant heroin but there were no Protestants in the days of shivalry. I might have asked Lofty John last year but this year I cant because I've never

156

spoken to him since he played that horrid joke on me about the apple.

"When I meet him on the road I lok straight ahead just as lofty as he does. I have called my pig after him to get square. Cousin Jimmy has given me a little pig for my own. When it is sold I am to have the money. I mean to give some for missionaries and put the rest in the bank to go to my educashun. And I thought if I ever had a pig I would call it Uncle Wallace. But now it does not seem to me proper to call pigs after your uncles even if you dont like them.

"Teddy and Perry and Ilse and I play we are living in the days of shivalry and Ilse and I are distressed damsels reskued by galant knites. Teddy made a splendid suit of armour out of old barrel staves and then Perry made a better one out of old tin boilers hammered flat with a broken saucepan for a helmit. Sometimes we play at the Tansy Patch. I have a queer feeling that Teddy's mother hates me this summer. Last summer she just didnt like me. Smoke and Buttercup are not there now. They disappeared misteriously in the winter. Teddy says he feels sure his mother poisoned them because she thought he was getting too fond of them. Teddy is teaching me to whistle but Aunt Laura says it is unladylike. So many jolly things seem to be unladylike. Sometimes I almost wish my aunts were infidels like Dr Burnley. *He* never bothers whether Ilse is unladylike or not. But no, it would not be good manners to be an infidel. It would not be a New Moon tradishun.

"To-day I taught Perry that he must not eat with his knife. He wants to learn all the *rules of etiket*. And I am helping him learn a recitation for school examination day. I wanted Ilse to do it but she was mad because he asked me first and she wouldnt. But she should because she is a far better reciter than I am. I am too nervus.

"JUNE 14.

"Dear Father, we have composition in school now and I learned to-day that you put things in like this ' ' when you write anything anybody has said. I didnt know that before. I must go over all my letters to you and put them in. And after a question you must put a mark like this ? and when a letter is left out a postroffe which is a comma up in the air. Miss Brownell is sarcastic but she *does* teach you things. I am putting that down because I want to be fair even if I do hate her. And she is interesting although she is not nice. I have written a descripshun of her on a letter-bill. I like writing about people I don't like better than about those I do like. Aunt Laura is nicer to live with than Aunt

Elizabeth, but Aunt Elizabeth is nicer to write about. I can deskribe *her* fawlts but I feel wikked and ungrateful if I say anything that is not complementary about dear Aunt Laura. Aunt Elizabeth has locked your books away and says I'm not to have them till I'm grown up. Just as if I wouldn't be careful of them, dear Father. She says I wouldn't because she found that when I was reading one of them I put a tiny pencil dot under every beautiful word. It didn't hurt the book a bit, dear Father. Some of the words were dingles, pearled, musk, dappled, intervales, glen, bosky, piping, shimmer, crisp, beechen, ivory. I think those are all lovely words, Father.

"Aunt Laura lets me read her copy of A Pilgrims Progress on Sundays. I call the big hill on the road to White Cross the Delectable Mountain because it is such a beautiful one.

"Teddy lent me 3 books of poetry. One of them was Tennyson and I have learned The Bugle Song off by heart so I will always have it. One was Mrs Browning. She is lovely. I would like to meet her. I suppose I will when I die but that may be a long time away. The other was just one poem called Sohrab and Rustum. After I went to bed I cried over it. Aunt Elizabeth said "what are you sniffling about?" I wasn't sniffling—I was weeping sore. She made me tell her and then she said "You must be crazy." But I couldn't go to sleep until I had thought out a different end for it—a happy one.

"JUNE 25.

DEAR FATHER:

"There has been a dark shadow over this day. I dropped my cent in church. It made a dreadful noise. I felt as if everybody looked at me. Aunt Elizabeth was much annoyed. Perry dropped his too soon after. He told me after church he did it on purpose because he thought it would make me feel better but it didn't because I was afraid the people would think it was me dropping mine again. Boys do such queer things. I hope the minister did not hear because I am beginning to like him. I never liked him much before last Tuesday. His family are all boys and I suppose he doesn't understand little girls very well. Then he called at New Moon. Aunt Laura and Aunt Elizabeth were both away and I was in the kitchen alone. Mr Dare came in and sat down on Saucy Sal who was asleep in the rocking-chair. He was comfortable but Saucy Sal wasn't. He didn't sit on her stomach. If he had I suppose he would have killed her. He just sat on her legs and tail. Sal yowled but Mr Dare is a little deaf and didn't hear her and I was too shy to tell him. But Cousin Jimmy came in just as he was asking me if I knew my catechism and said "Catechism, is it? Lawful heart, man, listen to that poor dum beast. Get up if you're a Christian." So Mr Dare got up and said, "Dear me, this is very remarkable. I thought I felt something moving."

"I thought I would write this to you, dear Father, because it struck me as humerus.

"When Mr Dare finished asking me questions I thought it was my turn and I would ask him some about some things I've wanted to know for years. I asked him if he thought God was very perticular about every little thing I did and if he thought my cats would go to heaven. He said he hoped I never did wrong things and that animals had no souls. And I asked him why we shouldn't put new wine in old bottles. Aunt Elizabeth does with her dandelion wine and the old bottles do just as well as new ones. He explained quite kindly that the Bible bottles were made of skins and got rotten when they were old. It made it quite clear to me. Then I told him I was worried because I knew I ought to love God better than anything but there were things I loved better than God. He said "What things?" and I said flowers and stars and the Wind Woman and the Three Princesses and things like that. And he smiled and said "But they are just a part of God, Emily—every beautiful thing is." And all at once I liked him ever so much and didn't feel shy with him any more. He preached a sermon on heaven last Sunday. It seemed like a dull place. I think it must be more exciting than that. I wonder what I will do when I go to heaven since I cant sing. I wonder if they will let me write poetry. But I think church is interesting. Aunt Elizabeth and Aunt Laura always read their Bibles before the servis begins but I like to stare around and see everybody and wonder what they are thinking of. It's so nice to hear the silk dresses swishing up the isles. Bustles are very fashunable now but Aunt Elizabeth will not wear them. I think Aunt Elizabeth *would* look funny with a bustle. Aunt Laura wears a very little one.

"Your lovingest daughter,

"*Emily B. Starr.*

"P. S. Dear Father, it is lovely to write to you. But O, I never get an answer back.

159

"*E. B. S.*"

FATHER CASSIDY

Consternation reigned at New Moon. Everybody was desperately unhappy. Aunt Laura cried. Aunt Elizabeth was so cantankerous that there was no living with her. Cousin Jimmy went about as one distracted and Emily gave up worrying about Ilse's mother and Silas Lee's remorseful ghost after she went to bed, and worried over this new trouble. For it had all originated in her disregard of New Moon tradition in making calls on Lofty John, and Aunt Elizabeth did not mince matters in telling her so. If she, Emily Byrd Starr, had never gone to Lofty John's she would never have eaten the Big Sweet apple, and if she had never eaten the Big Sweet apple Lofty John would not have played a joke on her and if he had not played a joke on her Aunt Elizabeth would never have gone and said bitter, Murray-like things to him; and if Aunt Elizabeth had never said bitter Murray-like things to him Lofty John would not have become offended and revengeful; and if Lofty John had not become offended and revengeful he would never have taken it into his lofty head to cut down the beautiful grove to the north of New Moon.

For this was exactly where this house-that-jack-built progression had landed them all. Lofty John had announced publicly in the Blair Water blacksmith shop that he was going to cut down the bush as soon as harvest was over—every last tree and sapling was to be laid low. The news was promptly carried to New Moon and upset the inhabitants thereof as they had not been upset for years. In their eyes it was nothing short of a catastrophe.

Elizabeth and Laura could hardly bring themselves to believe it. The thing was incredible. That big, thick, protecting bush of spruce and hardwood had *always* been there; it belonged to New Moon *morally*; even Lofty John Sullivan would not *dare* to cut it down. But Lofty John had an uncomfortable reputation for doing what he said he would do;

160

that was a part of his loftiness; and if he did—if he did—

"New Moon will be ruined," wailed poor Aunt Laura. "It will look *dreadful—all* its beauty will go—and we will be left open to the north wind and the sea storms—we have always been so warm and sheltered here. And Jimmy's garden will be ruined too."

"This is what comes of bringing Emily here," said Aunt Elizabeth.

It was a cruel thing to say, even when all allowances were made—cruel and unjust, since her own sharp tongue and Murray sarcasm had had quite as much to do with it as Emily. But she said it and it pierced Emily to the heart with a pang that left a scar for years. Poor Emily did not feel as if she needed any additional anguish. She was already feeling so wretched that she could not eat or sleep. Elizabeth Murray, angry and unhappy as she was, slept soundly at nights; but beside her in the darkness, afraid to move or turn, lay a slender little creature whose tears, stealing silently down her cheeks, could not ease her breaking heart. For Emily thought her heart *was* breaking; she couldn't go on living and suffering like this. Nobody could.

Emily had lived long enough at New Moon for it to get pretty thoroughly into her blood. Perhaps it had even been born there. At any rate, when she came to it she fitted into its atmosphere as a hand into a glove. She loved it as well as if she had lived there all her short life—loved every stick and stone and tree and blade of grass about it—every nail in the old, kitchen floor, every cushion of green moss on the dairy roof, every pink and white columbine that grew in the old orchard, every "tradition" of its history. To think of its beauty being in a large measure reft from it was agony to her. And to think of Cousin Jimmy's garden being ruined! Emily loved that garden almost as much as he did; why, it was the pride of Cousin Jimmy's life that he could grow there plants and shrubs that would winter nowhere else in P. E. Island; if the northern shelter were removed they would die. And to think of that beautiful bush itself being cut down—the To-day Road and the Yesterday Road and the To-morrow Road being swept out of existence—the stately Monarch of the Forest discrowned—the little playhouse where she and Ilse had such glorious hours destroyed—the whole lovely, ferny, intimate place torn out of her life at one fell swoop.

Oh, Lofty John had chosen and timed his vengeance well!

When would the blow fall? Every morning Emily listened miserably as she stood on the sandstone doorstep of the kitchen, for the sound of axe blows on the clear September air. Every evening when she returned from school she dreaded to see that the work of destruction had begun. She pined and fretted. There were times when it seemed to her she couldn't bear her life any longer. Every day Aunt Elizabeth said something imputing the whole blame to her and the child grew morbidly sensitive about it. Almost she wished Lofty John would begin and be done with it. If Emily had ever heard the classic story of Damocles she would have heartily sympathized with him. If she had had any hope that it would do any good she would have swallowed Murray pride and Starr pride and every other kind of pride and gone on her knees to Lofty John to entreat him to hold his revengeful hand. But she believed it would not. Lofty John had left no doubt in anybody's mind as to his bitter determination in the matter. There was much talk about it in Blair Water and some were very well pleased at this blow to New Moon pride and prestige, and some held that it was low and unclean behaviour on Lofty John's part, and all agreed that this was what they had prophesied all along as bound to happen some day when the old Murray-Sullivan feud of three generations should have come to its inevitable head. The only surprising thing was that Lofty John hadn't done it long ago. He had always hated Elizabeth Murray since their school-days, when her tongue had not spared him.

One day by the banks of Blair Water Emily sat down and wept. She had been sent to trim the dead blossoms off the rosebushes on Grandmother Murray's grave; having finished her task she had not the heart to go back to the house where Aunt Elizabeth was making everybody miserable because she was herself so unhappy. Perry had reported that Lofty John had stated the day before at the blacksmith's that he was going to begin cutting down the big bush on Monday morning.

"I *can't* bear it," sobbed Emily to the rose-bushes.

A few late roses nodded at her; the Wind Woman combed and waved and stirred the long green grasses on the graves where proud Murrays, men and women, slept calmly, unstirred by old feuds and passions; the September sunlight shone beyond on old harvest fields mellowly bright and serene, and very softly against its green, shrub-hung bank, purred and lapped the blue Blair Water.

"I don't see why God doesn't *stop* Lofty John," said Emily

passionately. Surely the New Moon Murrays had a right to expect that much from Providence.

Teddy came whistling down the pasture, the notes of his tune blowing across the Blair Water like elfin drops of sound, vaulted the graveyard fence and perched his lean, graceful body irreverently on the "Here I stay" of Great-Grandrnother Murray's flat tombstone.

"What's the matter?" he said.

"Everything's the matter," said Emily, a little crossly. Teddy had no business to be looking so cheerful. She was used to more sympathy from Teddy and it aggravated her not to find it. "Don't you know Lofty John is going to begin cutting down the bush Monday?"

Teddy nodded.

"Yep. Ilse told me. But look here, Emily, I've thought of something. Lofty John wouldn't dare cut down that bush if the priest told him not to, would he?"

"Why?"

"Because the Catholics have to do just what their priests tell them to, haven't they?"

"I don't know—I don't know anything about them. *We* are Presbyterians."

Emily gave her head a little toss. Mrs Kent was known to be an "English Church" woman and though Teddy went to the Presbyterian Sunday-school, that fact gave him scanty standing among bred-in-the-bone Presbyterian circles.

"If your Aunt Elizabeth went to Father Cassidy at White Cross and asked him to stop Lofty John, maybe he'd do it," persisted Teddy.

"Aunt Elizabeth would never do that," said Emily positively. "I'm sure of it. She's too proud."

"Not even to save the bush?"

"Not even for that."

"Then I guess nothing can be done," said Teddy rather crestfallen. "Look here—see what I've made. This is a picture of Lofty John in purgatory, with three little devils sticking red-hot pitchforks into him. I copied some of it out of one of Mother's books—Dante's Infernal, I think it was—but I put Lofty John in place of the man in the book. You can have it."

"I don't want it." Emily uncoiled her legs and got up. She was past the stage when inflicting imaginary torments on Lofty John could comfort her. She had already slain him in several agonizing ways during her night vigils. But an idea had come to her—a daring, breathless idea. "I must go home now, Teddy—it's supper-time."

Teddy pocketed his despised sketch—which was really a wonderful bit of work if either of them had had the sense to know it: the expression of anguish in Lofty John's face as a merry little devil touched him up with a pitchfork would have been the despair of many a trained artist. He went home wishing he could help Emily; it was all wrong that a creature like Emily—with soft purple-gray eyes and a smile that made you think of all sorts of wonderful things you couldn't put into words—should be unhappy. Teddy felt so worried about it that he added a few more devils to his sketch of Lofty John in purgatory and lengthened the prongs of their pitchforks quite considerably.

Emily went home with a determined twist to her mouth. She ate as much supper as she could—which wasn't much, for Aunt Elizabeth's face would have destroyed her appetite if she had had any—and then sneaked out of the house by the front door. Cousin Jimmy was working in his garden but he did not call her. Cousin Jimmy was always very sorrowful now. Emily stood a moment on the Grecian porch and looked at Lofty John's bush—green-bosomed, waving, all lovely. Would it be a desecrated waste of stumps by Monday night? Goaded by the thought Emily cast fear and hesitation to the winds and started briskly off down the lane. When she reached the gate she turned to the left on the long red road of mystery that ran up the Delectable Mountain. She had never been on that road before; it ran straight to White Cross; Emily was going to the parish house there to interview Father Cassidy. It was two miles to White Cross and Emily walked it all too soon— not because it was a beautiful road of wind and wild fern, haunted by little rabbits—but because she dreaded what awaited her at the end. She had been trying to think what she should say—how she should say it; but her invention failed her. She had no acquaintance with Catholic priests, and couldn't imagine how you should talk to them at all. They were even more mysterious and unknowable than ministers. Suppose Father Cassidy should be dreadfully angry at her daring to come there and ask a favour. Perhaps it *was* a dreadful thing to do from every point of view. And very likely it would do no good. Very likely Father Cassidy would refuse to interfere with Lofty John, who was a good

Catholic, while she was, in his opinion, a heretic. But for any chance, even the faintest, of averting the calamity impending over New Moon, Emily would have faced the entire Sacred College. Horribly frightened, miserably nervous as she was, the idea of turning back never occurred to her. She was only sorry that she hadn't put on her Venetian beads. They might have impressed Father Cassidy.

Although Emily had never been to White Cross she knew the parish house when she saw it—a fine, tree-embowered residence near the big white chapel with the flashing gilt cross on its spire and the four gilt angels, one on each of the little spires at the corners. Emily thought them very beautiful as they gleamed in the light of the lowering sun, and wished they could have some on the plain white church at Blair Water. She couldn't understand why Catholics should have all the angels. But there was not time to puzzle over this, for the door was opening and the trim little maid was looking a question.

"Is—Father Cassidy—at—home?" asked Emily, rather jerkily.

"Yes."

"Can—I—see—him?"

"Come in," said the little maid. Evidently there was no difficulty about seeing Father Cassidy—no mysterious ceremonies such as Emily had half expected, even if she were allowed to see him at all. She was shown into a book-lined room and left there, while the maid went to call Father Cassidy, who, she said, was working in the garden. *That* sounded quite natural and encouraging. If Father Cassidy worked in a garden, he could not be so very terrible.

Emily looked about her curiously. She was in a very pretty room— with cosy chairs, and pictures and flowers. Nothing alarming or uncanny about it—except a huge black cat who was sitting on the top of one of the bookcases. It was really an enormous creature. Emily adored cats and had always felt at home with any of them. But she had never seen such a cat as this. What with its size and its insolent, gold-hued eyes, set like living jewels in its black velvet face, it did not seem to belong to the same species as nice, cuddly, respectable kittens at all. Mr Dare would never have had such a beast about his manse. All Emily's dread of Father Cassidy returned.

And then in came Father Cassidy, with the friendliest smile in the world. Emily took him in with her level glance as was her habit—or gift—and never again in the world was she the least bit afraid of Father

Cassidy. He was big and broad-shouldered, with brown eyes and brown hair; and his very face was so deeply tanned from his inveterate habit of going about bareheaded in merciless sunshine, that it was brown, too. Emily thought he looked just like a big nut—a big, brown, wholesome nut.

Father Cassidy looked at her as he shook hands; Emily had one of her visitations of beauty just then. Excitement had brought a wildrose hue to her face, the sunlight brought out the watered-silk gloss of her black hair; her eyes were softly dark and limpid; but it was at her ears Father Cassidy suddenly bent to look. Emily had a moment of agonized wonder if they were clean.

"She's got pointed ears," said Father Cassidy, in a thrilling whisper. "Pointed ears! I *knew* she came straight from fairyland the minute I saw her. Sit down, Elf—if elves do sit—sit down and give me the latest news av Titania's court."

Emily's foot was now on her native heath. Father Cassidy talked her language, and he talked it in such a mellow, throaty voice, slurring his "ofs" ever so softly as became a proper Irishman. But she shook her head a little sadly. With the burden of her errand on her soul she could not play the part of ambassadress from Elfland.

"I'm only Emily Starr of New Moon," she said; and then gasped hurriedly, because there must be no deception—no sailing under false colours, "and I'm a Protestant."

"And a very nice little Protestant you are," said Father Cassidy. "But for sure I'm a bit disappointed. I'm used to Protestants—the woods hereabouts being full av them—but it's a hundred years since the last elf called on me."

Emily stared. Surely Father Cassidy wasn't a hundred years old. He didn't look more than fifty. Perhaps, though, Catholic priests did live longer than other people. She didn't know exactly what to say so she said, a bit lamely,

"I see you have a cat."

"Wrong." Father Cassidy shook his head and groaned dismally. "A cat has me."

Emily gave up trying to understand Father Cassidy. He was nice but ununderstandable. She let it go at that. And she must get on with her errand.

166

"You are a kind of minister, aren't you?" she asked timidly. She didn't know whether Father Cassidy would like being called a minister.

"Kind av," he agreed amiably. "And you see ministers and priests can't do their own swearing. They have to keep cats to do it for them. I never knew any cat that could sware as genteelly and effectively as the B'y."

"Is that what you call him?" asked Emily, looking at the black cat in some awe. It seemed hardly safe to discuss him right before his face.

"That's what he calls himself. My mother doesn't like him because he steals the cream. Now, *I* don't mind his doing that; no, it's his way av licking his jaws after it that I can't stand. Oh, B'y, we've a fairy calling on us. Be excited for once, I implore you—there's a duck av a cat."

The B'y refused to be excited. He winked an insolent eye at Emily.

"Have you any idea what goes on in the head av a cat, elf?"

What queer questions Father Cassidy asked. Yet Emily thought she would like his questions if she were not so worried. Suddenly Father Cassidy leaned across the table and said,

"Now, just what's bothering you?"

"I'm so unhappy," said Emily piteously.

"So are lots av other people. Everybody is unhappy by spells, But creatures who have pointed ears shouldn't be unhappy. It's only mortals who should be that."

"Oh, please—please—" Emily wondered what she should call him. Would it offend him if a Protestant called him "Father"? But she had to risk it—"please, Father Cassidy, I'm in such trouble and I've come to ask a *great favour* of you."

Emily told him the whole tale from beginning to end—the old Murray-Sullivan feud, her erstwhile friendship with Lofty John, the Big Sweet apple, the unhappy consequence, and Lofty John's threatened revenge. The B'y and Father Cassidy listened with equal gravity until she had finished. Then the B'y winked at her, but Father Cassidy put his long brown fingers together.

"Humph," he said.

("That's the first time," reflected Emily, "that I've ever heard anyone outside of a book say 'Humph.'")

"Humph," said Father Cassidy again. "And you want me to put a stop to this nefarious deed?"

"If you can," said Emily. "Oh, it would be so splendid if you could.

Will you—will you?"

Father Cassidy fitted his fingers still more carefully together.

"I'm afraid I can hardly invoke the power av the keys to prevent Lofty John from disposing as he wishes av his own lawful property, you know, elf."

Emily didn't understand the allusion to the keys but she did understand that Father Cassidy was declining to bring the lever of the Church to bear on Lofty John. There was no hope, then. She could not keep the tears of disappointment out of her eyes.

"Oh, come now, darling, don't cry," implored Father Cassidy. "Elves never cry—they can't. It would break my heart to discover you weren't av the Green Folk. You may call yourself av New Moon and av any religion you like, but the fact remains that you belong to the Golden Age and the old gods. That's why I must save your precious bit av greenwood for you."

Emily stared.

"I think it can be done," Father Cassidy went on. "I think if I go to Lofty John and have a heart-to-heart talk with him I can make him see reason. Lofty John and I are very good friends. He's a reasonable creature, if you know how to take him—which means to flatter his vanity judiciously. I'll put it to him, not as priest to parishioner, but as man to man, that no decent Irishman carries on a feud with women and that no sensible person is going to destroy for nothing but a grudge those fine old trees that have taken half a century to grow and can never be replaced. Why the man who cuts down such a tree except when it is really necessary should be hanged as high as Haman on a gallows made from the wood av it."

(Emily thought she would write that last sentence of Father Cassidy's down in Cousin Jimmy's blank book when she got home.)

"But I won't say *that* to Lofty John," concluded Father Cassidy. "Yes, Emily av New Moon, I think we can consider it a settled thing that your bush will not be cut down."

Suddenly Emily felt very happy. Somehow she had entire confidence in Father Cassidy. She was sure he would twist Lofty John around his little finger.

"Oh, I can never thank you enough!" she said earnestly.

"That's true, so don't waste breath trying. And now tell me things.

Are there any more av you? And how long have you been yourself?"

"I'm twelve years old—I haven't any brothers or sisters. And I *think* I'd better be going home."

"Not till you've had a bite av lunch."

"Oh, thank you, I've had my supper."

"Two hours ago and a two-mile walk since. Don't tell me. I'm sorry I haven't any nectar and ambrosia on hand—such food as elves eat—and not even a saucer av moonshine—but my mother makes the best plum cake av any woman in P. E. Island. And we keep a cream cow. Wait here a bit. Don't be afraid av the B'y. He eats tender little Protestants sometimes, but he never meddles with leprechauns."

When Father Cassidy came back his mother came with him, carrying a tray. Emily had expected to see her big and brown too, but she was the tiniest woman imaginable, with snow-white, silky hair, mild blue eyes, and pink cheeks.

"Isn't she the sweetest thing in the way av mothers?" asked Father Cassidy. "I keep her to look at. Av course—" Father Cassidy dropped his voice to a pig's whisper—"there's something odd about her. I've known that woman to stop right in the middle av housecleaning, and go off and spend an afternoon in the woods. Like yourself, I'm thinking she has some truck with fairies."

Mrs Cassidy smiled, kissed Emily, said she must go out and finish her preserving, and trotted off.

"Now you sit right down here, Elf, and be human for ten minutes and we'll have a friendly snack."

Emily *was* hungry—a nice comfortable feeling she hadn't experienced for a fortnight. Mrs Cassidy's plum cake was all her reverend son claimed, and the cream cow seemed to be no myth.

"What do you think av me now?" asked Father Cassidy suddenly, finding Emily's eyes fixed on him speculatively.

Emily blushed. She had been wondering if she dared ask another favour of Father Cassidy.

"I think you are awfully good," she said.

"I *am* awfully good," agreed Father Cassidy. "I'm so good that I'll do what you want me to do—for I feel there's something else you want me to do."

"I'm in a scrape and I've been in it all summer. You see"—Emily was very sober—"I am a poetess."

"Holy Mike! That *is* serious. I don't know if I can do much for you. How long have you been that way?"

"Are you making fun of me?" asked Emily gravely.

Father Cassidy swallowed something besides plum cake.

"The saints forbid! It's only that I'm rather overcome. To be after entertaining a lady av New Moon—and an elf—and a poetess all in one is a bit too much for a humble praste like meself. Have another slice av cake and tell me all about it."

"It's like this—I'm writing an epic."

Father Cassidy suddenly leaned over and gave Emily's wrist a little pinch.

"I just wanted to see if you were real," he explained. "Yes—yes, you're writing an epic—go on. I think I've got my second wind now."

"I began it last spring. I called it *The White Lady* first but now I've changed it to *The Child of the Sea*. Don't you think that's a better title?"

"Much better."

"I've got three cantos done, and I can't get any further because there's something I don't know and can't find out. I've been so worried about it."

"What is it?"

"My epic," said Emily, diligently devouring plum cake, "is about a very beautiful high-born girl who was stolen away from her real parents when she was a baby and brought up in a woodcutter's hut."

"One av the seven original plots in the world," murmured Father Cassidy.

"What?"

"Nothing. Just a bad habit av thinking aloud. Go on."

"She had a lover of high degree but his family did not want him to marry her because she was only a woodcutter's daughter—"

"Another of the seven plots—excuse me."

"—so they sent him away to the Holy Land on a crusade and word came back that he was killed and then Editha—her name was Editha—went into a convent—"

Emily paused for a bite of plum cake and Father Cassidy took up the strain.

"And now her lover comes back very much alive, though covered with Paynim scars, and the secret av her birth is discovered through the dying confession av the old nurse and the birthmark on her arm."

"How did you know?" gasped Emily in amazement.

"Oh, I guessed it—I'm a good guesser. But where's your bother in all this?"

"I don't know how to get her out of the convent," confessed Emily. "I thought perhaps you would know how it could be done."

Again Father Cassidy fitted his fingers.

"Let us see, now. It's no light matter you've undertaken, young lady. How stands the case? *Editha* has taken the veil, not because she has a religious vocation but because she imagines her heart is broken. The Catholic Church does not release its nuns from their vows because they happen to think they've made a little mistake av that sort. No, no—we must have a better reason. Is this Editha the sole child av her real parents?"

"Yes."

"Oh, then the way is clear. If she had had any brothers or sisters you would have had to kill them off, which is a messy thing to do. Well, then, she is the sole daughter and heiress av a noble family who have for years been at deadly feud with another noble family—the family av the lover. Do you know what a feud is?"

"Of course," said Emily disdainfully. "And I've got all that in the poem already."

"So much the better. This feud has rent the kingdom in twain and can only be healed by an alliance between Capulet and Montague."

"Those aren't their names."

"No matter. This, then, is a national affair, with far-reaching issues, therefore an appeal to the Supreme Pontiff is quite in order. What you want," Father Cassidy nodded solemnly, "is a dispensation from Rome."

"Dispensation is a hard word to work into a poem," said Emily.

"Undoubtedly. But young ladies who *will* write epic poems and who *will* lay the scenes thereof amid times and manners av hundreds av years ago, and *will* choose heroines of a religion quite unknown to them, *must* expect to run up against a few snags."

"Oh, I think I'll be able to work it in," said Emily cheerfully. "And I'm so much obliged to you. You don't know what a relief it is to my mind. I'll finish the poem right up now in a few weeks. I haven't done a thing at it all summer. But then of course I've been busy. Ilse Burnley

171

and I have been making a new language."

"Making a—new—excuse me. *Did* you say *language*?"

"Yes."

"What's the matter with English? Isn't it good enough for you, you incomprehensible little being?"

"Oh, yes. *That* isn't why we're making a new one. You see in the spring, Cousin Jimmy got a lot of French boys to help plant the potatoes. I had to help too, and Ilse came to keep me company. And it was so annoying to hear those boys talking French when we couldn't understand a word of it. They did it just to make us mad. Such jabbering! So Ilse and I just made up our minds we'd invent a new language that *they* couldn't understand. We're getting on fine and when the potato picking time comes we'll be able to talk to each other and those boys won't be able to understand a word we're saying. Oh, it will be great fun!"

"I haven't a doubt. But two girls who will go to all the trouble av inventing a new language just to get square with some poor little French boys—you're beyond me," said Father Cassidy, helplessly. "Goodness knows what you'll be doing when you grow up. You'll be Red Revolutionists. I tremble for Canada."

"Oh, it isn't a trouble—it's fun. And all the girls in school are just wild because they hear us talking in it and can't make it out. We can talk secrets right before them."

"Human nature being what it is, I can see where the fun comes in all right. Let's hear a sample av your language."

"Nat millan O ste dolman bote ta Shrewsbury fernas ta poo litanos," said Emily glibly. "That means, 'Next summer I am going to Shrewsbury woods to pick strawberries.' I yelled that across the playground to Ilse the other day at recess and oh, how everybody stared."

"Staring, is it? I should say so. My own poor old eyes are all but dropping out av me head. Let's hear a bit more av it."

"Mo tral li dead seb ad li mo trene. Mo bertral seb mo bertrene das sten dead e ting setra. *That* means 'My father is dead and so is my mother. My grandfather and grandmother have been dead a long time.' We haven't invented a word for 'dead' yet. I think I will soon be able to write my poems in our language and then Aunt Elizabeth will not be able to read them if she finds them."

"Have you written any other poetry besides your epic?"

"Oh, yes—but just short pieces—dozens of them."

"H'm. Would you be so kind as to let me hear one av them?"

Emily was greatly flattered. And she did not mind letting Father Cassidy hear her precious stuff.

"I'll recite my last poem," she said, clearing her throat importantly. "It's called *Evening Dreams.*"

Father Cassidy listened attentively. After the first verse a change came over his big brown face, and he began patting his finger tips together. When Emily finished she hung down her lashes and waited tremblingly. What if Father Cassidy said it was no good? No, he wouldn't be so impolite—but if he bantered her as he had done about her epic—she would know what *that* meant.

Father Cassidy did not speak all at once. The prolonged suspense was terrible to Emily. She was afraid he could not praise and did not want to hurt her feelings by dispraise. All at once her "Evening Dreams" seemed trash and she wondered how she could ever have been silly enough to repeat it to Father Cassidy.

Of course, it *was* trash. Father Cassidy knew that well enough. All the same, for a child like this—and rhyme and rhythm were flawless— and there was one line—just one line—"the light of faintly golden stars"—for the sake of that line Father Cassidy suddenly said,

"Keep on—keep on writing poetry."

"You mean—?" Emily was breathless.

"I mean you'll be able to do something by and by. Something—I don't know how much—but keep on—keep on."

Emily was so happy she wanted to cry. It was the first word of commendation she had ever received except from her father—and a father might have too high an opinion of one. *This* was different. To the end of her struggle for recognition Emily never forgot Father Cassidy's "Keep on" and the tone in which he said it.

"Aunt Elizabeth scolds me for writing poetry," she said wistfully. "She says people will think I'm as simple as Cousin Jimmy."

"The path of genius never did run smooth. But have another piece av cake—do, just to show there's something human about you."

"Ve, merry ti. O del re dolman cosey aman ri sen ritter. *That* means, 'No, thank you. I must be going home before it gets dark.'"

"I'll drive you home."

"Oh, no, no. It's very kind of you"—the English language was quite good enough for Emily now, "but I'd rather *walk*. "It's—it's—such good exercise."

"Meaning," said Father Cassidy with a twinkle in his eye, "that we must keep it from the old lady? Good-bye, and may you always see a happy face in your looking-glass!"

Emily was too happy to be tired on the way home. There seemed to be a bubble of joy in her heart—a shimmering, prismatic bubble. When she came to the top of the big hill and looked across to New Moon, her eyes were satisfied and loving. How beautiful it was, lying embowered in the twilight of the old trees; the tips of the loftiest spruces came out in purple silhouette against the north-western sky of rose and amber; down behind it the Blair Water dreamed in silver; the Wind Woman had folded her misty bat-wings in a valley of sunset and stillness lay over the world like a blessing. Emily felt sure everything would be all right. Father Cassidy would manage it in some way.

And he had told her to "keep on."

FRIENDS AGAIN

Emily listened very anxiously on Monday morning, but "no sound of axe, no ponderous hammer rang" in Lofty John's bush. That evening on her way home from school, Lofty John himself overtook her in his buggy and for the first time since the night of the apple stopped and accosted her.

"Will ye take a lift, Miss Emily av New Moon?" he asked affably.

Emily climbed in, feeling a little bit foolish. But Lofty John looked quite friendly as he clucked to his horse.

"So you've clean wiled the heart out av Father Cassidy's body, 'The sweetest scrap av a girl I've iver seen,' says he to me. Sure an' ye might lave the poor prastes alone."

Emily looked at Lofty John out of the corner of her eye. He did not seem angry.

"Ye've put *me* in a nice tight fix av it," he went on. "I'm as proud

174

as any New Moon Murray av ye all and your Aunt Elizabeth said a number av things that got under my skin. I've many an old score to settle with her. So I thought I'd get square by cutting av the bush down. And you had to go and quare me wid me praste bekase av it and now I make no doubt I'll not be after daring to cut a stick av kindling to warm me shivering carcase without asking lave av the Pope."

"Oh, Mr Sullivan, are you going to leave the bush alone?" said Emily breathlessly.

"It all rests with yourself, Miss Emily av New Moon. Ye can't be after expecting a Lofty John to be too humble. I didn't come by the name bekase av me makeness."

"What do you want me to do?"

"First, then, I'm wanting you to let bygones be bygones in that matter av the apple. And be token av the same come over and talk to me now and then as ye did last summer. Sure now, and I've missed ye—ye and that spit-fire av an Ilse who's never come aither bekase she thinks I mistrated you."

"I'll come of course," said Emily doubtfully, "if only Aunt Elizabeth will let me."

"Tell her if she don't the bush'll be cut down—ivery last stick av it. That'll fetch her. And there's wan more thing. Ye must ask me rale make and polite to do ye the favour av not cutting down the bush. If ye do it pretty enough sure niver a tree will I touch. But if ye don't down they go, praste or no praste," concluded Lofty John.

Emily summoned all her wiles to her aid. She clasped her hands, she looked up through her lashes at Lofty John, she smiled as slowly and seductively as she knew how—and Emily had considerable native knowledge of that sort. "Please, Mr Lofty John," she coaxed, "won't you leave me the dear bush I love?"

Lofty John swept off his crumpled old felt hat. "To be sure an' I will. A proper Irishman always does what a lady asks him. Sure an' it's been the ruin av us. We're at the mercy av the petticoats. If ye'd come and said that to me afore ye'd have had no need av your walk to White Cross. But mind ye keep the rest av the bargain. The reds are ripe and the scabs soon will be—and all the rats have gone to glory."

Emily flew into the New Moon kitchen like a slim whirlwind.

"Aunt Elizabeth, Lofty John isn't going to cut down the bush—he told me he wouldn't—but I have to go and see him sometimes—if you

175

don't object."

"I suppose it wouldn't make much difference to you if I did," said Aunt Elizabeth. But her voice was not so sharp as usual. She would not confess how much Emily's announcement relieved her; but it mellowed her attitude considerably. "There's a letter here for you. I want to know what it means."

Emily took the letter. It was the first time she had ever received a real letter through the mail and she tingled with the delight of it. It was addressed in a heavy black hand to "Miss Emily Starr, New Moon, Blair Water." But—

"You opened it!" she cried indignantly.

"Of course I did. You are not going to receive letters I am not to see, Miss. What I want to know is—how comes Father Cassidy to be writing to you—and writing such nonsense?"

"I went to see him Saturday," confessed Emily, realizing that the cat was out of the bag. "And I asked him if he couldn't prevent Lofty John from cutting down the bush."

"Emily—Byrd—Starr!"

"I *told* him I was a Protestant," cried Emily. "He understands all about it. And he was just like anybody else. I like him *better* than Mr Dare."

Aunt Elizabeth did not say much more. There did not seem to be much she *could* say. Besides the bush wasn't going to be cut down. The bringer of good news is forgiven much. She contented herself with glaring at Emily—who was too happy and excited to mind glares. She carried her letter off to the garret dormer and gloated over the stamp and the superscription a bit before she took out the enclosure.

"Dear Pearl of Emilys," wrote Father Cassidy. "I've seen our lofty friend and I feel sure your green outpost of fairyland will be saved for your moonlit revels. I know you *do* dance there by light o' moon when mortals are snoring. I think you'll have to go through the form of asking Mr Sullivan to spare those trees, but you'll find him quite reasonable. It's all in the knowing how and the time of the moon. How goes the epic and the language? I hope you'll have no trouble in freeing the *Child of the Sea* from her vows. Continue to be the friend of all good elves, and of

"Your admiring friend,

"*James Cassidy*.

"P.S. The B'y sends respects. What word have you for 'cat' in your language? Sure and you can't get anything cattier than 'cat' can you, now?"

Lofty John spread the story of Emily's appeal to Father Cassidy far and wide, enjoying it as a good joke on himself. Rhoda Stuart said she always knew Emily Starr was a bold thing and Miss Brownell said she would be surprised at *nothing* Emily Starr would do, and Dr Burnley called her a Little Devil more admiringly than ever, and Perry said she had pluck and Teddy took credit for suggesting it, and Aunt Elizabeth endured, and Aunt Laura thought it might have been worse. But Cousin Jimmy made Emily feel very happy.

"It would have spoiled the garden and broken my heart, Emily," he told her. "You're a little darling girl to have prevented it."

One day a month later, when Aunt Elizabeth had taken Emily to Shrewsbury to fit her out with a winter coat, they met Father Cassidy in a store. Aunt Elizabeth bowed with great stateliness, but Emily put out a slender paw.

"What about the dispensation from Rome?" whispered Father Cassidy.

One Emily was quite horrified lest Aunt Elizabeth should overhear and think she was having sly dealings with the Pope, such as no good Presbyterian half-Murray of New Moon should have. The other Emily thrilled to her toes with the dramatic delight of a secret understanding of mystery and intrigue. She nodded gravely, her eyes eloquent with satisfaction.

"I got it without any trouble," she whispered back.

"Fine," said Father Cassidy. "I wish you good luck, and I wish it hard. Good-bye."

"Farewell," said Emily, thinking it a word more in keeping with dark secrets than good-bye. She tasted the flavour of that half-stolen interview all the way home, and felt quite as if she were living in an epic herself. She did not see Father Cassidy again for years—he was soon afterwards removed to another parish; but she always thought of him as a very agreeable and understanding person.

BY AERIAL POST

"DEAREST FATHER:

"My heart is very sore to-night. Mike died this morning. Cousin Jimmy says he must have been poisoned. Oh, Father dear, I felt so bad. He was such a lovely cat. I cried and cried and cried. Aunt Elizabeth was disgusted. She said, 'You did not make half so much fuss when your father died.' What a crewel speech. Aunt Laura was nicer but when she said, 'Don't cry, dear. I will get you another kitten,' I saw she didn't understand either. I don't want another kitten. If I had *millions* of kittens they wouldn't make up for Mike.

"Ilse and I buried him in Lofty John's bush. I am so thankful the ground wasn't frozen yet. Aunt Laura gave me a shoe box for a coffin, and some pink tissue paper to wrap his poor little body in. And we put a stone over the grave and I said 'Blessed are the dead who die in the Lord.' When I told Aunt Laura about it she was horrified and said, 'Oh, Emily, that was a dreadful thing. You should not have said that over a cat.' And Cousin Jimmy said, 'Don't you think, Laura, that an innocent little dum creature has a share in God? Emily loved him and all love is part of God.' And Aunt Laura said, 'Maybe you are right, Jimmy. But I am thankful Elizabeth did not hear her.'

"Cousin Jimmy may not be all there, but what is there is very nice.

"But oh, Father, I am so lonesome for Mike to-night. Last night he was here playing with me, so cunning and pretty and *smee,* and now he is cold and dead in Lofty John's bush.

"December 18.

"DEAR FATHER:

"I am here in the garret. The Wind Woman is very sorry about something to-night. She is sying so sadly around the window. And yet the first time I heard her to-night the flash came—I felt as if I had just seen something that happened long, long ago—something so lovely that it hurt me.

"Cousin Jimmy says there will be a snow storm to-night. I am glad. I like to hear a storm at night. It's so cosy to snuggle down among the blankets and feel it can't get at you. Only when I snuggle Aunt Elizabeth says I skwirm. The idea of any one not knowing the difference between snuggling and skwirming.

"I am glad we will have snow for Christmas. The Murray dinner is to be at New Moon this year. It is our turn. Last year it was at Uncle Oliver's but Cousin Jimmy had grippe and couldn't go so I stayed home with him. I will be right in the thick of it this year and it excites me. I will write you all about it after it is over, dearest.

"I want to tell you something, Father. I am ashamed of it, but I think I'll feel better if I tell you all about it. Last Saturday Ella Lee had a birthday party and I was invited. Aunt Elizabeth let me put on my new blue cashmere dress. It is a very pretty dress. Aunt Elizabeth wanted to get a dark brown but Aunt Laura insisted on blue. I looked at myself in my glass and I remembered that Ilse had told me her father told her I would be handsome if I had more colour. So I pinched my cheeks to make them red. I looked ever so much nicer but it didn't last. Then I took an old red velvet flower that had once been in Aunt Laura's bonnet and wet it and then rubbed the red on my cheeks. I went to the party and the girls all *looked* at me but nobody said anything, only Rhoda Stuart giggled and giggled. I meant to come home and wash the red off before Aunt Elizabeth saw me. But she took a notion to call for me on her way home from the store. She did not say anything there but when we got home she said, 'What have you been doing to your face, Emily?' I told her and I expected an awful scolding, but all she said was, 'Don't you know that you have made yourself *cheap*?' I did know it, too. I had felt that all along although I couldn't think of the right word for it before. 'I will never do such a thing again, Aunt Elizabeth,' I said. 'You'd better not,' she said. 'Go and wash your face this instant.' I did and I was not half so pretty but I felt ever so much better. Strange to relate, dear Father, I heard Aunt Elizabeth laughing about it in the pantry to Aunt Laura afterwards. You never can tell what will make Aunt Elizabeth laugh. I am sure it was ever so much funnier when Saucy Sal followed me to prayer-meeting last Wednesday night, but Aunt Elizabeth never laughed a bit then. I don't often go to prayer-meeting but Aunt Laura couldn't go that night so Aunt Elizabeth took me because she doesn't like to go alone. I didn't know Sal was following us till just as we got to the church I saw her. I shooed her away but after we went in I suppose Sal sneaked in when some one opened the door and got upstairs into the galery. And just as soon as Mr Dare began to pray Sal began to yowl. It sounded awful up in that big empty galery. I felt so gilty and miserable. I did not need to paint my face. It was just burning red and Aunt Elizabeth's eyes glittered feendishly. Mr Dare prayed a long time. He is deaf, so he did not hear Sal any more than when he sat on her. But every one else did and the boys giggled. After the prayer Mr Morris went up to the galery and chased Sal out. We could hear her skrambling over the seats and Mr Morris after her. I was wild for fear he'd hurt her. I ment to spank her myself with a shingle next day but I did not want her to be kicked. After a long time he got her out of the galery and she tore down the stairs and into the church, up one isle and down the other two or three times, as fast as she could go and Mr Morris after her with a broom. It is awfully funny to think of it now but I did not think it so funny at the time I was so ashamed and so afraid Sal would be hurt.

"Mr Morris chased her out at last. When he sat down I made a face at him behind my hymn-book. Coming home Aunt Elizabeth said, 'I hope you have disgraced us enough to-night, Emily Starr. I shall never take you to prayer-meeting again.' I am sorry I disgraced the Murrays but I don't see how I was to blame and anyway I don't like prayer-meeting because it is dull.

"But it wasn't dull that night, dear Father.

"Do you notice how my spelling is improved? I have thought of such a good plan. I write my letter first and then I look up all the words I'm not sure of and correct them. Sometimes though I think a word is all right when it isn't.

"Ilse and I have given up our language. We fought over the verbs. Ilse didn't want to have any tenses for the verbs. She just wanted to have a different word altogether for every tense. I said if I was going to make a language it was going to be a proper one and Ilse got mad and said she had enough bother with grammer in English and I could go and make my old language by myself. But that is no fun so I let it go too. I was sorry because it was very interesting and it was such fun to puzzle the other girls in school. We weren't able to get square with the French boys after all for Ilse had sore throat all through potato-picking time and couldn't come over. It seems to me that life is full of disappointments.

"We had examinations in school this week. I did pretty well in all except arithmetic. Miss Brownell explained something about the questions but I was busy composing a story in my mind and did not hear her so I got poor marks. The story is called *Madge MacPherson's Secret*. I am going to buy four sheets of foolscap with my egg money and sew them into a book and write the story in it. I can do what I like with my egg money. I think maybe I'll write novels when I grow up as well as poetry. But Aunt Elizabeth won't let me read any novels so how can I find out how to write them? Another thing that worries me, if I do grow up and write a wonderful poem, perhaps people won't see how wonderful it is.

"Cousin Jimmy says that a man in Priest Pond says the end of the world is coming soon. I hope it won't come till I've seen everything in it.

"Poor Elder MacKay has the mumps.

"I was over sleeping with Ilse the other night because her father was away. Ilse says her prayers now and she said she'd bet me anything she could pray longer than me. I said she couldn't and I prayed ever so long about everything I could think of and when I couldn't think of anything more I thought at first I'd begin over again. Then I thought, 'No, that would not be honorable. A Starr must be honorable.' So I got up and said 'You win' and Ilse never answered. I went around the bed and there she was asleep on her knees. When I woke her up she said we'd have to call the bet off because she could have gone on praying for ever so long if she hadn't fell asleep.

"After we got into bed I told her a lot of things I wished afterwards I hadn't. Secrets.

"The other day in history class Miss Brownell read that Sir Walter Raleigh had to lie in the Tower for fourteen years. Perry said, 'Wouldn't they let him get up sometimes?' Then Miss Brownell punished him for impertinence, but Perry was in earnest. Ilse was mad at Miss Brownell for whipping Perry and mad at Perry for asking such a fool question as if he didn't know anything. But Perry says he is going to write a history book some day that won't have such puzzling things in it."

"I am finishing the Disappointed House in my mind. I'm furnishing the rooms like flowers. I'll have a rose room all pink and a lily room all white and silver and a pansy room, blue and gold. I wish the Disappointed House could have a Christmas. It never has any Christmases.

"Oh, Father, I've just thought of something nice. When I grow up and write a great novel and make lots of money, I will buy the Disappointed House and finish it. Then it won't be Disappointed any more.

"Ilse's Sunday-school teacher, Miss Willeson, gave her a Bible for learnig 200 verses. But when she took it home her father laid it on the floor and kicked it out in the yard. Mrs Simms says a judgment will come on him but nothing has happened yet. The poor man is warped. That is why he did such a wicked thing.

"Aunt Laura took me to old Mrs Mason's funeral last Wednesday. I like funerals. They are so dramatic.

"My pig died last week. It was a *great finanshul loss* to me. Aunt Elizabeth says Cousin Jimmy fed it too well. I suppose I should not have called it after Lofty John.

"We have maps to draw in school now. Rhoda Stuart always gets the most marks. Miss Brownell doesn't know that Rhoda just puts the map up against a window pane and the paper over it and copies it off. I like drawing maps. Norway and Sweden look like a tiger with mountains for stripes and Ireland looks like a little dog with its back turned on England, and its paws held up against its breast, and Africa looks like a big pork ham. Australia is a lovely map to draw.

"Ilse is getting on real well in school now. She says she isn't going to have me beating her. She can learn like the dickens as Perry says, when she tries, and she has won the silver medal for Queen's County. The W.C.T.U. in Charlottetown gave it for the best reciter. They had the contest in Shrewsbury and Aunt Laura took Ilse because Dr Burnley wouldn't and Ilse won it. Aunt Laura told Dr Burnley when he was here one day that he ought to give Ilse a good education. He said, 'I'm not going to waste money educating any she-thing.' And he looked black as a thunder cloud. Oh, I wish Dr Burnley would love Ilse. I'm so glad *you* loved *me*, Father.

"DEC. 22.

"Dear Father: We had our school examination to-day. It was a great occasion. Almost everybody was there except Dr Burnley and Aunt Elizabeth. All the girls wore their best dresses but me. I knew Ilse had nothing to wear but her shabby old last winter's plaid that is too short for her, so to keep her from feeling bad, I put on my old brown dress, too. Aunt Elizabeth did not want to let me do it at first because New Moon Murrays should be well dressed but when I explained about Ilse she looked at Aunt Laura and then said I might.

"Rhoda Stuart made fun of Ilse and me but I heaped coals of fire on her head. (That is what is called a figure of speech.) She got stuck in her recitation. She had left the book home and nobody else knew the piece but me. At first I looked at her triumphantly. But then a queer feeling came into me and I thought 'What would I feel like if I was stuck before a big crowd of people like this? And besides the honour of the school is at stake,' so I whispered it to her because I was quite close. She got through the rest all right. The strange thing is, dear Father, that now I don't feel any more as if I hated her. I feel quite kindly to her and it is much nicer. It is uncomfortable to hate people.

"DEC. 28.

"DEAR FATHER:

"Christmas is over. It was pretty nice. I never saw so many good things cooked all at once. Uncle Wallace and Aunt Eva and Uncle Oliver and Aunt Addie and Aunt Ruth were here. Uncle Oliver didn't bring any of his children and I was much disappointed. We had Dr Burnley and Ilse too. Every one was dressed up. Aunt Elizabeth wore her black satin dress with a pointed lace collar and cap. She looked quite handsome and I was proud of her. You like your relations to look well even if you don't like *them*. Aunt Laura wore her brown silk and Aunt Ruth had on a grey dress. Aunt Eva was *very* elegant. Her dress had a train. But it smelled of moth balls.

"I had on my blue cashmere and wore my hair tied with blue ribbons, and Aunt Laura let me wear mother's blue silk sash with the pink daisies on it that she had when she was a little girl at New Moon. Aunt Ruth sniffed when she saw me. She said, 'You have grown a good deal, Em'ly. I hope you are a better girl.'

"But she *didn't* hope it (really). I saw that quite plain. Then she told me my bootlace was untyed.

"'She looks better,' said Uncle Oliver. 'I wouldn't wonder if she grew up into a strong, healthy girl after all.'

"Aunt Eva sighed and shook her head. Uncle Wallace didn't say anything but shook hands with me. His hand was as cold as a fish.

When we went out to the sitting-room for dinner I stepped on Aunt Eva's train and I could hear some stitches rip somewhere. Aunt Eva pushed me away and Aunt Ruth said, 'What a very awkward child you are, Em'ly.' I stepped behind Aunt Ruth and stuck out my tongue at her. Uncle Oliver makes a noise eating his soup. We had all the good silver spoons out. Cousin Jimmy carved the turkeys and he gave me two slices of the breast because he knows I like the white meat best. Aunt Ruth said 'When I was a little girl the wing was good enough for me,' and Cousin Jimmy put *another* white slice on my plate. Aunt Ruth didn't say anything more then till the carving was done, and then she said, 'I saw your school teacher in Shrewsbury last Saturday, Em'ly, and she did not give me a very good account of you. If you were *my* daughter I would expect a different report.'

"'I am very glad I am not your daughter,' I said in my mind. I didn't say it out loud of course but Aunt Ruth said, 'Please do not look so sulky when I speak to you, Em'ly.' And Uncle Wallace said, 'It is a pity she has such an unattractive expression.'

"'*You* are conceited and domineering and stingy,' I said, still in my mind. 'I heard Dr Burnley say you were.'

"'I see there is an ink-stain on her finger,' said Aunt Ruth. (I had been writing a poem before dinner.)

"And then a most surprising thing happened. Relations are always surprising you. Aunt Elizabeth spoke up and said, '*I do wish, Ruth, that you and Wallace would leave that child alone.*' I could hardly believe my ears. Aunt Ruth looked annoyed but she *did* leave me alone after that and only sniffed when Cousin Jimmy slipped a bit more white meat on my plate.

"After that the dinner was nice. And when they got as far as the pudding they all began to talk and it was splendid to listen to. They told stories and jokes about the Murrays. Even Uncle Wallace laughed and Aunt Ruth told some things about Great-Aunt Nancy. They were sarcastic but they were interesting. Aunt Elizabeth opened Grandfather Murray's desk and took out an old poem that had been written to Aunt Nancy *by a lover* when she was young and Uncle Oliver read it. Great-Aunt Nancy must have been very beautiful. I wonder if anyone will ever write a poem to me. If I could have a bang somebody might. I said, 'Was Great-Aunt Nancy really as pretty as that?' and Uncle Oliver said, 'They say she was seventy years ago' and Uncle Wallace said, 'She hangs on well—she'll see the century mark yet,' and Uncle Oliver said, 'Oh, she's got so in the habit of living she'll never die.'

"Dr Burnley told a story I didn't understand. Uncle Wallace hawhawed right out and Uncle Oliver put his napkin up to his face. Aunt Addie and Aunt Eva looked at each other sidewise and then at their plates and smiled a little bit. Aunt Ruth seemed offended and Aunt Elizabeth looked *coldly* at Dr Burnley and said, 'I think you forget that there are children present.' Dr Burnley said, 'I beg your pardon, Elizabeth,' *very* politely. He can speak with a *grand air* when he likes. He is very handsome when he is dressed up and shaved. Ilse says she is proud of him even if he hates her.

"After dinner was over the presents were given. That is a Murray tradishun. We never have stockings or trees but a big bran pie is passed all around with the presents buried in it and ribbons hanging out with names on them. It was fun. My relations all give me useful presents except Aunt Laura. She gave me a bottle of perfume. I love it. I love nice smells. Aunt Elizabeth does not approve of perfumes. She gave me a new apron but I am thankful to say not a baby one. Aunt Ruth gave me a New Testament and said 'Em'ly, I hope you will read a portion of that every day until you have read it through,' and I said, 'Why, Aunt Ruth, I've read the whole New Testament a dozen times (and so I have.) I *love* Revelations.' (And I *do*. When I read the verse 'and the twelve gates were twelve pearls,' I just *saw* them and the flash came.) 'The Bible is not to be read as a story-book,' Aunt Ruth said coldly. Uncle Wallace and Aunt Eva gave me a pair of black mits and Uncle Oliver and Aunt Addie gave me a whole dollar in nice new silver dimes and Cousin Jimmy gave me a hair-ribbon. Perry had left a silk bookmark for me. He had to go home to spend Christmas day with his Aunt Tom at Stovepipe Town but I saved a lot of nuts and raisins for him. I gave him and Teddy handkerchiefs (Teddy's was a *little* the nicest) and I gave Ilse a hair-ribbon. I bought them myself out of my egg money. (I will not have any more egg money for a long time because my hen has stopped laying.) Everybody was happy and once Uncle Wallace smiled right at me. I did not think him so ugly when he smiled.

"After dinner Ilse and I played games in the kitchen and Cousin Jimmy helped us make taffy. We had a big supper but nobody could eat much because they had had such a dinner. Aunt Eva's head ached and Aunt Ruth said she didn't see why Elizabeth made the sausages so rich. But the rest were good humoured and Aunt Laura kept things pleasant. She is good at making things pleasant. And after it was all over Uncle Wallace said (this is another Murray tradishun) 'Let us think for a few moments of those who have gone before.' I liked the way he said it—very solemnly and kind. It was one of the times when I am glad the blood of the Murrays flows in my vains. And I thought of *you,* darling Father, and Mother and poor little Mike and Great-great-Grandmother Murray, and of my old account-book that Aunt Elizabeth burned, because it seemed just like a person to me. And then we all joined hands and sung 'For Auld Lang Syne' before they went home. I didn't feel like a stranger among the Murrays any more. Aunt Laura and I stood out on the porch to watch them go. Aunt Laura put her arm around me and said, 'Your mother and I used to stand like this long ago, Emily, to watch the Christmas guests go away.' The snow creaked and the bells rang back through the trees and the frost on the pighouse roof sparkled in the moonlight. And it was all so lovely (the bells and the frost and the big shining white night) that the *flash* came and that was best of all."

"ROMANTIC BUT NOT COMFORTABLE"

A certain thing happened at New Moon because Teddy Kent paid Ilse Burnley a compliment one day and Emily Starr didn't altogether like it. Empires have been overturned for the same reason.

Teddy was skating on Blair Water and taking Ilse and Emily out in turns for "slides." Neither Ilse nor Emily had skates. Nobody was sufficiently interested in Ilse to buy skates for her, and as for Emily, Aunt Elizabeth did not approve of girls skating. New Moon girls had never skated. Aunt Laura had a revolutionary idea that skating would be good exercise for Emily and would, moreover, prevent her from wearing out the soles of her boots sliding. But neither of these arguments was sufficient to convince Aunt Elizabeth, in spite of the thrifty streak that came to her from the Burnleys. The latter, however, caused her to issue an edict that Emily was not to "slide." Emily took this very hardly. She moped about in a woe-begone fashion and she wrote to her father, "I *hate* Aunt Elizabeth. She is so unjust. She never plays fair." But one day Dr Burnley stuck his head in at the door of the New Moon kitchen and said gruffly, "What's this I hear about you not letting Emily slide, Elizabeth?"

"She wears out the soles of her boots," said Elizabeth.

"Boots be ———" the doctor remembered that ladies were present just in time. "Let the creature slide all she wants to. She ought to be in the open air all the time. She ought"—the doctor stared at Elizabeth ferociously—"she ought to sleep out of doors."

Elizabeth trembled lest the doctor should go on to insist on this unheard-of proceeding. She knew he had absurd ideas about the proper treatment of consumptives and those who might become such. She was glad to appease him by letting Emily stay out of doors in daytime and do what seemed good to her, if only he would say no more about staying out all night too.

"He is much more concerned about Emily than he is about his own child," she said bitterly to Laura.

"Ilse is too healthy," said Aunt Laura with a smile. "If she were a delicate child Allan might forgive her for—for being her mother's daughter."

"S—s—h," said Aunt Elizabeth. But she "s—s—s—h'd" too late. Emily, coming into the kitchen, had heard Aunt Laura and puzzled over what she had said all day in school. Why had Ilse to be forgiven for being her mother's daughter? Everybody was her mother's daughter, wasn't she? Wherein did the crime consist? Emily worried over it so much that she was inattentive to her lessons and Miss Brownell raked her fore and aft with sarcasm.

It is time we got back to Blair Water where Teddy was just bringing Emily in from a glorious spin clear round the great circle of ice. Ilse was waiting for her turn, on the bank. Her golden cloud of hair aureoled her face and fell in a shimmering wave over her forehead under the faded, little red tam she wore. Ilse's clothes were always faded. The stinging kiss of the wind had crimsoned her cheeks and her eyes were glowing like amber pools with fire in their hearts. Teddy's artistic perception saw her beauty and rejoiced in it.

"Isn't Ilse handsome?" he said.

Emily was not jealous. It never hurt her to hear Ilse praised. But somehow she did not like this. Teddy was looking at Ilse altogether *too* admiringly. It was all, Emily believed, due to that shimmering fringe on Ilse's white brows.

"If *I* had a bang Teddy might think me handsome too," she thought resentfully. "Of course, black hair isn't as pretty as gold. But my forehead is too high—everybody says so. And I *did* look nice in Teddy's picture because he drew some curls over it."

The matter rankled. Emily thought of it as she went home over the sheen of the crusted snow-field slanting to the light of the winter sunset, and she could not eat her supper because she did not have a bang. All her long hidden yearning for a bang seemed to come to a head at once. She knew there was no use in coaxing Aunt Elizabeth for one. But when she was getting ready for bed that night she stood on a chair so that she could see little Emily-in-the-glass, then lifted the curling ends of her long braid and laid them over her forehead. The effect, in Emily's eyes at least, was very alluring. She suddenly thought—what if she cut a bang herself? It would take only a minute. And once done what could Aunt Elizabeth do? She would be very angry and doubtless inflict some kind of punishment. But the bang would be there—at least until it grew out long.

Emily, her lips set, went for the scissors. She unbraided her hair and parted the front tresses. Snip—snip—went the scissors. Glistening locks fell at her feet. In a minute Emily had her long-desired bang. Straight across her brows fell the lustrous, softly curving fringe. It changed the whole character of her face. It made it arch, provocative, elusive. For one brief moment Emily gazed at her reflection in triumph.

And then—sheer terror seized her. Oh, what had she done? How angry Aunt Elizabeth would be! Conscience suddenly awoke and added its pang also. She had been wicked. It was wicked to cut a bang when Aunt Elizabeth had forbidden it. Aunt Elizabeth had given her a home at New Moon—hadn't Rhoda Stuart that very day in school twitted her again with "living on charity?" And she was repaying her by disobedience and ingratitude. A Starr should not have done that. In a panic of fear and remorse Emily snatched the scissors and cut the bang off—cut it close against the hair-line. Worse and worse! Emily beheld the result in dismay. Any one could see that a bang *had* been cut, so Aunt Elizabeth's anger was still to face. And she had made a terrible fright of herself. Emily burst into tears, snatched up the fallen locks and crammed them into the waste-basket, blew out her candle and sprang into bed, just as Aunt Elizabeth came in.

Emily burrowed face downward in the pillows, and pretended to be asleep. She was afraid Aunt Elizabeth would ask her some question and insist on her looking up while she answered it. That was a Murray tradition—you looked people in the face when you spoke to them. But Aunt Elizabeth undressed in silence and came to bed. The room was in darkness—thick darkness. Emily sighed and turned over. There was a hot gin-jar in the bed, she knew, and her feet were cold. But she did not think she ought to have the privilege of the gin-jar. She was too wicked—too ungrateful.

"*Do* stop squirming," said Aunt Elizabeth.

Emily squirmed no more—physically at least. Mentally she continued to squirm. She could not sleep. Her feet or her conscience— or both—kept her awake. And fear, also. She dreaded the morning. Aunt Elizabeth would see then what had happened. If it were only over—if the revelation were only over. Emily forgot and squirmed.

"What makes you so restless to-night?" demanded Aunt Elizabeth, in high displeasure. "Are you taking a cold?"

"No, ma'am."

"Then go to sleep. I can't bear such wriggling. One might as well have an eel in bed—O—W!"

Aunt Elizabeth, in squirming a bit herself, had put her own foot against Emily's icy ones.

"Goodness, child, your feet are like snow. Here, put them on the gin-jar."

Aunt Elizabeth pushed the gin-jar over against Emily's feet. How lovely and warm and comforting it was!

Emily worked her toes against it like a cat. But she suddenly knew she could not wait for morning.

"Aunt Elizabeth, I've got something to confess."

Aunt Elizabeth was tired and sleepy and did not want confessions just then. In no very gracious tone she said:

"What have you been doing?"

"I—I cut a bang, Aunt Elizabeth."

"A bang?"

Aunt Elizabeth sat up in bed.

"But I cut it off again," cried Emily hurriedly. "Right off—close to my head."

Aunt Elizabeth got out of bed, lit a candle, and looked Emily over.

"Well you *have* made a sight of yourself," she said grimly. "I never saw any one as ugly as you are this minute. And you have behaved in a most underhanded fashion."

This was one of the times Emily felt compelled to agree with Aunt Elizabeth.

"I'm sorry," she said, lifting pleading eyes.

"You will eat your supper in the pantry for a week," said Aunt Elizabeth. "And you will not go to Uncle Oliver's next week when I go. I had promised to take you. But I shall take no one who looks as you do anywhere with me."

This was hard. Emily had looked forward to that visit to Uncle Oliver's. But on the whole she was relieved. The worst was over and her feet were getting warm. But there was one thing yet. She might as well unburden her heart completely while she was at it.

"There's another thing I feel I ought to tell you."

Aunt Elizabeth got into bed again with a grunt. Emily took it for permission.

"Aunt Elizabeth, you remember that book I found in Dr Burnley's bookcase and brought home and asked you if I could read it? It was called *The History of Henry Esmond*. You looked at it and said you had no objections to my reading history. So I read it. But, Aunt Elizabeth, it wasn't history—it was a novel. And I *knew it when I brought it home*."

"You know that I have forbidden you to read novels, Emily Starr. They are wicked books and have ruined many souls."

"It was very dull," pleaded Emily, as if dullness and wickedness were quite incompatible. "And it made me feel unhappy. Everybody seemed to be in love with the wrong person. I have made up my mind, Aunt Elizabeth, that I will never fall in love. It makes too much trouble."

"Don't talk of things you can't understand, and that are not fit for children to think about. This is the result of reading novels. I shall tell Dr Burnley to lock his bookcase up."

"Oh, don't do that, Aunt Elizabeth," exclaimed Emily. "There are no more novels in it. But I'm reading such an interesting book over there. It tells about everything that's inside of you. I've got as far along as the liver and its diseases. The pictures are so interesting. Please let me finish it." This was worse than novels. Aunt Elizabeth was truly horrified. Things that were inside of you were not to be read about.

"Have you no shame, Emily Starr? If you have not I am ashamed for you. Little girls do not read books like that."

"But, Aunt Elizabeth, why not? I *have* a liver, haven't I—and heart and lungs—and stomach—and—"

"That will do, Emily. Not another word."

Emily went to sleep unhappily. She wished she had never said a word about "Esmond." And she knew she would never have a chance to finish that other fascinating book. Nor had she. Dr Burnley's bookcase was locked thereafter and the doctor gruffly ordered her and Ilse to keep out of his office. He was in a very bad humour about it for he had words with Elizabeth Murray over the matter.

Emily was not allowed to forget her bang. She was twitted and teased in school about it and Aunt Elizabeth looked at it whenever she looked at Emily and the contempt in her eyes burned Emily like a flame. Nevertheless, as the mistreated hair grew out and began to curl in soft little ringlets, Emily found consolation. The bang was tacitly permitted, and she felt that her looks were greatly improved thereby. Of course, as soon as it grew long enough she knew Aunt Elizabeth would make her brush it back. But for the time being she took comfort in her added beauty.

The bang was just about at its best when the letter came from Great-Aunt Nancy.

It was written to Aunt Laura—Great-Aunt Nancy and Aunt Elizabeth were not over-fond of each other—and in it Great-Aunt Nancy said, "If you have a photograph of that child Emily send it along. I don't want to see *her;* she's stupid—I know she's stupid. But I want to see what Juliet's child looks like. Also the child of that fascinating young man, Douglas Starr. He *was* fascinating. What fools you all were to make such a fuss about Juliet running away with him. If you and Elizabeth had *both* run away with somebody in your running days it would have been better for you."

This letter was not shown to Emily. Aunt Elizabeth and Aunt Laura had a long secret consultation and then Emily was told that she was to be taken to Shrewsbury to have her picture taken for Aunt Nancy. Emily was much excited over this. She was dressed in her blue cashmere and Aunt Laura put a point lace collar on it and hung her Venetian beads over it. And new buttoned boots were got for the occasion.

"I'm so glad this has happened while I still have my bang," thought Emily happily.

But in the photographer's dressing-room, Aunt Elizabeth grimly proceeded to brush back her bang and pin it with hairpins.

"Oh, please, Aunt Elizabeth, let me have it down," Emily begged. "Just for the picture. After this I'll brush it back."

Aunt Elizabeth was inexorable. The bang was brushed back and the photograph taken. When Aunt Elizabeth saw the finished result she was satisfied.

"She looks sulky; but she is neat; and there is a resemblance to the Murrays I never noticed before," she told Aunt Laura. "That will please Aunt Nancy. She is very clannish under all her oddness."

Emily would have liked to throw every one of the photographs in the fire. She hated them. They made her look hideous. Her face seemed to be *all* forehead. If they sent Aunt Nancy that Aunt Nancy would think her stupider than ever. When Aunt Elizabeth did the photograph up in cardboard and told Emily to take it to the office Emily already knew what she meant to do. She went straight to the garret and took out of her box the water-colour Teddy had made of her. It was just the same size as the photograph. Emily removed the latter from its wrappings, spurning it aside with her foot.

"That isn't *me*," she said. "I looked sulky because I felt sulky about the bang. But I hardly ever look sulky, so it isn't fair."

She wrapped Teddy's sketch up in the cardboard and then sat down and wrote a letter.

"DEAR GREAT-AUNT NANCY:

"Aunt Elizabeth had my picture taken to send you but I don't like it because it makes me look too ugly and I am putting another picture in instead. An *artist friend* made it for me. It is just like me when I am smiling and have a bang. I am only *lending* it to you, not *giving* it, because I valew it very highly.

"Your obedient grand niece,

"EMILY BYRD STARR.

"P.S. I am not so stupid as you think.

"E. B. S.

"P. S. No. 2. I am not stupid *at all.*"

Emily put her letter in with the picture—thereby unconsciously cheating the post-office—and slipped out of the house to mail it. Once it was safely in the post-office she drew a breath of relief. She found the walk home very enjoyable. It was a bland day in early April and spring was looking at you round the corners. The Wind Woman was laughing and whistling over the wet sweet fields; freebooting crows held conferences in the tree-tops; little pools of sunshine lay in the mossy hollows; the sea was a blaze of sapphire beyond the golden dunes; the maples in Lofty John's bush were talking about red buds. Everything Emily had ever read of dream and myth and legend seemed a part of the charm of that bush. She was filled to her finger-tips with a rapture of living.

"Oh, I smell spring!" she cried as she danced along the brook path.

Then she began to compose a poem on it. Everybody who has ever lived in the world and could string two rhymes together has written a poem on spring. It is the most be-rhymed subject in the world—and always will be, because it is poetry incarnate itself. You can never be a real poet if you haven't made at least one poem about spring.

Emily was wondering whether she would have elves dancing on the brookside by moonlight, or pixies sleeping in a bed of ferns in her poem, when something confronted her at a bend in the path which was neither elf nor pixy, but seemed odd and weird enough to belong to some of the tribes of Little People. Was it a witch? Or an elderly fay of evil intentions—the bad fairy of all christening tales?

"I'm the b'y's Aunt Tom," said the appearance, seeing that Emily was too amazed to do anything but stand and stare.

"Oh!" Emily gasped in relief. She was no longer frightened. But what a *very* peculiar looking lady Perry's Aunt Tom was. Old—so old that it seemed quite impossible that she could ever have been young; a bright red hood over crone-like, fluttering grey locks; a little face seamed by a thousand fine, criss-cross wrinkles; a long nose with a knob on the end of it; little twinkling, eager, grey eyes under bristly brows; a ragged man's coat covering her from neck to feet; a basket in one hand and a black knobby stick in the other.

"Staring wasn't thought good breeding in my time," said Aunt Tom.

"Oh!" said Emily again. "Excuse me—How do you do!" she added, with a vague grasp after her manners.

"Polite—and not too proud," said Aunt Tom, peering curiously at her. "I've been up to the big house with a pair of socks for the b'y but 'twas yourself I wanted to see."

"Me?" said Emily blankly.

"Yis. The b'y has been talking a bit of you and a plan kem into my head. Thinks I to myself it's no bad notion. But I'll make sure before I waste my bit o' money. Emily Byrd Starr is your name and Murray is your nature. If I give the b'y an eddication will ye marry him when ye grow up?"

"Me!" said Emily again. It seemed to be all she could say. Was she dreaming? She *must* be.

"Yis—you. You're half Murray and it'll be a great step up f'r the b'y. He's smart and he'll be a rich man some day and boss the country. But divil a cent will I spend on him unless you promise."

"Aunt Elizabeth wouldn't let me," cried Emily, too frightened of this odd old body to refuse on her own account.

"If you've got any Murray in you you'll do your own choosing," said Aunt Tom, thrusting her face so close to Emily's that her bushy eyebrows tickled Emily's nose. "Say you'll marry the b'y and to college he goes."

Emily seemed to be rendered speechless. She could think of nothing to say—oh, if she could *only* wake up! She could not even run.

"Say it!" insisted Aunt Tom, thumping her stick sharply on a stone in the path.

Emily was so horrified that she might have said something—anything—to escape. But at this moment Perry bounded out of the spruce copse, his face white with rage, and seized his Aunt Tom most disrespectfully by the shoulder.

"You go home!" he said furiously.

"Now, b'y dear," quavered Aunt Tom deprecatingly. "I was only trying to do you a good turn. I was asking her to marry ye after a bit an—"

"I'll do my own asking!" Perry was angrier than ever. "You've likely spoiled everything. Go home—go home, I say!"

Aunt Tom hobbled off muttering, "Then I'll know better than to waste me bit o' money. No Murray, no money, me b'y."

When she had disappeared down the brook path Perry turned to Emily. From white he had gone very red.

"Don't mind her—she's cracked," he said. "Of course, when I grow up I mean to ask you to marry me but—"

"I couldn't—Aunt Elizabeth—"

"Oh, she will then. I'm going to be premier of Canada some day."

"But I wouldn't want—I'm sure I wouldn't—"

"You will when you grow up. Ilse is better looking of course, and I don't know why I like you best but I do."

"Don't you ever talk to me like this again!" commanded Emily, beginning to recover her dignity.

"Oh, I won't—not till we grow up. I'm as ashamed of it as you are," said Perry with a sheepish grin. "Only I had to say something after Aunt Tom butted in like that. I ain't to blame for it so don't you hold it against me. But just you remember that I'm going to ask you some day. And I believe Teddy Kent is too."

Emily was walking haughtily away but she turned at this to say coolly over her shoulder.

"If he does I'll marry him."

"If you do I'll knock his head off," shouted Perry in a prompt rage.

But Emily walked steadily on home and went to the garret to think things over.

"It has been romantic but not comfortable," was her conclusion. And that particular poem on spring was never finished.

WYTHER GRANGE

No reply or acknowledgment came from Great-Aunt-Nancy Priest regarding Emily's picture. Aunt Elizabeth and Aunt Laura, knowing Great-Aunt Nancy's ways tolerably well, were not surprised at this, but Emily felt rather worried over it. Perhaps Great-Aunt Nancy did not approve of what she had done; or perhaps she still thought her too stupid to bother with.

Emily did not like to lie under the imputation of stupidity. She wrote a scathing epistle to Great-Aunt Nancy on a letter-bill in which she did not mince her opinions as to that ancient lady's knowledge of the rules of epistolary etiquette; the letter was folded up and stowed away on the little shelf under the sofa but it served its purpose in blowing off steam and Emily had ceased to think about the matter when a letter came from Great-Aunt Nancy in July.

Elizabeth and Laura talked the matter over in the cookhouse, forgetful or ignorant of the fact that Emily was sitting on the kitchen doorstep just outside. Emily was imagining herself attending a drawing-room of Queen Victoria. Robed in white, with ostrich plumes, veil, and court train, she had just bent to kiss the Queen's hand when Aunt Elizabeth's voice shattered her dream as a pebble thrown into a pool scatters the fairy reflection.

"What is your opinion, Laura," Aunt Elizabeth was saying, "of letting Emily visit Aunt Nancy?"

Emily pricked up her ears. What was in the wind now?

"From her letter she seems very anxious to have the child," said Laura.

Elizabeth sniffed.

"A whim—a whim. You know what her whims are. Likely by the time Emily got there she'd be quite over it and have no use for her."

"Yes, but on the other hand if we don't let her go she will be dreadfully offended and never forgive us—or Emily. Emily should have her chance."

"I don't know that her chance is worth much. If Aunt Nancy really has any money beyond her annuity—and that's what neither you nor I nor any living soul knows, unless it's Caroline—she'll likely leave it all to some of the Priests—Leslie Priest's a favourite of hers, I understand. Aunt Nancy always liked her husband's family better than her own, even though she's always slurring at them. Still—she *might* take a fancy to Emily—they're both so odd they might suit each other—but you know the way she talks—she and that abominable old Caroline."

"Emily is too young to understand," said Aunt Laura.

"I understand more than you think," cried Emily indignantly.

Aunt Elizabeth jerked open the cook-house door.

"Emily Starr, haven't you learned by this time not to listen?"

"I wasn't listening. I thought you knew I was sitting here—I can't help my ears *hearing*. Why didn't you *whisper*? When you whisper I know you're talking secrets and I don't try to hear them. Am I going to Great-Aunt Nancy's for a visit?"

"We haven't decided," said Aunt Elizabeth coldly, and that was all the satisfaction Emily got for a week. She hardly knew herself whether she wanted to go or not. Aunt Elizabeth had begun making cheese—New Moon was noted for its cheeses—and Emily found the whole process absorbing, from the time the rennet was put in the warm new milk till the white curds were packed away in the hoop and put under the press in the old orchard, with the big, round, grey "cheese" stone to weight it down as it had weighed down New Moon cheeses for a hundred years. And then she and Ilse and Teddy and Perry were absorbed heart and soul in "playing out" the *Midsummer Night's Dream* in Lofty John's bush and it was very fascinating. When they entered Lofty John's bush they went out of the realm of daylight and things known into the realm of twilight and mystery and enchantment. Teddy had painted wonderful scenery on old boards and pieces of sails, which Perry had got at the Harbour. Ilse had fashioned delightful fairy wings from tissue paper and tinsel, and Perry had made an ass's head for *Bottom* out of an old calfskin that was very realistic. Emily had toiled happily for many weeks copying out the different parts and adapting them to circumstances. She had "cut" the play after a fashion that would have harrowed Shakespeare's soul, but after all the result was quite pretty and coherent. It did not worry them that four small actors had to take six times as many parts. Emily was *Titania* and *Hermia* and a job lot of fairies besides, Ilse was *Hippolyta* and *Helena,* plus some more fairies, and the boys were anything that the dialogue required. Aunt Elizabeth knew nothing of it all; she would promptly have put a stop to the whole thing, for she thought play-acting exceedingly wicked; but Aunt Laura was privy to the plot, and Cousin Jimmy and Lofty John had already attended a moonlight rehearsal.

To go away and leave all this, even for a time, would be a hard wrench, but on the other hand Emily had a burning curiosity to see Great-Aunt Nancy and Wyther Grange, her quaint, old house at Priest Pond with the famous stone dogs on the gate-posts. On the whole, she thought she would like to go; and when she saw Aunt Laura doing up her starched white petticoats and Aunt Elizabeth grimly dusting off a small, black, nail-studded trunk in the garret she knew, before she was told, that the visit to Priest Pond was going to come off; so she took out the letter she had written to Aunt Nancy and added an apologetic postscript.

Ilse chose to be disgruntled because Emily was going for a visit. In reality Ilse felt appalled at the lonely prospects of a month or more without her inseparable chum. No more jolly evenings of play-acting in Lofty John's bush, no more pungent quarrels. Besides, Ilse herself had never been anywhere for a visit in her whole life and she felt sore over this fact.

"*I* wouldn't go to Wyther Grange for anything," said Ilse. "It's haunted."

"'Tisn't."

"Yes! It's haunted by a ghost you can *feel* and *hear* but never *see*. Oh, I wouldn't be *you* for the world! Your Great-Aunt Nancy is an *awful crank*, and the old woman who lives with her is a *witch*. She'll put a spell on you. You'll pine away and die."

"I won't—she isn't!"

"*Is!* Why, she makes the stone dogs on the gate-posts howl every night if any one comes near the place. They go, '*Wo-or-oo-oo*.'"

Ilse was not a born elocutionist for nothing. Her "wo-or-oo-oo" was extremely gruesome. But it was daylight, and Emily was as brave as a lion in daylight.

"You're jealous," she said, and walked off.

"I'm not, you blithering centipede," Ilse yelled after her. "Putting on airs because your aunt has stone dogs on her gateposts! Why, I know a woman in Shrewsbury who has dogs on her posts that are ten times stonier than your aunt's!"

But next morning Ilse was over to bid Emily good-bye and entreat her to write every week. Emily was going to drive to Priest Pond with Old Kelly. Aunt Elizabeth was to have driven her but Aunt Elizabeth was not feeling well that day and Aunt Laura could not leave her. Cousin Jimmy had to work at the hay. It looked as if she could not go, and this was rather serious, for Aunt Nancy had been told to expect her that day and Aunt Nancy did not like to be disappointed. If Emily did not turn up at Priest Pond on the day set Great-Aunt Nancy was quite capable of shutting the door in her face when she did appear and telling her to go back home. Nothing less than this conviction would have induced Aunt Elizabeth to fall in with Old Kelly's suggestion that Emily should ride to Priest Pond with him. His home was on the other side of it and he was going straight there.

Emily was quite delighted. She liked Old Kelly and thought that a drive on his fine red waggon would be quite an adventure. Her little black box was hoisted to the roof and tied there and they went clinking and glittering down the New Moon lane in fine style. The tins in the bowels of the waggon behind them rumbled like a young earthquake.

"Get up, my nag, get up," said Old Kelly. "Sure, an' I always like to drive the pretty gurrls. An' when is the wedding to be?"

"Whose wedding?"

"The slyness av her? Your own, av coorse."

"I have no intention of being married—immediately," said Emily, in a very good imitation of Aunt Elizabeth's tone and manner.

"Sure, and ye're a chip av the ould block. Miss Elizabeth herself couldn't have said it better. Get up, my nag, get up."

"I only meant," said Emily, fearing that she had insulted Old Kelly, "that I am too young to be married."

"The younger the better—the less mischief ye'll be after working with them come-hither eyes. Get up, my nag, get up. The baste is tired. So we'll let him go at his own swate will. Here's a bag av swaties for ye. Ould Kelly always trates the ladies. Come now, tell me all about him."

"About whom?"—but Emily knew quite well.

"Your beau, av coorse."

"I haven't *any* beau. Mr Kelly, I wish you wouldn't talk to me about such things."

"Sure, and I won't if 'tis a sore subject. Don't ye be minding if ye haven't got one—there'll be scads av them after a while. And if the right one doesn't know what's good for him, just ye come to Ould Kelly and get some toad ointment."

Toad ointment! It sounded horrible. Emily shivered. But she would rather talk about toad ointment than beaux.

"What is that for?"

"It's a love charm," said Old Kelly mysteriously. "Put a li'l smooch on his eyelids and he's yourn for life with never a squint at any other gurrl."

"It doesn't *sound* very nice," said Emily. "How do you make it?"

"You bile four toads alive till they're good and soft and then mash—"

"Oh, stop, stop!" implored Emily, putting her hands to her ears. "I don't want to hear any more—you couldn't be so cruel!"

"Cruel is it? You were after eating lobsters this day that were biled alive—"

"I don't believe it. I don't. If it's true I'll never, never eat one again. Oh, Mr Kelly, I thought you were a nice kind man—but those poor toads!"

"Gurrl dear, it was only me joke. An' you won't be nading toad ointment to win your lad's love. Wait you now—I've something in the till behind me for a prisent for you."

Old Kelly fished out a box which he put into Emily's lap. She found a dainty little hair-brush in it.

"Look at the back av it," said Old Kelly. "You'll see something handsome—all the love charm ye'll ever nade."

Emily turned it over. Her own face looked back at her from a little inset mirror surrounded by a scroll of painted roses.

"Oh, Mr Kelly—how pretty—I mean the roses and the glass," she cried. "Is it really for me? Oh, thank you, thank you! Now, I can have Emily-in-the-glass whenever I want her. Why, I can carry her round with me. And you were really only in fun about the toads!"

"Av coorse. Get up, my nag, get up. An' so ye're going to visit the ould lady over at Praste Pond? Ever been there?"

"No."

"It's full of Prastes. Ye can't throw a stone but ye hit one. And hit one—hit all. They're as proud and lofty as the Murrays themselves. The only wan I know is Adam Praste—the others hold too high. He's the black shape and quite sociable. But if ye want to see how the world looked on the morning after the flood, go into his barnyard on a rainy day. Look a-here, gurrl dear"—Old Kelly lowered his voice mysteriously—"don't ye ever marry a Praste."

"Why not?" asked Emily, who had never thought of marrying a Priest but was immediately curious as to why she shouldn't.

"They're ill to marry—ill to live with. The wives die young. The ould lady of the Grange fought her man out and buried him but she had the Murray luck. I wouldn't trust it too far. The only dacent Praste among them is the wan they call Jarback Praste and he's too auld for you."

"Why do they call him Jarback?"

"Wan av his shoulders is a l'il bit higher than the other. He's got a bit of money and doesn't be after having to work. A book worrum, I'm belaving. Have ye got a bit av cold iron about you?"

"No; why?"

"Ye should have. Old Caroline Praste at the Grange is a witch if ever there was one."

"Why, that's what Ilse said. But there are no such thing as witches really, Mr Kelly."

"Maybe that's thrue but it's better to be on the safe side. Here, put this horseshoe-nail in your pocket and don't cross her if ye can help it. Ye don't mind if I have a bit av a smoke, do ye?"

Emily did not mind at all. It left her free to follow her own thoughts, which were more agreeable than Old Kelly's talk of toads and witches. The road from Blair Water to, Priest Pond was a very lovely one, winding along the gulf shore, crossing fir-fringed rivers and inlets, and coming ever and anon on one of the ponds for which that part of the north shore was noted—Blair Water, Derry Pond, Long Pond, Three Ponds where three blue laolets were strung together like three great sapphires held by a silver thread; and then Priest Pond, the largest of all, almost as round as Blair Water. As they drove down towards it Emily drank the scene in with avid eyes—as soon as possible she must write a description of it; she had packed the Jimmy blank book in her box for just such purposes.

The air seemed to be filled with opal dust over the great pond and the bowery summer homesteads around it. A western sky of smoky red was arched over the big Malvern Bay beyond. Little grey sails were drifting along by the fir-fringed shores. A sequestered side road, fringed thickly with young maples and birches, led down to Wyther Grange. How damp and cool the air was in the hollows! And how the ferns did smell! Emily was sorry when they reached Wyther Grange and climbed in between the gate-posts whereon the big stone dogs sat very stonily, looking grim enough in the twilight.

The wide hall door was open and a flood of light streamed out over the lawn. A little old woman was standing in it. Old Kelly seemed suddenly in something of a hurry. He swung Emily and her box to the ground, shook hands hastily and whispered, "Don't lose that bit av a nail. Good-bye. I wish ye a cool head and a warm heart," and was off before the little old woman could reach them.

"So this is Emily of New Moon!" Emily heard a rather shrill, cracked voice saying. She felt a thin, claw-like hand grasp hers and draw her towards the door. There were no witches, Emily knew—but she thrust her hand into her pocket and touched the horseshoe-nail.

DEALS WITH GHOSTS

"Your aunt is in the back parlour," said Caroline Priest. "Come this way. Are you tired?"

"No," said Emily, following Caroline and taking her in thoroughly. If Caroline were a witch she was a very small one. She was really no taller than Emily herself. She wore a black silk dress and a little string cap of black net edged with black ruching on her yellowish white hair. Her face was more wrinkled than Emily had ever supposed a face could be and she had the peculiar grey-green eyes which, as Emily afterwards discovered, "ran" in the Priest clan.

"You may be a witch," thought Emily, "but I think I can manage *you*."

They went through the spacious hall, catching glimpses on either side of large, dim, splendid rooms, then through the kitchen end out of it into an odd little back hall. It was long and narrow and dark. On one side was a row of four, square, small-paned windows, on the other were cupboards, reaching from floor to ceiling, with doors of black shining wood. Emily felt like one of the heroines in Gothic romance, wandering at midnight through a subterranean dungeon, with some unholy guide. She had read *The Mysteries of Udolpho* and *The Romance of the Forest* before the taboo had fallen on Dr Burnley's bookcase. She shivered. It was awful but interesting.

At the end of the hall a flight of four steps led up to a door. Beside the steps was an immense black grandfather's clock reaching almost to the ceiling.

"We shut little girls up in that when they're bad," whispered

Caroline, nodding at Emily, as she opened the door that led into the back parlour.

"I'll take good care you won't shut *me* up in it," thought Emily.

The back parlour was a pretty, quaint old room where a table was laid for supper. Caroline led Emily through it and knocked at another door, using a quaint old brass knocker that was fashioned like a chessy-cat, with such an irresistible grin that you wanted to grin, too, when you saw it. Somebody said, "Come in," and they went down another four steps—was there ever such a funny house?—into a bedroom. And here at last was Great-Aunt Nancy Priest, sitting in her arm-chair, with her black stick leaning against her knee, and her tiny white hands, still pretty, and sparkling with fine rings, lying on her purple silk apron.

Emily felt a distinct shock of disappointment. After hearing that poem in which Nancy Murray's beauty of nut-brown hair and starry brown eyes and cheek of satin rose had been be-rhymed she had somehow expected Great-Aunt Nancy, in spite of her ninety years, to be beautiful still. But Aunt Nancy was white-haired and yellow-skinned and wrinkled and shrunken, though her brown eyes were still bright and shrewd. Somehow, she looked like an old fairy—an impish, tolerant old fairy, who might turn suddenly malevolent if you rubbed her the wrong way—only fairies never wore long, gold-tasselled earrings that almost touched their shoulders, or white lace caps with purple pansies in them.

"So this is Juliet's girl!" she said, giving Emily one of her sparkling hands. "Don't look so startled, child. I'm not going to kiss you. I never held with inflicting kisses on defenceless creatures simply because they were so unlucky as to be my relatives. Now, who does she look like, Caroline?"

Emily made a mental grimace. Now for another ordeal of comparisons, wherein dead-and-gone noses and eyes and foreheads would be dragged out and fitted on her. She was thoroughly tired of having her looks talked over in every gathering of the clans.

"Not much like the Murrays," said Caroline, peering so closely into her face that Emily involuntarily drew back. "Not so handsome as the Murrays."

"Nor the Starrs either. Her father was a handsome man—so handsome that I'd have run away with him myself if I'd been fifty years younger. There's nothing of Juliet in her that I can see. Juliet was pretty.

You are not as good-looking as that picture made you out but I didn't expect you would be. Pictures and epitaphs are never to be trusted. Where's your bang gone, Emily?"

"Aunt Elizabeth combed it back."

"Well, you comb it down again while you're in my house. There's something of your Grandfather Murray about your eyebrows. Your grandfather was a handsome man—and a darned bad-tempered one—almost as bad-tempered as the Priests—hey, Caroline?"

"If you please, Great-Aunt Nancy," said Emily deliberately, "I don't like to be told I look like other people. I look just like myself."

Aunt Nancy chuckled.

"Spunk, I see. Good. I never cared for meek youngsters. So you're not stupid, eh?"

"No, I'm not."

Great-Aunt Nancy grinned this time. Her false teeth looked uncannily white and young in her old, brown face.

"Good. If you've brains it's better than beauty—brains last, beauty doesn't. Me, for example. Caroline here, now, never had either brains nor beauty, had you, Caroline? Come, let's go to supper. Thank goodness, my stomach has stood by me if my good looks haven't."

Great-Aunt Nancy hobbled, by the aid of her stick, up the steps and over to the table. She sat at one end, Caroline at the other, Emily between, feeling rather uncomfortable. But the ruling passion was still strong in her and she was already composing a description of them for the blank book.

"I wonder if anybody will be sorry when you die," she thought, looking intently at Caroline's wizened old face.

"Come now, tell me," said Aunt Nancy. "If you're not stupid, why did you write me such a stupid letter that first time. Lord, but it was stupid! I read it over to Caroline to punish her whenever she is naughty."

"I couldn't write any other kind of a letter because Aunt Elizabeth said she was going to read it."

"Trust Elizabeth for that. Well, you can write what you like here—and say what you like—and do what you like. Nobody will interfere with you or try to bring you up. I asked you for a visit, not for discipline. Thought likely you'd have enough of that at New Moon. You can have the run of the house and pick a beau to your liking from the Priest boys—not that the young fry are what they were in my time."

"I don't want a beau," retorted Emily. She felt rather disgusted. Old Kelly had ranted about beaux half the way over and here was Aunt Nancy beginning on the same unnecessary subject.

"Don't you tell me," said Aunt Nancy, laughing till her gold tassels shook. "There never was a Murray of New Moon that didn't like a beau. When I was your age I had half a dozen. All the little boys in Blair Water were fighting about me. Caroline here now never had a beau in her life, had you, Caroline?"

"Never wanted one," snapped Caroline.

"Eighty and twelve say the same thing and both lie," said Aunt Nancy. "What's the use of being hypocrites among ourselves? I don't say it isn't well enough when men are about. Caroline, do you notice what a pretty hand Emily has? As pretty as mine when I was young. And an elbow like a cat's. Cousin Susan Murray had an elbow like that. It's odd—she has more Murray points than Starr points and yet she looks like the Starrs and not like the Murrays. What odd sums in addition we all are—the answer is never what you'd expect. Caroline, what a pity Jarback isn't home. He'd like Emily—I have a feeling he'd like Emily. Jarback's the only Priest that'll ever go to heaven, Emily. Let's have a look at your ankles, puss."

Emily rather unwillingly put out her foot. Aunt Nancy nodded her satisfaction.

"Mary Shipley's ankle. Only one in a generation has it. I had it. The Murray ankles are thick. Even your mother's ankles were thick. Look at that instep, Caroline. Emily, you're not a beauty but if you learn to use your eyes and hands and feet properly you'll pass for one. The men are easily fooled and if the women say you're not 'twill be held for jealousy."

Emily decided that this was a good opportunity to find out something that had puzzled her.

"Old Mr Kelly said I had come-hither eyes, Aunt Nancy. Have I? And *what* are come-hither eyes?"

"Jock Kelly's an old ass. You haven't come-hither eyes—it wouldn't be a Murray tradish." Aunt Nancy laughed. "The Murrays have keep-your-distance eyes—and so have you—though your lashes contradict them a bit. But sometimes eyes like that—combined with certain other points—are quite as effective as come-hither eyes. Men go by contraries oftener than not—if you tell them to keep off they'll come on. My own Nathaniel now—the only way to get him to do anything was to coax him to do the opposite. Remember, Caroline? Have another cooky, Emily?"

"I haven't had one yet," said Emily, rather resentfully.

Those cookies looked very tempting and she had been wishing they might be passed. She didn't know why Aunt Nancy and Caroline both laughed. Caroline's laugh was unpleasant—a dry, rusty sort of laugh—"no juice in it," Emily decided. She thought she would write in her description that Caroline had a "thin, rattling laugh."

"What do you think of us?" demanded Aunt Nancy. "Come now, what *do* you think of us?"

Emily was dreadfully embarrassed. She had just been thinking of writing that Aunt Nancy looked "withered and shrivelled;" but one couldn't say that—one *couldn't*.

"Tell the truth and shame the devil," said Aunt Nancy.

"That isn't a fair question," cried Emily.

"You think," said Aunt Nancy, grinning, "that I'm a hideous old hag and that Caroline isn't quite human. She isn't. She never was—but you should have seen *me* seventy years ago. I was handsomest of all the handsome Murrays. The men were mad about me. When I married Nat Priest his three brothers could have cut his throat. One cut his own. Oh, I played havoc in my time. All I regret is I can't live it over. 'Twas a grand life while it lasted. I queened it over them. The women hated me, of course—all but Caroline here. You worshipped me, didn't you, Caroline? And you worship me yet, don't you, Caroline? Caroline, I *wish* you didn't have a wart on your nose."

"I wish you had one on your tongue," said Caroline waspishly.

Emily was beginning to feel tired and bewildered. It was interesting—and Aunt Nancy was kind enough in her queer way; but at home Ilse and Perry and Teddy would be foregathering in Lofty John's bush for their evening revel, and Saucy Sal would be sitting on the dairy steps, waiting for Cousin Jimmy to give her the froth. Emily suddenly realized that she was as homesick for New Moon as she had been for Maywood her first night at New Moon.

"The child's tired," said Aunt Nancy. "Take her to bed, Caroline. Put her in the Pink Room."

Emily followed Caroline through the back hall, through the kitchen, through the front hall, up the stairs, down a long hall, through a long side hall. Where on earth was she being taken? Finally they reached a large room. Caroline set down the lamp, and asked Emily if she had a nightgown.

"Of course I have. Do you suppose Aunt Elizabeth would have let me come without one?"

Emily was quite indignant.

"Nancy says you can sleep as long as you like in the morning," said Caroline. "Good night. Nancy and I sleep in the old wing, of course, and the rest of us sleep well in our graves."

With this cryptic remark Caroline trotted out and shut the door.

Emily sat down on an embroidered ottoman and looked about her. The window curtains were of faded pink brocade and the walls were hung with pink paper decorated with diamonds of rose chains. It made a very pretty fairy paper, as Emily found by cocking her eyes at it. There was a green carpet on the floor, so lavishly splashed with big pink roses that Emily was almost afraid to walk on it. She decided that the room was a very splendid one.

"But I have to sleep here alone, so I must say my prayers very carefully," she reflected.

She undressed rather hastily, blew out the light and got into bed. She covered herself up to her chin and lay there, staring at the high, white ceiling. She had grown so used to Aunt Elizabeth's curtained bed that she felt curiously unsheltered in this low, modern one. But at least the window was wide open—evidently Aunt Nancy did not share Aunt Elizabeth's horror of night air. Through it Emily could see summer fields lying in the magic of a rising yellow moon. But the room was big and ghostly. She felt horribly far away from everybody. She was lonesome—homesick. She thought of Old Kelly and his toad ointment. Perhaps he *did* boil the toads alive after all. This hideous thought tormented her. It was *awful* to think of toads—or anything—being boiled alive. She had never slept alone before. Suddenly she was frightened. How the window rattled. It sounded terribly as if somebody—or *something*—were trying to get in. She thought of Ilse's ghost—a ghost you couldn't *see* but could *hear* and *feel* was something especially spooky in the way of ghosts—she thought of the stone dogs that went "Wo—or—oo—oo" at midnight. A dog *did* begin to howl somewhere. Emily felt a cold perspiration on her brow. *What* had Caroline meant about the rest of them sleeping well in their graves? The floor creaked. Wasn't there somebody—or *something*—tiptoeing round outside the door? Did something move in the corner? There were mysterious sounds in the long hall.

"I *won't* be scared," said Emily. "I *won't* think of those things, and to-morrow I'll write down all about how I feel now."

And then—she *did* hear something—right behind the wall at the head of her bed. There was no mistake about it. It was not imagination. She heard distinctly strange uncanny rustles—as if stiff silk dresses were rubbing against each other—as if fluttering wings fanned the air—and there were soft, low, muffled sounds like tiny children's cries or moans. They lasted—they kept on. Now and then they would die away—then start up again.

Emily cowered under the bedclothes, cold with real terror. Before, her fright had been only on the surface—she had *known* there was nothing to fear, even while she feared. Something in her braced her to endure. But *this* was no mistake—no imagination. The rustles and flutterings and cries and moans were all too real. Wyther Grange suddenly became a dreadful, uncanny place. Ilse was right—it *was* haunted. And she was all alone here, with miles of rooms and halls between her and any human being. It was cruel of Aunt Nancy to put her in a haunted room. Aunt Nancy must have known it was haunted— cruel old Aunt Nancy with her ghoulish pride in men who had killed themselves for her. Oh, if she were back in dear New Moon, with Aunt Elizabeth beside her. Aunt Elizabeth was not an ideal bedfellow but she was flesh-and-blood. And if the windows were hermetically sealed they kept out spooks as well as night air.

"Perhaps it won't be so bad if I say my prayers over again," thought Emily.

But even this didn't help much.

To the end of her life Emily never forgot that first horrible night at Wyther Grange. She was so tired that sometimes she dozed fitfully off only to be awakened in a few minutes in panic horror, by the rustling and muffled moans behind her bed. Every ghost and groan, every tortured spirit and bleeding nun of the books she had read came into her mind.

"Aunt Elizabeth was right—novels aren't fit to read," she thought. "Oh, I will die here—of fright—I know I will. I know I'm a coward—I can't be brave."

When morning came the room was bright with sunshine and free from mysterious sounds. Emily got up, dressed and found her way to the old wing. She was pale, with black-ringed eyes, but resolute.

"Well, and how did you sleep?" asked Aunt Nancy graciously.

Emily ignored the question.

"I want to go home to-day," she said.

Aunt Nancy stared.

"Home? Nonsense! Are you such a homesick baby as that?"

"I'm not homesick—not *very*—but I must go home."

"You can't—there's no one here to take you. You don't expect Caroline can drive you to Blair Water, do you?"

"Then I will walk."

Aunt Nancy thumped her stick angrily on the floor.

"You will stay right here until I'm ready for you to go, Miss Puss. I never tolerate any whims but my own. Caroline knows that, don't you, Caroline? Sit down to your breakfast—and eat—*eat*."

Aunt Nancy glared at Emily.

"I won't stay here," said Emily. "I won't stay another night in that horrible haunted room. It was cruel of you to put me there. If—" Emily gave Aunt Nancy glare for glare—"if I was Salome I'd ask for *your* head on a charger."

"Hoity-toity! What nonsense is this about a haunted room? We've no ghosts at Wyther Grange. Have we, Caroline? We don't consider them hygienic."

"You have something *dreadful* in that room—it rustled and moaned and cried all night long right in the wall behind my bed. I won't stay—I won't—"

Emily's tears came in spite of her efforts to repress them. She was so unstrung nervously that she couldn't help crying. It lacked but little of hysterics with her already.

Aunt Nancy looked at Caroline and Caroline looked back at Aunt Nancy.

"We should have told her, Caroline. It's all our fault. I clean forgot— it's so long since any one slept in the Pink Room. No wonder she was frightened. Emily, you poor child, it was a shame. It would serve me right to have my head on a charger, you vindictive scrap. We should have told you."

"Told me—what?"

"About the swallows in the chimney. That was what you heard. The big central chimney goes right up through the walls behind your bed. It is never used now since the fireplaces were built in. The swallows nest there—hundreds of them. They do make an uncanny noise—fluttering and quarrelling as they do."

Emily felt foolish and ashamed—much more ashamed than she needed to feel, for her experience had really been a very trying one, and older folk than she had been woefully frightened o' nights in the Pink Room at Wyther Grange. Nancy Priest *had* put people into that room sometimes expressly to scare them. But to do her justice she really had forgotten in Emily's case and was sorry.

Emily said no more about going home; Caroline and Aunt Nancy were both very kind to her that day; she had a good nap in the afternoon; and when the second night came she went straight to the Pink Room and slept soundly the night through. The rustles and cries were as distinct as ever but swallows and spectres were two entirely different things.

"After all, I think I'll like Wyther Grange," said Emily.

A DIFFERENT KIND OF HAPPINESS

"JULY 20TH.

"DEAR FATHER:

"I have been a fortnight at Wyther Grange and I have not written to you once. But I thought of you every day. I had to write to Aunt Laura and Ilse and Teddy and Cousin Jimmy and Perry and between times I am having such fun. The first night I was here I did not think I was going to be happy. But I am—only it's a different kind from New Moon happiness.

"Aunt Nancy and Caroline are very good to me and let me do

210

exactly as I like. This is very agreeable. They are very sarcastic to each other. But I think they are a good bit like Ilse and me—they fight quite frequently but love each other very hard between times. I am sure Caroline isn't a witch but I would like to know what she thinks of when she is all alone by herself. Aunt Nancy is not pretty any longer but she is very *aristocratic looking*. She doesn't walk much because of her roomatism, so she sits mostly in her back parlour and reads and knits lace or plays cards with Caroline. I talk to her a great deal because she says it amuses her and I have told her a great many things but I have never told her that I write poetry. If I did I know she would make me recite it to her and I feel she is not the right person to recite your poetry to. And I do not talk about you or Mother to her, though she tries to make me. I told her all about Lofty John and his bush and going to Father Cassidy. She chuckled over that and said she always liked to talk to the Catholic Priests because they were the only men in the world a woman could talk to for more than ten minutes without other women saying she was throwing herself at their heads.

"Aunt Nancy says a great many things like that. She and Caroline talk a great deal to each other about things that happened in the Priest and Murray families. I like to sit and listen. They don't stop just as things are getting interesting the way Aunt Elizabeth and Aunt Laura do. A good many things I don't understand but I will remember them and will find out about them sometime. I have written descriptions of Aunt Nancy and Caroline in my Jimmy-book. I keep the book hid behind the wardrobe in my room because I found Caroline rummidging in my trunk one day. I must not call Aunt Nancy Great-Aunt. She says it makes her feel like Methoosaleh. She tells me all about the men who were in love with her. It seems to me they all behaved pretty much the same. I don't think that was exciting but she says it was. She tells me about all the parties and dances they used to have here long ago. Wyther Grange is bigger than New Moon and the furniture is much handsomer but it is harder to feel acquainted with it.

"There are many interesting things in this house. I love to look at them. There is a Jakobite glass on a stand in the parlour. It was a glass *an old ancester* of the Priests had long ago in Scotland and it has a thistle and a rose on it and they used it to drink Prince Charlie's health with and for *no other purpose*. It is a very *valewable airloom* and Aunt Nancy prizes it highly. And she has a pickled snake in a big glass jar in the china cabinet. It is hideous but fascinating. I shiver when I see it but yet I go to look at it every day. Something seems to drag me to it. Aunt Nancy has a bureau in her room with *glass knobs* and a vase shaped like a green fish sitting up on end and a Chinese draggon with a curly tail, and a case of sweet little stuffed humming-birds and a sand-glass for boiling eggs by and a framed wreath made out of the hair of all the dead Priests and lots of old dagerrotipes. But the thing I like the best of all is a great silvery shining ball hanging from the lamp in the parlour. It reflects everything like a little fairy world. Aunt Nancy calls it a gazing-ball, and says that when she is dead I am to have it. I wish she hadn't said that because I want the ball so much that I can't help wondering when she will die and that makes me feel wicked. I am to have the chessy-cat door knocker and her gold ear-rings, too. These are Murray airlooms. Aunt Nancy says the Priest airlooms must go to the Priests. I will like the chessy-cat but I don't want the ear-rings. I'd rather not have people notice my ears.

"I have to sleep alone. I feel frightened but I think if I could get over being frightened I'd like it. I don't mind the swallows now. It's just being alone so far away from any one. But it is lovely to be able to stretch out your legs just as you like and not have anybody scold you for skwirming. And when I wake up in the night and think of a splendid line of poetry (because the things that you think of like that always seem the best) I can get right out of bed and write it down in my Jimmy-book. I couldn't do that at home and then by morning I'd likely forget it. I thought of such a nice line last night. "Lilies lifted pearly chaluses (a chalus is a kind of cup only more poetical) where bees were drowned in sweetness" and I felt happy because I was sure they were two better lines than any I had composed yet.

"I am allowed to go into the kitchen and help Caroline cook. Caroline is a good cook but sometimes she makes a mistake and this vexes Aunt Nancy because she likes nice things to eat. The other day Caroline made the barley soup far too thick and when Aunt Nancy looked at her plate she said 'Lord, is this a dinner or a poltis?' Caroline said 'It is good enough for a Priest and what is good enough for a Priest is good enough for a Murray,' and Aunt Nancy said 'Woman, the Priests eat of the crumbs that fall from the Murrays' tables,' and Caroline was so mad she cried. And Aunt Nancy said to me 'Emily, never marry a Priest'—just like Old Kelly, when I have no notion of marrying one of them. I don't like any of them I've seen very much but they seem to me a good deal like other people. Jim is the best of them but impident.

"I like the Wyther Grange breakfasts better than the New Moon breakfasts. We have toast and bacon and marmalade—nicer than porridge.

"Sunday is more amusing here than at New Moon but not so holy. Nice for a change. Aunt Nancy can't go to church or knit lace so she and Caroline play cards all day but she says I must never do it—that she is just a bad example. I love to look at Aunt Nancy's big parlour Bible because there are so many interesting things in it—pieces of dresses and hair and poetry and old tintipes and accounts of deaths and weddings. I found a piece about my own birth and it gave me a queer feeling.

"In the afternoon some of the Priests come to see Aunt Nancy and to stay to supper. Leslie Priest always comes. He is Aunt Nancy's favourite neffew, so Jim says. I think that is because he pays her compliments. But I saw him wink at Isaac Priest once when he paid her one. I don't like him. He treats me as if I were a meer child. Aunt Nancy says terrible things to them all but they just laugh. When they go away Aunt Nancy makes fun of them to Caroline. Caroline doesn't like it, because she is a Priest and so she and Aunt Nancy always quarrel Sunday evening and don't speak again till Monday morning.

"I can read all the books in Aunt Nancy's bookcase except the row on the top shelf. I wonder why I can't read them. Aunt Nancy said they were French novels but I just peeped into one and it was English. I wonder if Aunt Nancy tells lies.

"The place I love best is down at bay shore. Some parts of the shore are very steep and there are such nice, woodsy, *unexpected* places all along it. I wander there and compose poetry. I miss Ilse and Teddy and Perry and Saucy Sal a great deal. I had a letter from Ilse to-day. She wrote me that they couldn't do anything more about the Midsummer Night's Dream till I got back. It is nice to feel so necessary.

"Aunt Nancy doesn't like Aunt Elizabeth. She called her a 'tyrant' one day and then she said 'Jimmy Murray was a very clever boy. Elizabeth Murray killed his intellect in her temper—and nothing was done to her. If she had killed his body she would have been a murderess.

The other was worse, if you ask me.' I do not like Aunt Elizabeth at times myself but I felt, dear Father, that I must stand up for *my family* and I said 'I do not want to hear such things said of my Aunt Elizabeth.'

"And I just gave Aunt Nancy a *look*. She said 'Well, Saucebox, my brother Archibald will never be dead as long as you're alive. If you don't want to hear things don't hang around when Caroline and I are talking. I notice there are plenty of things you like to hear.'

"This was sarcasm, dear Father, but still I feel Aunt Nancy likes me but perhaps she will not like me very long. Jim Priest says she is fickle and never liked any one, even her husband, very long. But after she had been sarcastic to me she always tells Caroline to give me a piece of pie so I don't mind the sarcasm. She lets me have real tea, too. I like it. At New Moon Aunt Elizabeth won't give me anything but cambric tea because it is best for my health. Aunt Nancy says the way to be healthy is to eat just what you want and never think about your stomach. But then she was never threttened with consumption. She says I needn't be a bit frightened of dying of consumption because I have too much ginger in me. That is a comfortable thought. The only time I don't like Aunt Nancy is when she begins talking about the different parts of me and the effect they will have on the men. It makes me feel so silly.

"I will write you oftener after this, dear Father. I feel I have been neglecting you.

"P. S. I am afraid there are some mistakes in spelling in this letter. I forgot to bring my dictionary with me.

"JULY 22.

"Oh, dear Father, I am in a dreadful scrape. I don't know what I am to do. Oh, Father, I have broken Aunt Nancy's Jakobite glass. It seems to me like a dreadful dream.

"I went into the parlour to-day to look at the pickled snake and just as I was turning away my sleeve caught the Jakobite glass and over it went on the harth and *shivered into fragments*. At first I rushed out and left them there but afterwards I went back and carefully gathered them up and hid them in a box behind the sofa. Aunt Nancy never goes into the parlour now and Caroline not very often and perhaps they may not miss the glass until I go home. But it *haunts* me. I keep thinking of it all the time and I cannot enjoy anything. I know Aunt Nancy will be furious and never forgive me if she finds out. I could not sleep all night for worrying about it. Jim Priest came down to play with me today but he said there was no fun in me and went home. The Priests mostly say what they think. Of course there was no fun in me. How could there be? I wonder if it would do any good to pray about it. I don't feel as if it would be right to pray because I am deceiving Aunt Nancy.

"JULY 24.

"Dear Father, this is a very strange world. Nothing ever turns out just like what you expect. Last night I couldn't sleep again. I was so worried. I thought I was a coward, and doing an underhanded thing and not living up to my tradishuns. At last it got so bad I couldn't stand it. I can bear it when other people have a bad opinion of me but it hurts too much when I have a bad opinion of myself. So I got out of bed and went right back through all those halls to the back parlour. Aunt Nancy was still there all alone playing Solitare. She said what on earth was I out of bed for at such an hour. I just said, short and quick to get the worst over, 'I broke your Jakobite glass yesterday and hid the pieces behind the sofa.' Then I waited for the *storm to burst*. Aunt Nancy said 'What a blessing. I've often wanted to smash it but never had the courage. All the Priest clan are waiting for me to die to get that glass and quarrel over it and I'm tickled to think none of them can have it now and yet can't pick a fuss with me over smashing it. Get off to bed and get your beauty sleep.' I said 'And you aren't mad at all, Aunt Nancy?' 'If it had been a Murray airloom I'd have torn up the turf' Aunt Nancy said. 'But I don't care a hoot about the Priest things.'

"So I went back to bed, dear Father, and felt very much releeved, but not so heroyik.

"I had a letter from Ilse to-day. She says Saucy Sal has had kittens at last. I feel that I ought to be home to see about them. Likely Aunt Elizabeth will have them all drowned before I get back. I had a letter from Teddy too, not much of a letter but all filled with dear little pictures of Ilse and Perry and the Tansy Patch and Lofty John's bush. They made me feel homesick.

"JULY 28.

"Oh, Father dear, I have found out all about the mistery of Ilse's mother. It is so terrible I can't write it down even to you. I cannot believe it but Aunt Nancy says it is true. I did not think there could be such terrible things in the world. No, I can't believe it and I won't believe it no matter who says it is true. I *know* Ilse's mother *couldn't* have done anything like that. There must have been a fearful mistake somewhere. I am so unhappy and feel as if I could never be happy any more. Last night I wept on my pilllow, like the heroins in Aunt Nancy's books do."

"SHE COULDN'T HAVE DONE IT"

Great-aunt Nancy and Caroline Priest were wont to colour their grey days with the remembered crimsons of old, long-past delights and merry-makings, but they went further than this and talked over any number of old family histories before Emily with a total disregard of her youth. Loves, births, deaths, scandals, tragedies—anything that came into their old heads. Nor did they spare details. Aunt Nancy revelled in details. She forgot nothing, and sins and weaknesses that death had covered and time shown mercy to were ruthlessly dragged out and dissected by this ghoulish old lady.

Emily was not quite certain whether she really liked it or not. It *was* fascinating—it fed some dramatic hunger in her—but it made her feel unhappy somehow, as if something very ugly were concealed in the darkness of the pit they opened before her innocent eyes. As Aunt Laura had said, her youth protected her to some extent, but it could not save her from a dreadful understanding of the pitiful story of Ilse's mother on the afternoon when it seemed good to Aunt Nancy to resurrect that tale of anguish and shame.

Emily was curled up on the sofa in the back parlour, reading *The Scottish Chiefs* because it was a breathlessly hot July afternoon—too hot to haunt the bay shore. Emily was feeling very happy. The Wind Woman was ruffling over the big maple grove behind the Grange, turning the leaves until every tree seemed to be covered with strange, pale, silvery blossoms; fragrances drifted in from the garden; the world was lovely; she had had a letter from Aunt Laura saying that one of Saucy Sal's kittens had been saved for her. Emily had felt when Mike II died that she would never want another cat. But now she found she did.

Everything suited her very well; she was so happy that she should have sacrificed her dearest possession to the jealous gods if she had known anything about the old pagan belief.

Aunt Nancy was tired of playing solitaire. She pushed the cards away and took up her knitting.

"Emily," she said, "has your Aunt Laura any notion of marrying Dr Burnley?"

Emily, recalled thus abruptly from the field of Bannockburn, looked bored. Blair Water gossip had often asked or hinted this question; and now it met her in Priest Pond.

"No, I'm sure she hasn't," she said. "Why, Aunt Nancy, Dr Burnley *hates* women."

Aunt Nancy chuckled.

"Thought perhaps he'd got over that. It's eleven years now since his wife ran away. Few men hold to one idea for anything like eleven years. But Allan Burnley always was stubborn in anything—love or hate. He still loves his wife—and that is why he hates her memory and all other women."

"I never heard the rights of that story," said Caroline. "Who was his wife?"

"Beatrice Mitchell—one of the Shrewsbury Mitchells. She was only eighteen when Allan married her. He was thirty-five. Emily, never you be fool enough to marry a man much older than yourself."

Emily said nothing. *The Scottish Chiefs* was forgotten. Her finger-tips were growing cold as they always did in excitement, her eyes turning black. She felt that she was on the verge of solving the mystery that had so long worried and puzzled her. She was desperately afraid that Aunt Nancy would branch off to something else.

"I've heard she was a great beauty," said Caroline.

Aunt Nancy sniffed.

"Depends on your taste in style. Oh, she was pretty—one of your golden-haired dolls. She had a little birthmark over her left eyebrow—just like a tiny red heart—I never could see anything but that mark when I looked at her. But her flatterers told her it was a beauty spot—'the Ace of Hearts' they called her. Allan was mad about her. She had been a flirt before her marriage. But I *will* say—for justice among women is a rare thing, Caroline—*you,* for instance, are an unjust old hag—that she didn't flirt after marrying—openly, at least. She was a sly puss—always

217

laughing and singing and dancing—no wife for Allan Burnley if you ask me. And he could have had Laura Murray. But between a fool and a sensible woman did a man ever hesitate? The fool wins every time, Caroline. That's why *you* never got a husband. You were too sensible. I got mine by pretending to be a fool. Emily, you remember that. You have brains—hide them. Your ankles will do more for you than your brains ever will."

"Never mind Emily's ankles," said Caroline, keen on a scandal hunt. "Go on about the Burnleys."

"Well, there was a cousin of hers—Leo Mitchell from Shrewsbury. You remember the Mitchells, don't you, Caroline? This Leo was a handsome fellow—a sea-captain. He had been in love with Beatrice, so gossip ran. Some said Beatrice wanted him but that her people made her marry Allan Burnley because he was the better match. Who knows? Gossip lies nine times and tells a half truth the tenth. She pretended to be in love with Allan anyhow, and he believed it. When Leo came home from a voyage and found Beatrice married he took it coolly enough. But he was always over at Blair Water. Beatrice had plenty of excuses. Leo was her cousin—they had been brought up together— they were like brother and sister—she was so lonesome in Blair Water after living in a town—he had no home except with a brother. Allan took it all down—he was so infatuated with her she could have made him believe anything. She and Leo were always together there when Allan was away seeing his patients. Then came the night Leo's vessel— *The Lady of Winds*—was to sail from Blair Harbour for South America. He went—and my Lady Beatrice went with him."

A queer little strangled sound came from Emily's corner. If Aunt Nancy or Caroline had looked at her they would have seen that the child was white as the dead, with wide, horror-filled eyes. But they did not look. They knitted and gossiped on, enjoying themselves hugely.

"How did the doctor take it?" asked Caroline.

"Take it—take it—nobody knows. Everybody knows what kind of a man he's been ever since, though. He came home that night at dusk. The baby was asleep in its crib and the servant girl was watching it. She told Allan that Mrs Burnley had gone to the harbour with her cousin for a good-bye walk and would be back at ten. Allan waited for her easily enough—he never doubted her—but she didn't come back. She had never intended to come back. In the morning the *Lady of Winds* was gone—had sailed out of the harbour at dark the night before. Beatrice had gone on board with him—that was all anybody knew. Allan Burnley *said* nothing, beyond forbidding her name ever to be mentioned in his hearing again. But *The Lady of Winds* was lost with all on board off Hatteras and that was the end of that elopement, and the end of Beatrice with her beauty and her laughter and her Ace of Hearts."

"But not the end of the shame and wretchedness she brought to her home," said Caroline shrewishly. "I'd tar and feather such a woman."

"Nonsense—if a man can't look after his wife—if he blinds his own eyes—Mercy on us, child, what is the matter?"

For Emily was standing up, holding out her hands as if pushing some loathly thing from her.

"I don't believe it," she cried, in a high, unnatural voice. "I don't believe Ilse's mother did *that*. She didn't—she couldn't have—not Ilse's *mother*."

"Catch her, Caroline!" cried Aunt Nancy.

But Emily, though the back parlour had whirled about her for a second, had recovered herself.

"Don't touch me!" she cried passionately. "Don't touch me! You—you—you *liked* hearing that story!"

She rushed out of the room. Aunt Nancy looked ashamed for a moment. For the first time it occurred to her that her scandal-loving old tongue had done a black thing. Then she shrugged her shoulders.

"She can't go through life in cotton-wool. Might as well learn spades are spades now as ever. I would have thought she'd have heard it all long ago if Blair Water gossip is what it used to be. If she goes home and tells this I'll have the indignant virgins of New Moon coming down on me in holy horror as a corrupter of youth. Caroline, don't you ask me to tell you any more family horrors before my niece, you scandalous old woman. At your age! I'm surprised at you!"

Aunt Nancy and Caroline returned to their knitting and their spicy reminiscences, and upstairs in the Pink Room Emily lay face downwards on her bed and cried for hours. It was so horrible—Ilse's mother had run away and left her little baby. To Emily that was the awful thing—the strange, cruel, heartless thing that Ilse's mother had done. She could not bring herself to believe it—there was some mistake somewhere—there *was.*

"Perhaps she was kidnapped," said Emily, trying desperately to explain it. "She just went on board to look around—and he weighed anchor and carried her off. She *couldn't* have gone away of her own accord and left her dear little baby."

The story haunted Emily in good earnest. She could think of nothing else for days. It took possession of her and worried and gnawed at her with an almost physical pain. She dreaded going back to New Moon and meeting Ilse with this consciousness of a dark secret which she must hide from her. Ilse knew nothing. She had asked Ilse once where her mother was buried and Ilse had said, "Oh, I don't know. At Shrewsbury, I guess—that's where all the Mitchells are buried."

Emily wrung her slim hands together. She was as sensitive to ugliness and pain as she was to beauty and pleasure, and this thing was both hideous and agonizing. Yet she could not keep from thinking about it, day and night. Life at Wyther Grange suddenly went stale. Aunt Nancy and Caroline all at once gave up talking family history, even harmless history, before her. And as it was painful repression for them, they did not encourage her hanging round. Emily began to feel that they were glad when she was out of hearing, so she kept away and spent most of her days wandering on the bay shore. She could not compose any poetry—she could not write in her Jimmy-book—she could not even write to her father. Something seemed to hang between her and her old delights. There was a drop of poison in every cup. Even the filmy shadows on the great bay, the charm of its fir-hung cliffs and its little purple islets that looked like outposts of fairyland, could not bring to her the old "fine, careless rapture." She was afraid she could never be happy again—so intense had been her reaction to her first revelation of the world's sin and sorrow. And under it all, persisted the same incredulity—Ilse's mother *couldn't* have done it—and the same helpless longing to prove she couldn't have done it. But how could it be proved? It couldn't. She had solved one "mystery" but she had stumbled into a darker one—the reason why Beatrice Burnley had never come back on that summer twilight of long ago. For, all the evidence of facts to the contrary notwithstanding, Emily persisted in her secret belief that whatever the reason *was,* it was *not* that she had gone away in *The Lady of Winds* when that doomed ship sailed out into the starlit wonder of the gulf beyond Blair Harbour.

ON THE BAY SHORE

"I wonder," thought Emily, "how much longer I have to live."

She had prowled that evening farther down the bay shore than she had ever gone before. It was a warm, windy evening, the air was resinous and sweet; the bay a misty turquoise. That part of the shore whereon she found herself seemed as lonely and virgin as if no human foot had ever trodden it, save for a tiny, tricksy path, slender as red thread and bordered by great, green, velvety sheets of moss, that wound in and out of the big firs and scrub spruces. The banks grew steeper and rockier as she went on and finally the little path vanished altogether in a plot of bracken. Emily was just turning to go back when she caught sight of a magnificent spray of farewell-summer, growing far out on the edge of the bank. She must get it—she had never seen farewell-summers of so dark and rich a purple. She stepped out to reach them—the treacherous mossy soil gave way under her feet and slid down the steep slope. Emily made a frantic attempt to scramble back but the harder she tried, the faster went the landslide, carrying her with it. In a moment it would pass the slope and go over the brink of the rocks, straight to the boulder-strewn shore thirty feet below. Emily had one dreadful moment of terror and despair; and then she found that the clump of mossy earth which had broken away had held on a narrow ledge of rock, half hanging over it; and she was lying on the clump. It seemed to her that the slightest movement on her part would send it over, straight to the cruel boulders underneath.

She lay very still, trying to think—trying not to be afraid. She was far, far away from any house—nobody could hear her if she screamed. And she did not even dare to scream lest the motion of her body dislodge the fragment on which she lay. How long could she lie there motionless? Night was coming on. Aunt Nancy would grow anxious when the dark fell and would send Caroline to look for her. But Caroline would never find her here. Nobody would ever think of looking here for her, so far away from the Grange, in the spruce barrens of the Lower Bay. To lie there alone all night—to fancy the earth was slipping over—waiting for help that would never come—Emily could hardly restrain a shudder that might have been ruinous.

She had faced death once before, or thought she had, on the night when Lofty John had told her she had eaten a poisoned apple—but this was even harder. To die here, all alone, far away from home! They might never know what had become of her—never find her. The crows or the gulls would pick her eyes out. She dramatized the thing so vividly that she almost screamed with the horror of it. She would just disappear from the world as Ilse's mother had disappeared.

What had become of Ilse's mother? Even in her own desperate plight Emily asked herself that question. And she would never see dear New Moon again and Teddy and the dairy and the Tansy Patch and Lofty John's bush and the mossy old sundial and her precious little heap of manuscripts on the sofa shelf in the garret.

"I must be very brave and patient," she thought. "My only chance is to lie still. And I can pray in my mind—I'm sure God can hear thoughts as well as words. It is nice to think He can hear me if nobody else can. O God—Father's God—please work a miracle and save my life, because I don't think I'm fit to die yet. Excuse my not being on my knees—You see I can't move. And if I die please don't let Aunt Elizabeth find my letter-bills ever. Please let Aunt Laura find them. And please don't let Caroline move out the wardrobe when she house-cleans because then she would find my Jimmy-book and read what I wrote about her. Please forgive all my sins, especially not being grateful enough and cutting a bang, and please don't let Father be very far away. Amen."

Then, characteristically she thought of a postscript. "And oh, *please* let somebody find out that Ilse's mother didn't do *that*."

She lay very still. The light on the water began to turn warm gold and rose. A great pine on a bluff in front of her overflowed in a crest of dark boughs against the amber splendour behind it—a part of the beauty of the beautiful world that was slipping away from her. The chill of the evening gulf breeze began to creep over her. Once a bit of earth broke off at her side and went down—Emily heard the thud of the little pebbles in it on the boulders below. The portion upon which one of her legs lay was quite loose and pendent also. She knew it might break off, too, at any moment. It would be very dreadful to be there when it got dark. She could see the big spray of farewell-summer that had lured her to her doom, waving unplucked above her, wonderfully purple and lovely.

Then, beside it, she saw a man's face looking down at her!

She heard him say, "My God!" softly to himself. She saw that he was slight and that one shoulder was a trifle higher than the other. This must be Dean Priest—Jarback Priest. Emily dared not call to him. She lay still and her great, grey-purple eyes said, "Save me."

"How can I help you?" said Dean Priest hoarsely, as if to himself. "I cannot reach you—and it looks as if the slightest touch or jar would send that broken earth over the brink. I must go for a rope—and to leave you here alone—like this. Can you wait, child?"

"Yes," breathed Emily. She smiled at him to encourage him—the little soft smile that began at the corners of her mouth and spread over her face. Dean Priest never forgot that smile—and the steadfast child-eyes looking out through it from the little face that seemed so perilously near the brink.

"I'll be as quick as I can," he said. "I can't go very fast—I'm a bit lame, you see. But don't be frightened—I'll save you. I'll leave my dog to keep you company. Here, Tweed."

He whistled—a great, tawny-gold dog came in sight.

"Sit right there, Tweed, till I come back. Don't stir a paw—don't wag a tail—talk to her only with your eyes."

Tweed sat down obediently and Dean Priest disappeared.

Emily lay there and dramatized the whole incident for her Jimmy-book. She was a little frightened still, but not too frightened to see herself writing it all out the next day. It would be quite a thrilling bit.

She liked to know the big dog was there. She was not so learned in lore of dogs as in lore of cats. But he looked very human and trusty watching her with great kindly eyes. A grey kitten was an adorable thing—but a grey kitten would not have sat there and encouraged her. "I believe," thought Emily, "that a dog is better than a cat when you're in trouble."

It was half an hour before Dean Priest returned.

"Thank God you haven't gone over," he muttered. "I hadn't to go as far as I feared—I found a rope in an empty boat up-shore and took it. And now—if I drop the rope down to you, are you strong enough to hold it while the earth goes and then hang on while I pull you up?"

"I'll try," said Emily.

Dean Priest knotted a loop at the end and slid it down to her. Then he wound the rope around the trunk of a heavy fir.

"Now," he said.

Emily said inwardly, "Dear God, *please*—" and caught the swaying loop. The next moment the full weight of her body swung from it, for at her first movement the broken soil beneath her slipped down—slipped over. Dean Priest sickened and shivered. Could she cling to the rope while he drew her up?

Then he saw she had got a little knee-hold on the narrow shelf. Carefully he drew on the rope. Emily, full of pluck, helped him by digging her toes into the crumbling bank. In a moment she was within his reach. He grasped her arms and pulled her up beside him into safety. As he lifted her past the farewell-summer Emily reached out her hand and broke off the spray.

"I've got it, anyhow," she said jubilantly. Then she remembered her manners. "I'm much obliged to you. You saved my life. And—and—I think I'll sit down a moment. My legs feel funny and trembly."

Emily sat down, all at once more shaky than she had been through all the danger. Dean Priest leaned against the gnarled old fir. He seemed "trembly" too. He wiped his forehead with his handkerchief. Emily looked curiously at him. She had learned a good deal about him from Aunt Nancy's casual remarks—not always good-natured remarks, for Aunt Nancy did not wholly like him, it seemed. She always called him "Jarback" rather contemptuously, while Caroline scrupulously called him Dean. Emily knew he had been to college, that he was thirty-six years old—which to Emily seemed a venerable age— and well-off; that he had a malformed shoulder and limped slightly; that he cared for nothing save books nor ever had; that he lived with an older brother and travelled a great deal; and that the whole Priest clan stood somewhat in awe of his ironic tongue. Aunt Nancy had called him a "cynic." Emily did not know what a cynic was but it sounded interesting. She looked him over carefully and saw that he had delicate, pale features and tawny-brown hair. His lips were thin and sensitive, with a whimsical curve. She liked his mouth. Had she been older she would have known why—because it connoted strength and tenderness and humour.

In spite of his twisted shoulder there was about him a certain aloof dignity of presence which was characteristic of many of the Priests and which was often mistaken for pride. The green Priest eyes, that were peering and uncanny in Caroline's face and impudent in Jim Priest's, were remarkably dreamy and attractive in his.

"Well, do you think me handsome?" he said, sitting down on another stone and smiling at her. His voice was beautiful—musical and caressing.

Emily blushed. She knew staring was not etiquette, and she did not think him at all handsome, so she was very thankful that he did not press his question, but asked another.

"Do you know who your knightly rescuer is?"

"I think you must be Jar—Mr Dean Priest." Emily flushed again with vexation. She had come so near to making another terrible hole in her manners.

"Yes, Jarback Priest. You needn't mind the nickname. I've heard it often enough. It's a Priest idea of humour." He laughed rather unpleasantly. "The reason for it is obvious enough, isn't it? I never got anything else at school. How came you to slide over that cliff?"

"I wanted this," said Emily, waving her farewell-summer.

"And you have it! Do you always get what you go after, even with death slipping a thin wedge between? I think you're born lucky. I see the signs. If that big aster lured you into danger it saved you as well, for it was through stepping over to investigate it that I saw you. Its size and colour caught my eye. Otherwise I should have gone on and you—what would have become of you? Whom do you belong to that you are let risk your life on these dangerous banks? What is your name—if you have a name! I begin to doubt you—I see you have pointed ears. Have I been tricked into meddling with fairies, and will I discover presently that twenty years have passed and that I am an old man long since lost to the living world with nothing but the skeleton of my dog for company?"

"I am Emily Byrd Starr of New Moon," said Emily, rather coldly. She was beginning to be sensitive about her ears. Father Cassidy had remarked on them—and now Jarback Priest. Was there really something uncanny about them?

And yet there was a flavour about the said Jarback that she liked—

liked decidedly. Emily never was long in doubt about anyone she met. In a few minutes she always knew whether she liked, disliked, or was indifferent to them. She had a queer feeling that she had known Jarback Priest for years—perhaps because it seemed so long when she was lying on that crumbling earth waiting for him to return. He was not handsome but she liked that lean, clever face of his with its magnetic green eyes.

"So you're the young lady visitor at the Grange!" said Dean Priest, in some astonishment. "Then my dear Aunt Nancy should look after you better—my *very* dear Aunt Nancy."

"You don't like Aunt Nancy, I see," said Emily coolly.

"What is the use of liking a lady who won't like me? You have probably discovered by this time that my Lady Aunt detests me."

"Oh, I don't think it's as bad as that," said Emily. "She must have some good opinions about you—she says you're the only Priest who will ever go to heaven."

"She doesn't mean that as a compliment, whatever you in your innocence believe it to be. And you are Douglas Starr's daughter? I knew your father. We were boys together at Queen's Academy—we drifted apart after we left it—he went into journalism, I to McGill. But he was the only friend I had at school—the only boy who would bother himself about Jarback Priest, who was lame and hunchbacked and couldn't play football or hockey. Emily Byrd Starr—Starr should be your first name. You look like a star—you have a radiant sort of personality shining through you—your proper habitat should be the evening sky just after sunset—or the morning sky just before sunrise. Yes. You'd be more at home in the morning sky. I think I shall call you Star."

"Do you mean that you think me pretty?" asked Emily directly.

"Why, it hadn't occurred to me to wonder whether you were pretty or not. Do you think a star should be pretty?"

Emily reflected.

"No," she said finally, "the word doesn't suit a star."

"I perceive you are an artist in words. Of course it doesn't. Stars are prismatic—palpitating—elusive. It is not often we find one made of flesh and blood. I think I'll wait for you."

"Oh, I'm ready to go now," said Emily, standing up.

"H'm. That wasn't what I meant. Never mind. Come along, Star—if you don't mind walking a bit slowly. I'll take you back from the wilderness at least—I don't know that I'll venture to Wyther Grange to-night. I don't want Aunt Nancy to take the edge off you. And so you don't think me handsome?"

"I didn't say so," cried Emily.

"Not in words. But I can read your thoughts, Star—it won't ever do to think anything you don't want me to know. The gods gave me that gift—when they kept back everything else I wanted. You don't think me handsome but you think me nice. Do you think you are pretty yourself?"

"A little—since Aunt Nancy lets me wear my bang," said Emily frankly.

Jarback Priest made a grimace.

"Don't call it by such a name. It's a worse name even than bustle. Bangs and bustles—they hurt me. I like that black wave breaking on your white brows—but don't call it a bang—ever again."

"It *is* a very ugly word. I never use it in my poetry, of course."

Whereby Dean Priest discovered that Emily wrote poetry. He also discovered pretty nearly everything else about her in that charming walk back to Priest Pond in the fir-scented dusk, with Tweed walking between them, his nose touching his master's hand softly every now and then, while the robins in the trees above them whistled blithely in the afterlight.

With nine out of ten people Emily was secretive and reserved, but Dean Priest was sealed of her tribe and she divined it instantly. He had a right to the inner sanctuary and she yielded it unquestionably. She talked to him freely.

Besides, she felt *alive* again—she felt the wonderful thrill of living again, after that dreadful space when she had seemed to hang between life and death. She felt, as she wrote to her father afterwards, "as if a little bird was singing in my heart." And oh, how good the green sod felt under her feet!

She told him all about herself and her doings and beings. Only one thing she did not tell him—her worry over Ilse's mother. *That* she could not speak of to any one. Aunt Nancy need not have been frightened that she would carry tales to New Moon.

"I wrote a whole poem yesterday when it rained and I couldn't get out," she said. "It began,

> I sit by the western window
>
> That looks on Malvern Bay—"

"Am I not to hear the whole of it?" asked Dean, who knew perfectly well that Emily was hoping that he would ask it.

Emily delightedly repeated the whole poem. When she came to the two lines she liked best in it,

> Perhaps in those wooded islands
>
> That gem the proud bay's breast—

she looked up sidewise at him to see if he admired them. But he was walking with eyes cast down and an absent expression on his face. She felt a little disappointed.

"H'm," he said when she had finished. "You're twelve, didn't you say? When you're ten years older I shouldn't wonder—but let's not think of it."

"Father Cassidy told me to keep on," cried Emily.

"There was no need of it. You *would* keep on anyhow—you have the itch for writing born in you. It's quite incurable. What are you going to do with it?"

"I think I shall be either a great poetess or a distinguished novelist," said Emily reflectively.

"Having only to choose," remarked Dean dryly. "Better be a novelist—I hear it pays better."

"What worries me about writing novels," confided Emily "is the love talk in them. I'm sure I'll never be able to write it. I've tried," she concluded candidly, "and I can't think of *anything* to say."

"Don't worry about that. *I'll* teach you some day," said Dean.

"Will you—will you really?" Emily was very eager. "I'll be so obliged if you will. I *think* I could manage *everything* else very nicely."

"It's a bargain then—don't forget it. And don't go looking for another teacher, mind. What do you find to do at the Grange besides writing poetry? Are you never lonesome with only those two old survivals?"

"No. I enjoy my own company," said Emily gravely.

"You would. Stars are said to dwell apart, anyhow, sufficient unto themselves—ensphered in their own light. Do you really like Aunt Nancy?"

"Yes, indeed. She is very kind to me. She doesn't make me wear sunbonnets and she lets me go barefooted in the forenoons. But I have to wear my buttoned boots in the afternoons, and I hate buttoned boots."

"Naturally. You should be shod with sandals of moonshine and wear a scarf of sea-mist with a few fire-flies caught in it over your hair. Star, you don't look like your father, but you suggest him in several ways. Do you look like your mother? I never saw her."

All at once Emily smiled demurely. A real sense of humour was born in her at that moment. Never again was she to feel quite so unmixedly tragic over anything.

"No," she said, "it's only my eyelashes and smile that are like Mother's. But I've got Father's forehead, and Grandma Starr's hair and eyes, and Great-Uncle George's nose, and Aunt Nancy's hands, and Cousin Susan's elbows, and Great-great-Grandmother Murray's ankles, and Grandfather Murray's eyebrows."

Dean Priest laughed.

"A rag-bag—as we all are," he said. "But your soul is your own, and fire-new, I'll swear to that."

"Oh, I'm so glad I like you," said Emily impulsively. "It would be *hateful* to think any one I didn't like had saved my life. I don't mind *your* saving it a bit."

"That's good. Because you see your life belongs to me henceforth. Since I saved it it's mine. Never forget that."

Emily felt an odd sensation of rebellion. She didn't fancy the idea of her life belonging to anybody but herself—not even to anybody she liked as much as she liked Dean Priest. Dean, watching her, saw it and smiled his whimsical smile that always seemed to have so much more in it than mere smiling.

"That doesn't quite suit you? Ah, you see one pays a penalty when one reaches out for something beyond the ordinary. One pays for it in bondage of some kind or other. Take your wonderful aster home and keep it as long as you can. It has cost you your freedom."

He was laughing—he was only joking, of course—yet Emily felt as if a cobweb fetter had been flung round her. Yielding to a sudden impulse she flung the big aster on the ground and set her foot on it.

Dean Priest looked on amusedly. His strange eyes were very kindly as he met hers.

"You rare thing—you vivid thing—you starry thing! We are going to be good friends—we *are* good friends. I'm coming up to Wyther Grange to-morrow to see those descriptions you've written of Caroline and my venerable Aunt in your Jimmy-book. I feel sure they're delicious. Here's your path—don't go roaming again so far from civilization. Goodnight, My Star of the Morning."

He stood at the cross-road and watched her out of sight.

"What a child!" he muttered. "I'll never forget her eyes as she lay there on the edge of death—the dauntless little soul—and I've never seen a creature who seemed so full of sheer joy in existence. She is Douglas Starr's child—*he* never called me Jarback."

He stooped and picked up the broken aster. Emily's heel had met it squarely and it was badly crushed. But he put it away that night between the leaves of an old volume of *Jane Eyre,* where he had marked a verse,

All glorious rose upon my sight

That child of shower and gleam.

THE VOW OF EMILY

In Dean Priest Emily found, for the first time since her father had died, a companion who could fully sympathize. She was always at her best with him, with a delightful feeling of being understood. To love is easy and therefore common—but to *understand*—how rare it is! They roamed wonderlands of fancy together in the magic August days that followed upon Emily's adventure on the bay shore, talked together of exquisite, immortal things, and were at home with "nature's old felicities" of which Wordsworth so happily speaks.

Emily showed him all the poetry and "descriptions" in her "Jimmy-book" and he read them gravely, and, exactly as Father had done, made little criticisms that did not hurt her because she knew they were just. As for Dean Priest, a certain secret well-spring of fancy that had long seemed dry bubbled up in him sparklingly again.

"You make me believe in fairies, whether I will or no," he told her, "and that means youth. As long as you believe in fairies you can't grow old."

"But I can't believe in fairies myself," protested Emily sorrowfully. "I wish I could."

"But *you* are a fairy yourself—or you wouldn't be able to find fairyland. You can't buy a ticket there, you know. Either the fairies themselves give you your passport at your christening—or they don't. That is all there is to it."

"Isn't 'Fairyland' the *loveliest* word?" said Emily dreamily.

"Because it means everything the human heart desires," said Dean.

When he talked to her Emily felt as if she were looking into some enchanted mirror where her own dreams and secret hopes were reflected back to her with added charm. If Dean Priest were a cynic he showed no cynicism to Emily. But in her company he was not a cynic; he had shed his years and became a boy again with a boy's untainted visions. She loved him for the world he opened to her view.

There was such fun in him, too—such sly, surprising fun. He told her jokes—he made her laugh. He told her strange old tales of forgotten gods who were very beautiful—of court festivals and the bridals of kings. He seemed to have the history of the whole world at his fingers' ends. He described things to her in unforgettable phrases as they walked by the bay shore or sat in the overgrown, shadowy old garden of Wyther Grange. When he spoke of Athens as "the City of the Violet Crown" Emily realized afresh what magic is made when the right words are wedded; and she loved to think of Rome as "the City of the Seven Hills." Dean had been in Rome and Athens—and almost everywhere else.

"I didn't know any one ever talked as you do except in books," she told him.

Dean laughed—with a little note of bitterness that was so often present in his laughter—though less often with Emily than with other people. It was really his laughter that had won Dean his reputation for cynicism. People so often felt that he was laughing *at* them instead of *with* them.

"I've had only books for companions most of my life," he said. "Is it any wonder I talk like them?"

"I'm sure I'll like studying history after this," said Emily; "except Canadian History. I'll never like *it*—it's so dull. Not just at the first, when we belonged to France and there was plenty of fighting, but after that it's nothing but politics."

"The happiest countries, like the happiest women, have no history," said Dean.

"I hope I'll have a history," cried Emily. "I want a *thrilling* career."

"We all do, foolish one. Do you know what makes history? Pain—and shame—and rebellion—and bloodshed and heartache. Star, ask yourself how many hearts ached—and broke—to make those crimson and purple pages in history that you find so enthralling. I told you the story of Leonidas and his Spartans the other day. They had mothers, sisters and sweethearts. If they could have fought a bloodless battle at the polls wouldn't it have been better—if not so dramatic."

"I—can't—*feel*—that way," said Emily confusedly. She was not old enough to think or say, as she would say ten years later, "The heroes of Thermopylae have been an inspiration to humanity for centuries. What squabble around a ballot-box will ever be that?"

"And, like all female creatures, you form your opinions by your feelings. Well, hope for your thrilling career—but remember that if there is to be drama in your life *somebody* must pay the piper in the coin of suffering. If not you—then someone else."

"Oh, no, I wouldn't like *that*."

"Then be content with fewer thrills. What about your tumble over the bank down there? That came near being a tragedy. What if I hadn't found you?"

"But you *did* find me," cried Emily. "I like near escapes—after they're over," she added. "If everybody had always been happy there'd be nothing to read about."

Tweed made a third in their rambles and Emily grew very fond of him, without losing any of her loyalty to the pussy folk.

"I like cats with one part of my mind and dogs with another part," she said.

"I like cats but I never keep one," Dean said. "They're too exacting—they ask too much. Dogs want only love but cats demand worship. They have never got over the Bubastis habit of godship."

Emily understood this—he had told her all about old Egypt and the goddess Pasht—but she did not quite agree with him.

"Kittens don't want to be worshipped," she said. "They just want to be cuddled."

"By their priestesses—yes. If you had been born on the banks of the Nile five thousand years ago, Emily, you would have been a priestess of Pasht—an adorable, slim, brown creature with a fillet of gold around your black hair and bands of silver on those ankles Aunt Nancy admires, with dozens of sacred little godlings frisking around you under the palms of the temple court."

"Oh," gasped Emily rapturously, "that gave me *the flash*. And," she added wonderingly, "just for a moment it made me *homesick,* too. Why?"

"Why? Because I haven't a doubt you *were* just such a priestess in a former incarnation and my words reminded your soul of it. Do you believe in the doctrine of the transmigration of souls, Star? But of course not—brought up by the true-blue Calvinists of New Moon."

"What does it mean?" asked Emily, and when Dean explained it to her she thought it a very delightful belief but was quite sure Aunt Elizabeth would not approve of it.

"So I won't believe it—yet," she said gravely.

Then it all came to an end quite suddenly. It had been taken for granted by all concerned that Emily was to stay at Wyther Grange until the end of August. But in mid-August Aunt Nancy said suddenly to her one day:

"Go home, Emily. I'm tired of you. I like you very well—you're not stupid and you're passably pretty and you've behaved exceedingly well—tell Elizabeth you do the Murrays credit—but I'm tired of you. Go home."

Emily's feelings were mixed. It hurt her to be told Aunt Nancy was tired of her—it would hurt any one. It rankled in her for several days until she thought of a sharp answer she might have made Aunt Nancy and wrote it down in her Jimmy-book. She felt quite as relieved then as if she had really said it.

And she was sorry to leave Wyther Grange; she had grown to love the old beautiful house, with its flavour of hidden secrets—a flavour that was wholly a trick of its architecture, for there had never been anything in it but the simple tale of births and deaths and marriages and everyday living that most houses have. She was sorry to leave the bay shore and the quaint garden and the gazing-ball and the chessy-cat and the Pink Room bed of freedom; and most of all she was sorry to leave Dean Priest. But on the other hand it was delightful to think of going back to New Moon and all the loved ones there—Teddy and his dear whistle, Ilse and her stimulating comradeship, Perry with his determined reaching up for higher things, Saucy Sal and the new kitten that must be needing proper training now, and the fairy world of the *Midsummer Night's Dream*. Cousin Jimmy's garden would be in its prime of splendour, the August apples would be ripe. Suddenly, Emily was very ready to go. She packed her little black box jubilantly and found it an excellent chance to work in neatly a certain line from a poem Dean had recently read to her which had captured her fancy.

"'Good-bye, proud world, I'm going home,'" she declaimed feelingly, standing at the top of the long, dark, shining staircase and apostrophizing the row of grim Priest photographs hanging on the wall.

But she was much annoyed over one thing. Aunt Nancy would not give her back the picture Teddy had painted.

"I'm going to keep it," Aunt Nancy said, grinning and shaking her gold tassels. "Some day that picture will be worth something as the early effort of a famous artist."

"I only lent it to you—I told you I only lent it to you," said Emily indignantly.

"I'm an unscrupulous old demon," said Aunt Nancy coolly. "That is what the Priests all call me behind my back. Don't they, Caroline? May as well have the game as the name. I happen to have a fancy for that picture, that's all. I'm going to frame it and hang it here in my parlour. But I'll leave it to you in my will—that and the chessy-cat and the gazing-ball and my gold ear-rings. Nothing else—I'm not going to leave you a cent of my money—never count on that."

"I don't want it," said Emily loftily. "I'm going to earn heaps of money for myself. But it isn't fair of you to keep my picture. It was given to me."

"I never was fair," said Aunt Nancy. "Was I, Caroline?"

"No," said Caroline shrewishly.

"You see. Now don't make a fuss, Emily. You've been a very good child but I feel that I've done my duty by you for this year. Go back to New Moon and when Elizabeth won't let you do things tell her *I* always let you. I don't know if it will do any good but try it. Elizabeth, like every one else related to me, is always wondering what I'm going to do with my money."

Cousin Jimmy came over for Emily. How glad she was to see his kind face with its gentle, elfish eyes and forked beard again! But she felt very badly when she turned to Dean.

"If you like I'll kiss you good-bye," she said chokily.

Emily did not like kissing people. She did not really want to kiss Dean but she liked him so much she thought she ought to extend all the courtesies to him.

Dean looked down smiling into her face, so young, so pure, so softly curved.

"No, I don't want you to kiss me—yet. And our first kiss mustn't have the flavour of good-bye. It would be a bad omen. Star o' Morning, I'm sorry you're going. But I'll see you again before long. My oldest sister lives in Blair Water, you know, and I feel a sudden access[???] of brotherly affection towards her. I seem to see myself visiting her very often henceforth. In the meantime remember you have promised to write me every week. And I'll write you."

"Nice fat letters," coaxed Emily. "I love fat letters."

"Fat! They'll be positively corpulent, Star. Now, I'm not even going to *say* good-bye. Let's make a pact, Star. We'll never *say* good-bye to each other. We'll just smile and go."

Emily made a gallant effort—smiled—and went. Aunt Nancy and Caroline returned to the back parlour and their cribbage. Dean Priest whistled for Tweed and went to the bay shore. He was so lonely that he laughed at himself.

Emily and Cousin Jimmy had so much to talk of that the drive home seemed very short.

New Moon was white in the evening sunshine which also lay with exceeding mellowness on the grey old barns. The Three Princesses, shooting up against the silvery sky, were as remote and princessly as ever. The old gulf was singing away down over the fields.

Aunt Laura came running out to meet them, her lovely blue eyes shining with pleasure. Aunt Elizabeth was in the cookhouse preparing supper and only shook hands with Emily, but looked a trifle less grim and stately than usual, and she had made Emily's favourite cream-puffs for supper. Perry was hanging about barefooted and sunburned, to tell her all the gossip of kittens and calves and little pigs and the new foal. Ilse came swooping over, and Emily discovered she had forgotten how vivid Ilse was—how brilliant her amber eyes, how golden her mane of spun-silk hair, looking more golden than ever under the bright blue silk tam Mrs Simms had bought her in Shrewsbury. As an article of dress, that loud tam made Laura Murray's eyes and sensibilities ache, but its colour certainly did set off Ilse's wonderful hair. She engulfed Emily in a rapturous embrace and quarrelled bitterly with her ten minutes later over the fact that Emily refused to give her Saucy Sal's sole surviving kitten.

"I ought to have it, you doddering hyena," stormed Ilse. "It's as much mine as yours, pig! Our old barn cat is its father."

"Such talk is not decent," said Aunt Elizabeth, pale with horror. "And if you two children are going to quarrel over that kitten I'll have it drowned—remember that."

Ilse was finally appeased by Emily's offering to let her name the kitten and have a half-interest in it. Ilse named it Daffodil. Emily did not think this suitable, since, from the fact of Cousin Jimmy referring to it as Little Tommy, she suspected it was of the sterner sex. But rather than again provoke Aunt Elizabeth's wrath by discussing tabooed subjects, she agreed.

"I can call it Daff," she thought. "That sounds more *masculine*."

The kitten was a delicate bit of striped greyness that reminded Emily of her dear lost Mikes. And it smelled so nice—of warmth and clean furriness, with whiffs of the clover hay where Saucy Sal had made her mother-nest.

After supper she heard Teddy's whistle in the old orchard—the same enchanting call. Emily flew out to greet him—after all, there was nobody just like Teddy in the world. They had an ecstatic scamper up to the Tansy Patch to see a new puppy that Dr Burnley had given

Teddy. Mrs Kent did not seem very glad to see Emily—she was colder and more remote than ever, and she sat and watched the two children playing with the chubby little pup with a smouldering fire in her dark eyes that made Emily vaguely uncomfortable whenever she happened to glance up and encounter it. Never before had she sensed Mrs Kent's dislike for her so keenly as that night.

"Why doesn't your mother like me?" she asked Teddy bluntly, when they carried little Leo to the barn for the night.

"Because *I* do," said Teddy briefly. "She doesn't like *anything* I like. I'm afraid she'll poison Leo very soon. I—I wish she wasn't so fond of me," he burst out, in the beginning of a revolt against this abnormal jealousy of love, which he felt rather than understood to be a fetter that was becoming galling. "She says she won't let me take up Latin and Algebra this year—you know Miss Brownell said I might—because I'm not to go to college. She says she can't bear to part from me—ever. I don't care about the Latin and stuff—but I want to learn to be an artist—I want to go away some day to the schools where they teach that. She won't let me—she hates my pictures now because she thinks I like them better than her. I *don't*—I love Mother—she's awful sweet and good to me every other way. But she thinks I do—and she's burned some of them. I know she has. They're missing from the barn wall and I can't find them anywhere. If she does anything to Leo—I'll—I'll *hate* her."

"Tell her that," said Emily coolly, with some of the Murray shrewdness coming uppermost in her. "She doesn't know that *you* know she poisoned Smoke and Buttercup. Tell her you do know it and that if she does anything to Leo you won't love her any more. She'll be so frightened of your *not* loving her that she won't meddle with Leo—I *know*. Tell her gently—don't hurt her feelings—but *tell* her. It will," concluded Emily, with a killing imitation of Aunt Elizabeth delivering an ultimatum, "be better for all concerned."

"I believe I will," said Teddy, much impressed. "I *can't* have Leo disappear like my cats did—he's the only dog I've ever had and I've always wanted a dog. Oh, Emily, I'm glad you're back!"

It was very nice to be told this—especially by Teddy. Emily went home to New Moon happily. In the old kitchen the candles were lighted and their flames were dancing in the winds of the August night blowing through door and window.

"I suppose you'll not like candles very well, Emily, after being used to lamps at Wyther Grange," said Aunt Laura with a little sigh. It was one of the bitter, small things in Laura Murray's life that Elizabeth's tyranny extended to candles.

Emily looked around her thoughtfully. One candle sputtered and bobbed at her as if greeting her. One, with a long wick, glowed and smouldered like a sulky little demon. One had a tiny flame—a sly, meditative candle. One swayed with a queer fiery grace in the draught from the door. One burned with a steady upright flame like a faithful soul.

"I—don't know—Aunt Laura," she answered slowly. "You can be— friends—with candles. I believe I like the candles best after all."

Aunt Elizabeth, coming in from the cook-house, heard her. Something like pleasure gleamed in her gulf-blue eyes.

"You have some sense in you," she said.

"That's the second compliment she has paid me," thought Emily.

"I think Emily has grown taller since she went to Wyther Grange," Aunt Laura said, looking at her rather wistfully.

Aunt Elizabeth, snuffing the candles, glanced sharply over her glasses.

"I can't see it," she said. "Her dress is just the same length on her."

"I'm sure she has," persisted Laura.

Cousin Jimmy, to settle the dispute, measured Emily by the sitting-room door. She just touched the former mark.

"You see," said Aunt Elizabeth triumphantly, liking to be right even in this small matter.

"She looks—different," said Laura with a sigh.

Laura, after all, was right. Emily *had* grown, taller and older, in soul, if not in body. It was this change which Laura felt, as close and tender affection swiftly feels. The Emily who returned from Wyther Grange was not the Emily who had gone there. She was no longer wholly the child. Aunt Nancy's family histories over which she had pondered, her enduring anguish over the story of Ilse's mother, that terrible hour when she had lain cheek by jowl with death on the cliffs of the bay shore, her association with Dean Priest, all had combined to mature her intelligence and her emotions. When she went to the garret next morning and pulled out her precious little bundle of manuscripts to read them lovingly over she was amazed and rather grieved to find that they were not half so good as she had believed they were. Some of them were positively silly, she thought; she was ashamed of them—so ashamed that she smuggled them down to the cook-house stove and burned them, much to Aunt Elizabeth's annoyance when she came to prepare dinner and found the fire-box all choked up with charred paper.

Emily no longer wondered that Miss Brownell had made fun of them—though this did not mellow her bitterness of remembrance in regard to that lady in any degree. The rest she put back on the sofa shelf, including "The Child of the Sea," which still impressed her as fairly good, though not just the wonderful composition she had once deemed it. She felt that many passages could be re-written to their advantage. Then she immediately began writing a new poem, "On Returning Home After Weeks' Absence." As everything and everybody connected with New Moon had to be mentioned in this poem it promised to be quite long and to furnish agreeable occupation for spare minutes in many weeks to come. It was very good to be home again.

"There is no place just like dear New Moon," thought Emily.

One thing that marked her return—one of those little household "epochs" that make a keener impression on the memory and imagination than perhaps their real importance warrants—was the fact that she was given a room of her own. Aunt Elizabeth had found her unshared slumber too sweet a thing to be again surrendered. She decided that she could not put up any longer with a squirming bedfellow who asked unearthly questions at any hour of the night she took it into her head to do so.

So, after a long conference with Laura, it was settled that Emily was to have her mother's room—the "lookout" as it was called, though it was not really a lookout. But it occupied the place in New Moon, looking over the front door to the garden, that the real lookouts did in other Blair Water houses, so it went by that name. It had been prepared for Emily's occupancy in her absence and when bedtime came on the first evening of her return Aunt Elizabeth curtly told her that henceforth she was to have her mother's room.

"All to myself?" exclaimed Emily.

"Yes. We will expect you to take care of it yourself and keep it very tidy."

"It has never been slept in since the night before your mother—went away," said Aunt Laura, with a queer sound in her voice—a sound of which Aunt Elizabeth disapproved.

"Your mother," she said, looking coldly at Emily over the flame of the candle—an attitude that gave a rather gruesome effect to her aquiline features—"*ran* away—flouted her family and broke her father's heart. She was a silly, ungrateful, disobedient girl. I hope *you* will never disgrace your family by such conduct."

"Oh, Aunt Elizabeth," said Emily breathlessly, "when you hold the candle down like that it makes your face look just like a corpse! Oh, it's so interesting."

Aunt Elizabeth turned and led the way upstairs in grim silence. There was no use in wasting perfectly good admonitions on a child like this.

Left alone in her lookout, lighted dimly by the one small candle, Emily gazed about her with keen and thrilling interest. She could not get into bed until she had explored every bit of it. The room was very old-fashioned, like all New Moon rooms. The walls were papered with a design of slender gilt diamonds enclosing golden stars and hung with worked woollen mottoes and pictures that had been "supplements" in the girlhood of her aunts. One of them, hanging over the head of the bed, represented two guardian angels. In its day this had been much admired but Emily looked at it with distaste.

"I don't like feather wings on angels," she said decidedly. "Angels should have rainbowy wings."

On the floor was a pretty homespun carpet and round braided rugs. There was a high black bedstead with carved posts, a fat feather-bed, and an Irish chain quilt, but, as Emily was glad to see, no curtains. A little table, with funny claw-feet and brass-knobbed drawers, stood by the window, which was curtained with muslin frills; one of the window-panes contorted the landscape funnily, making a hill where no hill was. Emily liked this—she couldn't have told why, but it was really because it gave the pane an individuality of its own. An oval mirror in a tarnished gilt frame hung above the table; Emily was delighted to find she could see herself in it—"all but my boots"— without craning or tipping it. "And it doesn't twist my face or turn my complexion green," she thought happily. Two high-backed, black chairs with horsehair seats, a little washstand with a blue basin and pitcher, and a faded ottoman with woollen roses cross-stitched on it, completed the furnishing. On the little mantel were vases full of dried and coloured grasses and a fascinating pot-bellied bottle filled with West Indian shells. On either side were lovable little cupboards with leaded-glass doors like those in the sitting-room. Underneath was a small fireplace.

"I wonder if Aunt Elizabeth will ever let me have a little fire here," thought Emily.

The room was full of that indefinable charm found in all rooms where the pieces of furniture, whether old or new, are well acquainted with each other and the walls and floors are on good terms. Emily felt it all over her as she flitted about examining everything. This was her room—she loved it already—she felt perfectly at home.

"I belong here," she breathed happily.

She felt deliciously *near* to her mother—as if Juliet Starr had suddenly become real to her. It thrilled her to think that her mother had probably crocheted the lace cover on the round pincushion on the table. And that flat, black jar of pot-pourri on the mantel—her mother must have compounded it. When Emily lifted the lid a faint spicy odour floated out. The souls of all the roses that had bloomed through many olden summers at New Moon seemed to be prisoned there in a sort of flower purgatory. Something in the haunting, mystical, elusive odour gave Emily *the flash*—and her room had received its consecration.

There was a picture of her mother hanging over the mantel—a large daguerreotype taken when she was a little girl. Emily looked at it lovingly. She had the picture of her mother which her father had left, taken after their marriage. But when Aunt Elizabeth had brought that from Maywood to New Moon she had hung it in the parlour where Emily seldom saw it. This picture, in her bedroom, of the golden-haired, rose-cheeked girl, was all her own. She could look at it—talk to it at will.

"Oh, Mother," she said, "what did you think of when you were a little girl here like me? I wish I could have known you *then*. And to think nobody has ever slept here since that last night you did before you ran away with Father. Aunt Elizabeth says you were wicked to do it but *I* don't think you were. It wasn't as if you were running away with a *stranger*. Anyway, I'm glad you *did,* because if you hadn't there wouldn't have been any *me*."

Emily, very glad that there was an Emily, opened her lookout window as high as it would go, got into bed and drifted off to sleep, feeling a happiness that was so deep as to be almost pain as she listened to the sonorous sweep of the night wind among the great trees in Lofty John's bush. When she wrote to her father a few days later she began the letter, "Dear Father and Mother."

"And I'll always write the letter to *you* as well as Father after this, Mother. I'm sorry I left you out so long. But you didn't seem *real* till that night I came home. I made the bed beautifully next morning—Aunt Elizabeth didn't find a bit of fault with it—and I dusted *everything*—and when I went out I knelt down and kissed the doorstep. I didn't think Aunt Elizabeth saw me but she did and said had I gone crazy. Why does Aunt Elizabeth think any one is crazy who does something she never does? I said 'No, it's only because I love my room so much' and she sniffed and said 'You'd better love your God.' But so I do, dear Father—and Mother—and I love Him better than ever since I have my dear room. I can see all over the garden from it and into Lofty John's bush and one little bit of the Blair Water through the gap in the trees where the Yesterday Road runs. I like to go to bed early now. I love to lie all alone in my own room and make poetry and think out descriptions of things while I look through the open window at the stars and the nice, big, kind, quiet trees in Lofty John's bush.

"Oh, Father dear and Mother, we are going to have a new teacher. Miss Brownell is not coming back. She is going to be married and Ilse says that when her father heard it he said 'God help the man.' And the new teacher is a Mr Carpenter. Ilse saw him when he came to see her father about the school—because Dr Burnley is a trustee this year—and she says he has bushy grey hair and whiskers. He is married, too, and is going to live in that little old house down in the hollow below the school. It seems so funny to think of a teacher having a wife and whiskers.

"I am glad to be home. But I miss Dean and the gazing-ball. Aunt Elizabeth looked very cross when she saw my bang but didn't say anything. Aunt Laura says just to keep quiet and go on wearing it. But I don't feel comfortable going against Aunt Elizabeth so I have combed it all back except a *little* fringe. I don't feel *quite* comfortable about it even yet, but I have to put up with being a little uncomfortable for the sake of my looks. Aunt Laura says bustles are going out of style so I'll never be able to have one but I don't care because I think they're ugly. Rhoda Stuart will be cross because she was just longing to be old enough to wear a bustle. I hope I'll be able to have a gin-jar all to myself when the weather gets cold. There is a row of gin-jars on the high shelf in the cook-house.

"Teddy and I had the nicest *adventure* yesterday evening. We are going to keep it a secret from everybody—partly because it was so nice, and partly because we think we'd get a fearful scolding for one thing we did.

"We went up to the Disappointed House, and we found one of the boards on the windows loose. So we pried it off and crawled in and went all over the house. It is lathed but not plastered, and the shavings are lying all over the floors just as the carpenters left them years ago. It seemed more disappointed than ever. I just felt like crying. There was a dear little fireplace in one room so we went to work and kindled a fire in it with shavings and pieces of boards (this is the thing we would be scolded for, likely) and then sat before it on an old carpenter's bench and talked. We decided that when we grew up we would buy the Disappointed House and live here together. Teddy said he supposed we'd have to get married, but I thought maybe we could find a way to manage without going to all that bother. Teddy will paint pictures and I will write poetry and we will have toast and bacon and marmalade *every* morning for breakfast—just like Wyther Grange—but *never* porridge. And we'll always have lots of nice things to eat in the pantry and I'll make lots of jam and Teddy is always going to help me wash the dishes and we'll hang the gazing-ball from the middle of the ceiling in the fireplace room—because likely Aunt Nancy will be dead by then.

"When the fire burned out we jammed the board into place in the window and came away. Every now and then to-day Teddy would say to me "Toast and bacon and marmalade" in the *most* mysterious tones and Ilse and Perry are wild because they can't find out what he means.

"Cousin Jimmy has got Jimmy Joe Belle to help with the harvest. Jimmy Joe Belle comes from over Derry Pond way. There are a great many French there and when a French girl marries they call her mostly by her husband's first name instead of Mrs like the English do. If a girl named Mary marries a man named Leon she will always be called

Mary Leon after that. But in Jimmy Joe Belle's case, it is the other way and he is called by his wife's names. I asked Cousin Jimmy why, and he said it was because Jimmy Joe was a poor stick of a creature and Belle wore the britches. But still I don't understand. Jimmy Joe wears britches himself—that means trousers—and why should he be called Jimmy Joe Bell instead of her being called Belle Jimmy Joe just because she wears them too! I won't rest till I find out.

"Cousin Jimmy's garden is splendid now. The tiger lilies are out. I am trying to love them because nobody seems to like them at all but deep down in my heart I know I love the late roses best. You just can't help loving the roses best.

"Ilse and I hunted all over the old orchard to-day for a four-leaved clover and couldn't find one. Then I found one in a clump of clover by the dairy steps to-night when I was straining the milk and never thinking of clovers. Cousin Jimmy says that is the way luck always comes, and it is no use to look for it.

"It is lovely to be with Ilse again. We have only fought twice since I came home. I am going to try not to fight with Ilse any more because I don't think it is dignified, although quite interesting. But it is hard not to because even when I keep quiet and don't say a word Ilse thinks that's a way of fighting and gets madder and says worse things than ever. Aunt Elizabeth says it always takes two to make a quarrel but she doesn't know Ilse as I do. Ilse called me a sneaking albatross to-day. I wonder how many animals are left to call me. She never repeats the same one twice. I wish she wouldn't clapper-claw Perry so much. (Clapper-claw is a word I learnt from Aunt Nancy. Very striking, I think.) It seems as if she couldn't bear him. He dared Teddy to jump from the henhouse roof across to the pighouse roof. Teddy wouldn't. He said he would try it if it had to be done or would do anybody any good but he wasn't going to do it just to show off. Perry did it and landed safe. If he hadn't he might have broken his neck. Then he bragged about it and said Teddy was afraid and Ilse turned red as a beet and told him to shut up or she would bite his snout off. She can't bear to have anything said against Teddy, but I guess he can take care of himself.

"Ilse can't study for the Entrance either. Her father won't let her. But she says she doesn't care. She says she's going to run away when she gets a little older and study for the stage. That sounds wicked, but interesting.

"I felt very queer and guilty when I saw Ilse first, because I knew about her mother. I don't know why I felt guilty because I had nothing to do with it. The feeling is wearing away a little now but I am so unhappy by spells over it. I wish I could either forget it altogether or find out the rights of it. Because I am sure nobody knows them.

"I had a letter from Dean to-day. He writes lovely letters—just as if I was grown up. He sent me a little poem he had cut out of a paper called *The Fringed Gentian*. He said it made him think of me. It is all lovely but I like the last verse best of all. This is it:

Then whisper, blossom, in thy sleep

How I may upward climb

The Alpine Path, so hard, so steep,

That leads to heights sublime.

How I may reach that far-off goal

Of true and honoured fame

And write upon its shining scroll

A woman's humble name.

"When I read that *the flash* came, and I took a sheet of paper—I forgot to tell you Cousin Jimmy gave me a little box of paper and envelopes—*on the sly*—and I wrote on it:

I, Emily Byrd Starr, do solemnly vow this day that I will climb the Alpine Path and write my name on the scroll of fame.

"Then I put it in the envelope and sealed it up and wrote on it *The Vow of Emily Byrd Starr, aged 12 years and 3 months*, and put it away on the sofa shelf in the garret.

"I am writing a murder story now and I am trying to feel how a man would feel who was a murderer. It is creepy, but thrilling. I almost feel as if I *had* murdered somebody.

"Good night, dear Father and Mother.

"Your lovingest daughter, *Emily,*

"P.S. I have been wondering how I'll sign my name when I grow up and print my pieces. I don't know which would be best—Emily Byrd Starr in full or Emily B. Starr, or E. B. Starr, or E. Byrd Starr. Sometimes I think I'll have a *nom-de-plume*—that is, another name you pick for yourself. It's in my dictionary among the "French phrases" at the back. If I did that then I could hear people talking of my pieces right before me, never suspecting, and say just what they really thought of them. That would be interesting but perhaps not always comfortable. I think I'll be,

"*E. Byrd Starr.*"

A WEAVER OF DREAMS

It took Emily several weeks to make up her mind whether she liked Mr Carpenter or not. She knew she did not *dis*like him, not even though his first greeting, shot at her on the opening day of school in a gruff voice, accompanied by a startling lift of his spiky grey brows was, "So you're the girl that writes poetry, eh? Better stick to your needle and duster. Too many fools in the world trying to write poetry and failing. I tried it myself once. Got better sense now."

"You don't keep your nails clean," thought Emily.

But he upset every kind of school tradition so speedily and thoroughly that Ilse, who gloried in upsetting things and hated routine, was the only scholar that liked him from the start. Some never liked him—the Rhoda Stuart type for example—but most of them came to it after they got used to never being used to anything. And Emily finally decided that she liked him tremendously.

Mr Carpenter was somewhere between forty and fifty—a tall man, with an upstanding shock of bushy grey hair, bristling grey moustache and eyebrows, a truculent beard, bright blue eyes out of which all his wild life had not yet burned the fire, and a long, lean, greyish face, deeply lined. He lived in a little two-roomed house below the school with a shy mouse of a wife. He never talked of his past or offered any explanation of the fact that at his age he had no better profession than teaching a district school for a pittance of salary, but the truth leaked out after a while; for Prince Edward Island is a small province and everybody in it knows something about everybody else. So eventually Blair Water people, and even the school children, understood that Mr Carpenter had been a brilliant student in his youth and had had his eye on the ministry. But at college he had got in with a "fast set"—Blair Water people nodded heads slowly and whispered the dreadful phrase portentously—and the fast set had ruined him. He "took to drink" and went to the dogs generally. And the upshot of it all was that Francis Carpenter, who had led his class in his first and second years at McGill, and for whom his teachers had predicted a great career, was a country school-teacher at forty-five with no prospect of ever being anything else. Perhaps he was resigned to it—perhaps not. Nobody ever knew, not even the brown mouse of a wife. Nobody in Blair Water cared—he was a good teacher, and that was all that mattered. Even if he did go on occasional "sprees" he always took Saturday for them and was sober enough by Monday. Sober, and especially dignified, wearing a rusty black frock-coat which he never put on any other day of the week. He did not invite pity and he did not pose as a tragedy. But sometimes, when Emily looked at his face, bent over the arithmetic problems of Blair Water School, she felt horribly sorry for him without in the least understanding why.

He had an explosive temper which generally burst into flame at least once a day, and then he would storm about wildly for a few minutes, tugging at his beard, imploring heaven to grant him patience, abusing everybody in general and the luckless object of his wrath in particular. But these tempers never lasted long. In a few minutes Mr Carpenter would be smiling as graciously as a sun bursting through a storm-cloud on the very pupil he had been rating. Nobody seemed to cherish any grudge because of his scoldings. He never said any of the biting things Miss Brownell was wont to say, which rankled and festered for weeks; his hail of words fell alike on just and unjust and rolled off harmlessly.

He could take a joke on himself in perfect good nature. "Do you hear me? Do you hear me, sirrah?" he bellowed to Perry Miller one day. "Of course I hear you," retorted Perry coolly, "they could hear you in

Charlottetown." Mr Carpenter stared for a moment, then broke into a great, jolly laugh.

His methods of teaching were so different from Miss Brownell's that the Blair Water pupils at first felt as if he had stood them on their heads. Miss Brownell had been a martinet for order. Mr Carpenter never tried to keep order apparently. But somehow he kept the children so busy that they had no time to do mischief. He taught history tempestuously for a month, making his pupils play the different characters and enact the incidents. He never bothered any one to learn dates—but the dates stuck in the memory just the same. If, as Mary Queen of Scots, you were beheaded by the school axe, kneeling blindfolded at the doorstep, with Perry Miller, wearing a mask made out of a piece of Aunt Laura's old black silk, for executioner, wondering what would happen if he brought the axe down *too* hard, you did not forget the year it happened; and if you fought the battle of Waterloo all over the school playground, and heard Teddy Kent shouting, "Up, Guards and at 'em!" as he led the last furious charge you remembered 1815 without half trying to.

Next month history would be thrust aside altogether and geography would take its place, when school and playground were mapped out into countries and you dressed up as the animals inhabiting them or traded in various commodities over their rivers and cities. When Rhoda Stuart had cheated you in a bargain in hides, you remembered that she had bought the cargo from the Argentine Republic, and when Perry Miller would not drink any water for a whole hot summer day because he was crossing the Arabian Desert with a caravan of camels and could not find an oasis, and then drank so much that he took terrible cramps and Aunt Laura had to be up all night with him— you did not forget where the said desert was. The trustees were quite scandalized over some of the goings on and felt sure that the children were having too good a time to be really learning anything.

If you wanted to learn Latin and French you had to do it by talking your exercises, not writing them, and on Friday afternoons all lessons were put aside and Mr Carpenter made the children recite poems, make speeches and declaim passages from Shakespeare and the Bible. This was the day Ilse loved. Mr Carpenter pounced on her gift like a starving dog on a bone and drilled her without mercy. They had endless fights and Ilse stamped her foot and called him names while the other pupils wondered why she was not punished for it but at last had to give in and do as he willed. Ilse went to school regularly—something she had never done before. Mr Carpenter had told her that if she were absent for a day without good excuse she could take no part in the Friday "exercises" and this would have killed her.

One day Mr Carpenter had picked up Teddy's slate and found a sketch of himself on it, in one of his favourite if not exactly beautiful attitudes. Teddy had labelled it "The Black Death"—half of the pupils of the school having died that day of the Great Plague, and having been carried out on stretchers to the Potter's Field by the terrified survivors.

Teddy expected a roar of denunciation, for the day before Garrett Marshall had been ground into figurative pulp on being discovered with the picture of a harmless cow on his slate—at least, Garrett said he meant it for a cow. But now this amazing Mr Carpenter only drew his beetling brows together, looked earnestly at Teddy's slate, put it down on the desk, looked at Teddy, and said,

"I don't know anything about drawing—I can't help you, but, by gad, I think hereafter you'd better give up those extra arithmetic problems in the afternoon and draw pictures."

Whereupon Garrett Marshall went home and told his father that "old Carpenter" wasn't fair and "made favourites" over Teddy Kent.

Mr Carpenter went up to the Tansy Patch that evening and saw the sketches in Teddy's old barn-loft studio. Then he went into the house and talked to Mrs Kent. What he said and what she said nobody ever knew. But Mr Carpenter went away looking grim, as if he had met an unexpected match. He took great pains with Teddy's general school work after that and procured from somewhere certain elementary textbooks on drawing which he gave him, telling him not to take them home—a caution Teddy did not require. He knew quite well that if he did they would disappear as mysteriously as his cats had done. He had taken Emily's advice and told his mother he would not love *her* if anything happened to Leo, and Leo flourished and waxed fat and doggy. But Teddy was too gentle at heart and too fond of his mother to make such a threat more than once. He knew she had cried all that night after Mr Carpenter had been there, and prayed on her knees in her little bedroom most of the next day, and looked at him with bitter, haunting eyes for a week. He wished she was more like other fellows' mothers but they loved each other very much and had dear hours together in the little grey house on the tansy hill. It was only when other people were about that Mrs Kent was queer and jealous.

"She's always lovely when we're alone," Teddy had told Emily.

As for the other boys, Perry Miller was the only one Mr Carpenter bothered much with in the way of speeches—and he was as merciless with him as with Ilse. Perry worked hard to please him and practised his speeches in barn and field—and even by nights in the kitchen loft—until Aunt Elizabeth put a stop to *that*. Emily could not understand why Mr Carpenter would smile amiably and say, "Very good," when Neddy Gray rattled off a speech glibly, without any expression whatever, and then rage at Perry and denounce him as a dunce and a nincompoop, by gad, because he had failed to give just the proper emphasis on a certain word, or had timed his gesture a fraction of a second too soon.

Neither could she understand why he made red pencil corrections all over her compositions and rated her for split infinitives and too lavish adjectives and strode up and down the aisle and hurled objurgations at her because she didn't know "a good place to stop when she saw it, by gad," and then told Rhoda Stuart and Nan Lee that their compositions were very pretty and gave them back without so much as a mark on them. Yet, in spite of it all, she liked him more and more as time went on and autumn passed and winter came with its beautiful bare-limbed trees, and soft pearl-grey skies that were slashed with rifts of gold in the afternoons, and cleared to a jewelled pageantry of stars over the wide white hills and valleys around New Moon.

Emily shot up so that winter that Aunt Laura had to let down the tucks of her dresses. Aunt Ruth, who had come for a week's visit, said she was outgrowing her strength—consumptive children always did.

"I am *not* consumptive," Emily said. "The Starrs are tall," she added, with a touch of subtle malice hardly to be looked for in near-thirteen.

Aunt Ruth, who was sensitive in regard to her dumpiness, sniffed.

"It would be well if *that* were the only thing in which you resemble them," she said. "How are you getting on in school?"

"Very well. I am the smartest scholar in my class," answered Emily composedly.

"You conceited child!" said Aunt Ruth.

"I'm *not* conceited." Emily looked scornful indignation. "Mr Carpenter said it and *he* doesn't flatter. Besides, I can't help seeing it myself."

"Well, it is to be hoped you have some brains, because you haven't much in the way of looks," said Aunt Ruth. "You've no complexion to speak of—and that inky hair around your white face is startling. I see you're going to be a plain girl."

"You wouldn't say that to a grown-up person's face," said Emily with a deliberate gravity which always exasperated Aunt Ruth because she could not understand it in a child. "I don't think it would hurt you to be as polite to me as you are to other people."

"I'm telling you your faults so you may correct them," said Aunt Ruth frigidly.

"It *isn't* my fault that my face is pale and my hair black," protested Emily. "I can't correct that."

"If you were a different girl," said Aunt Ruth, "I would—"

"But I don't *want* to be a different girl," said Emily decidedly. She had no intention of lowering the Starr flag to Aunt Ruth. "I wouldn't want to be anybody but myself even if I am plain. Besides," she added impressively as she turned to go out of the room, "though I may not be very good-looking now, when I go to heaven I believe I'll be very beautiful."

"Some people think Emily quite pretty," said Aunt Laura, but she did not say it until Emily was out of hearing. She was Murray enough for that.

"I don't know where they see it," said Aunt Ruth. "She's vain and pert and says things to be thought smart. You heard her just now. But the thing I dislike most in her is that she is unchildlike—and deep as the sea. Yes, she is, Laura—deep as the sea. You'll find it out to your cost one day if you disregard my warning. She's capable of anything. Sly is no word for it. You and Elizabeth don't keep a tight enough rein over her."

"I've done my best," said Elizabeth stiffly. She herself did think she had been much too lenient with Emily—Laura and Jimmy were two to one—but it nettled her to have Ruth say so.

Uncle Wallace also had an attack of worrying over Emily that winter.

He looked at her one day when he was at New Moon and remarked that she was getting to be a big girl.

"How old are you, Emily?" He asked her that every time he came to

New Moon.

"Thirteen in May."

"H'm. What are you going to do with her, Elizabeth?"

"I don't know what you mean," said Aunt Elizabeth coldly—or as coldly as is possible to speak when one is pouring melted tallow into candle-moulds.

"Why, she'll soon be grown up. She can't expect you to provide for her indefinitely—"

"I don't," Emily whispered resentfully under her breath.

"—and it's time we decided what is best to be done for her."

"The Murray women have never had to work out for a living," said Aunt Elizabeth, as if that disposed of the matter.

"Emily is only half Murray," said Wallace. "Besides, times are changing. You and Laura will not live for ever, Elizabeth, and when you are gone New Moon goes to Oliver's Andrew. In my opinion Emily should be fitted to support herself if necessary."

Emily did not like Uncle Wallace but she was very grateful to him at that moment. Whatever his motives were he was proposing the very thing she secretly yearned for.

"I would suggest," said Uncle Wallace, "that she be sent to Queen's Academy to get a teacher's licence. Teaching is a genteel, ladylike occupation. *I* will do my share in providing for the expense of it."

A blind person might have seen that Uncle Wallace thought this very splendid of himself.

"If you do," thought Emily, "I'll pay every cent back to you as soon as I'm able to earn it."

But Aunt Elizabeth was adamant.

"I do not believe in girls going out into the world," she said. "I don't mean Emily to go to Queen's. I told Mr Carpenter so when he came to see me about her taking up the Entrance work. He was very rude—schoolteachers knew their place better in my father's time. But I made him understand, I think. I'm rather surprised at *you*, Wallace. You did not send your own daughter out to work."

"*My* daughter had parents to provide for her," retorted Uncle Wallace pompously. "Emily is an orphan. I imagined from what I had heard about her that she would prefer earning her own living to living on charity."

"So I would," cried out Emily. "So I would, Uncle Wallace. Oh, Aunt Elizabeth, please let me study for the Entrance. Please! I'll pay you back every cent you spend on it—I will indeed. I pledge you my word of honour."

"It does not happen to be a question of money," said Aunt Elizabeth in her stateliest manner. "I undertook to provide for you, Emily, and I will do it. When you are older I may send you to the High School in Shrewsbury for a couple of years. I am not decrying education. But you are not going to be a slave to the public—no Murray girl ever was *that*."

Emily realizing the uselessness of pleading, went out in the same bitter disappointment she had felt after Mr Carpenter's visit. Then Aunt Elizabeth looked at Wallace.

"Have you forgotten what came of sending Juliet to Queen's?" she asked significantly.

If Emily was not allowed to take up the Entrance classes, Perry had no one to say him nay and he went at them with the same dogged determination he showed in all other matters. Perry's status at New Moon had changed subtly and steadily. Aunt Elizabeth had ceased to refer scornfully to him as "a hired boy." Even she recognized that though he was still undubitably a hired boy he was not going to remain one, and she no longer objected to Laura's patching up his ragged bits of clothing, or to Emily's helping him with his lessons in the kitchen after supper, nor did she growl when Cousin Jimmy began to pay him a certain small wage—though older boys than Perry were still glad to put in the winter months choring for board and lodging in some comfortable home. If a future premier was in the making at New Moon Aunt Elizabeth wanted to have some small share in the making. It was credible and commendable that a boy should have ambitions. A girl was an entirely different matter. A girl's place was at home.

Emily helped Perry work out algebra problems and heard his lessons in French and Latin. She picked up more thus than Aunt Elizabeth would have approved and more still when the Entrance pupils talked those languages in school. It was quite an easy matter for a girl who had once upon a time invented a language of her own. When George Bates, by way of showing off, asked her one day in French—*his* French, of which Mr Carpenter had once said doubtfully that perhaps God might understand it—"Have you the ink of my grandmother and the shoebrush of my cousin and the umbrella of my aunt's *husband* in your desk?" Emily retorted quite as glibly and *quite* as Frenchily, "No, but I have the pen of your father and the cheese of the innkeeper and the towel of your uncle's maidservant in my basket."

To console herself for her disappointment in regard to the Entrance class Emily wrote more poetry than ever. It was especially delightful to write poetry on a winter evening when the storm winds howled without and heaped the garden and orchard with big ghostly drifts, starred over with rabbits' candles. She also wrote several stories—desperate love affairs wherein she struggled heroically against the difficulties of affectionate dialogue; tales of bandits and pirates—Emily liked these because there was no necessity for bandits and pirates to converse lovingly; tragedies of earls and countesses whose conversation she dearly loved to pepper with scraps of French; and a dozen other subjects she didn't know anything about. She also meditated beginning a novel but decided it would be too hard to get enough paper for it. The letter-bills were all done now and the Jimmy-books were not big enough, though a new one always appeared mysteriously in her school basket when the old one was almost full. Cousin Jimmy seemed to have an uncanny prescience of the proper time—that was part of his Jimmyness.

Then one night, as she lay in her lookout bed and watched a full moon gleaming lustrously from a cloudless sky across the valley, she had a sudden dazzling idea.

She would send her latest poem to the Charlottetown *Enterprise*.

The *Enterprise* had a Poet's Corner where "original" verses were frequently printed. Privately Emily thought her own were quite as good—as probably they were, for most of the *Enterprise* "poems" were sad trash.

Emily was so excited over the idea that she could not sleep for the greater part of the night—and didn't want to. It was glorious to lie there, thrilling in the darkness, and picture the whole thing out. She saw her verses in print signed E. Byrd Starr—she saw Aunt Laura's eyes shining with pride—she saw Mr Carpenter pointing them out to strangers—"the work of a pupil of mine, by gad"—she saw all her schoolmates envying her or admiring, according to type—she saw herself with one foot at least firmly planted on the ladder of fame—one hill at least of the Alpine Path crested, with a new and glorious prospect opening therefrom.

Morning came. Emily went to school, so absent-minded because of her secret that she did badly in everything and was raged at by Mr Carpenter. But it all slipped off her like the proverbial water off a duck's back. Her body was in Blair Water school but her spirit was in kingdoms empyreal.

As soon as school was out she betook herself to the garret with half a sheet of blue-lined notepaper. Very painstakingly she copied down the poem, being especially careful to dot every *i* and cross every *t*. She wrote it on both sides of the paper, being in blissful ignorance of any taboo thereon. Then she read it aloud delightedly, not omitting the title *Evening Dreams*. There was one line in it she tasted two or three times:

The haunting elfin music of the air.

"I think that line is *very* good," said Emily. "I wonder now how I happened to think of it."

She mailed her poem the next day and lived in a delicious mystic rapture until the following Saturday. When the *Enterprise* came she opened it with tremulous eagerness and ice-cold fingers, and turned to the Poet's Corner. Now for her great moment!

There was not a sign of an Evening Dream about it!

Emily threw down the *Enterprise* and fled to the garret dormer where, face downward on the old hair-cloth sofa, she wept out her bitterness of disappointment. She drained the draught of failure to the very dregs. It was horribly real and tragic to her. She felt exactly as if she had been slapped in the face. She was crushed in the very dust of humiliation and was sure she could never rise again.

How thankful she was that she hadn't told Teddy anything about it—she had been so strongly tempted to, and only refrained because she didn't want to spoil the dramatic surprise of the moment when she would show him the verses with her name signed to them. She *had* told Perry, and Perry was furious when he saw her tear-stained face later on in the dairy, as they strained the milk together. Ordinarily Emily loved this, but to-night the savour had gone out of the world. Even the milky splendour of the still, mild winter evening and the purple bloom over the hillside woods that presaged a thaw could not give her the accustomed soul-thrill.

"I'm going to Charlottetown if I have to walk and I'll bust that *Enterprise* editor's head," said Perry, with the expression which, thirty

255

years later, warned the members of his party to scatter for cover.

"That wouldn't be any use," said Emily drearily. "He didn't think it good enough to print—that is what hurts me so, Perry—he didn't think it any good. Busting his head wouldn't change *that*."

It took her a week to recover from the blow. Then she wrote a story in which the editor of the *Enterprise* played the part of a dark and desperate villain who found lodging eventually behind prison bars. This got the venom out of her system and she forgot all about him in the delight of writing a poem addressed to "Sweet Lady April." But I question if she ever really forgave him—even when she discovered eventually that you must *not* write on both sides of the paper—even when she read over *Evening Dreams* a year later and wondered how she could ever have thought it any good.

This sort of thing was happening frequently now. Every time she read her little hoard of manuscripts over she found some of which the fairy gold had unaccountably turned to withered leaves, fit only for the burning. Emily burned them—but it hurt her a little. Outgrowing things we love is never a pleasant process.

SACRILEGE

There had been several clashes between Aunt Elizabeth and Emily that winter and spring. Generally Aunt Elizabeth came out victorious; there was that in her that would not be denied the satisfaction of having her own way even in trifling matters. But once in a while she came up against that curious streak of granite in Emily's composition which was unyielding and unbendable and unbreakable. Mary Murray, of a hundred years agone, had been, so family chronicle ran, a gentle and submissive creature generally; but she had that same streak in her, as her "Here I Stay" abundantly testified. When Aunt Elizabeth tried conclusions with that element in Emily she always got the worst of it. Yet she did not learn wisdom therefrom but pursued her policy of repression all the more rigorously; for it occasionally came home to her, as Laura let down tucks, that Emily was on the verge of beginning to grow up and that various breakers and reefs loomed ahead, ominously magnified in the mist of unseen years, Emily must not be allowed to get out of hand now, lest later on she make shipwreck as her mother had done—or as Elizabeth Murray firmly believed she had done. There were, in short, to be no more elopements from New Moon.

One of the things they fell out about was the fact that Emily, as Aunt Elizabeth discovered one day, was in the habit of using more of her egg money to buy paper than Aunt Elizabeth approved of. What did Emily do with so much paper? They had a fuss over this and eventually Aunt Elizabeth discovered that Emily was writing stories. Emily had been writing stories all winter under Aunt Elizabeth's very nose and Aunt Elizabeth had never suspected it. She had fondly supposed that Emily was writing school compositions. Aunt Elizabeth knew in a vague way that Emily wrote silly rhymes which she called "poetry" but this did not worry her especially. Jimmy made up a lot of similar trash. It was foolish but harmless and Emily would doubtless outgrow it. Jimmy had not outgrown it, to be sure, but then his accident—Elizabeth always went a little sick in soul when she remembered it—had made him more or less a child for life.

But writing stories was a very different thing and Aunt Elizabeth was horrified. Fiction of any kind was an abominable thing. Elizabeth Murray had been trained up in this belief in her youth and in her age she had not departed from it. She honestly thought that it was a wicked and sinful thing in any one to play cards, dance, or go to the theatre, read or write novels, and in Emily's case there was a worse feature—it was the Starr coming out in her—Douglas Starr especially. No Murray of New Moon had ever been guilty of writing "stories" or of ever wanting to write them. It was an alien growth that must be pruned off ruthlessly. Aunt Elizabeth applied the pruning shears; and found no pliant, snippable root but that same underlying streak of granite. Emily was respectful and reasonable and above-board; she bought no more paper with egg money; but she told Aunt Elizabeth that she could not give up writing stories and she went right on writing them, on pieces of brown wrapping paper and the blank backs of circulars which agricultural machinery firms sent Cousin Jimmy.

"Don't you know that it is wicked to write novels?" demanded Aunt Elizabeth.

"Oh, I'm not writing novels—yet," said Emily. "I can't get enough paper. These are just short stories. And it isn't wicked—Father liked novels."

"Your father—" began Aunt Elizabeth, and stopped. She remembered that Emily had "acted up" before now when anything derogatory was said of her father. But the very fact that she felt mysteriously compelled to stop annoyed Elizabeth, who had said what seemed good to her all her life at New Moon without much regard for other people's feelings.

"You will not write any more of *this stuff*," Aunt Elizabeth contemptuously flourished "The Secret of the Castle" under Emily's nose, "I forbid you—remember, I forbid you."

"Oh, I must write, Aunt Elizabeth," said Emily gravely, folding her slender, beautiful hands on the table and looking straight into Aunt Elizabeth's angry face with the steady, unblinking gaze which Aunt Ruth called unchildlike. "You see, it's this way. It is *in* me. I can't help it. And Father said I was *always* to keep on writing. He said I would be famous some day. Wouldn't you like to have a famous niece, Aunt Elizabeth?"

"I am not going to argue the matter," said Aunt Elizabeth.

"I'm not arguing—only explaining." Emily was exasperatingly respectful. "I just want you to understand how it is that I *have* to go on writing stories, even though I am so very sorry you don't approve."

"If you don't give up this—this worse than nonsense, Emily, I'll—I'll—"

Aunt Elizabeth stopped, not knowing what to say she would do. Emily was too big now to be slapped or shut up; and it was no use to say, as she was tempted to, "I'll send you away from New Moon," because Elizabeth Murray knew perfectly well she would not send Emily away from New Moon—*could* not send her away, indeed, though this knowledge was as yet only in her feelings and had not been translated into her intellect. She only felt that she was helpless and it angered her; but Emily was mistress of the situation and calmly went on writing stories. If Aunt Elizabeth had asked her to give up crocheting lace or making molasses taffy, or eating Aunt Laura's delicious drop cookies, Emily would have done so wholly and cheerfully, though she loved these things. But to give up writing stories—why, Aunt Elizabeth might as well have asked her to give up breathing. *Why* couldn't she understand? It seemed so simple and indisputable to Emily.

"Teddy can't help making pictures and Ilse can't help reciting, and I can't help writing. *Don't* you see, Aunt Elizabeth?"

"I see that you are an ungrateful and disobedient child," said Aunt Elizabeth.

This hurt Emily horribly, but she could not give in; and there continued to be a sense of soreness and disapproval between her and Aunt Elizabeth in all the little details of daily life that poisoned existence more or less for the child, who was so keenly sensitive to her environment and to the feelings with which her kindred regarded her. Emily felt it all the time—except when she was writing her stories. *Then* she forgot everything, roaming in some enchanted country between the sun and moon, where she saw wonderful beings whom she tried to describe and wonderful deeds which she tried to record, coming back to the candle-lit kitchen with a somewhat dazed sense of having been years in No-Man's Land.

She did not even have Aunt Laura to back her up in the matter. Aunt Laura thought Emily ought to yield in such an unimportant matter and please Aunt Elizabeth.

"But it's not unimportant," said Emily despairingly. "It's the most important thing in the world to me, Aunt Laura. Oh, I thought *you* would understand."

"I understand that you like to do it, dear, and I think it's a harmless enough amusement. But it seems to annoy Elizabeth some way and I do think you might give it up on that account. It is not as if it was anything that mattered much—it *is* really a waste of time."

"No—no," said distressed Emily. "Why, some day, Aunt Laura, I'll write real books—and make lots of money," she added, sensing that the businesslike Murrays measured the nature of most things on a cash basis.

Aunt Laura smiled indulgently.

"I'm afraid you'll never grow rich that way, dear. It would be wiser to employ your time preparing yourself for some useful work."

It was maddening to be condescended to like this—maddening that nobody could see that she *had* to write—maddening to have Aunt Laura so sweet and loving and stupid about it.

"Oh," thought Emily bitterly, "if that hateful *Enterprise* editor had printed my piece they'd have believed *then*."

"At any rate," advised Aunt Laura, "don't let Elizabeth *see* you writing them."

But somehow Emily could not take this prudent advice. There *had* been occasions when she had connived with Aunt Laura to hoodwink Aunt Elizabeth on some little matter, but she found she could not do it in this. *This* had to be open and above-board. She *must* write stories—and Aunt Elizabeth *must* know it—that was the way it had to be. She could not be false to herself in this—she could not *pretend* to be false.

She wrote her father all about it—poured out her bitterness and perplexity to him in what, though she did not suspect it at the time, was the last letter she was to write him. There was a large bundle of letters by now on the old sofa shelf in the garret—for Emily had written many letters to her father besides those which have been chronicled in this history. There were a great many paragraphs about Aunt Elizabeth in them, most of them very uncomplimentary and some of them, as Emily herself would have owned when her first bitterness was past, overdrawn and exaggerated. They had been written in moments when her hurt and angry soul demanded some outlet for its emotion and barbed her pen with venom. Emily was mistress of a subtly malicious style when she chose to be. After she had written them the hurt had ceased and she thought no more about them. But they remained.

And one spring day, Aunt Elizabeth, house-cleaning in the garret while Emily played happily with Teddy at the Tansy Patch, found the bundle of letters on the sofa shelf, sat down, and read them all.

Elizabeth Murray would never have read any writing belonging to a grown person. But it never occurred to her that there was anything dishonourable in reading the letters wherein Emily, lonely and—sometimes—misunderstood, had poured out her heart to the father she had loved and been loved by, so passionately and understandingly. Aunt Elizabeth thought she had a right to know everything that this pensioner on her bounty did, said, or thought. She read the letters and she found out what Emily thought of her—of her, Elizabeth Murray, autocrat unchallenged, to whom no one had ever dared to say anything uncomplimentary. Such an experience is no pleasanter at sixty than at sixteen. As Elizabeth Murray folded up the last letter her hands trembled—with anger, and something underneath it that was not anger.

"Emily, your Aunt Elizabeth wants to see you in the parlour," said Aunt Laura, when Emily returned from the Tansy Patch, driven home by the thin grey rain that had begun to drift over the greening fields. Her tone—her sorrowful look—warned Emily that mischief was in the wind. Emily had no idea what mischief—she could not recall anything she had done recently that should bring her up before the tribunal Aunt Elizabeth occasionally held in the parlour. It must be serious when it was in the parlour. For reasons best known to herself Aunt Elizabeth held super-serious interviews like this in the parlour. Possibly it was because she felt obscurely that the photographs of the Murrays on the walls gave her a backing she needed when dealing with this hop-out-of-kin; for the same reason Emily detested a trial in the parlour. She always felt on such occasions like a very small mouse surrounded by a circle of grim cats.

Emily skipped across the big hall, pausing, in spite of her alarm, to glance at the charming red world through the crimson glass; then pushed open the parlour door. The room was dim, for only one of the slat blinds was partially raised. Aunt Elizabeth was sitting bolt upright in Grandfather Murray's black horsehair chair. Emily looked at her stern, angry face first—and then at her lap.

Emily understood.

The first thing she did was to retrieve her precious letters. With the quickness of light she sprang to Aunt Elizabeth, snatched up the bundle and retreated to the door; there she faced Aunt Elizabeth, her face blazing with indignation and outrage. Sacrilege had been committed—the most sacred shrine of her soul had been profaned.

"How dare you?" she said. "How dare you touch *my private papers,* Aunt Elizabeth?"

Aunt Elizabeth had not expected *this.* She had looked for confusion—dismay—shame—fear—for anything but this righteous indignation, as if *she,* forsooth, were the guilty one. She rose.

"Give me those letters, Emily."

"No, I will not," said Emily, white with anger, as she clasped her hands around the bundle. "They are mine and Father's—not yours. You had no right to touch them. I will *never* forgive you!"

This was turning the tables with a vengeance. Aunt Elizabeth was so dumbfounded that she hardly knew what to say or do. Worst of all, a most unpleasant doubt of her own conduct suddenly assailed her—driven home perhaps by the intensity and earnestness of Emily's accusation. For the first time in her life it occurred to Elizabeth Murray to wonder if she had done rightly. For the first time in her life she felt ashamed; and the shame made her furious. It was intolerable that *she* should be made to feel ashamed.

For the moment they faced each other, not as aunt and niece, not as child and adult, but as two human beings each with hatred for the other in her heart—Elizabeth Murray, tall and austere and thin-lipped; Emily Starr, white of face, her eyes pools of black flame, her trembling arms hugging her letters.

"So *this* is your gratitude," said Aunt Elizabeth. "You were a penniless orphan—I took you to my home—I have given you shelter and food and education and kindness—and *this* is my thanks."

As yet Emily's tempest of anger and resentment prevented her from feeling the sting of this.

"You did not *want* to take me," she said. "You made me draw lots and you took me because the lot fell to you. You knew some of you had to take me because you were the proud Murrays and couldn't let a relation go to an orphan asylum. Aunt Laura loves me now but you don't. So why should I love you?"

"Ungrateful, thankless child!"

"I'm *not* thankless. I've tried to be good—I've tried to obey you and please you—I do all the chores I can to help pay for my keep. And you had *no business* to read my letters to Father."

"They are disgraceful letters—and must be destroyed," said Aunt Elizabeth.

"No," Emily clasped them tighter. "I'd sooner burn myself. You shall not have them, Aunt Elizabeth."

She felt her brows drawing together—she felt the Murray look on her face—she knew she was conquering.

Elizabeth Murray turned paler, if that were possible. There were times when she could give the Murray look herself; it was not that which dismayed her—it was the uncanny something which seemed to peer out behind the Murray look that always broke her will. She trembled—faltered—yielded.

"Keep your letters," she said bitterly, "and scorn the old woman who opened her home to you."

262

She went out of the parlour. Emily was left mistress of the field. And all at once her victory turned to dust and ashes in her mouth.

She went up to her own room, hid her letters in the cupboard over the mantel, and then crept up on her bed, huddling down in a little heap with her face buried in her pillow. She was still sore with a sense of outrage—but underneath another pain was beginning to ache terribly.

Something in her was hurt because she had hurt Aunt Elizabeth—for she felt that Aunt Elizabeth, under all her anger, was *hurt*. This surprised Emily. She would have expected Aunt Elizabeth to be angry, of course, but she would never have supposed it would affect her in any other way. Yet she had seen something in Aunt Elizabeth's eyes when she had flung that last stinging sentence at her—something that spoke of bitter hurt.

"Oh! Oh!" gasped Emily. She began to cry chokingly into her pillow. She was so wretched that she could not get out of herself and watch her own suffering with a sort of enjoyment in its drama—set her mind to analyse her feelings—and when Emily was as wretched as that she was very wretched indeed and wholly comfortless. Aunt Elizabeth would not keep her at New Moon after a poisonous quarrel like this. She would send her away, of course. Emily believed this. Nothing was too horrible to believe just then. How could she live away from dear New Moon?

"And I may have to live eighty years," Emily moaned.

But worse even than this was the remembrance of that look in Aunt Elizabeth's eyes.

Her own sense of outrage and sacrilege ebbed away under the remembrance. She thought of all the things she had written her father about Aunt Elizabeth—sharp, bitter things, some of them just, some of them unjust. She began to feel that she should not have written them. It was true enough that Aunt Elizabeth had not loved her—had not wanted to take her to New Moon. But she *had* taken her and though it had been done in duty, not in love, the fact remained. It was no use for her to tell herself that it wasn't as if the letters were written to any one living, to be seen and read by others. While she was under Aunt Elizabeth's roof—while she owed the food she ate and the clothes she wore to Aunt Elizabeth—she should not say, even to her father, harsh things of her. A Starr should not have done it.

"I must go and ask Aunt Elizabeth to forgive me," thought Emily at last, all the passion gone out of her and only regret and repentance left. "I suppose she never will—she'll hate me always now. But I must go."

She turned herself about—and then the door opened and Aunt Elizabeth entered. She came across the room and stood at the side of the bed, looking down at the grieved little face on the pillow—a face that in the dim, rainy twilight, with its tear-stains and black shadowed eyes, looked strangely mature and chiselled.

Elizabeth Murray was still austere and cold. Her voice sounded stern; but she said an amazing thing:

"Emily, I had no right to read your letters. I admit I was wrong. Will you forgive me?"

"Oh!" The word was almost a cry. Aunt Elizabeth had at last discerned the way to conquer Emily. The latter lifted herself up, flung her arms about Aunt Elizabeth, and said chokingly:

"Oh—Aunt Elizabeth—I'm sorry—I'm sorry—I shouldn't have written those things—but I wrote them when I was vexed—and I didn't mean them *all*—truly, I didn't mean the worst of them. Oh, you'll believe *that,* won't you, Aunt Elizabeth?"

"I'd like to believe it, Emily." An odd quiver passed through the tall, rigid form. "I—don't like to think you—*hate me*—my sister's child— little Juliet's child."

"I don't—oh, I don't," sobbed Emily. "And I'll *love* you, Aunt Elizabeth, if you'll let me—if you *want* me to. I didn't think you cared. *Dear* Aunt Elizabeth."

Emily gave Aunt Elizabeth a fierce hug and a passionate kiss on the white, fine-wrinkled cheek. Aunt Elizabeth kissed her gravely on the brow in return and then said, as if closing the door on the whole incident,

"You'd better wash your face and come down to supper."

But there was yet something to be cleared up.

"Aunt Elizabeth," whispered Emily. "I *can't* burn those letters, you know—they belong to Father. But I'll tell you what I will do. I'll go over them all and put a star by anything I said about you and then I'll add an explanatory footnote saying that I was mistaken."

Emily spent her spare time for several days putting in her "explanatory footnotes," and then her conscience had rest. But when she again tried to write a letter to her father she found that it no longer meant anything to her. The sense of reality—nearness—of close communion had gone. Perhaps she had been outgrowing it gradually, as childhood began to merge into girlhood—perhaps the bitter scene with Aunt Elizabeth had only shaken into dust something out of which the spirit had already departed. But, whatever the explanation, it was not possible to write such letters any more. She missed them terribly but she could not go back to them. A certain door of life was shut behind her and could not be reopened.

WHEN THE CURTAIN LIFTED

It would be pleasant to be able to record that after the reconciliation in the lookout Emily and Aunt Elizabeth lived in entire amity and harmony. But the truth was that things went on pretty much the same as before. Emily went softly, and tried to mingle serpent's wisdom and dove's harmlessness in practical proportions, but their points of view were so different that there were bound to be clashes; they did not speak the same language, so there was bound to be misunderstanding.

And yet there was a difference—a very vital difference. Elizabeth Murray had learned an important lesson—that there was not one law of fairness for children and another for grown-ups. She continued to be as autocratic as ever—but she did not do or say to Emily anything she would not have done or said to Laura had occasion called for it.

Emily, on her side, had discovered the fact that, under all her surface coldness and sternness, Aunt Elizabeth really had an affection for her; and it was wonderful what a difference this made. It took the sting out of Aunt Elizabeth's "ways" and words and healed entirely a certain little half-conscious sore spot that had been in Emily's heart ever since the incident of the drawn slips at Maywood.

"I don't believe I'm a duty to Aunt Elizabeth any more," she thought exultantly.

Emily grew rapidly that summer in body, mind and soul. Life was delightful, growing richer every hour, like an unfolding rose. Forms of beauty filled her imagination and were transferred as best she could to paper, though they were never so lovely there, and Emily had the heartbreaking moments of the true artist who discovers that

Never on painter's canvas lives

The charm of his fancy's dream.

Much of her "old stuff" she burned; even the *Child of the Sea* was reduced to ashes. But the little pile of manuscripts in the mantel cupboard of the lookout was growing steadily larger. Emily kept her scribblings there now; the sofa shelf in the garret was desecrated; and, besides, she felt somehow that Aunt Elizabeth would never meddle with her "private papers" again, no matter where they were kept. She did not go now to the garret to read or write or dream; her own dear lookout was the best place for that. She loved that quaint, little old room intensely; it was almost like a living thing to her—a sharer in gladness—a comforter in sorrow.

Ilse was growing, too, blossoming out into strange beauty and brilliance, knowing no law but her own pleasure, recognizing no authority but her own whim. Aunt Laura worried over her.

"She will be a woman so soon—and *who* will look after her? Allan won't."

"I've no patience with Allan," said Aunt Elizabeth grimly. "He is always ready to hector and advise other people. He'd better look at home. He'll come over here and order me to do this or that, or *not* to do it, for Emily; but if I say one word to him about Ilse he blows the roof off. The idea of a man turning against his daughter and neglecting her as he has neglected Ilse simply because her mother wasn't all she ought to be—as if the poor child was to blame for *that*."

"S-s-sh," said Aunt Laura, as Emily crossed the sitting-room on her way upstairs.

Emily smiled sadly to herself. Aunt Laura needn't be "s-s-sh'ing." There was nothing left for her to find out about Ilse's mother—nothing, except the most important thing of all, which neither she nor anybody else living knew. For Emily had never surrendered her conviction that the whole truth about Beatrice Burnley was not known. She often worried about it when she lay curled up in her black walnut bed o'nights, listening to the moan of the gulf and the Wind Woman singing in the trees, and drifted into sleep wishing intensely that she could solve the dark old mystery and dissolve its legend of shame and bitterness.

Emily went rather languidly upstairs to the lookout. She meant to write some more of her story, *The Ghost of the Well*, wherein she was weaving the old legend of the well in the Lee field; but somehow interest was lacking; she put the manuscript back into the mantel cupboard; she read over a letter from Dean Priest which had come that day, one of his fat, jolly, whimsical, delightful letters wherein he had told her that he was coming to stay a month with his sister at Blair Water. She wondered why this announcement did not excite her more. She was tired—her head was aching. Emily couldn't remember ever having had a headache before. Since she could not write she decided to lie down and be *Lady Trevanion* for awhile. Emily was *Lady Trevanion* very often that summer, in one of the dream lives she had begun to build up for herself. *Lady Trevanion* was the wife of an English earl and, besides being a famous novelist, was a member of the British House of Commons—where she always appeared in black velvet with a stately coronet of pearls on her dark hair. She was the only woman in the House and, as this was before the days of the suffragettes, she had to endure many sneers and innuendoes and insults from the ungallant males around her. Emily's favourite dream scene was where she rose to make her first speech—a wonderfully thrilling event. As Emily found it difficult to do justice to the scene in any ideas of her own, she always fell back on "Pitt's reply to Walpole," which she had found in her *Royal Reader*, and declaimed it, with suitable variations. The insolent speaker who had provoked *Lady Trevanion* into speech had sneered at her as a *woman*, and *Lady Trevanion*, a magnificent creature in her velvet and pearls, rose to her feet, amid hushed and dramatic silence, and said,

"The atrocious crime of being a *woman* which the honourable member has, with such spirit and decency, charged upon me, I shall attempt neither to palliate nor deny, but shall content myself with wishing that I may be one of those whose follies cease with their *sex* and *not* one of that number who are ignorant in spite of *manhood* and experience."

(Here she was always interrupted by thunders of applause.)

But the savour was entirely lacking in this scene to-day and by the time Emily had reached the line, "But *womanhood*, Sir, is not my only crime"—she gave up in disgust and fell to worrying over Ilse's mother again, mixed up with some uneasy speculations regarding the climax of her story about the ghost of the well, mingled with her unpleasant physical sensations.

Her eyes hurt her when she moved them. She was chilly, although the July day was hot. She was still lying there when Aunt Elizabeth came up to ask why she hadn't gone to bring the cows home from the pasture.

"I—I didn't know it was so late," said Emily confusedly. "I—my head aches, Aunt Elizabeth."

Aunt Elizabeth rolled up the white cotton blind and looked at Emily. She noted her flushed face—she felt her pulse. Then she bade her shortly to stay where she was, went down, and sent Perry for Dr Burnley.

"Probably she's got the measles," said the doctor as gruffly as usual. Emily was not yet sick enough to be gentle over. "There's an outbreak of them at Derry Pond. Has she had any chance to catch them?"

"Jimmy Joe Belle's two children were here one afternoon, about ten days ago. She played with them—she's always playing round with people she's no business to associate with. I haven't heard that they were or have been sick though."

Jimmy Joe Belle, when asked plainly, confessed that his "young ones" had come out with measles the very day after they had been at New Moon. There was therefore not much doubt as to Emily's malady.

"It's a bad kind of measles apparently," the doctor said. "Quite a number of the Derry Pond children have died of it. Mostly French though—the kids would be out of bed when they had no business to be and caught cold. I don't think you need worry about Emily. She might as well have measles and be done with it. Keep her warm and keep the room dark. I'll run over in the morning."

For three or four days nobody was much alarmed. Measles was a disease everybody had to have. Aunt Elizabeth looked after Emily well and slept on a sofa which had been moved into the lookout. She even left the window open at night. In spite of this—perhaps Aunt Elizabeth thought because of it—Emily grew steadily sicker, and on the fifth day a sharp change for the worse took place. Her fever went up rapidly, delirium set in; Dr Burnley came, looked anxious, scowled, changed

268

the medicine.

"I'm sent for to a bad case of pneumonia at White Cross," he said, "and I have to go to Charlottetown in the morning to be present at Mrs Jackwell's operation. I promised her I would go. I'll be back in the evening. Emily is very restless—that high-strung system of hers is evidently very sensitive to fever. What's that nonsense she's talking about the Wind Woman?"

"Oh, I don't know," said Aunt Elizabeth worriedly. "She's always talking nonsense like that, even when she's well. Allan, tell me plainly— is there any danger?"

"There's always danger in this type of measles. I don't like these symptoms—the eruption should be out by now and there's no sign of it. Her fever is very high—but I don't think we need be alarmed yet. If I thought otherwise I wouldn't go to town. Keep her as quiet as possible—humour her whims if you can—I don't like that mental disturbance. She looks terribly distressed—seems to be worrying over something. Has she had anything on her mind of late?"

"Not that I know of," said Aunt Elizabeth. She had a sudden bitter realization that she really did not know much about the child's mind. Emily would never have come to her with any of her little troubles and worries.

"Emily, what is bothering you?" asked Dr Burnley softly—very softly. He took the hot, tossing, little hand gently, oh, so gently, in his big one.

Emily looked up with wild, fever-bright eyes.

"She couldn't have done it—she *couldn't* have done it."

"Of course she couldn't," said the doctor cheerily. "Don't worry— she didn't do it."

His eyes telegraphed, "What does she mean?" to Elizabeth, but Elizabeth shook her head.

"Who are you talking about—dear?" she asked Emily. It was the first time she had called Emily "dear."

But Emily was off on another track. The well in Mr Lee's field was open, she declared. Some one would be sure to fall into it. Why didn't Mr Lee shut it up? Dr Burnley left Aunt Elizabeth trying to reassure Emily on that point and hurried away to White Cross.

At the door he nearly fell over Perry who was curled up on the sandstone slab, hugging his sunburned legs desperately. "How is

Emily?" he demanded, grasping the skirt of the doctor's coat.

"Don't bother me—I'm in a hurry," growled the doctor.

"You tell me how Emily is or I'll hang on to your coat till the seams go," said Perry stubbornly. "I can't get one word of sense out of them old maids. *You* tell me."

"She's a sick child but I'm not seriously alarmed about her yet." The doctor gave his coat another tug—but Perry held on for a last word.

"You've *got* to cure her," he said. "If anything happens to Emily I'll drown myself in the pond—mind that."

He let go so suddenly that Dr Burnley nearly went headlong on the ground. Then Perry curled up on the doorstep again. He watched there until Laura and Cousin Jimmy had gone to bed and then he sneaked through the house and sat on the stairs, where he could hear any sound in Emily's room. He sat there all night, with his fists clenched, as if keeping guard against an unseen foe.

Elizabeth Murray watched by Emily until two o'clock and then Laura took her place.

"She has raved a great deal," said Aunt Elizabeth. "I wish I knew what is worrying her—there *is* something, I feel sure. It isn't all mere delirium. She keeps repeating 'She couldn't have done it' in such imploring tones. I wonder oh, Laura, you remember the time I read her letters? Do you think she means me?"

Laura shook her head. She had never seen Elizabeth so moved.

"If the child—doesn't get—better—" said Aunt Elizabeth.

She said no more but went quickly out of the room.

Laura sat down by the bed. She was pale and drawn with her own worry and fatigue—for she had not been able to sleep. She loved Emily as her own child and the awful dread that had possessed her heart would not lift for an instant. She sat there and prayed mutely. Emily fell into a troubled slumber which lasted until the grey dawn crept into the lookout. Then she opened her eyes and looked at Aunt Laura—looked through her—looked beyond her.

"I see her coming over the fields," she said in a high, clear voice. "She is coming so gladly—she is singing—she is thinking of her baby—oh, keep her back—keep her back—she doesn't see the well—it's so dark she doesn't see it—oh, she's gone into it—she's gone into it!"

Emily's voice rose in a piercing shriek which penetrated to Aunt

Elizabeth's room and brought her flying across the hall in her flannel nightgown.

"What is wrong, Laura?" she gasped.

Laura was trying to soothe Emily, who was struggling to sit up in bed. Her cheeks were crimson and her eyes had still the same far, wild look.

"Emily—Emily, darling, you've just had a bad dream. The old Lee well isn't open—nobody has fallen into it."

"Yes, somebody has," said Emily shrilly. "*She* has—I saw her—I saw her—with the ace of hearts on her forehead. Do you think I don't know her?"

She fell back on her pillow, moaned, and tossed the hands which Laura Murray had loosened in her surprise.

The two ladies of New Moon looked at each other across her bed in dismay—and something like terror.

"Who did you see, Emily?" asked Aunt Elizabeth.

"Ilse's mother—of course. I always knew she didn't do that dreadful thing. She fell into the old well—she's there now—go—go and get her out, Aunt Laura. *Please.*"

"Yes—yes, of course we'll get her out, darling," said Aunt Laura, soothingly.

Emily sat up in bed and looked at Aunt Laura again. This time she did not look through her—she looked into her. Laura Murray felt that those burning eyes read her soul.

"You are lying to me," cried Emily. "You don't mean to try to get her out. You are only saying it to put me off. Aunt Elizabeth," she suddenly turned and caught Aunt Elizabeth's hand, "you'll do it for me, won't you? You'll go and get her out of the old well, won't you?"

Elizabeth remembered that Dr Burnley had said that Emily's whims must be humoured. She was terrified by the child's condition.

"Yes, I'll get her out if she is in there," she said.

Emily released her hand and sank down. The wild glare left her eyes. A great sudden calm fell over her anguished little face.

"I know *you'll* keep your word," she said. "You are very hard—but *you* never lie, Aunt Elizabeth."

Elizabeth Murray went back to her own room and dressed herself with her shaking fingers. A little later, when Emily had fallen into a quiet sleep, Laura went downstairs and heard Elizabeth giving Cousin

Jimmy some orders in the kitchen.

"Elizabeth, you don't really mean to have that old well searched?"

"I do," said Elizabeth resolutely. "I know it's nonsense as well as you do. But I had to promise it to quiet her down—and I'll keep my promise. You heard what she said—she believed I wouldn't lie to her. Nor will I. Jimmy, you will go over to James Lee's after breakfast and ask him to come here."

"How has she heard the story?" said Laura.

"I don't know—oh, some one has told her, of course—perhaps that old demon of a Nancy Priest. It doesn't matter who. She *has* heard it and the thing is to keep her quiet. It isn't so much of a job to put ladders in the well and get some one to go down it. The thing that matters is the absurdity of it."

"We'll be laughed at for a pair of fools," protested Laura, whose share of Murray pride was in hot revolt. "And besides, it will open up all the old scandal again."

"No matter. I'll keep my word to the child," said Elizabeth stubbornly.

Allan Burnley came to New Moon at sunset, on his way home from town. He was tired, for he had been going night and day for over a week; he was more worried than he had admitted over Emily; he looked old and rather desolate as he stepped into the New Moon kitchen.

Only Cousin Jimmy was there. Cousin Jimmy did not seem to have much to do, although it was a good hay-day and Jimmy Joe Belle and Perry were hauling in the great fragrant, sun-dried loads. He sat by the western window with a strange expression on his face.

"Hello, Jimmy, where are the girls? And how is Emily?"

"Emily is better," said Cousin Jimmy. "The rash is out and her fever has gone down. I think she's asleep."

"Good. We couldn't afford to lose that little girl, could we, Jimmy?"

"No," said Jimmy. But he did not seem to want to talk about it. "Laura and Elizabeth are in the sitting-room. They want to see you." He paused a minute and then added in an eerie way. "There is nothing hidden that shall not be revealed."

It occurred to Allan Burnley that Jimmy was acting mysteriously. And if Laura and Elizabeth wanted to see him why didn't they come out? It wasn't like them to stand on ceremony in this fashion. He pushed open the sitting-room door impatiently.

Laura Murray was sitting on the sofa, leaning her head on its arm. He could not see her face but he felt that she was crying. Elizabeth was sitting bolt upright on a chair. She wore her second-best black silk and her second-best lace cap. And she, too, had been crying. Dr Burnley never attached much importance to Laura's tears, easy as those of most women, but that Elizabeth Murray should cry—had he ever seen her cry before?

The thought of Ilse flashed into his mind—his little neglected daughter. Had anything happened to Ilse? In one dreadful moment Allan Burnley paid the price of his treatment of his child.

"What is wrong?" he exclaimed in his gruffest manner.

"Oh, Allan," said Elizabeth Murray. "God forgive us—God forgive us all!"

"It—is—Ilse," said Dr Burnley, dully.

"No—no—not Ilse."

Then she told him—she told him what had been found at the bottom of the old Lee well—she told him what had been the real fate of the lovely, laughing young wife whose name for twelve bitter years had never crossed his lips.

It was not until the next evening that Emily saw the doctor. She was lying in bed, weak and limp, red as a beet with the measles rash, but quite herself again. Allan Burnley stood by the bed and looked down at her.

"Emily—dear little child—do you know what you have done for me? God knows how you did it."

"I thought you didn't believe in God," said Emily, wonderingly.

"You have given me back my faith in Him, Emily."

"Why, what have I done?"

Dr Burnley saw that she had no remembrance of her delirium. Laura had told him that she had slept long and soundly after Elizabeth's promise and had awakened with fever gone and the eruption fast coming out. She had asked nothing and they had said nothing.

"When you are better we will tell you all," he said, smiling down at her. There was something very sorrowful in the smile—and yet something very sweet.

"He is smiling with his eyes as well as his mouth now," thought Emily.

"How—how did she know?" whispered Laura Murray to him when he went down. "I—can't understand it, Allan."

"Nor I. These things are beyond us, Laura," he answered gravely. "I only know this child has given Beatrice back to me, stainless and beloved. It can be explained rationally enough perhaps. Emily has evidently been told about Beatrice and worried over it—her repeated 'she couldn't have done it' shows that. And the tales of the old Lee well naturally made a deep impression on the mind of a sensitive child keenly alive to dramatic values. In her delirium she mixed this all up with the well-known fact of Jimmy's tumble into the New Moon well— and the rest was coincidence. I would have explained it all so myself once—but now—now, Laura, I only say humbly, 'A little child shall lead them.'"

"Our stepmother's mother was a Highland Scotchwoman. They said she had the second sight," said Elizabeth. "I never believed in it— before."

The excitement of Blair Water had died away before Emily was deemed strong enough to hear the story. That which had been found in the old Lee well had been buried in the Mitchell plot at Shrewsbury and a white marble shaft, "Sacred to the memory of Beatrice Burnley, beloved wife of Allan Burnley," had been erected. The sensation caused by Dr Burnley's presence every Sunday in the old Burnley pew had died away. On the first evening that Emily was allowed to sit up Aunt Laura told her the whole story. Her manner of telling stripped it for ever of the taint and innuendo left by Aunt Nancy.

"I *knew* Ilse's mother couldn't have done it," said Emily triumphantly.

"We blame ourselves now for our lack of faith," said Aunt Laura. "We should have known too—but it *did* seem black against her at the time, Emily. She was a bright, beautiful, merry creature—we thought her close friendship with her cousin natural and harmless. We know now it was so—but all these years since her disappearance we have believed differently. Mr James Lee remembers clearly that the well was open the night of Beatrice's disappearance. His hired man had taken the old rotten planks off it that evening, intending to put the new ones on at once. Then Robert Greerson's house caught fire and he ran with everybody else to help save it. By the time it was out it was too dark to finish the well, and the man said nothing about it until the morning.

Mr Lee was angry with him—he said it was a scandalous thing to leave a well uncovered like that. He went right down and put the new planks in place himself. He did not look down in the well—had he looked he could have seen nothing, for the ferns growing out from the sides screened the depths. It was just after harvest. No one was in the field again before the next spring. He never connected Beatrice's disappearance with the open well—he wonders now that he didn't. But you see—dear—there had been much malicious gossip—and Beatrice was *known* to have gone on board *The Lady of Winds*. It was taken for granted she never came off again. But she did—and went to her death in the old Lee field. It was a dreadful ending to her bright young life— but not so dreadful, after all, as what we believed. For twelve years we have wronged the dead. But—Emily—how could you *know*?"

"I—don't—know. When the doctor came in that day I couldn't remember anything—but now it seems to me that I remember something—just as if I'd dreamed it—of *seeing* Ilse's mother coming over the fields, singing. It was dark—and yet I could see the ace of hearts—oh, Aunty, I don't know—I don't like to think of it, some way."

"We won't talk of it again," said Aunt Laura gently. "It is one of the things best not talked of—one of God's secrets."

"And Ilse—does her father love her now?" asked Emily eagerly.

"Love her! He can't love her enough. It seems as if he were pouring out on her at once all the shut-up love of those twelve years."

"He'll likely spoil her now as much with indulgence as he did before with neglect," said Elizabeth, coming in with Emily's supper in time to hear Laura's reply.

"It will take a lot of love to spoil Ilse," laughed Laura. "She's drinking it up like a thirsty sponge. And she loves him wildly in return. There isn't a trace of grudge in her over his long neglect."

"All the same," said Elizabeth grimly, tucking pillows behind Emily's back with a very gentle hand, oddly in contrast with her severe expression, "he won't get off so easily. Ilse has run wild for twelve years. He won't find it so easy to make her behave properly now—if he ever does."

"Love will do wonders," said Aunt Laura softly. "Of course, Ilse is dying to come and see you, Emily. But she must wait until there is no danger of infection. I told her she might write—but when she found I would have to read it because of your eyes she said she'd wait till you

275

could read it yourself. Evidently"—Laura laughed again—"evidently Ilse has much of importance to tell you."

"I didn't know anybody could be so happy as I am now," said Emily. "And oh, Aunt Elizabeth, it is *so* nice to feel hungry again and to have something to *chew*."

EMILY'S GREAT MOMENT

Emily's convalescence was rather slow. Physically she recovered with normal celerity but a certain spiritual and emotional langour persisted for a time. One cannot go down to the depths of hidden things and escape the penalty. Aunt Elizabeth said she "moped." But Emily was too happy and contented to mope. It was just that life seemed to have lost its savour for a time, as if some spring of vital energy had been drained out of it and refilled slowly.

She had, just then, no one to play with. Perry, Ilse and Teddy had all come down with measles the same day. Mrs Kent at first declared bitterly that Teddy had caught them at New Moon, but all three had contracted them at a Sunday-school picnic where Derry Pond children had been. That picnic infected all Blair Water. There was a perfect orgy of measles. Teddy and Ilse were only moderately ill, but Perry, who had insisted on going home to Aunt Tom at the first symptoms, nearly died. Emily was not allowed to know his danger until it had passed, lest it worry her too much. Even Aunt Elizabeth worried over it. She was surprised to discover how much they missed Perry round the place.

It was fortunate for Emily that Dean Priest was in Blair Water during this forlorn time. His companionship was just what she needed and helped her wonderfully on the road to complete recovery. They went for long walks together all over Blair Water, with Tweed woofing around them, and explored places and roads Emily had never seen before. They watched a young moon grow old, night by night; they talked in dim scented chambers of twilight over long red roads of mystery; they followed the lure of hill winds; they saw the stars rise and Dean told her all about them—the great constellations of the old myths. It was a wonderful month; but on the first day of Teddy's convalescence Emily was off to the Tansy Patch for the afternoon and Jarback Priest walked—if he walked at all—alone.

Aunt Elizabeth was extremely polite to him, though she did not like the Priests of Priest Pond overmuch, and never felt quite comfortable under the mocking gleam of "Jarback's" green eyes and the faint derision of his smile, which seemed to make Murray pride and Murray traditions seem much less important than they really were.

"He has the Priest flavour," she told Laura, "though it isn't as strong in him as in most of them. And he's certainly helping Emily—she has begun to spunk up since he came."

Emily continued to "spunk up" and by September, when the measles epidemic was spent and Dean Priest had gone on one of his sudden swoops over to Europe for the autumn, she was ready for school again—a little taller, a little thinner, a little less childlike, with great grey shadowy eyes that had looked into death and read the riddle of a buried thing, and henceforth would hold in them some haunting, elusive remembrance of that world behind the veil. Dean Priest had seen it—Mr Carpenter saw it when she smiled at him across her desk at school.

"She's left the childhood of her soul behind, though she is still a child in body," he muttered.

One afternoon amid the golden days and hazes of October he asked her gruffly to let him see some of her verses.

"I never meant to encourage you in it," he said. "I don't mean it now. Probably you can't write a line of real poetry and never will. But let me see your stuff. If it's hopelessly bad I'll tell you so. I won't have you wasting years striving for the unattainable—at least I won't have it on my conscience if you do. If there's any promise in it, I'll tell you so just as honestly. And bring some of your stories, too—*they're* trash yet, that's certain, but I'll see if they show just and sufficient cause for going on."

Emily spent a very solemn hour that evening, weighing, choosing, rejecting. To the little bundle of verse she added one of her Jimmy-books which contained, as she thought, her best stories. She went to school next day, so secret and mysterious that Ilse took offence, started in to call her names—and then stopped. Ilse had promised her father that she would try to break herself of the habit of calling names. She was making fairly good headway and her conversation, if less vivid, was beginning to approximate to New Moon standards.

Emily made a sad mess of her lessons that day. She was nervous and frightened. She had a tremendous respect for Mr Carpenter's opinion. Father Cassidy had told her to keep on—Dean Priest had told her that some day she might really write—but perhaps they were only trying to be encouraging because they liked her and didn't want to hurt her feelings. Emily knew Mr Carpenter would not do this. No matter if he did like her he would nip her aspirations mercilessly if he thought the root of the matter was not in her. If, on the contrary, he bade her God-speed, she would rest content with that against the world and never lose heart in the face of any future criticism. No wonder the day seemed fraught with tremendous issues to Emily.

When school was out Mr Carpenter asked her to remain. She was so white and tense that the other pupils thought she must have been found out by Mr Carpenter in some especially dreadful behaviour and knew she was going to "catch it." Rhoda Stuart flung her a significantly malicious smile from the porch—which Emily never even saw. She was, indeed, at a momentous bar, with Mr Carpenter as supreme judge, and her whole future career—so she believed—hanging on his verdict.

The pupils disappeared and a mellow, sunshiny stillness settled over the old schoolroom. Mr Carpenter took the little packet she had given him in the morning out of his desk, came down the aisle and sat in the seat before her, facing her. Very deliberately he settled his glasses astride his hooked nose, took out her manuscripts and began to read— or rather to glance over them, flinging scraps of comments, mingled with grunts, sniffs and hoots, at her as he glanced. Emily folded her cold hands on her desk and braced her feet against the legs of it to keep her knees from trembling. This was a very terrible experience. She wished she had never given her verses to Mr Carpenter. They were no good—of course they were no good. Remember the editor of the *Enterprise*.

"Humph!" said Mr Carpenter. "*Sunset*—Lord, how many poems have been written on 'Sunset'—

The clouds are massed in splendid state

At heaven's unbarred western gate

Where troops of star-eyed spirits wait—

By gad, what does that mean?"

"I—I—don't know," faltered startled Emily, whose wits had been scattered by the sudden swoop of his spiked glance.

Mr Carpenter snorted.

"For heaven's sake, girl, don't write what you can't understand yourself. And this—*To Life*—'Life, as thy gift I ask no rainbow joy'—is that sincere? Is it, girl? Stop and think. *Do* you ask 'no rainbow joy' of life?"

He transfixed her with another glare. But Emily was beginning to pick herself up a bit. Nevertheless, she suddenly felt oddly ashamed of the very elevated and unselfish desires expressed in that sonnet.

"No—o," she answered reluctantly, "I *do* want rainbow joy—lots of it."

"Of course you do. We all do. We don't get it—you won't get it—but don't be hypocrite enough to pretend you don't want it, even in a sonnet. *Lines to a Mountain Cascade*—'On its dark rocks like the whiteness of a veil around a bride'—Where did you see a mountain cascade in Prince Edward Island?"

"Nowhere—there's a picture of one in Dr Burnley's library."

"A Wood Stream—

The threading sunbeams quiver,

The bending bushes shiver,

O'er the little shadowy river—

There's only one more rhyme that occurs to me and that's 'liver.' Why did you leave it out?"

Emily writhed.

"Wind Song—

279

I have shaken the dew in the meadows

From the clover's creamy gown—

Pretty, but weak. *June*—June, for heaven's sake, girl, don't write poetry on June. It's the sickliest subject in the world. It's been written to death."

"No, June is immortal," cried Emily suddenly, a mutinous sparkle replacing the strained look in her eyes. She was not going to let Mr Carpenter have it all his own way.

But Mr Carpenter had tossed *June* aside without reading a line of it.

"'I weary of the hungry world'—what do you know of the hungry world?—you in your New Moon seclusion of old trees and old maids—but it *is* hungry. *Ode to Winter*—the seasons are a sort of disease all young poets must have, it seems—ha! 'Spring will not forget'—*that's* a good line—the only good line in it. H'm'm—*Wanderings*—

I've heard the secret of the rune

That the somber pines on the hillside croon—

Have you—*have* you learned that secret?"

"I think I've always known it," said Emily dreamily. That flash of unimaginable sweetness that sometimes surprised her had just come and gone. "*Aim and Endeavour*—too didactic—too didactic. You've no right to try to teach until you're old—and then you won't want to—

Her face was like a star all pale and fair—

Were you looking in the glass when you composed that line?"

"No—" indignantly.

"'When the morning light is shaken like a banner on the hill'—a good line—a good line—

Oh, on such a golden morning

To be living is delight—

Too much like a faint echo of Wordsworth. *The Sea in September*—

'blue and austerely bright'—'austerely bright'—child, how can you marry the right adjectives like that? *Morning*—'all the secret fears that haunt the night'—what do *you* know of the fears that haunt the night?"

"I know something," said Emily decidedly, remembering her first night at Wyther Grange.

"*To a Dead Day*—

With the chilly calm on her brow

That only the dead may wear—

Have you even *seen* the chilly calm on the brow of the dead, Emily?"

"Yes," said Emily softly, recalling that grey dawn in the old house in the hollow.

"I thought so—otherwise you couldn't have written *that*—and even as it is—how old are you, jade?"

"Thirteen, last May."

"Humph! *Lines to Mrs George Irving's Infant Son*—you should study the art of titles, Emily—there's a fashion in them as in everything else. Your titles are as out of date as the candles of New Moon—

Soundly he sleeps with his red lips pressed

Like a beautiful blossom close to her breast—

The rest isn't worth reading. *September*—is there a month you've missed?—'Windy meadows harvest-deep'—good line. *Blair Water by Moonlight*—gossamer, Emily, nothing but gossamer. *The Garden of New Moon*—

Beguiling laughter and old song

Of merry maids and men—

Good line—I suppose New Moon *is* full of ghosts. 'Death's fell minion well fulfilled its part'—that might have passed in Addison's day but not now—not now, Emily—

Your azure dimples are the graves

Where million buried sunbeams play—

Atrocious, girl—atrocious. Graves aren't playgrounds. How much would *you* play if you were buried?"

Emily writhed and blushed again. *Why* couldn't she have seen that herself? *Any* goose could have seen it.

"Sail onward, ships—white wings, sail on,

Till past the horizon's purple bar

You drift from sight.—In flush of dawn

Sail on, and 'neath the evening star—

Trash—trash—and yet there's a picture in it—

Lap softly, purple waves. I dream,

And dreams are sweet—I'll wake no more—

Ah, but you'll have to wake if you want to accomplish anything. Girl, you've used *purple* twice in the same poem.

Buttercups in a golden frenzy—

'a golden frenzy'—girl, I *see* the wind shaking the buttercups, From the purple gates of the west I come— You're too fond of purple, Emily."

"It's such a lovely word," said Emily.

"Dreams that seem too bright to die—

Seem but never *are,* Emily—

The luring voice of the echo, fame—

So you've heard it, too? It *is* a lure and for most of us only an echo. And that's the last of the lot."

Mr Carpenter swept the little sheets aside, folded his arms on the desk, and looked over his glasses at Emily.

Emily looked back at him mutely, nervelessly. All the life seemed to have been drained out of her body and concentrated in her eyes.

"Ten good lines out of four hundred, Emily—comparatively good, that is—and all the rest balderdash—balderdash, Emily."

"I—suppose so," said Emily faintly.

Her eyes brimmed with tears—her lips quivered. She could not help it. Pride was hopelessly submerged in the bitterness of her disappointment. She felt exactly like a candle that somebody had blown out.

"What are you crying for?" demanded Mr Carpenter.

Emily blinked away the tears and tried to laugh.

"I—I'm sorry—you think it's no good—" she said.

Mr Carpenter gave the desk a mighty thump.

"No good! Didn't I tell you there were ten good lines? Jade, for ten righteous men Sodom had been spared."

"Do you mean—that—after all—" The candle was being relighted again.

"Of course, I mean. If at thirteen you can write ten good lines, at twenty you'll write ten times ten—if the gods are kind. Stop messing over months, though—and don't imagine you're a genius either, if you *have* written ten decent lines. I think there's *something* trying to speak through you—but you'll have to make yourself a fit instrument for it. You've got to work hard and sacrifice—by gad, girl, you've chosen a jealous goddess. And she never lets her votaries go—even when she shuts her ears for ever to their plea. What have you there?"

Emily, her heart thrilling, handed him her Jimmy-book. She was so happy that it shone through her whole being with a positive radiance. She saw her future, wonderful, brilliant—oh, her goddess would listen to *her*—"Emily B. Starr, the distinguished poet"—"E. Byrd Starr, the rising young novelist."

She was recalled from her enchanting reverie by a chuckle from Mr Carpenter. Emily wondered a little uneasily what he was laughing at. She didn't think there was anything funny in *that* book. It contained only three or four of her latest stories—*The Butterfly Queen,* a little fairy tale; *The Disappointed House,* wherein she had woven a pretty dream of hopes come true after long years; *The Secret of the Glen,* which, in spite of its title, was a fanciful little dialogue between the Spirit of the Snow, the Spirit of the Grey Rain, the Spirit of Mist, and the Spirit of Moonshine.

"So you think I am not beautiful when I say my prayers?" said Mr Carpenter.

Emily gasped—realized what had happened—made a frantic grab at her Jimmy-book—missed it. Mr Carpenter held it up beyond her reach and mocked at her.

She had given him the wrong Jimmy-book! And this one, oh, horrors, what was in it? Or rather, what wasn't in it? Sketches of every one in Blair Water—and a full—a very full—description of Mr Carpenter himself. Intent on describing him exactly, she had been as mercilessly lucid as she always was, especially in regard to the odd faces he made on mornings when he opened the school day with a prayer. Thanks to her dramatic knack of word painting, Mr Carpenter *lived* in that sketch. Emily did not know it, but *he* did—he saw himself as in a glass and the artistry of it pleased him so that he cared for nothing else. Besides, she had drawn his good points quite as clearly as his bad ones. And there were some sentences in it—"He looks as if he knew a great deal that can never be any use to him"—"I think he wears the black coat Mondays because it makes him feel that he hasn't been drunk at all." Who or what had taught the little jade these things? Oh, her goddess would not pass Emily by!

"I'm—sorry," said Emily, crimson with shame all over her dainty paleness.

"Why, I wouldn't have missed this for all the poetry you've written or ever will write! By gad, its literature—*literature*—and you're only thirteen. But you don't know what's ahead of you—the stony hills—the steep ascents—the buffets—the discouragements. Stay in the valley if you're wise. Emily, *why* do you want to write? Give me your reason."

"I want to be famous and rich," said Emily coolly.

"Everybody does. Is that all?"

"No. I just *love* to write."

"A better reason—but not enough—not enough. Tell me this—if you knew you would be poor as a church mouse all your life—if you knew you'd never have a line published—would you still go on writing—*would* you?"

"Of course I would," said Emily disdainfully. "Why, I *have* to write—I can't help it at times—I've just *got* to."

"Oh—then I'd waste my breath giving advice at all. If it's *in* you to climb you must—there are those who *must* lift their eyes to the hills— they can't breathe properly in the valleys. God help them if there's some weakness in them that prevents their climbing. You don't understand a word I'm saying—yet. But go on—climb! There, take your book and go home. Thirty years from now I will have a claim to distinction in the fact that Emily Byrd Starr was once a pupil of mine. Go—go—before I remember what a disrespectful baggage you are to write such stuff about me and be properly enraged."

Emily went, still a bit scared but oddly exultant behind her fright. She was so happy that her happiness seemed to irradiate the world with its own splendour. All the sweet sounds of nature around her seemed like the broken words of her own delight. Mr Carpenter watched her out of sight from the old worn threshold.

"Wind—and flame—and sea!" he muttered. "Nature is always taking us by surprise. This child has—what I have never had and would have made any sacrifice to have. But 'the gods don't allow us to be in their debt'—she will pay for it—she will pay."

At sunset Emily sat in the lookout room. It was flooded with soft splendour. Outside, in sky and trees, were delicate tintings and aerial sounds. Down in the garden Daffy was chasing dead leaves along the red walks. The sight of his sleek, striped sides, the grace of his movements, gave her pleasure—as did the beautiful, even, glossy furrows of the ploughed fields beyond the lane, and the first faint white star in the crystal-green sky.

The wind of the autumn night was blowing trumpets of fairyland on the hills; and over in Lofty John's bush was laughter—like the laughter of fauns. Ilse and Perry and Teddy were waiting there for her—they had made a tryst for a twilight romp. She would go to them—presently— not yet. She was so full of rapture that she must write it out before she went back from her world of dreams to the world of reality. Once she would have poured it into a letter to her father. She could no longer do that. But on the table before her lay a brand-new Jimmy-book. She pulled it towards her, took up her pen, and on its first virgin page she wrote,

New moon,

Blair water,

P. E. island.

October 8th.
I am going to write a diary, that it may be published when I die.

THE END

EMILY CLIMBS

WRITING HERSELF OUT

Emily Byrd Starr was alone in her room, in the old New Moon farmhouse at Blair Water, one stormy night in a February of the olden years before the world turned upside down. She was at that moment as perfectly happy as any human being is ever permitted to be. Aunt Elizabeth, in consideration of the coldness of the night, had allowed her to have a fire in her little fireplace—a rare favour. It was burning brightly and showering a red-golden light over the small, immaculate room, with its old-time furniture and deep-set, wide-silled windows, to whose frosted, blue-white panes the snowflakes clung in little wreaths. It lent depth and mystery to the mirror on the wall which reflected Emily as she sat coiled on the ottoman before the fire, writing, by the light of two tall, white candles—which were the only approved means of illumination at New Moon—in a brand-new, glossy, black "Jimmy-book" which Cousin Jimmy had given her that day. Emily had been very glad to get it, for she had filled the one he had given her the preceding autumn, and for over a week she had suffered acute pangs of suppression because she could not write in a nonexistent "diary."

Her diary had become a dominant factor in her young, vivid life. It had taken the place of certain "letters" she had written in her childhood to her dead father, in which she had been wont to "write out" her problems and worries—for even in the magic years when one is almost fourteen one has problems and worries, especially when one is under the strict and well-meant but not over-tender governance of an Aunt Elizabeth Murray. Sometimes Emily felt that if it were not for her diary she would have flown into little bits by reason of consuming her own smoke. The fat, black "Jimmy-book" seemed to her like a

287

personal friend and a safe confidant for certain matters which burned for expression and yet were too combustible to be trusted to the ears of any living being. Now blank books of any sort were not easy to come by at New Moon, and if it had not been for Cousin Jimmy, Emily might never have had one. Certainly Aunt Elizabeth would not give her one—Aunt Elizabeth thought Emily wasted far too much time "over her scribbling nonsense" as it was—and Aunt Laura did not dare to go contrary to Aunt Elizabeth in this—more by token that Laura herself really thought Emily might be better employed. Aunt Laura was a jewel of a woman, but certain things were holden from her eyes.

Now Cousin Jimmy was never in the least frightened of Aunt Elizabeth, and when the notion occurred to him that Emily probably wanted another "blank book," that blank book materialized straightway, in defiance of Aunt Elizabeth's scornful glances. He had gone to Shrewsbury that very day, in the teeth of the rising storm, for no other reason than to get it. So Emily was happy, in her subtle and friendly firelight, while the wind howled and shrieked through the great old trees to the north of New Moon, sent huge, spectral wreaths of snow whirling across Cousin Jimmy's famous garden, drifted the sundial completely over, and whistled eerily through the Three Princesses—as Emily always called the three tall Lombardies in the corner of the garden.

"I love a storm like this at night when I don't have to go out in it," wrote Emily. "Cousin Jimmy and I had a splendid evening planning out our garden and choosing our seeds and plants in the catalogue. Just where the biggest drift is making, behind the summer-house, we are going to have a bed of pink asters, and we are going to give the Golden Ones—who are dreaming under four feet of snow—a background of flowering almond. I love to plan out summer days like this, in the midst of a storm. It makes me feel as if I were winning a victory over something ever so much bigger than myself, just because *I* have a brain and the storm is nothing but blind, white force—terrible, but blind. I have the same feeling when I sit here cosily by my own dear fire, and hear it raging all around me, and *laugh* at it. And *that* is just because over a hundred years ago great-great-grandfather Murray built this house and built it well. I wonder if, a hundred years from now, anybody will win a victory over anything because of something *I* left or did. It is an *inspiring thought.*

"I drew that line of italics before I thought. Mr. Carpenter says I use far too many italics. He says it is an Early Victorian obsession, and I must strive to cast it off. I concluded I would when I looked in the dictionary, for it is evidently not a nice thing to be obsessed, though it doesn't seem quite so bad as to be *possessed*. There I go again: but I think the italics are all right this time.

"I read the dictionary for a whole hour—till Aunt Elizabeth got suspicious and suggested that it would be much better for me to be knitting my ribbed stockings. She couldn't see exactly why it was wrong for me to be poring over the dictionary but she felt sure it must be because *she* never wants to do it. I *love* reading the dictionary. (Yes, those italics are *necessary*, Mr. Carpenter. An ordinary 'love' wouldn't express my feeling at all!) Words are such *fas*cinating things. (I caught myself at the first syllable that time!) The very sound of some of them—'haunted'—'mystic'—for example, gives me *the flash*. (Oh, dear! But I *have* to italicize *the flash*. *It* isn't ordinary—it's the most extraordinary and wonderful thing in my whole life. When it comes I feel as if a door had swung open in a wall before me and given me a glimpse of—yes, of *heaven*. *More italics!* Oh, I see why Mr, Carpenter scolds! I *must* break myself of the habit.)

"Big words are never beautiful—'incriminating'—'obstreperous'—'international'—'unconstitutional.' They make me think of those horrible big dahlias and chrysanthemums Cousin Jimmy took me to see at the exhibition in Charlottetown last fall. We couldn't see anything lovely in them, though some people thought them wonderful. Cousin Jimmy's little yellow 'mums, like pale, fairy-like stars shining against the fir copse in the north-west corner of the garden, were ten times more beautiful. But I am wandering from my subject—also a bad habit of mine, according to Mr. Carpenter. He says I *must* (the italics are his this time!) learn to concentrate—another big word and a very ugly one.

"But I had a good time over that dictionary—much better than I had over the ribbed stockings. I wish I could have a pair—just one pair—of silk stockings. Ilse has three. Her father gives her everything she wants, now that he has learned to love her. But Aunt Elizabeth says silk stockings are *immoral*. I wonder why—any more than silk dresses.

"Speaking of silk dresses, Aunt Janey Milburn, at Derry Pond—she isn't any relation really, but everybody calls her that—has made a vow that she will never wear a silk dress until the whole heathen world is converted to Christianity. That is very fine. I wish *I* could be as good as that, but I couldn't—I love silk too much. It is so rich and sheeny. I would like to dress in it all the time, and if I could afford to I would—though I suppose every time I thought of dear old Aunt Janey and the unconverted heathen I would feel conscience-stricken. However, it will be years, if ever, before I can afford to buy even one silk dress, and meanwhile I give some of my egg money every month to missions. (I have five hens of my own now, all descended from the gray pullet Perry gave me on my twelfth birthday.) If ever I can buy that one silk dress I know what it is going to be like. Not black or brown or navy blue—sensible, serviceable colours, such as New Moon Murrays always wear—oh, dear, no! It is to be of shot silk, blue in one light, silver in others, like a twilight sky, glimpsed through a frosted window-pane—with a bit of lace-foam here and there, like those little feathers of snow clinging to my window-pane. Teddy says he will paint me in it and call it 'The Ice Maiden,' and Aunt Laura smiles and says, sweetly and condescendingly, in a way I hate even in dear Aunt Laura,

"'What use would such a dress be to you, Emily?'

"It mightn't be of any use, but I would feel it as if it were a part of me—that it *grew* on me and wasn't just bought and put on. I want *one* dress like that in my life-time. And a silk petticoat underneath it—and silk stockings!

"Ilse has a silk dress now—a bright pink one. Aunt Elizabeth says Dr. Burnley dresses Ilse far too old and rich for a child. But he wants to make up for all the years he didn't dress her at all. (I don't mean she went naked, but she might have as far as Dr. Burnley was concerned. Other people had to see to her clothes.) He does everything she wants him to do now, and gives her her own way in everything. Aunt Elizabeth says it is very bad for her, but there are times when I envy Ilse a little. I know it is wicked, but I cannot help it.

"Dr. Burnley is going to send Ilse to Shrewsbury High School next fall, and after that to Montreal to study elocution. That is why I envy her—not because of the silk dress. I wish Aunt Elizabeth would let me go to Shrewsbury, but I fear she never will. She feels she can't trust me out of her sight because my mother eloped. But she need not be afraid I will ever elope. I have made up my mind that I will never marry. I shall be *wedded to my art.*

"Teddy wants to go to Shrewsbury next fall, but his mother won't let him go, either. Not that she is afraid of his eloping, but because she loves him so much she can't part with him. Teddy wants to be an artist, and Mr. Carpenter says he has genius and should have his chance, but everybody is afraid to say anything to Mrs. Kent. She is a little bit of a woman—no taller than I am, really, quiet and shy—and yet every one is afraid of her. *I* am—dreadfully afraid. I've always known she didn't like me—ever since those days long ago when Ilse and I first went up to the Tansy Patch, to play with Teddy. But now she hates me—I feel sure of it—just because Teddy likes me. She can't bear to have him like anybody or anything but her. She is even jealous of his pictures. So there is not much chance of his getting to Shrewsbury. Perry is going. He hasn't a cent, but he is going to work his way through. That is why he thinks he will go to Shrewsbury in place of Queen's Academy. He thinks it will be easier to get work to do in Shrewsbury, and board is cheaper there.

"'My old beast of an Aunt Tom has a little money,' he told me, 'but she won't give me any of it—unless—unless—'

"Then he looked at me *significantly*.

"I blushed because I couldn't help it, and then I was furious with myself for blushing, and with Perry—because he referred to something I didn't want to hear about—that time ever so long ago when his Aunt Tom met me in Lofty John's bush and nearly frightened me to death by demanding that I promise to *marry Perry when we grew up*, in which case she would educate him. I never told anybody about it—being ashamed—except Ilse, and she said,

"'The idea of old Aunt Tom aspiring to a Murray for Perry!'

"But then, Ilse is awfully hard on Perry and quarrels with him half the time, over things *I* only smile at. Perry never likes to be outdone by anyone in anything. When we were at Amy Moore's party last week, her uncle told us a story of some remarkable freak calf he had seen, with three legs, and Perry said,

"'Oh, *that's* nothing to a duck I saw once in Norway.'

"(Perry really was in Norway. He used to sail everywhere with his father when he was little. But I don't believe one word about that duck. He wasn't *lying*—he was just *romancing*. Dear Mr. Carpenter, I *can't* get along without italics.)

"Perry's duck had four legs, according to him—two where a proper duck's legs should be, and two sprouting from its back. And when it got tired of walking on its ordinary pair it flopped over on its back and walked on the other pair!

"Perry told this yarn with a sober face, and everybody laughed, and Amy's uncle said, 'Go up head, Perry.' But Ilse was furious and wouldn't speak to him all the way home. She said he had made a fool of himself, trying to 'show off' with a silly story like that, and that *no gentleman* would act so.

"Perry said: 'I'm no gentleman, yet, only a hired boy, but some day, Miss Ilse, I'll be a finer gentleman than anyone *you* know.'

"'Gentlemen,' said Ilse in a nasty voice, 'have to be *born*. They can't be *made*, you know.'

"Ilse has almost given up calling names, as she used to do when she quarrelled with Perry or me, and taken to saying cruel, cutting things. They hurt far worse than the names used to, but I don't really mind them—much—or long—because I know Ilse doesn't mean them and really loves me as much as I love her. But Perry says they stick in his crop. They didn't speak to each other the rest of the way home, but next day Ilse was at him again about using bad grammar and not standing up when a lady enters the room.

"'Of course you couldn't be expected to know *that*,' she said in her nastiest voice, 'but I am sure Mr. Carpenter has done his best to teach you grammar.'

"Perry didn't say one word to Ilse, but he turned to me.

"'Will *you* tell me my faults?' he said. 'I don't mind *you* doing it—it will be *you* that will have to put up with me when we're grown up, not Ilse.'

"He said that to make Ilse angry, but it made me angrier still, for it was an allusion to a *forbidden topic*. So we neither of us spoke to him for two days and he said it was a good rest from Ilse's slams anyway.

"Perry is not the only one who gets into disgrace at New Moon. I said something silly yesterday evening which makes me blush to recall it. The Ladies' Aid met here and Aunt Elizabeth gave them a supper and the husbands of the Aid came to it. Ilse and I waited on the table, which was set in the kitchen because the dining-room table wasn't long enough. It was exciting at first and then, when every one was served, it was a little dull and I began to compose some poetry in my mind as I stood by the window looking out on the garden. It was so interesting that I soon forgot everything else until suddenly I heard Aunt Elizabeth say, 'Emily,' very sharply, and then she looked significantly at Mr. Johnson, our new minister. I was confused and I snatched up the teapot and exclaimed,

"'Oh, Mr. *Cup,* will you have your *Johnson* filled?'

"Everybody roared and Aunt Elizabeth looked disgusted and Aunt Laura ashamed, and I felt as if I would sink through the floor. I couldn't sleep half the night for thinking over it. The strange thing was that I do believe I felt worse and more ashamed than I would have felt if I had done something really wrong. This is the 'Murray pride' of course, and I suppose it is very wicked. Sometimes I am afraid Aunt Ruth Dutton is right in her opinion of me after all.

"No, she isn't!

"But it is a tradition of New Moon that its women should be equal to any situation and always be graceful and dignified. Now, there was nothing graceful or dignified in asking such a question of the new minister. I am sure he will never see me again without thinking of it and I will always writhe when I catch his eye upon me.

"But now that I have written it out in my diary I don't feel so badly over it. *Nothing* ever seems as big or as terrible—oh, nor as beautiful and grand, either, alas!—when it is written out, as it does when you are thinking or feeling about it. It seems to *shrink* directly you put it into words. Even the line of poetry I had made just before I asked that absurd question won't seem half as fine when I write it down:

"Where the velvet feet of darkness softly go.

"It *doesn't.* Some bloom seems gone from it. And yet, while I was standing there, behind all those chattering, eating people, and *saw* darkness stealing so softly over the garden and the hills, like a beautiful woman robed in shadows, with stars for eyes, the *flash* came and I forgot everything but that I wanted to put something of the beauty I felt into the words of my poem. When that line came into my mind it didn't seem to me that *I* composed it at all—it seemed as if *Something Else* were trying to speak through me—and it was that *Something Else* that made the line seem wonderful—and now when it is gone the words seem flat and foolish and the picture I tried to draw in them not so wonderful after all.

"Oh, if I could only put things into words as I *see* them! Mr. Carpenter says, 'Strive—strive—keep on—words are your medium—make them your slaves—until they will say for you what you want

293

them to say.' That is true—and I do try—but it seems to me there is something *beyond* words—any words—all words—something that always escapes you when you try to grasp it—and yet leaves something in your hand which you wouldn't have had if you hadn't reached for it.

"I remember one day last fall when Dean and I walked over the Delectable Mountain to the woods beyond it—fir woods mostly, but with one corner of splendid old pines. We sat under them and Dean read *Peveril of the Peak* and some of Scott's poems to me; and then he looked up into the big, plumy boughs and said,

"'The gods are talking in the pines—gods of the old northland—of the viking sagas. Star, do you know Emerson's lines?'

"And then he quoted them—I've remembered and loved them ever since.

"The gods talk in the breath of the wold,

They talk in the shaken pine,

And they fill the reach of the old seashore

With dialogue divine;

And the poet who overhears

One random word they say

Is the fated man of men

Whom the ages must obey.

"Oh, that 'random word'—that is the *Something* that escapes me. I'm always listening for it—I know I can never hear it—my ear isn't attuned to it—but I am sure I hear at times a little, faint, far-off echo of it—and it makes me feel a delight that is like pain and a despair of ever being able to translate its beauty into any words I know.

"Still, it *is* a pity I made such a goose of myself immediately after that wonderful experience.

"If I had just floated up behind Mr. Johnson, as velvet-footedly as darkness herself, and poured his tea gracefully from Great-grandmother Murray's silver teapot, like my shadow-woman pouring night into the white cup of Blair Valley, Aunt Elizabeth would be far better pleased with me than if I could write the most wonderful poem in the world.

"Cousin Jimmy is so different. I recited my poem to him this evening after we had finished with the catalogue and he thought it was beautiful. *(He* couldn't know how far it fell short of what I had seen in my mind.) Cousin Jimmy composes poetry himself. He is very clever in spots. And in other spots, where his brain was hurt when Aunt Elizabeth pushed him into our New Moon well, he isn't *anything.* There's just *blankness* there. So people call him simple, and Aunt Ruth dares to say he hasn't sense enough to shoo a cat from cream. And yet if you put all his clever spots together there isn't anybody in Blair Water has half as much real cleverness as he has—not even Mr. Carpenter. The trouble is you can't put his clever spots together—there are always those gaps between. But I love Cousin Jimmy and I'm never in the least afraid of him when his queer spells come on him. Everybody else is—even Aunt Elizabeth, though perhaps it is remorse with her, instead of fear—except Perry. Perry always brags that he is never afraid of anything—doesn't know what fear is. I think that is very wonderful. I wish I could be so fearless. Mr. Carpenter says fear is a vile thing, and is at the bottom of almost every wrong and hatred of the world.

"'Cast it out, Jade,' he says—'cast it out of your heart. Fear is a confession of weakness. What you fear is stronger than you, or you think it is, else you wouldn't be afraid of it. Remember your Emerson—"always do what you are afraid to do."'

"But that is a counsel of perfection, as Dean says, and I don't believe I'll ever be able to attain to it. To be honest, I am afraid of a good many *things,* but there are only two people in the world I'm truly afraid of. One is Mrs. Kent, and the other is Mad Mr. Morrison. I'm terribly afraid of him and I think almost every one is. His home is in Derry Pond, but he hardly ever stays there—he roams over the country looking for his lost bride. He was married only a few weeks when his young wife died, many years ago, and he has never been right in his mind since. He insists she is not dead, only lost, and that he will find her some time. He has grown old and bent, looking for her, but to him she is still young and fair.

"He was here one day last summer, but would not come in—just peered into the kitchen wistfully and said, 'Is Annie here?' He was quite gentle that day, but sometimes he is very wild and violent. He declares he always hears Annie calling to him—that her voice flits on before him—always before him, like my random word. His face is wrinkled and shrivelled and he looks like an old, old monkey. But the thing I hate most about him is his right hand—it is a deep blood-red all over—birth-marked. I can't tell why, but that hand fills me with horror. I could not bear to touch it. And sometimes he laughs to himself very horribly. The only living thing he seems to care for is his old black dog that always is with him. They say he will never ask for a bite of food for himself. If people do not offer it to him he goes hungry, but he will beg for his dog.

"Oh, I am terribly afraid of him, and I was so glad he didn't come into the house that day. Aunt Elizabeth looked after him, as he went away with his long, gray hair streaming in the wind, and said,

"'Fairfax Morrison was once a fine, clever, young man, with excellent prospects. Well, God's ways are very mysterious.'

"'That is why they are interesting,' I said.

"But Aunt Elizabeth frowned and told me not to be irreverent, as she always does when I say anything about God. I wonder why. She won't let Perry and me talk about Him, either, though Perry is really very much interested in Him and wants to find out all about Him. Aunt Elizabeth overheard me telling Perry one Sunday afternoon what I thought God was like, and she said it was scandalous.

"It wasn't! The trouble is, Aunt Elizabeth and I have different Gods, that is all. Everybody has a different God, I think. Aunt Ruth's, for instance, is one that punishes her enemies—sends 'judgments' on them. That seems to me to be about all the use He really is to her. Jim Cosgrain uses his to swear by. But Aunt Janey Milburn walks in the light of her God's countenance, every day, and shines with it.

"I have written myself out for to-night, and am going to bed. I know I have 'wasted words' in this diary—another of my literary faults, according to Mr. Carpenter.

"'You waste words, Jade—you spill them about too lavishly. Economy and restraint—that's what you need.

"He's right, of course, and in my essays and stories I try to practise what he preaches. But in my diary, which nobody sees but myself, or ever will see until after I'm dead, I like just to let myself go."

****

Emily looked at her candle—it, too, was almost burned out. She knew she could not have another that night—Aunt Elizabeth's rules were as those of Mede and Persian: she put away her diary in the little right-hand cupboard above the mantel, covered her dying fire, undressed and blew out her candle. The room slowly filled with the faint, ghostly snow-light of a night when a full moon is behind the driving storm-clouds. And just as Emily was ready to slip into her high black bedstead a sudden inspiration came—a splendid new idea for a story. For a minute she shivered reluctantly: the room was getting cold. But the idea would not be denied. Emily slipped her hand between the feather tick of her bed and the chaff mattress and produced a half-burned candle, secreted there for just such an emergency.

It was not, of course, a proper thing to do. But then I have never pretended, nor ever will pretend, that Emily was a proper child. Books are not written about proper children. They would be so dull nobody would read them.

She lighted her candle, put on her stockings and a heavy coat, got out another half-filled Jimmy-book, and began to write by the single, uncertain candle which made a pale oasis of light in the shadows of the room. In that oasis Emily wrote, her black head bent over her book, as the hours of night crept away and the other occupants of New Moon slumbered soundly; she grew chill and cramped, but she was quite unconscious of it. Her eyes burned—her cheeks glowed—words came like troops of obedient genii to the call of her pen. When at last her candle went out with a splutter and a hiss in its little pool of melted tallow, she came back to reality with a sigh and a shiver. It was two, by the clock, and she was very tired and very cold; but she had finished her story and it was the best she had ever written. She crept into her cold nest with a sense of completion and victory, born of the working out of her creative impulse, and fell asleep to the lullaby of the waning storm.

SALAD DAYS

This book is not going to be wholly, or even mainly, made up of extracts from Emily's diary; but, by way of linking up matters unimportant enough for a chapter in themselves, and yet necessary for a proper understanding of her personality and environment, I am going to include some more of them. Besides, when one has material ready to hand, why not use it? Emily's "diary," with all its youthful crudities and italics, really gives a better interpretation of her and of her imaginative and introspective mind, in that, her fourteenth spring, than any biographer, however sympathetic, could do. So let us take another peep into the yellowed pages of that old "Jimmy-book," written long ago in the "look-out" of New Moon.

****

"February 15, 19—

"I have decided that I will write down, in this journal, every day, all my good deeds and all my bad ones. I got the idea out of a book, and it appeals to me. I mean to be as honest about it as I can. It will be easy, of course, to write down the good deeds, but not so easy to record the bad ones.

"I did only one bad thing to-day—only one thing I think bad, that is. I was impertinent to Aunt Elizabeth. She thought I took too long washing the dishes. I didn't suppose there was any hurry and I was composing a story called *The Secret of the Mill*. Aunt Elizabeth looked at me and then at the clock, and said in her most disagreeable way,

"'Is the snail your sister, Emily?'

"'No! Snails are no relation to *me*,' I said *haughtily*.

"It was not what I said, but the way I said it that was impertinent. *And I meant it to be*. I was very angry—sarcastic speeches always aggravate me. Afterwards I was very sorry that I had been in a temper—but I was sorry because it was *foolish* and *undignified*, not because it was *wicked*.

298

So I suppose that was not true repentance.

"As for my good deeds, I did two to-day. I saved two little lives. Saucy Sal had caught a poor snowbird and I took it from her. It flew off quite briskly, and I am sure it felt wonderfully happy. Later on I went down to the cellar cupboard and found a mouse caught in a trap by its foot. The poor thing lay there, almost exhausted from struggling, with *such* a look in its black eyes. I *couldn't* endure it so I set it free, and it managed to get away quite smartly in spite of its foot. I do not feel *sure* about *this* deed. I know it was a good one from the mouse's point of view, but what about Aunt Elizabeth's?

"This evening Aunt Laura and Aunt Elizabeth read and burned a boxful of old letters. They read them aloud and commented on them, while I sat in a corner and knitted my stockings. The letters were very interesting and I learned a great deal about the Murrays I had never known before. I feel that it is quite wonderful to belong to a family like this. No wonder the Blair Water folks call us 'the Chosen People'— though *they* don't mean it as a compliment. I feel that I must live up to the traditions of my family.

"I had a long letter from Dean Priest to-day. He is spending the winter in Algiers. He says he is coming home in April and is going to take rooms with his sister, Mrs. Fred Evans, for the summer. I am so glad. It will be splendid to have him in Blair Water all summer. Nobody ever talks to me as Dean does. He is the nicest and most interesting old person I know. Aunt Elizabeth says he is selfish, as all the Priests are. But then she does not like the Priests. And she always calls him Jarback, which somehow sets my teeth on edge. One of Dean's shoulders *is* a little higher than the other, but that is not his fault. I told Aunt Elizabeth once that I wished she would not call my friend that, but she only said,

"'*I* did not nickname *your friend,* Emily. His own clan have always called him Jarback. The Priests are not noted for delicacy!"

"Teddy had a letter from Dean, too, and a book—*The Lives of Great Artists*—Michael Angelo, Raphael, Velasquez, Rembrandt, Titian. He says he dare not let his mother see him reading it—she would burn it. I am sure if Teddy could only have his chance he would be as great an artist as any of them.

****

"February 18, 19—

"I had a lovely time with myself this evening, after school, walking on the brook road in Lofty John's bush. The sun was low and creamy and the snow so white and the shadows so slender and blue. I think there is nothing so beautiful as tree shadows. And when I came out into the garden my own shadow looked so funny—so long that it stretched right across the garden. I immediately made a poem of which two lines were,

"If we were as tall as our shadows

How tall our shadows would be.

"I think there is a good deal of *philosophy* in that.

"To-night I wrote a story and Aunt Elizabeth knew what I was doing and was very much annoyed. She scolded me for wasting time. But it *wasn't* wasted time. I *grew* in it—I know I did. And there was something about some of the sentences I liked. '*I am afraid of the grey wood*'—that pleased me very much. And—'white and stately she walked the dark wood like a moonbeam.' I think that is rather fine. Yet Mr. Carpenter tells me that whenever I think a thing especially fine I am to cut it out. But oh, I *can't* cut that out—not yet, at least. The strange part is that about three months after Mr. Carpenter tells me to cut a thing out I come round to his point of view and feel ashamed of it. Mr. Carpenter was quite merciless over my essay to-day. Nothing about it suited him.

"'Three *alas's* in one paragraph, Emily. One would have been too many in this year of grace!' '*More irresistible*—Emily, for heaven's sake, write English! That is unpardonable.'

"It *was*, too. I saw it for myself and I felt shame going all over me from head to foot like a red wave. Then, after Mr. Carpenter had blue-pencilled almost every sentence and sneered at all my fine phrases and found fault with most of my constructions and told me I was too fond of putting 'cleverisms' into everything I wrote, he flung my exercise book down, tore at his hair and said,

"'You write! Jade, get a spoon and learn to cook!'

"Then he strode off, muttering maledictions 'not loud but deep.' I picked up my poor essay and didn't feel very badly. I *can* cook already, and I have learned a thing or two about Mr. Carpenter. The better my essays are the more he rages over them. This one must have been quite good. But it makes him so angry and impatient to see where I might have made it *still better* and didn't—through carelessness or laziness or indifference—as he thinks. And he can't tolerate a person who *could* do better and doesn't. And he wouldn't bother with me at all if he didn't think I may amount to something by and by.

"Aunt Elizabeth does not approve of Mr. Johnson. She thinks his theology is not sound. He said in his sermon last Sunday that there was some good in Buddhism.

"'He will be saying that there is some good in Popery next,' said Aunt Elizabeth indignantly at the dinner-table.

"There *may* be some good in Buddhism. I must ask Dean about it when he comes home.

****

"March 2, 19—

"We were all at a funeral to-day—old Mrs. Sarah Paul. I have always liked going to funerals. When I said that, Aunt Elizabeth looked shocked and Aunt Laura said, 'Oh, Emily *dear!*' I rather like to shock Aunt Elizabeth, but I never feel comfortable if I worry Aunt Laura—she's *such* a darling—so I explained—or tried to. It is sometimes very hard to explain things to Aunt Elizabeth.

"'Funerals are interesting,' I said. 'And humorous, too.'

"I think I only made matters worse by saying *that*. And yet Aunt Elizabeth knew as well as I did that it was funny to see some of those relatives of Mrs. Paul, who have fought with and hated her for years—she *wasn't* amiable, if she is dead!—sitting there, holding their handkerchiefs to their faces and pretending to cry. I knew quite well what each and every one was thinking in his heart. Jake Paul was wondering if the old harridan had by any chance left him anything in her will—and Alice Paul, who knew *she* wouldn't get anything, was hoping Jake Paul wouldn't either. That would satisfy *her*. And Mrs. Charles Paul was wondering how soon it would be decent to do the house over the way she had always wanted it and Mrs. Paul *hadn't*. And Aunty Min was worrying for fear there wouldn't be enough baked meats for such a mob of fourth cousins that they'd never expected and didn't want, and Lisette Paul was counting the people and feeling vexed because there wasn't as large an attendance as there was at Mrs. Henry Lister's funeral last week. When I told Aunt Laura this, she said gravely,

"'All this may be true, Emily'—(she knew it was!)—'but somehow it doesn't seem quite right for so young a girl as you, to—to—to be able to see these things, in short.'

"However, I can't help seeing them. Darling Aunt Laura is always so sorry for people that she can't see their humorous side. But I saw other things too. I saw that little Zack Fritz, whom Mrs. Paul adopted and was very kind to, was almost broken-hearted, and I saw that Martha Paul was feeling sorry and ashamed to think of her bitter old quarrel with Mrs. Paul—and I saw that Mrs. Paul's face, that looked so discontented and thwarted in life, looked peaceful and majestic and even beautiful—as if Death had *satisfied* her at last.

"Yes, funerals *are* interesting.

****

"March 5, 19—

"It is snowing a little to-night. I love to see the snow coming down in slanting lines against the dark trees.

"I *think* I did a good deed to-day. Jason Merrowby was here helping Cousin Jimmy saw wood—and I *saw him sneak into the pighouse, and take a swig from a whisky bottle.* But I did not say one word about it to anyone—that is my good deed.

"Perhaps I *ought* to tell Aunt Elizabeth, but if I did she would never have him again, and he needs all the work he can get, for his poor wife's and children's sakes. I find it is not always easy to be sure whether your deeds are good or bad.

****

"March 20, 19—

"Yesterday Aunt Elizabeth was very angry because I would not write an 'obituary poem' for old Peter DeGeer who died last week. Mrs. DeGeer came here and asked me to do it. I wouldn't—I felt very indignant at such a request. I felt it would be *a desecration of my art* to do such a thing—though of course I didn't say that to Mrs. DeGeer. For one thing it would have hurt her feelings, and for another she wouldn't have had the faintest idea what I meant. Even Aunt Elizabeth hadn't when I told her my reasons for refusing, after Mrs. DeGeer had gone.

"'You are always writing yards of trash that nobody wants,' she said. 'I think you might write something that *is* wanted. It would have pleased poor old Mary DeGeer. "Desecration of your art" indeed. If you *must* talk, Emily, why not talk sense?'

"I proceeded to talk sense.

"'Aunt Elizabeth,' I said seriously, 'how could I write that obituary poem for her? I couldn't write an *untruthful* one to please anybody. And you know yourself that nothing good *and* truthful could be said about old Peter DeGeer!'

"Aunt Elizabeth did know it, and it posed her, but she was all the more displeased with me for that. She vexed me so much that I came up to my room and wrote an 'obituary poem' about Peter, just for my own satisfaction. It is certainly great fun to write a *truthful* obituary of some one you don't like. Not that I *disliked* Peter DeGeer; I just despised him as everybody did. But Aunt Elizabeth had annoyed me, and when I am annoyed I can write very sarcastically. And again I felt that *Something* was writing through me—but a very different *Something* from the usual one—a malicious, mocking *Something* that *enjoyed* making fun of poor, lazy, shiftless, lying, silly, hypocritical, old Peter DeGeer. Ideas—words—rhymes—all seemed to drop into place while that *Something* chuckled.

"I thought the poem was so clever that I couldn't resist the temptation to take it to school to-day and show it to Mr Carpenter. I thought he would enjoy it—and I think he *did,* too, in a way, but after he had read it he laid it down and looked at me.

"'I suppose there *is* a pleasure in satirizing a failure,' he said. 'Poor old Peter was a failure—and he is dead—and His Maker may be merciful to him, but his fellow creatures will not. When *I* am dead, Emily, will you write like this about me? You have the power—oh, yes, it's all here—this *is* very clever. You can paint the weakness and foolishness and wickedness of a character in a way that is positively uncanny, in a girl of your age. But—is it worth while, Emily?'

"'No—no,' I said. I was so ashamed and sorry that I wanted to get away and cry. It was terrible to think Mr. Carpenter imagined I would ever write so about *him,* after all he has done for me.

"'It isn't,' said Mr. Carpenter. 'There is a place for satire—there are gangrenes that can only be burned out—but leave the burning to the great geniuses. It's better to heal than hurt. We failures know that.'

"'Oh, Mr. Carpenter!' I began. I wanted to say *he* wasn't a failure—I wanted to say a hundred things—but he wouldn't let me.

"'There—there, we won't talk of it, Emily. When *I* am dead say, "He was a failure, and none knew it more truly or felt it more bitterly than himself." Be merciful to the failures, Emily. Satirize wickedness if you must—but pity weakness.'

"He stalked off then, and called school in. I've felt wretched ever since and I won't sleep to-night. But here and now I record this vow, most solemnly, in my diary, *My pen shall heal, not hurt.* And I write it in italics, Early Victorian or not, because I am tremendously in earnest.

"I didn't tear that poem up, though—I couldn't—it really *was* too good to destroy. I put it away in my literary cupboard to read over once in a while for my own enjoyment, but I will never show it to anybody.

"Oh, how I wish I hadn't hurt Mr. Carpenter!

****

"April 1, 19—

"Something I heard a visitor in Blair Water say today annoyed me very much. Mr. and Mrs. Alec Sawyer, who live in Charlottetown, were in the post office when I was there. Mrs. Sawyer is very handsome and fashionable and condescending. I heard her say to her husband, '*How* do the natives of this sleepy place continue to live here year in and year out? *I* should go mad. *Nothing* ever happens here.'

"I would dearly have liked to tell her a few things about Blair Water. I could have been sarcastic with a vengeance. But, of course, New Moon people *do not make scenes in public.* So I contented myself with bowing *very coldly* when she spoke to me and *sweeping past* her. I heard Mr. Sawyer say, 'Who is that girl?' and Mrs. Sawyer said, 'She must be that Starr puss—she has the Murray trick of holding her head, all right.'

"The idea of saying 'nothing ever happens here'! Why, things are happening right along—*thrilling* things. I think life here is *extremely* wonderful. We have always so much to laugh and cry and talk about.

"Look at all the things that have happened in Blair Water in just the last three weeks—comedy and tragedy all mixed up together. James Baxter has suddenly stopped speaking to his wife and *nobody knows why. She* doesn't, poor soul, and she is breaking her heart about it. Old Adam Gillian, who hated pretence of any sort, died two weeks ago and his last words were, 'See that there isn't any howling and sniffling at my funeral.' So nobody howled or sniffled. Nobody wanted to, and since he had forbidden it nobody pretended to. There never was such a cheerful funeral in Blair Water. I've seen weddings that were more melancholy—Ella Brice's, for instance. What cast a cloud over hers was that she forgot to put on her white slippers when she dressed, and went down to the parlour in a pair of old, faded, bedroom shoes with holes in the toes. Really, people couldn't have talked more about it if she had gone down without *anything* on. Poor Ella cried all through the wedding-supper about it.

"Old Robert Scobie and his half-sister have quarrelled, after living together for thirty years without a fuss, although she is said to be a very aggravating woman. Nothing she did or said ever provoked Robert into an outburst, but it seems that there was just one doughnut left from supper one evening recently, and Robert is very fond of doughnuts. He put it away in the pantry for a bedtime snack, and when he went to get it he found that Matilda had eaten it. He went into a terrible rage, pulled her nose, called her a *she-deviless,* and ordered her out of his house. She has gone to live with her sister at Derry Pond, and Robert is going to bach it. Neither of them will ever forgive the other, Scobie-like, and neither will ever be happy or contented again.

"George Lake was walking home from Derry Pond one moonlit evening two weeks ago, and *all at once* he saw another *very black* shadow going along beside his, on the moonlit snow.

"And there was nothing to cast that shadow.

He rushed to the nearest house, nearly dead with fright, and they say he will never be the same man again.

"This is the most *dramatic* thing that has happened. It makes me shiver as I write of it. Of course George *must* have been mistaken. But hc is a truthful man, and hc docsn't drink. I don't know what to think of it.

"Arminius Scobie is a *very mean man* and always buys his wife's hats for her, lest she pay too much for them. They know this in the Shrewsbury stores, and laugh at him. One day last week he was in Jones and McCallum's, buying her a hat, and Mr. Jones told him that if he would *wear the hat* from the store to the station he would let him have it for nothing. Arminius did. It was a quarter of a mile to the station and all the small boys in Shrewsbury ran after him and hooted him. But Arminus didn't care. He had saved three dollars and forty-nine cents.

"*And,* one evening, right here at New Moon, I dropped a soft-boiled egg on Aunt Elizabeth's second-best cashmere dress. That *was* a happening. A kingdom might have been upset in Europe, and it wouldn't have made such a commotion at New Moon.

"So, Mistress Sawyer, you are vastly mistaken. Besides, apart from all happenings, the folks here are interesting in themselves. I don't *like* every one but I find every one interesting—Miss Matty Small, who is forty and wears *outrageous* colours—she wore an old-rose dress and a scarlet hat to church all last summer—old Uncle Reuben Bascom, who is so lazy that he held an umbrella over himself all one rainy night in bed, when the roof began to leak, rather than get out and move the bed—Elder McCloskey, who thought it wouldn't do to say 'pants' in a story he was telling about a missionary, at prayer-meeting, so always said politely 'the clothes of his lower parts'—Amasa Derry, who carried off four prizes at the Exhibition last fall, with vegetables he stole from Ronnie Bascom's field, while Ronnie didn't get one prize—Jimmy Joe Belle, who came here from Derry Pond yesterday to get some lumber 'to beeld a henhouse for my leetle dog'—old Luke Elliott, who is such a systematic fiend that he even draws up a schedule of the year on New Year's day, and charts down all the days he means to get drunk on—*and sticks to it:*—they're all interesting and amusing and delightful.

"There, I've proved Mrs. Alex Sawyer to be so completely wrong that I feel quite kindly towards her, even though she did call me a puss.

"Why don't I like being called a puss, when cats are such nice things? And I like being called *pussy.*

****

"April 28, 19—

"Two weeks ago I sent my very best poem, *Wind Song,* to a magazine in New York, and to-day it came back with just a little *printed slip* saying, 'We regret we cannot use this contribution.'

306

"I feel dreadfully. I suppose I can't really write anything that is any good.

"I *can*. That magazine will be *glad* to print my pieces some day!

"I didn't tell Mr. Carpenter I sent it. I wouldn't get any sympathy from him. *He* says that five years from now will be time enough to begin pestering editors. But I *know* that some poems I've read in that very magazine were not a bit better than *Wind Song*.

"I feel more like writing poetry in spring than at any other time. Mr. Carpenter tells me to fight against the impulse. He says spring has been responsible for more trash than anything else in the universe of God.

"Mr. Carpenter's way of talking has a *tang* to it.

****

"May 1, 19—

"Dean is home. He came to his sister's yesterday and this evening he was here and we walked in the garden, up and down the sundial walk, and talked. It was splendid to have him back, with his mysterious green eyes and his nice mouth.

"We had a long conversation. We talked of Algiers and the transmigration of souls and of being cremated and of profiles—Dean says I have a good profile—'pure Greek.' I always like Dean's compliments.

"'Star o' Morning, how you have grown!' he said. 'I left a child last autumn—and I find a woman!'

"(I will be fourteen in three weeks, and I am tall for my age. Dean seems to be glad of this—quite unlike Aunt Laura who always sighs when she lengthens my dresses, and thinks children grow up too fast.)

"'So goes time by,' I said, quoting the motto on the sundial, and feeling *quite sophisticated*.

"'You are almost as tall as I am,' he said; and then added *bitterly,* 'to be sure Jarback Priest is of no very stately height.'

"I have always shrunk from referring to his shoulder in any way, but now I said,

"'Dean, please don't sneer at yourself like that—not with me, at least. I *never* think of you as Jarback.'

"Dean took my hand and looked right into my eyes as if he were trying to *read my very soul*.

"'Are you sure of that, Emily? Don't you often wish that I wasn't lame—and crooked?'

"'For your sake I do,' I answered, 'but as far as I am concerned it doesn't make a bit of difference—and never will.'

"'And never will!' Dean repeated the words emphatically. 'If I were sure of that, Emily—if I were only sure of that.'

"'You *can* be sure of it,' I declared quite warmly. I was vexed because he seemed to doubt it—and yet something in his expression made me feel a little uncomfortable. It suddenly made me think of the time he rescued me from the cliff on Malvern Bay and told me my life belonged to him since he had saved it. I don't like the thought of my life belonging to any one but myself—not *any one,* even Dean, much as I like him. And *in some ways* I like Dean better than any one in the world.

"When it got darker the stars came out and we studied them through Dean's splendid new field-glasses. It was very fascinating. Dean knows all about the stars—it seems to me he knows all about everything. But when I said so, he said,

"'There is one secret I do not know—I would give everything else I *do* know for it—one secret—perhaps I shall never know it. The way to win—the way to win—'

"'What?' I asked curiously.

"'My heart's desire,' said Dean dreamily, looking at a shimmering star that seemed to be hung on the very tip of one of the Three Princesses. 'It seems now as desirable and unobtainable as that gem-like star, Emily. But—who knows?'

"I wonder what it is Dean wants so much.

****

"May 4, 19—

"Dean brought me a lovely portfolio from Paris, and I have copied my favourite verse from *The Fringed Gentian* on the inside of the cover. I will read it over every day and remember my vow to 'climb the Alpine Path.' I begin to see that I will have to do a good bit of scrambling, though I once expected, I think, to soar right up to 'that far-off goal' on shining wings. Mr. Carpenter has banished that fond dream.

"'Dig in your toes and hang on with your teeth—that's the only way,' he says.

"Last night in bed I thought out some lovely titles for the books I'm going to write in the future—*A Lady of High Degree, True to Faith and Vow, Oh, Rare Pale Margaret* (I got that from Tennyson), *The Caste of Vere de Vere* (ditto) and *A Kingdom by the Sea.*

"Now, if I can only get ideas to match the titles!

"I am writing a story called *The House Among the Rowans*—also a very good title, I think. But the love talk still bothers me. Everything of the kind I write seems so stiff and silly the minute I write it down that it infuriates me. I asked Dean if he could teach me how to write it properly because he promised long ago that he would, but he said I was too young yet—said it in that mysterious way of his which always seems to convey the idea that there is so much more in his words than the mere sound of them expresses. I wish I could speak so *significantly,* because it makes you *very interesting.*

"This evening after school Dean and I began to read *The Alhambra* over again, sitting on the stone bench in the garden. That book always makes me feel as if I had opened a little door and stepped straight into fairyland.

"'How I would love to see the Alhambra!' I said.

"'We will go to see it sometime—together,' said Dean.

"'Oh, that would be *lovely,*' I cried. 'Do you think we can ever manage it, Dean?'

"Before Dean could answer I heard Teddy's whistle in Lofty John's bush—the dear little whistle of two short high notes and one long low one, that is *our signal.*

"'Excuse me—I must go—Teddy's calling me,' I said.

"'Must you always go when Teddy calls?' asked Dean.

"I nodded and explained,

"'He only calls like that when he wants me *especially* and I have promised I will always go if I possibly can.'

"'*I* want you *especially!*' said Dean. 'I came up this evening on purpose to read *The Alhambra* with you.'

"Suddenly I felt very unhappy. I wanted to stay with Dean dreadfully, and yet I felt as if I must go to Teddy. Dean looked at me piercingly. Then he shut up *The Alhambra.*

"'Go,' he said.

"I went—but things seemed spoiled, somehow.

****

"May 10, 19—

"I have been reading three books Dean lent me this week. One was like a rose garden—very pleasant, but just a little too sweet. And one was like a pine wood on a mountain—full of balsam and tang—I loved it, and yet it filled me with a sort of despair. It was written so beautifully—I can *never* write like that, I feel sure. And one—it was just like a pigsty. Dean gave me that one by mistake. He was very angry with himself when he found it out—angry and distressed.

"'Star—Star—I would *never* have given you a book like that—my confounded carelessness—forgive me. That book is a faithful picture of one world—but not your world, thank God—nor any world you will ever be a citizen of. Star, promise me you will forget that book.'

"'I'll forget it if I can,' I said.

"But I don't know if I can. It was so ugly. I have not been so happy since I read it. I feel as if my hands were soiled somehow and I couldn't wash them clean. And I have another queer feeling, as if *some gate had been shut behind me,* shutting me into a new world I don't quite understand or like, but through which I must travel.

"To-night I tried to write a description of Dean in my Jimmy-book of character sketches. But I didn't succeed. What I wrote seemed like a photograph—not a portrait. There is something in Dean that is beyond me.

"Dean took a picture of me the other day with his new camera, but he wasn't pleased with it.

"'It doesn't look like you,' he said, 'but of course one can never photograph starlight.'

"Then he added, quite sharply, I thought,

"'Tell that young imp of a Teddy Kent to keep your face out of his pictures. He has no business to put *you* into every one he draws.'

"'He doesn't!' I cried. 'Why, Teddy never made but the one picture of me—the one Aunt Nancy *stole.*'

"I said it quite viciously and unashamed, for I've never forgiven Aunt Nancy for keeping that picture.

"'He's got *something* of you in every picture,' said Dean stubbornly—'your eyes—the curve of your neck—the tilt of your head—your personality. That's the worst—I don't mind your eyes and curves

310

so much, but I won't have that cub putting a bit of your soul into everything he draws. Probably he doesn't know he's doing it—which makes it all the worse.'

"'I don't understand you,' I said, *quite haughtily.* 'But Teddy is *wonderful*—Mr. Carpenter says so.'

"'And Emily of New Moon echoes it! Oh, the kid has talent—he'll do something some day if his morbid mother doesn't ruin his life. But let him keep his pencil and brush off *my* property.'

"Dean laughed as he said it. But I held my head high. I am not anybody's 'property,' not even in fun. And I *never* will be.

****

"May 12, 19—

"Aunt Ruth and Uncle Wallace and Uncle Oliver were all here this afternoon. I like Uncle Oliver, but I am not much fonder of Aunt Ruth and Uncle Wallace than I ever was. They held some kind of family conclave in the parlour with Aunt Elizabeth and Aunt Laura. Cousin Jimmy was allowed in but I was excluded, although I feel perfectly certain that it had something to do with me. I think Aunt Ruth didn't get her own way, either, for she snubbed me continually all through supper, and said I was growing weedy! Aunt Ruth generally snubs me and Uncle Wallace patronizes me. I prefer Aunt Ruth's snubs because I don't have to look as if I liked them. I endured them to a certain point, and then the lid flew off. Aunt Ruth said to me,

"'Em'ly, don't contradict,' just as she might have spoken to a *mere child.* I looked her right in the eyes and said *coldly,*

"'Aunt Ruth, I think I am too old to be spoken to in that fashion now.'

"'You are not too old to be very rude and impertinent,' said Aunt Ruth, with a sniff, 'and if *I* were in Elizabeth's place I would give you a sound box on the ear, Miss.'

"I hate to be Em'ly'd and Miss'd and sniffed at! It seems to me that Aunt Ruth has *all* the Murray faults, and *none* of their virtues.

"Uncle Oliver's son Andrew came with him and is going to stay for a week. He is four years older than I am.

****

"May 19, 19—

"This is my birthday. I am fourteen years old today. I wrote a letter 'From myself at fourteen to myself at twenty-four,' sealed it up and put it away in my cupboard, to be opened on my twenty-fourth birthday. I made some predictions in it. I wonder if they will have come to pass when I open it.

"Aunt Elizabeth gave me back all Father's books today. I was so glad. It seems to me that a part of Father is in those books. His name is in each one in his own handwriting, and the notes he made on the margins. They seem like little bits of letters from him. I have been looking over them all the evening, and Father seems so *near* to me again, and I feel both happy and sad.

"One thing spoiled the day for me. In school, when I went up to the blackboard to work a problem, everybody suddenly began to titter. I could not imagine why. Then I discovered that some one had pinned a sheet of foolscap to my back, on which was printed in big, black letters: *'Emily Byrd Starr, Authoress of The Four-Legged Duck.'* They laughed more than ever when I snatched it off and threw it in the coal-scuttle. It infuriates me when anyone ridicules my ambitions like that. I came home angry and sore. But when I had sat on the steps of the summer-house and looked at one of Cousin Jimmy's big purple pansies for five minutes all my anger went away. Nobody can keep on being angry if she looks into the heart of a pansy for a little while.

"Besides, *the time will come when they will not laugh at me!*

"Andrew went home yesterday. Aunt Elizabeth asked me how I liked him. She never asked me how I liked anyone before—my likings were not important enough. I suppose she is beginning to realize that I am no *longer a child*.

"I said I thought he was good and kind and stupid and uninteresting.

"Aunt Elizabeth was so annoyed she would not speak to me the whole evening. Why? I had to tell the truth. And Andrew *is*.

****

"May 21, 19—

"Old Kelly was here to-day for the first time this spring, with a load of shining new tins. He brought me a bag of candies as usual—and teased me about getting married, also as usual. But he seemed to have

312

something on his mind, and when I went to the dairy to get him the drink of milk he had asked for, he followed me.

"'Gurrl dear,' he said mysteriously. 'I met Jarback Praste in the lane. Does he be coming here much?'

"I cocked my head at the Murray angle.

"'If you mean Mr. Dean Priest,' I said, 'he comes often. He is a particular friend of mine.'

"Old Kelly shook his head.

"'Gurrl dear—I warned ye—niver be after saying I didn't warn ye. I towld ye the day I took ye to Praste Pond niver to marry a Praste. Didn't I now?'

"'Mr. Kelly, you're too ridiculous,' I said—angry and yet feeling it was absurd to be angry with Old Jock Kelly. 'I'm not going to marry anybody. Mr. Priest is old enough to be my father, and I am just a little girl he helps in her studies.'

"Old Kelly gave his head another shake.

"'I know the Prastes, gurrl dear—and when they do be after setting their minds on a thing ye might as well try to turn the wind. This Jarback now—they tell me he's had his eye on ye iver since he fished ye up from the Malvern rocks—he's just biding his time till ye get old enough for coorting. They tell me he's an infidel, and it's well known that whin he was being christened he rached up and clawed the spectacles off av the minister. So what wud ye ixpect? I nadn't be telling ye he's lame and crooked—ye can see that for yerself. Take foolish Ould Kelly's advice and cut loose while there's time. Now, don't be looking at me like the Murrays, gurrl dear. Shure, and it's for your own good I do be spaking.'

"I walked off and left him. One *couldn't* argue with him over such a thing. I *wish* people wouldn't put such ideas into my mind. They stick there like burrs. I won't feel as comfortable with Dean for weeks now, though I know perfectly well every word Old Kelly said was nonsense.

"After Old Kelly went away I came up to my room and wrote a full description of him in a Jimmy-book.

"Ilse has got a new hat trimmed with clouds of blue tulle, and red cherries, with big blue tulle bows under the chin. I did not like it and told her so. She was furious and said I was jealous and hasn't spoken to me for two days. I thought it all over. I knew I was not jealous, but I concluded I had made a mistake. I will never again tell anyone a thing like that. It was true but it was not tactful.

"I hope Ilse will have forgiven me by to-morrow. I miss her horribly when she is offended with me. She's such a dear thing and so jolly, and splendid, when she isn't vexed.

"Teddy is a little squiffy with me, too, just now. I *think* it is because Geoff North walked home with me from prayer-meeting last Wednesday night. I *hope* that is the reason. I like to feel that I *have that much power* over Teddy.

"I wonder if I ought to have written that down. But it's *true*.

"If Teddy only knew it, I have been very unhappy and ashamed over that affair. At first, when Geoff singled me out from all the girls, I was quite proud of it. It was the very first time I had had an *escort home,* and Geoff is a town boy, *very handsome and polished,* and all the older girls in Blair Water are quite foolish about him. So I sailed away from the church door with him, feeling as if I had grown up all at once. But we hadn't gone far before I was hating him. He was so *condescending.* He seemed to think I was a simple little country girl who must be quite overwhelmed with the *honour* of his company.

"And that was true at first! *That* was what stung me. To think I had been such a little fool!

"He kept saying, 'Really, you surprise me,' in an affected, drawling kind of way, whenever I made a remark. And he *bored* me. He couldn't talk sensibly about anything. Or else he wouldn't try to with me. I was quite savage by the time we got to New Moon. And then *that insufferable creature* asked me to kiss him!

"I drew myself up—oh, I was Murray clear through at that moment, all right. I *felt* I was looking exactly like Aunt Elizabeth.

"'I do not kiss young men,' I said disdainfully.

"Geoff laughed and caught my hand.

"'Why, you little goose, what do you suppose I came home with you for?' he said.

"I pulled my hand away from him, and walked into the house. But before I did that, I did something else.

"I slapped his face!

"Then I came up to my room and cried with shame over being insulted, and having been so undignified in resenting it. Dignity is a tradition of New Moon, and I felt that I had been false to it.

"But I think I 'surprised' Geoff North in right good earnest!

****

"May 24, 19—

"Jennie Strang told me to-day that Geoff North told her brother that I was 'a regular spitfire' and he had had enough of me.

"Aunt Elizabeth has found out that Geoff came home with me, and told me to-day that I would not be 'trusted' to go alone to prayer-meeting again.

****

"May 25, 19—

"I am sitting here in my room at twilight. The window is open and the frogs are singing of something that happened very long ago. All along the middle garden walk the Gay Folk are holding up great fluted cups of ruby and gold and pearl. It is not raining now, but it rained all day—a rain scented with lilacs. I like all kinds of weather and I like rainy days—soft, misty, rainy days when the Wind Woman just shakes the tops of the spruces gently; and wild, tempestuous, streaming rainy days. I like being shut in by the rain—I like to hear it thudding on the roof, and beating on the panes and pouring off the eaves, while the Wind Woman skirls like a mad old witch in the woods, and through the garden.

"Still, if it rains when I want to go anywhere I growl just as much as anybody!

"An evening like this always makes me think of that spring Father died, three years ago, and that dear little, old house down at Maywood. I've never been back since. I wonder if anyone is living in it now. And if Adam-and-Eve and the Rooster Pine and the Praying Tree are just the same. And who is sleeping in my old room there, and if anyone is loving the little birches and playing with the Wind Woman in the spruce barrens. Just as I wrote the words 'spruce barrens' an old memory came back to me. One spring evening, when I was eight years old, I was running about the barrens playing hide-and-seek with the Wind Woman, and I found a little hollow between two spruces that was just carpeted with tiny, bright-green leaves, when everything else was still brown and faded. They were so beautiful that *the flash* came as I looked at them—it was the very first time it ever came to me. I

315

suppose that is why I remember those little green leaves so distinctly. No one else remembers them—perhaps no one else ever saw them. I have forgotten other leaves, but I remember them every spring and with each remembrance I feel again the wonder-moment they gave me."

IN THE WATCHES OF THE NIGHT

Some of us can recall the exact time in which we reached certain milestones on life's road—the wonderful hour when we passed from childhood to girlhood—the enchanted, beautiful—or perhaps the shattering and horrible—hour when girlhood was suddenly womanhood—the chilling hour when we faced the fact that youth was definitely behind us—the peaceful, sorrowful hour of the realization of age. Emily Starr never forgot the night when she passed the first milestone, and left childhood behind her for ever.

Every experience enriches life and the deeper such an experience, the greater the richness it brings. That night of horror and mystery and strange delight ripened her mind and heart like the passage of years.

It was a night early in July. The day had been one of intense heat. Aunt Elizabeth had suffered so much from it that she decided she would not go to prayer-meeting. Aunt Laura and Cousin Jimmy and Emily went. Before leaving Emily asked and obtained Aunt Elizabeth's permission to go home with Ilse Burnley after meeting, and spend the night. This was a rare treat. Aunt Elizabeth did not approve of all-night absences as a general thing.

But Dr. Burnley had to be away, and his housekeeper was temporarily laid up with a broken ankle. Ilse had asked Emily to come over for the night, and Emily was to be permitted to go. Ilse did not know this— hardly hoped for it, in fact—but was to be informed at prayer-meeting. If Ilse had not been late Emily would have told her before meeting "went in," and the mischances of the night would probably have been averted; but Ilse, as usual, *was* late, and everything else followed in course.

Emily sat in the Murray pew, near the top of the church by the window that looked out into the grove of fir and maple that surrounded the little white church. This prayer-meeting was not the ordinary weekly sprinkling of a faithful few. It was a "special meeting," held in view of the approaching communion Sunday, and the speaker was not young, earnest Mr. Johnson, to whom Emily always liked to listen, in spite of her blunder at the Ladies' Aid Supper but an itinerant evangelist lent by Shrewsbury for one night. His fame brought out a churchful of people, but most of the audience declared afterwards that they would much rather have heard their own Mr. Johnson. Emily looked at him with her level, critical gaze, and decided that he was oily and unspiritual. She heard him through a prayer, and thought,

"Giving God good advice, and abusing the devil isn't praying."

She listened to his discourse for a few minutes and made up her mind that he was blatant and illogical and sensational, and then proceeded, coolly, to shut mind and ears to him and disappear into dreamland—something which she could generally do at will when anxious to escape from discordant realities.

Outside, moonlight was still sifting in a rain of silver through the firs and maples, though an ominous bank of cloud was making up in the north-west, and repeated rumblings of thunder came on the silent air of the hot summer night—a windless night for the most part, though occasionally a sudden breath that seemed more like a sigh than a breeze brushed through the trees, and set their shadows dancing in weird companies. There was something strange about the night in its mingling of placid, accustomed beauty with the omens of rising storm, that intrigued Emily, and she spent half the time of the evangelist's address in composing a mental description of it for her Jimmy-book. The rest of the time she studied such of the audience as were within her range of vision.

This was something that Emily never wearied of, in public assemblages, and the older she grew the more she liked it. It was fascinating to study those varied faces, and speculate on the histories written in mysterious hieroglyphics over them. They had all their inner, secret lives, those men and women, known to no one but themselves and God. Others could only guess at them, and Emily loved this game of guessing. At times it seemed veritably to her that it was more than guessing—that in some intense moments she could pass into their souls and read therein hidden motives and passions that were, perhaps, a mystery even to their possessors. It was never easy for Emily to resist the temptation to do this when the power came, although she never yielded to it without an uneasy feeling that she was committing trespass. It was quite a different thing from soaring on the wings of fancy into an ideal world of creation—quite different from the exquisite, unearthly beauty of "the flash;" neither of these gave her any moments of pause or doubt. But to slip on tiptoe through some momentarily unlatched door, as it were, and catch a glimpse of masked, unuttered, unutterable things in the hearts and souls of others, was something that always brought, along with its sense of power, a sense of the forbidden—a sense even of sacrilege. Yet Emily did not know if she would ever be able to resist the allure of it—she had always peered through the door and seen the things before she realized that she was doing it. They were nearly always terrible things. Secrets are generally terrible. Beauty is not often hidden—only ugliness and deformity.

"Elder Forsyth would have been a persecutor in old times," she thought. "He has the face of one. This very minute he is loving the preacher because he is describing hell, and Elder Forsyth thinks all his enemies will go there. Yes, that is why he is looking pleased. I think Mrs. Bowes flies off on a broomstick o' nights. She *looks* it. Four hundred years ago she would have been a witch, and Elder Forsyth would have burned her at the stake. She hates everybody—it must be terrible to hate everybody—to have your soul full of hatred. I must try to describe such a person in my Jimmy-book. I wonder if hate has driven *all* love out of her soul, or if there is a little bit left in it for any one or any thing. If there is it might save her. That would be a good idea for a story. I must jot it down before I go to bed—I'll borrow a bit of paper from Ilse. No—here's a bit in my hymn-book. I'll write it now.

"I wonder what all these people would say if they were suddenly asked what they wanted most, and *had* to answer truthfully. I wonder how many of these husbands and wives would like a change? Chris Farrar and Mrs. Chris would—everybody knows that. I can't think why I feel so sure that James Beatty and *his* wife would, too. They *seem* to be quite contented with each other—but once I saw her look at him when she did not know anyone was watching—oh, it seemed to me I saw right into her soul, through her eyes, and she hated him—and feared him. She is sitting there now, beside him, little and thin and dowdy, and her face is grey and her hair is faded—but she, herself, is one red flame of rebellion. What *she* wants most is to be free from him—or just to *strike back once*. That would satisfy her.

"There's Dean—I wonder what brought him to prayer-meeting? His face is very solemn, but his eyes are mocking Mr. Sampson—what's that Mr. Sampson's saying?—oh, something about the wise virgins. I hate the wise virgins—I think they were horribly selfish. They *might* have given the poor foolish ones a little oil. I don't believe Jesus meant to praise them any more than He meant to praise the unjust steward—I think he was just trying to warn foolish people that they must not *be* careless, and foolish, because if they were, prudent, selfish folks would never help them out. I wonder if it's very wicked to feel that I'd rather be outside with the foolish ones trying to help and comfort them, than inside feasting with the wise ones. It would be *more interesting*, too.

"There's Mrs. Kent and Teddy. Oh, *she* wants something terribly—I don't know what it is but it's something she can never get, and the hunger for it goads her night and day. That is why she holds Teddy so closely—I know. But I don't know what it is that makes her so different from other women. I can never get a peep into *her* soul—she shuts every one out—the door is never unlatched.

"What do *I* want most? It is to climb the Alpine Path to the very top,

"And write upon its shining scroll

A woman's humble name.

"We're all hungry. We all want some bread of life—but Mr. Sampson can't give it to us. I wonder what *he* wants most? His soul is so muggy I can't see into it. He has a lot of sordid wants—he doesn't want *anything* enough to dominate him. Mr. Johnson wants to help people and preach truth—he really does. And Aunt Janey wants most of all to see the whole heathen world Christianized. Her soul hasn't any dark wishes in it. I know what Mr. Carpenter wants—his one lost chance again. Katherine Morris wants her youth back—she hates us younger girls *because* we are young. Old Malcolm Strang just wants to live—just one more year—always just one more year—just to live—just not to die. It must be horrible to have nothing to live for except just to escape dying. Yet he believes in heaven—he thinks he will go there. If he could see

319

my flash just once he wouldn't hate the thought of dying so, poor old man. And Mary Strang wants to die—before something terrible she is afraid of tortures her to death. They say it's cancer. There's Mad Mr. Morrison up in the gallery—we all know what *he* wants—to find his Annie. Tom Sibley wants the moon, I think—and knows he can never get it—that's why people say he's not all there. Amy Crabbe wants Max Terry to come back to her—nothing else matters to her.

"I must write all these things down in my Jimmy-book to-morrow. They are fascinating—but, after all, I like writing of beautiful things better. Only—these things have a *tang* beautiful things don't have some way. Those woods out there—how wonderful they are in their silver and shadow. The moonlight is doing strange things to the tombstones—it makes even the ugly ones beautiful. But it's terribly hot—it is smothering here—and those thunder-growls are coming nearer. I hope Ilse and I will get home before the storm breaks. Oh, Mr. Sampson, Mr. Sampson, God isn't an angry God—you don't know anything about Him if you say that—He's sorrowful, I'm sure, when we're foolish and wicked, but He doesn't fly into tantrums. Your God and Ellen Greene's God are exactly alike. I'd like to get up and tell you so, but it isn't a Murray tradition to sass back in church. You make God ugly—and He's beautiful. I hate you for making God ugly, you fat little man."

Whereupon Mr. Sampson, who had several times noted Emily's intent, probing gaze, and thought he was impressing her tremendously with a sense of her unsaved condition, finished with a final urgent whoop of entreaty, and sat down. The audience in the close, oppressive atmosphere of the crowded, lamplit church gave an audible sigh of relief, and scarcely waited for the hymn and benediction before crowding out to purer air. Emily, caught in the current, and parted from Aunt Laura, was swept out by way of the choir door to the left of the pulpit. It was some time before she could disentangle herself from the throng and hurry around to the front where she expected to meet Ilse. Here was another dense, though rapidly thinning crowd, in which she found no trace of Ilse. Suddenly Emily noticed that she did not have her hymn-book. Hastily she dashed back to the choir door. She must have left her hymn-book in the pew—and it would never do to leave it there. In it she had placed for safe-keeping a slip of paper on which she had furtively jotted down some fragmentary notes during the last hymn—a rather biting description of scrawny Miss Potter in the choir—a couple of satiric sentences regarding Mr. Sampson himself—and a few random fancies which she desired most of all to hide because there was in them something of dream and vision which would have made the reading of them by alien eyes a sacrilege.

Old Jacob Banks, the sexton, a little blind and more than a little deaf, was turning out the lamps as she went in. He had reached the two on the wall behind the pulpit. Emily caught her hymn-book from the rack—her slip of paper was not in it. By the faint gleam of light, as Jacob Banks turned out the last lamp, she saw it on the floor, under the seat of the pew in front. She kneeled down and reached after it. As she did so Jacob went out and locked the choir door. Emily did not notice his going—the church was still faintly illuminated by the moon that as yet outrode the rapidly climbing thunder-heads. That was not the right slip of paper after all—*where* could it be?—oh, here, at last. She caught it up and ran to the door which would not open.

For the first time Emily realized that Jacob Banks had gone—that she was alone in the church. She wasted time trying to open the door—then in calling Mr. Banks. Finally she ran down the aisle into the front porch. As she did so she heard the last buggy turn gridingly at the gate and drive away: at the same time the moon was suddenly swallowed up by the black clouds and the church was engulfed in darkness—close, hot, smothering, almost tangible darkness. Emily screamed in sudden panic—beat on the door—frantically twisted the handle—screamed again. Oh, everybody could not have gone—surely somebody would hear her! "Aunt Laura"—"Cousin Jimmy"—"Ilse"—then finally in a wail of despair—"Oh, Teddy—Teddy!"

A blue-white stream of lightning swept the porch, followed by a crash of thunder. One of the worst storms in Blair Water annals had begun—and Emily Starr was locked alone in the dark church in the maple woods—she, who had always been afraid of thunderstorms with a reasonless, instinctive fear which she could never banish and only partially control.

She sank, quivering, on a step of the gallery stairs, and huddled there in a heap. Surely some one would come back when it was discovered she was missing. But *would* it be discovered? Who would miss her? Aunt Laura and Cousin Jimmy would suppose she was with Ilse, as had been arranged. Ilse, who had evidently gone, believing that Emily was not coming with her, would suppose she had gone home to New Moon. Nobody knew where she was—nobody would come back for her. She must stay here in this horrible, lonely, black, echoing place— for now the church she knew so well and loved for its old associations of Sunday-school and song and homely faces of dear friends had become a ghostly, alien place full of haunting terrors. There was no escape. The windows could not be opened. The church was ventilated by transom-like panes near the top of them, which were opened and shut by pulling a wire. She could not get up to them, and she could not have got through them if she had.

She cowered down on the step, shuddering from head to foot. By now the thunder and lightning were almost incessant: rain blew against the windows, not in drops but sheets, and intermittent volleys of hail bombarded them. The wind had risen suddenly with the storm and shrieked around the church. It was not her old dear friend of childhood, the bat-winged, misty "Wind Woman," but a legion of yelling witches. "The Prince of the Power of the Air rules the wind," she had heard Mad Mr. Morrison say once. Why should she think of Mad Mr. Morrison now? How the windows rattled as if demon riders of the storm were shaking them! She had heard a wild tale of some one hearing the organ play in the empty church one night several years ago. *Suppose it began playing now!* No fancy seemed too grotesque or horrible to come true. Didn't the stairs creak? The blackness between the lightnings was so intense that it looked *thick*. Emily was frightened of it touching her and buried her face in her lap.

Presently, however, she got a grip on herself and began to reflect that she was not living up to Murray traditions. Murrays were not supposed to go to pieces like this. Murrays were not foolishly panicky in thunderstorms. Those old Murrays sleeping in the private graveyard across the pond would have scorned her as a degenerate descendant. Aunt Elizabeth would have said that it was the Starr coming out in her. She must be brave: after all, she had lived through worse hours than this— the night she had eaten of Lofty John's poisoned apple*—the afternoon she had fallen over the rocks of Malvern Bay. This had come so suddenly on her that she had been in the throes of terror before she could brace herself against it. She *must* pick up. Nothing dreadful was going to happen to her—nothing worse than staying all night in the church. In the morning she could attract the attention of some one passing.

She had been here over an hour now, and nothing had happened to her—unless indeed her hair had turned white, as she understood hair sometimes did. There had been such a funny, crinkly, crawly feeling at the roots of it at times. Emily held out her long braid, ready for the next flash. When it came she saw that her hair was still black. She sighed with relief and began to chirk up. The storm was passing. The thunder-peals were growing fainter and fewer, though the rain continued to fall and the wind to drive and shriek around the church, whining through the big keyhole eerily.

* See *Emily of New Moon*.

Emily straightened her shoulders and cautiously let down her feet to a lower step. She thought she had better try to get back into the church. If another cloud came up, the steeple might be struck—steeples were always getting struck, she remembered: it might come crashing down on the, porch right over her. She would go in and sit down in the Murray pew: she would be cool and sensible and collected: she was ashamed of her panic—but it *had* been terrible.

All around her now was a soft, heavy darkness, still with that same eerie sensation of something you could touch, born perhaps of the heat and humidity of the July night. The porch was so small and narrow— she would not feel so smothered and oppressed in the church.

She put out her hand to grasp a stair rail and pull herself to her cramped feet. Her hand touched—not the stair rail—merciful heavens, what was it?—something *hairy*—Emily's shriek of horror froze on her lips—padding footsteps passed down the steps beside her; a flash of lightning came and at the bottom of the steps was a huge black dog, which had turned and was looking up at her before he was blotted out in the returning darkness. Even then for a moment she saw his eyes blazing redly at her, like a fiend's.

Emily's hair roots began to crawl and crinkle again—a very large, very cold caterpillar began to creep slowly up her spine. She could not have moved a muscle had life depended on it. She could not even cry out. The only thing she could think of at first was the horrible demon hound of the Manx Castle in *Peveril of the Peak*. For a few minutes her terror was so great that it turned her physically sick. Then, with an effort which was unchild-like in its determination—I think it was at that moment Emily wholly ceased to be a child—she recovered her self-control. She *would not* yield to fear—she set her teeth and clenched her trembling hands; she *would* be brave—sensible. That was only a commonplace Blair Water dog which had followed its owner—some rapscallion boy—into the gallery, and got itself left behind. The thing had happened before. A flash of lightning showed her that the porch was empty. Evidently the dog had gone into the church. Emily decided that she would stay where she was. She had recovered from her panic, but she did not want to feel the sudden touch of a cold nose or a hairy flank in the darkness. She could never forget the awfulness of the moment when she *had* touched the creature.

It must be all of twelve o'clock now—it had been ten when the meeting came out. The noise of the storm had for the most part died away. The drive and shriek of the wind came occasionally, but between its gusts there was a silence, broken only by the diminishing raindrops. Thunder still muttered faintly and lightning came at frequent intervals, but of a paler, gentler flame—not the rending glare that had seemed to wrap the very building in intolerable blue radiance, and scorch her eye. Gradually her heart began to beat normally. The power of rational thought returned. She did not like her predicament, but she began to find dramatic possibilities in it. Oh, what a chapter for her diary—or her Jimmy-book—and, beyond it, for that novel she would write some day! It was a situation expressly shaped for the heroine—who must, of course, be rescued by the hero. Emily began constructing the scene—adding to it—intensifying it—hunting for words to express it. This was rather—interesting—after all. Only she wished she knew just where the dog was. How weirdly the pale lightning gleamed on the gravestones which she could see through the porch window opposite her! How strange the familiar valley beyond looked in the recurrent illuminations! How the wind moaned and sighed and complained— but it was her own Wind Woman again. The Wind Woman was one of her childish fancies that she had carried over into maturity, and it comforted her now, with a sense of ancient companionship. The wild riders of the storm were gone—her fairy friend had come back. Emily gave a sigh that was almost of contentment. The worst was over—and really, hadn't she behaved pretty well? She began to feel quite self-respecting again.

All at once Emily knew she was not alone!

How she knew it she could not have told. She had heard nothing— seen nothing—felt nothing: and yet she knew, beyond all doubt or dispute, that there was a Presence in the darkness above her on the stairs.

She turned and looked up. It was horrible to look, but it was less horrible to feel that—Something—was in front of you than that it was behind you. She stared with wildly dilated eyes into the darkness, but she could see nothing. Then—she heard a low laugh above her—a laugh that almost made her heart stop beating—the very dreadful, inhuman laughter of the unsound in mind. She did not need the lightning flash that came then to tell her that Mad Mr. Morrison was somewhere on the stairs above her. But it came—she saw him—she felt as if she were sinking in some icy gulf of coldness—she could not even scream.

The picture of him, etched on her brain by the lightning, never left her. He was crouched five steps above her, with his gray head thrust forward. She saw the frenzied gleam of his eyes—the fang-like yellow teeth exposed in a horrible smile—the long, thin, blood-red hand outstretched towards her, almost touching her shoulder.

Sheer panic shattered Emily's trance. She bounded to her feet with a piercing scream of terror.

"Teddy! Teddy! Save me!" she shrieked madly.

She did not know why she called for Teddy—she did not even realize that she *had* called him—she only remembered it afterwards, as one might recall the waking shriek in a nightmare—she only knew that she *must* have help—that she would die if that awful hand touched her. *It must not touch her.*

She made a mad spring down the steps, rushed into the church, and up the aisle. She must hide before the next flash came—but not in the Murray pew. He might look for her there. She dived into one of the middle pews and crouched down in its corner on the floor. Her body was bathed in an ice-cold perspiration. She was wholly in the grip of uncontrollable terror. All she could think of was that it must not touch her—that blood-red hand of the mad old man.

Moments passed that seemed like years. Presently she heard footsteps—footsteps that came and went yet seemed to approach her slowly. Suddenly she knew what he was doing. He was going into every pew, not waiting for the lightning, to feel about for her. He *was* looking for her, then—she had heard that sometimes he followed young girls, thinking they were Annie. If he caught them he held them with one hand and stroked their hair and faces fondly with the other, mumbling foolish, senile endearments. He had never harmed anyone, but he had never let anyone go until she was rescued by some other person. It was said that Mary Paxton of Derry Pond had never been quite the same again; her nerves never recovered from the shock.

Emily knew that it was only a question of time before he would reach the pew where she crouched—feeling about with those hands! All that kept her senses in her frozen body was the thought that if she lost consciousness those hands would touch her—hold her—caress her. The next lightning flash showed him entering the adjoining pew. Emily sprang up and out and rushed to the other side of the church. She hid again: he would search her out, but she could again elude him: this might go on all night: a madman's strength would outlast hers: at last she might fall exhausted and he would pounce on her.

For what seemed hours to Emily, this mad game of hide-and-seek lasted. It was in reality about half an hour. She was hardly a rational creature at all, any more than her demented pursuer. She was merely a crouching, springing, shrieking thing of horror. Time after time he hunted her out with his cunning, implacable patience. The last time she was near one of the porch doors, and in desperation she sprang through it and slammed it in his face. With the last ounce of her strength she tried to hold the knob from turning in his grasp. And as she strove she heard—was she dreaming?—Teddy's voice calling to her from the steps outside the outer door.

"Emily—Emily—are you there?"

She did not know how he had come—she did not wonder—she only knew he *was* there!

"Teddy, I'm locked in the church!" she shrieked—"and Mad Mr. Morrison is here—oh—quick—quick—save me—save me!"

"The key of the door is hanging up in there on a nail at the right side!" shouted Teddy. "Can you get it and unlock the door? If you can't I'll smash the porch window."

The clouds broke at that moment and the porch was filled with moonlight. In it she saw plainly the big key, hanging high on the wall beside the front door. She dashed at it and caught it as Mad Mr. Morrison wrenched upon the door and sprang into the porch, his dog behind him. Emily unlocked the outer door and stumbled out into Teddy's arms just in time to elude that outstretched, blood-red hand. She heard Mad Mr. Morrison give a wild, eerie shriek of despair as she escaped him.

Sobbing, shaking, she clung to Teddy.

"Oh, Teddy, take me away—take me quick—oh, don't let him touch me, Teddy—don't let him touch me!"

Teddy swung her behind him and faced Mad Mr. Morrison on the stone step.

"How dare you frighten her so?" he demanded angrily.

Mad Mr. Morrison smiled deprecatingly in the moonlight. All at once he was not wild or violent—only a heart-broken old man who sought his own.

"I want Annie," he mumbled. "Where is Annie? I thought I had found her in there. I only wanted to find my beautiful Annie."

"Annie isn't here," said Teddy, tightening his hold on Emily's cold little hand.

"Can you tell me where Annie is?" entreated Mad Mr. Morrison, wistfully. "Can you tell me where my dark-haired Annie is?"

Teddy was furious with Mad Mr. Morrison for frightening Emily, but the old man's piteous entreaty touched him—and the artist in him responded to the values of the picture presented against the background of the white, moonlit church. He thought he would like to paint Mad Mr. Morrison as he stood there, tall and gaunt, in his gray "duster" coat, with his long white hair and beard, and the ageless quest in his hollow, sunken eyes.

"No—no—I don't know where she is," he said gently, "but I think you will find her sometime."

Mad Mr. Morrison sighed.

"Oh, yes. Sometime I will overtake her. Come, my dog, we will seek her."

Followed by his old black dog he went down the steps, across the green and down the long, wet, tree-shadowed road. So going, he passed out of Emily's life. She never saw Mad Mr. Morrison again. But she looked after him understandingly, and forgave him. To himself he was not the repulsive old man he seemed to her; he was a gallant young lover seeking his lost and lovely bride. The pitiful beauty of his quest intrigued her, even in the shaking reaction from her hour of agony.

"Poor Mr. Morrison," she sobbed, as Teddy half led, half carried her to one of the old flat gravestones at the side of the church.

They sat there until Emily recovered composure and managed to tell her tale—or the outlines of it. She felt she could never tell—perhaps not even write in a Jimmy-book—the whole of its racking horror. *That* was beyond words.

"And to think," she sobbed, "that the key was there all the time. I never knew it."

"Old Jacob Banks always locks the front door with its big key on the inside, and then hangs it up on that nail," said Teddy. "He locks the choir door with a little key, which he takes home. He has always done that since the time, three years ago, when he lost the big key and was weeks before he found it."

Suddenly Emily awoke to the strangeness of Teddy's coming.

"How did you happen to come, Teddy?"

"Why, I heard you call me," he said. "You did call me, didn't you?"

"Yes," said Emily, slowly, "I called for you when I saw Mad Mr. Morrison first. But, Teddy, you couldn't have heard me—you *couldn't*. The Tansy Patch is a mile from here."

"I *did* hear you," said Teddy, stubbornly. "I was asleep and it woke me up. You called 'Teddy, Teddy, save me'—it was your voice as plain as I ever heard it in my life. I got right up and hurried on my clothes and came here as fast as I could."

"How did you know I was here?"

"Why—I don't know," said Teddy confusedly. "I didn't stop to think—I just seemed to *know* you were in the church when I heard you calling me, and I must get here as quick as I could. It's—it's all— funny," he concluded lamely.

"It's—it's—it frightens me a little." Emily shivered. "Aunt Elizabeth says I have second sight—you remember Ilse's mother? Mr. Carpenter says I'm psychic—I don't know just what that means, but think I'd rather not be it."

She shivered again. Teddy thought she was cold and, having nothing else to put around her, put his arm—somewhat tentatively, since Murray pride and Murray dignity might be outraged. Emily was not cold in body, but a little chill had blown over her soul. Something supernatural—some mystery she could not understand—had brushed too near her in that strange summoning. Involuntarily she nestled a little closer to Teddy, acutely conscious of the boyish tenderness she sensed behind the aloofness of his boyish shyness. Suddenly she knew that she liked Teddy better than anybody—better even than Aunt

Laura or Ilse or Dean.

Teddy's arm tightened a little.

"Anyhow, I'm glad I got here in time," he said. "If I hadn't that crazy old man might have frightened you to death."

They sat so for a few minutes in silence. Everything seemed very wonderful and beautiful—and a little unreal. Emily thought she must be in a dream, or in one of her own wonder tales. The storm had passed, and the moon was shining clearly once more. The cool fresh air was threaded with beguiling voices—the fitful voice of raindrops falling from the shaken boughs of the maple woods behind them—the freakish voice of the Wind Woman around the white church—the far-off, intriguing voice of the sea—and, still finer and rarer, the little, remote, detached voices of the night. Emily heard them all, more with the ears of her soul than of her body, it seemed, as she had never heard them before. Beyond were fields and groves and roads, pleasantly suggestive and elusive, as if brooding over elfish secrets in the moonlight. Silver-white daisies were nodding and swaying all over the graveyard above graves remembered and graves forgotten. An owl laughed delightfully to itself in the old pine. At the magical sound Emily's mystic flash swept over her, swaying her like a strong wind. She felt as if she and Teddy were all alone in a wonderful new world, created for themselves only out of youth and mystery and delight. They seemed, themselves, to be part of the faint, cool fragrance of the night, of the owl's laughter, of the daisies blowing in the shadowy air.

As for Teddy, he was thinking that Emily looked very sweet in the pale moonshine, with her fringed, mysterious eyes and the little dark love-curls clinging to her ivory neck. He tightened his arm a little more—and still Murray pride and Murray dignity made not a particle of protest.

"Emily," whispered Teddy, "you're the sweetest girl in the world."

The words have been said so often by so many millions of lads to so many millions of lasses, that they ought to be worn to tatters. But when you hear them for the first time, in some magic hour of your teens, they are as new and fresh and wondrous as if they had just drifted over the hedges of Eden. Madam, whoever you are, and however old you are, be honest, and admit that the first time you heard those words on the lips of some shy sweetheart, was the great moment of your life. Emily thrilled, from the crown of her head to the toes of her slippered feet, with a sensation of hitherto unknown and almost terrifying sweetness—a sensation that was to sense what her "flash" was to spirit. It is quite conceivable and not totally reprehensible that the next thing that happened might have been a kiss. Emily thought Teddy was going to kiss her: Teddy knew he was: and the odds are that he wouldn't have had his face slapped as Geoff North had had.

But it was not to be. A shadow that had slipped in at the gate and drifted across the wet grass, halted beside them, and touched Teddy's shoulder, just as he bent his glossy black head. He looked up, startled. Emily looked up. Mrs. Kent was standing there, bareheaded, her scarred face clear in the moonlight, looking at them tragically.

Emily and Teddy both stood up so suddenly that they seemed veritably to have been jerked to their feet. Emily's fairy world vanished like a dissolving bubble. She was in a different world altogether—an absurd, ridiculous one. Yes, ridiculous. Everything had suddenly become ridiculous. *Could* anything be more ridiculous than to be caught here with Teddy, *by his mother,* at two o'clock at night—what was that horrid word she had lately heard for the first time?—oh, yes, *spooning*—that was it—spooning on George Horton's eighty-year-old tombstone? That was how other people would look at it. How could a thing be so beautiful one moment and so absurd the next? She was one horrible scorch of shame from head to feet. And Teddy—she knew Teddy was feeling like a fool.

To Mrs. Kent it was not ridiculous—it was dreadful. To her abnormal jealousy the incident had the most sinister significance. She looked at Emily with her hollow, hungry eyes.

"So you are trying to steal my son from me," she said. "He is all I have and you are trying to steal him."

"Oh, Mother, for goodness' sake, be sensible!" muttered Teddy.

"He—he tells me to be sensible," Mrs. Kent echoed tragically to the moon. "Sensible!"

"Yes, sensible," said Teddy angrily. "There's nothing to make such a fuss about. Emily was locked in the church by accident and Mad Mr. Morrison was there, too, and nearly frightened her to death. I came to let her out and we were sitting here for a few minutes until she got over her fright and was able to walk home. That's all."

"How did you know she was here?" demanded Mrs. Kent.

How indeed! This was a hard question to answer. The truth sounded like a silly, stupid invention. Nevertheless, Teddy told it.

"She called me," he said bluntly.

"And you heard her—a mile away. Do you expect me to believe that?" said Mrs. Kent, laughing wildly.

Emily had by this time recovered her poise. At no time in her life was Emily Byrd Starr ever disconcerted for long. She drew herself up proudly and in the dim light, in spite of her Starr features, she looked much as Elizabeth Murray must have looked thirty years before.

"Whether you believe it or not it is true, Mrs. Kent," she said haughtily. "I am not stealing your son—I do not want him—he can go."

"I'm going to take you home first, Emily," said Teddy. He folded his arms and threw back his head and tried to look as stately as Emily. He felt that he was a dismal failure at it, but it imposed on Mrs. Kent. She began to cry.

"Go—go," she said. "Go to her—desert me."

Emily was thoroughly angry now. If this irrational woman persisted in making a scene, very well: a scene she should have.

"I won't let him take me home," she said, freezingly. "Teddy, go with your mother."

"Oh, you command him, do you? He must do as you tell him, must he?" cried Mrs. Kent, who now seemed to lose all control of herself. Her tiny form was shaken with violent sobs. She wrung her hands.

"He shall choose for himself," she cried. "He shall go with you—or come with me. Choose, Teddy, for yourself. You shall not do her bidding. Choose!"

She was fiercely dramatic again, as she lifted her hand and pointed it at poor Teddy.

Teddy was feeling as miserable and impotently angry as any male creature does when two women are quarrelling about him in his presence. He wished himself a thousand miles away. What a mess to be in—and to be made ridiculous like this before Emily! Why on earth couldn't his mother behave like other boys' mothers? Why must she be so intense and exacting? He knew Blair Water gossip said she was "a little touched." He did not believe that. But—but—well, in short here *was* a mess. You came back to that every time. What on earth was he to do? If he took Emily home he knew his mother would cry and pray for days. On the other hand to desert Emily after her dreadful experience in the church, and leave her to traverse that lonely road alone was unthinkable. But Emily now dominated the situation. She was very angry, with the icy anger of old Hugh Murray that did not dissipate itself in idle bluster, but went straight to the point.

"You are a foolish, selfish woman," she said, "and you will make your son hate you."

"Selfish! You call me selfish," sobbed Mrs. Kent. "I live only for Teddy—he is all I have to live for."

"You *are* selfish." Emily was standing straight: her eyes had gone black: her voice was cutting: "the Murray look" was on her face, and in the pale moonlight it was a rather fearsome thing. She wondered, as she spoke, how she knew certain things. But she *did* know them. "You think you love him—it is only yourself you love. You are determined to spoil his life. You won't let him go to Shrewsbury because it will hurt you to let him go away from you. You have let your jealousy of everything he cares for eat your heart out, and master you. You won't bear a little pain for his sake. You are not a mother at all. Teddy has a great talent—every one says so. You ought to be proud of him—you ought to give him his chance. But you won't—and some day he will hate you for it—yes, he will."

"Oh, no, no," moaned Mrs. Kent. She held up her hands as if to ward off a blow and shrank back against Teddy. "Oh, you are cruel—cruel. You don't know what I've suffered—you don't know what ache is always at my heart. He is all I have—all. I have nothing else—not even a memory. You don't understand. I can't—I can't give him up."

"If you let your jealousy ruin his life you will lose him," said Emily inexorably. She had always been afraid of Mrs. Kent. Now she was suddenly no longer afraid of her—she knew she would never be afraid of her again. "You hate everything he cares for—you hate his friends and his dog and his drawing. You know you do. But you can't keep him that way, Mrs. Kent. And you will find out when it is too late. Good night, Teddy. Thank you again for coming to my rescue. Good night, Mrs. Kent."

Emily's good night was very final. She turned and stalked across the green without another glance, holding her head high. Down the wet road she marched—at first very angry—then, as anger ebbed, very tired—oh, horribly tired. She discovered that she was fairly shaking with weariness. The emotions of the night had exhausted her, and now—what to do? She did not like the idea of going home to New

Moon. Emily felt that she could never face outraged Aunt Elizabeth if the various scandalous doings of this night should be discovered. She turned in at the gate of Dr. Burnley's house. His doors were never locked. Emily slipped into the front hall as the dawn began to whiten in the sky and curled up on the lounge behind the staircase. There was no use in waking Ilse. She would tell her the whole story in the morning and bind her to secrecy—all, at least, except one thing Teddy had said, and the episode of Mrs. Kent. One was too beautiful, and the other too disagreeable to be talked about. Of course, Mrs. Kent wasn't like other women and there was no use in feeling too badly about it. Nevertheless, she had wrecked and spoiled a frail, beautiful something—she had blotched with absurdity a moment that should have been eternally lovely. And she had, of course, made poor Teddy feel like an ass. *That,* in the last analysis, was what Emily really could not forgive.

As she drifted off to sleep she recalled drowsily the events of that bewildering night—her imprisonment in the lonely church—the horror of touching the dog—the worse horror of Mad Mr. Morrison's pursuit—her rapture of relief at Teddy's voice—the brief little moonlit idyll in the graveyard—of all places for an idyll!—the tragi-comic advent of poor morbid, jealous Mrs. Kent.

"I hope I wasn't too hard on her," thought Emily as she drifted into slumber. "If I was I'm sorry. I'll have to write it down as a bad deed in my diary. I feel somehow as if I'd grown up all at once tonight—yesterday seems years away. But what a chapter it will make for my diary. I'll write it all down—all but Teddy's saying I was the sweetest girl in the world. *That's* too—dear—to write. I'll—just—*remember* it."

"AS ITHERS SEE US"

Emily had finished mopping up the kitchen floor at New Moon and was absorbed in sanding it in the beautiful and complicated "herring-bone pattern" which was one of the New Moon traditions, having been invented, so it was said, by great-great-grandmother of "Here I stay" fame. Aunt Laura had taught Emily how to do it and Emily was proud of her skill. Even Aunt Elizabeth had condescended to say that Emily sanded the famous pattern very well, and when Aunt Elizabeth praised, further comment was superfluous. New Moon was the only place in Blair Water where the old custom of sanding the floor was kept up; other housewives had long ago begun to use "new-fangled" devices and patent cleaners for making their floors white. But Dame Elizabeth Murray would none of such; as long as she reigned at New Moon so long should candles burn and sanded floors gleam whitely. Aunt Elizabeth had exasperated Emily somewhat by insisting that the latter should put on Aunt Laura's old "Mother Hubbard" while she was scrubbing the floor. A "Mother Hubbard," it may be necessary to explain to those of this generation, was a loose and shapeless garment which served principally as a sort of morning gown and was liked in its day because it was cool and easily put on. Aunt Elizabeth, it is quite unnecessary to say, disapproved entirely of Mother Hubbards. She considered them the last word in slovenliness, and Laura was never permitted to have another one. But the old one, though its original pretty lilac tint had faded to a dingy white, was still too "good" to be banished to the rag bag; and it was this which Emily had been told to put on.

Emily detested Mother Hubbards as heartily as Aunt Elizabeth herself did. They were worse, she considered, even than the hated "baby aprons" of her first summer at New Moon. She knew she looked ridiculous in Aunt Laura's Mother Hubbard, which came to her feet, and hung in loose, unbeautiful lines from her thin young shoulders; and Emily had a horror of being "ridiculous." She had once shocked Aunt Elizabeth by coolly telling her that she would "rather be bad than ridiculous." Emily had scrubbed and sanded with one eye on the door, ready to run if any stranger loomed up while she had on that hideous wrapper.

It was not, as Emily very well knew, a Murray tradition to "run." At New Moon you stood your ground, no matter what you had on—the presupposition being that you were always neatly and properly habited for the occupation of the moment. Emily recognized the propriety of this, yet was, nevertheless, foolish and young enough to feel that she would die of shame if seen by anyone in Aunt Laura's Mother Hubbard. It was neat—it was clean—but it was "ridiculous." There you were!

Just as Emily finished sanding and turned to place her can of sand in the niche under the kitchen mantel, where it had been kept from time immemorial, she heard strange voices in the kitchen yard. A hasty glimpse through the window revealed to her the owners of the voices—Miss Beulah Potter, and Mrs. Ann Cyrilla Potter, calling, no doubt, in regard to the projected Ladies' Aid Social. They were coming to the back door as was the Blair Water custom when running in to see your neighbours, informally or on business; they were already past the gay platoons of hollyhocks with which Cousin Jimmy had flanked the stone path to the dairy, and of all the people in Blair Water and out of it they were the two whom Emily would least want to see her in any ridiculous plight whatever. Without stopping to think, she darted into the boot closet and shut the door.

Mrs. Ann Cyrilla knocked twice at the kitchen door, but Emily did not budge. She knew Aunt Laura was weaving in the garret—she could hear the dull thud of the treadles overhead—but she thought Aunt Elizabeth was concocting pies in the cook-house and would see or hear the callers. She would take them into the sitting-room and then Emily could make her escape. And on one thing she was determined— they should not see her in that Mother Hubbard. Miss Potter was a thin, venomous, acidulated gossip who seemed to dislike everybody in general and Emily in particular; and Mrs. Ann Cyrilla was a plump, pretty, smooth, amiable gossip who, by very reason of her smoothness and amiability, did more real harm in a week than Miss Potter did in a year. Emily distrusted her even while she could not help liking her. She had so often heard Mrs. Ann Cyrilla make smiling fun of people, to whose "faces" she had been very sweet and charming, and Mrs. Ann Cyrilla, who had been one of the "dressy Wallaces" from Derry Pond, was especially fond of laughing over the peculiarities of other people's clothes.

Again the knock came—Miss Potter's this time, as Emily knew by the staccato raps. They were getting impatient. Well, they might knock there till the cows come home, vowed Emily. She would not go to the door in the Mother Hubbard. Then she heard Perry's voice outside explaining that Miss Elizabeth was away in the stumps behind the barn picking raspberries, but that he would go and get her if they would walk in and make themselves at home. To Emily's despair, this was just what they did. Miss Potter sat down with a creak and Mrs. Ann Cyrilla with a puff, and Perry's retreating footsteps died away in the yard. Emily realized that she was by way of being in a plight. It was very hot and stuffy in the tiny boot closet—where Cousin Jimmy's working clothes were kept as well as boots. She hoped earnestly that Perry would not be long in finding Aunt Elizabeth.

"My, but it's awful hot," said Mrs. Ann Cyrilla, with a large groan.

Poor Emily—no, no, we must not call her poor Emily; she does not deserve pity—she has been very silly and is served exactly right; Emily, then, already violently perspiring in her close quarters, agreed wholly with her.

"*I* don't feel the heat as fat people do," said Miss Potter. "I hope Elizabeth won't keep us waiting long. Laura's weaving—I hear the loom going in the garret. But there would be no use in seeing her—Elizabeth would override anything Laura might promise, just because it wasn't *her* arrangement. I see somebody has just finished sanding the floor. Look at those worn boards, will you? You'd think Elizabeth Murray would have a new floor laid down; but she is too mean, of course. Look at that row of candles on the chimney-piece—all that trouble and poor light because of the little extra coal-oil would cost. Well, she can't take her money with her—she'll have to leave it all behind at the golden gate even if she *is* a Murray."

Emily experienced a shock. She realized that not only was she being half suffocated in the boot closet, but that she was an eavesdropper—something she had never been since the evening at Maywood when she had hidden under the table to hear her aunts and uncles discussing her fate. To be sure, that had been voluntary, while this was compulsory—at least, the Mother Hubbard had made it compulsory. But that would not make Miss Potter's comments any pleasanter to hear. What business had she to call Aunt Elizabeth mean? Aunt Elizabeth *wasn't* mean. Emily was suddenly very angry with Miss Potter. She, herself, often criticized Aunt Elizabeth in secret, but it was intolerable that an outsider should do it. And that little sneer at the Murrays! Emily could imagine the shrewish glint in Miss Potter's eye as she uttered it. As for the candles—

"The Murrays can see farther by candle-light than *you* can by sunlight, Miss Potter," thought Emily disdainfully—or at least as disdainfully as it is possible to think when a river of perspiration is running down your back, and you have nothing to breathe but the aroma of old leather.

"I suppose it's because of the expense that she won't send Emily to school any longer than this year," said Mrs. Ann Cyrilla. "Most folks think she ought to give her a year at Shrewsbury, anyhow—you'd think she would for pride's sake, if nothing else. But I am told she has decided against it."

Emily's heart sank. She hadn't been quite sure till now that Aunt Elizabeth wouldn't send her to Shrewsbury. The tears sprang to her eyes—burning, stinging tears of disappointment.

"Emily ought to be taught something to earn a living by," said Miss Potter. "Her father left nothing."

"He left *me*," said Emily below her breath, clenching her fists. Anger dried up her tears.

"Oh," said Mrs. Ann Cyrilla, laughing with tolerant derision, "I hear that Emily is going to make a living by writing stories—not only a living but a fortune, I believe."

She laughed again. The idea was so exquisitely ridiculous. Mrs. Ann Cyrilla hadn't heard anything so funny for a long time.

"They say she wastes half her time scribbling trash," agreed Miss Potter. "If I was her Aunt Elizabeth I would soon cure her of that nonsense."

"You mightn't find it so easy. I understand she has always been a difficult girl to manage—so very pig-headed, Murray-like. The whole clamjamfry of them are as stubborn as mules."

(*Emily, wrathfully:* "What a disrespectful way to speak of us! Oh, if I only hadn't on this Mother Hubbard I'd fling this door open and confront them.")

"She needs a tight rein, if *I* know anything of human nature," said Miss Potter. "She's going to be a flirt—anyone can see that. She'll be Juliet over again. You'll see. She makes eyes at every one and her only fourteen!"

(*Emily, sarcastically:* "I do *not*! And Mother wasn't a flirt. She *could* have been, but she wasn't. *You* couldn't flirt, even if you wanted to—you respectable old female!")

"She isn't pretty as poor Juliet was, and she's very sly—sly and deep. Mrs. Dutton says she's the slyest child she ever saw. But still there are things I like about poor Emily."

Mrs. Ann Cyrilla's tone was very patronizing. "Poor" Emily writhed among the boots.

"The thing *I* don't like in her is that she is always trying to be smart," said Miss Potter decidedly. "She says clever things she has read in books and passes them off as her own—"

(Emily, outraged: "I don't!")

"And she's very sarcastic and touchy, and of course as proud as Lucifer," concluded Miss Potter.

Mrs. Ann Cyrilla laughed pleasantly and tolerantly again.

"Oh, that goes without saying in a Murray. But their worst fault is that they think nobody can do anything right but themselves, and Emily is full of it. Why, she even thinks she can preach better than Mr. Johnson."

(Emily: "That is because I said he contradicted himself in one of his sermons—and he *did*. And I've heard *you* criticize dozens of sermons, Mrs. Ann Cyrilla.")

"She's jealous, too," continued Mrs. Ann Cyrilla. "She can't bear to be beaten—she wants to be first in everything. I understand she actually shed tears of mortification the night of the concert because Ilse Burnley carried off the honours in the dialogue. Emily did very poorly—she was a perfect *stick*. And she contradicts older people continually. It would be funny if it weren't so ill-bred."

"It's odd Elizabeth doesn't cure her of *that*. The Murrays think their breeding is a little above the common," said Miss Potter.

(Emily, wrathfully, to the boots: "It *is*, too.")

"Of course," said Mrs. Ann Cyrilla, "I think a great many of Emily's faults come from her intimacy with Ilse Burnley. She shouldn't be allowed to run about with Ilse as she does. Why, they say Ilse is as much an infidel as her father. I have always understood she doesn't believe in God at all—or the Devil either."

(Emily: "Which is a far worse thing in *your* eyes.")

"Oh, the doctor's training her a little better now since he found out his precious wife didn't elope with Leo Mitchell," sniffed Miss Potter. "He makes her go to Sunday-school. But she's no fit associate for Emily. She swears like a trooper, I'm told. Mrs. Mark Burns was in the doctor's office one day and heard Ilse in the parlour say distinctly 'out, damned Spot!' probably to the dog."

"Dear, dear," moaned Mrs. Ann Cyrilla.

"Do you know what *I* saw her do one day last week—saw her with my own eyes!" Miss Potter was very emphatic over this. Ann Cyrilla need not suppose that she had been using any other person's eyes.

"You couldn't surprise me," gurgled Mrs. Ann Cyrilla. "Why, they say she was at the charivari at Johnson's last Tuesday night, dressed as a boy."

"Quite likely. But this happened in my own front yard. She was there with Jen Strang, who had come to get a root of my Persian rose-bush for her mother. I asked Ilse if she could sew and bake and a few other things that I thought she ought to be reminded of. Ilse said 'No' to them all, quite brazenly, and then *she* said—*what* do you think that girl said?"

"Oh, what?" breathed Mrs. Ann Cyrilla eagerly.

"She said, 'Can *you* stand on one foot and lift your other to a level with your eyes, Miss Potter? I can.' And"—Miss Potter hushed her tone to the proper pitch of horror—*"she did it!"*

The listener in the closet stifled a spasm of laughter in Cousin Jimmy's grey juniper. How madcap Ilse did love to shock Miss Potter!

"Good gracious, were there any men around?" entreated Mrs. Ann Cyrilla.

"No—fortunately. But it's my belief she would have done it just the same no matter who was there. We were close to the road—*anybody* might have been passing. I felt so ashamed. In *my* time a young girl would have *died* before she would have done a thing like that."

"It's no worse than her and Emily bathing by moonlight up on the sands *without a stitch on*," said Mrs. Ann Cyrilla. *"That* was the most scandalous thing. Did you hear about it?"

"Oh, yes, that story's all over Blair Water. Everybody's heard it but Elizabeth and Laura. I can't find out how it started. Were they *seen?"*

"Oh, dear no, not so bad as that. Ilse told it herself. She seemed to think it was quite a matter of course. *I* think some one ought to tell Laura and Elizabeth."

"Tell them yourself," suggested Miss Potter.

"Oh, no, *I* don't want to get in wrong with my neighbours. *I* am not responsible for Emily Starr's training, thank goodness. If I were I wouldn't let her have so much to do with Jarback Priest, either. He's the queerest of all those queer Priests. I'm sure he must have a bad influence over her. Those green eyes of his positively give me the creeps. I can't find out that he believes in *anything."*

(*Emily, sarcastically again:* "Not even the Devil?")

"There's a queer story going around about him and Emily," said Miss Potter. "I can't make head or tail of it. They were seen on the big hill last Wednesday evening at sunset, behaving in a most extraordinary fashion. They would walk along with their eyes fixed on the sky—then suddenly stop—grasp each other by the arm and point upward. They did it time and again. Mrs. Price was watching them from the window and she can't imagine what they were up it. It was too early for stars, and *she* couldn't see a solitary thing in the sky. She laid awake all night wondering about it."

"Well, it all comes to this—Emily Starr needs looking after," said Mrs. Ann Cyrilla. "I sometimes feel that it would be wiser to stop Muriel and Gladys from going about so much with her."

(*Emily, devoutly:* "I wish you *would*. They are so stupid and silly and they just stick around Ilse and me all the time.")

"When all is said and done, I pity her," said Miss Potter. "She's so foolish and high-minded that she'll get in wrong with every one, and no decent, sensible man will ever be bothered with her. Geoff North says he went home with her once and that was enough for *him*."

(*Emily, emphatically:* "I believe you! Geoff showed almost human intelligence in *that* remark.")

"But then she probably won't live through her teens. She looks very consumptive. Really, Ann Cyrilla, I *do* feel sorry for the poor thing."

This was the proverbial last straw for Emily. *She,* whole Starr and half Murray to be pitied by Beulah Potter! Mother Hubbard or no Mother Hubbard, it could not be borne! The closet door suddenly opened wide and Emily stood revealed, Mother Hubbard and all, against a background of boots and jumpers. Her cheeks were crimson, her eyes black. The mouths of Mrs. Ann Cyrilla and Miss Beulah Potter fell open and stayed open; their faces turned dull red; they were dumb.

Emily looked at them steadily for a minute of scornful, eloquent silence. Then, with the air of a queen, she swept across the kitchen and vanished through the sitting-room door, just as Aunt Elizabeth came up the sandstone steps with dignified apologies for keeping them waiting. Miss Potter and Mrs. Ann Cyrilla were so dumbfounded that they were hardly able to talk about the Ladies' Aid, and got themselves confusedly away after a few jerky questions and answers. Aunt Elizabeth did not know what to make of them and thought they must have been unreasonably offended over having to wait. Then she dismissed the matter from her mind. A Murray did not care what Potters thought or did. The open closet door told no tales, and she did not know that up in the lookout chamber Emily was lying face downward across the bed crying passionately for shame and anger and humiliation. She felt degraded and hurt. It had all been the outcome of her own silly vanity in the beginning—she acknowledged that—but her punishment had been *too* severe.

She did not mind so much what Miss Potter had said, but Mrs. Ann Cyrilla's tiny barbs of malice *did* sting. She had liked pretty, pleasant Mrs. Ann Cyrilla, who had always seemed kind and friendly and had paid her many compliments. She had thought Mrs. Ann Cyrilla had really liked her. And now to find out that she would talk about her like this!

"Couldn't they have said *one* good thing of me?" she sobbed. "Oh, I feel *soiled,* somehow—between my own silliness and their malice— and all dirty and messed-up mentally. Will I ever feel *clean* again?"

She did not feel "clean" until she had written it all out in her diary. Then she took a less distorted view of it and summoned philosophy to her aid.

"Mr. Carpenter says we should make every experience teach us something," she wrote. "He says every experience, no matter whether it is pleasant or unpleasant, has something for us if we are able to view it dispassionately. 'That,' he added bitterly, 'is one of the pieces of good advice I have kept by me all my life and never been able to make any use of myself.'

"Very well, I shall try to view this dispassionately! I suppose the way to do it is to consider all that was said of me and decide just what was *true* and what false, and what merely distorted—which is worse than the false, I think.

"To begin with: hiding in the closet at all, just out of vanity, comes under my heading of bad deeds. And I *suppose* that appearing as I did, after I *had* stayed there so long, and covering them with confusion, was another. But if so, I can't feel it 'dispassionately' yet, because I am sinfully glad I did it—yes, even if they did see me in the Mother Hubbard! I shall never forget their faces! Especially Mrs. Ann Cyrilla's. Miss Potter won't worry over it long—she will say it served me right— but Mrs. Ann Cyrilla will never, to her dying day, get over being *found out* like that.

"Now for a review of their criticisms of Emily Byrd Starr and the decision as to whether said Emily Byrd Starr deserved the said criticisms, wholly or in part. Be honest now, Emily, 'look then into thy heart' and try to see yourself, not as Miss Potter sees you or as you see yourself, but as you really are.

"(I think I'm going to find this interesting!)

"In the first place, Mrs. Ann Cyrilla said I was pig-headed.

"*Am* I pig-headed?

"I know I am determined, and Aunt Elizabeth says I am stubborn. But pig-headedness is worse than either of those. Determination is a good quality and even stubbornness has a saving grace in it if you have a little gumption as well. But a pig-headed person is one who is too stupid to see or understand the foolishness of a certain course and insists on taking it—insists, in short, on running full tilt into a stone wall.

"No, I am *not* pig-headed. I accept stone walls.

"But I take a good deal of convincing that they *are* stone walls and not cardboard imitations. Therefore, I *am* a little stubborn.

"Miss Potter said I was a flirt. This is wholly untrue, so I won't discuss it. But she also said I 'made eyes.' Now do I? I don't mean to—I know that; but it seems you can 'make eyes' without being conscious of it, so how am I going to prevent that? I can't go about all the days of my life with my eyes dropped down. Dean said the other day:

"'When you look at me like that, Star, there is nothing for me but to do as you ask.'

"And Aunt Elizabeth was quite annoyed last week because she said I was looking 'improperly' at Perry when I was coaxing him to go to the Sunday-school picnic. (Perry hates Sunday-school picnics.)

"Now, in both cases I thought I was only looking *beseechingly*.

"Mrs. Ann Cyrilla said I wasn't pretty. Is that true?"

Emily laid down her pen, went over to the mirror and took a "dispassionate" stock of her looks. Black of hair—smoke-purple of eye—crimson of lip. So far, not bad. Her forehead was too high, but the new way of doing her hair obviated that defect. Her skin was very white and her cheeks, which had been so pale in childhood, were now as delicately hued as a pink pearl. Her mouth was too large, but her teeth were good. Her slightly pointed ears gave her a fawn-like charm. Her neck had lines that she could not help liking. Her slender, immature figure was graceful; she knew, for Aunt Nancy had told her, that she had the Shipley ankle and instep. Emily looked very earnestly at Emily-in-the-Glass from several angles, and returned to her diary.

"I have decided that I am not pretty," she wrote. "I think I *look* quite pretty when my hair is done a certain way, but a really pretty girl would be pretty no matter how her hair was done, so Mrs. Ann Cyrilla was right. But I feel sure that I am not so plain as she implied, either.

"Then she said I was sly—and *deep*. I don't think it is any fault to be 'deep,' though she spoke as if she thought it was. I would rather be deep than shallow. But am I sly? *No*. I am *not*. Then what is it about me that makes people think I am sly? Aunt Ruth always insists that I am. *I* think it is because I have a habit, when I am bored or disgusted with people, of stepping suddenly into my own world and shutting the door. People resent this—I suppose it is only natural to resent a door being shut in your face. They call it slyness when it is only self-defence. So I won't worry over that.

"Miss Potter said an abominable thing—that I passed off clever speeches I had read in books, as my own—trying to be smart. That is *utterly false*. Honestly, I never 'try to be smart.' But—I *do* try often to see how a certain thing I've thought out sounds when it is put into words. Perhaps this is a kind of showing-off. I must be careful about it.

"Jealous: no, I'm not that. I *do* like to be first, I admit. But it wasn't because I was jealous of Ilse that I cried that night at the concert. I cried because I felt I had made a mess of my part. I *was* a stick, just as Mrs. Ann Cyrilla said. I can't *act* a part somehow. Sometimes a certain part seems to suit me and then I can *be* it, but if not I'm no good in a dialogue. I only went in it to oblige Mrs. Johnson, and I felt horribly mortified because I knew she was disappointed.

"And I suppose my pride suffered a bit, but I never thought of being jealous of Ilse. I was proud of her—she does magnificently in a play.

"Yes, I contradict. I admit that *is* one of my faults. But people do say such outrageous things! And why isn't it as bad for people to contradict me? They do it continually—and I am *right* just as often as they are.

"Sarcastic? Yes, I'm afraid that is another of my faults. Touchy—no, I'm *not*. I'm only *sensitive*. And proud? Well, yes, I *am* a little proud—but not nearly as proud as people think me. I can't help carrying my head at a certain angle and I can't help feeling it is a great thing to have a century of good, upright people with fine traditions and considerable brains behind you. Not like the Potters—upstarts of yesterday!

"Oh, how those women garbled things about poor Ilse. We couldn't, I suppose, expect a Potter or the wife of a Potter to recognize the sleep-walking scene from *Lady Macbeth*. I have told Ilse repeatedly that she ought to see that all doors are shut when she tries it over. She is quite wonderful in it. She *never* was at that charivari—she only said she'd *like* to go. And as for the moonlight bathing—that was true enough except that we had *some* stitches on. There was nothing dreadful about it. It was perfectly beautiful—though now it is all spoiled and degraded by being dragged about in common gossip. I wish Ilse hadn't told about it.

"We had gone away up the sandshore for a walk. It was a moonlit night and the sandshore was wonderful. The Wind Woman was rustling in the grasses on the dunes and there was a long, gentle wash of little gleaming waves on the shore. We wanted to bathe, but at first we thought we couldn't because we didn't have our bathing dresses. So we sat on the sands and we just talked. The great gulf stretched out before us, silvery, gleaming, alluring, going farther and farther into the mists of the northern sky. It was like an ocean in 'fairylands forlorn.'

"I said:

"'I would like to get into a ship and sail straight out there—out—out—where would I land?'

"'Anticosti, I expect,' said Ilse—a bit too prosaically, I thought.

"'No—no—Ultima Thule, I think,' I said dreamily. 'Some beautiful unknown shore where "the rain never falls, and the wind never blows." Perhaps the country back of the North Wind where *Diamond* went. One could sail to it over that silver sea on a night like this.'

"'*That* was heaven, I think,' said Ilse.

"Then we talked about immortality, and Ilse said she was afraid of it—afraid of living for ever and for ever; she said she was sure she would get awfully tired of herself. I said I thought I liked Dean's idea of a succession of lives—I can't make out from him whether he really believes that or not—and Ilse said that might be all very well if you were sure of being born again as a decent person, but how about it if you weren't?

"'Well, you have to take some risk in any kind of immortality,' I said.

"'Anyhow,' said Ilse, 'whether I am myself or somebody else next time, I do hope I won't have such a dreadful temper. If I just go on being myself I'll smash my harp and tear my halo to pieces and pull all the feathers out of the other angels' wings half an hour after getting to heaven. You know I will, Emily. I can't help it. I had a fiendish quarrel with Perry yesterday again. It was all my fault—but of course he vexed me by his boasting. I *wish* I could control my temper.'

"I don't mind Ilse's rages one bit now—I know she never means anything she says in them. I never say anything back. I just smile at her and if I've a bit of paper handy I jot down the things she says. This infuriates her so that she chokes with anger and can't say anything more. At all other times Ilse is a darling and such good fun.

"'You can't control your rages because you like going into them,' I said.

"Ilse stared at me.

"'I don't—I don't.'

"'You do. You enjoy them,' I insisted.

"'Well, of course,' said Ilse, grinning, "I *do* have a good time while they last. It's awfully *satisfying* to say the most insulting things and call the worst names. I believe you're right, Emily. I *do* enjoy them. Queer I never thought of it. I suppose if I really were unhappy in them I wouldn't go into them. But after they're over—I'm so remorseful. I cried for an hour yesterday after fighting with Perry.'

"'Yes, and you enjoyed that, too—didn't you?'

"Ilse reflected.

"'I guess so, Emily; you're an uncanny thing. I won't talk about it any more. Let's go bathing. No dresses? What does it matter. There isn't a soul for miles. I can't resist those waves. They're *calling* me.'

"I felt just as she did, and bathing by moonlight seemed such a lovely, romantic thing—and it *is*, when the Potters of the world don't know of it. When they do, they smudge it. We undressed in a little hollow among the dunes—that was like a bowl of silver in the moonlight— but we kept our petticoats on. We had the loveliest time splashing and swimming about in that silver-blue water and those creamy little waves, like mermaids or sea nymphs. It was like living in a poem or a fairy tale. And when we came out I held out my hands to Ilse and said:

"Come unto these yellow sands

Curtseyed when we have and kissed,

The wild winds whist,

Foot it featly here and there

And, sweet sprites, the burden bear.

"Ilse took my hands and we danced in rings over the moonlit sands, and then we went up to the silver bowl and dressed and went home perfectly happy. Only, of course, we had to carry our wet petticoats rolled up under our arms, so we looked rather slinky, but nobody saw us. And *that* is what Blair Water is so scandalized about.

"All the same, I hope Aunt Elizabeth won't hear of it.

"It is too bad Mrs. Price lost so much sleep over Dean and me. We were not performing any weird incantations—we were simply walking over the Delectable Mountain and tracing pictures in the clouds. Perhaps it was childish—but it was great fun. That is one thing I like about Dean—he isn't afraid of doing something harmless and pleasant just because it's childish. One cloud he pointed out to me looked exactly like an angel flying along the pale, shining sky and carrying a baby in its arms. There was a filmy blue veil over its head with a faint, first star gleaming through it. Its wings were tipped with gold and its white robe flecked with crimson.

"'There goes the Angel of the Evening Star with to-morrow in its arms,' said Dean.

"It was so beautiful that it gave me one of my wonder moments. But ten seconds later it had changed into something that looked like a camel with an exaggerated hump!

"We had a wonderful half hour, even if Mrs. Price, who couldn't see anything in the sky, did think us quite mad.

"Well, it all comes to this, there's no use trying to live in other people's opinions. The only thing to do is to live in your own. After all, I believe in myself. I'm not so bad and silly as they think me, and I'm not consumptive, and I *can* write. Now that I've written it all out I feel differently about it. The only thing that still aggravates me is that Miss

Potter *pitied* me—pitied by a Potter!

"I looked out of my window just now and saw Cousin Jimmy's nasturtium bed—and suddenly the flash came—and Miss Potter and her pity, and her malicious tongue seemed to matter not at all. Nasturtiums, who coloured you, you wonderful, glowing things? You must have been fashioned out of summer sunsets.

"I help Cousin Jimmy a great deal with his garden this summer. I think I love it as much as he does. Every day we make new discoveries of bud and bloom.

"So Aunt Elizabeth won't send me to Shrewsbury! Oh, I feel as disappointed as if I'd really hoped she would. Every door in life seems shut to me.

"Still, after all, I've lots to be thankful for. Aunt Elizabeth will let me go to school another year here, I think, and Mr. Carpenter can teach me heaps yet; I'm not hideous; moonlight is still a fair thing; I'm going to do something with my pen some day—*and* I've got a lovely, grey, moon-faced cat who has just jumped up on my table and poked my pen with his nose as a signal that I've written enough for one sitting.

"The only real cat is a grey cat!"

HALF A LOAF

One late August evening Emily heard Teddy's signal whistle from the To-morrow Road, and slipped out to join him. He had news—that was evident from his shining eyes.

"Emily," he cried excitedly, "I'm going to Shrewsbury after all! Mother told me this evening she had made up her mind to let me go!"

Emily was glad—with a queer sorriness underneath, for which she reproached herself. How lonesome it would be at New Moon when her three old pals were gone! She had not realized until that moment how much she had counted on Teddy's companionship. He had always been there in the background of her thoughts of the coming year. She had always taken Teddy for granted. Now there would be nobody—not even Dean, for Dean was going away for the winter as usual—to Egypt or Japan, as he might decide at the last moment. What would she do? Would all the Jimmy-books in the world take the place of her flesh-and-blood chums?

"If you were only going, too!" said Teddy, as they walked along the To-morrow Road—which was almost a To-day Road now, so fast and so tall had the leafy young maples grown.

"There's no use wishing it—don't speak of it—it makes me unhappy," said Emily jerkily.

"Well, we'll have week-ends anyhow. And it's you I have to thank for going. It was what you said to Mother that night in the graveyard that made her let me go. I know she's been thinking of it ever since, by things she would say every once in a while. One day last week I heard her muttering: 'It's awful to be a mother—awful to be a mother and suffer like this.' Yet she called me selfish!' And another time she said, 'Is it selfish to want to keep the only thing you have left in the world?' But she was lovely to-night when she told me I could go. I know folks say Mother isn't quite right in her mind—and sometimes she *is* a little queer. But it's only when other people are around. You've no idea, Emily, how nice and dear she is when we're alone. I hate to leave her. But I *must* get some education!"

"I'm very glad if what I said has made her change her mind, but she will never forgive me for it. She has hated me ever since—you know she has. You know how she *looks* at me whenever I'm at the Tansy Patch—oh, she's very polite to me. But her eyes, Teddy."

"I know," said Teddy, uncomfortably. "But don't be hard on Mother, Emily. I'm sure she wasn't always like that—though she has been ever since I can remember. I don't know *anything* of her before that. She never tells me anything—I don't know a thing about my father. She won't talk about him. I don't even know how she got that scar on her face."

"I don't think there's anything the matter with your mother's mind, really," said Emily slowly. "But I think there's something troubling it—always troubling it—something she can't forget or throw off. Teddy, I'm sure your mother is *haunted*. Of course, I don't mean by a ghost or anything silly like that. But by some terrible *thought*."

"She isn't happy, I know," said Teddy, "and, of course, we're poor. Mother said to-night she could only send me to Shrewsbury for three years—that was all she could afford. But that will give me a start—I'll get on somehow after that. I *know* I can. I'll make it up to her yet."

"You will be a great artist some day," said Emily dreamily.

They had come to the end of the To-morrow Road. Before them was the pond pasture, whitened over with a drift of daisies. Farmers hate the daisies as a pestiferous weed, but a field white with them on a summer twilight is a vision from the Land of Lost Delight. Beneath them Blair Water shone like a great golden lily. Up on the eastern hill the little Disappointed House crouched amid its shadows, dreaming, perhaps, of the false bride that had never come to it. There was no light at the Tansy Patch. Was lonely Mrs. Kent crying there in the darkness, with only her secret, tormenting heart-hunger for companion?

Emily was looking at the sunset sky—her eyes rapt, her face pale and seeking. She felt no longer blue or depressed—somehow she never could feel that way long in Teddy's company. In all the world there was no music like his voice. All good things seemed suddenly possible with him. She could not go to Shrewsbury—but she could work and study at New Moon—oh, how she would work and study. Another year with Mr. Carpenter would do a great deal for her—as much as Shrewsbury, perhaps. She, too, had her Alpine Path to climb—she *would* climb it, no matter what the obstacles in the way—no matter whether there was any one to help her or not.

"When I am I'll paint you just as you're looking now," said Teddy, "and call it Joan of Arc—with a face all spirit—listening to her voices."

In spite of her voices Emily went to bed that night feeling rather down-hearted—and woke in the morning with an unaccountable conviction that some good news was coming to her that day—a conviction that did not lessen as the hours passed by in the commonplace fashion of Saturday hours at New Moon—busy hours in which the house was made immaculate for Sunday, and the pantry replenished. It was a cool, damp day when the fogs were coming up from the shore on the east wind, and New Moon and its old garden were veiled in mist.

At twilight a thin, grey rain began to fall, and still the good news had not come. Emily had just finished scouring the brass candlesticks and composing a poem called *Rain Song,* simultaneously, when Aunt Laura told her that Aunt Elizabeth wanted to see her in the parlour.

Emily's recollections of parlour interviews with Aunt Elizabeth were not especially pleasant. She could not recall any recent deed, done or left undone, which would justify this summons, yet she walked into the parlour quakingly: whatever Aunt Elizabeth was going to say to her it must have some special significance or it would not be said in the parlour. This was just one of Aunt Elizabeth's little ways. Daffy, her big cat, slipped in beside her like a noiseless, grey shadow. She hoped Aunt Elizabeth would not shoo him out: his presence was a certain comfort: a cat is a good backer when he is on your side!

Aunt Elizabeth was knitting; she looked solemn but not offended or angry. She ignored Daff, but thought that Emily seemed very tall in the old, stately, twilit room. How quickly children grew up! It seemed but the other day since fair, pretty Juliet—Elizabeth Murray shut her thoughts off with a click.

"Sit down, Emily," she said. "I want to have a talk with you."

Emily sat down. So did Daffy, wreathing his tail comfortably about his paws. Emily suddenly felt that her hands were clammy and her mouth dry. She wished that she had knitting, too. It was nasty to sit there, unoccupied, and wonder what was coming. What *did* come was the one thing she had never thought of. Aunt Elizabeth, after knitting a deliberate round on her stocking, said directly:

"Emily, would you like to go to Shrewsbury next week?"

Go to Shrewsbury? Had she heard aright?

"Oh, Aunt Elizabeth!" she said.

"I have been talking the matter over with your uncles and aunts," said Aunt Elizabeth. "They agree with me that you should have some further education. It will be a considerable expense, of course—no, don't interrupt. I don't like interruptions—but Ruth will board you for half-price, as her contribution to your up-bringing—Emily, *I* will *not* be interrupted! Your Uncle Oliver will pay the other half; your Uncle Wallace will provide your books, and I will see to your clothes. You will, of course, help your Aunt Ruth about the house in every way possible as some return for her kindness. You may go to Shrewsbury for three years on a certain condition."

What was the condition? Emily, who wanted to dance and sing and laugh through the old parlour as no Murray, not ever her mother, had ever ventured to dance and laugh before, constrained herself to sit rigidly on her ottoman and ask herself that question. Behind her suspense she felt that the moment was quite dramatic.

"Three years at Shrewsbury," Aunt Elizabeth went on, "will do as much for you as three at Queen's—except, of course, that you don't get a teacher's licence, which doesn't matter in your case, as you are not under the necessity of working for your living. But, as I have said, there is a condition."

Why didn't Aunt Elizabeth name the condition? Emily felt that the suspense was unendurable. Could it be possible that Aunt Elizabeth was a little *afraid* to name it? It was not like her to talk for time. Was it so very terrible?

"You must promise," said Aunt Elizabeth sternly, "that for the three years you are at Shrewsbury you will give up entirely this writing nonsense of yours—*entirely,* except in so far as school compositions may be required."

Emily sat very still—and cold. No Shrewsbury on the one hand— on the other no more poems, no more stories and "studies," no more delightful Jimmy-books of miscellany. She did not take more than one instant to make up her mind.

"I can't promise that, Aunt Elizabeth," she said resolutely.

Aunt Elizabeth dropped her knitting in amazement. She had not expected this. She had thought Emily was so set on going to Shrewsbury that she would do anything that might be asked of her in order to go—especially such a trifling thing as this—which, so Aunt Elizabeth thought, involved only a surrender of stubbornness.

"Do you mean to say you won't give up your foolish scribbling for the sake of the education you've always pretended to want so much?" she demanded.

"Not that I *won't*—it's just that I *can't,*" said Emily despairingly. She knew Aunt Elizabeth could not understand—Aunt Elizabeth never had understood *this.* "I *can't* help writing, Aunt Elizabeth. It's in my blood. There's no use in asking me. I *do* want an education—it isn't pretending—but I can't give up my writing to get it. I *couldn't* keep such a promise—so what use would there be in making it?"

"Then you can stay home," said Aunt Elizabeth angrily.

Emily expected to see her get up and walk out of the room. Instead, Aunt Elizabeth picked up her stocking and wrathfully resumed her knitting. To tell the truth, Aunt Elizabeth was absurdly taken aback. She really wanted to send Emily to Shrewsbury. Tradition required so much of her, and all the clan were of opinion she should be sent. This condition had been her own idea. She thought it a good chance to break Emily of a silly un-Murray-like habit of wasting time and paper, and she had never doubted that her plan would succeed, for she knew how much Emily wanted to go. And now this senseless, unreasoning, ungrateful obstinacy—"the Starr coming out," thought Aunt Elizabeth rancorously, forgetful of the Shipley inheritance! What was to be done? She knew too well from past experience that there would be no moving Emily once she had taken up a position, and she knew that Wallace and Oliver and Ruth, though they thought Emily's craze for writing as silly and untraditional as she did, would not back her—Elizabeth—up in her demand. Elizabeth Murray foresaw a complete right-about-face before her, and Elizabeth Murray did not like the prospect. She could have shaken, with a right good will, the slim, pale thing sitting before her on the ottoman. The creature was so slight—and young—and indomitable. For over three years Elizabeth Murray had tried to cure Emily of this foolishness of writing and for over three years she, who had never failed in anything before, had failed in this. One couldn't starve her into submission—and nothing short of it would seem to be efficacious.

Elizabeth knitted furiously in her vexation, and Emily sat motionless, struggling with her bitter disappointment and sense of injustice. She was determined she would not cry before Aunt Elizabeth, but it was hard to keep the tears back. She wished Daff wouldn't purr with such resounding satisfaction, as if everything were perfectly delicious from a grey cat's point of view. She wished Aunt Elizabeth would tell her to go. But Aunt Elizabeth only knitted furiously and said nothing. It all seemed rather nightmarish. The wind was rising and the rain began to drive against the pane, and the dead-and-gone Murrays looked down accusingly from their dark frames. *They* had no sympathy with flashes and Jimmy-books and Alpine paths—with the pursuit of unwon, alluring divinities. Yet Emily couldn't help thinking, under all her disappointment, what an excellent setting it would make for some tragic scene in a novel.

The door opened and Cousin Jimmy slipped in. Cousin Jimmy knew what was in the wind and had been coolly and deliberately listening outside the door. *He* knew Emily would never promise such a thing— he had told Elizabeth so at the family council ten days before. *He* was only simply Jimmy Murray, but he understood what sensible Elizabeth Murray could not understand.

"What is wrong?" he asked, looking from one to the other.

"Nothing is wrong," said Aunt Elizabeth haughtily. "I have offered Emily an education and she has refused it. She is free to do so, of course."

"No one can be free who has a thousand ancestors," said Cousin Jimmy in the eerie tone in which he generally said such things. It always made Elizabeth shiver—she could never forget that his eeriness was *her* fault. "Emily can't promise what you want. Can you, Emily?"

"No." In spite of herself a couple of big tears rolled down Emily's cheeks.

"If you *could*," said Cousin Jimmy, "you *would* promise it for *me*, wouldn't you?"

Emily nodded.

"You've asked too much, Elizabeth," said Cousin Jimmy to the angry lady of the knitting-needles. "You've asked her to give up *all* her writing—now, if you'd just asked her to give up *some*—Emily, what if she just asked you to give up *some*? You might be able to do that, mightn't you?"

"What *some?*" asked Emily cautiously.

"Well, anything that wasn't *true*, for instance." Cousin Jimmy sidled over to Emily and put a beseeching hand on her shoulder. Elizabeth did not stop knitting, but the needles went more slowly. "*Stories*, for instance, Emily. She doesn't like your writing stories, especially. She thinks they're lies. She doesn't mind other things so much. Don't you think, Emily, you could give up writing stories for three years? An education is a great thing. Your grandmother Archibald would have lived on herring tails to get an education—many a time I've heard her say it. Come, Emily?"

Emily thought rapidly. She loved writing stories: it would be a hard thing to give them up. But if she could still write air-born fancies in verse—and weird little Jimmy-book sketches of character—and accounts of everyday events—witty—satirical—tragic—as the humour took her—she might be able to get along.

"Try her—try her," whispered Cousin Jimmy. "Propitiate her a little. You do owe her a great deal, Emily. Meet her half-way."

"Aunt Elizabeth," said Emily tremulously, "if you will send me to Shrewsbury I promise you that for three years I won't write anything that isn't *true*. Will that do? Because it's *all* I can promise."

Elizabeth knitted two rounds before deigning to reply. Cousin

Jimmy and Emily thought she was not going to reply at all. Suddenly she folded up her knitting and rose.

"Very well. I will let it go at that. It is, of course, your stories I object to most: as for the rest, I fancy Ruth will see to it that you have not much time to waste on it."

Aunt Elizabeth swept out, much relieved in her secret heart that she had not been utterly routed, but had been enabled to retreat from a perplexing position with some of the honours of war. Cousin Jimmy patted Emily's black head.

"That's good, Emily. Mustn't be too stubborn, you know. And three years isn't a lifetime, pussy."

No: but it seems like one at fourteen. Emily cried herself to sleep when she went to bed—and woke again at three by the clock, of that windy, dark-grey night on the old north shore—rose—lighted a candle—sat down at her table and described the whole scene in her Jimmy-book; being exceedingly careful to write therein no word that was not strictly true!

SHREWSBURY BEGINNINGS

Teddy and Ilse and Perry whooped for joy when Emily told them she was going to Shrewsbury. Emily, thinking it over, was reasonably happy. The great thing was that she was going to High School. She did not like the idea of boarding with Aunt Ruth. This was unexpected. She had supposed Aunt Ruth would never be willing to have *her* about and that, if Aunt Elizabeth *did* decide to send her to Shrewsbury, she would board elsewhere—probably with Ilse. Certainly, she would have greatly preferred this. She knew quite well that life would not be very easy under Aunt Ruth's roof. And then she must write no more stories.

To feel within her the creative urge and be forbidden to express it—to tingle with delight in the conception of humorous or dramatic characters, and be forbidden to bring them into existence—to be suddenly seized with the idea of a capital plot and realize immediately afterward that you couldn't develop it. All this was a torture which no one who has not been born with the fatal itch for writing can realize. The Aunt Elizabeths of the world can never understand it. To them, it is merely foolishness.

Those last two weeks of August were busy ones at New Moon. Elizabeth and Laura held long conferences over Emily's clothes. She must have an outfit that would cast no discredit on the Murrays, but common sense and not fashion was to give the casting vote. Emily herself had no say in the matter. Laura and Elizabeth argued "from noon to dewy eve" one day as to whether Emily might have a taffeta silk blouse—Ilse had three—and decided against it, much to Emily's disappointment. But Laura had her way in regard to what she dared not call an "evening dress," since the name would have doomed it in Elizabeth's opinion: it was a pretty crepe thing, of a pinkish-grey—the shade, I think, which was then called ashes-of-roses—and was made collarless—a great concession on Elizabeth's part—with the big puffed sleeves that look very absurd to-day, but which, like every other fashion, were pretty and piquant when worn by the youth and beauty of their time. It was the prettiest dress Emily had ever had—and the longest, which meant much in those days, when you could not be grown up until you had put on "long" dresses. It came to her pretty ankles.

She put it on one evening, when Laura and Elizabeth were away, because she wanted Dean to see her in it. He had come up to spend the evening with her—he was off the next day, having decided on Egypt— and they walked in the garden. Emily felt quite old and sophisticated because she had to lift her shimmering skirt clear of the ribbon grasses. She had a little greyish-pink scarf wound around her head and looked more like a star than ever, Dean thought. The cats were in attendance— Daffy, sleek and striped, Saucy Sal, who still reigned supreme in the New Moon barns. Cats might come and cats might go, but Saucy Sal went on for ever. They frisked over the grass plots and pounced on each other from flowery jungles and rolled insinuatingly around Emily's feet. Dean was going to Egypt but he knew that nowhere, even amid the strange charm of forgotten empires, would he see anything he liked better than the pretty picture Emily and her little cats made in the prim, stately, scented old garden of New Moon.

They did not talk as much as usual and the silences did queer things to both of them. Dean had one or two mad impulses to throw up the trip to Egypt and stay home for the winter—go to Shrewsbury perhaps;

he shrugged his shoulders and laughed at himself. This child did not need his looking after—the ladies of New Moon were competent guardians. She was only a child yet—in spite of her slim height and her unfathomable eyes. But how perfect the white line of her throat—how kissable the sweet red curve of her mouth. She would be a woman soon—but not for him—not for lame Jarback Priest of her father's generation. For the hundredth time Dean told himself that he was not going to be a fool. He must be content with what fate had given him—the friendship and affection of this exquisite, starry creature. In the years to come her love would be a wonderful thing—for some other man. No doubt, thought Dean cynically, she would waste it on some good-looking young manikin who wasn't half worthy of it.

Emily was thinking how dreadfully she was going to miss Dean—more than she had ever missed him before. They had been such good pals that summer. She had never had a talk with him, even if it were only for a few minutes, without feeling that life was richer. His wise, witty, humorous, satiric sayings were educative. They stimulated—stung—inspired her. And his occasional compliments gave her self-confidence. He had a certain strange fascination for her that no one else in the world possessed. She felt it though she could not analyse it. Teddy, now—she knew perfectly well why she liked Teddy. It was just because of his Teddyness. And Perry—Perry was a jolly, sunburned, outspoken, boastful rogue you couldn't help liking. But Dean was different. Was his charm the allure of the unknown—of experience—of subtle knowledge—of a mind grown wise on bitterness—of things Dean knew that she could never know? Emily couldn't tell. She only knew that everybody tasted a little flat after Dean—even Teddy, though she liked him best.

Oh, yes, Emily never had any doubt at all that she liked Teddy best. And yet Dean seemed to satisfy some part of her subtle and intricate nature that always went hungry without him.

"Thank you for all you've taught me, Dean," she said as they stood by the sundial.

"Do you think you have taught me nothing, Star?"

"How could I? I'm so young—so ignorant—"

"You've taught me how to laugh without bitterness, I hope you'll never realize what a boon that is. Don't let them spoil you at Shrewsbury, Star. You're so pleased over going that I don't want to throw cold water.

But you'd be just as well off—better—here at New Moon."

"Dean! I want *some* education—"

"Education! Education isn't being spoon-fed with algebra and second-rate Latin. Old Carpenter could teach you more and better than the college cubs, male and female, in Shrewsbury High School."

"I can't go to school any more here," protested Emily. "I'd be all alone. All the pupils of my age are going to Queen's or Shrewsbury or staying home. I don't understand you, Dean. I thought you'd be so glad they're letting me go to Shrewsbury."

"I *am* glad—since it pleases you. Only—the lore I wished for you isn't learned in High Schools or measured by terminal exams. Whatever of worth you get at any school you'll dig out for yourself. Don't let them make anything of you but yourself, that's all. I don't think they will."

"No, they won't," said Emily decidedly. "I'm like Kipling's cat—I walk by my wild lone and wave my wild tail where so it pleases me. That's why the Murrays look askance at me. They think I should only run with the pack. Oh, Dean, you'll write me often, won't you? Nobody understands like you. And you've got to be such a habit with me I can't do without you."

Emily said—and meant—it lightly enough; but Dean's thin face flushed darkly. They did not say good-bye—that was an old compact of theirs. Dean waved his hand at her.

"May every day be kind to you," he said.

Emily gave him only her slow, mysterious smile—he was gone. The garden seemed very lonely in the faint blue twilight, with the ghostly blossoms of the white phlox here and there. She was glad when she heard Teddy's whistle in Lofty John's Bush.

On her last evening at home she went to see Mr. Carpenter and get his opinion regarding some manuscripts she had left with him for criticism the preceding week. Among them were her latest stories, written before Aunt Elizabeth's ultimatum. Criticism was something Mr. Carpenter could give with a right good will and he never minced matters; but he was just, and Emily had confidence in his verdicts, even when he said things that raised temporary blisters on her soul.

"This love story is no good," he said bluntly.

"I know that it isn't what I wanted to make it," sighed Emily.

"No story ever is," said Mr. Carpenter. "You'll never write anything that really satisfies you though it may satisfy other people. As for love

357

stories, you can't write them because you can't feel them. Don't try to write anything you can't feel—it will be a failure—'echoes nothing worth.' This other yarn now—about this old woman. It's not bad. The dialogue is clever—the climax simple and effective. And thank the Lord you've got a sense of humour. *That's* mainly why you're no good at love stories, I believe. Nobody with any real sense of humour *can* write a love story."

Emily didn't see why this should be. She liked writing love stories—and terribly sentimental, tragical stories they were.

"Shakespeare could," she said defiantly.

"You're hardly in the Shakespeare class," said Mr. Carpenter dryly. Emily blushed scorchingly.

"I *know* I'm not. But you said *nobody*."

"And I maintain it. Shakespeare is the exception that proves the rule. Though *his* sense of humour was certainly in abeyance when he wrote *Romeo and Juliet*. However, let's come back to Emily of New Moon. *This* story—well, a young person might read it without contamination."

Emily knew by the inflection of Mr. Carpenter's voice that he was not praising her story. She kept silence and Mr. Carpenter went on, flicking her precious manuscripts aside irreverently.

"This one sounds like a weak imitation of Kipling. Been reading him lately?"

"Yes."

"I thought so. Don't try to imitate Kipling. If you *must* imitate, imitate Laura Jean Libbey. Nothing good about this but its title. A priggish little yarn. And *Hidden Riches* is not a story—it's a machine. It creaks. It never made me forget for one instant that it *was* a story. Hence it *isn't* a story."

"I was trying to write something very true to life," protested Emily.

"Ah, that's why. We all see life through an illusion—even the most disillusioned of us. That's why things aren't convincing if they're too true to life. Let me see—*The Madden Family*—another attempt at realism. But it's only photography—not portraiture."

"What a lot of disagreeable things you've said," sighed Emily.

"It might be a nice world if nobody ever said a disagreeable thing, but it would be a dangerous one," retorted Mr. Carpenter. "You told me you wanted criticism, not taffy. However, here's a bit of taffy for you. I kept it for the last. *Something Different* is comparatively good and if I wasn't afraid of ruining you I'd say it was absolutely good. Ten years from now you can rewrite it and make something of it. Yes, ten years—don't screw up your face, Jade. You have talent—and you've got a wonderful feeling for words—you get the inevitable one every time— that's a priceless thing. But you have some vile faults, too. Those cursed italics—forswear them, Jade, forswear them. And your imagination needs a curb when you get away from realism."

"It's to have one now," said Emily, gloomily.

She told him of her compact with Aunt Elizabeth. Mr. Carpenter nodded.

"Excellent."

"Excellent!" echoed Emily blankly.

"Yes. It's just what you need. It will teach you restraint and economy. Stick to facts for three years and see what you can make of them. Leave the realm of imagination severely alone and confine yourself to ordinary life."

"There isn't any such thing as ordinary life," said Emily.

Mr. Carpenter looked at her for a moment.

"You're right—there isn't," he said slowly. "But one wonders a little how you know it. Well, go on—go on—walk in your chosen path—and 'thank whatever gods there be' that you're free to walk it."

"Cousin Jimmy says nobody can be free who has a thousand ancestors."

"And yet people call that man simple," muttered Mr. Carpenter. "However, your ancestors don't seem to have wished any special curse on you. They've simply laid it on you to aim for the heights and they'll give you no peace if you don't. Call it ambition—aspiration—*cacoëthes scribendi*—any name you will. Under its sting—or allure—one has to go on climbing—until one fails—or—"

"Succeeds," said Emily, flinging back her dark head.

"Amen," said Mr. Carpenter.

Emily wrote a poem that night—*Farewell to New Moon*—and shed tears over it. She felt every line of it. It was all very well to be going to school—but to leave dear New Moon! Everything at New Moon was linked with her life and thoughts—was a part of her.

"It's not only that I love my room and trees and hills—they love me," she thought.

Her little black trunk was packed. Aunt Elizabeth had seen that everything necessary was in it, and Aunt Laura and Cousin Jimmy had seen that one or two unnecessary things were in it. Aunt Laura had told Emily that she would find a pair of black lace stockings inside her strap slippers—even Laura did not dare go so far as silk stockings—and Cousin Jimmy had given her three Jimmy-books and an envelope with a five-dollar bill in it.

"To get anything you want with, Pussy. I'd have made it ten but five was all Elizabeth would advance me on next month's wages. I think she suspected."

"Can I spend a dollar of it for American stamps if I can find a way to get them?" whispered Emily anxiously.

"Anything you like," repeated Cousin Jimmy loyally—though even to him it did not appear an unaccountable thing that any one should want to buy American stamps. But if dear little Emily wanted American stamps, American stamps she should have.

The next day seemed rather dream-like to Emily—the bird she heard singing rapturously in Lofty John's bush when she woke at dawn—the drive to Shrewsbury in the early crisp September morning—Aunt Ruth's cool welcome—the hours at a strange school—the organization of the "Prep" classes—home to supper—surely it must all have taken more than a day.

Aunt Ruth's house was at the end of a residential side street—almost out in the country. Emily thought it a very ugly house, covered as it was with gingerbread-work of various kinds. But a house with white wooden lace on its roof and its bay windows was the last word of elegance in Shrewsbury. There was no garden—nothing but a bare, prim, little lawn; but one thing rejoiced Emily's eyes. Behind the house was a big plantation of tall, slender fir-trees—the tallest, straightest, slenderest firs she had ever seen, stretching back into long, green, gossamered vistas.

Aunt Elizabeth had spent the day in Shrewsbury and went home after supper. She shook hands with Emily on the doorstep and told her to be a good girl and do exactly as Aunt Ruth bade her. She did not kiss Emily, but her tone was very gentle for Aunt Elizabeth. Emily choked up and stood tearfully on the doorstep to watch Aunt Elizabeth out of sight—Aunt Elizabeth going back to dear New Moon.

"Come in," said Aunt Ruth, and *"please* don't slam the door."

Now, Emily never slammed doors.

"We will wash the supper dishes," said Aunt Ruth. "You will always do that after this. I will show you where everything is put. I suppose Elizabeth told you I would expect you to do a few chores for your board."

"Yes," said Emily briefly.

She did not mind doing chores, any number of them—but it was Aunt Ruth's *tone*.

"Of course your being here will mean a great deal of extra expense for me," continued Aunt Ruth. "But it is only fair that we should all contribute something to your bringing up. *I* think, and I have always thought, that it would have been much better to send you to Queen's to get a teacher's licence."

"I wanted that, too," said Emily.

"M—m." Aunt Ruth pursed her mouth. "So you tell me. In that case I don't see why Elizabeth didn't send you to Queen's. She has pampered you enough in other ways, I'm sure—I would expect her to give in about this, too, if she thought you really wanted it. You will sleep in the kitchen chamber. It is warmer in winter than the other rooms. There is no gas in it but I could not afford to let you have gas to study by in any case. You must use candles—you can burn two at a time. I shall expect you to keep your room neat and tidy and to be here at my exact hours for meals. I am very particular about that. And there is another thing you might as well understand at once. You must not bring your friends here. I do not propose to entertain them."

"Not Ilse—or Perry—or Teddy?"

"Well, Ilse is a Burnley and a distant connection. She might come in once in a while—I can't have her running in at all times. From all I hear of her she isn't a very suitable companion for you. As for the boys—certainly not. I know nothing of Teddy Kent—and you ought to be too proud to associate with Perry Miller."

"I'm too proud *not* to associate with him," retorted Emily.

"Don't be pert with *me*, Em'ly. You might as well understand right away that you are not going to have things all your own way, *here*, as you had at New Moon. You have been badly spoiled. But I will not have hired boys calling on my niece. I don't know where you get your low tastes from, I'm sure. Even your father *seemed* like a gentleman. Go upstairs and unpack your trunk. Then do your lessons. We go to bed at nine o'clock!"

Emily felt very indignant. Even Aunt Elizabeth had never dreamed of forbidding Teddy to come to New Moon. She shut herself in her room and unpacked drearily. The room was such an ugly one. She hated it at sight. The door wouldn't shut tight; the slanting ceiling was rain stained, and came down so close to the bed that she could touch it with her hand. On the bare floor was a large "hooked" mat which made Emily's eyes ache. It was not in Murray taste—nor in Ruth Dutton's taste either, to be just. A country cousin of the deceased Mr. Dutton had given it to her. The centre, of a crude, glaring scarlet, was surrounded by scrolls of militant orange and violent green. In the corners were bunches of purple ferns and blue roses.

The woodwork was painted a hideous chocolate brown, and the walls were covered with paper of still more hideous design. The pictures were in keeping, especially a chromo of Queen Alexandra, gorgeously bedizened with jewels, hung at such an angle that it seemed the royal lady must certainly fall over on her face. Not even a chromo could make Queen Alexandra ugly or vulgar, but it came piteously near it. On a narrow, chocolate shelf sat a vase filled with paper flowers that had been paper flowers for twenty years. One couldn't believe that *anything* could be as ugly and depressing as they were.

"This room is unfriendly—it—doesn't want me—I can *never* feel at home here," said Emily.

She was horribly homesick. She wanted the New Moon candle-lights shining out on the birch-trees—the scent of hop-vines in the dew—her purring pussy cats—her own dear room, full of dreams—the silences and shadows of the old garden—the grand anthems of wind and billow in the gulf—that sonorous old music she missed so much in this inland silence. She missed even the little graveyard where slept the New Moon dead.

"I'm *not* going to cry." Emily clenched her hands. "Aunt Ruth will laugh at me. There's nothing *in* this room I can ever love. Is there anything *out* of it?"

She pushed up the window. It looked south into the fir grove and its balsam blew in to her like a caress. To the left there was an opening in the trees like a green, arched window, and one saw an enchanting little moonlit landscape through it. And it would let in the splendour of sunset. To the right was a view of the hill-side along which West Shrewsbury straggled: the hill was dotted with lights in the autumn dusk, and had a fairy-like loveliness. Somewhere near by there was a drowsy twittering, as of little, sleepy birds swinging on a shadowy bough.

"Oh, *this* is beautiful," breathed Emily, bending out to drink in the balsam-scented air. "Father told me once that one could find something beautiful to love *everywhere*. I'll love this."

Aunt Ruth poked her head in at the door, unannounced.

"Em'ly, why did you leave that antimacassar crooked on the sofa in the dining-room?"

"I—don't—know," said Emily confusedly. She hadn't even known she had disarranged the antimacassar. Why did Aunt Ruth ask such a question, as if she suspected her of some dark, deep, sinister design?

"Go down and put it straight."

As Emily turned obediently Aunt Ruth exclaimed,

"Em'ly Starr, put that window down at once! Are you crazy?"

"The room is so close," pleaded Emily.

"You can air it in the daytime but *never* have that window open after sundown. *I* am responsible for your health now. You must know that consumptives have to avoid night air and draughts."

"I'm not a consumptive," cried Emily rebelliously.

"Contradict, of course."

"And if I *were,* fresh air any time is the best thing for me. Dr. Burnley says so. I *hate* being smothered."

"'Young people *think* old people to be fools and old people *know* young people to be fools.'" Aunt Ruth felt that the proverb left nothing to be said. "Go and straighten that antimacassar, Em'ly."

"Em'ly" swallowed something and went. The offending antimacassar was mathematically corrected.

Emily stood for a moment and looked about her. Aunt Ruth's dining-room was much more splendid and "up-to-date" than the "sitting-room" at New Moon where they had "company" meals. Hardwood floor—Wilton rug—Early English oak furniture. But it was not half as "friendly" as the old New Moon room, Emily thought. She was more homesick than ever. She did not believe she was going to like *anything* in Shrewsbury—living with Aunt Ruth, or going to school. The teachers all seemed flat and insipid after pungent Mr. Carpenter and there was a girl in the Junior class she had hated at sight. And she had thought it would be all so delightful—living in pretty Shrewsbury and going to

High School. Well, nothing ever *is* exactly like what you expect it to be, Emily told herself in temporary pessimism as she went back to her room. Hadn't Dean told her once that he had dreamed all his life of rowing in a gondola through the canals of Venice on a moonlit night? And when he did he was almost eaten alive by mosquitoes.

Emily set her teeth as she crept into bed.

"I shall just have to fix my thoughts on the moonlight and romance and ignore the mosquitoes," she thought. "Only—Aunt Ruth *does* sting so."

POT-POURRI

"September 20, 19—

"I have been neglecting my diary of late. One does not have a great deal of spare time at Aunt Ruth's. But it is Friday night and I couldn't go home for the week-end so I come to my diary for comforting. I can spend only alternate week-ends at New Moon. Aunt Ruth wants me every other Saturday to help 'houseclean.' We go over this house from top to bottom whether it needs it or not, as the tramp said when he washed his face every month, and then rest from our labours for Sunday.

"There is a hint of frost in the air to-night. I am afraid the garden at New Moon will suffer. Aunt Elizabeth will begin to think it is time to give up the cookhouse for the season and move the Waterloo back into the kitchen. Cousin Jimmy will be boiling the pigs' potatoes in the old orchard and reciting his poetry. Likely Teddy and Ilse and Perry—who have all gone home, lucky creatures—will be there and Daff will be prowling about. But I must not think of it. That way homesickness lies.

"I am beginning to like Shrewsbury and Shrewsbury school and Shrewsbury teachers—though Dean was right when he said I would not find anyone here like Mr. Carpenter. The Seniors and Juniors look down on the Preps and are very condescending. Some of them condescended to *me*, but I do not think they will try it again—except Evelyn Blake, who condescends every time we meet, as we do quite often, because her chum, Mary Carswell, rooms with Ilse at Mrs. Adamson's boarding-house.

"I hate Evelyn Blake. There is no doubt at all about that. And there is as little doubt that she hates me. We are instinctive enemies—we looked at each other the first time we met like two strange cats, and that was enough. I never really hated any one before. I thought I did but now I know it was only dislike. Hate is rather interesting for a change. Evelyn is a Junior—tall, clever, rather handsome. Has long, bright, *treacherous* brown eyes and talks through her nose. She has *literary ambitions,* I understand, and considers herself the best dressed girl in High School. Perhaps she is; but somehow her clothes seem to make more impression on you than *she* does. People criticize Ilse for dressing too richly and too *old* but *she dominates* her clothes for all that. Evelyn doesn't. You always think of her clothes before you think of her. The difference seems to be that Evelyn dresses for other people and Ilse dresses for herself. I must write a character sketch of her when I have studied her a little more. What a satisfaction that will be!

"I met her first in Ilse's room and Mary Carswell introduced us. Evelyn looked down at me—she is a little taller, being a year older— and said,

"'Oh, yes, Miss Starr? I've heard my aunt, Mrs. Henry Blake, talking about you.'

Mrs. Henry Blake was once Miss Brownell. I looked straight into Evelyn's eyes and said,

"'No doubt Mrs. Henry Blake painted a very flattering picture of me.'

"Evelyn laughed—with a kind of laugh I don't like. It gives you the feeling that she is laughing at *you,* not at what you've said.

"'You didn't get on very well with her, did you? I understand you are quite literary. What papers do you write for?'

"She asked the question sweetly but she knew perfectly well that I don't write for any—yet.

"'The Charlottetown *Enterprise* and the Shrewsbury *Weekly Times,*' I said with a wicked grin. 'I've just made a bargain with them. I'm to get two cents for every news item I send the *Enterprise* and twenty-five cents a week for a society letter for the *Times.*'

"My grin worried Evelyn. Preps aren't supposed to grin like that at Juniors. It isn't done.

"'Oh, yes, I understand you are working for your board,' she said. 'I suppose every little helps. But I meant real literary periodicals.'

"'*The Quill?*' I asked with another grin.

"*The Quill* is the High School paper, appearing monthly. It is edited by the members of the *Skull and Owl,* a 'literary society' to which only Juniors and Seniors are eligible. The contents of *The Quill* are written by the students and in theory any student can contribute but in practice hardly anything is ever accepted from a Prep. Evelyn is a Skull and Owlite and her cousin is editor of *The Quill.* She evidently thought I was waxing sarcastic at her expense and ignored me for the rest of her call, except for one dear little jab when dress came up for discussion.

"'I want one of the new ties,' she said. 'There are some sweet ones at Jones and McCallum's and they are awfully smart. The little black velvet ribbon you are wearing around your neck, Miss Starr, is rather becoming. I used to wear one myself when they were in style.'

"I couldn't think of anything clever to say in retort. I can think of clever things so easily when there is no one to say them to. So I said nothing but merely smiled *very* slowly and *disdainfully.* That seemed to annoy Evelyn more than speech, for I heard she said afterwards that 'that Emily Starr' had a very affected smile.

"Note:—One can do a great deal with appropriate smiles. I must study the subject carefully. The friendly smile—the scornful smile—the detached smile—the entreating smile—the common or garden grin.

"As for Miss Brownell—or rather Mrs. Blake—I met *her* on the street a few days ago. After she passed she said something to her companion and they both laughed. Very bad manners, *I* think.

"I like Shrewsbury and I like school but I shall never like Aunt Ruth's house. It has a disagreeable personality. Houses are like people—some you like and some you don't like—and once in a while there is one you love. Outside, this house is covered with frippery. I feel like getting a broom and sweeping it off. Inside, its rooms are all square and proper and soulless. Nothing you could put into them would ever seem to belong to them. There are no nice romantic corners in it, as there are at New Moon. My room hasn't improved on acquaintance, either. The ceiling oppresses me—it comes down so low over my bed—and Aunt Ruth won't let me move the bed. She looked amazed when I suggested it.

"'The bed has *always* been in that corner,' she said, just as she might have said, 'The sun has always risen in the east.'

"But the pictures are really the worst thing about this room—chromos of the most aggravated description. Once I turned them all to the wall and of course Aunt Ruth walked in—she *never* knocks—and noticed them at once.

"'Em'ly, why have you meddled with the pictures?'

"Aunt Ruth is always asking 'why' I do this and that. Sometimes I can explain and sometimes I can't. This was one of the times I couldn't. But of course I had to answer Aunt Ruth's question. No disdainful smile would do here.

"'Queen Alexandra's dog collar gets on my nerves,' I said, 'and Byron's expression on his death-bed at Missolonghi hinders me from studying.'

"'Em'ly,' said Aunt Ruth, 'you might try to show a *little* gratitude.'

"I wanted to say,

"'To whom—Queen Alexandra or Lord Byron?' but of course I didn't. Instead I meekly turned all the pictures right side out again.

"'You haven't told me the real reason why you turned those pictures,' said Aunt Ruth sternly. 'I suppose you don't mean to tell me. Deep and sly—deep and sly—I always said you were. The very first time I saw you at Maywood I said you were the slyest child I had ever seen.'

"'Aunt Ruth, why do you say such things to me?' I said, in exasperation. 'Is it because you love me and want to improve me—or hate me and want to hurt me—or just because you can't help it?'

"'Miss Impertinence, please remember that this is my house. And you will leave *my* pictures alone after this. I will forgive you for meddling with them this time but don't let it happen again. I will find out yet your motive in turning them around, clever as you think yourself.'

"Aunt Ruth stalked out but I know she listened on the landing quite a while to find out if I would begin talking to myself. She is always watching me—even when she says nothing—does nothing—I know she is watching me. I feel like a little fly under a microscope. Not a word or action escapes her criticism, and, though she can't read my thoughts, she attributes thoughts to me that I never had any idea of thinking. I hate that worse than anything else.

"Can't I say anything good of Aunt Ruth? Of course I can.

"She is honest and virtuous and truthful and industrious and of her pantry she needeth not to be ashamed. But she hasn't any lovable virtues—and she will never give up trying to find out why I turned the pictures. She will never believe that I told her the simple truth.

"Of course, things 'might be worse.' As Teddy says, it might have been Queen Victoria instead of Queen Alexandra.

"I have some pictures of my own pinned up that save me—some lovely sketches of New Moon and the old orchard that Teddy made for me, and an engraving Dean gave me. It is a picture in soft, dim colours of palms around a desert well and a train of camels passing across the sands against a black sky gemmed with stars. It is full of lure and mystery and when I look at it I forget Queen Alexandra's jewellery and Lord Byron's lugubrious face, and my soul slips out—out—through a little gateway into a great, vast world of freedom and dream.

"Aunt Ruth asked me where I got that picture. When I told her she sniffed and said,

"'I can't understand how you have such a liking for Jarback Priest. He's a man I've no use for.'

"I shouldn't think she would have.

"But if the house is ugly and my room unfriendly, the Land of Uprightness is beautiful and saves my soul alive. The Land of Uprightness is the fir grove behind the house. I call it that because the firs are all so exceedingly tall and slender and straight. There is a pool in it, veiled with ferns, with a big grey boulder beside it. It is reached by a little, winding, capricious path so narrow that only one can walk in it. When I'm tired or lonely or angry or too ambitious I go there and sit for a few minutes. Nobody can keep an upset mind looking at those slender, crossed tips against the sky. I go there to study on fine evenings, though Aunt Ruth is suspicious and thinks it is just another manifestation of my slyness. Soon it will be dark too early to study there and I'll be so sorry. Somehow, my books have a *meaning* there they never have anywhere else.

"There are so many dear, green corners in the Land of Uprightness, full of the aroma of sun-steeped ferns, and grassy, open spaces where pale asters feather the grass, swaying gently towards each other when the Wind Woman runs among them. And just to the left of my window there is a group of tall old firs that look, in moonlight or twilight, like a group of witches weaving spells of sorcery. When I first saw them, one windy night against the red sunset, with the reflection of my candle, like a weird, signal flame, suspended in the air among their boughs, the *flash* came—for the first time in Shrewsbury—and I felt so happy that nothing else mattered. I have written a poem about them.

"But oh, I burn to write stories. I knew it would be hard to keep my promise to Aunt Elizabeth but I didn't know it would be *so* hard. Every day it seems harder—such splendid ideas for plots pop into my mind. Then I have to fall back on character studies of the people I know. I have written several of them. I always feel so strongly tempted to *touch them up a bit*—deepen the shadows—bring out the highlights a little more vividly. But I remember that I promised Aunt Elizabeth never to write anything that wasn't true so I stay my hand and try to paint them exactly as they are.

"I have written one of Aunt Ruth. Interesting but dangerous. I never leave my Jimmy-book or my diary in my room. I know Aunt Ruth rummages through it when I'm out. So I always carry them in my book-bag.

"Ilse was up this evening and we did our lessons together. Aunt Ruth frowns on this—and, to be strictly just, I don't know that she is wrong. Ilse is so jolly and comical that we laugh more than we study, I'm afraid. We don't do as well in class next day—and besides, this house disapproves of laughter.

"Perry and Teddy like the High School. Perry earns his lodging by looking after the furnace and grounds and his board by waiting on the table. Besides, he gets twenty-five cents an hour for doing odd jobs. I don't see much of him or Teddy, except in the week-ends home, for it is against the school rules for boys and girls to walk together to and from school. Lots *do* it, though. I had several chances to but I concluded that it would not be in keeping with New Moon traditions to break the rule. Besides, Aunt Ruth asks me every blessed night when I come home from school if I've walked with anybody. I think she's sometimes a little disappointed when I say 'No.'

"Besides, I didn't much fancy any of the boys who wanted to walk with me.

****

"October 20, 19—

"My room is full of boiled cabbage smells to-night but I dare not open my window. Too much night air outside. I would risk it for a little while if Aunt Ruth hadn't been in a very bad humour all day. Yesterday was my Sunday in Shrewsbury and when we went to church I sat in the corner of the pew. I did not know that Aunt Ruth must always sit there but she thought I did it on purpose. She read her Bible all the afternoon. I *felt* she was reading it *at* me, though I couldn't imagine why. This morning she asked me why I did it.

"'Did what?' I said in bewilderment.

"'Em'ly, you know what you did. I will not tolerate this slyness. What was your motive?'

"'Aunt Ruth, I haven't the slightest idea what you mean,' I said— quite haughtily, for I felt I was not being treated fairly.

"'Em'ly, you sat in the corner of the pew yesterday just to keep me out of it. *Why* did you do it?"

"I looked down at Aunt Ruth—I am taller than she is now and I can do it. She doesn't like it, either. I was angry and I *think* I had a little of the Murray look on my face. The whole thing seemed so contemptible to be making a fuss over.

"'If I did it to keep you out of it, isn't that *why?*' I said as contemptuously as I felt. I picked up my book-bag and stalked to the door. There I stopped. It occurred to me that, whatever the Murrays might or might not do, I was not behaving as a Starr should. Father wouldn't have approved of my behaviour. So I turned and said, very politely,

"'I should not have spoken like that, Aunt Ruth, and I beg your pardon. I didn't mean anything by sitting in the corner. It was just because I happened to go into the pew first. I didn't know you preferred the corner.'

"Perhaps I overdid the politeness. At any rate, my apology only seemed to irritate Aunt Ruth the more. She sniffed and said,

"'I will forgive you this time, but don't let it happen again. Of course I didn't expect you would tell me your reason. You are too sly for that.'

"Aunt Ruth, Aunt Ruth! If you keep on calling me sly you'll drive me into being sly in reality and *then* watch out. If I choose to be sly I can twist you round my finger! It's only because I'm straightforward that you can manage me at all.

"I have to go to bed every night at nine o'clock—'people who are threatened with consumption require a great deal of sleep.' When I come from school there are chores to be done and I must study in the evenings. So I haven't a moment of time for writing anything. I know Aunt Elizabeth and Aunt Ruth have had a conference on the subject. But I *have* to write. So I get up in the morning as soon as it is daylight, dress, and put on a coat—for the mornings are cold now—sit down and scribble for a priceless hour. I didn't choose that Aunt Ruth should discover it and call me sly so I told her I was doing it. She gave me to understand that I was mentally unsound and would make a bad end in some asylum, but she didn't actually forbid me—probably because she thought it would be of no use. It wouldn't. I've *got* to write, that is all there is to it. That hour in the grey morning is the most delightful one in the day for me.

"Lately, being forbidden to write stories, I've been *thinking* them out. But one day it struck me that I was breaking my compact with Aunt Elizabeth in spirit if not in letter. So I have stopped it.

"I wrote a character study of Ilse to-day. Very fascinating. It is difficult to analyse her. She is so different and unexpectable. (I coined that word myself.) She doesn't even get mad like anybody else. I enjoy her tantrums. She doesn't say so many awful things in them as she used to but she is *piquant*. (Piquant is a new word for me. I like using a new word. I never think I really own a word until I've spoken or written it.)

"I am writing by my window. I love to watch the Shrewsbury lights twinkle out in the dusk over that long hill.

"I had a letter from Dean to-day. He is in Egypt—among ruined shrines of old gods and the tombs of old kings. I saw that strange land through his eyes—I seemed to go back with him through the old centuries—I knew the magic of its skies. I was Emily of Karnak or Thebes—not Emily of Shrewsbury at all. That is a trick Dean has.

"Aunt Ruth insisted on seeing his letter and when she read it she said it was impious!

"I should never have thought of that adjective.

****

"October 21, 19—

"I climbed the steep little wooded hill in the Land of Uprightness to-night and had an exultation on its crest. There's always something satisfying in climbing to the top of a hill. There was a fine tang of frost in the air, the view over Shrewsbury Harbour was very wonderful, and the woods all about me were expecting something to happen soon—at least that is the only way I can describe the effect they had on me. I forgot *everything*—Aunt Ruth's stings and Evelyn Blake's patronage and Queen Alexandra's dog collar—everything in life that isn't just right. Lovely thoughts came flying to meet me like birds. They weren't *my* thoughts. I couldn't think anything half so exquisite. They *came* from somewhere.

"Coming back, on that dark little path, where the air was full of nice, whispering sounds, I heard a chuckle of laughter in a fir copse just behind me. I was startled—and a little bit alarmed. I knew at once it wasn't human laughter—it was more like the Puckish mirth of fairy folk, with just a faint hint of malice in it. I can no longer believe in wood elves—alas, one loses so much when one becomes incredulous—so this laughter puzzled me—and, yes, a horrid, crawly feeling began in my spine. Then, suddenly, I thought of owls and knew it for what it was—a truly delightful sound, as if some survival of the Golden Age were chuckling to himself there in the dark. There were two of them, I think, and they were certainly having a good time over some owlish joke. I must write a poem about it—though I'll never be able to put into words half the charm and devilry of it.

"Ilse was up on the carpet in the principal's room yesterday for walking home from school with Guy Lindsay. Something Mr. Hardy said made her so furious that she snatched up a vase of chrysanthemums that was on his desk and hurled it against the wall, where of course it was smashed to pieces.

"'If I hadn't thrown it at the wall I'd have had to have thrown it at *you*,' she told him.

"It would have gone hard with some girls but Mr. Hardy is a friend of Dr. Burnley's. Besides, there is something about those yellow eyes of Ilse's that do things to you. I know exactly how she would look at Mr. Hardy after she had smashed the vase. All her rage would be gone and her eyes would be laughing and daring—impudent, Aunt Ruth would call it. Mr. Hardy merely told her she was acting like a baby and would have to pay for the vase, since it was school property. That rather squelched Ilse; she thought it a tame ending to her heroics.

"I scolded her roundly. Really, somebody *has* to bring Ilse up and nobody but me seems to feel any responsibility in the matter. Dr. Burnley will just roar with laughter when she tells him. But I might as well have scolded the Wind Woman. Ilse just laughed and hugged me.

"'Honey, it made such a jolly smash. When I heard it I wasn't a bit mad any more.'

"Ilse recited at our school concert last week and everybody thought her wonderful.

"Aunt Ruth told me to-day that she expected me to be a star pupil. She wasn't punning on my name—oh, no, Aunt Ruth hasn't a nodding acquaintance with puns. All the pupils who make ninety per cent average at the Christmas exams and do not fall below eighty in any subject are called 'Star' pupils and are given a gold star-pin to wear for the rest of the term. It is a coveted distinction and of course not many win it. If I fail Aunt Ruth will rub it in to the bone. I must *not* fail.

****

"October 30, 19—

"The November *Quill* came out to-day. I sent my owl poem in to the editor a week ago but he didn't use is. And he *did* use one of Evelyn Blake's—a silly, simpering little rhyme about *Autumn Leaves*—very much the sort of thing *I* wrote three years ago.

"And Evelyn *condoled* with me before the whole roomful of girls because *my* poem hadn't been taken. I suppose Tom Blake had told her about it.

"'You mustn't feel badly about it, Miss Starr. Tom said it wasn't half bad but of course not up to *The Quill's* standard. Likely in another year or two you'll be able to get in. Keep on trying.'

"'Thanks,' I said. 'I'm not feeling badly. Why should I? I didn't make "beam" rhyme with "green" in my poem. If I had I'd be feeling very badly indeed.'

"Evelyn coloured to her eyes.

"'Don't show your disappointment so plainly, *child,*' she said.

"But I noticed she dropped the subject after that.

"For my own satisfaction I wrote a criticism of Evelyn's poem in my Jimmy-book as soon as I came from school. I modelled it on Macaulay's essay on poor Robert Montgomery, and I got so much fun out of it that I didn't feel sore and humiliated any more. I must show it to Mr. Carpenter when I go home. He'll chuckle over it.

****

"November 6, 19—

"I noticed this evening in glancing over my journal that I soon gave up recording my good and bad deeds. I suppose it was because so many of my doings were half-and-half. I never could decide in what class they belonged.

"We are expected to answer roll-call with a quotation on Monday mornings. This morning I repeated a verse from my own poem *A Window that Faces the Sea*. When I left Assembly to go down to the Prep classroom Miss Aylmer, the Vice-Principal, stopped me.

"'Emily, that was a beautiful verse you gave at roll-call. Where did you get it? And do you know the whole poem?'

"I was so elated I could hardly answer,

"'Yes, Miss Aylmer,' *very* demurely.

"'I would like a copy of it,' said Miss Aylmer. 'Could you write me off one? And who is the author?'

"'The author,' I said laughing, 'is Emily Byrd Starr. The truth is, Miss Aylmer, that I forgot to look up a quotation for roll-call and couldn't think of any in a hurry, so just fell back on a bit of my own.'

"Miss Aylmer didn't say anything for a moment. She just looked at me. She is a stout, middle-aged woman with a square face and nice, wide, grey eyes.

"'Do you still want the poem, Miss Aylmer?' I said, smiling.

"'Yes,' she said, still looking at me in that funny way, as if she had never seen me before. 'Yes—and autograph it, please.'

"I promised and went on down the stairs. At the foot I glanced back. She was still looking after me. Something in her look made me feel glad and proud and happy and humble—and—and—*prayerful*. Yes, that was just how I felt.

"Oh, this has been a wonderful day. What care I now for *The Quill* or Evelyn Blake?

"This evening Aunt Ruth marched up town to see Uncle Oliver's Andrew, who is in the bank here now. She made me go along. She gave Andrew lots of good advice about his morals and his meals and his underclothes and asked him to come down for an evening whenever he wished. Andrew is a Murray, you see, and can therefore rush in where Teddy and Perry dare not tread. He is quite good-looking, with straight, well-groomed, red hair. But he always looks as if he'd just been starched and ironed.

"I thought the evening not wholly wasted, for Mrs. Garden, his landlady, has an interesting cat who made certain advances to me. But when Andrew patted him and called him 'Poor pussy' the intelligent animal hissed at him.

"'You mustn't be too familiar with a cat,' I advised Andrew. 'And you must speak respectfully *to* and *of* him.'

"'Piffle!' said Aunt Ruth.

"But a cat's a cat for a' that.

****

"November 8, 19—

"The nights are cold now. When I came back Monday I brought one of the New Moon gin jars for my comforting. I cuddle down with it in bed and enjoy the contrasting roars of the storm wind outside in the Land of Uprightness, and the rain whirling over the room. Aunt Ruth worries for fear the cork will come out and deluge the bed. That would be almost as bad as what really did happen night before last. I woke up about midnight with the most wonderful idea for a story. I felt that I must rise at once and jot it down in a Jimmy-book before I forgot it. Then I could keep it until my three years are up and I am free to write it.

"I hopped out of bed and, in pawing around my table to find my candle, I upset my ink-bottle. Then of course I went mad and couldn't find *anything!* Matches—candles—everything had disappeared. I set the ink-bottle up, but I knew there was a pool of ink on the table. I had ink all over my fingers and dare not touch anything in the dark and couldn't find anything to wipe it off. And all the time I heard that ink drip-dripping on the floor.

"In desperation I opened the door—with my *toes* because I dare not touch it with my inky hands—and went downstairs where I wiped my hands on the stove rag and got some matches. But this time, of course, Aunt Ruth was up, demanding whys and motives. She took my matches, lighted her candle, and marched me upstairs. Oh, 'twas a gruesome sight! How could a small stone ink-bottle hold a quart of ink? There *must* have been a quart to have made the mess it did.

"I felt like the old Scotch emigrant who came home one evening, found his house burned down and his entire family scalped by Indians and said, 'This is pairfectly redeeclous.' The table cover was ruined— the carpet was soaked—even the wall-paper was bespattered. But Queen Alexandra smiled benignly over all and Byron went on dying.

"Aunt Ruth and I had an hour's seance with salt and vinegar. Aunt Ruth wouldn't believe me when I said I got up to jot down the plot of a story. She knew I had some other motive and it was just some more of my deepness and slyness. She also said a few other things which I won't write down. Of course I deserved a scolding for leaving that ink-bottle uncorked; but I *didn't* deserve all she said. However, I took it all very meekly. For one thing I *had* been careless: and for another I had my bedroom shoes on. Anyone can overcrow me when I'm wearing bedroom shoes. Then she wound up by saying she would forgive me this time, but it was not to happen again.

"Perry won the mile race in the school sports and broke the record. He bragged too much about it and Ilse raged at him.

****

"November 11, 19—

"Last night Aunt Ruth found me reading *David Copperfield* and crying over *Davy's* alienation from his mother, with a black rage against *Mr. Murdstone* in my heart. She must know *why* I was crying and wouldn't believe me when I told her.

"'Crying over people who never existed!' said my Aunt Ruth incredulously.

"'Oh, but they *do* exist,' I said. 'Why, they are as real as *you* are, Aunt Ruth. Do you mean to say that Miss Betsy Trotwood is a delusion?'

"I thought perhaps I could have *real* tea when I came to Shrewsbury, but Aunt Ruth says it is not healthy. So I drink cold water for I will *not* drink cambric tea any longer. As if I were a child!

****

"November 30, 19—

376

"Andrew was in to-night. He always comes the Friday night I don't go to New Moon. Aunt Ruth left us alone in the parlour and went out to a meeting of the Ladies' Aid. Andrew, being a Murray, can be trusted.

"I don't dislike Andrew. It would be impossible to dislike so harmless a being. He is one of those good, talkative, awkward dears who goad you irresistibly into tormenting them. Then you feel remorseful afterwards because they *are* so good.

"To-night, Aunt Ruth being out, I tried to discover how little I could really say to Andrew, while I pursued my own train of thought. I discovered that I could get along with very few words—'Yes'—'No'— in several inflections, with or without a little laugh—'I don't know'— 'Really?'—'Well, well'—'How wonderful!'—especially the last. Andrew talked on, and when he stopped for breath I stuck in 'How wonderful.' I did it exactly eleven times. Andrew liked it. I know it gave him a nice, flattering feeling that *he* was wonderful, and his conversation wonderful. Meanwhile I was living a splendid imaginary dream-life by the River of Egypt in the days of Thotmes I.

"So we were both very happy. I think I'll try it again. Andrew is too stupid to catch me at it.

"When Aunt Ruth came home she asked, 'Well, how did you and Andrew get along?'

"She asks that every time he comes down. I *know why.* I know the little scheme that is understood among the Murrays, even though I don't believe any of them have ever put it into words.

"'Beautifully,' I said. 'Andrew is improving. He said *one* interesting thing to-night, and he hadn't so many feet and hands as usual.'

"I don't know *why* I say things like that to Aunt Ruth occasionally. It would be so much better for me if I didn't. But *something*—whether it's Murray or Starr or Shipley or Burnley, or just pure cussedness I know not—*makes* me say them before I've time to reflect.

"'No doubt you would find more congenial company in Stovepipe Town,' said Aunt Ruth.

NOT PROVEN

Emily regretfully left the "Booke Shoppe," where the aroma of books and new magazines was as the savour of sweet incense in her nostrils, and hastened down cold and blustery Prince Street. Whenever possible she slipped into the Booke Shoppe and took hungry dips into magazines she could not afford to buy, avid to learn what kind of stuff they published—especially poetry. She could not see that many of the verses in them were any better than some of her own, yet editors sent hers back religiously. Emily had already used a considerable portion of the American stamps she had bought with Cousin Jimmy's dollar in paying the homeward way of her fledgelings, accompanied by only the cold comfort of rejection slips. Her *Owl's Laughter* had already been returned six times, but Emily had not wholly lost faith in it yet. That very morning she had dropped it again into the letter-box at the Shoppe.

"The seventh time brings luck," she thought as she turned down the street leading to Ilse's boarding-house. She had her examination in English at eleven o'clock and she wanted to glance over Ilse's note-book before she went for it. The Preps were almost through their terminal examinations, taking them by fits and starts when the class-rooms were free from Seniors and Juniors—a thing that always made the Preps furious. Emily felt comfortably certain she would get her star pin. The examinations in her hardest subjects were over and she did not believe she had fallen below eighty in any of them. To-day was English, in which she ought to go well over ninety. Remained only history, which she also loved. Everybody expected her to win the star pin. Cousin Jimmy was intensely excited over it, and Dean had sent her premature congratulations from the top of a pyramid, so sure was he of her success. His letter had come the previous day, along with the packet containing his Christmas gift.

"I send you a little gold necklace that was taken from the mummy of a dead princess of the nineteenth dynasty," wrote Dean. "Her name was Mena and it said in her epitaph that she was 'sweet of heart.' So I think she fared well in the Hall of Judgment and that the dread old gods smiled indulgently upon her. This little amulet lay on her dead breast for thousands of years. I send it to you weighted with centuries of love. I think it must have been a love gift. Else why should it have rested on her heart all this time? It must have been her own choice. Others would have put a finer thing on the neck of a king's daughter."

The little trinket intrigued Emily with its charm and mystery, yet she was almost afraid of it. She gave a slight ghostly shudder as she clasped it around her slim white throat and wondered about the royal girl who had worn it in those days of a dead empire. What was its history and its secret?

Naturally Aunt Ruth had disapproved. What business had Emily to be getting Christmas presents from Jarback Priest?

"At least he might have sent you something *new* if he had to send anything," she said.

"A souvenir of Cairo, made in Germany," suggested Emily gravely.

"Something like that," agreed Aunt Ruth unsuspiciously. "Mrs. Ayers has a handsome, gold-mounted glass paper-weight with a picture of the Sphinx in it that her brother brought *her* from Egypt. That battered thing looks positively cheap."

"Cheap! Aunt Ruth, do you realize that this necklace was made by hand and worn by an Egyptian princess before the days of Moses?"

"Oh, well—if you want to believe Jarback Priest's fairy tales," said Aunt Ruth, much amused. "I wouldn't wear it in public if I were you, Em'ly. The Murrays never wear shabby jewellery. You're not going to leave it on to-night, child?"

"Of course I am. The last time it was worn was probably at the court of Pharaoh in the days of the oppression. Now, it will go to Kit Barrett's snow-shoe dance. What a difference! I hope the ghost of Princess Mena won't haunt me to-night. She may resent my sacrilege—who knows? But it was not *I* who rifled her tomb, and somebody would have this if I didn't—somebody who mightn't think of the little princess at all. I'm sure she would rather that it was warm and shining about my neck than in some grim museum for thousands of curious, cold eyes to stare at. She was 'sweet of heart,' Dean says—she won't grudge me her pretty pendant. Lady of Egypt, whose kingdom has been poured on the desert sands like spilled wine, I salute you across the gulf of time."

Emily bowed deeply and waved her hand adown the vistas of dead centuries.

"Such high-falutin' language is very foolish," sniffed Aunt Ruth.

"Oh, most of that last sentence was a quotation from Dean's letter," said Emily candidly.

"Sounds like him," was Aunt Ruth's contemptuous agreement. "Well, *I* think your Venetian beads would be better than that heathenish-looking thing. Now, mind you don't stay too late, Em'ly. Make Andrew bring you home not later than twelve."

Emily was going with Andrew to Kitty Barrett's dance—a privilege quite graciously accorded since Andrew was one of the elect people. Even when she did not get home until one o'clock Aunt Ruth overlooked it. But it left Emily rather sleepy for the day, especially as she had studied late the two previous nights. Aunt Ruth relaxed her rigid rules in examination time and permitted an extra allowance of candles. What she would have said had she known that Emily used some of the extra candle-light to write a poem on *Shadows* I do not know and cannot record. But no doubt she would have considered it an added proof of slyness. Perhaps it was sly. Remember that I am only Emily's biographer, not her apologist.

Emily found Evelyn Blake in Ilse's room and Evelyn Blake was secretly much annoyed because *she* had not been invited to the snowshoe dance and Emily Starr had. Therefore Evelyn, sitting on Ilse's table and swinging her high, silken-sheathed instep flauntingly in the face of girls who had no silk stockings, was prepared to be disagreeable.

"I'm glad you've come, trusty and well-beloved," moaned Ilse. "Evelyn has been clapper-clawing me all the morning. Perhaps she'll whirl in at you now and give me a rest."

"I have been telling her that she should learn to control her temper," said Evelyn virtuously. "Don't you agree with me, Miss Starr?"

"What have you been doing now, Ilse?" asked Emily.

"Oh, I had a large quarrel with Mrs. Adamson this morning. It was bound to come sooner or later. I've been good so long there was an awful lot of wickedness bottled up in me. Mary knew that, didn't you, Mary? Mary felt quite sure an explosion was due to happen. Mrs. Adamson began it by asking disagreeable questions. She's always doing that—isn't she, Mary? After that she started in scolding—and finally she cried. *Then* I slapped her face."

"You see," said Evelyn, significantly.

"I couldn't help it," grinned Ilse. "I could have endured her impertinence and her scolding—but when she began to cry—she's so *ugly* when she cries—well, I just slapped her."

"I suppose you felt better after that," said Emily, determined not to show any disapproval before Evelyn.

Ilse burst out laughing.

"Yes, at first. It stopped her yowling, anyway. But afterwards came remorse. I'll apologize to her, of course. I *do* feel real sorry—but I'm quite likely to do it again. If Mary here weren't so good I wouldn't be half as bad. I have to even the balance up a bit. Mary is meek and humble and Mrs. Adamson walks all over her. You should hear her scold Mary if Mary goes out more than one evening a week."

"She is right," said Evelyn. "It would be much better if *you* went out less. You're getting talked about, Ilse."

"You weren't out last night, anyhow, were you, dear?" asked Ilse with another unholy grin.

Evelyn coloured and was haughtily silent. Emily buried herself in her note-book and Mary and Ilse went out. Emily wished Evelyn would go, too. But Evelyn had no intention of going.

"Why don't you make Ilse behave herself?" she began in a hatefully confidential sort of way.

"*I* have no authority over Ilse," said Emily coldly. "Besides, I don't think she misbehaves."

"Oh, my dear girl—why, you heard her yourself saying she slapped Mrs. Adamson."

"Mrs. Adamson *needed* it. She's an odious woman—*always* crying when there's no need in the world for her to cry. There's nothing more aggravating."

"Well, Ilse skipped French *again* yesterday afternoon and went for a walk up-river with Ronnie Gibson. If she does that too often she's going to get caught."

"Ilse is very popular with the boys," said Emily, who knew that Evelyn wanted to be.

"She's popular in the wrong quarters." Evelyn was condescending now, knowing by instinct that Emily Starr hated to be condescended to. "She always has a ruck of wild boys after her—the nice ones don't bother with her, you notice."

"Ronnie Gibson's nice, isn't he?"

"Well, what do you say to Marshall Orde?"

"Ilse has nothing to do with Marshall Orde."

"Oh, hasn't she! She was driving with him till twelve o'clock last Tuesday night—and he was drunk when he got the horse from the livery stable."

"I don't believe a word of it! Ilse never went driving with Marsh Orde." Emily was white-lipped with indignation.

"I was told by a person who *saw* them. Ilse is being talked about *everywhere*. Perhaps you have no authority over her but surely you have some *influence*. Though *you* do foolish things yourself sometimes, don't you? Not meaning any harm perhaps. That time you went bathing on the Blair Water sands without any clothes on, for instance? *That's* known all through the school. I heard Marsh's brother laughing about it. Now, *wasn't* that foolish, my dear?"

Emily blushed with anger and shame—though quite as much over being my-deared by Evelyn Blake as anything else. That beautiful bathing by moonlight—what a thing of desecration it had been made by the world! She would *not* discuss it with Evelyn—she would not even tell Evelyn they had their petticoats on. Let her think what she would.

"I don't think you quite understand some things, Miss Blake," she said, with a certain fine, detached irony of tone and manner which made very commonplace words seem charged, with meanings unutterable.

"Oh, you belong to the Chosen People, don't you?" Evelyn laughed her malicious little laugh.

"I do," said Emily calmly, refusing to withdraw her eyes from her note-book.

"Well, don't get so vexed, dear. I only spoke because I thought it a pity to see poor Ilse getting in wrong everywhere. I rather like her, poor soul. And I wish she would tone down her taste in colours a bit. That scarlet evening dress she wore at the Prep concert—really, you know, it's weird."

"She looked like a tall golden lily in a scarlet sheath, *I* thought," said Emily.

"What a loyal friend you are, dear. I wonder if Ilse would stand up for *you* like that. Well, I suppose I ought to let you study. You have English at ten, haven't you? Mr. Scoville is going to watch the room—

Mr. Travers is sick. Don't you think Mr. Scoville's hair is wonderful? Speaking of hair, dear, why don't you dress yours low enough at the sides to hide your ears—the tips, anyway? I think it would become you so much better."

Emily decided that if Evelyn Blake called her "dear" again she would throw an ink-bottle at her. *Why* didn't she go away and let her study?

Evelyn had another shot in her locker.

"That callow young friend of yours from Stovepipe Town has been trying to get into *The Quill*. He sent in a patriotic poem. Tom showed it to me. It was a scream. One line especially was delicious—'Canada, like a *maiden,* welcomes back her sons.' You should have heard Tom howl."

Emily could hardly help smiling herself, though she was horribly annoyed with Perry for making such a target of himself. *Why* couldn't he learn his limitations and understand that the slopes of Parnassus were not for him?

"I do not think the editor of *The Quill* has any business to show rejected contributions to outsiders," she said coldly.

"Oh, Tom doesn't look on *me* as an outsider. And that really *was* too good to keep. Well, I think I'll run down to the Shoppe."

Emily sighed with relief as Evelyn took her departure. Presently Ilse returned.

"Evelyn gone? Sweet temper she was in this morning. I can't understand what Mary sees in her. Mary's a decent sort though she isn't exciting."

"Ilse," said Emily seriously. "Were you out driving with Marsh Orde one night last week?"

Ilse stared.

"No, you dear young ass, I wasn't. I can guess where you heard *that* yarn. I don't know who the girl was."

"But you cut French and went up-river with Ronnie Gibson?"

"Peccavi."

"Ilse—you shouldn't—really—"

"Now, don't make me mad, Emily!" said Ilse shortly. "You're getting too smug—something ought to be done to cure you before it gets chronic. I hate prunes and prisms. I'm off—I want to run round to the Shoppe before I go to the school."

Ilse gathered up her books pettishly and flounced out. Emily yawned and decided she was through with the note-book. She had half an hour yet before it was necessary to go to the school. She would lie down on Ilse's bed for just a moment.

It seemed the next minute when she found herself sitting up, staring with dismayed face at Mary Carswell's clock. Five minutes to eleven—five minutes to cover a quarter of a mile and be at her desk for examination. Emily flung on coat and cap, caught up her note-books and fled. She arrived at the High School out of breath, with a nasty subconsciousness that people had looked at her queerly as she tore through the streets, hung up her wraps without a glance at the mirror, and hurried into the class-room.

A stare of amazement followed by a ripple of laughter went over the room. Mr. Scoville, tall, slim, elegant, was giving out the examination papers. He laid one down before Emily and said gravely,

"Did you look in your mirror before you came to class, Miss Starr?"

"No," said Emily resentfully, sensing something fearfully wrong somewhere.

"I—think—I would look—now—if I were—you." Mr. Scoville seemed to be speaking with difficulty.

Emily got up and went back to the girls' dressing-room. She met Principal Hardy in the Hall and Principal Hardy stared at her. Why Principal Hardy stared—why the Preps had laughed—Emily understood when she confronted the dressing-room looking-glass.

Drawn skilfully and blackly across her upper lip and her cheeks was a moustache—a flamboyant, very black moustache, with fantastically curled ends. For a moment Emily gaped at herself in blank horror— why—what—*who* had done it?

She whirled furiously about. Evelyn Blake had just entered the room.

"*You*—you did this!" panted Emily.

Evelyn stared for a moment—then went off into a peal of laughter.

"Emily Starr! You look like a nightmare. Do you mean to tell me you went into class with *that* on your face?"

Emily clenched her hands.

"*You* did it," she said again.

Evelyn drew herself up very haughtily.

"Really, Miss Starr, I hope you don't think I'd *stoop* to such a trick. I suppose your dear friend Ilse thought she'd play a joke on you—she was chuckling over something when she came in a few minutes ago."

384

"Ilse never did it," cried Emily.

Evelyn shrugged her shoulders.

"I'd wash it off first and find out who did it afterward," she said with a twitching face as she went out

Emily, trembling from head to foot with anger, shame and the most intense humiliation she had ever suffered, washed the moustache off her face. Her first impulse was to go home—she could not face that roomful of Preps again. Then she set her teeth and went back, holding her black head very high as she walked down the aisle to her desk. Her face was burning and her spirit was aflame. In the corner she saw Ilse's yellow head bent over her paper. The others were smiling and tittering. Mr. Scoville was insultingly grave. Emily took up her pen but her hand shook over her paper.

If she could have had a good cry there and then her shame and anger would have found a saving vent. But that was impossible. She would *not* cry. She would not let them see the depths of her humiliation. If Emily could have laughed off the malicious joke it would have been better for her. Being Emily—and being one of the proud Murrays—she could not. She resented the indignity to the very core of her passionate soul.

As far as the English paper was concerned she might almost as well have gone home. She had lost twenty minutes already. It was ten minutes more before she could steady her hand sufficiently to write. Her thoughts she could not command at all. The paper was a difficult one, as Mr. Travers' papers always were. Her mind seemed a chaos of jostling ideas spinning around a fixed point of torturing shame. When she handed in her paper and left the class-room she knew she had lost her star. That paper would be no more than a pass, if it were that. But in her turmoil of feeling she did not care. She hurried home to her unfriendly room, thankful that Aunt Ruth was out, threw herself on the bed and wept. She felt sore, beaten, bruised—and under all her pain was a horrible, teasing little doubt.

Did Ilse do it—no, she *didn't*—she *couldn't* have. Who then? Mary? The idea was absurd. It must have been Evelyn—Evelyn had come back and played that cruel trick on her out of spite and pique. Yet she had denied it, with seemingly insulted indignation, and eyes that were perhaps a shade too innocent. *What* had Ilse said—"You are getting positively smug—something ought to be done to cure you before it gets chronic." Had Ilse taken that abominable way of curing her?

"No—no—no!" Emily sobbed fiercely into her pillow. But the doubt persisted.

Aunt Ruth had no doubt. Aunt Ruth was calling on her friend, Mrs. Ball, and her friend, Mrs. Ball, had a daughter who was a Prep. Anita Ball came home with the tale that had been well laughed over in Prep and Junior and Senior classes, and Anita Ball said that Evelyn Blake had said Ilse Burnley had done the deed.

"Well," said Aunt Ruth, invading Emily's room on her return home, "I hear Ilse Burnley decorated you beautifully to-day. I hope you realize what she is now."

"Ilse didn't do it," said Emily.

"Have you asked her?"

"No. I wouldn't insult her with such a question."

"Well, I believe she did do it. And she is not to come here again. Understand that."

"Aunt Ruth—"

"You've heard what I said, Em'ly. Ilse Burnley is no fit associate for you. I've heard too many tales about her lately. But this is unpardonable."

"Aunt Ruth, if I ask Ilse if she did it and she says she did not, won't you believe her?"

"No, I wouldn't believe any girl brought up as Ilse Burnley was. It's my belief she'd do anything and say anything. Don't let me see her in my house again."

Emily stood up and tried to summon the Murray look into a face distorted by weeping.

"Of course, Aunt Ruth," she said coldly, "I won't bring Ilse here if she is not welcome. But I shall go to see her. And if you forbid me—I'll—I'll go home to New Moon. I feel as if I wanted to go anyhow now. Only—I *won't* let Evelyn Blake drive me away."

Aunt Ruth knew quite well that the New Moon folks would not agree to a complete divorce between Emily and Ilse. They were too good friends with the doctor for that. Mrs. Dutton had never liked Dr. Burnley. She had to be content with the excuse for keeping Ilse away from her house, for which she had long hankered. Her own annoyance over the matter was not born out of any sympathy with Emily but solely from anger at a Murray being made ridiculous.

"I would have thought you'd had enough of going to see Ilse. As for Evelyn Blake, she is too clever and sensible a girl to have played a silly trick like that. I know the Blakes. They are an excellent family and Evelyn's father is well-to-do. Now, stop crying. A pretty face you've got. What sense is there in crying?"

"None at all," agreed Emily drearily, "only I can't help it. I can't *bear* to be made ridiculous. I can endure anything but that. Oh, Aunt Ruth, *please* leave me alone. I can't eat any supper."

"You've got yourself all worked up—Starr-like. We Murrays conceal our feelings."

"I don't believe you've any to conceal—some of you," thought Emily rebelliously.

"Keep away from Ilse Burnley after this, and you'll not be so likely to be publicly disgraced," was Aunt Ruth's parting advice.

Emily, after a sleepless night—during which it seemed to her that if she couldn't push that ceiling farther from her face she would surely smother—went to see Ilse the next day and reluctantly told her what Aunt Ruth had said. Ilse was furious—but Emily noted with a pang that she did not assert any innocence of the crayon trick.

"Ilse, you—you didn't really do that?" she faltered. She *knew* Ilse hadn't—she was *sure* of it—but she wanted to hear her say so. To her surprise, a sudden blush swept over Ilse's face.

"Is thy servant a dog?" she said, rather confusedly. It was very unlike straightforward, outspoken Ilse to be so confused. She turned her face away and began fumbling aimlessly with her book-bag. "You don't suppose I'd do anything like that to you, Emily?"

"No, of course not," said Emily, slowly. The subject was dropped. But the little doubt and distrust at the bottom of Emily's mind came out of its lurking-place and declared itself. Even yet she couldn't believe Ilse could do such a thing—and lie about it afterward. But why was she so confused and shamefaced? Would not an innocent Ilse have stormed about according to form, berated Emily, roundly, for mere suspicion, and aired the subject generally until all the venom had been blown out of it?

It was not referred to again. But the shadow was there and spoiled, to a certain extent, the Christmas holidays at New Moon. Outwardly, the girls were the friends they had always been, but Emily was acutely conscious of a sudden rift between them. Strive as she would she could not bridge it. The seeming unconsciousness of any such severance on Ilse's part served to deepen it. Hadn't Ilse cared enough for her and her friendship to *feel* the chill that had come over it? Could she be so shallow and indifferent as not to perceive it? Emily brooded and grew morbid over it. A thing like that—a dim, poisonous thing that lurked in shadow and dared not come into the open—always played havoc with her sensitive and passionate temperament. No open quarrel with Ilse could have affected her like this—she had quarrelled with Ilse scores of times and made up the next minute with no bitterness or backward glance. *This* was different. The more Emily brooded over it the more monstrous it grew. She was unhappy, absent, restless. Aunt Laura and Cousin Jimmy noticed it but attributed it to her disappointment over the star pin. She had told them she was sure she would not win. But Emily had ceased to care about the star pin.

To be sure, she had a bad time of it, when she went back to High School and the examination results were announced. She was not one of the envied four who flaunted star pins and Aunt Ruth rubbed it in for weeks. Aunt Ruth felt that she had lost family prestige in Emily's failure and she was very bitter about it. Altogether Emily felt that the New Year had come in very inauspiciously for her. The first month of it was a time she never liked to recall. She was very lonely. Ilse could not come to see her, and though she made herself go to see Ilse the subtle little rift between them was slowly widening. Ilse still gave no sign of feeling it; but then, somehow, she was seldom alone with Ilse now. The room was always filled with girls, and there was a good deal of noise and laughter and jokes and school gossip—all very harmless and even jolly, but very different from the old intimacy and understanding comradeship with Ilse. Formerly it used to be a chummy jest between them that they could walk or sit for hours together and say no word and yet feel that they had had a splendid time. There were no such silences now: when they did happen to be alone together they both chattered gaily and shallowly, as if each were secretly afraid that there might come a moment for the silence that betrays.

Emily's heart ached over their lost friendship: every night her pillow was wet with tears. Yet there was nothing she could do: she could not, try as she would, banish the doubt that possessed her. She made many an honest effort to do so. She told herself every day that Ilse Burnley could never have played that trick—that she was constitutionally incapable of it—and went straightway to Ilse with the firm determination to be just what she had always been to her. With the result that she was unnaturally cordial and friendly—even gushing—and no more like her real self than she was like Evelyn Blake. Ilse was just as cordial and friendly—and the rift was wider still.

"Ilse never goes into a tantrum with me now," Emily reflected sadly.

It was quite true. Ilse was always good-tempered with Emily, presenting a baffling front of politeness unbroken by a single flash of her old wild spirit. Emily felt that nothing could have been more welcome than one of Ilse's stormy rages. It might break the ice that was forming so relentlessly between them, and release the pent-up flood of old affection.

One of the keenest stings in the situation was that Evelyn Blake was quite well aware of the state of affairs between Ilse and Emily. The mockery of her long brown eyes and the hidden sneer in her casual sentences betrayed her knowledge and her enjoyment of it. This was gall and wormwood to Emily, who felt that she had no defence against it. Evelyn was a girl whom intimacies between other girls annoyed, and the friendship between Ilse and Emily had annoyed her especially. It had been so complete—so absorbing. There had been no place in it for anyone else. And Evelyn did not like to feel that she was barred out—that there was some garden enclosed, into which she might not enter. She was therefore hugely delighted to think that this vexingly beautiful friendship between two girls she secretly hated was at an end.

A SUPREME MOMENT

Emily came downstairs laggingly, feeling that all the colour and music had somehow gone out of life, and that it stretched before her in unbroken greyness. Ten minutes later she was encompassed by rainbows and the desert of her future had blossomed like the rose.

The cause of this miracle of transformation was a thin letter which Aunt Ruth handed to her with an Aunt Ruthian sniff. There was a magazine, too, but Emily did not at first regard it. She saw the address of a floral firm on the corner of the envelope, and sensed at touch the promising thinness of it—so different from the plump letters full of rejected verses.

Her heart beat violently as she tore it open and glanced over the typewritten sheet.

MISS EMILY B. STARR,

Shrewsbury, P.E. Island,

Can.

DEAR MISS STARR:

It gives us great pleasure to tell you that your poem, *Owl's Laughter* has been found available for use in *Garden and Woodland*. It appears in the current issue of our magazine, a copy of which we are sending you. Your verses have the true ring and we shall be glad to see more of your work.

It is not our custom to pay cash for our contributions but you may select two dollars' worth of seeds or plants from our catalogue to be sent to your address prepaid.

Thanking you,

We remain,

Yours truly,

THOS. E. CARLTON & CO.

Emily dropped the letter and seized upon the magazine with trembling fingers. She grew dizzy—the letters danced before her eyes—she felt a curious sensation of choking—for there on the front page, in a fine border of curlicues, was her poem—*Owl's Laughter*, by Emily Byrd Starr.

It was the first sweet bubble on the cup of success and we must not think her silly if it intoxicated her. She carried the letter and magazine off to her room to gloat over it, blissfully unconscious that Aunt Ruth was doing an extra deal of sniffing. Aunt Ruth felt very suspicious of suddenly crimsoned cheek and glowing eye and general air of rapture and detachment from earth.

In her room Emily sat down and read her poem as if she had never seen it before. There was, to be sure, a printer's error in it that made the flesh creep on her bones—it was awful to have *hunter's moon* come out as *hunter's moan*—but it was her poem—*hers*—accepted by and printed in a *real* magazine.

And *paid* for! To be sure a cheque would have been more acceptable—two dollars all her own, earned by her own pen, would have seemed like riches to Emily. But what fun she and Cousin Jimmy would have selecting the seeds! She could see in imagination that beautiful flower-bed next summer in the New Moon garden—a glory of crimson and purple and blue and gold.

And what was it the letter said?

"Your verses have the true ring and we shall be glad to see more of your work."

Oh, bliss—oh, rapture! The world was hers—the *Alpine Path* was as good as climbed—what signified a few more scrambles to the summit?

Emily could not remain in that dark little room with its oppressive ceiling and unfriendly furniture. Lord Byron's funereal expression was an insult to her happiness. She threw on her wraps and hurried out to the Land of Uprightness.

As she went through the kitchen, Aunt Ruth, naturally more suspicious than ever, inquired with markedly bland sarcasm,

"Is the house on fire? Or the harbour?"

"Neither. It's my soul that's on fire," said Emily with an inscrutable smile. She shut the door behind her and at once forgot Aunt Ruth and every other disagreeable thing and person. How beautiful the world was—how beautiful life was—how wonderful the Land of Uprightness was! The young firs along the narrow path were lightly powdered with snow, as if, thought Emily, a veil of aerial lace had been tricksily flung over austere young Druid priestesses foresworn to all such frivolities of vain adornment. Emily decided she would write that sentence down in her Jimmy-book when she went back. On and on she flitted to the crest of the hill. She felt as if she were flying—her feet *couldn't* really be touching the earth. On the hill she paused and stood, a rapt, ecstatic figure with clasped hands and eyes of dream. It was just after sunset. Out, over the ice-bound harbour, great clouds piled themselves up in dazzling, iridescent masses. Beyond were gleaming white hills with early stars over them. Between the dark trunks of the old fir trees to her right, far away through the crystal evening air, rose a great, round, full moon.

"'It has the true ring,'" murmured Emily, tasting the incredible words anew. "They want to see more of my work! Oh, if only Father could see my verses in print!"

Years before, in the old house at Maywood, her father, bending over her as she slept had said, "She will love deeply—suffer terribly—she will have glorious moments to compensate."

This was one of her glorious moments. She felt a wonderful lightness of spirit—a soul-stirring joy in mere existence. The creative faculty, dormant through the wretched month just passed, suddenly burned in her soul again like a purifying flame. It swept away all morbid, poisonous, rankling things. All at once Emily *knew* that Ilse had never done *that*. She laughed joyously—amusedly.

"What a little fool I've been! Oh, *such* a little fool! Of course, Ilse never did it. There's nothing between us now—it's gone—gone—gone. I'll go right to her and tell her so."

Emily hurried back adown her little path. The Land of Uprightness lay all about her, mysterious in the moonlight, wrapped in the exquisite reticence of winter woods. She seemed one with its beauty and charm and mystery. With a sudden sigh of the Wind Woman through the shadowy aisles came "the flash" and Emily went dancing to Ilse with the afterglow of it in her soul.

She found Ilse alone—threw her arms around her—hugged her fiercely.

"Ilse, do forgive me," she cried. "I shouldn't have doubted you—I *did* doubt you—but now I know—I *know*. You *will* forgive me?"

"You young goat," said Ilse.

Emily loved to be called a young goat. This was the old Ilse—*her* Ilse.

"Oh, Ilse, I've been so unhappy."

"Well, don't bawl over it," said Ilse. "I haven't been very hilarious myself. Look here, Emily, I've got something to tell you. Shut up and listen. That day I met Evelyn at the Shoppe and we went back for some book she wanted and we found you sound asleep—so sound asleep that you never stirred when I pinched your cheek. Then, just for devilment I picked up a black crayon and said, 'I'm going to draw a moustache on her'—shut up! Evelyn pulled a long face and said, 'Oh, no! that would be *mean*, don't you think?' I hadn't had the slightest intention of doing it—I'd only spoken in fun—but that shrimp Evelyn's ungodly affectation of righteousness made me so mad that I decided I would do it—shut *up*!—I meant to wake you right up and hold a glass before you, that was all. But before I could do it Kate Errol came in and wanted us to go along with her and I threw down the chalk and went out. That's all, Emily, honest to Caesar. But it made me feel ashamed and silly later on—I'd say a bit conscience-stricken if I had such a thing as a conscience, because I felt that *I* must have put the idea into the head of whoever did do it, and so was responsible in a way. And then I saw you distrusted me—and that made me mad—not tempery-mad, you see, but a nasty, cold, *inside* sort of madness. I thought you had no business even to suspect that I could have done such a thing as let you go to class like that. And I thought, since you did, you could go on doing it—*I* wouldn't say one word to put matters straight. Golly, but I'm glad you're through with seein' things."

"Do you think Evelyn Blake did it?"

"No. Oh, she's quite capable of it, of course, but I don't see how it could have been she. She went to the Shoppe with Kate and me and we left her there. She was in class fifteen minutes later, so I don't think she'd have had time to go back and do it. I really think it was that little devil of a May Hilson. She'd do anything and she was in the hall when I was flourishing the crayon. She'd 'take the suggestion as a cat laps milk.' But it couldn't have been Evelyn."

Emily retained her belief that it could have been and was. But the only thing that mattered now was the fact that Aunt Ruth still believed Ilse guilty and would continue so to believe.

"Well, that's a rotten shame," said Ilse. "We can't have any real chum-talks here—Mary always has such a mob in and E. B. pervades the place."

"I'll find out who did it yet," said Emily darkly, "and *make* Aunt Ruth give in."

On the next afternoon Evelyn Blake found Ilse and Emily in a beautiful row. At least Ilse was rowing while Emily sat with her legs crossed and a bored, haughty expression in her insolently half-shut eyes. It should have been a welcome sight to a girl who disliked the intimacies of other girls. But Evelyn Blake was not rejoiced. Ilse was quarrelling with Emily again—*ergo*, Ilse and Emily were on good terms once more.

"I'm so glad to see you've forgiven Ilse for that mean trick," she said sweetly to Emily the next day. "Of course, it was just pure thoughtlessness on her part—I've always insisted on *that*—she never stopped to think what ridicule she was letting you in for. Poor Ilse is like that. You know I tried to stop her—I didn't tell you this before, of course—*I* didn't want to make any more trouble than there was—but I *told* her it was a horribly mean thing to do to a friend. I thought I *had* put her off. It's sweet of you to forgive her, Emily dear. You *are* better-hearted than I am. I'm afraid I could *never* pardon anyone who had made me such a laughing-stock."

"Why didn't you slay her in her tracks?" said Ilse when she heard of it from Emily.

"I simply half-shut my eyes and looked at her like a Murray," said Emily, "and that was more bitter than death."

THE MADNESS OF AN HOUR

The High School concert in aid of the school library was an annual event in Shrewsbury, coming off in early April, before it was necessary to settle down to hard study for spring examinations. This year it was at first intended to have the usual programme of music and readings with a short dialogue. Emily was asked to take part in the latter and agreed, after securing Aunt Ruth's very grudging consent, which would probably never have been secured if Miss Aylmer had not come in person to plead for it. Miss Aylmer was a granddaughter of Senator Aylmer and Aunt Ruth yielded to family what she would have yielded to nothing else. Then Miss Aylmer suggested cutting out most of the music and all of the readings and having a short play instead. This found favour in the eyes of the students and the change was made forthwith. Emily was cast for a part that suited her, so she became keenly interested in the matter and enjoyed the practices, which were held in the school building two evenings of the week under the chaperonage of Miss Aylmer.

The play created quite a stir in Shrewsbury. Nothing so ambitious had been undertaken by the High School students before: it became known that many of the Queen's Academy students were coming up from Charlottetown on the evening train to see it. This drove the performers half wild. The Queen's students were old hands at putting on plays. Of course they came to criticize. It became a fixed obsession with each member of the cast to make the play as good as any of the Queen's Academy plays had been, and every nerve was strained to that end. Kate Errol's sister, who was a graduate of a school of oratory, coached them and when the evening of the performance arrived there was burning excitement in the various homes and boarding-houses of Shrewsbury.

Emily, in her small, candle-lighted room, looked at Emily-in-the-Glass with considerable satisfaction—a satisfaction that was quite justifiable. The scarlet flush of her cheeks, the deepening darkness of her grey eyes, came out brilliantly above the ashes-of-roses gown, and the little wreath of silver leaves, twisted around her black hair, made her look like a young dryad. She did not, however, *feel* like a dryad. Aunt Ruth had made her take off her lace stockings and put on cashmere ones—had tried, indeed, to make her put on woollen ones, but had gone down in defeat on that point, retrieving her position, however, by insisting on a flannel petticoat.

"Horrid bunchy thing," thought Emily resentfully—meaning the petticoat, of course. But the skirts of the day were full and Emily's slenderness could carry even a thick flannel petticoat.

She was just fastening her Egyptian chain around her neck when Aunt Ruth stalked in.

One glance was sufficient to reveal that Aunt Ruth was very angry.

"Em'ly, Mrs. Ball has just called. She told me something that amazed me. Is this a *play* you're taking part in to-night?"

"Of course it's a play, Aunt Ruth. Surely you knew that."

"When you asked my permission to take part in this concert you told me it was a *dialogue*," said Aunt Ruth icily.

"O-o-h—but Miss Aylmer decided to have a little play in place of it. I *thought* you knew, Aunt Ruth—truly I did. I thought I mentioned it to you."

"You didn't think anything of the kind, Em'ly—you deliberately kept me in ignorance because you knew I wouldn't have allowed you to take part in a *play*."

"Indeed, no, Aunt Ruth," pleaded Emily, gravely. "I never thought of hiding it. Of course, I didn't feel like talking much to you about it because I knew you didn't approve of the concert at all."

When Emily spoke gravely Aunt Ruth always thought she was impudent.

"This crowns all, Em'ly. Sly as I've always known you to be I wouldn't have believed you could be as sly as this."

"There was nothing of the kind about it, Aunt Ruth!" said Emily impatiently. "It would have been silly of me to try to hide the fact that we were getting up a play when all Shrewsbury is talking of it. I don't see how you could *help* hearing of it."

"You knew I wasn't going anywhere because of my bronchitis. Oh, I see through it all, Em'ly. You cannot deceive *me*."

"I haven't tried to deceive you. I thought you knew—that is all there is to it. I thought the reason you never spoke of it was because you were opposed to the whole thing. That is the truth, Aunt Ruth. What difference is there between a dialogue and a play?"

"There is *every* difference," said Aunt Ruth. "Plays are wicked."

"But this is such a *little* one," pleaded Emily despairingly—and then laughed because it sounded so ridiculously like the nursemaid's excuse in *Midshipman Easy*. Her sense of humour was untimely; her laughter infuriated Aunt Ruth.

"Little or big, you are not going to take part in it."

Emily stared again, paling a little.

"Aunt Ruth—I *must*—why, the play would be ruined."

"Better a play ruined than a soul ruined," retorted Aunt Ruth.

Emily dared not smile. The issue at stake was too serious.

"Don't be so—so—indignant, Aunt Ruth"—she had nearly said unjust. "I am sorry you don't approve of plays—I won't take part in any more—but you can see I *must* do it to-night."

"Oh, my dear Em'ly, I don't think you are quite as indispensable as all *that*."

Certainly Aunt Ruth was very maddening. How disagreeable the word "dear" could be! Still was Emily patient.

"I really am—to-night. You see, they couldn't get a substitute at the last moment. Miss Aylmer would never forgive me."

"Do you care more about Miss Aylmer's forgiveness than God's?" demanded Aunt Ruth with the air of one stating a decisive position.

"Yes—than *your* God's," muttered Emily, unable to keep her patience under such insensate questions.

"Have you no respect for your forefathers?" was Aunt Ruth's next relevant query. "Why, if they knew a descendant of theirs was play-acting they would turn over in their graves!"

Emily favoured Aunt Ruth with a sample of the Murray look.

"It would be excellent exercise for them. I am going to take my part in the play to-night, Aunt Ruth."

Emily spoke quietly, looking down from her young height with resolute eyes. Aunt Ruth felt a nasty sense of helplessness: there was no lock to Emily's door—and she couldn't detain her by physical force.

"If you go, you needn't come back here to-night," she said, pale with rage. "This house is locked at nine o'clock."

"If I don't come back here to-night, I won't come at all." Emily was too angry over Aunt Ruth's unreasonable attitude to care for consequences. "If you lock me out I'll go back to New Moon. They know all about the play there—even Aunt Elizabeth was willing for me to take part."

She caught up her coat and jammed the little red-feather hat, which Uncle Oliver's wife had given her at Christmas, down on her head. Aunt Addie's taste was not approved at New Moon but the hat was very becoming and Emily loved it. Aunt Ruth suddenly realized that Emily looked oddly mature and grown-up in it. But the knowledge did not as yet dampen her anger. Em'ly was gone—Em'ly had dared to defy her and disobey her—sly, underhand Em'ly—Em'ly must be taught a lesson.

At nine o'clock a stubborn, outraged Aunt Ruth locked all the doors and went to bed.

The play was a big success. Even the Queen's students admitted that and applauded generously. Emily threw herself into her part with a fire and energy generated by her encounter with Aunt Ruth, which swept away all hampering consciousness of flannel petticoats and agreeably astonished Miss Errol, whose one criticism of Emily's acting had been that she was rather cold and reserved in a part that called for more abandon. Emily was showered with compliments at the close of the performance. Even Evelyn Blake said graciously,

"Really, dear, you are quite wonderful—a star actress—a poet—a budding novelist—what surprise will you give us next?"

Thought Emily, "Condescending, insufferable creature!"

Said Emily, "*Thank* you!"

There was a happy, triumphant walk home with Teddy, a gay good night at the gate, and then—the locked door.

Emily's anger, which had been sublimated during the evening into energy and ambition, suddenly flared up again, sweeping everything before it. It was unbearable to be treated thus. She had endured enough at Aunt Ruth's hands—this was the proverbial last straw. One could not put up with *everything,* even to get an education. One owed *something* to one's dignity and self-respect.

There were three things she could do. She could thump the old-fashioned brass knocker on the door until Aunt Ruth came down and let her in, as she had done once before—and then endure weeks of slurs because of it. She could fly up-street and down-street to Ilse's boarding-house—the girls wouldn't be in bed yet—as she had likewise done once before, and as no doubt Aunt Ruth would expect her to do now; and then Mary Carswell would tell Evelyn Blake and Evelyn Blake would laugh maliciously and tell it all through the school. Emily had no intention of doing either of these things; she knew from the moment she found the door locked just what she would do. She would walk to New Moon—and stay there! Months of suppressed chafing under Aunt Ruth's perpetual stings burst into a conflagration of revolt. Emily marched out of the gate, slammed it shut behind her with no Murray dignity but plenty of Starr passion, and started on her seven-mile walk through the midnight. Had it been three times seven she would have started just the same.

So angry was she, and so angry she continued to be, that the walk did not seem long, nor, though she had no wrap save her cloth coat, did she feel the cold of the sharp April night.

The winter's snow had gone but the bare road was hard-frozen and rough—no dainty footing for the thin kid slippers of Cousin Jimmy's Christmas box. Emily reflected with what she considered a grim, sarcastic laugh that it was well, after all, that Aunt Ruth had insisted on cashmere stockings and flannel petticoat.

There was a moon that night, but the sky was covered with curdled grey clouds, and the harsh, bleak landscape lay dourly in the pallid grey light. The wind came across it in sudden, moaning gusts. Emily felt with considerable dramatic satisfaction that the night harmonized with her stormy, tragic mood.

She would *never* go back to Aunt Ruth's that was certain. No matter what Aunt Elizabeth might say—and she *would* say aplenty, no doubt of that—no matter what anyone would say. If Aunt Elizabeth would not let her go anywhere else to board she would give up school altogether. She knew it would cause a tremendous upheaval at New Moon. Never mind. In her very reckless mood upheavals seemed welcome things. It was time somebody upheaved. She would not humiliate herself another day—that she would not! Aunt Ruth had gone too far at last. You could not safely drive a Starr to desperation.

"I have done with Ruth Dutton for ever," vowed Emily, feeling a tremendous satisfaction in leaving off the "Aunt."

As she drew near home the clouds cleared away suddenly, and when she turned into the New Moon lane the austere beauty of the three tall Lombardies against the moonlit sky made her catch her breath. Oh, how wonderful! For a moment she almost forgot her wrongs and Aunt Ruth. Then bitterness rushed over her soul again—not even the magic of the Three Princesses could charm it away.

There was a light shining out of the New Moon kitchen window, falling on the tall, white birches in Lofty John's bush with spectral effect. Emily wondered who could be up at New Moon: she had expected to find it in darkness and had meant to slip in by the front door and up to her own dear room, leaving explanations to the morning. Aunt Elizabeth always locked and barred the kitchen door every night with great ceremony before retiring, but the front door was never locked. Tramps and burglars would surely never be so ill-mannered as to come to the front door of New Moon.

Emily crossed the garden and peeped through the kitchen window. Cousin Jimmy was there alone, sitting by the table, with two candles for company. On the table was a stoneware crock and just as Emily looked in he absently put his hand into it and drew out a chubby doughnut. Cousin Jimmy's eyes were fixed on a big beef ham hanging from the ceiling and Cousin Jimmy's lips moved soundlessly. There was no reasonable doubt that Cousin Jimmy was composing poetry, though why he was doing it at that hour o' night was a puzzle.

Emily slipped around the house, opened the kitchen door gently, and walked in. Poor Cousin Jimmy in his amazement tried to swallow half a doughnut whole and then couldn't speak for several seconds. Was *this* Emily—or an apparition? Emily in a dark-blue coat, an enchanting little red-feather hat—Emily with windblown night-black hair and tragic eyes—Emily with tattered kid slippers on her feet—Emily in this plight at New Moon when she should have been sound asleep on her maiden couch in Shrewsbury?

Cousin Jimmy seized the cold hands Emily held out to him.

"Emily, dear child, what has happened?"

"Well, just to jump into the middle of things—I've left Aunt Ruth's and I'm not going back."

Cousin Jimmy didn't say anything for a few moments. But he did a few things. First he tiptoed across the kitchen and carefully shut the sitting-room door; then he gently filled the stove up with wood, drew a chair up to it, pushed Emily into it and lifted her cold, ragged feet to the hearth. Then he lighted two more candles and put them on the chimney-piece. Finally he sat down in his chair again and put his hands on his knees.

"Now, tell me all about it."

Emily, still in the throes of rebellion and indignation, told it pretty fully.

As soon as Cousin Jimmy got an inkling of what had really happened he began to shake his head slowly—continued to shake it— shook it so long and gravely that Emily began to feel an uncomfortable conviction that instead of being a wronged, dramatic figure she was by way of being a bit of a little fool. The longer Cousin Jimmy shook his head the smaller grew her heroics. When she had finished her story with a defiant, conclusive "I'm *not* going back to Aunt Ruth's, anyhow," Cousin Jimmy gave a final wag to his head and pushed the crock across the table.

"Have a doughnut, pussy."

Emily hesitated. She was very fond of doughnuts—and it had been a long time since she had her supper. But doughnuts seemed out of keeping with rebellion and tumult. They were decidedly reactionary in their tendencies. Some vague glimmering of this made Emily refuse the doughnut.

Cousin Jimmy took one himself.

"So you're not going back to Shrewsbury?"

"Not to Aunt Ruth's," said Emily.

"It's the same thing," said Cousin Jimmy.

Emily knew it was. She knew it was of no use to hope that Aunt Elizabeth would let her board elsewhere.

"And you walked all the way home over those roads." Cousin Jimmy shook his head. "Well, you *have* spunk. Heaps of it," he added meditatively between bites.

"Do you blame me?" demanded Emily passionately—all the more passionately because she felt some inward support had been shaken away by Cousin Jimmy's head.

"No-o-o, it was a durn mean shame to lock you out—just like Ruth Dutton."

"And you see—don't you—that I can't go back after such an insult?"

Cousin Jimmy nibbled at the doughnut cautiously, as if bent on trying to see how near he could nibble to the hole without actually breaking through.

"I don't think any of your grandmothers would have given up a chance for an education so easily," he said. "Not on the Murray side, anyhow," he added after a moment's reflection, which apparently reminded him that he knew too little about the Starrs to dogmatize concerning them.

Emily sat very still. As Teddy would have said in cricket parlance, Cousin Jimmy had got her middle wicket with the first ball. She felt at once that when Cousin Jimmy, in that diabolical fit of inspiration, dragged her grandmothers in, everything was over but the precise terms of surrender. She could see them all around her—the dear, dead ladies of New Moon—Mary Shipley and Elizabeth Burnley, and all the rest—mild, determined, restrained, looking down with something of contemptuous pity on her, their foolish, impulsive descendant. Cousin Jimmy appeared to think there might be some weakness on the Starr side. Well, there wasn't—she would show him!

She *had* expected more sympathy from Cousin Jimmy. She had known Aunt Elizabeth would condemn her and even Aunt Laura would look disappointed question. But she had counted on Cousin Jimmy taking her part. He always had before.

"My grandmothers never had to put up with Aunt Ruth," she flung at him.

"They had to put up with your grandfathers." Cousin Jimmy appeared to think that this was conclusive—as anyone who had known Archibald and Hugh Murray might have very well thought.

"Cousin Jimmy, do you think I ought to go back and accept Aunt Ruth's scolding and go on as if this had never happened?"

"What do *you* think about it?" asked Cousin Jimmy. "*Do* take a doughnut, pussy."

This time Emily took the doughnut. She might as well have some comfort. Now, you can't eat doughnuts and remain dramatic. Try it.

Emily slipped from her peak of tragedy to the valley of petulance.

"Aunt Ruth has been *abominable* these past two months—ever since her bronchitis has prevented her from going out. You don't know *what* it's been like."

"Oh, I do—I do. Ruth Dutton never made anyone feel better pleased with herself. Feet getting warm, Emily?"

"I *hate* her," cried Emily, still grasping after self-justification. "It's horrible to live in the same house with anyone you hate—"

"Poisonous," agreed Cousin Jimmy.

"And it *isn't* my fault. I *have* tried to like her—tried to please her—she's always twitting me—she attributes mean motives to everything I do or say—or *don't* do or say. I've never heard the last of sitting in the corner of the pew—and failing to get a star pin. She's always *hinting* insults to my father and mother. And she's always *forgiving* me for things I haven't done—or that don't need forgiveness."

"Aggravating—very," conceded Cousin Jimmy.

"Aggravating—you're right. I know if I go back she'll say 'I'll forgive you this time, but don't let it happen again.' And she will *sniff*—oh, Aunt Ruth's sniff is the hatefulest sound in the world!"

"Ever hear a dull knife sawing through thick cardboard?" murmured Cousin Jimmy.

Emily ignored him and swept on.

"I can't be *always* in the wrong—but Aunt Ruth thinks I am—and says she has 'to make allowances' for me. She doses me with cod-liver oil—she never lets me go out in the evening if she can help it— 'consumptives should never be out after eight o clock.' If *she* is cold, *I* must put on an extra petticoat. She is always asking disagreeable questions and refusing to believe my answers. She believes and always will believe that I kept this play a secret from her because of slyness. I never thought of such a thing. Why, the Shrewsbury *Times* referred to it last week. Aunt Ruth doesn't often miss anything in the *Times*. She twitted me for days because she found a composition of mine that I had signed 'Emilie.' 'Better try to spell your name after some unheard-of-twist,' she sneered!"

"Well, wasn't it a bit silly, pussy?"

"Oh, I suppose my grandmothers wouldn't have done it! But Aunt Ruth needn't have kept it up as she did. *That* is what is so dreadful—if she'd speak her mind on a thing and have done with it. Why, I got a little spot of iron-rust on my white petticoat and Aunt Ruth harped on it for weeks. She was determined to find out *when* it was rusted and *how*—and I hadn't the least idea. Really, Cousin Jimmy, when this had gone on for three weeks I thought I'd have to scream if she mentioned it again."

"*Any* proper person would feel the same," said Cousin Jimmy to the beef ham.

"Oh, any *one* of these things is only a pin-prick, I know—and you think I'm silly to mind it—but—"

"No, no. A hundred pin-pricks would be harder to put up with than a broken leg. *I'd* sooner be knocked on the head and be done with it."

"Yes, that's it—nothing but pin-pricks all the time. She won't let Ilse come to the house—or Teddy, or Perry—nobody but that stupid Andrew. I'm so tired of him. She wouldn't let me go to the Prep dance. They had a sleigh drive and supper at the Brown Teapot Inn and a little dance—everybody went but me—it was the event of the winter. If I go for a walk in the Land of Uprightness at sunset she is sure there is something sinister in it—*she* never wants to walk in the Land of Uprightness, so why should *I*? She says I have got too high an opinion of myself. I *haven't*—have I, Cousin Jimmy?"

"No," said Cousin Jimmy thoughtfully. "High—but not *too* high."

"She says I'm always displacing things—if I look out of a window she'll trot across the room and mathematically match the corners of the curtains again. And it's 'Why—why—why'—all the time, *all* the time, Cousin Jimmy."

"I know you feel a lot better now that you've got all that out of your system," said Cousin Jimmy. "'Nother doughnut?"

Emily, with a sigh of surrender, took her feet off the stove and moved over to the table. The crock of doughnuts was between her and Cousin Jimmy. She *was* very hungry.

"Ruth give you enough to eat?" queried Cousin Jimmy anxiously.

"Oh, yes. Aunt Ruth keeps up one New Moon tradish at least. She has a good table. But there are no snacks."

"And you always liked a tasty bite at bed-time, didn't you? But you took a box back last time you were home?"

"Aunt Ruth confiscated it. That is, she put it in the pantry and served its contents up at meal times. These doughnuts *are* good. And there is always something exciting and lawless about eating at unearthly hours like this, isn't there? How did you happen to be up, Cousin Jimmy?"

"A sick cow. Thought I'd better sit up and look after her."

"It was lucky for me you were. Oh, I'm in my proper senses again, Cousin Jimmy. Of course, I know you think I've been a little fool."

"Everybody's a fool in some particular," said Cousin Jimmy.

"Well, I'll go back and bite the sour apple without a grimace."

"Lie down on the sofa and have a nap. I'll hitch up the grey mare and drive you back as soon as it begins to be daylight."

"No, that won't do at all. Several reasons. In the first place, the roads aren't fit for wheels or runners. In the second place we couldn't drive away from here without Aunt Elizabeth hearing us, and then she'd find out all about it and I don't want her to. We'll keep my foolishness a dark and deadly secret between you and me, Cousin Jimmy."

"Then how are you going to get back to Shrewsbury?"

"Walk."

"Walk? To Shrewsbury? At this hour of the night?"

"Haven't I just walked from Shrewsbury at this hour? I can do it again and it won't be any harder than bumping over those awful roads behind the grey mare. Of course, I'll put something on my feet that will be a little more protection than kid slippers. I've ruined your Christmas present in my brain-storm. There is a pair of my old boots in the closet there. I'll put them on—and my old ulster. I'll be back in Shrewsbury by daylight. I'll start as soon as we finish the doughnuts. Let's lick the platter clean, Cousin Jimmy."

Cousin Jimmy yielded. After all, Emily was young and wiry, the night was fine, and the less Elizabeth knew about some things the better for all concerned. With a sigh of relief that the affair had turned out so well—he had really been afraid at first that Emily's underlying "stubbornness" had been reached and then, whew!—Cousin Jimmy settled down to doughnuts.

"How's the writing coming on?" he asked.

"I've written a good deal lately—though it's pretty cold in my room mornings, but I love it so—it's my dearest dream to do something worth while some day."

"So you will. *You* haven't been pushed down a well," said Cousin Jimmy.

Emily patted his hand. None realized better than she what Cousin Jimmy might have done if *he* had not been pushed down a well.

When the doughnuts were finished Emily donned her old boots and

404

ulster. It was a very shabby garment but her young-moon beauty shone over it like a star in the old, dim, candle-lighted room.

Cousin Jimmy looked up at her. He thought that she was a gifted, beautiful, joyous creature and that some things were a shame.

"Tall and stately—tall and stately like all our women," he murmured dreamily. "Except Aunt Ruth," he added.

Emily laughed—and "made a face."

"Aunt Ruth will make the most of her inches in our forthcoming interview. This will last her the rest of the year. But don't worry, Cousin darling, I won't do any more foolish things for quite a long time now. This has cleared the air. Aunt Elizabeth will think it was dreadful of you to eat a whole crockful of doughnuts yourself, you greedy Cousin Jimmy."

"Do you want another blank-book?"

"Not yet. The last one you gave me is only half-full yet. A blank-book lasts me quite a while when I can't write stories. Oh, I wish I could, Cousin Jimmy."

"The time will come—the time will come," said Cousin Jimmy encouragingly. "Wait a while—just wait a while. If we don't chase things—sometimes the things following us can catch up. 'Through wisdom is an house builded, and by understanding is it established. And by knowledge shall the chambers be filled with all precious and pleasant riches'—all precious and pleasant riches, Emily. Proverbs twenty-fourth, third and fifth."

He let Emily out and bolted the door. He put out all the candles but one. He glared at it for a few moments, then, satisfied that Elizabeth could not hear him, Cousin Jimmy said fervently,

"Ruth Dutton can go to—to—to—" Cousin Jimmy's courage failed him, "—to heaven!"

Emily went back to Shrewsbury through the clear moonlight. She had expected the walk to be dreary and weary, robbed of the impetus anger and rebellion had given. But she found that it had become transmuted into a thing of beauty—and Emily was one of "the eternal slaves of beauty," of whom Carman sings, who are yet "masters of the world." She was tired, but her tiredness showed itself in a certain exaltation of feeling and imagination such as she often experienced when over-fatigued. Thought was quick and active. She had a series of brilliant imaginary conversations and thought out so many epigrams that she was agreeably surprised at herself. It was good to feel vivid and interesting and all-alive once more. She was alone but not lonely.

As she walked along she dramatized the night. There was about it a wild, lawless charm that appealed to a certain wild, lawless strain hidden deep in Emily's nature—a strain that wished to walk where it would with no guidance but its own—the strain of the gypsy and the poet, the genius and the fool.

The big fir-trees, released from their burden of snow, were tossing their arms freely and wildly and gladly across the moonlit fields. Was ever anything so beautiful as the shadows of those grey, clean-limbed maples on the road at her feet? The houses she passed were full of intriguing mystery. She liked to think of the people who lay there dreaming and saw in sleep what waking life denied them—of little children's dear hands folded in exquisite slumber—of hearts that, perhaps, kept sorrowful, wakeful vigils—of lonely arms that reached out in the emptiness of the night—all while she, Emily, flitted by like a shadowy wraith of the small hours.

And it was easy to think, too, that other things were abroad—things that were not mortal or human. She always lived on the edge of fairyland and now she stepped right over it. The Wind Woman was really whistling eerily in the reeds of the swamp—she was sure she heard the dear, diabolical chuckles of owls in the spruce copses—something frisked across her path—it might be a rabbit or it might be a Little Grey Person; the trees put on half-pleasing, half-terrifying shapes they never wore by day. The dead thistles of last year were goblin groups along the fences: that shaggy, old yellow birch was some satyr of the woodland: the footsteps of the old gods echoed around her: those gnarled stumps on the hill field were surely Pan piping through moonlight and shadow with his troop of laughing fauns. It was delightful to believe they were.

"One loses so much when one becomes incredulous," said Emily—and then thought that was a rather clever remark and wished she had a Jimmy-book to write it down.

So, having washed her soul free from bitterness in the aerial bath of the spring night and tingling from head to foot with the wild, strange, sweet life of the spirit, she came to Aunt Ruth's when the faint, purplish hills east of the harbour were growing clear under a whitening sky. She had expected to find the door still locked; but the knob turned as she tried it and she went in.

Aunt Ruth was up and was lighting the kitchen fire.

On the way from New Moon Emily had thought over a dozen different ways of saying what she meant to say—and now she used not one of them. At the last moment an impish inspiration came to her. Before Aunt Ruth could—or would—speak Emily said,

"Aunt Ruth, I've come back to tell you that I forgive you, but that this must not happen again."

To tell the truth, Mistress Ruth Dutton was considerably relieved that Emily *had* come back. She had been afraid of Elizabeth and Laura—Murray family rows were bitter things—and truly a little afraid of the results to Emily herself if she had really gone to New Moon in those thin shoes and that insufficient coat. For Ruth Dutton was not a fiend—only a rather stupid, stubborn little barnyard fowl trying to train up a skylark. She was honestly afraid that Emily might catch a cold and go into consumption. And if Emily took it into her head *not* to come back to Shrewsbury—well, that would "make talk" and Ruth Dutton hated "talk" when she or her doings was the subject. So, all things considered, she decided to ignore the impertinence of Emily's greeting.

"Did you spend the night on the streets?" she asked grimly.

"Oh, dear no—I went out to New Moon—had a chat with Cousin Jimmy and some lunch—then walked back."

"Did Elizabeth see you? Or Laura?"

"No. They were asleep."

Mrs. Dutton reflected that this was just as well.

"Well," she said coldly, "you have been guilty of great ingratitude, Em'ly, but I'll forgive you this time"—then stopped abruptly. Hadn't that been said already this morning? Before she could think of a substitute remark Emily had vanished upstairs. Mistress Ruth Dutton was left with the unpleasant sensation that, somehow or other, she had not come out of the affair quite as triumphantly as she should have.

HEIGHTS AND HOLLOWS

"April 28, 19—

"This was my week-end at New Moon and I came back this morning. Consequently this is blue Monday and I'm homesick. Aunt Ruth, too, is always a little more *unliveable* on Mondays—or seems so by contrast with Aunt Laura and Aunt Elizabeth. Cousin Jimmy wasn't quite so nice this week-end as he usually is. He had several of his queer spells and was a bit grumpy for two reasons: in the first place, several of his young apple-trees are dying because they were girdled by mice in the winter; and in the second place he can't induce Aunt Elizabeth to try the new creamers that every one else is using. For my own part I am secretly glad that she won't. I don't want our beautiful old dairy and the glossy brown milk pans to be improved out of existence. I can't think of New Moon without a dairy.

"When I could get Cousin Jimmy's mind off his grievances we explored the Carlton catalogue and discussed the best selections to make for my two dollars' worth of owl's laughter. We planned a dozen different combinations and beds, and got several hundred dollars' worth of fun out of it, but finally settled on a long, narrow bed full of asters—lavender down the middle, white around it and a border of pale pink, with clumps of deep purple for sentinels at the four corners. I am sure it will be beautiful: and I shall look at its September loveliness and think, 'This came out of my head!'

"I have taken another step in the Alpine Path. Last week the *Ladies' Own Journal* accepted my poem, *The Wind Woman,* and gave me two subscriptions to the *Journal* for it. No cash—but that may come yet. I *must* make enough money before very long to pay Aunt Ruth every cent my living with her has cost her. Then she won't be able to twit me with the expense I am to her. She hardly misses a day without some hint of it—'No, Mrs. Beatty, I feel I can't give quite as much to missions this year as usual—my expenses have been much heavier, you know'— 'Oh, no, Mr. Morrison, your new goods are beautiful but I can't afford a silk dress *this* spring'—'This davenport should really be upholstered again—it's getting fearfully shabby—but it's out of the question now for a year or two.' So it goes.

"But my soul doesn't belong to Aunt Ruth.

"*Owl's Laughter* was copied in the Shrewsbury *Times*—'hunter's moan' and all. Evelyn Blake, I understand, says she doesn't believe I wrote it at all—she's *sure* she read something exactly like it somewhere some years ago.

"Dear Evelyn!

"Aunt Elizabeth said nothing at all about it, but Cousin Jimmy told me she cut it out and put it in the Bible she keeps on the stand by her bed. When I told her I was to get two dollars' worth of seeds for it she said I'd likely find when I sent for them that the firm had gone bankrupt!

"I have a notion to send that little story about the child that Mr. Carpenter liked to *Golden Hours*. I wish I could get it typewritten, but that is impossible, so I shall have to write it very plainly. I wonder if I *dare*. They would surely pay for a story.

"Dean will soon be home. How glad I will be to see him! I wonder if he will think I have changed much. I have certainly grown taller. Aunt Laura says I will soon have to have really long dresses and put my hair up, but Aunt Elizabeth says fifteen is too young for that. She says girls are not so womanly at fifteen nowadays as they were in *her* time. Aunt Elizabeth is really frightened, I know, that if she lets me grow up I'll be eloping—'like Juliet.' But I'm in no hurry to grow up. It's nicer to be just like this—betwixt-and-between. Then, if I want to be childish I can be, none daring to make me ashamed; and if I want to behave maturely I have the authority of my extra inches.

"It's a gentle, rainy evening to-night. There are pussy willows out in the swamp and some young birches in the Land of Uprightness have cast a veil of transparent purple over their bare limbs. I think I will write a poem on *A Vision of Spring*.

****

"May 5, 19—
"There has been quite an outbreak of spring poetry in High School. Evelyn has one in the May *Quill* on *Flowers*. Very wobbly rhymes.

"And Perry! He also felt the annual spring urge, as Mr. Carpenter calls it, and wrote a dreadful thing called *The Old Farmer Sows His Seed*. He sent it to *The Quill* and *The Quill* actually printed it—in the 'jokes' column. Perry is quite proud of it and doesn't realize that he has made an ass of himself. Ilse turned pale with fury when she read it and hasn't spoken to him since. She says he isn't fit to associate with. Ilse is far too hard on Perry. And yet, when I read the thing, especially the verse,

"I've ploughed and harrowed and sown—

I've done my best,

Now I'll leave the crop alone

And let God do the rest.

I wanted to murder him myself. Perry can't understand what is wrong with it.

"'It rhymes, doesn't it?'

"Oh, yes, it rhymes!

"Ilse has also been raging at Perry lately because he has been coming to school with all but one button off his coat. I couldn't endure it myself, so when we came out of class I whispered to Perry to meet me for five minutes by the Fern Pool at sunset. I slipped out with needle, thread and buttons and sewed them on. He didn't see why it wouldn't have done to wait till Friday night and have Aunt Tom sew them on. I said,

"'Why didn't you sew them on yourself, Perry?'

"'I've no buttons and no money to buy any,' he said, 'but never mind, some day I will have gold buttons if I want them.'

"Aunt Ruth saw me coming in with thread and scissors, etc., and of course wanted to know where, what and why. I told her the whole tale and she said,

"'You'd better let Perry Miller's friends sew his buttons on for him.'

"I'm the best friend he's got," I said.

"'I don't know where you get your low tastes from,' said Aunt Ruth.

****

"May 7, 19—

"This afternoon after school Teddy rowed Ilse and me across the harbour to pick May-flowers in the spruce barrens up the Green River. We got basketfuls, and spent a perfect hour wandering about the barrens with the friendly murmur of the little fir-trees all around us. As somebody said of strawberries so say I of Mayflowers, 'God might have made a sweeter blossom, but never did.'

"When we left for home a thick white fog had come in over the bar and filled the harbour. But Teddy rowed in the direction of the train whistles, so we hadn't any trouble really and I thought the experience quite wonderful. We seemed to be floating over a white sea in an unbroken calm. There was no sound save the faint moan of the bar, the deep-sea call beyond, and the low dip of the oars in the glassy water. We were alone in a world of mist on a veiled, shoreless sea. Now and then, for just a moment, a cool air current lifted the mist curtain and dim coasts loomed phantom-like around us. Then the blank whiteness shut down again. It was as though we sought some strange, enchanted shore that ever receded farther and farther. I was really sorry when we got to the wharf, but when I reached home I found Aunt Ruth all worked up on account of the fog.

"'I knew I shouldn't have allowed you to go,' she said.

"'There wasn't any danger really, Aunt Ruth,' I protested, 'and look at my lovely May-flowers.'

"Aunt Ruth wouldn't look at the May-flowers.

"'No danger—in a white fog! Suppose you had got lost and a wind had come up before you reached land?'

"'How could one get lost on little Shrewsbury harbour, Aunt Ruth?' I said. 'The fog was wonderful—wonderful. It just seemed as if we were voyaging over the planet's rim into the depth of space.'

"I spoke enthusiastically and I suppose I looked a bit wild with mist drops on my hair, for Aunt Ruth said coldly, pityingly,

"'It is unfortunate that you are *so excitable,* Emily.'

"It is maddening to be frozen and pitied, so I answered recklessly,

"'But think of the fun you miss when you're non-excitable, Aunt Ruth. There is nothing more wonderful than dancing around a blazing fire. What matter if it end in ashes?'

"'When you are as old as I am,' said Aunt Ruth, you will have more sense than to go into ecstasies over white fogs.'

"It seems to me impossible that I shall either grow old or die. I *know* I will, of course, but I don't *believe* it. I didn't make any answer to Aunt Ruth, so she started on another tack.

"'I was watching Ilse go past. Em'ly, does that girl wear *any* petticoats?'

"'*Her clothing is silk and purple,*' I murmured, quoting the Bible verse simply because there is something in it that charms me. One couldn't imagine a finer or simpler description of a gorgeously dressed woman. I don't think Aunt Ruth recognized the quotation: she thought I was just trying to be smart.

"'If you mean that she wears a purple silk petticoat, Em'ly, say so in plain English. Silk petticoats, indeed. If *I* had anything to do with her I'd silk petticoat her.'

"'Some day *I* am going to wear silk petticoats,' I said.

"'Oh, indeed, miss. And may I ask what *you* have got to get silk petticoats with?'

"'I've got a *future*,' I said, as proudly as the Murrayest of all Murrays could have said it.

"Aunt Ruth sniffed.

"I have filled my room with May-flowers and even Lord Byron looks as if there might be a chance of recovery.

****

"May 13, 19—

"I have made the plunge and sent my story *Something Different* to *Golden Hours*. I actually trembled as I dropped it into the box at the Shoppe. Oh, if it should be accepted!

"Perry has set the school laughing again. He said in class that France *exported fashions*. Ilse walked up to him when class came out and said, 'You *spawn!*' She hasn't spoken to him since.

"Evelyn continues to say sweet cutting things and laugh. I might forgive her the cutting things but never the laugh.

****

"May 15, 19—

"We had our Prep 'pow-wow' last night. It always comes off in

May. We had it in the Assembly room of the school and when we got
there we found we couldn't light the gas. We didn't know what was the
matter but suspected the Juniors. (To-day we discovered they had cut
off the gas in the basement and locked the basement doors.) At first
we didn't know what to do: then I remembered that Aunt Elizabeth
had brought Aunt Ruth a big box of candles last week for my use. I
tore home and got them—Aunt Ruth being out—and we stuck them
all around the room. So we had our Pow-wow after all and it was a
brilliant success. We had such fun improvising candle holders that we
got off to a good start, and somehow the candle-light was so much
more friendly and inspiring than gas. We all seemed to be able to think
of wittier things to say. Everybody was supposed to make a speech on
any subject he or she wished. Perry made the speech of the evening.
He had prepared a speech on 'Canadian History'—very sensible and, I
suspect, dull; but at the last minute he changed his mind and spoke on
'candles'—just making it up as he went along, telling of all the candles
he saw in different lands when he was a little boy sailing with his father.
It was so witty and interesting that we sat enthralled and I think the
students will forget about French fashions and the old farmer who left
the hoeing and weeding to God.

"Aunt Ruth hasn't found out about the candles yet, as the old box
isn't quite empty. When I go to New Moon to-morrow night I'll coax
Aunt Laura to give me another box—I know she will—and I'll bring
them to Aunt Ruth.

****

"May 22, 19—

"To-day there was a hateful, long, fat envelope for me in the mail.
Golden Hours had sent my story back. The accompanying rejection slip
said:

"We have read your story with interest, and regret to say that we
cannot accept it for publication at the present time.

"At first I tried to extract a little comfort from the fact that they had
read it with 'keen interest.' Then it came home to me that the rejection
slip was a printed one, so of course it is just what they send with *all*
rejected manuscripts.

"The worst of it was that Aunt Ruth had seen the packet before I got home from school and had opened it. It was humiliating to have *her* know of my failure.

"'I hope *this* will convince you that you'd better waste no more stamps on such nonsense, Em'ly. The idea of your thinking *you* could write a story fit to be published.'

"'I've had two poems published,' I cried.

"Aunt Ruth sniffed.

"'Oh, *poems.* Of course they have to have something to fill up the corners.'

"Perhaps it's so. I felt very flat as I crawled off to my room with my poor story. I was quite 'content to fill a little space' then. You could have packed me in a thimble.

"My story is all dog-eared and smells of tobacco. I've a notion to burn it.

"No, I *wont!!* I'll copy it out again and try somewhere else. I *will* succeed!

"I think, from glancing over the recent pages of this journal, that I am beginning to be able to do without italics. But sometimes they are necessary.

****

"New Moon, Blair Water.

"May 24, 19—

"'For lo, the winter is past: the rain is over and gone: the flowers appear on the earth: the time of the singing of birds has come.'

"I'm sitting on the sill of my open window in my own dear room. It's so lovely to get back to it every now and then. Out there, over Lofty John's bush, is a soft yellow sky and one very white little star is just visible where the pale yellow shades off into paler green. Far off, down in the south 'in regions mild of calm and serene air' are great cloud-palaces of rosy marble. Leaning over the fence is a choke-cherry tree that is a mass of blossoms like creamy caterpillars. Everything is so lovely—'the eye is not satisfied with seeing nor the ear with hearing.'

"Sometimes I think it really isn't worth while to try to write anything when everything is already so well expressed in the Bible. That verse I've just quoted for instance—it makes me feel like a pigmy in the presence of a giant. Only twelve simple words—yet a dozen pages

414

couldn't have better expressed the feeling one has in spring.

"This afternoon Cousin Jimmy and I sowed our aster bed. The seeds came promptly. Evidently the firm has not gone bankrupt yet. But Aunt Elizabeth thinks they are old stock and won't grow.

"Dean is home; he was down to see me last night—dear old Dean. He hasn't changed a bit. His green eyes are as green as ever and his nice mouth as nice as ever and his interesting face as interesting as ever. He took both my hands and looked earnestly at me.

"'You have changed, Star,' he said. 'You look more like spring than ever. But don't grow any taller,' he went on. 'I don't want to have you looking down on me.'

"I don't want to, either. I'd hate to be taller than Dean. It wouldn't seem right at all.

"Teddy is an inch taller than I am. Dean says he has improved greatly in his drawing this past year. Mrs. Kent still hates me. I met her to-night, when I was out for a walk with myself in the spring twilight, and she would not even stop to speak to me—just slipped by me like a shadow in the twilight. She looked at me for a second as she passed me, and her eyes were pools of hatred. I think she grows more unhappy every year.

"In my walk I went and said good evening to the Disappointed House. I am always so sorry for it—it is a house that has never lived—that has not fulfilled its destiny. Its blind windows seem peering wistfully from its face as if seeking vainly for what they cannot find. No homelight has ever gleamed through them in summer dusk or winter darkness. And yet I feel, somehow, that the little house has kept its dream and that sometime it will come true.

"I wish I owned it.

"I dandered around all my old haunts to-night—Lofty John's bush—Emily's Bower—the old orchard—the pond graveyard—the To-day Road—I love that little road. It's like a personal friend to me.

"I think 'dandering' is a lovely word of its kind—not in itself exactly, like some words, but because it is so perfectly expressive of its own meaning. Even if you'd never heard it before you'd know exactly what it meant—*dandering* could mean *only* dandering.

"The discovery of beautiful and interesting words always gives me joy. When I find a new, charming word I exult as a jewel-seeker and am unhappy until I've set it in a sentence.

415

****

"May 29, 19—

"To-night Aunt Ruth came home with a portentous face.

"'Em'ly, what does this story mean that is all over Shrewsbury—that you were seen standing on Queen-street last night *with a man's arms around you, kissing him?*'

"I knew in a minute what had happened. I wanted to stamp—I wanted to laugh—I wanted to tear my hair. The whole thing was so absurd and ludicrous. But I had to keep a grave face and explain to Aunt Ruth.

"This is the dark, unholy tale.

"Ilse and I were 'dandering' along Queen-street last night at dusk. Just by the old Taylor house we met a man. I do not know the man—not likely I shall ever know him. I do not know if he was tall or short, old or young, handsome or ugly, black or white, Jew or Gentile, bond or free. But I *do* know he hadn't shaved that day!

"He was walking at a brisk pace. Then something happened which passed in the wink of an eye, but takes several seconds to describe. I stepped aside to let him pass—he stepped in the same direction—I darted the other way—so did he—then I thought I saw a chance of getting past and I made a wild dash—he made a dash—with the result that I ran full tilt against him. He had thrown out his arms when he realized a collision was unavoidable—I went right between them—and in the shock of the encounter they involuntarily closed around me for a moment while my nose came into violent contact with his chin.

"'I—I—beg your pardon,' the poor creature gasped, dropped me as if I were a hot coal, and tore off around the corner.

"Ilse was in fits. She said she had never seen anything so funny in her life. It had all passed so quickly that to a bystander it looked exactly as if that man and I had stopped, gazed at each other for a moment, and then rushed madly into each other's arms.

"My nose ached for blocks. Ilse said she saw Miss Taylor peering from the window just as it happened. Of course that old gossip has spread the story with her own interpretation of it.

"I explained all this to Aunt Ruth, who remained incredulous and seemed to consider it a very limping tale indeed.

"'It's a *very* strange thing that on a sidewalk twelve feet wide you

416

couldn't get past a man without embracing him,' she said.

"'Come now, Aunt Ruth,' I said, 'I know you think me sly and deep and foolish and ungrateful. But you know I am half Murray, and *do* you think anyone with *any* Murray in her would embrace a gentleman friend on the public street?'

"'Oh, I *did* think you could hardly be so brazen,' admitted Aunt Ruth. 'But Miss Taylor said she *saw* it. Every one has heard it. I do *not* like to have one of my family talked about like that. It would not have occurred if you had not been out with Ilse Burnley in defiance of my advice. Don't let anything like this happen again.'

"'Things like that don't happen,' I said. 'They are foreordained.'

******

"June 3, 19—

"The Land of Uprightness is a thing of beauty. I can go to the Fern Pool to write again. Aunt Ruth is very suspicious of this performance. She has never forgotten that I 'met Perry' there one evening. The pool is very lovely now under its new young ferns. I look into it and imagine it is the legendary pool in which one could see the future. I picture myself tiptoeing to it at midnight by full o' moon—casting something precious into it—then looking timidly at what I saw.

"What would it show me? The Alpine Path gloriously climbed? Or failure?

"No, never failure!

******

"June 9, 19—

"Last week Aunt Ruth had a birthday and I gave her a centre-piece which I had embroidered. She thanked me rather stiffly and didn't seem to care anything about it.

"To-night I was sitting in the bay window recess of the dining-room, doing my algebra by the last light. The folding-doors were open and Aunt Ruth was talking to Mrs. Ince in the parlour. I thought they knew I was in the bay, but I suppose the curtains hid me. All at once I heard my name. Aunt Ruth was showing the centre-piece to Mrs. Ince—quite proudly.

"'My niece Em'ly gave me this on my birthday. See how beautifully it is done—she is very skilful with her needle.'

"Could this be Aunt Ruth? I was so petrified with amazement that I could neither move nor speak.

"'She is clever with more than her needle,' said Mrs. Ince. 'I hear Principal Hardy expects her to head her class in the terminal examinations.'

"'Her mother—my sister Juliet—was a *very* clever girl,' said Aunt Ruth.

"'And she's quite pretty, too,' said Mrs. Ince.

"'Her father, Douglas Starr, was a remarkably handsome man,' said Aunt Ruth.

"They went out then. For once an eavesdropper heard something good of herself!

"But from Aunt Ruth!!

****

"June 17, 19—

"My 'candle goeth not out by night' now—at least not until quite late. Aunt Ruth lets me sit up because the terminal examinations are on. Perry infuriated Mr. Travers by writing at the end of his algebra paper, Matthew 7:5. When Mr. Travers turned it up he read: 'Thou hypocrite, first cast out the beam out of thine own eye, and then shalt thou see clearly to cast out the mote out of thy brother's eye.' Mr. Travers is credited with knowing much less about mathematics than he pretends to. So he was furious and threw Perry's paper out 'as a punishment for impertinence.' The truth is poor Perry made a mistake. He *meant* to write Matthew 5:7. 'Blessed are the merciful for they shall obtain mercy.' He went and explained to Mr. Travers but Mr. Travers wouldn't listen. Then Ilse bearded the lion in his den—that is, went to Principal Hardy, told him the tale and induced him to intercede with Mr. Travers. As a result Perry got his marks, but was warned not to juggle with Scripture texts again.

****

"June 28, 19—

418

"School's out. I have won my star pin. It has been a great old year of fun and study and *stings*. And now I'm going back to dear New Moon for two splendid months of freedom and happiness.

"I'm going to write a Garden Book in vacation. The idea has been sizzling in my brain for some time and since I can't write stories I shall try my hand at a series of essays on Cousin Jimmy's garden, with a poem for a tail-piece to each essay. It will be good practice and will please Cousin Jimmy."

AT THE SIGN OF THE HAYSTACK

"*Why* do you want to do a thing like that?" said Aunt Ruth—sniffing, of course. A sniff may always be taken for granted with each of Aunt Ruth's remarks, even when the present biographer omits mention of it.

"To poke some dollars into my slim purse," said Emily.

Holidays were over—the Garden Book had been written and read in instalments to Cousin Jimmy, in the dusks of July and August, to his great delight; and now it was September, with its return to school and studies, the Land of Uprightness, and Aunt Ruth. Emily, with skirts a fraction longer and her hair clubbed up so high in the "Cadogan Braid" of those days, that it really was almost "up," was back in Shrewsbury for her Junior year; and she had just told Aunt Ruth what she meant to do on her Shrewsbury Saturdays, for the autumn.

The editor of the Shrewsbury *Times* was planning a special illustrated Shrewsbury edition and Emily was going to canvass as much of the country as she could cover for subscriptions to it. She had wrung a rather reluctant consent from Aunt Elizabeth—a consent which could never have been extorted if Aunt Elizabeth had been paying all Emily's expenses at school. But there was Wallace paying for her books and tuition fees, and occasionally hinting to Elizabeth that he was a very fine, generous fellow to do so. Elizabeth, in her secret heart, was not overfond of her brother Wallace and resented his splendid airs over the little help he was extending to Emily. So, when Emily pointed out that she could easily earn, during the fall, at least half enough to pay for her books for the whole year, Elizabeth yielded. Wallace would have been offended, if *she,* Elizabeth, had insisted on paying Emily's expenses when *he* took a notion to do it, but he could not reasonably resent Emily earning part for herself. He was always preaching that girls should be self-reliant, and able to earn their own way in life.

Aunt Ruth could not refuse when Elizabeth had assented, but she did not approve.

"The idea of your wandering over the country alone!"

"Oh, I'll not be alone. Ilse is going with me," said Emily.

Aunt Ruth did not seem to consider this much of an improvement.

"We're going to begin Thursday," said Emily. "There is no school Friday, owing to the death of Principal Hardy's father, and our classes are over at three on Thursday afternoon. We are going to canvass the Western Road that evening."

"May I ask if you intend to camp on the side of the road?"

"Oh, no. We'll spend the night with Ilse's aunt at Wiltney. Then, on Friday, we'll cut back to the Western Road, finish it that day and spend Friday night with Mary Carswell's people at St. Clair—then work home Saturday by the River Road."

"It's perfectly absurd," said Aunt Ruth. "No Murray ever did such a thing. I'm surprised at Elizabeth. It simply isn't decent for two young girls like you and Ilse to be wandering alone over the country for three days."

"What do you suppose could happen to us?' asked Emily.

"A good many things might happen," said Aunt Ruth severely.

She was right. A good many things might—and did—happen in that excursion; but Emily and Ilse set off in high spirits Thursday afternoon, two graceless schoolgirls with an eye for the funny side of everything and a determination to have a good time. Emily especially was feeling uplifted. There had been another thin letter in the mail that day, with the address of a third-rate magazine in the corner, offering her three subscriptions to the said magazine for her poem *Night in the Garden,* which had formed the conclusion of her Garden Book and was considered both by herself and Cousin Jimmy to be the gem of the volume. Emily had left the Garden Book locked up in the mantel cupboard of her room at New Moon, but she meant to send copies of its "tail pieces" to various publications during the fall. It augured well that the first one sent had been accepted so promptly.

"Well, we're off," she said, "'over the hills and far away'—what an alluring old phrase! *Anything* may be beyond those hills ahead of us."

"I hope we'll get lots of material for our essays," said Ilse practically. Principal Hardy had informed the Junior English class that he would require several essays from them during the fall term and Emily and Ilse had decided that one at least of their essays should recount their experiences in canvassing for subscriptions, from their separate points of view. Thus they had two strings to their bow.

"I suggest we work along the Western Road and its branches as far as Hunter's Creek, to-night," said Emily. "We ought to get there by sunset. Then we can hit the gypsy trail across the country, through the Malvern woods and come out on the other side of them, quite near Wiltney. It's only half an hour's walk, while around by the Malvern Road it's an hour. What a lovely afternoon this is!"

It was a lovely afternoon—such an afternoon as only September can produce when summer has stolen back for one more day of dream and glamour. Harvest fields drenched in sunshine lay all around them: the austere charm of northern firs made wonderful the ways over which they walked: goldenrod beribboned the fences and the sacrificial fires of willow-herb were kindled on all the burnt lands along the sequestered roads back among the hills. But they soon discovered that canvassing for subscriptions was not all fun—though, to be sure, as Ilse said, they found plenty of human nature for their essays.

There was the old man who said "Humph" at the end of every remark Emily made. When finally asked for a subscription he gruffly said "No."

"I'm glad you didn't say 'Humph' this time," said Emily. "It was getting monotonous."

The old fellow stared—then chuckled.

"Are ye any relation to the proud Murrays? I worked at a place they call New Moon when I was young and one of the Murray gals—Elizabeth her name was—had a sort of high-and-lofty way o' looking at ye, just like yours."

"My mother was a Murray."

"I was thinkin' so—ye bear the stamp of the breed. Well, here's two dollars an' ye kin put my name down. I'd ruther see the special edition 'fore I subscribe. I don't favour buying bearskins afore I see the bear. But it's worth two dollars to see a proud Murray coming down to askin' old Billy Scott fer a subscription."

"Why didn't you slay him with a glance?" asked Ilse as they walked away.

Emily was walking savagely, with her head held high and her eyes snapping.

"I'm out to get subscriptions, not to make widows. I didn't expect it would be all plain sailing."

There was another man who growled all the way through Emily's explanations—and then, when she was primed for refusal, gave her five subscriptions.

"He likes to disappoint people," she told Ilse, as they went down the lane. "He would rather disappoint them agreeably than not at all."

One man swore volubly—"not at anything in particular, but just at large," as Ilse said; and another old man was on the point of subscribing when his wife interfered.

"I wouldn't if I was you, Father. The editor of that paper is an infidel."

"Very impident of him, to be sure," said "Father," and put his money back in his wallet.

"Delicious!" murmured Emily when she was out of ear-shot. "I must jot that down in my Jimmy-book." As a rule the women received them more politely than the men, but the men gave them more subscriptions. Indeed, the only woman who subscribed, was an elderly dame whose heart Emily won by listening sympathetically to a long account of the beauty and virtues of the said elderly lady's deceased pet Thomas-cat—though it must be admitted that she whispered aside to Ilse at its conclusion,

"Charlottetown papers please copy."

Their worst experience was with a man who treated them to a tirade of abuse because his politics differed from the politics of the *Times* and he seemed to hold them responsible for it. When he halted for breath Emily stood up.

"Kick the dog—then you'll feel better," she said calmly, as she stalked out. Ilse was white with rage. "Could you have believed people could be so detestable?" she exploded. "To rate *us* as if we were responsible for the politics of the *Times*! Well—*Human Nature from a Canvasser's Point of View* is to be the subject of my essay. I'll describe that man and picture myself telling him all the things I wanted to and didn't!"

Emily broke into laughter—and found her temper again.

"*You* can. *I* can't even take that revenge—my promise to Aunt Elizabeth binds me. I shall have to stick to facts. Come, let's not think of the brute. After all, we've got quite a lot of subscriptions already—and there's a clump of white birches in which it is reasonably certain a dryad lives—and that cloud over the firs looks like the faint, golden ghost of a cloud."

"Nevertheless, I should have liked to reduce that old vampire to powder," said Ilse.

At the next place of call, however, their experience was pleasant and they were asked to stay for supper. By sunset they had done reasonably well in the matter of subscriptions and had accumulated enough private jokes and by-words to furnish fun for many moons of reminiscence. They decided to canvass no more that night. They had not got quite as far as Hunter's Creek but Emily thought it would be safe to make a cross-cut from where they were. The Malvern woods were not so very extensive and no matter where they came out on the northern side of them, they would be able to see Wiltney.

They climbed a fence, went up across a hill pasture-field feathered with asters, and were swallowed up by the Malvern woods, crossed and recrossed by dozens of trails. The world disappeared behind them and they were alone in a realm of wild beauty. Emily thought the walk through the woods all too short, though tired Ilse, whose foot had turned on a pebble earlier in the day, found it unpleasantly long. Emily liked everything about it—she liked to see that shining gold head of Ilse's slipping through the grey-green trunks, under the long, swaying boughs—she liked the faint dream-like notes of sleepy birds—she liked the little wandering, whispering, tricksy wind o' dusk among the tree crests—she liked the incredibly delicate fragrance of wood flowers and growths—she liked the little ferns that brushed Ilse's silken ankles—she liked that slender, white, tantalizing thing which gleamed out for a moment adown the dim vista of a winding path—was it a birch or a wood-nymph? No matter—it had given her that stab of poignant rapture she called "the flash"—her priceless thing whose flitting, uncalculated moments were worth cycles of mere existence. Emily wandered on, thinking all of the loveliness of the road and nothing of the road itself, absently following limping Ilse, until at last the trees suddenly fell away before them and they found themselves in the open, with a wild sort of little pasture before them, and beyond, in the clear afterlight, a long, sloping valley, rather bare and desolate, where the farmsteads had no great appearance of thrift or comfort.

"Why—where are we?" said Ilse blankly. "I don't see anything like Wiltney."

Emily came abruptly out of her dreams and tried to get her bearings. The only landmark visible was a tall spire on a hill ten miles away.

"Why, there's the spire of the Catholic church at Indian Head," she said flatly. "And that must be Hardscrabble Road down there. We must have taken a wrong turning somewhere, Ilse—we've come out on the east side of the woods instead of the north."

"Then we're five miles from Wiltney," said Ilse despairingly. "I can never walk that far—and we can't go back through those woods—it will be pitch dark in a quarter of an hour. What on earth can we do?"

"Admit we're lost and make a beautiful thing of it," said Emily, coolly.

"Oh, we're lost all right, to all intents and purposes," moaned Ilse, climbing feebly up on the tumbledown fence and sitting there, "but I don't see how we're going to make it beautiful. We can't stay here all night. The only thing to do is to go down and see if they'll put us up at any of those houses. I don't like the idea. If that's Hardscrabble Road the people are all poor—and *dirty*. I've heard Aunt Net tell weird tales of Hardscrabble Road."

"Why can't we stay here all night?" said Emily. Ilse looked at Emily to see if she meant it—saw that she did.

"Where can we sleep? Hang ourselves over this fence?"

"Over on that haystack," said Emily. "It's only half finished—Hardscrabble fashion. The top is flat—there's a ladder leaning against it—the hay is dry and clean—the night is summer warm—there are no mosquitoes this time of year—we can put our raincoats over us to keep off the dew. Why not?"

Ilse looked at the haystack in the corner of the little pasture—and began to laugh assentingly.

"What will Aunt Ruth say?"

"Aunt Ruth need never know it. I'll be sly for once with a vengeance. Besides, I've always longed to sleep out in the open. It's been one of the secret wishes I believed were for ever unattainable, hedged about as I am with aunts. And now it has tumbled into my lap like a gift thrown down by the gods. It's really such good luck as to be uncanny."

"Suppose it rains," said Ilse, who, nevertheless, found the idea very alluring

"It won't rain—there isn't a cloud in sight except those great fluffy rose-and-white ones piling up over Indian Head. They're the kind of clouds that always make me feel that I'd love to soar up on wings as eagles and swoop right down into the middle of them."

It was easy to ascend the little haystack. They sank down on its top with sighs of content, realizing that they were tireder than they had thought. The stack was built of the wild, fragrant grasses of the little pasture, and yielded an indescribably alluring aroma, such as no cultivated clover can give. They could see nothing but a great sky of faint rose above them, pricked with early stars, and the dim fringe of tree-tops around the field. Bats and swallows swooped darkly above them against the paling western gold—delicate fragrances exhaled from the mosses and ferns just over the fence under the trees—a couple of aspen poplars in the corner talked in silvery whispers, of the gossip of the woods. They laughed together in sheer lawless pleasure. An ancient enchantment was suddenly upon them, and the white magic of the sky and the dark magic of the woods wove the final spell of a potent incantation.

"Such loveliness as this doesn't seem real," murmured Emily. "It's so wonderful it *hurts* me. I'm afraid to speak out loud for fear it will vanish. Were we vexed with that horrid old man and his beastly politics to-day, Ilse? Why, he doesn't exist—not in *this* world, anyway. I hear the Wind Woman running with soft, soft footsteps over the hill. I shall always think of the wind as a personality. She is a shrew when she blows from the north—a lonely seeker when she blows from the east—a laughing girl when she comes from the west—and to-night from the south a little grey fairy."

"How do you think of such things?" asked Ilse. This was a question which, for some mysterious reason, always annoyed Emily.

"I don't think of them—they *come*," she answered rather shortly.

Ilse resented the tone.

"For heaven's sake, Emily, don't be such a crank!" she exclaimed.

For a second the wonderful world in which Emily was at the moment living, trembled and wavered like a disturbed reflection in water. Then—

"Don't let's quarrel *here*," she implored. "One of us might push the other off the haystack."

Ilse burst out laughing. Nobody can really laugh and keep angry. So their night under the stars was not spoiled by a fight. They talked for a while in whispers, of schoolgirl secrets and dreams and fears. They even talked of getting married some time in the future. Of course they shouldn't have, but they *did*. Ilse, it appeared, was slightly pessimistic in regard to her matrimonial chances.

"The boys like me as a pal but I don't believe any one will ever really fall in love with me."

"Nonsense," said Emily reassuringly. "Nine out of ten men will fall in love with you."

"But it will be the tenth I'll want," persisted Ilse gloomily.

And then they talked of almost everything else in the world. Finally, they made a solemn compact that whichever one of them died first was to come back to the other if it were possible. How many such compacts have been made! And has even one ever been kept?

Then Ilse grew drowsy and fell asleep. But Emily did not sleep—did not want to sleep. It was too dear a night to go to sleep, she felt. She wanted to lie awake for the pleasure of it and think over a thousand things.

Emily always looked back to that night spent under the stars as a sort of milestone. Everything in it and of it ministered to her. It filled her with its beauty, which she must later give to the world. She wished that she could coin some magic word that might express it.

The round moon rose. Did an old witch in a high-crowned hat ride past it on a broomstick? No, it was only a bat and the little tip of a hemlock-tree by the fence. She made a poem on it at once, the lines singing themselves through her consciousness without effort. With one side of her nature she liked writing prose best—with the other she liked writing poetry. This side was uppermost to-night and her very thoughts ran into rhyme. A great, pulsating star hung low in the sky over Indian Head. Emily gazed on it and recalled Teddy's old fancy of his previous existence in a star. The idea seized on her imagination and she spun a dream-life, lived in some happy planet circling round that mighty, far-off sun. Then came the northern lights—drifts of pale fire over the sky—spears of light, as of empyrean armies—pale, elusive hosts retreating and advancing. Emily lay and watched them in rapture. Her soul was washed pure in that great bath of splendour.

She was a high priestess of loveliness assisting at the divine rites of her worship—and she knew her goddess smiled.

She was glad Ilse was asleep. Any human companionship, even the dearest and most perfect, would have been alien to her then. She was sufficient unto herself, needing not love nor comradeship nor any human emotion to round out her felicity. Such moments come rarely in any life, but when they do come they are inexpressibly wonderful—as if the finite were for a second infinity—as if humanity were for a space uplifted into divinity—as if all ugliness had vanished, leaving only flawless beauty. Oh—beauty—Emily shivered with the pure ecstasy of it. She loved it—it filled her being to-night as never before. She was afraid to move or breathe lest she break the current of beauty that was flowing through her. Life seemed like a wonderful instrument on which to play supernal harmonies.

"Oh, God, make me worthy of it—oh, make me worthy of it," she prayed. Could she ever be worthy of such a message—could she dare try to carry some of the loveliness of that "dialogue divine" back to the everyday world of sordid market-place and clamorous street? She *must* give it—she could not keep it to herself. Would the world listen—understand—feel? Only if she were faithful to the trust and gave out that which was committed to her, careless of blame or praise. High priestess of beauty—yes, she would serve at no other shrine!

She fell asleep in this rapt mood—dreamed that she was Sappho springing from the Leucadian rock—woke to find herself at the bottom of the haystack with Ilse's startled face peering down at her. Fortunately so much of the stack had slipped down with her that she was able to say cautiously,

"I think I'm all in one piece still."

HAVEN

When you have fallen asleep listening to the hymns of the gods it is something of an anti-climax to be awakened by an ignominious tumble from a haystack. But at least it had aroused them in time to see

427

the sunrise over Indian Head, which was worth the sacrifice of several hours of inglorious ease.

"Besides, I might never have known what an exquisite thing a spider's web beaded with dew is," said Emily. "*Look* at it—swung between those two tall, plumy grasses."

"Write a poem on it," jeered Ilse, whose alarm made her fleetingly cross.

"How's your foot?"

"Oh, it's all right. But my hair is sopping wet with dew."

"So is mine. We'll carry our hats for a while and the sun will soon dry us. It's just as well to get an early start. We can get back to civilization by the time it's safe for us to be seen. Only we'll have to breakfast on the crackers in my bag. It won't do for us to be looking for breakfast, with no rational account to give of where we spent the night. Ilse, swear you'll never mention this escapade to a living soul. It's been beautiful—but it will remain beautiful just as long as only we two know of it. Remember the result of your telling about our moonlit bath."

"People have such beastly minds," grumbled Ilse, sliding down the stack.

"Oh, *look* at Indian Head. I could be a sun worshipper this very moment."

Indian Head was a flaming mount of splendour. The far-off hills turned beautifully purple against the radiant sky. Even the bare, ugly Hardscrabble Road was transfigured and luminous in hazes of silver. The fields and woods were very lovely in the faint pearly lustre.

"The world is always young again for just a few moments at the dawn," murmured Emily.

Then she pulled her Jimmy-book out of her bag and wrote the sentence down!

They had the usual experiences of canvassers the world over that day. Some people refused to subscribe, ungraciously: some subscribed graciously: some refused to subscribe so pleasantly that they left an agreeable impression: some consented to subscribe so unpleasantly that Emily wished they had refused. But on the whole they enjoyed the forenoon, especially when an excellent early dinner in a hospitable farmhouse on the Western Road filled up the aching void left by a few crackers and a night on a haystack.

"S'pose you didn't come across any stray children to-day?" asked their host.

"No. Have any been lost?"

"Little Allan Bradshaw—Will Bradshaw's son, down-river at Malvern Point—has been missing ever since Tuesday morning. He walked out of the house that morning, singing, and hasn't been seen or heard of since."

Emily and Ilse exchanged shocked glances.

"How old was he?"

"Just seven—and an only child. They say his poor ma is plumb distracted. All the Malvern Point men have been s'arching for him for two days, and not a trace of him kin they discover."

"What can have happened to him!" said Emily, pale with horror.

"It's a mystery. Some think he fell off the wharf at the Point—it was only about a quarter of a mile from the house and he used to like sitting there and watching the boats. But nobody saw anything of him 'round the wharf or the bridge that morning. There's a lot of marshland west of the Bradshaw farm, full of bogs and pools. Some think he must have wandered there and got lost and perished—ye remember Tuesday night was terrible cold. *That's* where his mother thinks he is—and if you ask *me,* she's right. If he'd been anywhere else he'd have been found by the s'arching parties. They've combed the country."

The story haunted Emily all the rest of the day and she walked under its shadow. Anything like that always took almost a morbid hold on her. She could not bear the thought of the poor mother at Malvern Point. And the little lad—where was he? Where had he been the previous night when she had lain in the ecstasy of wild, free hours? That night had not been cold—but Wednesday night had. And she shuddered as she recalled Tuesday night, when a bitter autumnal windstorm had raged till dawn, with showers of hail and stinging rain. Had he been out in that—the poor lost baby?

"Oh, I can't *bear* it!" she moaned.

"It's dreadful," agreed Ilse, looking rather sick, "but *we* can't do anything. There's no use in thinking of it. Oh"—suddenly Ilse stamped her foot—"I believe Father used to be right when he didn't believe in God. Such a hideous thing as *this*—how could it happen if there *is* a God—a *decent* God, anyway?"

"God hadn't anything to do with *this,*" said Emily. "You *know* the

Power that made last night couldn't have brought about this monstrous thing."

"Well, He didn't prevent it," retorted Ilse—who was suffering so keenly that she wanted to arraign the universe at the bar of her pain.

"Little Allan Bradshaw may be found yet—he *must* be," exclaimed Emily.

"He won't be found alive," stormed Ilse. "No, don't talk to me about God. And don't talk to me of this. I've got to forget it—I'll go crazy if I don't."

Ilse put the matter out of her mind with another stamp of her foot and Emily tried to. She could not quite succeed but she forced herself to concentrate superficially on the business of the day, though she knew the horror lurked in the back of her consciousness. Only once did she really forget it—when they came around a point on the Malvern River Road and saw a little house built in the cup of a tiny bay, with a steep grassy hill rising behind it. Scattered over the hill were solitary, beautifully shaped young fir-trees like little green, elongated pyramids. No other house was in sight. All about it was a lovely autumnal solitude of grey, swift-running, windy river, and red, spruce-fringed points.

"That house belongs to me," said Emily.

Ilse stared.

"To you?"

"Yes. Of course, I don't *own* it. But haven't you sometimes seen houses that you knew belonged to you no matter who owned them?"

No, Ilse hadn't. She hadn't the least idea what Emily meant.

"I know who owns that house," she said. "It's Mr. Scobie of Kingsport. He built it for a summer cottage. I heard Aunt Net talking of it the last time I was in Wiltney. It was finished a few weeks ago. It's a pretty little house, but too small for me. *I* like a big house—I don't want to feel cramped and crowded—especially in summer."

"It's hard for a big house to have any personality," said Emily thoughtfully. "But little houses almost always have. That house is full of it. There isn't a line or a corner that isn't eloquent, and those casement windows are lovable—especially that little one high up under the eaves over the front door. It's absolutely smiling at me. Look at it glowing like a jewel in the sunshine out of the dark shingle setting. The little house is greeting us. You dear friendly thing, I love you—I understand you. As Old Kelly would say, 'may niver a tear be shed under your roof.' The people who are going to live in you must be nice people or they would never have *thought* you. If I lived in you, beloved, I'd always stand at that western window at evening to wave to some one coming home. That is just exactly what that window was built for—a frame for love and welcome."

"When you get through with talking to your house we'd better hurry on," warned Ilse. "There's a storm coming up. See those clouds— and those sea-gulls. Gulls never come up this far except before a storm. It's going to rain any minute. We'll not sleep on a haystack to-night, Friend Emily."

Emily loitered past the little house and looked at it lovingly as long as she could. It *was* such a dear little place with its dubbed-off gables and rich, brown shingle tints, and its general intimate air of sharing mutual jokes and secrets. She turned around half a dozen times to look upon it, as they climbed the steep hill, and when at last it dipped below sight she sighed.

"I hate to leave it. I have the oddest feeling, Ilse, that it's *calling* to me—that I ought to go back to it."

"Don't be silly," said Ilse impatiently. "There—it's sprinkling now! If you hadn't poked so long looking at your blessed little hut we'd have been out on the main road now, and near shelter. Wow, but it's cold!"

"It's going to be a dreadful night," said Emily in a low voice. "Oh, Ilse, where is that poor little lost boy to-night? I wish I knew if they had found him."

"Don't!" said Ilse savagely, "Don't say another word about him. It's awful—it's hideous—but what can *we* do?"

"Nothing. That's the dreadful thing about it. It seems wicked to go on about our own business, asking for subscriptions, when that child is not found."

By this time they had reached the main road. The rest of the afternoon was not pleasant. Stinging showers came at intervals: between them the world was raw and damp and cold, with a moaning wind that came in ominous sighing gusts under a leaden sky. At every house where they called they were reminded of the lost baby, for there were only women to give or refuse subscriptions. The men were all away searching for him.

"Though it isn't any use *now*," said one woman gloomily, "except that they may find his little body. He can't have lived this long. I jest can't eat or cook for thinking of his poor mother. They say she's nigh crazy—I don't wonder."

"They say old Margaret McIntyre is taking it quite calmly," said an older woman, who was piecing a log-cabin quilt by the window. "I'd have thought she'd be wild, too. She seemed real fond of little Allan."

"Oh, Margaret McIntyre has never got worked up about anything for the past five years—ever since her own son Neil was frozen to death in the Klondyke. Seems as if her feelings were frozen then, too—she's been a little mad ever since. *She* won't worry none over this—she'll just smile and tell you she spanked the King."

Both women laughed. Emily, with the story-teller's nose, scented a story instantly, but though she would fain have lingered to hunt it down Ilse hustled her away.

"We *must* get on, Emily, or we'll never reach St. Clair before night."

They soon realized that they were not going to reach it. At sunset St. Clair was still three miles away and there was every indication of a wild evening.

"We can't get to St. Clair, that's certain," said Ilse. "It's going to settle down for a steady rain and it'll be as black as a million black cats in a quarter of an hour. We'd better go to that house over there and ask if we can stay all night. It looks snug and respectable—though it certainly is the jumping-off place."

The house at which Ilse pointed—an old whitewashed house with a grey roof—was set on the face of a hill amid bright green fields of clover aftermath. A wet red road wound up the hill to it. A thick grove of spruces shut it off from the gulf shore, and beyond the grove a tiny dip in the land revealed a triangular glimpse of misty, white-capped, grey sea. The near brook valley was filled with young spruces, dark-green in the rain. The grey clouds hung heavily over it. Suddenly the sun broke through the clouds in the west for one magical moment. The hill of clover meadows flashed instantly into incredibly vivid green. The triangle of sea shimmered into violet. The old house gleamed like white marble against the emerald of its hilly background, and the inky black sky over and around it.

"Oh," gasped Emily, "I never saw anything so wonderful!"

She groped wildly in her bag and clutched her Jimmy-book. The post of a field-gate served as a desk—Emily licked a stubborn pencil and wrote feverishly. Ilse squatted on a stone in a fence corner and waited with ostentatious patience. She knew that when a certain look appeared on Emily's face she was not to be dragged away until she was ready to go. The sun had vanished and the rain was beginning to fall again when Emily put her Jimmy-book back into her bag, with a sigh of satisfaction.

"I *had* to get it, Ilse."

"Couldn't you have waited till you got to dry land and wrote it down from memory?" grumbled Ilse, uncoiling herself from her stone.

"No—I'd have missed some of the flavour then. I've got it all now—and in just exactly the right words. Come on—I'll race you to the house. Oh, smell that wind—there's nothing in all the world like a salt sea-wind—a savage salt sea-wind. After all, there's something delightful in a storm. There's always *something*—deep down in me—that seems to rise and leap out to meet a storm—wrestle with it."

"I feel that way sometimes—but not to-night," said Ilse. "I'm tired—and that poor baby—"

"Oh!" Emily's triumph and exultation went from her in a cry of pain. "Oh—Ilse—I'd forgotten for a moment—how could I! *Where* can he be?"

"Dead," said Ilse harshly. "It's better to think so—than to think of him alive still—out to-night. Come, we've got to get in somewhere. The storm is on for good now—no more showers."

An angular woman panoplied in a white apron so stiffly starched that it could easily have stood alone, opened the door of the house on the hill and bade them enter.

"Oh, yes, you can stay here, I reckon," she said, not inhospitably, "if you'll excuse things being a bit upset. They're in sad trouble here."

"Oh—I'm sorry," stammered Emily. "We won't intrude—we'll go somewhere else."

"Oh, we don't mind *you,* if you don't mind *us.* There's a spare room. You're welcome. You can't go on in a storm like this—there isn't another house for some ways. I advise you to stop here. I'll get you a bit of supper—I don't live here—I'm just a neighbour come to help 'em out a bit. Hollinger's my name—Mrs. Julia Hollinger. Mrs. Bradshaw ain't good for anything—you've heard of her little boy mebbe."

"Is this where—and—he—hasn't—been found?"

"No—never will be. I'm not mentioning it to her"—with a quick glance over her shoulder along the hall—"but it's my opinion he got in the quicksands down by the bay. That's what *I* think. Come in and lay off your things. I s'pose you don't mind eating in the kitchen. The room is cold—we haven't the stove up in it yet. It'll have to be put up soon if there's a funeral. I s'pose there won't be if he's in the quicksand. You can't have a funeral without a body, can you?"

All this was very gruesome. Emily and Ilse would fain have gone elsewhere—but the storm had broken in full fury and darkness seemed to pour in from the sea over the changed world. They took off their drenched hats and coats and followed their hostess to the kitchen, a clean, old-fashioned spot which seemed cheerful enough in lamp-light and fire-glow.

"Sit up to the fire. I'll poke it a bit. Don't mind Grandfather Bradshaw—Grandfather, here's two young ladies that want to stay all night."

Grandfather stared stonily at them out of little, hazy, blue eyes and said not a word.

"Don't mind him"—in a pig's whisper—"he's over ninety and he never was much of a talker. Clara—Mrs. Bradshaw—is in there"—nodding towards the door of what seemed a small bedroom off the kitchen. "Her brother's with her—Dr. McIntyre from Charlottetown. We sent for him yesterday. He's the only one that can do anything with her. She's been walking the floor all day but we've got her persuaded to lie down a bit. Her husband's out looking for little Allan."

"A child *can't* be lost in the nineteenth century," said Grandfather Bradshaw, with uncanny suddenness and positiveness.

"There, there now, Grandfather, I advise *you* not to get worked up. And this is the twentieth century now. He's still living back there. His memory stopped a few years ago. What might your names be? Burnley? Starr? From Blair Water? Oh, then you'll know the Murrays? Niece? Oh!"

Mrs. Julia Hollinger's "Oh" was subtly eloquent. She had been setting dishes and food down at a rapid rate on the clean oil-cloth on the table. Now she swept them aside, extracted a table-cloth from a drawer of the cupboard, got silver forks and spoons out of another drawer, and a handsome pair of salt and pepper shakers from the shelves.

"Don't go to any trouble for us," pleaded Emily.

"Oh, it's no trouble. If all was well here you'd find Mrs. Bradshaw real glad to have you. She's a very kind woman, poor soul. It's awful hard to see her in such trouble. Allan was all the child she had, you see."

"A child can't be *lost* in the nineteenth century, I tell you," repeated Grandfather Bradshaw, with an irritable shift of emphasis.

"No—no," soothingly, "of course not, Grandfather. Little Allan'll turn up all right yet. Here's a hot cup o' tea for you. I advise you to drink it. *That'll* keep him quiet for a bit. Not that he's ever very fussy—only everybody's a bit upset—except old Mrs. McIntyre. Nothing ever upsets *her*. It's just as well, only it seems to me real unfeeling. 'Course, she isn't just right. Come, sit in and have a bite, girls. Listen to that rain, will you? The men will be soaked. They can't search much longer to-night—Will will soon be home. I sorter dread it—Clara'll go wild again when he comes home without little Allan. We had a terrible time with her last night, pore thing."

"A child can't be lost in the *nineteenth* century," said Grandfather Bradshaw—and choked over his hot drink in his indignation.

"No—nor in the twentieth neither," said Mrs. Hollinger, patting him on the back. "I advise you to go to bed, Grandfather. You're tired."

"I am *not* tired and I will go to bed when I choose, Julia Hollinger."

"Oh, very well, Grandfather. I advise you not to get worked up. I think I'll take a cup o' tea in to Clara. Perhaps she'll take it now. She hasn't eaten or drunk since Tuesday night. How can a woman stand that—I put it to you?"

Emily and Ilse ate their supper with what appetite they could summon up, while Grandfather Bradshaw watched them suspiciously, and sorrowful sounds reached them from the little inner room.

"It is wet and cold to-night—where is he—my little son?" moaned a woman's voice, with an undertone of agony that made Emily writhe as if she felt it herself.

"They'll find him soon, Clara," said Mrs. Hollinger, in a sprightly tone of artificial comfort. "Just you be patient—take a sleep, I advise you—they're bound to find him soon."

"They'll never find him." The voice was almost a scream, now. "He is dead—he is dead—he died that bitter cold Tuesday night so long ago. O God, have mercy! He was such a little fellow! And I've told him so often not to speak until he was spoken to—he'll never speak to me again. I wouldn't let him have a light after he went to bed—and he died in the dark, alone and cold. I wouldn't let him have a dog—he wanted one so much. But he wants nothing now—only a grave and a shroud."

"I can't endure this," muttered Emily. "I *can't*, Ilse. I feel as if I'd go mad with horror. I'd rather be out in the storm."

Lank Mrs. Hollinger, looking at once sympathetic and important, came out of the bedroom and shut the door.

"Awful, isn't it! She'll go on like that all night. Would you like to go to bed? Its quite airly, but mebbe you're tired an' 'ud ruther be where you can't hear her, pore soul. She wouldn't take the tea—she's scared the doctor put a sleeping pill in it. She doesn't want to sleep till he's found, dead or alive. If he's in the quicksands o' course he never *will* be found."

"Julia Hollinger, you are a fool and the daughter of a fool, but surely even you must see that a child *can't* be lost in the nineteenth century," said Grandfather Bradshaw.

"Well, if it was anybody but you called me a fool, Grandfather, I'd be mad," said Mrs. Hollinger, a trifle tartly. She lighted a lamp and took the girls upstairs. "I hope you'll sleep. I advise you to get in between the blankets though there's sheets on the bed. They wuz all aired to-day, blankets *and* sheets. I thought it'd be better to air 'em in case there was a funeral. I remember the New Moon Murrays wuz always particular about airing their beds, so I thought I'd mention it. Listen to that wind. We'll likely hear of awful damage from this storm. I wouldn't wonder if the roof blew off this house to-night. Troubles never come singly. I advise you not to git upset if you hear a noise through the night. If the men bring the body home Clara'll likely act like all possessed, pore thing. Mebbe you'd better turn the key in the lock. Old Mrs. McIntyre wanders round a bit sometimes. She's quite harmless and mostly sane enough but it gives folks a start."

The girls felt relieved as the door closed behind Mrs. Hollinger. She was a good soul, doing her neighbourly duty as she conceived it, faithfully, but she was not exactly cheerful company. They found themselves in a tiny, meticulously neat "spare room" under the sloping eaves. Most of the space in it was occupied by a big comfortable bed that looked as if it were meant to be slept in, and not merely to decorate the room. A little four-paned window, with a spotless white muslin frill, shut them in from the cold, stormy night that was on the sea.

"Ugh," shivered Ilse, and got into the bed as speedily as possible. Emily followed her more slowly, forgetting about the key. Ilse, tired out, fell asleep almost immediately, but Emily could not sleep. She lay and suffered, straining her ears for the sound of footsteps. The rain dashed against the window, not in drops, but sheets, the wind snarled and shrieked. Down below the hill she heard the white waves ravening along the dark shore. Could it be only twenty-four hours since that moonlit, summery glamour of the haystack and the ferny pasture? Why, that must have been in another world.

Where was that poor lost child? In one of the pauses of the storm she fancied she heard a little whimper overhead in the dark as if some lonely little soul, lately freed from the body, were trying to find its way to kin. She could discover no way of escape from her pain: her gates of dream were shut against her: she could not detach her mind from her feelings and dramatize them. Her nerves grew strained and tense. Painfully she sent her thoughts out into the storm, seeking, striving to pierce the mystery of the child's whereabouts. He *must* be found—she clenched her hands—he *must*. That poor mother!

"O God, let him be found, *safe*—let him be found, *safe*," Emily prayed desperately and insistently, over and over again—all the more desperately and insistently because it seemed a prayer so impossible of fulfilment. But she reiterated it to bar out of her mind terrible pictures of swamp and quicksand and river, until at last she was so weary that mental torture could no longer keep her awake, and she fell into a troubled slumber, while the storm roared on and the baffled searchers finally gave up their vain quest.

THE WOMAN WHO SPANKED THE KING

The wet dawn came up from the gulf in the wake of the spent storm and crept greyly into the little spare room of the whitewashed house on the hill. Emily woke with a start from a troubled dream of seeking— and finding—the lost boy. But where she had found him she could not now remember. Ilse was still asleep at the back of the bed, her pale-gold curls lying in a silken heap on the pillow. Emily, her thoughts still tangled in the cobweb meshes of her dream, looked around the

437

room—and thought she must be dreaming still.

By the tiny table, covered with its white, lace-trimmed cloth, a woman was sitting—a tall, stout, old woman, wearing over her thick grey hair a spotless white widow's cap, such as the old Highland Scotch-women still wore in the early years of the century. She had on a dress of plum-coloured drugget with a large, snowy apron, and she wore it with the air of a queen. A neat blue shawl was folded over her breast. Her face was curiously white and deeply wrinkled but Emily, with her gift for seeing essentials, saw instantly the strength and vivacity which still characterized every feature. She saw, too, that the beautiful, clear blue eyes looked as if their owner had been dreadfully hurt sometime. This must be the old Mrs. McIntyre of whom Mrs. Hollinger had spoken. And if so, then old Mrs. McIntyre was a very dignified personage indeed.

Mrs. McIntyre sat with her hands folded on her lap, looking steadily at Emily with a gaze in which there was something hard to define—something just a little strange. Emily recalled the fact that Mrs. McIntyre was supposed to be not "quite right." She wondered a little uneasily what she should do. Ought she to speak? Mrs. McIntyre saved her the trouble of deciding.

"You will be having Highlandmen for your forefathers?" she said, in an unexpectedly rich, powerful voice, full of the delightful Highland accent.

"Yes," said Emily.

"And you will be Presbyterian?"

"Yes."

"They will be the only decent things to be," remarked Mrs. McIntyre in a tone of satisfaction. "And will you please be telling me what your name is? Emily Starr! That will be a fery pretty name. I will be telling you mine—it iss Mistress Margaret McIntyre. I am no common person—I am the woman who spanked the King."

Again Emily, now thoroughly awake, thrilled with the story-teller's instinct. But Ilse, awakening at the moment, gave a low exclamation of surprise. Mistress McIntyre lifted her head with a quite regal gesture.

"You will not be afraid of me, my dear. I will not be hurting you although I will be the woman who spanked the King. That iss what the people say of me—oh, yess—as I walk into the church. 'She iss the woman who spanked the King.'"

"I suppose," said Emily hesitatingly, "that we'd better be getting up."

"You will not be rising until I haf told you my tale," said Mistress McIntyre firmly. "I will be knowing as soon as I saw you that you will be the one to hear it. You will not be having fery much colour and I will not be saying that you are fery pretty—oh, no. But you will be having the little hands and the little ears—they will be the ears of the fairies, I am thinking. The girl with you there, she iss a fery nice girl and will make a fery fine wife for a handsome man—she is clefer, oh, yes—but you haf the way and it is to you I will be telling my story."

"Let her tell it," whispered Ilse. "I'm dying of curiosity to hear about the King being spanked."

Emily, who realized that there was no "letting" in the case, only a matter of lying still and listening to whatever it seemed good to Mistress McIntyre to say, nodded.

"You will not be having the twa talks? I will be meaning the Gaelic."

Spellbound, Emily shook her black head.

"That iss a pity, for my story will not be sounding so well in the English—oh, no. You will be saying to yourself the old woman iss having a dream, but you will be wrong, for it iss the true story I will be telling you—oh, yess. I spanked the King. Of course he would not be the King then—he would be only a little prince and no more than nine years old—just the same age as my little Alec. But it iss at the beginning I must be or you will not be understanding the matter at all at all. It wass all a long, long time ago, before ever we left the Old Country. My husband would be Alistair McIntyre and he would be a shepherd near the Balmoral Castle. Alistair was a fery handsome man and we were fery happy. It wass not that we did not quarrel once in a while—oh, no, that would be fery monotonous. But when we made up it is more loving than ever we would be. And I would be fery good-looking myself. I will be getting fatter and fatter all the time now but I wass fery slim and peautiful then—oh, yess, it iss the truth I will be telling you though I will be seeing that you are laughing in your sleeves at me. When you will be eighty you will be knowing more about it.

"You will be remembering maybe that Queen Victoria and Prince Albert would be coming up to Balmoral efery summer and bringing their children with them, and they would not be bringing any more servants than they could help, for they would not be wanting fuss and pother, but just a quiet, nice time like common folks. On Sundays

439

they would be walking down sometimes to the church in the glen to be hearing Mr. Donald MacPherson preach. Mr. Donald MacPherson wass fery gifted in prayer and he would not be liking it when people would come in when he wass praying. He would be apt to be stopping and saying, 'O Lord, we will be waiting until Sandy Big Jim hass taken his seat'—oh, yes. I would be hearing the Queen laugh the next day—at Sandy Big Jim, you will be knowing, not at the minister.

"When they will be needing some more help at the Castle, they just sent for me and Janet Jardine. Janet's husband was a gillie on the estate. She would be always saying to me, 'Good-morning, *Mistress* McIntyre' when we would be meeting and I would be saying, 'Good-morning, *Janet*,' just to be showing the superiority of the McIntyres over the Jardines. But she wass a fery good creature in her place and we would be getting on fery well together when she would not be forgetting it.

"I wass fery good friends with the Queen—oh, yess. She wass not a proud woman whatefer. She would be sitting in my house at times and drinking a cup of tea and she would be talking to me of her children. She wass not fery handsome, oh, no, but she would be having a fery pretty hand. Prince Albert wass fery fine looking, so people would be saying, but to my mind Alistair wass far the handsomer man. They would be fery fine people, whatefer, and the little princes and princesses would be playing about with my children efery day. The Queen would be knowing they were in good company and she would be easier in her mind about them than I wass—for Prince Bertie was the daring lad if efer there wass one—oh, yess, and the tricky one—and I would be worrying all the time for the fear he and Alec would be getting into a scrape. They would be playing every day together—and quarrelling, too. And it would not always be Alec's fault either. But it wass Alec that would be getting the scolding, poor lad. Somebody would haf to be scolded and you will be knowing that I could not be scolding the prince, my dear.

"There wass one great worry I will be having—the burn behind the house in the trees. It wass fery deep and swift in places and if a child should be falling in he would be drowned. I would be telling Prince Bertie and Alec time after time that they must nefer be going near the banks of the burn. They would be doing it once or twice for all that and I would be punishing Alec for it, though he would be telling me that he did not want to go and Prince Bertie would be saying, 'Oh, come on, there will not be any danger, do not be a coward,' and Alec, he would be going because he would be thinking he had to do what Prince Bertie wanted, and not liking fery well either to be called a coward, and him a McIntyre. I would be worrying so much over it that I would not be sleeping at nights. And then, my dear, one day Prince Bertie would be falling right into the deep pool and Alec would be trying to pull him out and falling in after him. And they would haf been drowned together if I had not been hearing the skirls of them when I would be coming home from the Castle after taking some buttermilk up for the Queen. Oh, yess, it is quick I will be taking in what had happened and running to the burn and it will not be long before I wass fishing them out, fery frightened and dripping. I will be knowing something had to be done and I wass tired of blaming poor Alec, and besides it will be truth, my dear, that I wass fery, fery mad and I wass not thinking of princes and kings, but just of two fery bad little boys. Oh, it iss the quick temper I will be always having—oh, yess. I will be picking up Prince Bertie and turning him over my knee: and I will be giving him a sound spanking on the place the Good Lord will be making for spanks in princes as well as in common children. I will be spanking him *first* because he wass a prince. Then I spanked Alec and they made music together, for it wass fery angry I was and I will be doing what my hands will be finding to do with all my might, as the Good Book says.

"Then when Prince Bertie had gone home—fery mad—I will be cooling off and feeling a bit frightened. For I will not be knowing just how the Queen will be taking it, and I will not be liking the thought of Janet Jardine triumphing over me. But it iss a sensible woman Queen Victoria wass and she will be telling me next day that I did right: and Prince Albert will be smiling and joking to me about the laying on of hands. And Prince Bertie would not be disobeying me again about going to the burn—oh, no—and he could not be sitting down fery easy for some time. As for Alistair, I had been thinking he would be fery cross with me, but it will always be hard telling what a man will think of anything—oh, yess—for he would be laughing over it, too, and telling me that a day would come when I could be boasting that I had spanked the King. It wass all a long time ago now, but nefer will I be forgetting it. She would be dying two years ago and Prince Bertie would be the king at last. When Alistair and I came to Canada the Queen will be giving me a silk petticoat. It wass a very fine petticoat of the Victoria tartan. I haf nefer worn it, but I will be wearing it once—in my coffin, oh, yess. I will be keeping it in the chest in my room and they will be knowing what it iss for. I will be wishing Janet Jardine could have known that I wass to be buried in a petticoat of the Victoria tartan, but she hass been dead for a long while. She wass a fery good sort of creature, although she wass not a McIntyre."

Mistress McIntyre folded her hands and held her peace. Having told her story she was content. Emily had listened avidly. Now she said:

"Mrs. McIntyre, will you let me write that story down, and publish it?"

Mistress McIntyre leaned forward. Her white, shrivelled face warmed a little, her deep-set eyes shone.

"Will you be meaning that it will be printed in a paper?"

"Yes."

Mistress McIntyre rearranged her shawl over her breast with hands that trembled a little.

"It iss strange how our wishes will be coming true at times. It iss a pity that the foolish people who will be saying there iss no God could not be hearing of this. You will be writing it out and you will be putting it into proud words—"

"No, no," said Emily quickly. "I will not do that. I may have to make a few changes and write a framework, but most of it I shall write exactly as you told it. I could not better it by a syllable."

Mistress McIntyre looked doubtful for a moment—then gratified.

"It iss only a poor, ignorant body I am, and I will not be choosing my words fery well, but maybe you will be knowing best. You haf listened to me fery nicely and it is sorry I am to have kept you so long with my old tales. I will be going now and letting you get up."

"Have they found the lost child?" asked Ilse eagerly.

Mistress McIntyre shook her head, composedly.

"Oh, no. It is not finding him in a hurry they will be. I will be hearing Clara skirling in the night. She iss the daughter of my son Angus. He will be marrying a Wilson and the Wilsons will always be making a stramash over eferything. The poor thing will be worrying that she was not good enough to the little lad, but it would always be spoiling him she wass, and him that full of mischief. I will not be of much use to her—I haf not the second sight. You will be having a bit of that yourself, I am thinking, oh, yess."

"No—no," said Emily, hurriedly. She could not help recalling a certain incident of her childhood at New Moon, of which she somehow never liked to think.

Old Mistress McIntyre nodded sagely and smoothed her white apron.

"It will not be right for you to be denying it, my dear, for it iss a great gift and my Cousin Helen four times removed will be having it, oh, yess. But they will not be finding little Allan, oh, no. Clara will be loving him too much. It iss not a fery good thing to be loving any one too much. God will be a jealous God, oh, yess; it is Margaret McIntyre who knows it. I will be having six sons once, all fery fine men and the youngest would be Neil. He was six-feet-two in hiss stockings and there would be none of the others like him at all. There would be such fun in him—he would always be laughing, oh, yess, and the wiling tongue of him would be coaxing the birds off the bushes. He will be going to the Klondyke and he will be getting frozen to death out there one night, oh, yess. He will be dying while I wass praying for him. I haf not been praying since. Clara will be feeling like that now—she will be saying God does not hear. It iss a fery strange thing to be a woman, my dears, and to be loving so much for nothing. Little Allan was a fery pretty baby. He will be having a fat little brown face and fery big blue eyes, and it is a pity he will not be turning up, though they will not be finding my Neil in time, oh, no. I will be leaving Clara alone and not vexing her with comforting. I wass always the great hand to leave people alone—without it would be when I spanked the King. It iss Julia Hollinger who will be darkening council by words without knowledge. It iss the foolish woman she iss. She would be leaving her husband because he will not be giving up a dog he liked. I am thinking he wass wise in sticking to the dog. But I will always be getting on well with Julia because I will have learned to suffer fools gladly. She will enjoy giving advice so much and it will not be hurting me whatefer because I will never be taking it. I will be saying good-bye to you now, my dears, and it iss fery glad I am to haf seen you and I will be wishing that trouble may nefer sit on your hearthstones. And I will not be forgetting either that you listened to me very polite, oh, yess. I will not be of much importance to anybody now—but once I spanked the King."

"THE THING THAT COULDN'T"

When the door had closed behind Mistress McIntyre, the girls got up and dressed rather laggingly. Emily thought of the day before her with some distaste. The fine flavour of adventure and romance with which they had started out had vanished, and canvassing a country road for subscriptions had suddenly become irksome. Physically, they were both tireder than they thought.

"It seems like an age since we left Shrewsbury," grumbled Ilse as she pulled on her stockings.

Emily had an even stronger feeling of a long passage of time. Her wakeful, enraptured night under the moon had seemed in itself like a year of some strange soul-growth. And this past night had been wakeful also, in a very different way, and she had roused from her brief sleep at its close with an odd, rather unpleasant sensation of some confused and troubled journey—a sensation which old Mistress McIntyre's story had banished for a time, but which now returned as she brushed her hair.

"I feel as if I had been wandering—somewhere—for hours," she said. "And I dreamed I found little Allan—but I don't know where. It was horrible to wake up feeling that I *had* known just immediately before I woke and had forgotten."

"I slept like a log," said Ilse, yawning. "I didn't even dream. Emily, I want to get away from this house and this place as soon as I can. I feel as if I were in a nightmare—as if something horrible were pressing me down and I couldn't escape from it. It would be different if I could *do* anything—help in any way. But since I can't, I just want to escape from it. I forgot it for a few minutes while the old lady was telling her story— heartless old thing! *She* wasn't worrying one bit about poor little lost Allan."

"I think she stopped worrying long ago," said Emily dreamily. "That's what people mean when they say she isn't right. People who don't worry a little never *are* right—like Cousin Jimmy. But that was a great story. I'm going to write it for my first essay—and later on I'll see about having it printed. I'm sure it would make a splendid sketch for some magazine, if I can only catch the savour and vivacity she put into it. I think I'll jot down some of her expressions right away in my Jimmy-book before I forget them."

"Oh, drat your Jimmy-book!" said Ilse. "Let's get down—and eat breakfast if we have to—and get away."

But Emily, revelling again in her story-teller's paradise, had temporarily forgotten everything else.

"Where *is* my Jimmy-book?" she said impatiently. "It isn't in my bag—I know it was here last night. Surely I didn't leave it on that gate-post!"

"Isn't that it over on the table?" asked Ilse.

Emily gazed blankly at it.

"It can't be—it *is*—how did it get there? I *know* I didn't take it out of the bag last night."

"You must have," said Ilse indifferently.

Emily walked over to the table with a puzzled expression. The Jimmy-book was lying open on it, with her pencil beside it. Something on the page caught her eye suddenly. She bent over it.

"Why don't you hurry and finish your hair?" demanded Ilse a few minutes later. "I'm ready now—for pity's sake, tear yourself from that blessed Jimmy-book for long enough to get dressed!"

Emily turned around, holding the Jimmy-book in her hands. She was very pale and her eyes were dark with fear and mystery.

"Ilse, look at this," she said in a trembling voice.

Ilse went over and looked at the page of the Jimmy-book which Emily held out to her. On it was a pencil sketch, exceedingly well done, of the little house on the river shore to which Emily had been so attracted on the preceding day. A black cross was marked on a small window over the front door and opposite it, on the margin of the Jimmy-book, beside another cross, was written:

"Allan Bradshaw is here."

"'What does it mean?" gasped Ilse. "Who did it?"

"I—don't know," stammered Emily. "The writing—is *mine.*"

Ilse looked at Emily and drew back a little.

"You must have drawn it in your sleep," she said dazedly.

"I can't draw," said Emily.

445

"Who else could have done it? Mistress McIntyre couldn't—you know she couldn't. Emily, I never heard of such a strange thing. Do you think—do you think—he can be there?"

"How could he? The house must be locked up—there's no one working at it now. Besides, they must have searched all around there—he would be looking out of the window—it wasn't shuttered, you remember—calling—they would have seen—heard—him. I suppose I must have drawn that picture in my sleep—though I can't understand how I did it—because my mind was so filled with the thought of little Allan. It's so strange—it frightens me."

"You'll have to show it to the Bradshaws," said Ilse.

"I suppose so—and yet I hate to. It may fill them with a cruel false hope again—and there *can't* be anything in it. But I daren't risk *not* showing it. *You* show it—I can't, somehow. The thing has upset me—I feel frightened—childish—I could sit down and cry. If he *should* have been there—since Tuesday—he would be dead of starvation."

"Well, they'd *know*—I'll show it, of course. If it should turn out—Emily, you're an uncanny creature."

"Don't talk of it—I can't bear it," said Emily, shuddering.

There was no one in the kitchen when then entered it, but presently a young man came in—evidently the Dr. McIntyre of whom Mrs. Hollinger had spoken. He had a pleasant, clever face, with keen eyes behind his glasses, but he looked tired and sad.

"Good-morning," he said. "I hope you had a good rest and were not disturbed in any way. We are all sadly upset here, of course."

"They haven't found the little boy?" asked Ilse.

Dr. McIntyre shook his head.

"No. They have given up the search. He cannot be living yet—after Tuesday night and last night. The swamp will not give up its dead—I feel sure that is where he is. My poor sister is broken-hearted. I am sorry your visit should have happened at such a sorrowful time, but I hope Mrs. Hollinger has made you comfortable. Grandmother McIntyre would be quite offended if you lacked for anything. She was very famous for her hospitality in her day. I suppose you haven't seen her. She does not often show herself to strangers."

"Oh, we have seen her," said Emily absently. "She came into our room this morning and told us how she spanked the King."

Dr. McIntyre laughed a little.

"Then you have been honoured. It is not to every one Grandmother tells that tale. She's something of an Ancient Mariner and knows her predestined listeners. She is a little bit strange. A few years ago her favourite son, my Uncle Neil, met his death in the Klondyke under sad circumstances. He was one of the Lost Patrol. Grandmother never recovered from the shock. She has never *felt* anything since—feeling seems to have been killed in her. She neither loves nor hates nor fears nor hopes—she lives entirely in the past and experiences only one emotion—a great pride in the fact that she once spanked the King. But I am keeping you from your breakfast—here comes Mrs. Hollinger to scold me."

"Wait a moment please, Dr. McIntyre," said Ilse hurriedly. "I—you—we—there is something I want to show you."

Dr. McIntyre bent a puzzled face over the Jimmy-book.

"What is this? I don't understand—"

"We don't understand it, either—Emily drew it in her sleep."

"In her sleep?" Dr. McIntyre was too bewildered to be anything but an echo.

"She *must* have. There was nobody else—unless your Grandmother can draw."

"Not she. And she never saw this house—it's the Scobie cottage below Malvern Bridge, isn't it?"

"Yes. We saw it yesterday."

"But Allan can't be *there*—it's been locked for a month—the carpenters went away in August."

"Oh—I know," stammered Emily. "I was thinking so much of Allan before I went to sleep—I suppose it's only a dream—I don't understand it at all—but we *had* to show it to you."

"Of course. Well, I won't say anything to Will or Clara about it. I'll get Rob Mason from over the hill and we'll run down and have a look around the cottage. It would be odd if—but it couldn't possibly be. I don't see how we can get into the cottage. It's locked and the windows are shuttered."

"This one—over the front door—isn't."

"No—but that's a closet window at the end of the upstairs hall. I was over the house one day in August when the painters were at work in it. The closet shuts with a spring lock, so I suppose that is why they didn't put a shutter on that window. It's high up, close to the ceiling, I

447

remember. Well, I'll slip over to Rob's and see about this. It won't do to leave any stone unturned."

Emily and Ilse ate what breakfast they could, thankful that Mrs. Hollinger let them alone, save for a few passing remarks as she came and went at work.

"Turrible night last night—but the rain is over. I never closed an eye. Pore Clara didn't either, but she's quieter now—sorter despairing. I'm skeered for her mind—her Grandmother never was right after she heard of *her* son's death. When Clara heard they weren't going to search no more she screamed once and laid down on the bed with her face to the wall—hain't stirred since. Well, the world has to go on for other folks. Help yourselves to the toast. I'd advise ye not to be in too much of a hurry starting out till the wind dries the mud a bit."

"I'm not going to go until we find out if—" whispered Ilse inconclusively.

Emily nodded. She could not eat, and if Aunt Elizabeth or Aunt Ruth had seen her they would have sent her to bed at once with orders to stay there—and they would have been quite right. She had almost reached her breaking-point. The hour that passed after Dr. McIntyre's departure seemed interminable. Suddenly they heard Mrs. Hollinger, who was washing milk-pails at the bench outside the kitchen door, give a sharp exclamation. A minute later she rushed into the kitchen, followed by Dr. McIntyre, breathless from his mad run from Malvern Bridge.

"Clara must be told first," he said. "It is her right."

He disappeared into the inner room. Mrs. Hollinger dropped into a chair, laughing and crying.

"They've found him—they've found little Allan—on the floor of the hall closet—in the Scobie cottage!"

"Is—he—living?" gasped Emily.

"Yes, but no more—he couldn't even speak—but he'll come round with care, the doctor says. They carried him to the nearest house— that's all the doctor had time to tell me."

A wild cry of joy came from the bedroom—and Clara Bradshaw, with dishevelled hair and pallid lips, but with the light of rapture shining in her eyes, rushed through the kitchen—out and over the hill. Mrs. Hollinger caught up a coat and ran after her. Dr. McIntyre sank into a chair.

"I couldn't stop her—-and I'm not fit for another run yet—but joy doesn't kill. It would have been cruel to stop her, even if I could."

"Is little Allan all right?" asked Ilse.

"He will be. The poor kid was at the point of exhaustion, naturally. He wouldn't have lasted for another day. We carried him right up to Dr. Matheson at the Bridge and left him in his charge. He won't be fit to be brought home before to-morrow."

"Have you any idea how he came to be there?"

"Well, he couldn't tell us anything, of course, but I think I know how it happened. We found a cellar window about half an inch open. I fancy that Allan was poking about the house, boy fashion, and found that this window hadn't been fastened. He must have got entrance by it, pushed it almost shut behind him and then explored the house. He had pulled the closet door tight in some way and the spring lock made him a prisoner. The window was too high for him to reach or he might have attracted attention from it. The white plaster of the closet wall is all marked and scarred with his vain attempts to get up to the window. Of course, he must have shouted, but nobody has ever been near enough the house to hear him. You know, it stands in that bare little cove with nothing near it where a child could be hidden, so I suppose the searchers did not pay much attention to it. They didn't search the river banks until yesterday, anyhow, because it was never thought he would have gone away down there alone, and by yesterday he was past calling for help."

"I'm so—happy—since he's found," said Ilse, winking back tears of relief.

Grandfather Bradshaw suddenly poked his head out of the sitting-room doorway.

"I told ye a child *couldn't* be lost in the nineteenth century," he chuckled.

"He *was* lost, though," said Dr. McIntyre, "and he wouldn't have been found—in time—if it were not for this young lady. It's a very extraordinary thing."

"Emily is—psychic," said Ilse, quoting Mr. Carpenter.

"Psychic! Humph! Well, it's curious—very. I don't pretend to understand it. Grandmother would say it was second sight, of course. Naturally, she's a firm believer in that, like all the Highland folk."

"Oh—I'm sure I haven't second sight," protested Emily. "I must just

449

have dreamed it—and got up in my sleep—but, then, I can't draw."

"Something used you as an instrument then," said Dr. McIntyre. "After all, Grandmother's explanation of second sight is just as reasonable as anything else, when one is compelled to believe an unbelievable thing."

"I'd rather not talk of it," said Emily, with a shiver. "I'm so glad Allan has been found—but *please* don't tell people about my part in it. Let them think it just occurred to you to search inside the Scobie house. I—I couldn't bear to have this talked of all over the country."

When they left the little white house on the windy hill the sun was breaking through the clouds and the harbour waters were dancing madly in it. The landscape was full of the wild beauty that comes in the wake of a spent storm and the Western Road stretched before them in loop and hill and dip of wet, red allurement; but Emily turned away from it.

"I'm going to leave it for my next trip," she said. "I can't go canvassing to-day, somehow. Friend of my heart, let's go to Malvern Bridge and take the morning train to Shrewsbury."

"It—was—awfully funny—about your dream," said Ilse. "It makes me a little afraid of you, Emily—somehow."

"Oh, don't be afraid of me," implored Emily. "It was only a coincidence. I was thinking of him so much—and the house took possession of me yesterday—"

"Remember how you found out about Mother?" said Ilse, in a low tone. "You *have* some power the rest of us haven't."

"Perhaps I'll grow out of it," said Emily desperately. "I hope so—I don't *want* to have any such power—you don't know how I feel about it, Ilse. It seems to me a terrible thing—as if I were marked out in some uncanny way—I don't feel *human*. When Dr. McIntyre spoke about *something* using me as an instrument, I went cold all over. It seemed to me that while *I* was asleep some *other* intelligence must have taken possession of my body and drawn that picture."

"It was *your* writing," said Ilse.

"Oh, I'm not going to talk of it—or *think* of it. I'm going to forget it. Don't ever speak of it to me again, Ilse."

DRIFTWOOD

"Shrewsbury,

"October 3, 19—

"I have finished canvassing my allotted portion of our fair province—I have the banner list of all the canvassers—and I have made almost enough out of my commissions to pay for my books for my whole Junior year. When I told Aunt Ruth this she did *not* sniff. I consider that a fact worth recording.

"To-day my story, *The Sands of Time,* came back from *Merton's Magazine.* But the rejection slip was typewritten, not printed. Typewriting doesn't seem *quite* as insulting as print, some way.

"We have read your story with interest, and regret to say that we cannot accept it for publication at the present time.

"If they meant that 'with interest,' it is a little encouragement. But were they only trying to soften the blow?

"Ilse and I were notified recently that there were nine vacancies in the *Skull and Owl* and that we had been put on the list of those who might apply for membership. So we did. It is considered a great thing in school to be a Skull and Owl.

"The Junior year is in full swing now, and I find the work very interesting. Mr. Hardy has several of our classes, and I like him as a teacher better than anyone since Mr. Carpenter. He was very much interested in my essay, *The Woman Who Spanked the King.* He gave it first place and commented on it specially in his class criticisms. Evelyn Blake is sure, naturally, that I copied it out of something, and feels certain she has read it somewhere before. Evelyn is wearing her hair in the new pompadour style this year and I think it is very unbecoming to her. But then, of course, the only part of Evelyn's anatomy I like is her back.

"I understand that the Martin clan are furious with me. Sally Martin was married last week in the Anglican church here, and the *Times* editor asked me to report it. Of course, I went—though I *hate* reporting weddings. There are so many things I'd *like* to say sometimes that can't *be* said. But Sally's wedding was pretty and so was she, and I sent in quite a nice report of it, I thought, especially mentioning the bride's beautiful bouquet of 'roses and orchids'—the first bridal bouquet of orchids ever seen in Shrewsbury. I wrote as plain as print and there was no excuse whatever for that wretched typesetter on the *Times* turning 'orchids' into *sardines*. Of course, anybody with any sense would have known that it was only a printer's error. But the Martin clan have taken into their heads the absurd notion that I wrote *sardines* on purpose for a silly joke—because, it seems, it has been reported to them that I said once I was tired of the conventional reports of weddings and would like to write just one along different lines. I *did* say it—but my craving for originality would hardly lead me to report the bride as carrying a bouquet of sardines! Nevertheless, the Martins *do* think it, and Stella Martin didn't invite me to her thimble party—and Aunt Ruth says she doesn't wonder at it—and Aunt Elizabeth says I shouldn't have been so careless. *I*! Heaven grant me patience!

****

"October 5, 19—

"Mrs. Will Bradshaw came to see me this evening.

Luckily Aunt Ruth was out—I say luckily, for I don't want Aunt Ruth to find out about my dream and its part in finding little Allan Bradshaw. This may be 'sly,' as Aunt Ruth would say, but the truth is that, sly or not sly, I could *not* bear to have Aunt Ruth sniffing and wondering and pawing over the incident.

"Mrs. Bradshaw came to thank me. It embarrassed me—because, after all, what had *I* to do with it? I don't want to think of or talk of it at all. Mrs. Bradshaw says little Allan is all right again, now, though it was a week after they found him before he could sit up. She was very pale and earnest.

"'He would have died there if you hadn't come, Miss Starr—and *I* would have died. I couldn't have gone on living—not knowing—oh, I shall never forget the horror of those days. I *had* to come and try to utter a little of my gratitude—you were gone when I came back that morning—I felt that I had been very inhospitable—'

"She broke down and cried—and so did I—and we had a good howl

452

together. I am very glad and thankful that Allan was found, but I shall never like to think of the way it happened.

****

"New Moon,
"October 7, 19—
"I had a lovely walk and prowl this evening in the pond graveyard. Not exactly a cheerful place for an evening's ramble, one might suppose. But I always like to wander over that little westward slope of graves in the gentle melancholy of a fine autumn evening. I like to read the names on the stones and note the ages and think of all the loves and hates and hopes and fears that lie buried there. It was beautiful—and not sad. And all around were the red ploughed fields and the frosted, ferny woodsides and all the old familiar things I have loved—and love more and more it seems to me, the older I grow. Every week-end I come home to New Moon these things seem dearer to me—more a part of me. I love *things* just as much as *people*. I think Aunt Elizabeth is like this, too. That is why she will not have anything changed at New Moon. I am beginning to understand her better. I believe she likes me now, too. I was only a duty at first, but now I am something more.

"I stayed in the graveyard until a dull gold twilight came down and made a glimmering spectral place of it. Then Teddy came for me and we walked together up the field and through the To-morrow Road. It is really a To-day Road now, for the trees along it are above our heads, but we still call it the To-morrow Road—partly out of habit and partly because we talk so much on it of *our* to-morrows and what we hope to do in them. Somehow, Teddy is the only person I like to talk to about my to-morrows and my ambitions. There is no one else. Perry scoffs at my literary aspirations. He says, when I say anything about writing books, 'What is the good of that sort of thing?' And of course if a person can't see 'the good' for himself you can't explain it to him. I can't even talk to Dean about them—not since he said so bitterly one evening, 'I hate to hear of your to-morrows—they cannot be *my* tomorrows.' I think in a way Dean doesn't like to think of my growing up—I *think* he has a little of the Priest jealousy of sharing *anything*, especially friendship, with anyone else—or with the world. I feel thrown back on myself. Somehow, it has seemed to me lately that

Dean isn't interested any longer in my writing ambitions. He even, it seems to me, ridicules them slightly. For instance, Mr. Carpenter was delighted with my *Woman Who Spanked the King,* and told me it was excellent; but when Dean read it he smiled and said, 'It will do very well for a school essay, but—' and then he smiled again. It was not the smile I liked, either. It had 'too much Priest in it,' as Aunt Elizabeth would say. I felt—and feel—horribly cast down about it. It seemed to say, 'You can scribble amusingly, my dear, and have a pretty knack of phrase-turning; but I should be doing you an unkindness if I let you think that such a knack meant a very great deal.' If this is true—and it very likely is, for Dean is so clever and knows so much—then I can never accomplish anything worth while. I won't *try* to accomplish anything—I *won't* be just a 'pretty scribbler.'

"But it's different with Teddy."

"Teddy was wildly elated to-night—and so was I when I heard his news. He showed two of his pictures at the Charlottetown exhibition in September, and Mr. Lewes, of Montreal, has offered him fifty dollars apiece for them. That will pay his board in Shrewsbury for the winter and make it easier for Mrs. Kent. Although *she* wasn't glad when he told her. She said, 'Oh, yes, you think you are independent of me now'—and cried. Teddy was hurt, because he had never thought of such a thing. Poor Mrs. Kent. She must be very lonely. There is some strange barrier between her and her kind. I haven't been to the Tansy Patch for a long, long time. Once in the summer I went with Aunt Laura, who had heard Mrs. Kent was ill. Mrs. Kent was able to be up and she talked to Aunt Laura, but she never spoke to me, only looked at me now and then with a queer, smouldering fire in her eyes. But when we rose to come away, she spoke once—and said,

"'You are very tall. You will soon be a woman—and stealing some other woman's son from her.'

"Aunt Laura said, as we walked home, that Mrs. Kent had always been strange, but was growing stranger.

"'Some people think her mind is affected,' she said.

"'I don't think the trouble is in her mind. She has a sick soul,' I said.

"'Emily, dear, that is a dreadful thing to say,' said Aunt Laura.

"I don't see why. If bodies and minds can be sick, can't souls be, too? There are times when I feel as certain as if I had been told it that Mrs. Kent got some kind of terrible soul-wound some time, and it has never healed. I wish she didn't hate me. It hurts me to have Teddy's mother hate me. I don't know why this is. Dean is just as dear a friend as Teddy, yet I wouldn't care if all the rest of the Priest clan hated me.

****

"October 19, 19—

"Ilse and the other seven applicants were elected Skulls and Owls. I was black-beaned. We were notified to that effect Monday.

"Of course, I know it was Evelyn Blake who did it. There is nobody else who would do it. Ilse was furious: she tore into pieces the notification of her election and sent the scraps back to the secretary with a scathing repudiation of the *Skull and Owl* and all its works.

"Evelyn met me in the cloakroom to-day and assured me that she had voted for both Ilse and me.

"'Has anyone been saying you did not?' I asked, in my best Aunt Elizabethan manner.

"'Yes—Ilse has,' said Evelyn peevishly. 'She was very insolent to me about it. Do you want to know who I *think* put the black bean in?'

"I looked Evelyn straight in the eyes.

"'No, it is not necessary. I *know* who put it in'—and I turned and left her.

"Most of the Skulls and Owls are very angry about it—especially the Skulls. One or two Owls, I have heard, hoot that it is a good pill for the Murray pride. And, of course, several Seniors and Juniors who were not among the favoured nine are either gloatingly rejoiced or odiously sympathetic.

"Aunt Ruth heard of it to-day and wanted to know *why* I was black-beaned.

****

"New Moon,
"November 5, 19—

"Aunt Laura and I spent this afternoon, the one teaching, the other learning, a certain New Moon tradition—to wit, how to put pickles into glass jars in patterns. We stowed away the whole big crockful of new pickles, and when Aunt Elizabeth came to look them over she admitted she could not tell those which Aunt Laura had done from mine.

"This evening was very delightful. I had a good time with myself, out in the garden. It was lovely there to-night with the eerie loveliness of a fine November evening. At sunset there had been a wild little shower of snow, but it had cleared off, leaving the world just lightly covered, and the air clear and tingling. Almost all the flowers, including my wonderful asters, which were a vision all through the fall, were frozen black two weeks ago, but the beds still had white drifts of alyssum all around them. A big, smoky-red hunter's moon was just rising above the tree-tops. There was a yellow-red glow in the west behind the white hills on which a few dark trees grew. The snow had banished all the strange deep sadness of a dead landscape on a late fall evening, and the slopes and meadows of old New Moon farm were transformed into a wonderland in the faint, early moonlight. The old house had a coating of sparkling snow on its roof. Its lighted windows glowed like jewels. It looked exactly like a picture on a Christmas card. There was just a suggestion of grey-blue chimney smoke over the kitchen. A nice reek of burning autumn leaves came from Cousin Jimmy's smouldering bonfires in the lane. My cats were there, too, stealthy, goblin-eyed, harmonizing with the hour and the place. The twilight—appropriately called the cats' light—is the only time when a cat really reveals himself. Saucy Sal was thin and gleaming, like the silvery ghost of a pussy. Daff was like a dark-grey, skulking tiger. He certainly gives the world assurance of a cat: he doesn't condescend to every one—and he never talks too much. They pounced at my feet and tore off and frisked back and rolled each other over—and were all so a part of the night and the haunted place that they didn't disturb my thoughts at all. I walked up and down the paths and around the dial and the summer-house in exhilaration. Air such as I breathed then always makes me a little drunk, I verily believe. I laughed at myself for feeling badly over not being elected an *Owl*. An Owl! Why, I felt like a young eagle, soaring sunward. All the world was before me to see and learn, and I exulted in it. The future was mine—and the past, too. I felt as if I had been alive here always—as if I shared in all the loves and lives of the old house. I felt as if I would live always—always—always—I was sure of immortality then. I didn't just believe it—I *felt* it.

"Dean found me there: he was close beside me before I was aware of his presence.

"'You are smiling,' said Dean. 'I like to see a woman smiling to herself. Her thoughts must be innocent and pleasant. Has the day been kind to you, dear lady?'

"'Very kind—and this evening is its best gift. I'm *so* happy to-night, Dean—just to be alive makes me happy. I feel as if I were driving a team of stars. I wish such a mood could last, I feel so sure of myself to-night—so sure of my future. I'm not afraid of *anything*. At life's banquet of success I may not be the guest of honour, but I'll be among those present.'

"'You looked like a seeress gazing into the future as I came down the walk,' said Dean, 'standing here in the moonlight, white and rapt. Your skin is like a narcissus petal. You could dare to hold a white rose against your face—very few women can dare that. You aren't really very pretty, you know, Star, but your face makes people think of beautiful things—and that is a far rarer gift than mere beauty.'

"I like Dean's compliments. They are always different from anybody else's. And I like to be called a woman.

"'You'll make me vain,' I said.

"'Not with your sense of humour,' said Dean. 'A woman with a sense of humour is never vain. The most malevolent bad fairy in the world couldn't bestow two such drawbacks on the same christened babe.'

"'Do you call a sense of humour a drawback?' I asked.

"'To be sure it is. A woman who has a sense of humour possesses no refuge from the merciless truth about herself. She cannot think herself misunderstood. She cannot revel in self-pity. She cannot comfortably damn anyone who differs from her. No, Emily, the woman with a sense of humour isn't to be envied.'

"This view of it hadn't occurred to me. We sat down on the stone bench and thrashed it out. Dean is not going away this winter. I am glad—I would miss him horribly. If I can't have a good spiel with Dean at least once a fortnight, life seems faded. There's so much *colour* in our talks; and then at times he can be so eloquently quiet. Part of the time tonight he was like that: we just sat there in the dream and dusk and quiet of the old garden and *heard* each other's thoughts. Part of the time he told me tales of old lands and the gorgeous bazaars of the East. Part of the time he asked me about myself, and my studies and my doings. I like a man who gives me a chance now and then to talk about myself.

"'What have you been reading lately?' he asked.

"'This afternoon, after I finished the pickles, I read several of Mrs. Browning's poems. We have her in our English work this year, you know. My favourite poem is *The Lay of the Brown Rosary*—and I am much more in sympathy with *Onora* than Mrs. Browning was.'

"'You would be,' said Dean. 'That is because you are a creature of emotion yourself. *You* would barter heaven for love, just as *Onora* did.'

"'I will not love—to love is to be a slave,' I said.

"And the minute I said it I was ashamed of saying it—because I knew I had just said it to sound clever. I don't really believe that to love is to be a slave—not with Murrays, anyhow. But Dean took me quite seriously.

"'Well, one must be a slave to *something* in this kind of a world,' he said. 'No one is free. Perhaps, after all, O daughter of the Stars, love is the easiest master—easier than hate—or fear—or necessity—or ambition—or pride. By the way, how are you getting on with the love-making parts of your stories?'

"'You forget—I can't write stories just now. When I can—well, you know long ago you promised you would teach me how to make love artistically.'

"I said it in a teasing way, just for a joke. But Dean seemed suddenly to become very much in earnest.

"'Are you ready for the teaching?' he said, bending forward.

"For one crazy moment I really thought he was going to kiss me. I drew back—I felt myself flushing—all at once I thought of Teddy. I didn't know what to say—I picked up Daff—buried my face in his beautiful fur—listened to his inner purring. At that opportune moment Aunt Elizabeth came to the front door and wanted to know if I had my rubbers on. I hadn't—so I went in—and Dean went home. I watched him from my window, limping down the lane. He seemed very lonely, and all at once I felt terribly sorry for him. When I'm with Dean he's such good company, and we have such good times that I forget there must be another side to his life. I can fill only such a little corner of it. The rest must be very empty.

****

"November 14, 19—

"There is a fresh scandal about Emily of New Moon plus Ilse of Blair Water. I have just had an unpleasant interview with Aunt Ruth and must write it all out to rid my soul of bitterness. Such a tempest in a teapot over nothing! But Ilse and I *do* have the worst luck.

"I spent last Thursday evening with Ilse studying our English literature together. We did an evening of honest work and I left for home at nine. Ilse came out to the gate with me. It was a soft, dark, gentle, starry night. Ilse's new boarding-house is the last house on Cardigan-street, and beyond it the road veers over the little creek bridge into the park. We could see the park, dim and luring, in the starlight.

"'Let's go for a walk around it before you go home,' proposed Ilse.

"We went: of course, I shouldn't have: I should have come right home to bed, like any good consumptive. But I had just completed my autumnal course of cod-liver emulsion—ugh!—and thought I might defy the night air for once. So—we went. And it was delightful. Away over the harbour we heard the windy music of the November hills, but among the trees of the park it was calm and still. We left the road and wandered up a little side trail through the spicy fragrant evergreens on the hill. The firs and pines are always friendly, but they tell you no secrets as maples and poplars do: they never reveal their mysteries— never betray their long-guarded lore—and so, of course, they are more interesting than any other trees.

"The whole hillside was full of nice, elfish sounds and cool, elusive night smells—balsam and frosted fern. We seemed to be in the very heart of a peaceful hush. The night put her arms around us like a mother and drew us close together. We told each other everything. Of course, next day I repented me of this—though Ilse is a very satisfactory confidante and never betrays anything, even in her rages. But then it is not a Murray tradition to turn your soul inside out, even to your dearest friend. But darkness and fir balsam make people do such things. And we had lots of fun, too—Ilse is such an exhilarating companion. You're never dull a moment in her company. Altogether we had a lovely walk and came out of the park feeling dearer to each other than ever, with another beautiful memory to share. Just at the bridge we met Teddy and Perry coming off the Western Road. They'd been out for a constitutional hike. It happens to be one of the times Ilse and Perry are on speaking terms, so we all walked across the bridge together and then they went their way and we went ours. I was in bed and asleep by ten o'clock.

"But somebody saw us walking across the bridge. Next day it was all through the school: day after that all through the town: that Isle and I had been prowling in the park with Teddy Kent and Perry Miller till twelve o'clock at night. Aunt Ruth heard it and summoned me to the bar of judgment to-night. I told her the whole story, but of course she didn't believe it.

"'You know I was home at a quarter to ten last Thursday night, Aunt Ruth,' I said.

"'I suppose the time was exaggerated,' admitted Aunt Ruth. 'But there must have been *something* to start such a story. There's no smoke without *some* fire. Emily, you are treading in your mother's footsteps.'

"'Suppose we leave my mother out of the question—she's dead,' I said. 'The point is, Aunt Ruth, do you believe me or do you not?'

"'I don't believe it was as bad as the report,' Aunt Ruth said reluctantly. 'But you have got yourself talked about. Of course, you must expect that, as long as you run with Ilse Burnley and off-scourings of the gutter like Perry Miller. Andrew wanted you to go for a walk in the park last Friday evening and you refused—I heard you. That would have been too respectable, of course.'

"'Exactly,' I said. 'That was the very reason. There's no fun in anything that's too respectable.'

"'Impertinence, Miss, is not wit,' said Aunt Ruth.

"I didn't mean to be impertinent, but it does annoy me to have Andrew flung in my teeth like that. Andrew is going to be one of my problems. Dean thinks it's great fun—*he* knows what is in the wind as well as I do. He is always teasing me about my red-headed young man—my r.h.y.m. for short.

"'He's almost a rhyme,' said Dean.

"'But never a poem,' said I.

"Certainly poor, good, dear Andrew is the stodgiest of prose. Yet I'd like him well enough if the whole Murray clan weren't literally throwing him at my head. They want to get me safely engaged before I'm old enough to elope, and who so safe as Andrew Murray?

"Oh, as Dean says, nobody is free—never, except just for a few brief moments now and then, when the flash comes, or when, as on my haystack night, the soul slips over into eternity for a little space.

All the rest of our years we are slaves to something—traditions—conventions—ambitions—*relations*. And sometimes, as tonight, I think that last is the hardest bondage of all.

****

"New Moon,
"December 3, 19—

"I am here in my own dear room, with a fire in my little fireplace by the grace of Aunt Elizabeth. An open fire is always lovely, but it is ten times lovelier on a stormy night. I watched the storm from my window until darkness fell. There is a singular charm in snow coming gently down in slanting lines against dark trees. I wrote a description of it in my Jimmy-book as I watched. A wind has come up since and now my room is full of the soft forlorn sigh of snow, driving through Lofty John's spruce wood. It is one of the loveliest sounds in the world. Some sounds *are* so exquisite—far more exquisite than anything *seen*. Daff's purr there on my rug, for instance—and the snap and crackle of the fire—and the squeaks and scrambles of mice that are having a jamboree behind the wainscot. I love to be alone in my room like this. I like to think even the mice are having a good time. And I get so much pleasure out of all my little belongings. They have a meaning for me they have for no one else. I have never for one moment felt at home in my room at Aunt Ruth's, but as soon as I come *here* I enter into my kingdom. I love to read here—dream here—sit by the window and shape some airy fancy into verse.

"I've been reading one of Father's books to-night. I always feel so beautifully near to Father when I read his books—as if I might suddenly look over my shoulder and see him. And so often I come across his pencilled notes on the margin and they seem like a message from him. The book I'm reading to-night is a wonderful one—wonderful in plot and conception—wonderful in its grasp of motives and passions. As I read it I feel humbled and insignificant—which is good for me. I say to myself, 'You poor, pitiful, little creature, did you ever imagine *you* could write? If so, your delusion is now stripped away from you for ever and you behold yourself in your naked paltriness.' But I shall recover from this state of mind—and believe again that I *can* write a little—and go on cheerfully producing sketches and poems until I can do

461

better. In another year and a half my promise to Aunt Elizabeth will be out and I can write stories again. Meanwhile—patience! To be sure, I get a bit weary at times of saying 'patience and perseverance.' It is hard not to see all at once the results of those estimable virtues. Sometimes I feel that I want to tear around and be as impatient as I like. But not to-night. To-night I feel as contented as a cat on a rug. I would purr if I knew how.

****

"December 9, 19—
"This was Andrew-night. He came, all beautifully groomed up, as usual. Of course, I like a boy who gets himself up well, but Andrew really carries it too far. He always seems as if he had just been starched and ironed and was afraid to move or laugh for fear he'd crack. When I come to think of it, I've never heard Andrew give a hearty laugh yet. And I *know* he never hunted pirate gold when he was a boy. But he's good and sensible and tidy, and his nails are always clean, and the bank manager thinks a great deal of him. And he likes cats—in their place! Oh, I don't deserve such a cousin!"

****

"January 5, 19—
"Holidays are over. I had a beautiful two weeks at old white-hooded New Moon. The day before Christmas I had *five acceptances*. I wonder I didn't go crazy. Three of them were from magazines who don't pay anything, but subscriptions, for contributions. But the others were accompanied by *cheques*—one for two dollars for a poem and one for ten dollars for my *Sands of Time*, which has been taken at last—my first story acceptance. Aunt Elizabeth looked at the cheques and said wonderingly:

"'Do you suppose the bank will really pay you *money* for those?'

"She could hardly believe it, even after Cousin Jimmy took them to Shrewsbury and cashed them.

"Of course, the money goes to my Shrewsbury expenses. But I had no end of fun planning how I would have spent it if I had been free to spend.

"Perry is on the High School team who will debate with the Queen's Academy boys in February. Good for Perry—it's a great honour to be chosen on that team. The debate is a yearly occurrence and Queen's has won for three years. Ilse offered to coach Perry on the elocution of his speech and she is taking no end of trouble with him—especially in preventing him from saying *'devilopment'* when he means 'development.' It's awfully good of her, for she really doesn't like him. I do hope Shrewsbury will win.

"We have *The Idylls of the King* in English class this term. I like some things in them, but I detest Tennyson's *Arthur*. If I had been *Guinevere* I'd have boxed his ears—but I wouldn't have been unfaithful to him for *Lancelot,* who was just as odious in a different way. As for *Geraint,* if I had been *Enid* I'd have *bitten* him. These 'patient Griseldas' deserve all they get. Lady Enid, if you had been a Murray of New Moon you would have kept your husband in better order and he would have liked you all the better for it.

"I read a story to-night. It ended unhappily. I was wretched until I had invented a happy ending for it. I shall always end *my* stories happily. I don't care whether it's 'true to life' or not. It's true to life as it *should be* and that's a better truth than the other.

"Speaking of books. I read an old one of Aunt Ruth's the other day—The *Children of the Abbey.* The heroine fainted in every chapter and cried quarts if any one looked at her. But as for the trials and persecutions she underwent, in spite of her delicate frame, their name was Legion and no fair maiden of these degenerate days could survive half of them—not even the newest of new women. I laughed over the book until I amazed Aunt Ruth, who thought it a very sad volume. It is the only novel in Aunt Ruth's house. One of her beaux gave it to her when she was young. It seems impossible to think that Aunt Ruth ever had beaux. Uncle Dutton seems an unreality, and even his picture on the crepe-draped easel in the parlour cannot convince me of his existence.

****

"January 21, 19—

"Friday night the debate between Shrewsbury High and Queen's came off. The Queen's boys came up believing they were going to come, see and conquer—and went home like the proverbial dogs with carefully adjusted tails. It was really Perry's speech that won the debate. He was a wonder. Even Aunt Ruth admitted for the first time that there was something in him. After it was over he came rushing up to Ilse and me in the corridor.

"'Didn't I do great, Emily?' he demanded. 'I knew it was in me, but I didn't know if I could get it out. When I got up at first I felt tongue-tied—and then I saw *you,* looking at me as if you said, 'You can—you *must*'—and I went ahead full steam. *You* won that debate, Emily.'

"Now wasn't that a nice thing to say before Ilse, who had worked for hours with him and drilled and slaved? Never a word of tribute to *her*—everything to me who hadn't done a thing except look interested.

"'Perry, you're an ungrateful barbarian,' I said—and left him there, with his jaw dropping. Ilse was so furious she cried. She has never spoken to him since—and that ass of a Perry can't understand why.

"'What's she peeved about now? I *thanked* her for all her trouble at our last practice,' he says.

"Certainly, Stovepipe Town has its limitations.

****

"February 2, 19—

"Last night Mrs. Rogers invited Aunt Ruth and me to dinner to meet her sister and brother-in-law, Mr. and Mrs. Herbert. Aunt Ruth had her Sunday scallops in her hair and wore her brown velvet dress that reeked of moth-balls and her big oval brooch with Uncle Dutton's hair in it; and I put on my ashes-of-roses and Princess Mena's necklace and went, quivering with excitement, for Mr. Herbert is a member of the Dominion Cabinet and a man who stands in the presence of kings. He has a massive, silver head and eyes that have looked into people's thoughts so long that you have an uncanny feeling that they can see right into your soul and read motives you don't dare avow even to yourself. His face is a most interesting one. There is so much in it. All the varied experiences of his full, wonderful life had written it over. One could tell at sight that he was a born leader. Mrs. Rogers let me sit beside him at dinner. I was afraid to speak—afraid I'd say something stupid—afraid I'd make some ludicrous mistake. So I just sat quiet as a mouse and listened adoringly. Mrs. Rogers told me to-day that Mr.

464

Herbert said, after we had left,

"'That little Starr girl of New Moon is the best conversationalist of any girl of her age I ever met.'

"So even great statesmen—but there—I won't be horrid.

"And he *was* splendid: he was wise and witty and humorous. I felt as if I were drinking in some rare, stimulating, mental wine. I forgot even Aunt Ruth's moth-balls. What an event it is to meet such a man and take a peep through his wise eyes at the fascinating game of empire building!

"Perry went to the station to-day to get a glimpse of Mr. Herbert. Perry says he will be just as great a man some day. But, no. Perry can— and I believe will—go far—climb high. But he will be only a successful politician—never a statesman. Ilse flew into me when I said this.

"'I hate Perry Miller,' she fumed, 'but I hate snobbery worse. *You're* a snob, Emily Starr. You think just because Perry comes from Stovepipe Town that he can never be a great man. If he had been one of the sacred Murrays you would see no limits to his attainments!'

"I thought Ilse was unfair, and I lifted my head haughtily.

"'After all,' I said, 'there *is* a difference between New Moon and Stovepipe Town.'"

****

IF A BODY KISS A BODY

It was half-past ten o'clock and Emily realized with a sigh that she must go to bed. When she had come in at half-past nine from Alice Kennedy's thimble party, she had asked permission of Aunt Ruth to sit up an hour later to do some special studying. Aunt Ruth had consented reluctantly and suspiciously and had gone to bed herself, with sundry warnings regarding candles and matches. Emily had studied diligently for forty-five minutes and written poetry for fifteen. The poem burned for completion, but Emily resolutely pushed her portfolio away.

At that moment she remembered that she had left her Jimmy-book in her school-bag in the dining-room. This would never do. Aunt Ruth would be down before her in the morning and would inevitably examine the book-bag, find the Jimmy-book and read it. There were things in that Jimmy-book it was well Aunt Ruth should not see. She must slip down and bring it up.

Very quietly she opened her door and tiptoed downstairs, in anguish at every creaking step. Aunt Ruth, who slept in the big front bedroom at the other end of the hall, would surely hear those creaks. They were enough to waken the dead. They did not waken Aunt Ruth, however, and Emily reached the dining-room, found her book-bag, and was just going to return when she happened to glance at the mantelpiece. There, propped up against the clock, was a letter for her which had evidently come by the evening mail—a nice thin letter with the address of a magazine in the corner. Emily set her candle on the table, tore open the letter, found the acceptance of a poem and a cheque for three dollars. Acceptances—especially acceptances with cheque—were still such rare occurrences with our Emily that they always made her a little crazy. She forgot Aunt Ruth—she forgot that it was nearing eleven o'clock: she stood there entranced, reading over and over the brief editorial note—brief, but, oh, how sweet! "Your charming poem"—"we would like to see more of your work"—oh, yes, indeed, they *should* see more of it.

Emily turned with a start. Was that a tap at the door? No—at the window. Who? What? The next moment she was aware that Perry was standing on the side veranda, grinning at her through the window.

She was at it in a flash and without pausing to think, still in the exhilaration of her acceptance, she slipped the catch and pushed the window up. She knew where Perry had been and was dying to know how he had got along. He had been invited to dinner with Dr. Hardy, in the fine Queen-street house. This was considered a great honour and very few students ever received it. Perry owed the invitation to his brilliant speech at the inter-school debate. Dr. Hardy had heard it and decided that here was a coming man.

Perry had been enormously proud of the invitation and had bragged of it to Teddy and Emily—not to Ilse, who had not yet forgiven him for his tactlessness on the night of the debate. Emily had been pleased, but had warned Perry that he would need to watch his step at Dr. Hardy's.

She felt some qualms in regard to his etiquette, but Perry had felt none. *He* would be all right, he loftily declared. Perry perched himself on the window-pill and Emily sat down on the corner of the sofa, reminding herself that it could be only for a minute.

"Saw the light in the window as I went past," said Perry. "So I thought I'd just take a sneak round to the side and see if it was you. Wanted to tell you the tale while it was fresh. Say, Emily, you were right—r-i-g-h-t! I should smile. I wouldn't go through this evening again for a hundred dollars."

"How *did* you get along?" asked Emily anxiously. In a sense, she felt responsible for Perry's manners. Such as he had he had acquired at New Moon.

Perry grinned.

"It's a heart-rending tale. I've had a lot of conceit taken out of me. I suppose you'll say that's a good thing."

"You could spare some," said Emily coolly.

Perry shrugged his shoulders.

"Well, I'll tell you all about it if you won't tell Ilse or Teddy. I'm not going to have *them* laughing at me. I went to Queen-street at the proper time—I remembered all you'd said about boots and tie and nails and handkerchief and I was all right outside. When I got to the house my troubles began. It was so big and splendid I felt queer—not afraid—I wasn't afraid *then*—but just a bit as if I was ready to jump—like a strange cat when you try to pat it. I rang the bell; of course, it stuck and kept on ringing like mad. I could hear it away down the hall, and thinks I, 'They'll think I don't know any better than to keep on ringing it till somebody comes,' and that rattled me. The maid rattled me still more. I didn't know whether I ought to shake hands with her or not."

"Oh, Perry!"

"Well, I *didn't*. I never was to a house where there was a maid like that before, all dolled up with a cap and finicky little apron. She made me feel like thirty cents."

"*Did* you shake hands with her?"

"No."

Emily gave a sigh of relief.

"She held the door open and I went in. I didn't know what to do then. Guess I'd have stood there till I took root, only Dr. Hardy himself come—came—through the hall. *He* shook hands and showed me where to put my hat and coat and then he took me into the parlour to meet his wife. The floor was as slippery as ice—and just as I stepped on the rug inside the parlour door it went clean from under me and down I went and slid across the floor, feet foremost, right to Mrs. Hardy. I was on my back, not on my stomach, or it would have been quite the proper Oriental caper, wouldn't it?"

Emily couldn't laugh.

"Oh, *Perry!*"

"Great snakes, Emily, it wasn't my fault. All the etiquette in the world couldn't have prevented it. Of course, I felt like a fool, but I got up and laughed. Nobody else laughed. They were all decent. Mrs. Hardy was smooth as wax—hoped I hadn't hurt myself, and Dr. Hardy said *he* had slipped the same way more than once after they had given up their good old carpets and taken to rugs and hardwood. I was scared to move, so I sat down in the nearest chair, and there was a dog on it— Mrs. Hardy's Peke. Oh, I didn't kill it—*I* got the worst scare of the two. By the time I had made port in another chair the *sw*—perspiration was just pouring down my face. Some more folks arrived just then, so that kind of took the edge off me, and I had time to get my bearings. I found I had about ten pairs of hands and feet. And my boots were too big and coarse. Then I found myself with my hands in my pockets, *whistling.*"

Emily began to say, "Oh, Perry," but bit it off and swallowed it. What was the use of saying *anything?*

"I knew *that* wasn't proper, so I stopped and took my hands out— and began to bite my nails. Finally, I put my hands underneath me and sat on 'em. I doubled my feet back under my chair, and I sat like that till we went out to dinner—sat like that when a fat old lady waddled in and all the other fellows stood up. I didn't—didn't see any reason for it—there was plenty of chairs. But later on it occurred to me that it was some etiquette stunt and I ought to have got up, too. Should I?"

"Of course," said Emily, wearily. "Don't you remember how Ilse used to rag you about that very thing?"

"Oh, I'd forgotten—Ilse was always jawing about something. But live and learn. I won't forget again, you bet. There were three or four other boys there—the new French teacher and a couple of bankers— and some ladies. I got out to dinner without falling over the floor and got into a chair between Miss Hardy and the aforesaid old lady. I gave one look over that table—and then, Emily, I knew what it was to be

468

afraid at last, all right. I never knew it before, honest. It's an awful feeling. I was in a regular funk. I used to think you carried fierce style at New Moon when you had company, but I never saw anything like that table—and everything so dazzling and glittering, and enough forks and spoons and things at one place to fit everybody out. There was a piece of bread folded in my napkin and it fell out and went skating over the floor. I could feel myself turning red all over my face and neck. I s'pose you call it blushing. I never blushed afore—before—that I remember. I didn't know whether I ought to get up and go and pick it up or not. Then the maid brought me another one. I used the wrong spoon to eat my soup with, but I tried to remember what your Aunt Laura said about the proper way to eat soup. I'd get on all right for a few spoonfuls—then I'd get interested in something somebody was saying—and go *gulp*."

"Did you tilt your plate to get the last spoonful?" asked Emily despairingly.

"No, I was just going to when I remembered it wasn't proper. I hated to lose it, too. It was awful good soup and I was hungry. The good old dowager next to me *did*. I got on pretty well with the meat and vegetables, except once. I had packed a load of meat and potatoes on my fork and just as I lifted it I saw Mrs. Hardy eyeing it, and I remembered I oughtn't to have loaded up my fork like that—and I jumped—and it all fell off in my napkin. I didn't know whether it would be etiquette to scrape it up and put it back on my plate so I left it there. The pudding was all right—only I et it with a spoon—my soup spoon—and every one else et theirs with a fork. But it tasted just as good one way as another and I was getting reckless. You always use spoons at New Moon to eat pudding."

"Why didn't you watch what the others did and imitate them?"

"Too rattled. But I'll say this—for all the style, the eats weren't a bit better than you have at New Moon—no, nor as good, by a jugful. Your Aunt Elizabeth's cooking would knock the spots off the Hardys' every time—and they didn't give you too much of anything! After the dinner was over we went back to the parlour—*they* called it living-room—and things weren't so bad. I didn't do anything out of the way except knock over a bookcase."

"Perry!"

"Well, it was wobbly. I was leaning against it talking to Mr. Hardy, and I suppose I leaned too hard, for the blooming thing went over. But, righting it and getting the books back seemed to loosen me up and I wasn't so tongue-tied after that. I got on not too bad—only every once in a long while I'd let slip a bit of slang, before I could catch it. I tell you, I wished I'd taken your advice about talking slang. Once the fat old lady agreed with something I'd said—she had sense if she *did* have three chins—and I was so tickled to find her on my side that I got excited and said to her, 'You bet your boots' before I thought. And I guess I bragged a bit. *Do* I brag too much, Emily?"

This question had never presented itself to Perry before.

"You *do,*" said Emily candidly, "and it's *very* bad form."

"Well, I felt kind of cheap after I'd done it. I guess I've got an awful lot to learn yet, Emily. I'm going to buy a book on etiquette and learn it off by heart. No more evenings like this for me. But it was better at the last. Jim Hardy took me off to the den and we played checkers and I licked him dizzy. Nothing wrong with my checker etiquette, I tell *you.* And Mrs. Hardy said my speech at the debate was the best she had ever heard for a boy of my age, and she wanted to know what I meant to go in for. She's a great little dame and has the social end of things down fine. That is one reason I want you to marry me when the times comes, Emily—I've got to have a wife with brains."

"Don't talk nonsense, Perry," said Emily, haughtily.

"'Tisn't nonsense," said Perry, stubbornly. "And it's time we settled *something.* You needn't turn up your nose at me because you're a Murray. I'll be worth marrying some day—even for a Murray. Come, put me out of my misery."

Emily rose disdainfully. She had her dreams, as all girls have, the rose-red one of love among them, but Perry Miller had no share in those dreams.

"I'm *not* a Murray—and I'm going upstairs. Good night."

"Wait half a second," said Perry, with a grin. "When the clock strikes eleven I'm going to kiss you."

Emily did not for a moment believe that Perry had the slightest notion of doing anything of the kind—which was foolish of her, for Perry had a habit of always doing what he said he was going to do. But, then, he had never been sentimental. She ignored his remark, but lingered a moment to ask another question about the Hardy dinner. Perry did not answer the question: the clock began to strike eleven as she asked it—he flung his legs over the window-sill and stepped into the room. Emily realized too late that he meant what he said. She had only time to duck her head and Perry's hearty, energetic smack—there was nothing subtle about Perry's kisses—fell on her ear instead of her cheek.

At the very moment Perry kissed her and before her indignant protest could rush to her lips two things happened. A gust of wind swept in from the veranda and blew the little candle out, *and* the dining-room door opened and Aunt Ruth appeared in the doorway, robed in a pink flannel nightgown and carrying another candle, the light of which struck upward with gruesome effect on her set face with its halo of crimping-pins.

This is one of the places where a conscientious biographer feels that, in the good old phrase, her pen cannot do justice to the scene.

Emily and Perry stood as if turned to stone. So, for a moment, did Aunt Ruth. Aunt Ruth had expected to find Emily there, writing, as she had done one night a month previously when Emily had had an inspiration at bedtime and had slipped down to the warm dining-room to jot it down in a Jimmy-book. But *this!* I must admit it *did* look bad. Really, I think we can hardly blame Aunt Ruth for righteous indignation.

Aunt Ruth looked at the unlucky pair.

"What are you doing here?" she asked Perry.

Stovepipe Town made a mistake.

"Oh, looking for a round square," said Perry offhandedly, his eyes suddenly becoming limpid with mischief and lawless roguery.

Perry's "impudence"—Aunt Ruth called it that, and, really, I think he *was* impudent—naturally made a bad matter worse. Aunt Ruth turned to Emily.

"Perhaps *you* can explain how you came to be here, at this hour, kissing this fellow in the dark?"

Emily flinched from the crude vulgarity of the question as if Aunt Ruth had struck her. She forgot how much appearances justified Aunt Ruth, and let a perverse spirit enter into and possess her. She lifted her head haughtily.

"I have no explanation to give to such a question, Aunt Ruth."

"I didn't think you would have."

Aunt Ruth gave a very disagreeable laugh, through which a thin, discordant note of triumph sounded. One might have thought that, under all her anger, something pleased Aunt Ruth. It *is* pleasant to be justified in the opinion we have always entertained of anybody. "Well, perhaps you will be so good as to answer some questions. How did this fellow get here?"

"Window," said Perry laconically, seeing that Emily was not going to answer.

"I was not asking *you*, sir. Go," said Aunt Ruth, pointing dramatically to the window.

"I'm not going to stir a step out of this room until I see what you're going to do to Emily," said Perry stubbornly.

"*I*," said Aunt Ruth, with an air of terrible detachment, "am not going to do anything to Emily."

"Mrs. Dutton, be a good sport," implored Perry coaxingly. "It's all my fault—honest! Emily wasn't one bit to blame. You see, it was this way—"

But Perry was too late.

"I have asked my niece for an explanation and she has refused to give it. I do not choose to listen to yours."

"But—" persisted Perry.

"You had better go, Perry," said Emily, whose face was flying danger signals. She spoke quietly, but the Murrayest of all Murrays could not have expressed a more definite command. There was a quality in it Perry dared not disregard. He meekly scrambled out of the window into the night. Aunt Ruth stepped forward and shut the window. Then, ignoring Emily utterly, she marched her pink flanneled little figure back upstairs.

Emily did not sleep much that night—nor, I admit, did she deserve to. After her sudden anger died away, shame cut her like a whip. She realized that she had behaved very foolishly in refusing an explanation to Aunt Ruth. Aunt Ruth had a right to it, when such a situation developed in her own house, no matter how hateful and disagreeable she made her method of demanding it. Of course, she would not have believed a word of it; but Emily, if she had given it, would not have further complicated her false position.

Emily fully expected she would be sent home to New Moon in disgrace. Aunt Ruth would stonily decline to keep such a girl any longer in her house—Aunt Elizabeth would agree with her—Aunt

Laura would be heart-broken. Would even Cousin Jimmy's loyalty stand the strain? It was a very bitter prospect. No wonder Emily spent a white night. She was so unhappy that every beat of her heart seemed to hurt her. And again I say, most unequivocally, she deserved it. I haven't one word of pity or excuse for her.

CIRCUMSTANTIAL EVIDENCE

At the Saturday morning breakfast-table Aunt Ruth preserved a stony silence, but she smiled cruelly to herself as she buttered and ate her toast. Anyone might have seen clearly that Aunt Ruth was enjoying herself—and, with equal clearness, that Emily was *not*. Aunt Ruth passed Emily the toast and marmalade with killing politeness, as if to say,

"I will not abate one jot or tittle of the proper thing. I may turn you out of my house, but it will be your own fault if you go without your breakfast."

After breakfast Aunt Ruth went uptown. Emily suspected that she had gone to telephone to Dr. Burnley a message for New Moon. She expected when Aunt Ruth returned to be told to pack her trunk. But still Aunt Ruth spoke not. In the middle of the afternoon Cousin Jimmy arrived with the double-seated box-sleigh. Aunt Ruth went out and conferred with him. Then she came in and at last broke her silence.

"Put on your wraps," she said. "We are going to New Moon."

Emily obeyed mutely. She got into the back seat of the sleigh and Aunt Ruth sat beside Cousin Jimmy in front. Cousin Jimmy looked back at Emily over the collar of his fur coat and said, "Hello, Pussy," with just a shade too much of cheerful encouragement. Evidently Cousin Jimmy believed something very serious had happened, though he didn't know what.

It was not a pleasant drive through the beautiful greys and smokes and pearls of the winter afternoon. The arrival at New Moon was not pleasant. Aunt Elizabeth looked stern—Aunt Laura looked apprehensive.

"I have brought Emily here," said Aunt Ruth, "because I do not feel that I can deal with her alone. You and Laura, Elizabeth, must pass judgment on her behaviour yourselves."

So it was to be a domestic court, with her, Emily, at the bar of justice. Justice—would she get justice? Well, she would make a fight for it. She flung up her head and the colour rushed back into her face.

They were all in the sitting-room when she came down from her room. Aunt Elizabeth sat by the table. Aunt Laura was on the sofa ready to cry. Aunt Ruth was standing on the rug before the fire, looking peevishly at Cousin Jimmy, who, instead of going to the barn as he should have done, had tied the horse to the orchard fence and had seated himself back in the corner, determined, like Perry, to see what was going to be done to Emily. Ruth was annoyed. She wished Elizabeth would not always insist on admitting Jimmy to family conclaves when he desired to be present. It was absurd to suppose that a grown-up child like Jimmy had any right there.

Emily did not sit down. She went and stood by the window, where her black head came out against the crimson curtain as softly and darkly clear as a pine-tree against a sunset of spring. Outside a white, dead world lay in the chilly twilight of early March. Past the garden and the Lombardy poplars the fields of New Moon looked very lonely and drear, with the intense red streak of lingering sunset beyond them. Emily shivered.

"Well," said Cousin Jimmy, "let's begin and get it over. Emily must want her supper."

"When you know what *I* know about her, you will think she needs something besides supper," said Mrs. Dutton tartly.

"I know all anyone need know about Emily," retorted Cousin Jimmy.

"Jimmy Murray, you are an ass," said Aunt Ruth, angrily.

"Well, we're cousins," agreed Cousin Jimmy pleasantly.

"Jimmy, be silent," said Elizabeth, majestically. "Ruth, let us hear what you have to say."

Aunt Ruth told the whole story. She stuck to facts, but her manner of telling them made them seem even blacker than they were. She really contrived to make a very ugly story of it, and Emily shivered again as she listened. As the telling proceeded Aunt Elizabeth's face became harder and colder, Aunt Laura began to cry, and Cousin Jimmy began to whistle.

"He was kissing her *neck*," concluded Aunt Ruth. Her tone implied that, bad as it was to kiss on ordinary places for kissing, it was a thousand-fold more scandalous and disgraceful to kiss the neck.

"It was my ear, really," murmured Emily, with a sudden impish grin she could not check in time. Under all her discomfort and dread, there was *Something* that was standing back and *enjoying* this—the drama, the comedy of it. But this outbreak of it was most unfortunate. It made her appear flippant and unashamed.

"Now, I ask you," said Aunt Ruth, throwing out her pudgy hands, "if you can expect me to keep a girl like her any longer in my house?"

"No, I don't think we can," said Elizabeth slowly.

Aunt Laura began to sob wildly. Cousin Jimmy brought down the front legs of his chair with a bang.

Emily turned from the window and faced them all.

"I want to explain what happened, Aunt Elizabeth."

"I think we have heard enough about it," said Aunt Elizabeth icily—all the more icily because of a certain bitter disappointment that was filling her soul. She had been gradually becoming very fond and proud of Emily, in her reserved, undemonstrative Murray way: to find her capable of such conduct as this was a terrible blow to Aunt Elizabeth. Her very pain made her the more merciless.

"No, that won't do now, Aunt Elizabeth," said Emily quietly. "I'm too old to be treated like that. You *must* hear my side of the story."

The Murray look was on her face—the look Elizabeth knew and remembered so well of old. She wavered.

"You had your chance to explain last night," snapped Aunt Ruth, "and you wouldn't do it."

"Because I was hurt and angry over your thinking the worst of me," said Emily. "Besides, I knew *you* wouldn't believe me."

"I would have believed you if you had told the truth," said Aunt Ruth. "The reason you wouldn't explain last night was because you couldn't think up an excuse for your conduct on the spur of the moment. You've had time to invent something since, I suppose."

"Did you ever know Emily to tell a lie?" demanded Cousin Jimmy.

Mrs. Dutton opened her lips to say "Yes." Then closed them again. Suppose Jimmy should demand a specific instance? She felt sure Emily had told her—fibs—a score of times, but what proof had she of it?

"*Did* you?" persisted that abominable Jimmy.

"I am not going to be catechized by you." Aunt Ruth turned her back on him. "Elizabeth, I've always told you that girl was deep and sly, haven't I?"

"Yes," admitted poor Elizabeth, rather thankful that there need be no indecision on *that* point. Ruth had certainly told her so times out of number.

"And doesn't this show I was right?"

"I'm—afraid—so." Elizabeth Murray felt that it was a very bitter moment for her.

"Then it is for *you* to decide what is to be done about the matter," said Ruth triumphantly.

"Not yet," interposed Cousin Jimmy resolutely. "You haven't given Emily the ghost of a chance to explain. That's no fair trial. Now let her talk for ten minutes without interrupting her once."

"That is only fair," said Elizabeth with sudden resolution. She had a mad, irrational hope that, after all, Emily might be able to clear herself.

"Oh—well—" Mrs. Dutton yielded ungraciously and sat herself down with a thud on old Archibald Murray's chair.

"Now, Emily, tell us what really happened," said Cousin Jimmy.

"Well, upon my word!" exploded Aunt Ruth. "Do you mean to say *I* didn't tell what really happened?"

Cousin Jimmy lifted his hand.

"Now—now—you had your say. Come, Pussy."

Emily told her story from beginning to end. Something in it carried conviction. Three of her listeners at least believed her and felt an enormous load lifted from their minds. Even Aunt Ruth, deep down in her heart, knew Emily was telling the truth, but she would not admit it.

"A very ingenious tale, upon my word." she said derisively.

Cousin Jimmy got up and walked across the floor. He bent down before Mrs. Dutton and thrust his rosy face with its forked beard and child-like brown eyes under his shock of grey curls, very close to hers.

"Ruth Murray," he said, "do you remember the story that got around forty years ago about you and Fred Blair? *Do* you?"

Aunt Ruth pushed back her chair. Cousin Jimmy followed her.

"Do you remember that you were caught in a scrape that looked far worse than this? *Didn't* it?"

Again poor Aunt Ruth pushed back her chair. Again Cousin Jimmy followed.

"Do you remember how mad you were because people wouldn't believe you? But your father believed you—*he* had confidence in his own flesh and blood. *Hadn't* he?"

Aunt Ruth had reached the wall by this time and had to surrender at discretion.

"I—I—remember well enough," she said shortly.

Her cheeks were a curdled red. Emily looked at her interestedly. *Was* Aunt Ruth trying to blush? Ruth Dutton was, in fact, living over some very miserable months in her long past youth. When she was a girl of eighteen she had been trapped in a very ugly situation. And she had been innocent—absolutely innocent. She had been the helpless victim of a most impish combination of circumstances. Her father had believed her story and her own family had backed her up. But her contemporaries had believed the evidence of known facts for years— perhaps believed it yet, if they ever thought about the matter. Ruth Dutton shivered over the remembrance of her suffering under the lash of scandal. She no longer dared to refuse credence to Emily's story but she could not yield gracefully.

"Jimmy," she said sharply, "will you be good enough to go away and sit down? I suppose Emily *is* telling the truth—it's a pity she took so long deciding to tell it. And I'm sure that creature *was* making love to her."

"No, he was only asking me to marry him," said Emily coolly.

You heard three gasps in the room. Aunt Ruth alone was able to speak.

"Do you intend to, may I ask?"

"No. I've told him so half a dozen times."

"Well, I'm glad you had that much sense. Stovepipe Town, indeed!"

"Stovepipe Town had nothing to do with it. Ten years from now Perry Miller will be a man whom even a Murray would delight to honour. But he doesn't happen to be the type I fancy, that's all."

Could *this* be Emily—this tall young woman coolly giving her reasons for refusing an offer of marriage—and talking about the "types" she fancied? Elizabeth—Laura—even Ruth looked at her as if they had never seen her before. And there was a new respect in their eyes. Of course they knew that Andrew was—was—well, in short, that Andrew *was*. But years must doubtless pass before Andrew would— would—well, *would!* And now the thing had happened already with

477

another suitor—happened "half a dozen times" mark you! At that moment, although they were quite unconscious of it, they ceased to regard her as a child. At a bound she had entered their world and must henceforth be met on equal terms. There could be no more family courts. They *felt* this, though they did not perceive it. Aunt Ruth's next remark showed it. She spoke almost as she might have spoken to Laura or Elizabeth, if she had deemed it her duty to admonish them.

"Just suppose, Emily, if anyone passing had seen Perry Miller sitting in that window at that hour of night?"

"Yes, of course. I see your angle of it perfectly, Aunt Ruth. All I want is to get you to see *mine*. I was foolish to open the window and talk to Perry—I see that now. I simply didn't think—and then I got so interested in the story of his mishaps at Dr. Hardy's dinner that I forgot how time was going."

"Was Perry Miller to dinner at *Dr. Hardy's?*" asked Aunt Elizabeth. This was another staggerer for her. The world—the Murray world—must be literally turned upside-down if Stovepipe Town was invited to dinner on Queen Street. At the same moment Aunt Ruth remembered with a pang of horror that Perry Miller had seen her in her pink flannel nightgown. It hadn't mattered before—he had been only the help-boy at New Moon. *Now* he was Dr. Hardy's guest.

"Yes. Dr. Hardy thinks he is a very brilliant debater and says he has a future," said Emily.

"Well," snapped Aunt Ruth, "*I* wish you would stop prowling about my house at all hours, writing novels. If you had been in your bed, as you should have been, this would never have happened."

"I wasn't writing novels," cried Emily. "I've never written a word of fiction since I promised Aunt Elizabeth. I wasn't writing *anything*. I told you I just went down to get my Jimmy-book."

"*Why* couldn't you have left that where it was till morning?" persisted Aunt Ruth.

"Come, come," said Cousin Jimmy, "don't start up another argument. I want my supper. You girls go and get it."

Elizabeth and Laura left the room as meekly as if old Archibald Murray himself had commanded it. After a moment Ruth followed them. Things had not turned out just as she anticipated; but, after all, she was resigned. It would not have been a nice thing for a scandal like this concerning a Murray to be blown abroad, as must have happened if a verdict of guilty had been found against Emily.

"So *that's* settled," said Cousin Jimmy to Emily as the door closed.

Emily drew a long breath. The quiet, dignified old room suddenly seemed very beautiful and friendly to her.

"Yes, thanks to you," she said, springing across it to give him an impetuous hug. "Now, scold me, Cousin Jimmy, scold me *hard.*"

"No, no. But it *would* have been more prudent *not* to have opened that window, wouldn't it now, Pussy?"

"Of course it would. But prudence is such a shoddy virtue at times, Cousin Jimmy. One is ashamed of it—one likes to just go ahead and—and—"

"And hang consequences," supplied Cousin Jimmy.

"Something like that," Emily laughed. "I hate to go mincing through life, afraid to take a single long step for fear somebody is watching. I want to 'wave my wild tail and walk by my wild lone.' There wasn't a bit of real harm in my opening that window and talking to Perry. There wasn't even any harm in his trying to kiss me. He just did it to tease me. Oh, I *hate* conventions. As you say—hang consequences."

"But we can't hang 'em, Pussy—that's just the trouble. They're more likely to hang us. I put it to you, Pussy—suppose—there's no harm in supposing it—that you were grown up and married and had a daughter of your age, and you went downstairs one night and found her as Aunt Ruth found you and Perry. *Would* you like it? *Would* you be well pleased? Honest, now?"

Emily stared hard at the fire for a moment.

"No, I wouldn't," she said at last. "But then—that's different. I wouldn't *know.*"

Cousin Jimmy chuckled.

"That's the point, Pussy. Other people can't *know.* So we've got to watch our step. Oh, I'm only simple Jimmy Murray, but I can see we have to watch our step. Pussy, we're going to have roast spare-ribs for supper."

A savoury whiff crept in from the kitchen at that very moment—a homely, comfortable odour that had nothing in common with compromising situations and family skeletons. Emily gave Cousin Jimmy another hug.

"Better a dinner of herbs where Cousin Jimmy is than roast spare-ribs and Aunt Ruth therewith," she said.

"AIRY VOICES"

"April 3, 19—

"There *are* times when I am tempted to believe in the influence of evil stars or the reality of unlucky days. Otherwise how can such diabolical things happen as do happen to well-meaning people? Aunt Ruth has only just begun to grow weary of recalling the night she found Perry kissing me in the dining-room, and now I'm in another ridiculous scrape.

"I will be honest. It was not dropping my umbrella which was responsible for it, neither was it the fact that I let the kitchen mirror at New Moon fall last Saturday and crack. It was just my own carelessness.

"St. John's Presbyterian church here in Shrewsbury became vacant at New Year's and has been hearing candidates. Mr. Towers of the *Times* asked me to report the sermons for his paper on such Sundays as I was not in Blair Water. The first sermon was good and I reported it with pleasure. The second one was harmless, very harmless, and I reported it without pain. But the third, which I heard last Sunday, was ridiculous. I said so to Aunt Ruth on the way home from church and Aunt Ruth said, 'Do you think *you* are competent to criticize a sermon?'

"Well, yes, I do!

"That sermon was a most inconsistent thing. Mr. Wickham contradicted himself half a dozen times. He mixed his metaphors— he attributed something to St. Paul that belonged to Shakespeare— he committed almost every conceivable literary sin, including the unpardonable one of being deadly dull. However, it was my business to report the sermon, so report it I did. Then I had to do something to get it out of my system, so I wrote, for my own satisfaction, an analysis of it. It was a crazy but delightful deed. I showed up all the inconsistencies, the misquotations, the weaknesses and the wobblings. I enjoyed writing it—I made it as pointed and satirical and satanical as I could—oh, I admit it was a very vitriolic document.

"Then I handed *it* into the *Times* by mistake!

"Mr. Towers passed it over to the typesetter without reading it. He had a touching confidence in my work, which he will never have again. It came out the next day.

"I woke to find myself infamous.

"I expected Mr. Towers would be furious; but he is only mildly annoyed—and a little amused at the back of it. It isn't as if Mr. Wickham had been a settled minister here, of course. Nobody cared for him or his sermon and Mr. Towers is a Presbyterian, so the St. John's people can't accuse him of wanting to insult *them*. It is poor Emily B. on whom is laid the whole burden of condemnation. It appears most of them think I did it 'to show off.' Aunt Ruth is furious, Aunt Elizabeth outraged; Aunt Laura grieved, Cousin Jimmy alarmed. It is such a shocking thing to criticize a minister's sermon. It is a Murray tradition that ministers' sermons—Presbyterian Ministers' especially—are sacrosanct. My presumption and vanity will yet be the ruin of me, so Aunt Elizabeth coldly informs me. The only person who seems pleased is Mr. Carpenter. (Dean is away in New York. I know *he* would like it, too.) Mr. Carpenter is telling every one that my 'report' is the best thing of its kind he ever read. But Mr. Carpenter is suspected of heresy, so his commendation will not go far to rehabilitate me.

"I feel wretched over the affair. My mistakes worry me more than my sins sometimes. And yet, an unholy something, 'way back in me, is grinning over it all. Every word in that 'report' was true. And more than true—appropriate. *I* didn't mix my metaphors.

"Now, to live this down!

****

"April 20, 19—

"'Awake thou north wind and come thou south. Blow upon my garden that the spices thereof may flow out.'

"So chanted I as I went through the Land of Uprightness this evening—only I put 'woods' in place of garden. For spring is just around the corner and I have forgotten everything but gladness.

"We had a grey, rainy dawn but sunshine came in the afternoon and a bit of April frost to-night—just enough to make the earth firm. It seemed to me a night when the ancient gods might be met with in the lonely places. But I saw nothing except some sly things back among the fir copses that *may* have been companies of goblins, if they weren't merely shadows.

"(I wonder why *goblin* is such an enchanting word and *gobbling* such an ugly one. And why is *shadowy* suggestive of all beauty while umbrageous is so ugly?)

"But I heard all kinds of fairy sounds and each gave me an exquisite vanishing joy as I went up the hill. There is always something satisfying in climbing to the top of a hill. And that is a hill-top I love. When I reached it I stood still and let the loveliness of the evening flow through me like music. How the Wind Woman was singing in the bits of birchland around me—how she whistled in the serrated tops of the trees against the sky! One of the thirteen new silver moons of the year was hanging over the harbour. I stood there and thought of many, many beautiful things—of wild, free brooks running through starlit April fields—of rippled grey-satin seas—of the grace of an elm against the moonlight—of roots stirring and thrilling in the earth—owls laughing in darkness—a curl of foam on a long sandy shore—a young moon setting over a dark hill—the grey of gulf storms.

"I had only seventy-five cents in the world but Paradise isn't bought with money.

"Then I sat down on an old boulder and tried to put those moments of delicate happiness into a poem. I caught the shape of them fairly well, I think—but not their soul. It escaped me.

"It was quite dark when I came back and the whole character of my Land of Uprightness seemed changed. It was eerie—almost sinister. I would have run if I could have dared. The trees, my old well-known friends, were strange and aloof. The sounds I heard were not the cheery, companionable sounds of daytime—nor the friendly, fairy sounds of the sunset—they were creeping and weird, as if the life of the woods had suddenly developed something almost hostile to me—something at least that was furtive and alien and unacquainted. I could fancy that I heard stealthy footsteps all around me—that strange eyes were watching me through the boughs. When I reached the open space and hopped over the fence into Aunt Ruth's back yard I felt as if I were escaping from some fascinating but not altogether hallowed locality—a place given over to Paganism and the revels of satyrs. I don't believe the woods are ever wholly Christian in the darkness. There is always a lurking life in them that dares not show itself to the sun but regains its own with the night.

"'You should not be out in the damp with that cough of yours,' said Aunt Ruth.

"But it wasn't the damp that hurt me—for I *was* hurt. It was that little fascinating whisper of something unholy. I was afraid of it—and yet I loved it. The beauty I had loved on the hill-top seemed suddenly quite tasteless beside it. I sat down in my room and wrote another poem. When I had written it I felt that I had exorcised something out of my soul and Emily-in-the-Glass seemed no longer a stranger to me.

****

"Aunt Ruth has just brought in a dose of hot milk and cayenne pepper for my cough. It is on the table before me—I have to drink it— and it has made both Paradise and Pagan-land seem very foolish and unreal!

****

"May 25, 19—

"Dean came home from New York last Friday and that evening we walked and talked in New Moon garden in a weird, uncanny twilight following a rainy day. I had a light dress on and as Dean came down the path he said,

"'When I saw you first I thought you were a wild, white cherry-tree— like *that*'—and he pointed to one that was leaning and beckoning, ghost-fair in the dusk, from Lofty John's bush.

"It was such a beautiful thing that just to be distantly compared to it made me feel very well pleased with myself, and it was lovely to have dear old Dean back again. So we had a delightful evening, and picked a big bunch of Cousin Jimmy's pansies and watched the grey rain-clouds draw together in great purple masses in the east, leaving the western sky all clear and star-powdered.

"'There is something in your company,' said Dean, 'that makes stars seem starrier and pansies purpler.'

"Wasn't that nice of him! How is it that his opinion of me and Aunt Ruth's opinion of me are so very different?

"He had a little flat parcel under his arm and when he went away he handed it to me.

"'I brought you that to counteract Lord Byron,' he said.

"It was a framed copy of the 'Portrait of Giovanna Degli Albizzi, wife of Lorenzo Tornabuoni Ghirlanjo'—a Lady of the Quatro Cento. I brought it to Shrewsbury and have it hanging in my room. I love to look at the Lady Giovanna—that slim, beautiful young thing with her sleek coils of pale gold and her prim little curls and her fine, high-bred profile (*did* the painter flatter her?) and her white neck and open, unshadowed brow, with the indefinable air over it all of saintliness and remoteness and fate—for the Lady Giovanna died young.

"*And* her embroidered velvet sleeves, slashed and puffed, very beautifully made and fitting the arm perfectly. The Lady Giovanna must have had a good dressmaker and, in spite of her saintliness, one thinks she was quite aware of the fact. I am always wishing that she would turn her head and let me see her full face.

"Aunt Ruth thinks she is queer-looking and evidently doubts the propriety of having her in the same room with the jewelled chromo of Queen Alexandra.

"I doubt it myself.

****

"June 10, 19—

"I do all my studying now by the pool in the Land of Uprightness, among those wonderful, tall, slender trees. I'm a Druidess in the woods—I regard trees with something more than love—worship.

"And then, too, trees, unlike so many humans, always improve on acquaintance. No matter how much you like them at the start you are sure to like them much better further on, and best of all when you have known them for years and enjoyed intercourse with them in all seasons. I know a hundred dear things about these trees in the Land of Uprightness that I didn't know when I came here two years ago.

"Trees have as much individuality as human beings. Not even two spruces are alike. There is always some kink or curve or bend of bough to single each one out from its fellows. Some trees love to grow sociably together, their branches twining, like Ilse and me with our arms about each other, whispering interminably of their secrets. Then there are

484

more exclusive groups of four or five—clan-Murray trees; and there are hermits of trees who choose to stand apart in solitary state and who hold commune only with the winds of heaven. Yet these trees are often the best worth knowing. One feels it is more of a triumph to win their confidence than that of easier trees. To-night I suddenly saw a great, pulsating star resting on the very crest of the big fir that stands alone in the eastern corner and I had a sense of two majesties meeting that will abide with me for days and enchant everything—even classroom routine and dish-washing and Aunt Ruth's Saturday cleaning.

****

"June 25, 19—

"We had our history examination to-day—the Tudor period. I've found it very fascinating—but more because of what isn't in the histories than of what *is*. They don't—they *can't* tell you what you would really like to know. What did Jane Seymour think of when she was awake in the dark? Of murdered Anne, or of pale, forsaken Katherine? Or just about the fashion of her new ruff? Did she ever think she had paid too high for her crown or was she satisfied with her bargain? And was she happy in those few hours after her little son was born—or did she see a ghostly procession beckoning her onward with them? Was Lady Jane Gray 'Janie' to her friends and did she *ever* have a fit of temper? What did Shakespeare's wife actually think of him? And was any man ever *really* in love with Queen Elizabeth? I am always asking questions like this when I study that pageant of kings and queens and geniuses and puppets put down in the school curriculum as 'The Tudor Period.'

****

"July 7, 19—

"Two years of High School are over. The result of my exams was such as to please even Aunt Ruth, who condescended to say that she always knew I could study if I put my mind to it. In brief, I led my class. And I'm pleased. But I begin to understand what Dean meant when he said real education was what you dug out of life for yourself. After all, the things that have taught me the most these past two years have been my wanderings in the Land of Uprightness, and my night on the haystack, and the Lady Giovanna, and the old woman who spanked the King, and trying to write nothing but *facts,* and things like that. Even rejection slips and hating Evelyn Blake have taught me something. Speaking of Evelyn—she failed in her exams and will have to take her senior year over again. I am truly sorry.

"That sounds as if I were a most amiable, forgiving creature. Let me be perfectly frank. I am sorry she didn't pass, because if she had she wouldn't be in school next year.

****

"July, 20, 19—

"Ilse and I go bathing every day now. Aunt Laura is always very particular about seeing that we have our bathing suits with us. I wonder if she ever heard any faint, far-off echoes of our moonlit petticoatedness.

"But so far our dips have been in the afternoon. And afterwards we have a glorious wallow on sun-warm, golden sands, with the gauzy dunes behind us stretching to the harbour, and the lazy blue sea before us, dotted over with sails that are silver in the magic of the sunlight. Oh, life is good—good—good. In spite of three rejection slips that came to-day. Those very editors will be *asking* for my work some day! Meanwhile Aunt Laura is teaching me how to make a certain rich and complicated kind of chocolate cake after a recipe which a friend of hers in Virginia sent her thirty years ago. Nobody in Blair Water has ever been able to get it and Aunt Laura made me solemnly promise I would never reveal it.

"The real name of the cake is Devil's Food, but Aunt Elizabeth will not have it called that.

****

"Aug. 2, 19—

"I was down seeing Mr. Carpenter this evening. He has been laid up with rheumatism and one can see he is getting old. He was very cranky with the scholars last year and there was some protest against keeping him on, but it was done. Most of the Blair Water people have sense enough to realize that with all his crankiness Mr. Carpenter is a teacher in a thousand.

"'One can't teach fools amiably,' he growled, when the trustees told him there were complaints about his harshness.

"Perhaps it was his rheumatism that made Mr. Carpenter rather crusty over the poems I took to him for criticism. When he read the one I had composed that April night on a hill-top he tossed it back to me—'pretty little gossamer thing,' he said.

"And I had really thought the poem expressed in some measure the enchantment of that evening. How I must have failed!

"Then I gave him the poem I had written after I had come in that night. He read it over twice, then he deliberately tore it into strips.

"'Now—*why?*' I said, rather annoyed. 'There was nothing wrong about that poem, Mr. Carpenter.'

"'Not about its body,' he said. 'Every line of it, taken by itself, might be read in Sunday-school. But its *soul*—what mood were you in when you wrote that in heaven's name?'

"'The mood of the Golden Age,' I said.

"'No—of an age far before that. That poem was sheer Paganism, girl, though I don't think you realize it. To be sure, from the point of view of literature it's worth a thousand of your pretty songs. All the same, that way danger lies. Better stick to your own age. You're part of it and can possess it without its possessing you. Emily, there was a streak of diabolism in that poem. It's enough to make me believe that poets *are* inspired—by some spirits outside themselves. Didn't you feel *possessed* when you wrote it?'

"'Yes,' I said, remembering. I felt rather glad Mr. Carpenter had torn the poem up. I could never have done it myself. I have destroyed a great many of my poems that seemed trash on successive readings, but this one never seemed so and it always brought back the strange charm and terror of that walk. But Mr. Carpenter was right—I feel it.

"He also berated me because I happened to mention I had been reading Mrs. Hemans' poems. Aunt Laura has a cherished volume, bound in faded blue and gold, with an inscription from an admirer. In Aunt Laura's youth it was the thing to give your adored a volume of poetry on her birthday. The things Mr. Carpenter said about Mrs. Hemans were not fit to write in a young lady's diary. I suppose he is right in the main—yet I *do* like some of her poems. Just here and there comes a line or verse that haunts me for days, delightfully.

"The march of the hosts as Alaric passed
is one—though I can't give any *reason* for my liking it—one never
can give reasons for enchantment—and another is,

"The sounds of the sea and the sounds of the night

Were around Clotilde as she knelt to pray

In a chapel where the mighty lay

On the old Provencal shore.

"That isn't great poetry—but there's a bit of magic in it for all that—
concentrated in the last line, I think. I never read it without feeling that
I am *Clotilde,* kneeling there—'on the old Provencal shore'—with the
banners of forgotten wars waving over me.

"Mr. Carpenter sneered at my 'liking for slops' and told me to go
and read the Elsie books! But when I was coming away he paid me the
first personal compliment I ever had from him.

"'I like that blue dress you've got on. And you know how to wear it.
That's good. I can't bear to see a woman badly dressed. It hurts me—
and it must hurt God Almighty. I've no use for dowds and I'm sure He
hasn't. After all, if you know how to dress yourself it won't matter if you
do like Mrs. Hemans.'

"I met Old Kelly on the way home and he stopped and gave me a bag
of candy and sent his 'rispects to *him.*'

****

"August 15, 19—
"This is a wonderful year for columbines. The old orchard is full of
them—all in lovely white and purple and fairy blue and dreamy pink
colour. They are half wild and so have a charm no real tamed garden
flower ever has. And what a name—*columbine* is poetry itself. How
much lovelier the common names of flowers are than the horrid Latiny
names the florists stick in their catalogues. Heartsease and Bride's
Bouquet, Prince's Feather, Snap-dragon, Flora's Paint Brush, Dusty
Millers, Bachelor's Buttons, Baby's Breath, Love-in-a-mist—oh, I love

them all.

****

"September 1, 19—

"Two things happened to-day. One was a letter from Great-aunt Nancy to Aunt Elizabeth. Aunt Nancy has never taken any notice of my existence since my visit to Priest Pond four years ago. But she is still alive, ninety-four years old, and from all accounts quite lively yet. She wrote some sarcastic things in her letter, about both me and Aunt Elizabeth; but she wound up by offering to pay all my expenses in Shrewsbury next year, including my board to Aunt Ruth.

"I am very glad. In spite of Aunt Nancy's sarcasm I don't mind feeling indebted to her. *She* has never nagged or patronized me—or did anything for me because she felt it her 'duty.' 'Hang duty,' she said in her letter. 'I'm doing this because it will vex some of the Priests, and because Wallace is putting on too many airs about "helping to educate Emily." I dare say you feel yourself that you've done virtuously. Tell Emily to go back to Shrewsbury and learn all she can—but to hide it and show her ankles.' Aunt Elizabeth was horrified at this and wouldn't show me the letter. But Cousin Jimmy told me what was in it.

"The second thing was that Aunt Elizabeth informed me that, since Aunt Nancy was paying my expenses, she, Aunt Elizabeth, felt that she ought not to hold me any longer to my promise about writing fiction. I was, she told me, free to do as I chose about that matter.

"'Though I shall never approve of your writing fiction,' she said, gravely. 'At least I hope you will not neglect your studies.'

"Oh, no, dear Aunt Elizabeth, I won't neglect them. But I feel like a released prisoner. My fingers tingle to grasp a pen—my brain teems with plots. I've a score of fascinating dream characters I want to write about. Oh, if there only were not such a chasm between *seeing* a thing and getting it down on paper!

"'Ever since you got that cheque for a story last winter Elizabeth's been wondering if she oughtn't to let you write,' Cousin Jimmy told me. 'But she couldn't bring herself to back down till Aunt Nancy's letter gave her the excuse. Money makes the Murray mare go, Emily. Want some more Yankee stamps?'

"Mrs. Kent has told Teddy he can go for another year. After that he doesn't know what will happen. So we are all going back and I am so happy that I want to write it in Italics.

****

"September 10, 19—

"I have been elected president of the Senior class for this year. *And the Skulls and Owls* sent me a notice that I had been elected a member of their august fraternity without the formality of an application.

"Evelyn Blake, by the way, is at present laid up with tonsilitis!

"I accepted the presidency—but I wrote a note to the *Skull and Owl* declining membership with awful politeness.

"After black-beaning me last year, indeed!

****

"October 7, 19—

"There was great excitement to-day in class when Dr. Hardy made a certain announcement. Kathleen Darcy's uncle, who is a Professor of McGill, is visiting here, and he has taken it into his head to offer a prize for the best poem, written by a pupil of Shrewsbury High School—said prize being a complete set of Parkman. The poems must be handed in by the first of November, and are to be 'not less than twenty lines, and no more than sixty.' Sounds as if a tape-measure was the first requisite. I have been wildly hunting through my Jimmy-books to-night and have decided to send in *Wild Grapes.* It is my second best poem. *A Song of Sixpence* is my best, but it has only fifteen lines and to add any more would spoil it. I think I can improve *Wild Grapes* a bit. There are two or three words in it I've always been dubious about. They don't exactly express fully what I want to say, but I can't find any others that do, either. I wish one could coin words, as I used to do long ago when I wrote letters to Father and just invented a word whenever I wanted one. But then, Father would have understood the words if he had ever seen the letters—while I am afraid the judges in the contest wouldn't.

"*Wild Grapes* should certainly win the prize. This isn't conceit or vanity or presumption. It's just *knowing.* If the prize were for mathematics Kath Darcy should win it. If it were for beauty Hazel Ellis would win it. If it were for all round proficiency, Perry Miller—

490

for elocution, Ilse—for drawing, Teddy. But since it is for poetry, E. B. Starr is the one!

"We are studying Tennyson and Keats in Senior Literature this year. I like Tennyson but sometimes he enrages me. He is beautiful—not *too* beautiful, as Keats is—the Perfect Artist. But he never lets us forget the artist—we are always conscious of it—he is never swept away by some splendid mountain torrent of feeling. Not he—he flows on serenely between well-ordered banks and carefully laid-out gardens. And no matter how much one loves a garden one doesn't want to be cooped up in it *all* the time—one likes an excursion now and then into the wilderness. At least Emily Byrd Starr does—to the sorrow of her relations.

"Keats *is* too full of beauty. When I read his poetry I feel stifled in roses and long for a breath of frosty air or the austerity of a chill mountain peak. But, oh, he has *some* lines—

"Magic casements opening on the foam

Of perilous seas, in faerylands forlorn—

"When I read them I always feel a sort of despair! *What* is the use of trying to do what *has* been done, once and for all?

"But I found some other lines that inspire me—I have written them on the index-page of my new Jimmy-book.

"He ne'er is crowned

With immortality who fears to follow

Where airy voices lead.

"Oh, it's true. We must follow our 'airy voices,' follow them through every discouragement and doubt and disbelief till they lead us to our City of Fulfilment, wherever it may be.

"I had four rejections in the mail to-day, raucously shrieking failure at me. Airy Voices grow faint in such a clamour. But I'll hear them again. And I *will* follow—I will not be discouraged. Years ago I wrote a 'vow'—I found it the other day in an old packet in my cupboard—that I

would 'climb the Alpine Path and write my name on the scroll of fame.'
"I'll keep on climbing!

****

"October 20, 19—

"I read my *Chronicles of an Old Garden* over the other night. I think
I can improve it considerably, now that Aunt Elizabeth has lifted the
ban. I wanted Mr. Carpenter to read it, but he said,

"'Lord, girl, I can't wade through all that stuff. My eyes are bad.
What is it—a book? Jade, it will be time ten years from now for you to
be writing books.'

"'I've got to practise,' I said indignantly.

"'Oh, practise—practise—but don't try out the results on me. I'm
too old—I really am, Jade. I don't mind a short—a very short story—
now and then—but let a poor old devil off the books.'

"I might ask Dean what he thinks of it. But Dean *does* laugh now
at my ambitions—very cautiously and kindly—but he *does* laugh. And
Teddy thinks everything I write perfect, so he's no use as a critic. I
wonder—I wonder if any publisher would accept *The Chronicles?* I'm
sure I've seen books of the kind that weren't *much* better.

****

"November 11, 19—

"This evening I spent "expurgating" a novel for Mr. Towers' use and
behoof. When Mr. Towers was away in August on his vacation the sub-
editor, Mr. Grady, began to run a serial in the *Times* called *A Bleeding
Heart.* Instead of getting A. P. A. stuff, as Mr. Towers always does,
Mr. Grady simply bought the reprint of a sensational and sentimental
English novel at the Shoppe and began publishing it. It was very long
and only about half of it has appeared. Mr. Towers saw that it would
run all winter in its present form. So he bade me take it and cut out 'all
unnecessary stuff.' I have followed instruction mercilessly—'cutting
out' most of the kisses and embraces, two-thirds of the love-making
and all the descriptions, with the happy results that I have reduced it
to about a quarter of its normal length; and all I can say is may heaven
have mercy on the soul of the compositor who has to set it in its present

mutilated condition.

"Summer and autumn have gone. It seems to me they go more quickly than they used to. The golden-rod has turned white in the corners of the Land of Uprightness and the frost lies like a silver scarf on the ground o' mornings. The evening winds that go 'piping down the valleys wild' are heart-broken searchers, seeking for things loved and lost, calling in vain on elf and fay. For the fairy folk, if they be not all fled afar to the southlands, must be curled up asleep in the hearts of the firs or among the roots of the ferns.

"And every night we have murky red sunsets flaming in smoky crimson across the harbour, with a star above them like a saved soul gazing with compassionate eyes into pits of torment where sinful spirits are being purged from the stains of earthly pilgrimage.

"Would I dare to show the above sentence to Mr. Carpenter? I would *not*. Therefore there is something fearfully wrong with it.

"I know what's wrong with it, now that I've written it in cold blood. It's 'fine writing.' And yet it's just what I felt when I stood on the hill beyond the Land of Uprightness to-night and looked across the harbour. And who cares what this old journal thinks?

****

"December 2, 19—

"The results of the prize poem competition were announced to-day. Evelyn Blake is the winner with a poem entitled *A Legend of Abegweit*.

"There isn't anything to say—so I say it.

"Besides, Aunt Ruth has said everything!

****

"December 15, 19—

"Evelyn's prize poem was printed in the *Times* this week with her photograph and a biographical sketch. The set of Parkman is on exhibition in the windows of the Booke Shoppe.

"*A Legend of Abegweit is* a fairly good poem. It is in ballad style, and rhythm and rhyme are correct—which could not be said of any other poem of Evelyn's I've ever seen.

"Evelyn Blake has said of everything of mine she ever saw in print

493

that she was sure I copied it from somewhere. I hate to imitate her—but I *know* that *she* never wrote that poem. It isn't any expression of *her* at all. She might as well have imitated Dr. Hardy's handwriting and claimed it as her own. Her mincing, copperplate script is as much like Dr. Hardy's black, forcible scrawl as that poem is like *her*.

"Besides, though *A Legend of Abegweit* is fairly good it is *not* as good as *Wild Grapes*.

"I am not going to say so to anyone but down it goes in this journal. Because it's *true*.

****

"December 20, 19—

"I showed *A Legend of Abegweit* and *Wild Grapes* to Mr. Carpenter. When he had read them both he said, 'Who were the judges?'

"I told him.

"'Give them my compliments and tell them they're asses.' he said.

"I feel comforted. I won't tell the judges—or anyone—that they're asses. But it soothes me to know they are.

"The strange thing is—Aunt Elizabeth asked to see *Wild Grapes* and when she had read it she said,

"'I am no judge of poetry, of course, but it seems to me that *yours* is of a *higher order*.'

****

"Jan. 4, 19—

"I spent the Christmas week at Uncle Oliver's. I didn't like it. It was too noisy. I would have liked it years ago but they never asked me then. I had to eat when I wasn't hungry—play parchesi when I didn't want to—talk when I wanted to be silent. I was never alone for one moment all the time I was there. Besides, Andrew is getting to be such a nuisance. And Aunt Addie was odiously kind and motherly. I just felt all the time like a cat who is held on a lap where it doesn't want to be and gently, firmly stroked. I had to sleep with Jen, who is my first cousin and just my age, and who thinks in her heart I'm not half good enough for Andrew but is going to try, with the blessing of God, to make the best of it. Jen is a nice, sensible girl and she and I are friendish. That is a word of my own coining. Jen and I are more than mere acquaintances but not really friendly. We will always be friendish and never more than friendish. We don't talk the same language.

"When I got home to dear New Moon I went up to my room and shut the door and revelled in solitude.

"School opened yesterday. To-day in the Booke Shoppe I had an internal laugh. Mrs. Rodney and Mrs. Elder were looking over some books and Mrs. Elder said,

"'That story in the *Times—A Bleeding Heart*—was the strangest one I ever read. It wandered on, chapter after chapter, for weeks, and never seemed to get anywhere, and then it just finished up in eight chapters *lickety-split*. I can't understand it.'

"I could have solved the mystery for her but I didn't."

IN THE OLD JOHN HOUSE

When *The Woman Who Spanked the King* was accepted and published by a New York magazine of some standing, quite a sensation was produced in Blair Water and Shrewsbury, especially when the incredible news was whispered from lip to lip that Emily had actually been paid forty dollars for it. For the first time her clan began to take her writing mania with some degree of seriousness and Aunt Ruth gave up, finally and for ever, all slurs over wasted time. The acceptance came at the psychological moment when the sands of Emily's faith were running rather low. All the fall and winter her stuff had been coming back to her, except from two magazines whose editors evidently thought that literature was its own reward and quite independent of degrading monetary considerations. At first she had always felt dreadfully when a poem or story over which she had agonized came back with one of those icy little rejection slips or a few words of faint praise—the "but" rejections, Emily called these, and hated them worse than the printed ones. Tears of disappointment *would* come. But after a time she got hardened to it and didn't mind—so much. She only gave the editorial slip the Murray look and said "I will succeed." And never at any time had she any *real* doubt that she would. Down, deep down, something told her that her time would come. So, though she flinched momentarily at each rejection, as from the flick of a whip, she sat down and—wrote another story.

Still, her inner voice had grown rather faint under so many discouragements. The acceptance of *The Woman Who Spanked the King* suddenly raised it into a joyous paean of certainty again. The cheque meant much, but the storming of that magazine much more. She felt that she was surely winning a foothold. Mr. Carpenter chuckled over it and told her it really was "absolutely good."

"The best in this story belongs to Mistress McIntyre," said Emily ruefully. "I can't call it mine."

"The setting is yours—and what you've added harmonizes perfectly with your foundation. And you didn't polish hers up too much—*that* shows the artist. Weren't you tempted to?"

"Yes. There were so many places I thought I *could* improve it a good deal."

"But you didn't try to—*that* makes it yours," said Mr. Carpenter— and left her to puzzle his meaning out for herself.

Emily spent thirty-five of her dollars so sensibly that even Aunt Ruth herself couldn't find fault with her budget. But with the remaining five she bought a set of Parkman. It was a much nicer set than the prize one—which the donor had really picked out of a mail-order list—and Emily felt much prouder of it than if it had been the prize. After all, it was better to earn things for yourself. Emily has those Parkmans yet— somewhat faded and frayed now, but dearer to her than all the other volumes in her library. For a few weeks she was very happy and uplifted. The Murrays were proud of her. Principal Hardy had congratulated her, a local elocutionist of some repute had read her story at a concert in Charlottetown. And, most wonderful of all, a far-away reader in Mexico had written her a letter telling her what pleasure *The Woman Who Spanked the King* had given him. Emily read and re-read that letter until she knew it off by heart, and slept with it under her pillow. No lover's missive was ever more tenderly treated.

Then the affair of the old John house came up like a thunder-cloud and darkened all her cerulean sky.

There was a concert and "pie social" at Derry Pond one Friday night and Ilse had been asked to recite. Dr. Burnley took Ilse and Emily and Perry and Teddy over in his big, double-seated sleigh, and they had a gay and merry eight miles' drive through the soft snow that was beginning to fall. When the concert was half over, Dr. Burnley was summoned out. There was sudden and serious illness in a Derry Pond household. The doctor went, telling Teddy that he must drive the party home. Dr. Burnley made no bones about it. They might have silly rules about chaperonage in Shrewsbury and Charlottetown, but in Blair Water and Derry Pond they did not obtain. Teddy and Perry were decent boys—Emily was a Murray—Ilse was no fool. The doctor would have summed them up thus tersely if he had thought about it at all.

When the concert was over they left for home. It was snowing very thickly now and the wind was rising rapidly, but the first three miles of the road were through sheltering woods and were not unpleasant. There was a wild, weird beauty in the snow-coated ranks of trees, standing in the pale light of the moon behind the storm-clouds. The sleigh-bells laughed at the shriek of the wind far overhead. Teddy managed the doctor's team without difficulty. Once or twice Emily had a strong suspicion that he was using only one arm to drive them. She wondered if he had noticed that evening that she wore her hair really "up" for the first time—in a soft ebon "Psyche knot" under her crimson hat. Emily thought again that there was something quite delightful about a storm.

But when they left the woods their troubles began. The storm swooped down on them in all its fury. The winter road went through the fields and wound and twisted and doubled in and out and around corners and spruce groves—a road that would "break a snake's back," as Perry said. The track was already almost obliterated with the drift and the horses plunged to their knees. They had not gone a mile before Perry whistled in dismay.

"We'll never make Blair Water to-night, Ted."

"We've got to make somewhere," shouted Ted. "We can't camp *here*. And there's no house till we get back to the summer road, past Shaw's hill. Duck under the robes, girls. You'd better get back with Ilse, Emily, and Perry will come here with me."

The transfer was effected, Emily no longer thinking storms quite so delightful. Perry and Teddy were both thoroughly alarmed. They knew the horses could not go much farther in that depth of snow—the summer road beyond Shaw's hill would be blocked with drift—and it was bitterly cold on those high, bleak hills between the valleys of Derry

Pond and Blair Water.

"If we can only get to Malcolm Shaw's we'll be all right," muttered Perry.

"We'll never get that far. Shaw's hill is filled in by this time to the fence-tops," said Teddy. "Here's the old John house. Do you suppose we could stay here?"

"Cold as a barn," said Perry. "The girls would freeze. We must try to make Malcolm's."

When the plunging horses reached the summer road, the boys saw at a glance that Shaw's hill was a hopeless proposition. All traces of track were obliterated by drifts that were over the fence-tops. Telephone-posts were blown down across the road and a huge, fallen tree blocked the gap where the field road ran out to it.

"Nothing to do but go back to the old John house," said Perry. "We can't go wandering over the fields in the teeth of this storm, looking for a way through to Malcolm's. We'd get stuck and freeze to death."

Teddy turned the horses. The snow was thicker than ever. Every minute the drift deepened. The track was entirely gone, and if the old John house had been very far away they could never have found it. Fortunately, it was near, and after one last wild flounder through the unbroken drift around it, during which the boys had to get out and scramble along on their own feet, they reached the comparative calm of the little cleared space in the young spruce woods, wherein stood the old John house.

The "old John house" had been old when, forty years before, John Shaw had moved into it with his young bride. It had been a lonely spot even then, far back from the road, and almost surrounded by spruce woods. John Shaw had lived there five years; then his wife died; he had sold the farm to his brother Malcolm and gone West. Malcolm farmed the land and kept the little barn in good repair, but the house had never been occupied since, save for a few weeks in winter when Malcolm's boys camped there while they "got out" their firewood. It was not even locked. Tramps and burglars were unknown in Derry Pond. Our castaways found easy entrance through the door of the tumbledown porch and drew a breath of relief to find themselves out of the shrieking wind and driving snow.

"We won't freeze anyhow," said Perry. "Ted and I'll have to see if we can get the horses in the barn and then we'll come back and see if we can't make ourselves comfortable. I've got matches and I've never been stumped yet."

Perry met no great difficulties in making good his boast. His lighted match revealed a couple of half-burned candles in squat tin candlesticks, a cracked and rusty but still quite serviceable old Waterloo stove, three chairs, a bench, a sofa and a table.

"What's the matter with this?" demanded Perry.

"They'll be awfully worried about us at home, that's all," said Emily, shaking the snow off her wraps.

"Worry won't kill them in one night," said Perry. "We'll get home to-morrow somehow."

"Meanwhile, this is an adventure," laughed Emily. "Let's get all the fun out of it we can."

Ilse said nothing—which was very odd in Ilse. Emily, looking at her, saw that she was very pale and recalled that she had been unusually quiet ever since they had left the hall.

"Aren't you feeling all right, Ilse?" she asked anxiously.

"I'm feeling all wrong," said Ilse, with a ghastly smile. "I'm—I'm sick as a dog," she added, with more force than elegance.

"Oh, Ilse—"

"Don't hit the ceiling," said Ilse impatiently. "I'm not beginning pneumonia or appendicitis. I'm just plain *sick*. That pie I had at the hall was too rich, I suppose. It's turned my little tummy upside down. O—w—w."

"Lie down on the sofa," urged Emily. "Perhaps you'll feel better then."

Ilse, shuddering and abject, cast herself down. A "sick stomach" is not a romantic ailment or a very deadly one, but it certainly takes the ginger out of its victim for the time being.

The boys, finding a box full of wood behind the stove, soon had a roaring fire. Perry took one of the candles and explored the little house. In a small room opening off the kitchen was an old-fashioned wooden bedstead with a rope mattress. The other room—it had been Almira Shaw's parlour in olden days—was half filled with oat-straw. Upstairs there was nothing but emptiness and dust. But in the little pantry Perry made some finds.

"There's a can of pork and beans here," he announced, "and a tin box half full of crackers. I see our breakfast. I s'pose the Shaw boys left

EMILY CLIMBS

them here. And what's this?"

Perry brought out a small bottle, uncorked and sniffed it solemnly.

"Whisky, as I'm a living sinner. Not much, but enough. Here's your medicine, Ilse. You take it in some hot water and it'll settle your stomach in a jiffy."

"I hate the taste of whisky," moaned Ilse. "Father never uses it—he doesn't believe in it."

"Aunt Tom does," said Perry, as if that settled the matter. "It's a sure cure. Try it and see."

"But there isn't any water," said Ilse.

"You'll have to take it straight, then. There's only about two tablespoons in the bottle. Try it. It won't kill you if it doesn't cure you."

Poor Ilse was really feeling so abjectly wretched that she would have taken anything, short of poison, if she thought there was any chance of its helping her. She crawled off the sofa, sat down on a chair before the fire and swallowed the dose. It was good, strong whisky—Malcolm Shaw could have told you that. And I think there was really more than two tablespoonfuls in the bottle, though Perry always insisted that there wasn't. Ilse sat huddled in her chair for a few minutes longer, then she got up and put her hand uncertainly on Emily's shoulder.

"Do you feel worse?" asked Emily, anxiously.

"I'm—I'm drunk," said Ilse. "Help me back to the sofa, for mercy's sake. My legs are going to double up under me. Who was the Scotchman up at Malvern who said he never got drunk but the whisky always settled in his knees? But mine's in the head too. It's spinning round."

Perry and Teddy both sprang to help her and between them a very wobbly Ilse made safe port on the sofa again.

"Is there anything we can do?" implored Emily.

"Too much has already been done," said Ilse with preternatural solemnity. She shut her eyes and not another word would she say in response to any entreaty. Finally it was deemed best to let her alone.

"She'll sleep it off, and, anyway, I guess it'll settle her stomach," said Perry.

Emily could not take it so philosophically. Not until Ilse's quiet breathing half an hour later proved that she was really asleep could Emily begin to taste the flavour of their "adventure." The wind threshed about the old house and rattled the windows as if in a fury over their escape from it. It was very pleasant to sit before the stove and listen to

500

the wild melody of defeated storm—very pleasant to think about the vanished life of this old dead house, in the years when it had been full of love and laughter—very pleasant to talk of cabbages and kings with Perry and Teddy, in the faint glow of candlelight—very pleasant to sit in occasional silences, staring into the firelight, which flickered alluringly over Emily's milk-white brow and haunting, shadowy eyes. Once Emily, glancing up suddenly, found Teddy looking at her strangely. For just a moment their eyes met and locked—only a moment—yet Emily was never really to belong to herself again. She wondered dazedly what had happened. Whence came that wave of unimaginable sweetness that seemed to engulf her, body and spirit? She trembled—she was afraid. It seemed to open such dizzying possibilities of change. The only clear idea that emerged from her confusion of thought was that she wanted to sit with Teddy before a fire like this every night of their lives—and then a fig for the storms! She dared not look at Teddy again, but she thrilled with a delicious sense of his nearness; she was acutely conscious of his tall, boyish straightness, his glossy black hair, his luminous dark-blue eyes. She had always known she liked Teddy better than any other male creature in her ken—but *this* was something apart from liking altogether—this sense of belonging to him that had come in that significant exchange of glances. All at once she seemed to know why she had always snubbed any of the High School boys who wanted to be her beau.

The delight of the spell that had been suddenly laid on her was so intolerable that she must break it. She sprang up and went over to the window. The little hissing whisper of snow against the blue-white frost crystals on the pane seemed softly to scorn her bewilderment. The three big haystacks, thatched with snow, dimly visible at the corner of the barn, seemed to be shaking their shoulders with laughter over her predicament. The fire in the stove reflected out in the clearing seemed like a mocking goblin bonfire under the firs. Beyond it, through the woods, were unfathomable spaces of white storm. For a moment Emily wished she were out in them—there would be freedom there from this fetter of terrible delight that had so suddenly and inexplicably made her a prisoner—her, who hated bonds.

"Am I falling in love with Teddy?" she thought. "I won't—I won't."

Perry, quite unconscious of all that had happened in the wink of an eye to Teddy and Emily, yawned and stretched.

"Guess we'd better hit the hay—the candles are about done. I guess that straw will make a real good bed for us, Ted. Let's carry enough out and pile it on the bedstead in there to make a comfortable roost for the girls. With one of the fur rugs over it, it won't be so bad. We ought to have some high old dreams to-night—Ilse especially. Wonder if she's sober yet?"

"I've a pocket full of dreams to sell," said Teddy, whimsically, with a new, unaccountable gaiety of voice and manner. "What d'ye lack? What d'ye lack? A dream of success—a dream of adventure—a dream of the sea—a dream of the woodland—any kind of a dream you want at reasonable prices, including one or two unique little nightmares. What will you give me for a dream?"

Emily turned around—stared at him for a moment—then forgot thrills and pells and everything else in a wild longing for a Jimmy-book. As if his question, "What will you give me for a dream?" had been a magic formula opening some sealed chamber in her brain, she saw unrolling before her a dazzling idea for a story—complete even to the title—*A Seller of Dreams*. For the rest of that night Emily thought of nothing else.

The boys went off to their straw couch, and Emily, after deciding to leave Ilse, who seemed comfortable, on the sofa as long as she slept, lay down on the bed in the small room. But not to sleep. She had never felt less like sleeping. She did not want to sleep. She had forgotten that she had been falling in love with Teddy—she had forgotten everything but her wonderful idea; chapter by chapter, page by page, it unrolled itself before her in the darkness. Her characters lived and laughed and talked and did and enjoyed and suffered—she saw them on the background of the storm. Her cheeks burned, her heart beat, she tingled from head to foot with the keen rapture of creation—a joy that sprang fountain-like from the depths of being and seemed independent of all earthly things. Ilse had got drunk on Malcolm Shaw's forgotten Scotch whisky, but Emily was intoxicated with immortal wine.

THICKER THAN WATER

Emily did not sleep until nearly morning. The storm had ceased and the landscape around the old John house had a spectral look in the light of the sinking moon when she finally drifted into slumber, with a delightful sense of accomplishment—for she had finished thinking out her story. Nothing remained now except to jot its outlines down in her Jimmy-book. She would not feel safe until she had them in black and white. She would not try to write it yet—oh, not for years. She must wait until time and experience had made of her pen an instrument capable of doing justice to her conception—for it is one thing to pursue an idea through an ecstatic night and quite another to get it down on paper in a manner that will reproduce a tenth of its original charm and significance.

Emily was wakened by Ilse, who was sitting on the side of her bed, looking rather pale and seedy, but with amber eyes full of unconquerable laughter.

"Well, I've slept off my debauch, Emily Starr. And my tummy's all right this morning. Malcolm's whisky *did* settle it—though I think the remedy is worse than the disease. I suppose you wondered why I wouldn't talk last night."

"I thought you were too drunk to talk," said Emily candidly.

Ilse giggled.

"I was too drunk *not* to talk. When I got to that sofa, Emily, my giddiness passed off and I *wanted* to talk—oh, golly, but I wanted to talk! And I wanted to say the silliest things and tell everything I ever knew or thought. I'd just enough sense left to know I mustn't say those things or I'd make a fool of myself for ever—and I felt that if I said *one* word it would be like taking a cork out of a bottle—*everything* would gurgle out. So I just buttoned my mouth up and wouldn't say the one word. It gives me a chill to think of the things I *could* have said—and before Perry. You'll never catch your little Ilse going on a spree again. I'm a reformed character from this day forth."

"What I can't understand," said Emily, "is how such a small dose of *anything* could have turned your head like that."

"Oh, well, you know Mother was a Mitchell. It's a notorious fact that the Mitchells can't take a teaspoonful of booze without toppling. It's one of their family kinks. Well, rise up, my love, my fair one. The boys are getting a fire on and Perry says we can dope up a fair meal from the pork and beans and crackers. I'm hungry enough to eat the cans."

It was while Emily was rummaging in the pantry in search of some salt that she made a great discovery. Far back on the top shelf was a pile of dusty old books—dating back probably to the days of John and Almira Shaw—old, mildewed diaries, almanacs, account books. Emily knocked the pile down and when she was picking it up discovered that one of the books was an old scrap-book. A loose leaf had fallen out of it. As Emily replaced it, her eyes fell on the title of a poem pasted on it. She caught it up, her breath coming quickly. *A Legend of Abegweit*—the poem with which Evelyn had won the prize! Here it was in this old, yellowed scrap-book of twenty years' vintage—word for word, except that Evelyn had cut out two verses to shorten it to the required length.

"And the two best verses in it," thought Emily, contemptuously. "How like Evelyn! She has simply no literary judgment."

Emily replaced the books on the shelf, but she slipped the loose leaf into her pocket and ate her share of breakfast very absently. By this time men were on the roads breaking out the tracks. Perry and Teddy found a shovel in the barn and soon had a way opened to the road. They got home finally, after a slow but uneventful drive, to find the New Moon folks rather anxious as to their fate and mildly horrified to learn that they had had to spend the night in the old John house.

"You might have caught your deaths of cold," said Elizabeth, severely.

"Well, it was Hobson's choice. It was that or freeze to death in the drifts," said Emily, and nothing more was said about the matter. Since they had got home safe and nobody had caught cold, what more *was* there to say? That was the New Moon way of looking at it.

The Shrewsbury way was somewhat different. But the Shrewsbury way did not become apparent immediately. The whole story was over Shrewsbury by Monday night—Ilse told it in school and described her drunken orgy with great spirit and vivacity, amid shrieks of laughter from her classmates. Emily, who had called, for the first time, on

Evelyn Blake that evening, found Evelyn looking quite well pleased over something.

"Can't you stop Ilse from telling that story, my dear?"

"What story?"

"Why, about getting drunk last Friday night—the night you and she spent with Teddy Kent and Perry Miller in that old house up at Derry Pond," said Evelyn smoothly.

Emily suddenly flushed. There was *something* in Evelyn's tone— the innocent fact seemed all at once to take on shades of a sinister significance. Was Evelyn being deliberately insolent?

"I don't know why she shouldn't tell the story," said Emily, coldly. "It was a good joke on her."

"But you know how people will talk," said Evelyn, gently. "It's all rather—unfortunate. Of course, you couldn't help being caught in the storm—I suppose—but Ilse will only make matters worse. She is so indiscreet—haven't you *any* influence over her, Emily?"

"I didn't come here to discuss that," said Emily, bluntly. "I came to show you something I found in the old John house."

She held out the leaf of the scrap-book. Evelyn looked at it blankly for a moment. Then her face turned a curious mottled purple. She made an involuntary movement as if to snatch the paper, but Emily quickly drew it back. Their eyes met. In that moment Emily felt that the score between them was at last even.

She waited for Evelyn to speak. After a moment Evelyn did speak— sullenly:

"Well, what are you going to do about it?"

"I haven't decided yet," said Emily.

Evelyn's long, brown, treacherous eyes swept up to Emily's face with a crafty, seeking expression.

"I suppose you mean to take it to Dr. Hardy and disgrace me before the school?"

"Well, you deserve it, don't you?" said Emily, judicially.

"I—I wanted to win that prize because Father promised me a trip to Vancouver next summer if I won it," muttered Evelyn, suddenly crumpling. "I—I was crazy to go. Oh, *don't* betray me, Emily—Father will be furious. I—I'll give you the Parkman set—I'll do anything— only don't—"

Evelyn began to cry. Emily didn't like the sight.

"I don't want your Parkman," she said, contemptuously, "But there is one thing you must do. You will confess to Aunt Ruth that it was you who drew that moustache on my face the day of the English exam and not Ilse."

Evelyn wiped away her tears and swallowed something.

"That was only a joke," she sobbed.

"It was no joke to lie about it," said Emily, sternly.

"You're so—so—*blunt*." Evelyn looked for a dry spot on her handkerchief and found one. "It was all a joke. I just ran back from the Shoppe to do it. I thought, of course, you'd look in the glass when you got up. I d-didn't suppose you'd g-go to class like that. And I didn't know your Aunt took it so seriously. Of course—I'll tell her—if you'll—if you'll—"

"Write it out and sign it," said Emily, remorselessly.

Evelyn wrote it out and signed it.

"You'll give me—*that,*" she pleaded, with an entreating gesture towards the scrap-book leaf.

"Oh, no, I'll keep this," said Emily.

"And what assurance have I that you won't tell—some day—after all?" sniffed Evelyn.

"You have the word of a Starr," said Emily, loftily.

She went out with a smile. She had finally conquered in the long duel. And she held in her hand what would finally clear Ilse in Aunt Ruth's eyes.

Aunt Ruth sniffed a good deal over Evelyn's note and was inclined to ask questions as to how it had been extorted. But not getting much satisfaction out of Emily on this score and knowing that Allan Burnley had been sore at her ever since her banishment of his daughter, she secretly welcomed an excuse to recall it.

"Very well, then. I told you Ilse could come here when you could prove to my satisfaction that she had not played that trick on you. You have proved it, and I keep my word. I am a just woman," concluded Aunt Ruth—who was, perhaps, the most unjust woman on the earth at that time.

So far, well. But if Evelyn wanted revenge she tasted it to the full in the next three weeks, without raising a finger or wagging a tongue to secure it. All Shrewsbury burned with gossip about the night of the storm—insinuations, distortions, wholesale fabrications. Emily was so snubbed at Janet Thompson's afternoon tea that she went home white with humiliation. Ilse was furious.

"I wouldn't mind if I *had* been rip-roaring drunk and had the fun of it," she vowed with a stamp of her foot. "But I wasn't drunk enough to be happy—only just drunk enough to be silly. There are moments, Emily, when I feel that I could have a gorgeous time if I were a cat and these old Shrewsbury dames were mice. But let's keep our smiles pinned on. I really don't care a snap for them. This will soon die out. We'll fight."

"You can't fight insinuations," said Emily, bitterly.

Ilse did not care—but Emily cared horribly. The Murray pride smarted unbearably. And it smarted worse and worse as time went on. A sneer at the night of the storm was published in a rag of a paper that was printed in a town on the mainland and made up of "spicy" notes sent to it from all over the Maritimes. Nobody ever confessed to reading it, but almost everybody knew everything that was in it— except Aunt Ruth, who wouldn't have handled the sheet with the tongs. No names were mentioned, but every one knew who was referred to, and the venomous innuendo of the thing was unmistakable. Emily thought she would die of shame. And the worst sting was that it was so vulgar and ugly—and had made that beautiful night of laughter and revelation and rapturous creation in the old John house vulgar and ugly. She had thought it would always be one of her most beautiful memories. And now this!

Teddy and Perry saw red and wanted to kill somebody, but whom could they kill? As Emily told them, anything they said or did would only make the matter worse. It was bad enough after the publication of that paragraph. Emily was not invited to Florence Blake's dance the next week—the great social event of the winter. She was left out of Hattie Denoon's skating party. Several of the Shrewsbury matrons did not see her when they met her on the streets. Others set her a thousand miles away by bland, icy politeness. Some young men about town grew oddly familiar in look and manner. One of them, with whom she was totally unacquainted, spoke to her one evening in the Post Office. Emily turned and looked at him. Crushed, humiliated as she was, she was still Archibald Murray's granddaughter. The wretched youth was three blocks away from the Post Office before he came to himself and knew where he was. To this day he has not forgotten how Emily Byrd

Starr's eyes looked when she was angry.

But even the Murray look, while it might demolish a concrete offender, could not scotch scandalous stories. Everybody, she felt morbidly, believed them. It was reported to her that Miss Percy of the library said she had always distrusted Emily Starr's smile—she had always felt sure it was deliberately provocative and alluring. Emily felt that she, like poor King Henry, would never smile again. People remembered that old Nancy Priest had been a wild thing seventy years ago—and hadn't there been some scandal about Mrs. Dutton herself in her girlhood? What's bred in the bone, you understand. Her mother had eloped, hadn't she? And Ilse's mother? Of course, she had been killed by falling into the old Lee well, but who knew what she would have done if she hadn't? Then there was that old story of bathing on Blair Water sandshore, *au naturel*. In short, you didn't see ankles like Emily's on proper girls. They simply didn't have them.

Even harmless, unnecessary Andrew had ceased to call on Friday nights. There *was* a sting in this. Emily thought Andrew a bore and dreaded his Friday nights. She had always meant to send him packing as soon as he gave her an opportunity. But for Andrew to go packing of his own accord had a very different flavour, mark you. Emily clenched her hands when she thought of it.

A bitter report came to her ears that Principal Hardy had said she ought to resign from the presidency of the Senior Class. Emily threw up her head. Resign? Confess defeat and admit guilt? Not she!

"I could knock that man's block off," said Ilse. "Emily Starr, don't let yourself worry over this. What does it matter what a lot of doddering old donkeys think? I hereby devote them to the infernal gods. They'll have their maws full of something else in a month and they'll forget this."

"*I*'ll never forget it," said Emily, passionately. "To my dying day I'll remember the humiliation of these weeks. And now—Ilse, Mrs. Tolliver has written asking me to give up my stall at the St. John's bazaar."

"Emily Starr—she hasn't!"

"She has. Oh, of course, she cloaks it under an excuse that she'd like a stall for her cousin from New York, who is visiting her—but *I* understand. And it's 'Dear Miss Starr'—look you—when it was 'Dearest Emily' a few weeks ago. Everybody in St. John's will know why I've been asked to step out. And she almost went on her knees to

508

Aunt Ruth to let me take the stall. Aunt Ruth didn't want to let me."

"What will your Aunt Ruth say about this?"

"Oh, that's the worst of it, Ilse. She'll have to know now. She's never heard a word of this since she's been laid up with her sciatica. I've lived in dread of her finding out—for I know it will be hideous when she does. She's getting about now, so of course she'd soon hear it, anyway. And I haven't the spirit to stand up to her, Ilse. Oh, it all seems like a nightmare."

"They've got such mean, narrow, malicious, beastly little minds in this town," said Ilse—and was straightway comforted. But Emily could not ease her tortured spirit by a choice assortment of adjectives. Neither could she write out her misery and so rid herself of it. There were no more jottings in her Jimmy-book, no further entries in her journal, no new stories or poems. The flash never came now—never would come again. There would never again be wonderful little secret raptures of insight and creation which no one could share. Life had grown thin and poor, tarnished and unlovely. There was no beauty in anything—not even in the golden-white March solitudes of New Moon, when she went home for the week-end. She had longed to go home, where no one believed ill of her. No one at New Moon had heard anything of what was being whispered in Shrewsbury. But there very ignorance tortured Emily. Soon they *would* know; they would be hurt and grieved over the fact that a Murray, even an innocent Murray, had become a target for scandal. And who knew how they would regard Ilse's mishap with Malcolm's Scotch? Emily felt it almost a relief to go back to Shrewsbury.

She imagined slurs in everything Principal Hardy said—covert insults in every remark or look of her schoolmates. Only Evelyn Blake posed as friend and defender, and this was the most unkindest cut of all. Whether alarm or malice was beyond Evelyn's pose, Emily did not know—but she did know that Evelyn's parade of friendship and loyalty and staunch belief in the face of overwhelming evidence, was something that seemed to smirch her more than all the gossip could. Evelyn went about assuring every one that *she* wouldn't believe one word against "poor dear Emily." Poor dear Emily could have cheerfully watched her drown—or thought she could.

Meanwhile, Aunt Ruth, who had been confined to her house for several weeks with sciatica and had been so crusty with it that neither friends nor enemies had dared to hint anything to her of the gossip concerning her niece, was beginning to take notice. Her sciatica had departed and left her faculties free to concentrate on other things. She recalled that Emily's appetite had been poor for days and Aunt Ruth suspected that she had not been sleeping. The moment this suspicion occurred to Aunt Ruth she took action. Secret worries were not to be tolerated in her house.

"Emily, I want to know what is the matter with you," she demanded, one Saturday afternoon when Emily pale and listless, with purple smudges under her eyes, had eaten next to nothing for dinner.

A little colour came into Emily's face. The hour she had dreaded so was upon her. Aunt Ruth must be told all. And Emily felt miserably that she had neither the courage to endure the resultant heckling nor the spirit to hold her own against Aunt Ruth's whys and wherefores. She knew so well how it would all be: horror over the John house episode— as if anybody could have helped it: annoyance over the gossip—as if Emily were responsible for it: several assurances that she had always expected something like this: and then intolerable weeks of reminders and slurs. Emily felt a sort of mental nausea at the whole prospect. For a minute she could not speak.

"What have you been doing?" persisted Aunt Ruth.

Emily set her teeth. It was unendurable, but it must be endured. The story had to be told—the only thing to do was to get it told as soon as possible.

"I haven't done anything wrong, Aunt Ruth. I've just done something that has been misunderstood."

Aunt Ruth sniffed. But she listened without interruption to Emily's story. Emily told it as briefly as possible, feeling as if she were a criminal in the witness box with Aunt Ruth as judge, jury and prosecuting attorney all in one. When she had finished she sat in silence waiting for some characteristic Aunt Ruthian comment.

"And what are they making all the fuss about?" said Aunt Ruth.

Emily didn't know exactly what to say. She stared at Aunt Ruth.

"They—they're thinking—and saying all sorts of horrible things," she faltered. "You see—down here in sheltered Shrewsbury they didn't realize what a storm it was. And then, of course, every one who repeated the story coloured it a little—we were *all* drunk by the time it filtered through Shrewsbury."

"What exasperates me," said Aunt Ruth, "is to think you told about it in Shrewsbury at all. Why on earth didn't you keep it all quiet?"

"That would have been *sly*." Emily's demon suddenly prompted her to say this. Now that the story was out she felt a rebound of spirit that was almost laughter.

"Sly! It would have been common sense," snorted Aunt Ruth. "But, of course, Ilse couldn't hold her tongue. I've often told you, Emily, that a fool friend is ten times more dangerous than an enemy. But what are you killing yourself worrying for? *Your* conscience is clear. This gossip will soon die out."

"Principal Hardy says I ought to resign from the presidency of the class," said Emily.

"Jim Hardy! Why, his Father was a hired boy to my Grandfather for years," said Aunt Ruth in tones of ineffable contempt. "Does Jim Hardy imagine that *my niece* would behave improperly?"

Emily felt herself all at sea. She thought she really must be dreaming. Was this incredible woman Aunt Ruth? It couldn't be Aunt Ruth. Emily was up against one of the contradictions of human nature. She was learning that you may fight with your kin—disapprove of them—even hate them, but that there is a bond between you for all that. Somehow, your very nerves and sinews are twisted with theirs. Blood is always thicker than water. Let an outsider attack—that's all. Aunt Ruth had at least one of the Murray virtues—loyalty to clan.

"Don't worry over Jim Hardy," said Aunt Ruth. "I'll soon settle him. I'll teach people to keep their tongues off the Murrays."

"But Mrs. Tolliver has asked me to let her cousin take my stall in the bazaar," said Emily. "You know what that means."

"I know that Polly Tolliver is an upstart and a fool," retorted Aunt Ruth. "Ever since Nat Tolliver married his stenographer, St. John's Church hasn't been the same place. Ten years ago she was a barefooted girl running round the back streets of Charlottetown. The cats themselves wouldn't have brought her in. Now she puts on the airs of a queen and tries to run the church. I'll soon clip *her* claws. She was pretty thankful a few weeks ago to have a Murray in her stall. It was a rise in the world for *her*. Polly Tolliver, forsooth. What is this world coming to?"

Aunt Ruth sailed upstairs, leaving a dazed Emily looking at vanishing bogies. Aunt Ruth came down again, ready for the warpath.

She had taken out her crimps, put on her best bonnet, her best black silk, and her new sealskin coat. Thus arrayed she skimmed uptown to the Tolliver residence on the hill. She remained there half an hour closeted with Mrs. Nat Tolliver. Aunt Ruth was a short, fat, little woman, looking very dowdy and old-fashioned in spite of new bonnet and sealskin coat. Mrs. Nat was the last word in fashion and elegance, with her Paris gown, her lorgnette and her beautifully marcelled hair—marcels were just coming in then and Mrs. Nat's was the first in Shrewsbury. But the victory of the encounter did not perch on Mrs. Tolliver's standard. Nobody knows just what was said at that notable interview. Certainly Mrs. Tolliver never told. But when Aunt Ruth left the big house Mrs. Tolliver was crushing her Paris gown and her marcel waves among the cushions of her davenport while she wept tears of rage and humiliation; and Aunt Ruth carried a note in her muff to Mrs. Tolliver's "Dear Emily," saying that her cousin was not going to take part in the bazaar and would "Dear Emily" be so kind as to take the stall as at first planned. Dr. Hardy was next interviewed, and again Aunt Ruth went, saw, conquered. The maid in the Hardy household heard and reported one sentence of the confab, though nobody ever believed that Aunt Ruth really said to stately, spectacled Dr. Hardy,

"I know you're a fool, Jim Hardy, but for heaven's sake pretend you're not for five minutes!"

No, the thing was impossible. Of course, the maid invented it.

"You won't have much more trouble, Emily," said Aunt Ruth on her return home. "Polly and Jim have got their craws full. When people see you at the bazaar they'll soon realise what way the wind blows and trim their sails accordingly. I've a few things to say to some other folks when opportunity offers. Matters have come to a pretty pass if decent boys and girls can't escape freezing to death without being slandered for it. Don't you give this thing another thought, Emily. Remember, you've got a family behind you."

Emily went to her glass when Aunt Ruth had gone downstairs. She tilted it at the proper angle and smiled at Emily-in-the-Glass—smiled slowly, provocatively, alluringly.

"I wonder where I put my Jimmy-book," thought Emily. "I must add a few more touches to my sketch of Aunt Ruth."

"LOVE ME, LOVE MY DOG"

When Shrewsbury people discovered that Mrs. Dutton was backing her niece, the flame of gossip that had swept over the town died down in an incredibly short time. Mrs. Dutton gave more to the various funds of St. John's Church than any other member—it was a Murray tradition to support your church becomingly. Mrs. Dutton had lent money to half the business men in town—she held Nat Tolliver's note for an amount that kept him wakeful o' nights. Mrs. Dutton had a disconcerting knowledge of family skeletons—to which she had no delicacy in referring. Therefore, Mrs. Dutton was a person to be kept in good humour, and if people had made the mistake of supposing that because she was very strict with her niece, it was safe to snub that niece, why, the sooner they corrected that mistake the better for all concerned.

Emily sold baby jackets and blankets and bootees and bonnets in Mrs. Tolliver's stall at the big bazaar and wheedled elderly gentlemen into buying them, with her now famous smile; everybody was nice to her and she was happy again, though the experience had left a scar. Shrewsbury folks in after years said that Emily Starr had never really forgiven them for having talked about her—and added that the Murrays never did forgive, you know. But forgiveness did not enter into the matter. Emily had suffered so horribly that henceforth the sight of any one who had been connected with her suffering was hateful to her. When Mrs. Tolliver asked her, a week later, to pour tea at the reception she was giving her cousin, Emily declined politely, without troubling herself to give any excuse. And something in the tilt of her chin, or in the level glance of her eyes, made Mrs. Tolliver feel to her marrow that she was still Polly Riordan of Riordan Alley, and would never be anybody else in the sight of a Murray of New Moon.

But Andrew was welcomed quite sweetly when he somewhat sheepishly called the following Friday night. It may be that he felt a little doubtful of his reception, in spite of the fact that he was sealed

513

of the tribe. But Emily was markedly gracious to him. Perhaps she had her own reasons for it. Again, I call attention to the fact that I am Emily's biographer, not her apologist. If she took a way to get even with Andrew which I may not approve, what can I do but deplore it? For my own satisfaction, however, I may remark in passing that I do think Emily went too far when she told Andrew—after his report of some compliments his manager had paid him—that he was certainly a wonder. I cannot even excuse her by saying that she spoke in sarcastic tones. She did not: she said it most sweetly with an upward glance followed by a downward one that made even Andrew's well-regulated heart skip a beat. Oh, Emily, Emily!

Things went well with Emily that Spring. She had several acceptances and cheques, and was beginning to plume herself on being quite a literary person. Her clan began to take her scribbling mania somewhat seriously. Cheques were unanswerable things.

"Emily has made fifty dollars by her pen since New Year's," Aunt Ruth told Mrs. Drury. "I begin to think the child has an easy way of making a living."

An easy way! Emily, overhearing this as she went through the hall, smiled and sighed. What did Aunt Ruth—what did any one know of the disappointments and failures of the climbers on Alpine Paths? What did she know of the despairs and agonies of one who *sees* but cannot *reach*. What did she know of the bitterness of one who conceives a wonderful tale and writes it down, only to find a flat and flavourless manuscript as a reward for all her toil? What did she know of barred doors and impregnable editorial sanctums? Of brutal rejection slips and the awfulness of faint praise? Of hopes deferred and hours of sickening doubt and self-distrust?

Aunt Ruth knew of none of these things, but she took to having fits of indignation when Emily's manuscripts were returned.

"Impudence *I* call it," she said. "Don't send that editor another line. Remember, you're a Murray!"

"I'm afraid he doesn't know that," said Emily, gravely.

"Then why don't you tell him?" said Aunt Ruth.

Shrewsbury had a mild sensation in May when Janet Royal came home from New York with her wonderful dresses, her brilliant reputation, and her chow dog. Janet was a Shrewsbury girl, but she had never been home since she had "gone to the States" twenty years ago. She was clever and ambitious and she had succeeded. She was the literary editor of a big metropolitan woman's magazine and one of the readers for a noted publishing house. Emily held her breath when she heard of Miss Royal's arrival. Oh, if she could only see her—have a talk with her—ask her about a hundred things she wanted to know! When Mr. Towers told her in an off-hand manner to go and interview Miss Royal and write it up for the *Times,* Emily trembled between terror and delight. Here was her excuse. But *could* she—had she assurance enough? Wouldn't Miss Royal think her unbearably presumptuous? How could *she* ask Miss Royal questions about her career and her opinion of the United States' foreign policy and reciprocity? She could never have the courage.

"We both worship at the same altar—but she is high priestess and I am only the humblest acolyte," wrote Emily in her journal.

Then she indited a very worshipful letter to Miss Royal, and rewrote it a dozen times, asking permission to interview her. After she had mailed it she could not sleep all night because it occurred to her that she should have signed herself "yours truly" instead of "yours sincerely." "Yours sincerely" smacked of an acquaintanceship that did not exist. Miss Royal would surely think her presuming.

But Miss Royal sent back a charming letter—Emily has it to this day.

"Ashburn, Monday.

"DEAR MISS STARR:—

"Of course you may come and see me and I'll tell you everything you want to know for Jimmy Towers (God rest his soul, an' wasn't he my first beau!) and everything you want to know for yourself. I think half my reason for coming back to P. E. I. this spring was because I wanted to see the writer of *The Woman Who Spanked the King.* I read it last winter when it came out in *Roche's* and I thought it charming. Come and tell me all about yourself and your ambitions. You *are* ambitious, aren't you? And I think you're going to be able to realize your ambitions, too, and I want to help you if I can. You've got something I never had— real creative ability—but I've heaps of experience and what I've learned from it is yours for the asking. I *can* help you to avoid some snares and pitfalls, and I'm not without a bit of 'pull' in certain quarters. Come to Ashburn next Friday afternoon when 'school's out' and we'll have a heart-to-heart pow-wow.

"Yours fraternally,

"JANET ROYAL."

Emily thrilled to the ends of her toes when she read this letter. "Yours fraternally"—oh, heavenly! She knelt at her window and looked out with enraptured eyes into the slender firs of the Land of Uprightness and the dewy young clover-fields beyond. Oh, was it possible that some day she would be a brilliant, successful woman like Miss Royal? That letter made it seem possible—made every wonderful dream seem possible. And on Friday—four more days—she was going to see and talk intimately with her high priestess.

Mrs. Angela Royal, who called to see Aunt Ruth that evening, didn't exactly seem to think Janet Royal a high priestess or a wonder. But then, of course, a prophetess is apt to have scant honour in her own country and Mrs. Royal had brought Janet up.

"I don't say but what she's got on well," she confided to Aunt Ruth. "She gets a big salary. But she's an old maid for all that. And as odd in some ways as Dick's hat-band."

Emily, studying Latin in the bay window, went on fire with indignation. This was nothing short of *lese-majeste.*

"She is very fine looking yet," said Aunt Ruth. "Janet was always a nice girl."

"Oh, yes, she's nice enough. But I was always afraid she was too clever to get married, and I was right. And she's full of foreign notions. She's never on time for her meals—and it really makes me sick the fuss she makes over that dog of hers—Chu-Chin, she calls it. *He* rules the house. He does *exactly* as he likes and nobody dare say a word. My poor cat can't call her soul her own. Janet is so touchy about him. When I complained about him sleeping on the plush davenport she was so vexed she wouldn't speak for a day. That's a thing I don't like about Janet. She gets so high and mighty when she's offended. And she gets offended at things nobody else would dream of minding. And when she's offended with one she's offended with everybody. I hope nothing will upset her before you come on Friday, Emily. If she's out of humour she'll visit it on you. But I will say for her that she doesn't often get vexed and there's nothing mean or grudging about her. She'd work her fingers to the bone to serve a friend."

When Aunt Ruth had gone out to interview the grocer's boy, Mrs. Royal added hurriedly,

"She's greatly interested in you, Emily. She's always fond of having pretty, fresh girls about her—says it keeps her feeling young. She thinks your work shows real talent. If she takes a fancy to you it would be a great thing for you. But, for pity's sake, keep on good terms with that chow! If you offend *him,* Janet wouldn't have anything to do with you supposing you were Shakespeare himself."

Emily awoke Friday morning with the conviction that this was to be one of the crucial days of her life—a day of dazzling possibilities. She had had a terrible dream of sitting spellbound before Miss Royal, unable to utter one word except "Chu-Chin," which she repeated parrot-like whenever Miss Royal asked her a question.

It poured rain all the forenoon, much to her dismay, but at noon it cleared up brilliantly and the hills across the harbour scarfed themselves in fairy blue. Emily hurried home from school, pale with the solemnity of the occasion. Her toilet was an important rite. She must wear her new navy-blue silk—no question about that. It was positively long and made her look fully grown up. But how should she do her hair? The Psyche knot had more distinction, suited her profile, and showed to better advantage under her hat. Besides, perhaps a bare forehead made her look more intellectual. But Mrs. Royal had said that Miss Royal liked pretty girls. Pretty, therefore, she must be at all costs. The rich black hair was dressed low on her forehead and crowned by the new spring hat which Emily had dared to buy with her latest cheque, in spite of Aunt Elizabeth's disapproval and Aunt Ruth's unvarnished statement that a fool and her money were soon parted. But Emily was glad now that she had bought the hat. She *couldn't* have gone to interview Miss Royal in her plain black sailor. This hat was very becoming with its cascade of purple violets that fell from it over the lovely, unbroken waves of hair, just touching the milk-whiteness of her neck. Everything about her was exquisitely neat and dainty: she looked—I like the old phrase—as if she had just stepped from a band-box. Aunt Ruth, prowling about the hall, saw her coming downstairs and realized, with something of a shock, that Emily was a young woman.

"She carries herself like a Murray," thought Aunt Ruth.

The force of commendation could no further go, though it was really from the Starrs that Emily had inherited her slim elegance. The Murrays were stately and dignified, but stiff.

It was quite a little walk to Ashburn, which was a fine old white house set far back from the street amid great trees. Emily went up the gravel walk, edged with its fine-fringed shadows of spring, as a worshipper approaching a sacred fane. A fairly large, fluffy white dog was sitting half-way up the gravel walk. Emily looked at him curiously. She had never seen a chow dog. She decided that Chu-Chin was handsome, but not clean. He had evidently been having a glorious time in some mud puddle, for his paws and breast were reeking. Emily hoped he would approve of her, but keep his distance.

Evidently he approved of her, for he turned and trotted up the walk with her, amiably waving a plumy tail—or rather a tail that would have been plumy had it not been wet and muddy. He stood expectantly beside her while she rang the bell, and as soon as the door was opened he made a joyous bound on the lady who stood within, almost knocking her over.

Miss Royal herself had opened the door. She had, as Emily saw at once, no beauty, but unmistakable distinction, from the crown of her gold-bronze hair to the toes of her satin slippers. She was arrayed in some marvellous dress of mauve velvet and she wore pince-nez with tortoise-shell rims, the first of their kind to be seen in Shrewsbury.

Chu-Chin gave one rapturous, slobbery wipe at her face with his tongue, then rushed on into Mrs. Royal's parlour. The beautiful mauve dress was spotted from collar to hem with muddy paw-marks. Emily thought that Chu-Chin fully deserved Mrs. Royal's bad opinion and mentally remarked that if he were *her* dog he should behave better. But Miss Royal did not reprove him in any way, and perhaps Emily's secret criticism was subconsciously prompted by her instant perception that Miss Royal's greeting, while perfectly courteous, was very cold. From her letter Emily had somehow expected a warmer reception.

"Won't you come in and sit down?" said Miss Royal. She ushered Emily in, waved to a comfortable chair, and sat down on a stiff and uncompromising Chippendale one. Somehow, Emily, sensitive at all times and abnormally so just now, felt that Miss Royal's selection of a chair was ominous. Why hadn't she sunk chummily into the depths of the big velvet morris? But there she sat, a stately, aloof figure, having apparently paid not the slightest attention to the appalling mud-stains on her beautiful dress. Chu-Chin had jumped on the big plush davenport, where he sat, cockily looking from one to the other as if enjoying the situation. It was all too evident that, as Mrs. Royal had foreboded, something had "upset" Miss Royal, and Emily's heart suddenly sank like lead.

"It's—a lovely day," she faltered. She knew it was an incredibly stupid thing to say, but she had to say something when Miss Royal wouldn't say anything. The silence was too awful.

"Very lovely," agreed Miss Royal, not looking at Emily at all but at Chu-Chin, who was thumping a beautiful silk and lace cushion of Mrs. Royal's with his wet tail. Emily hated Chu-Chin. It was a relief to hate him, since as yet she did not dare to hate Miss Royal. But she wished herself a thousand miles away. Oh, if she only hadn't that little bundle of manuscripts on her lap! It was so evident what it was. She would never dare to show one of them to Miss Royal. Was this outraged empress the writer of that kind, friendly letter? It was impossible to believe it. This must be a nightmare. Her dream was "out" with a vengeance. She felt crude and bread-and-buttery and ignorant and dowdy—and young! Oh, so horribly young!

The moments passed—not so very many, perhaps, but seeming like hours to Emily. Her mouth was dry and parched, her brain paralysed. She couldn't think of a solitary thing to say. A horrible suspicion flashed across her mind that, since writing her letter, Miss Royal had heard the gossip about the night in the old John house and that her altered attitude was the result.

In her misery Emily squirmed in her chair and her little packet of manuscripts slipped to the floor. Emily stooped to retrieve it. At the same moment Chu-Chin made a flying leap from the davenport at it. His muddy paws caught the spray of violets hanging from Emily's hat and tore it loose. Emily let go of her packet and clutched her hat. Chu-Chin let go of the violets and pounced on the packet. Then, holding that in his mouth, he bolted out of the open glass door leading to the garden.

"Oh, what a relief it would be to tear my hair," thought Emily violently.

That diabolical chow had carried off her latest and best story and a number of choice poems. Heaven knew what he would do with them. She supposed she would never see them again. But, at least, there was fortunately now no question of showing them to Miss Royal.

Emily no longer cared whether Miss Royal was in a bad humour or not. She was no longer desirous of pleasing her—a woman who would let her dog behave like that to an invited guest and never reprove him! Nay, she even seemed to be amused at his antics. Emily was sure she had detected a fleeting smile on Miss Royal's arrogant face as she looked at the ruined violets scattered over the floor.

There suddenly popped into Emily's mind a story she had heard of Lofty John's father, who was in the habit of telling his wife,

"When people do be after snubbing you, Bridget, pull up your lip, Bridget, pull up your lip."

Emily pulled up her lip.

"A very playful dog," she said sarcastically.

"Very," agreed Miss Royal composedly.

"Don't you think a little discipline would improve him?" asked Emily.

"No, I do not think so," said Miss Royal meditatively.

Chu-Chin returned at this moment, capered about the room, knocked a small glass vase off a taboret with a whisk of his tail, sniffed at the ensuing fragments, then bounded up on the davenport again, where he sat panting. "Oh, what a good dog am I!"

Emily picked up her note-book and pencil.

"Mr. Towers sent me to interview you," she said.

"So I understand," said Miss Royal, never taking her eyes off her worshipped chow.

Emily: "May I trouble you to answer a few questions?"

Miss Royal, with exaggerated amiability: "Charmed."

(Chu-Chin, having saved enough breath, springs from the davenport and rushes through the half-opened folding doors of the dining-room.)

Emily, consulting note-book and recklessly asking the first question jotted down therein: "What do you think will be the result of the Presidential election this fall?"

(Emily, with compressed lips, writes down in her note-book: "She never thinks about it." Chu-Chin reappears, darts through parlour and out into the garden, carrying a roast chicken in his mouth.)

Miss Royal: "There goes my supper."

Emily, checking off first questions: "Is there any likelihood that the United States Congress will look favourably on the recent reciprocity proposals of the Canadian Government?"

Miss Royal: "*Is* the Canadian Government making reciprocity proposals? I never heard of them."

(Emily writes, "She never heard of them." Miss Royal refits her pince-nez.)

Emily, thinks: "With a chin and a nose like that you'll look very witch-like when you grow old." *Says:* "Is it your opinion that the historical novel has had its day?"

Miss Royal, languidly: "I always leave my opinions at home when I take a holiday."

(Emily writes, "She always leaves her opinions home when she takes a holiday," and wishes savagely she could write her own description of this interview, but knows Mr. Towers wouldn't print it. Then consoles herself by remembering that she has a virgin Jimmy-book at home and takes a wicked delight in thinking of the account that will be written in it that night. Chu-Chin enters. Emily wonders if he could have eaten the chicken in that short time. Chu-Chin, evidently feeling the need of some desert, helps himself to one of Mrs. Royal's crocheted tidies, crawls under the piano with it and falls to chewing rapturously.)

Miss Royal, fervently: "*Dear* dog!"

Emily, suddenly inspired: "What do you think of chow dogs?"

Miss Royal: "The most adorable creatures in the world."

Emily to herself: "So you've brought *one* opinion with you." *To Miss Royal:* "*I* do not admire them."

Miss Royal, with an icy smile: "It is evident that your taste in dogs must be quite different from mine."

Emily, to herself: "I wish Ilse were here to call you names for me."

(A large, motherly grey cat passes across the doorstep outside. Chu-Chin bolts out from under the piano, shoots between the legs of a tall plant stand, and pursues the flying cat. The plant stand has gone over with a crash and Mrs. Royal's beautiful rex begonia lies in ruins on the floor, amid a heap of earth and broken pottery.)

Miss Royal, unsympathetically: "Poor Aunt Angela! Her heart will be broken."

Emily: "But that doesn't matter, does it?"

Miss Royal, gently: "Oh, no; not at all."

Emily, consulting note-book: "Do you find many changes in Shrewsbury?"

Miss Royal: "I find a good many changes in the people. The younger

521

generation does not impress me favourably."

(Emily writes this down. Chu-Chin again reappears, evidently having chased the cat through a fresh mud puddle, and resumes his repast of the tidy, under the piano.)

Emily shut her note-book and rose. Not for any number of Mr. Towers would she prolong this interview. She looked like a young angel, but she was thinking terrible things. And she hated Miss Royal—oh, how she hated her!

"Thank you, that will be all," she said, with a haughtiness quite equal to Miss Royal's. "I'm sorry to have taken so much of your time. Good-afternoon."

She bowed slightly and went out to the hall. Miss Royal followed her to the parlour door.

"Hadn't you better take your dog, Miss Starr?" she asked sweetly.

Emily paused in the act of shutting the outer door and looked at Miss Royal.

"Pardon me."

"I said, hadn't you better take your dog?"

"My *dog?*"

"Yes. He hasn't quite finished the tidy, to be sure, but you might take it along. It won't be much good to Aunt Angela now."

"He—he—isn't *my* dog," gasped Emily.

"Not your dog? Whose dog is he then?" said Miss Royal.

"I—I thought he was yours—your chow," said Emily.

AN OPEN DOOR

Miss Royal looked at Emily for a moment. Then she seized her wrist, shut the door, drew her back to the parlour, and firmly pushed her down into the morris chair. This done, Miss Royal threw herself on the muddy davenport and began to laugh—long and helplessly. Once or twice she rocked herself forward, gave Emily's knee two wild whacks, then rocked back and continued to laugh. Emily sat, smiling faintly. Her feelings had been too deeply harrowed to permit of Miss Royal's convulsions of mirth, but already there was glimmering in her mind a sketch for her Jimmy-book. Meanwhile, the white dog, having chewed the tidy to tatters, spied the cat again, and again rushed after her.

Finally Miss Royal sat erect and wiped her eyes.

"Oh, this is priceless, Emily Byrd Starr—priceless! When I'm eighty I'll recall this and howl over it. Who will write it up, you or I? But *who* does own that brute?"

"I'm sure I don't know," said Emily demurely. "I never saw him in my life before."

"Well, let's shut the door before he can return. And now, dear thing, sit here beside me—there's one clean spot here under the cushion. We're going to have our real talk now. Oh, I was so beastly to you when you were trying to ask me questions. I was *trying* to be beastly. Why didn't you throw something at me, you poor insulted darling?"

"I wanted to. But now I think you let me off very easily, considering the behaviour of my supposed dog."

Miss Royal went off in another convulsion.

"I don't know if I can forgive you for thinking that horrid curly white creature was my glorious red-gold chow. I'll take you up to my room before you go and you shall apologize to him. He's asleep on my bed. I locked him there to relieve dear Aunt Angela's mind about her cat. Chu-Chin wouldn't hurt the cat—he merely wants to play with her, and the foolish old thing runs. Now, you know, when a cat runs, a dog simply can't help chasing her. As Kipling tells us, he wouldn't be a proper dog if he didn't. If only that white fiend had confined himself to chasing the cat!"

"It is too bad about Mrs. Royal's begonia," said Emily, regretfully.

"Yes, that *is* a pity. Aunt Angela's had it for years. But I'll get her a new one. When I saw you coming up the walk with that dog frisking around you, of course I concluded he was yours. I had put on my favourite dress because it really makes me look almost beautiful—and I wanted you to love me; and when the beast muddied it all over and you never said a word of rebuke or apology, I simply went into one of my cold rages. I *do* go into them—I can't help it. It's one of my little faults. But I soon thaw out if no fresh aggravation occurs. In this case fresh aggravation occurred every minute. I vowed to myself that if you did not even try to make your dog behave I would not suggest that you should. And I suppose *you* were indignant because I calmly let *my* dog spoil your violets and eat your manuscripts?"

"I was."

"It's too bad about the manuscripts. Perhaps we can find them—he can't really have swallowed them, but I suppose he has chewed them to bits."

"It doesn't matter. I have other copies at home."

"And your questions! Emily, you were too delicious. Did you really write down my answers?"

"Word for word. I meant to print them just so, too. Mr. Towers had given me a list of questions for you, but of course I didn't mean to fire them off point-blank like that. I meant to weave them artfully into our conversation as we went along. But here comes Mrs. Royal."

Mrs. Royal came in, smiling. Her face changed as she saw the begonia. But Miss Royal interposed quickly.

"Dearest Aunty, don't weep or faint—at least not before you've told me who around here owns a white, curly, utterly mannerless, devilish dog?"

"Lily Bates," said Mrs. Royal in a tone of despair. "Oh, has she let that creature out again? I had a most terrible time with him before you came. He's really just a big puppy and he *can't* behave. I told her finally if I caught him over here again I'd poison him. She's kept him shut up since then. But now—oh, my lovely rex.

"Well, this dog came in with Emily. I supposed he was her dog. Courtesy to a guest implies courtesy to her dog—isn't there an old proverb that expresses it more concisely? He embraced me fervently upon his entrance, as my dearest dress testifies. He marked up your davenport—he tore off Emily's violets—he chased your cat—he overturned your begonia—he broke your vase—he ran off with our chicken—ay, groan, Aunt Angela, he did!—and yet I, determinedly composed and courteous, said not a word of protest. I vow my behaviour was worthy of New Moon itself—wasn't it, Emily?"

"You were just too mad to speak," said Mrs. Royal ruefully, fingering her wrecked begonia.

Miss Royal stole a sly glance at Emily.

"You see, I can't put anything over on Aunt Angela. She knows me too well. I admit I was not my usual charming self. But, Aunty darling, I'll get you a new vase and a new begonia—think of all the fun you'll have coaxing it along. Anticipation is always so much more interesting than realization."

"*I*'ll settle Lily Bates," said Mrs. Royal, going out of the room to look for a dustpan.

"Now, dear thing. Let's gab," said Miss Royal, snuggling down beside Emily.

This was the Miss Royal of the letter. Emily found no difficulty in talking to *her*. They had a jolly hour and at the end of it Miss Royal made a proposition that took away Emily's breath.

"Emily, I want you to come back to New York with me in July. There's a vacancy on the staff of *The Ladies' Own*—no great thing in itself. You'll be sort of general handy-man, and all odd jobs will be turned over to you—but you'll have a chance to work up. And you'll be in the centre of things. You can write—I, realized that the moment I read *The Woman Who Spanked the King*. I know the editor of *Roche's* and I found out who you were and where you lived. That's really why I came down this spring—I wanted to get hold of you. You mustn't waste your life here—it would be a crime. Oh, of course, I know New Moon is a dear, quaint, lovely spot—full of poetry and steeped in romance, it was just the place for you to spend your childhood in. But you must have a chance to grow and develop and be yourself. You must have the stimulus of association with great minds—the training that only a great city can give. Come with me. If you do, I promise you that in ten years' time Emily Byrd Starr will be a name to conjure with among the magazines of America."

Emily sat in a maze of bewilderment, too confused and dazzled to think clearly. She had never dreamed of this. It was as if Miss Royal had suddenly put into her hand a key to unlock the door into the world of all her dreams, and hopes, and imaginings. Beyond that door was all she had ever hoped for of success and fame. And yet—and yet—what faint, odd, resentment stirred at the back of all her whirling sensations? Was there a sting in Miss Royal's calm assumption that if Emily did *not* go with her her name would forever remain unknown? Did the old dead-and-gone Murrays turn over in their graves at the whisper that one of their descendants could never succeed without the help and "pull" of a stranger? Or *had* Miss Royal's manner been a shade too patronizing? Whatever it was it kept Emily from figuratively flinging herself at Miss Royal's feet.

"Oh, Miss Royal, that would be wonderful," she faltered. "I'd love to go—but I'm afraid Aunt Elizabeth will never consent. She'll say I'm too young."

"How old *are* you?"

"Seventeen."

"I was eighteen when I went. I didn't know a soul in New York—I had just enough money to keep me for three months. I was a crude, callow little thing—yet I won out. *You* shall live with me. I'll look after you as well as Aunt Elizabeth herself could do. Tell her I'll guard you like the apple of my eye. I have a dear, cozy, little flat where we'll be as happy as queens, with my adored and adorable Chu-Chin. You'll love Chu-Chin, Emily."

"I think I'd like a cat better," said Emily firmly.

"Cats! Oh, we couldn't have a cat in a flat. It wouldn't be amenable enough to discipline. You must sacrifice your pussies on the altar of your art. I'm sure you'll like living with me. I'm *very* kind and amiable, dearest, when I feel like it—and I generally do feel like it—and I *never* lose my temper. It freezes up occasionally, but, as I told you, it thaws quickly. I bear other people's misfortunes with equanimity. And I *never* tell any one she has a cold or that she looks tired. Oh, I'd really make an adorable housemate."

"I'm sure you would," said Emily, smiling.

"I never saw a young girl before that I wanted to live with," said Miss Royal. "You have a sort of luminous personality, Emily. You'll give off light in dull places and empurple drab spots. Now, *do* make up your mind to come with me."

"It is Aunt Elizabeth's mind that must be made up," said Emily ruefully. "If she says I can go I'll—"

Emily found herself stopping suddenly.

"Go," finished Miss Royal joyfully. "Aunt Elizabeth will come around. I'll go and have a talk with her. I'll go out to New Moon with you next Friday night. You *must* have your chance."

"I can't thank you enough, Miss Royal, so I won't try. But I must go now. I'll think this all over—I'm too dazzled just now to think at all. You don't know what this means to me."

"I think I do," said Miss Royal gently. "I was once a young girl in Shrewsbury, eating my heart out because I had no chance."

"But you made your own chance—and won out," said Emily wistfully.

526

"Yes—but I had to go away to do it. I could never have got anywhere here. And it was a horribly hard climb at first. It took my youth. I want to save you some of the hardships and discouragements. You will go far beyond what I have done—you can create—I can only build with the materials others have made. But we builders have our place—we can make temples for our gods and goddesses if nothing else. Come with me, dear Girl Emily, and I will do all I can to help you in every way."

"Thank you—thank you," was all Emily could say. Tears of gratitude for this offer of ungrudging help and sympathy were in her eyes. She had not received too much of sympathy or encouragement in her life. It touched her deeply. She went away feeling that she *must* turn the key and open the magic door beyond which now seemed to lie all the beauty and allurement of life—if only Aunt Elizabeth would let her.

"I can't do it if she doesn't approve," decided Emily.

Half-way home she suddenly stopped and laughed. After all, Miss Royal had forgotten to show her Chu-Chin.

"But it doesn't matter," she thought, "because in the first place I can't believe that, after this, I'll ever feel any real interest in chow dogs. And in the second place I'll see him often enough if I go to New York with Miss Royal."

A VALLEY OF VISION

Would she go to New York with Miss Royal?

That was the question Emily had now to answer. Or rather, the question Aunt Elizabeth must answer. For on Aunt Elizabeth's answer, as Emily felt, everything depended. And she had no real hope that Aunt Elizabeth would let her go. Emily might look longingly towards those pleasant, far-off, green pastures pictured by Miss Royal, but she was quite sure she could never browse in them. The Murray pride—and prejudice—would be an impassable barrier.

Emily said nothing to Aunt Ruth about Miss Royal's offer. It was Aunt Elizabeth's due to hear it first. She kept her dazzling secret until the next week-end, when Miss Royal came to New Moon, very gracious and pleasant, and the wee-est bit patronizing, to ask Aunt Elizabeth to let Emily go with her.

Aunt Elizabeth listened in silence—a disapproving silence, as Emily felt.

"The Murray women have never had to work out for their living," she said coldly.

"It isn't exactly what you would call 'working out,' dear Miss Murray," said Miss Royal, with the courteous patience one must use to a lady whose viewpoint was that of an outlived generation. "Thousands of women are going into business and professional life, everywhere."

"I suppose it's all right for them if they don't get married," said Aunt Elizabeth.

Miss Royal flushed slightly. She knew that in Blair Water and Shrewsbury she was regarded as an old maid, and therefore a failure, no matter what her income and her standing might be in New York. But she kept her temper and tried another line of attack.

"Emily has an unusual gift for writing," she said. "I think she can do something really worth while if she gets a chance. She ought to have her chance, Miss Murray. You know there isn't any chance for that kind of work here."

"Emily has made ninety dollars this past year with her pen," said Aunt Elizabeth.

"Heaven grant me patience!" thought Miss Royal. Said Miss Royal,

"Yes, and ten years from now she may be making a few hundreds; whereas, if she comes with me, in ten years' time her income would probably be as many thousands."

"I'll have to think it over," said Aunt Elizabeth.

Emily felt surprised that Aunt Elizabeth had even consented to think it over. She had expected absolute refusal.

"She'll come round to it," whispered Miss Royal, when she went away. "I'm going to get you, darling Emily B. I know the Murrays of old. They always had an eye to the main chance. Aunty will let you come."

"I'm afraid not," said Emily ruefully.

When Miss Royal had gone Aunt Elizabeth looked at Emily.

"Would you like to go, Emily?"

"Yes—I think so—if you don't mind," faltered Emily. She was very pale—she did not plead or coax. But she had no hope—none.

Aunt Elizabeth took a week to think it over. She called in Ruth and Wallace and Oliver to help her. Ruth said dubiously,

"I suppose we ought to let her go. It's a splendid chance for her. It's not as if she were going alone—I'd never agree to that. Janet will look after her."

"She's too young—she's too young," said Uncle Oliver.

"It seems a good chance for her—Janet Royal has done well, they say," said Uncle Wallace.

Aunt Elizabeth even wrote to Great-aunt Nancy. The answer came back in Aunt Nancy's quavering hand:

"Suppose you let Emily decide for herself," suggested Aunt Nancy.

Aunt Elizabeth folded up Aunt Nancy's letter and called Emily into the parlour.

"If you wish to go with Miss Royal you may," she said. "I feel it would not be right for me to hinder you. We shall miss you—we would rather have you with us for a few years yet. I know nothing about New York. I am told it is a wicked city. But you have been brought up carefully. I leave the decision in your own hands. Laura, what are you crying about?"

Emily felt as if she wanted to cry herself. To her amazement she felt something that was *not* delight or pleasure. It was one thing to long after forbidden pastures. It seemed to be quite another thing when the bars were flung down and you were told to enter if you would.

Emily did not immediately rush to her room and write a joyous letter to Miss Royal—who was visiting friends in Charlottetown. Instead she went out into the garden and thought very hard—all that afternoon and all Sunday. During the week-end in Shrewsbury she was quiet and thoughtful, conscious that Aunt Ruth was watching her closely. For some reason Aunt Ruth did not discuss the matter with her. Perhaps she was thinking of Andrew. Or perhaps it was an understood thing among the Murrays that Emily's decision was to be entirely uninfluenced.

Emily couldn't understand why she didn't write Miss Royal at once. Of course she would go. Wouldn't it be terribly foolish not to? She would never have such a chance again. It *was* such a splendid chance—everything made easy—the Alpine Path no more than a smooth and gentle slope—success certain and brilliant and quick. Why, then, did she have to keep telling herself all this—why was she driven to seek Mr.

Carpenter's advice the next week-end? And Mr. Carpenter would not help her very much. He was rheumatic and cranky.

"Don't tell me the cats have been hunting again," he groaned.

"No. I haven't any manuscripts this time," said Emily, with a faint smile. "I've come for advice of a different kind."

She told him of her perplexity.

"It's such a splendid chance," she concluded.

"Of course it's a splendid chance—to go and be Yankeefied," grunted Mr. Carpenter.

"I wouldn't get Yankeefied," said Emily resentfully. "Miss Royal has been twenty years in New York and she isn't Yankeefied."

"Isn't she? I don't mean by Yankeefied what you think I do," retorted Mr. Carpenter. "I'm not referring to the silly girls who go up to "the States" to work and come back in six months with an accent that would raise blisters on your skin. Janet Royal *is* Yankeefied—her outlook and atmosphere and style are all U. S. And I'm not condemning them— they're all right. But—she isn't a Canadian any longer—and that's what I wanted you to be—pure Canadian through and through, doing something as far as in you lay for the literature of your own country, keeping your Canadian tang and flavour. But of course there's not many dollars in that sort of thing yet."

"There's no chance to do *anything* here," argued Emily.

"No—no more than there was in Haworth Parsonage," growled Mr. Carpenter.

"I'm not a Charlotte Bronte," protested Emily. "She had genius— it can stand alone. I have only talent—it needs help—and—and— guidance."

"In short, pull," said Mr. Carpenter.

"So you think I oughtn't to go," said Emily anxiously.

"Go if you want to. To be quickly famous we must all stoop a little. Oh, go—go—I'm telling you. I'm too old to argue—go in peace. You'd be a fool not to—only—fools do sometimes attain. There's a special Providence for them, no doubt."

Emily went away from the little house in the hollow with her eyes rather black. She met Old Kelly on her way up the hill and he pulled his plump nag and red chariot to a standstill and beckoned to her.

"Gurrl dear, here's some peppermints for you. And now, ain't it high time—eh—now, you know—" Old Kelly winked at her.

530

"Oh, I'm going to be an old maid, Mr. Kelly," smiled Emily.

Old Kelly shook his head as he gathered up his reins.

"Shure an' nothing like that will ever be happening to you. You're one av the folks God really loves—only don't be taking one av the Prastes now—never one av the Prastes, gurrl dear."

"Mr. Kelly," said Emily suddenly, "I've been offered a splendid chance—to go to New York and take a place on the staff of a magazine. I can't make up my mind. What do you think I'd better do?"

As she spoke she thought of the horror of Aunt Elizabeth at the idea of a Murray asking Old Jock Kelly's advice. She herself was a little ashamed of doing it.

Old Kelly shook his head again.

"What do the b'ys around here be thinking av? But what does the ould lady say?"

"Aunt Elizabeth says I can do as I like."

"Then I guess we'll be laving it at that," said Old Kelly—and drove off without another word. Plainly there was no help to be had in Old Kelly.

"Why should I want help?" thought Emily desperately. "What has got into me that I can't make up my own mind? Why can't I *say* I'll go? It doesn't seem to me now that I *want* to go—I only feel I *ought* to want to go."

She wished that Dean were home. But Dean had not got back from his winter in Los Angeles. And somehow she could not talk the matter over with Teddy. Nothing had come of that wonderful moment in the old John house—nothing except a certain constraint that had almost spoiled their old comradeship. Outwardly they were as good friends as ever; but something was gone—and nothing seemed to be taking its place. She would not admit to herself that she was afraid to ask Teddy. Suppose he told her to go? That would hurt unbearably—because it would show that he didn't care whether she went or stayed. But Emily would not glance at this at all.

"Of course I'll go," she said aloud to herself. Perhaps the spoken word would settle things. "What would I do next year if I didn't? Aunt Elizabeth will certainly never let me go anywhere else alone. Ilse will be away—and Perry—Teddy too, likely. He says he's bound to go and do something to earn money for his art study. I *must* go."

She said it fiercely, as if arguing against some invisible opponent.

531

When she reached home in the twilight, no one was there and she went restlessly all over the house. What charm and dignity and fineness the old rooms had, with their candles and their ladder-backed chairs and their braided rugs! How dear and entreating was her own little room with its diamond paper and its guardian angel, its fat black rose-jar and its funny, kinky window-pane! Would Miss Royal's flat be half so wonderful?"

"Of course I'll go," she said again—feeling that if she could only have left off the "of course" the thing *would* have been settled.

She went out into the garden, lying in the remote, passionless beauty of early spring moonlight, and walked up and down its paths. From afar came the whistle of the Shrewsbury train—like a call from the alluring world beyond—a world full of interest, charm, drama. She paused by the old lichened sun-dial and traced the motto on its border, "So goes Time by." Time did go by—swiftly, mercilessly, even at New Moon, unspoiled as it was by any haste or rush of modernity. Should she not take the current when it offered? The white June lilies waved in the faint breeze—she could almost see her old friend the Wind-Woman bending over them to tilt their waxen chins. Would the Wind Woman come to her in the crowded city streets? Could she be like Kipling's cat there?

"And I wonder if I'll ever have the flash in New York," she thought wistfully.

How beautiful was this old garden which Cousin Jimmy loved! How beautiful was old New Moon farm! Its beauty had a subtly romantic quality all its own. There was enchantment in the curve of the dark-red, dew-wet road beyond—remote, spiritual allurement in the Three Princesses—magic in the orchard—a hint of intriguing devilment in the fir wood. How could she leave this old house that had sheltered and loved her—never tell me houses do not love!—the graves of her kin by the Blair Water pond, the wide fields and haunted woods where her childhood dreams had been dreamed? All at once she knew she could not leave them—she knew she had never really wanted to leave them. *That* was why she had gone about desperately asking advice of impossible outsiders. She had really been hoping they would tell her not to go. That was why she had wished so wildly that Dean were home—he would certainly have told her not to go.

"I belong to New Moon—I stay among my own people," she said.

532

EMILY CLIMBS

There was no doubt about this decision—she did not want any one to help her to it. A deep, inner contentment possessed her as she went up the walk and into the old house which no longer looked reproachfully at her. She found Elizabeth and Laura and Cousin Jimmy in the kitchen full of its candle magic.

"I am not going to New York, Aunt Elizabeth," she said. "I am going to stay here at New Moon with you."

Aunt Laura gave a little cry of joy. Cousin Jimmy said, "Hurrah!" Aunt Elizabeth knitted a round of her stocking before she said anything. Then—

"I thought a Murray would," she said.

Emily went straight to Ashburn Monday evening. Miss Royal had returned and greeted her warmly.

"I hope you've come to tell me that Miss Murray has decided to be reasonable and let you come with me, honey-sweet."

"She told me I could decide for myself."

Miss Royal clapped her hands.

"Oh, goody, goody! Then it's all settled."

Emily was pale, but her eyes were black with earnestness and intense feeling.

"Yes, it's settled—I'm not going," she said. "I thank you with all my heart, Miss Royal, but I can't go."

Miss Royal stared at her—realized in a moment that it was not the slightest use to plead or argue—but began to plead and argue all the same.

"Emily—you can't mean it? Why can't you come?"

"I can't leave New Moon—I love it too much—it means too much to me."

"I thought you wanted to come with me, Emily," said Miss Royal reproachfully.

"I did. And part of me wants to yet. But away down under that another part of me will not go. Don't think me foolish and ungrateful, Miss Royal."

"Of course I don't think you're ungrateful," said Miss Royal, helplessly, "but I do—yes, I do think you are awfully foolish. You are simply throwing away your chances of a career. What can you ever do here that is worth while, child? You've no idea of the difficulties in your path. You can't get material here—there's no atmosphere—no—"

533

"I'll create my own atmosphere," said Emily, with a trifle of spirit. After all, she thought, Miss Royal's viewpoint was the just the same as Mrs. Alec Sawyer's, and her manner *was* patronizing. "And as for material—people *live* here just the same as anywhere else—suffer and enjoy and sin and aspire just as they do in New York."

"You don't know a thing about it," said Miss Royal, rather pettishly. "You'll never be able to write anything really worth while here—no big thing. There's no inspiration—you'll be hampered in every way—the big editors won't look farther than the address of P. E. Island on your manuscript. Emily, you're committing literary suicide. You'll realize that at three of the clock some white night, Emily B. Oh, I suppose, after some years you'll work up a clientele of Sunday-school and agricultural papers. But will that satisfy you? You know it won't. And then the petty jealousy of these small prunes-and-prisms places—if you do anything the people you went to school with can't do some of them will never forgive you. And they'll all think you're the heroine of your own stories—especially if you portray her beautiful and charming. If you write a love story they'll be sure it's your own. You'll get so tired of Blair Water—you'll know all the people in it—what they are and can be—it'll be like reading a book for the twentieth time. Oh, I know all about it. 'I was alive before you were borned,' as I said when I was eight, to a playmate of six. You'll get discouraged—the hour of three o'clock will gradually overwhelm you—there's a three o'clock every night, remember—you'll give up—you'll marry that cousin of yours—"

"Never."

"Well, some one like him, then, and 'settle down'—"

"No, I'll never 'settle down,'" said Emily decidedly. "Never as long as I live—what a stodgy condition!"

—"and you'll have a parlour like this of Aunt Angela's," continued Miss Royal relentlessly. "A mantelpiece crowded with photographs—an easel with an 'enlarged' picture in a frame eight inches wide—a red plush album with a crocheted doily on it, a crazy-quilt on your spare-room bed—a hand-painted banner in your hall—and, as a final touch of elegance, an asparagus fern will 'grace the centre of your dining-room table.'"

"No," said Emily gravely, "such things are not among the Murray traditions."

"Well, the spiritual equivalent of them, then. Oh, I can see your whole life, Emily, here in a place like this where people can't see a mile beyond their nose."

"I can see farther than that," said Emily, putting up her chin. "I can see to the stars."

"I was speaking figuratively, my dear."

"So was I. Oh, Miss Royal, I know life is rather cramped here in some ways—but the sky is as much mine as anybody's. I may not succeed here—but, if not, I wouldn't succeed in New York either. Some fountain of living water would dry up in my soul if I left the land I love. I know I'll have difficulties and discouragements here, but people have overcome far worse. You know that story you told me about Parkman—that for years he was unable to write for more than five minutes at a time—that he took three years to write one of his books—six lines per day for three years. I shall always remember that when I get discouraged. It will help me through any number of white nights."

"Well"—Miss Royal threw out her hands—"I give up. I think you're making a terrible mistake, Emily—but if in the years to come I find out I'm wrong I'll write and admit it. And if *you* find out you were wrong write me and admit it, and you'll find me as ready to help you as ever. I won't even say 'I told you so.' Send me any of your stories my magazine is fit for, and ask me for any advice I can give. I'm going right back to New York to-morrow. I was only going to wait till July to take you with me. Since you won't come I'm off. I detest living in a place where all they think is that I've played my cards badly, and lost the matrimonial game—where all the young girls—except *you*—are so abominably respectful to me—and where the old folks keep telling me I look so much like my mother. Mother was *ugly*. Let's say good-bye and make it snappy."

"Miss Royal," said Emily earnestly, "you do believe—don't you—that I appreciate your kindness? Your sympathy and encouragement have meant more to me—always will mean more to me than you can ever dream."

Miss Royal whisked her handkerchief furtively across her eyes and made an elaborate curtsey.

"Thank you for them kind words, lady," she said solemnly.

Then she laughed a little, put her hands on Emily's shoulders and kissed her cheek.

"All the good wishes ever thought, said, or written go with you," she said. "And I think it would be—nice—if any place could ever mean to me what it is evident New Moon means to you."

At three o'clock that night a wakeful but contented Emily remembered that she had never seen Chu-Chin.

APRIL LOVE

"June 10, 19—

"Yesterday evening Andrew Oliver Murray asked Emily Byrd Starr to marry him.

"The said Emily Byrd Starr told him she wouldn't.

"I'm glad it's over. I've felt it coming for some time. Every evening Andrew has been here I've felt that he was trying to bring the conversation around to some serious subject, but I have never felt quite equal to the interview, and always contrived to sidetrack him with frivolity.

"Yesterday evening I went to the Land of Uprightness for one of the last rambles I shall have in it. I climbed the hill of firs and looked down over the fields of mist and silver in the moonlight. The shadows of the ferns and sweet wild grasses along the edge of the woods were like a dance of sprites. Away beyond the harbour, below the moonlight, was a sky of purple and amber where a sunset had been. But behind me was darkness—a darkness which, with its tang of fir balsam, was like a perfumed chamber where one might dream dreams and see visions. Always when I go into the Land of Uprightness I leave behind the realm of daylight and things known and go into the realm of shadow and mystery and enchantment where anything might happen—anything might come true. I can *believe* anything there—old myths—legends—dryads—fauns—leprechauns. One of my wonder moments came to me—it seemed to me that I got out of my body and was *free*—I'm sure I heard an echo of that 'random word' of the gods—and I wanted some unused language to express what I saw and felt.

"Enter Andrew, spic and span, prim and gentlemanly.

"Fauns—fairies—wonder moments—random words—fled pell-

536

mell. No new language was needed now.

"'What a pity side-whiskers went out with the last generation—they would suit him so,' I said to myself in good plain English.

"I knew Andrew had come to say something special. Otherwise he would not have followed me into the Land of Uprightness, but have waited decorously in Aunt Ruth's parlour. I knew it had to come and I made up my mind to get it over and have done with it. The expectant attitude of Aunt Ruth and the New Moon folks has been oppressive lately. I believe they all feel quite sure that the real reason I wouldn't go to New York was that I couldn't bear to part with Andrew!

"But I was *not* going to have Andrew propose to me by moonlight in the Land of Uprightness. I might have been bewitched into accepting him. So when he said, 'It's nice here, let's stay here for a while—after all, I think there is nothing so pretty as nature,' I said gently but firmly that, though nature must feel highly flattered, it was too damp for a person with a tendency to consumption, and I must go in.

"In we went. I sat down opposite Andrew and stared at a bit of Aunt Ruth's crochet yarn on the carpet. I shall remember the colour and shape of that yarn to my dying day. Andrew talked jerkily about indifferent things and then began throwing out hints—he would get his managership in two years more—he believed in people marrying young—and, so on. He floundered badly. I suppose I could have made it easier for him but I hardened my heart, remembering how he had kept away in those dreadful weeks of the John house scandal. At last he blurted out,

"'Emily, let's get married when—when—as soon as I'm able to.'

"He seemed to feel that he ought to say something more but didn't know just what—so he repeated 'just as soon as I'm able to' and stopped.

"I don't believe I even went through the motions of a blush.

"'Why should we get married?' I said.

"Andrew looked aghast. Evidently this was not the Murray tradition of receiving a proposal.

"'Why? Why? Because—I'd like it,' he stammered.

"'*I* wouldn't,' I said.

"Andrew stared at me for a few moments trying to take in the amazing idea that he was being refused.

"'But *why?*' he asked—exactly in Aunt Ruth's tone and manner.

"'Because I don't love you,' I said.

"Andrew *did* blush. I know he thought I was immodest.

"'I—I—think—they'd all like it,' he stammered.

"*I* wouldn't,' I said again. I said it in a tone even Andrew couldn't mistake.

"He was so surprised I don't think he felt anything *but* surprise— not even disappointment. He didn't know what to do or say—a *Murray* couldn't coax—so he got up and went out without another word. I thought he banged the door but afterwards I discovered it was only the wind. I wish he *had* banged the door. It would have saved my self-respect. It is mortifying to refuse a man and then discover that his main feeling is bewilderment.

"Next morning Aunt Ruth, evidently suspecting something amiss from the brevity of Andrew's call, asked me point blank what had happened. There's nothing subtle about Aunt Ruth. I told her just as point blankly.

"'What fault have you to find with Andrew?' she asked icily.

"'No fault—but he tastes flat. He has all the virtues but the pinch of salt was left out,' I said, with my nose in the air.

"'I hope you don't go farther and fare worse,' said Aunt Ruth ominously—meaning, as I knew, Stovepipe Town. I could have reassured Aunt Ruth on that point, also, had I chosen. Last week Perry came to tell me that he is going into Mr. Abel's office in Charlottetown to study law. It's a splendid chance for him. Mr. Abel heard his speech the night of the inter-school debate and has had his eye on him ever since, I understand. I congratulated him heartily. I really was delighted.

"'He'll give me enough to pay my board,' said Perry, 'and I guess I can rustle my clothes on some side line. I've got to hoe my own row. Aunt Tom won't help me. *You* know why.'

"'I'm sorry, Perry,' I said, laughing a little.

"'*Won't* you, Emily?' he said. 'I'd like this thing settled.'

"'It is settled,' I said.

"'I suppose I've made an awful ass of myself about you,' grumbled Perry.

"'You have,' I said comfortingly—but still laughingly. Somehow I've never been able to take Perry seriously any more than Andrew. I've always got the feeling that he just imagines he's in love with me.

"'You won't get a cleverer man than me in a hurry,' warned Perry. 'I'm going to climb high.'

"'I'm sure you will,' I said warmly, 'and nobody will be more pleased than your friend, Emily B.'

"'Oh, *friends*,' said Perry sulkily. 'It's not for a friend I want you. But I've always heard it was no use to coax a Murray. Will you tell me one thing? It isn't my funeral—but are you going to marry Andrew Murray?'

"'It isn't your funeral—but I'm *not*,' I said.

"'Well,' said Perry, as he went out, 'if you ever change your mind, let me know. It will be all right—if I haven't changed mine.'

"I have written the account of this exactly as it happened. But—I have also written another account of it in my Jimmy-book as it *should* have happened. I find I am beginning to overcome my old difficulty of getting my dream people to make love fluently. In my imaginary account both Perry and I talked bee-yew-tifully.

"I think Perry really felt a little worse than Andrew did, and I felt sorry about it. I do like Perry so much as a chum and friend. I hate to disappoint him, but I know he will soon get over it.

"So I'll be the only one left at Blair Water next year. I don't know how I'll feel about that. I dare say I'll feel a little flat by times—perhaps at three o' the night I'll wish I had gone with Miss Royal. But I'm going to settle down to hard, serious work. It's a long climb to the crest of the Alpine Path.

"But I believe in myself, and there is always my world behind the curtain.

****

"New Moon,
"June 21, 19—

"As soon as I arrived home to-night I felt a decided atmosphere of disapproval, and realized that Aunt Elizabeth knew all about Andrew. She was angry and Aunt Laura was sorry; but nobody has said anything. At twilight I talked it over in the garden with Cousin Jimmy. Andrew, it seems, *has* been feeling quite badly since the numbness of shock wore off. His appetite has failed; and Aunt Addie indignantly wants to know if I expect to marry a prince or a millionaire since *her* son is not good enough for me.

"Cousin Jimmy thinks I did perfectly right. Cousin Jimmy would

539

think I had done perfectly right if I had murdered Andrew and buried him in the Land of Uprightness. It's very nice to have *one* friend like that, though too many wouldn't be good for you.

****

"June 22, 19—

"I don't know which is worse—to have somebody you *don't* like ask you to marry him or *not* have some one you *do* like. Both are rather unpleasant.

"I have decided that I only imagined certain things in the old John house. I'm afraid Aunt Ruth was right when she used to say my imagination needed a curb. This evening I loitered in the garden. In spite of the fact that it was June it was cold and raw, and I felt a little lonely and discouraged and flat—perhaps because two stories of which I had hoped a good deal came back to me to-day. Suddenly I heard Teddy's signal whistle in the old orchard. Of course I went. It's always a case of 'Oh, whistle and I'll come to you, my lad' with me—though I would die before I would admit it to any one but my journal. As soon as I saw his face I knew he had some great news.

"He had. He held out a letter, 'Mr. Frederick Kent.' I never can remember that Teddy's name is Frederick—he can never be anything but Teddy to me. He has won a scholarship at the School of Design in Montreal—five hundred dollars for two years. I was instantly as excited as he was—with a queer feeling behind the excitement which was so compounded of fear and hope and expectancy that I couldn't tell which predominated.

"'How splendid for you, Teddy!' I said, a little tremulously. 'Oh, I'm so glad! But your mother—what does she think of it?'

"'She'll let me go—but she'll be very lonely and unhappy,' said Teddy, growing very sober instantly. 'I want her to come with me, but she won't leave the Tansy Patch. I hate to think of her living there all alone. I—I wish she didn't feel as she does about you, Emily. If she didn't—you could be such a comfort to her.'

"I wondered if it occurred to Teddy that I might need a little comforting too. A queer silence fell between us. We walked along the To-morrow Road—it has grown so beautiful that one wonders if any to-morrow can make it more beautiful—until we reached the fence of the pond-pasture and stood there under the grey-green gloom of the firs. I felt suddenly very happy and in those few minutes part of me planted a garden and laid out beautiful closets and bought a dozen solid silver teaspoons and arranged my attic and hemstitched a double damask table-cloth—and the other part of me just *waited*. Once I said it was a lovely evening—it wasn't—and a few minutes later I said it looked like rain—it didn't.

"But one *had* to say something.

"'I'm going to work hard—I'm going to get everything possible out of those two years,' Teddy said at last, staring at Blair Water and at the sky and at the sandhills, and at the green leisurely meadows, and at everything but me. 'Then, perhaps, when they're up I'll manage to get to Paris. To go abroad—to see the masterpieces of great artists—to live in their atmosphere—to see the scenes their genius immortalized—all I've been hungry for all my life. And when I come back—'

"Teddy stopped abruptly and turned to me. From the look in his eyes I thought he was going to kiss me—I really did. I don't know what I would have done if I couldn't have shut my own eyes.

"'And when I come back—' he repeated—stopped again.

"'Yes?' I said. I don't deny to this my journal that I said it a trifle expectantly.

"'I'll make the name of Frederick Kent mean something in Canada!' said Teddy.

"I opened my eyes.

"Teddy was looking at the dim gold of Blair Water and scowling. Again I had a feeling that night air was not good for me. I shivered, said a few polite commonplaces, and left him there scowling. I wonder if he was too shy to kiss me—or just didn't want to.

"I *could* care tremendously for Teddy Kent if I let myself—if he wanted me to. It is evident he doesn't want me to. He is thinking of nothing but success and ambition and a career. He has forgotten our exchange of glances in the old John house—he has forgotten that he told me three years ago, on George Horton's tombstone, that I was the sweetest girl in the world. He will meet hundreds of wonderful girls out in the world—he will never think of me again.

"So be it.

"If Teddy doesn't want me I won't want him. That is a Murray tradition. But then I'm only half Murray. There is the Starr half to

541

be considered. Luckily *I* have a career and an ambition also to think about, and a jealous goddess to serve, as Mr. Carpenter once told me. I think she might not tolerate a divided allegiance.

"I am conscious of three sensations.

"On top I am sternly composed and traditional.

"Underneath that, something that would hurt horribly if I let it is being kept down.

"And underneath that again is a queer feeling of relief that I still have my freedom.

****

"June 26, 19—

"All Shrewsbury is laughing over Ilse's last exploit and half Shrewsbury is disapproving. There is a certain very pompous young Senior who acts as usher in St. John's Church on Sundays, who takes himself very seriously and whom Ilse hates. Last Sunday she dressed herself up as an old woman, borrowing the toggery from a poor relation of Mrs. Adamson's who boards with her—a long, full, black skirt, bordered with crape, a widow's bonnet, and a heavy crape widow's veil. Arrayed thus, she tottered down the street and paused wistfully at the church steps as if she couldn't possibly climb them. Young Pomposity saw her, and, having some decent instincts behind his pomposity, went gallantly to her assistance. He took her shaking, mittened hand—it *was* shaking all right—Ilse was in spasms of laughter behind her veil— and assisted her frail, trembling feet up the steps, through the porch, up the aisle and into a pew. Ilse murmured a broken blessing on him, handed him a tract, sat through the service and then tottered home. Next day, of course, the story was all through the school and the poor lad was so guyed by the other boys that all his pomposity oozed out— temporarily at least—under the torture. Perhaps the incident may do him a world of good.

"Of course I scolded Ilse. She is a glad, daring creature and counts no cost. She will always do whatever she takes it into her head to do, even if it were to turn a somersault in the church aisle. I love her—love her—love her; and what I will do without her next year I do not know. Our to-morrows will always be separated after this—and grow apart— and when we meet occasionally it will be as strangers. Oh, I know—I know.

"Ilse was furious over what she called Perry's 'presumption' in thinking I could ever marry him.

"'Oh, it was not presumption—it was condescension,' I said, laughing. 'Perry belongs to the great ducal house of Carabas.'

"'Oh, he'll succeed, of course. But there'll always be a flavour of Stovepipe Town about him,' retorted Ilse.

"'Why have you always been so hard on Perry, Ilse?' I protested.

"'He's such a cackling oaf,' said Ilse morosely.

"'Oh, well, he's just at the age when a boy knows everything,' I said, feeling quite wise and elderly. 'He will grow more ignorant and endurable after a while,' I went on, feeling epigrammatic. 'And he has improved in these Shrewsbury years,' I concluded, feeling smug.

"'You talk as if he were a cabbage,' fumed Ilse. 'For heaven's sake, Emily, don't be so superior and patronizing!'

"There are times when Ilse is good for me. I know I deserved that.

****

"June 27, 19—

"Last night I dreamed I stood in the old summer-house at New Moon and saw the Lost Diamond sparkling on the floor at my feet. I picked it up in delight. It lay in my hand for a moment—then it seemed to elude my grasp, flash through the air, leaving a long, slender trail of brilliance behind it, and become a star in the western sky, just above the edge of the world. 'It is my star—I must reach it before it sets,' I thought, and started out. Suddenly Dean was beside me—and he, too, was following the star. I felt I must go slowly because he was lame and could not go fast—and all the time the star sank lower and lower. Yet I felt I couldn't leave Dean. Then just as suddenly—things *do* happen like that in dreams—so nice—without a bit of trouble—Teddy was beside me, too, holding out his hands to me, with the look in his eyes I had seen twice before. I put my hands in his—and he drew me towards him—I was holding up my face—then Dean gave a bitter cry, 'My star has set.' I turned my head for just a glance—the star was gone—and I woke up in a dull, ugly, rainy dawn with no star—no Teddy—no kiss.

"I wonder what the dream meant—if it meant anything. I must not think it did. It is a Murray tradition not to be superstitious.

543

****

"June 28, 19—

"This is my last night in Shrewsbury. 'Good-bye, proud world, I'm going home'—to-morrow, when Cousin Jimmy is coming for me and my trunk in the old express waggon and I will ride back in that chariot of state to New Moon.

"These three Shrewsbury years seemed so long to me when I looked ahead to them. And now, looking back, they seem as yesterday when it has passed. I think I've won something in them. I don't use so many italics—I've acquired a little poise and self-control—I've got a bit of bitter worldly wisdom—and I've learned to smile over a rejection slip. I think that has been the hardest lesson of all to learn—and doubtless the most necessary.

"As I look back over these three years some things stand out so much more clearly and significantly than others, as if they had a special meaning all their own. And not always the things one might expect either. For instance, Evelyn's enmity and even that horrible moustache incident seem faded and unimportant. But the moment I saw my first poem in *Garden and Woodland*—oh, that *was* a moment— my walk to New Moon and back the night of the play—the writing of that queer little poem of mine that Mr. Carpenter tore up—my night on the haystack under the September moon—that splendid old woman who spanked the King—the moment in class when I discovered Keats' lines about the 'airy voices'—and that other moment in the old John house when Teddy looked into my eyes—oh, it seems to me these are the things I will remember in the halls of Eternity when Evelyn Blake's sneers and the old John house scandal and Aunt Ruth's nagging and the routine of lessons and examinations have been for ever forgotten. And my promise to Aunt Elizabeth *has* helped me, as Mr. Carpenter predicted. Not in my diary perhaps—I just let myself *go* here—one must have a 'vent'—but in my stories and Jimmy-books.

"We had our class day exercises this afternoon. I wore my new cream organdy with the violets in it and carried a big bouquet of pink peonies. Dean, who is in Montreal on his way home, wired the florist here for a bouquet of roses for me—seventeen roses—one for each year of my life—and it was presented to me when I went up for my diploma. That was dear of Dean.

"Perry was class orator and made a fine speech. And he got the medal for general proficiency. It has been a stiff pull between him and Will Morris, but Perry has won out.

"I wrote and read the class day prophecy. It was very amusing and the audience seemed to enjoy it. I had another one in my Jimmy-book at home. It was much *more* amusing but it wouldn't have done to read it.

"I wrote my last society letter for Mr. Towers tonight. I've always hated that stunt but I wanted the few pennies it brought in and one mustn't scorn the base degrees by which one ascends young ambition's ladder.

"I've also been packing up. Aunt Ruth came up occasionally and looked at me as I packed but was oddly silent. Finally she said, with a sigh,

"'I shall miss you awfully, Emily.'

"I never dreamed of her saying and feeling anything like that. And it made me feel uncomfortable. Since Aunt Ruth was so decent about the John house scandal I've felt differently towards her. But I couldn't say I'd miss her.

"Yet something had to be said.

"'I shall always be very grateful to you, Aunt Ruth, for what you have done for me these past three years.'

"'I've tried to do my duty,' said Aunt Ruth virtuously.

****

"I find I'm oddly sorry to leave this little room I've never liked and that has never liked me, and that long hill starred with lights—after all, I've had some wonderful moments here. And even poor dying Byron! But by no stretch of sentiment can I regret parting from Queen Alexandra's chromo, or the vase of paper flowers. Of course, the Lady Giovanna goes with me. She *belongs* in my room at New Moon. She has always seemed like an exile here. It hurts me to think I shall never again hear the night wind in the Land of Uprightness. But I'll have my night wind in Lofty John's bush; I think Aunt Elizabeth means to let me have a kerosene lamp to write by—my door at New Moon shuts *tight*—and I will not have to drink cambric tea. I went at dusk to-night

545

to that little pearly pool which has always been such a witching spot to linger near on spring evenings. Through the trees that fringed it faint hues of rose and saffron from the west stole across it. It was unruffled by a breath and every leaf and branch and fern and blade of grass was mirrored in it. I looked in—and saw my face; and by an odd twist of reflection from a bending bough I seemed to wear a leafy garland on my head—like a laurel crown.

"I took it as a good omen.

"Perhaps Teddy was only shy!"

THE END

EMILY'S QUEST

CHAPTER I

I

"No more cambric-tea" had Emily Byrd Starr written in her diary when she came home to New Moon from Shrewsbury, with high school days behind her and immortality before her.

Which was a symbol. When Aunt Elizabeth Murray permitted Emily to drink real tea—as a matter of course and not as an occasional concession—she thereby tacitly consented to let Emily grow up. Emily had been considered grownup by other people for some time, especially by Cousin Andrew Murray and Friend Perry Miller, each of whom had asked her to marry him and been disdainfully refused for his pains. When Aunt Elizabeth found this out she knew it was no use to go on making Emily drink cambric-tea. Though, even then, Emily had no real hope that she would ever be permitted to wear silk stockings. A silk petticoat might be tolerated, being a hidden thing, in spite of its seductive rustle, but silk stockings were immoral.

So Emily, of whom it was whispered somewhat mysteriously by people who knew her to people who didn't know her, "she *writes*," was accepted as one of the ladies of New Moon, where nothing had ever changed since her coming there seven years before and where the carved ornament on the sideboard still cast the same queer shadow of an Ethiopian silhouette on exactly the same place on the wall where she had noticed it delightedly on her first evening there. An old house that had lived its life long ago and so was very quiet and wise and a little mysterious. Also a little austere, but very kind. Some of the Blair Water and Shrewsbury people thought it was a dull place and outlook

547

for a young girl and said she had been very foolish to refuse Miss Royal's offer of "a position on a magazine" in New York. Throwing away such a good chance to make something of herself! But Emily, who had very clear-cut ideas of what she was going to make of herself, did not think life would be dull at New Moon or that she had lost her chance of Alpine climbing because she had elected to stay there.

She belonged by right divine to the Ancient and Noble Order of Story-tellers. Born thousands of years earlier she would have sat in the circle around the fires of the tribe and enchanted her listeners. Born in the foremost files of time she must reach her audience through many artificial mediums.

But the materials of story weaving are the same in all ages and all places. Births, deaths, marriages, scandals—these are the only really interesting things in the world. So she settled down very determinedly and happily to her pursuit of fame and fortune—and of something that was neither. For writing, to Emily Byrd Starr, was not primarily a matter of worldly lucre or laurel crown. It was something she *had* to do. A thing—an idea—whether of beauty or ugliness, tortured her until it was "written out." Humorous and dramatic by instinct, the comedy and tragedy of life enthralled her and demanded expression through her pen. A world of lost but immortal dreams, lying just beyond the drop-curtain of the real, called to her for embodiment and interpretation—called with a voice she could not—dared not—disobey.

She was filled with youth's joy in mere existence. Life was for ever luring and beckoning her onward. She knew that a hard struggle was before her; she knew that she must constantly offend Blair Water neighbours who would want her to write obituaries for them and who, if she used an unfamiliar word would say contemptuously that she was "talking big;" she knew there would be rejection slips galore; she knew there would be days when she would feel despairingly that she could not write and that it was of no use to try; days when the editorial phrase, "not necessarily a reflection on its merits," would get on her nerves to such an extent that she would feel like imitating Marie Bashkirtseff and hurling the taunting, ticking, remorseless sitting-room clock out of the window; days when everything she had done or tried to do would slump—become mediocre and despicable; days when she would be tempted to bitter disbelief in her fundamental conviction that there was as much truth in the poetry of life as in the prose; days when the echo of that "random word" of the gods, for which she so avidly listened, would only seem to taunt her with its suggestions of unattainable perfection and loveliness beyond the reach of mortal ear or pen.

She knew that Aunt Elizabeth tolerated but never approved her mania for scribbling. In her last two years in Shrewsbury High School Emily, to Aunt Elizabeth's almost incredulous amazement, had actually earned some money by her verses and stories. Hence the toleration. But no Murray had ever done such a thing before. And there was always that sense, which Dame Elizabeth Murray did not like, of being shut out of something. Aunt Elizabeth really resented the fact that Emily had another world, apart from the world of New Moon and Blair Water, a kingdom starry and illimitable, into which she could enter at will and into which not even the most determined and suspicious of aunts could follow her. I really think that if Emily's eyes had not so often seemed to be looking at something dreamy and lovely and secretive Aunt Elizabeth might have had more sympathy with her ambitions. None of us, not even self-sufficing Murrays of New Moon, like to be barred out.

II

Those of you who have already followed Emily through her years of New Moon and Shrewsbury* must have a tolerable notion what she looked like. For those of you to whom she comes as a stranger let me draw a portrait of her as she seemed to the outward eye at the enchanted portal of seventeen, walking where the golden chrysanthemums lighted up an old autumnal, maritime garden. A place of peace, that garden of New Moon. An enchanted pleasaunce, full of rich, sensuous colours and wonderful spiritual shadows. Scents of pine and rose were in it; boom of bees, threnody of wind, murmurs of the blue Atlantic gulf; and always the soft sighing of the firs in Lofty John Sullivan's "bush" to the north of it. Emily loved every flower and shadow and sound in it, every beautiful old tree in and around it, especially her own intimate, beloved trees—a cluster of wild cherries in the south-west corner, Three Princesses of Lombardy, a certain maiden-like wild plum on the brook path, the big spruce in the centre of the garden, a silver maple and a pine farther on, an aspen in another corner always coquetting with gay little winds, and a whole row of stately white birches in Lofty John's bush.

* See *Emily of New Moon* and *Emily Climbs*.

Emily was always glad that she lived where there were many trees—old ancestral trees, planted and tended by hands long dead, bound up with everything of joy and sorrow that visited the lives in their shadows.

A slender, virginal young thing. Hair like black silk. Purplish-grey eyes, with violet shadows under them that always seemed darker and more alluring after Emily had sat up to some unholy and un-Elizabethan hour completing a story or working out the skeleton of a plot; scarlet lips with a Murray-like crease at the corners; ears with Puckish, slightly pointed tips. Perhaps it was the crease and the ears that made certain people think her something of a puss. An exquisite line of chin and neck; a smile with a trick in it; such a slow-blossoming thing with a sudden radiance of fulfilment. And ankles that scandalous old Aunt Nancy Priest of Priest Pond commended. Faint stains of rose in her rounded cheeks that sometimes suddenly deepened to crimson. Very little could bring that transforming flush—a wind off the sea, a sudden glimpse of blue upland, a flame-red poppy, white sails going out of the harbour in the magic of morning, gulf-waters silver under the moon, a Wedgwood-blue columbine in the old orchard. Or a certain whistle in Lofty John's bush.

With all this—pretty? I cannot tell you. Emily was never mentioned when Blair Water beauties were being tabulated. But no one who looked upon her face ever forgot it. No one, meeting Emily the second time ever had to say "Er—your face seems familiar but—" Generations of lovely women were behind her. They had all given her something of personality. She had the grace of running water. Something, too, of its sparkle and limpidity. A thought swayed her like a strong wind. An emotion shook her as a tempest shakes a rose. She was one of those vital creatures of whom, when they do die, we say it seems impossible that they can be dead. Against the background of her practical, sensible clan she shone like a diamond flame. Many people liked her, many disliked her. No one was ever wholly indifferent to her.

Once, when Emily had been very small, living with her father down in the little old house at Maywood, where he had died, she had started out to seek the rainbow's end. Over long wet fields and hills she ran, hopeful, expectant. But as she ran the wonderful arch was faded—was dim—was gone. Emily was alone in an alien valley, not too sure in which direction lay home. For a moment her lips quivered, her eyes filled. Then she lifted her face and smiled gallantly at the empty sky.

"There will be other rainbows," she said.

Emily was a chaser of rainbows.

III

Life at New Moon had changed. She must adjust herself to it. A certain loneliness must be reckoned with. Ilse Burnley, the madcap pal of seven faithful years, had gone to the School of Literature and Expression in Montreal. The two girls parted with the tears and vows of girlhood. Never to meet on quite the same ground again. For, disguise the fact as we will, when friends, even the closest—perhaps the more because of that very closeness—meet again after a separation there is always a chill, lesser or greater, of change. Neither finds the other *quite* the same. This is natural and inevitable. Human nature is ever growing or retrogressing—never stationary. But still, with all our philosophy, who of us can repress a little feeling of bewildered disappointment when we realize that our friend is not and never can be just the same as before—even though the change may be by way of improvement? Emily, with the strange intuition which supplied the place of experience, felt this as Ilse did not, and felt that in a sense she was bidding good-bye for ever to the Ilse of New Moon days and Shrewsbury years.

Perry Miller, too, former "hired boy" of New Moon, medalist of Shrewsbury High School, rejected but not quite hopeless suitor of Emily, butt of Ilse's rages, was gone. Perry was studying law in an office in Charlottetown, with his eye fixed firmly on several glittering legal goals. No rainbow ends—no mythical pots of gold for Perry. He knew what *he* wanted would stay put and he was going after it. People were beginning to believe he would get it. After all, the gulf between the law clerk in Mr. Abel's office and the Supreme Court Bench of Canada was no wider than the gulf between that same law clerk and the barefoot gamin of Stovepipe Town-by-the-Harbour.

There was more of the rainbow-seeker in Teddy Kent, of the Tansy Patch. He, too, was going. To the School of Design in Montreal. He, too, knew—had known for years—the delight and allurement and despair and anguish of the rainbow quest.

"Even if we never find it," he said to Emily, as they lingered in the New Moon garden under the violet sky of a long, wondrous, northern twilight, on the last evening before he went away, "there's something in the search for it that's better than even the finding would be."

"But we *will* find it," said Emily, lifting her eyes to a star that glittered over the tip of one of the Three Princesses. Something in Teddy's use of "we" thrilled her with its implications. Emily was always very honest with herself and she never attempted to shut her eyes to the knowledge that Teddy Kent meant more to her than anyone else in the world. Whereas she—what did she mean to him? Little? Much? Or nothing?

She was bareheaded and she had put a star-like cluster of tiny yellow 'mums in her hair. She had thought a good deal about her dress before she decided on her primrose silk. She thought she was looking very well, but what difference did that make if Teddy didn't notice it? He always took her so for granted, she thought a little rebelliously. Dean Priest, now, would have noticed it and paid her some subtle compliment about it.

"I don't know," said Teddy, morosely scowling at Emily's topaz-eyed grey cat, Daffy, who was fancying himself as a skulking tiger in the spirea thicket. "I don't know. Now that I'm really flying the Blue Peter I feel—flat. After all—perhaps I can never do anything worth while. A little knack of drawing—what does it amount to? Especially when you're lying awake at three o'clock at night?"

"Oh, I know that feeling," agreed Emily. "Last night I mulled over a story for hours and concluded despairingly that I could *never* write— that it was no use to try—that I couldn't do anything really worth while. I went to bed on that note and drenched my pillow with tears. Woke up at three and couldn't even cry. Tears seemed as foolish as laughter—or ambition. I was quite bankrupt in hope and belief. And then I got up in the chilly grey dawn and began a new story. Don't let a three-o'clock-at-night feeling fog your soul."

"Unfortunately there's a three o'clock every night," said Teddy. "At that ungodly hour I am always convinced that if you want things *too* much you're not likely ever to get them. And there are two things that I want tremendously. One, of course, is to be a great artist. I never supposed I was a coward, Emily, but I'm afraid now. If I don't make

good! Everybody'll laugh at me. Mother will say she knew it. She hates
to see me go really, you know. To go and fail! It would be better not to
go."

"No, it wouldn't," said Emily passionately, wondering at the same
time in the back of her head what was the *other* thing Teddy wanted so
tremendously. "You must not be afraid. Father said I wasn't to be afraid
of anything in that talk I had with him the night he died. And isn't it
Emerson who said, 'Always do what you are afraid to do?'"

"I'll bet Emerson said that when he'd got through with being afraid
of things. It's easy to be brave when you're taking off your harness."

"You know I believe in you, Teddy," said Emily softly.

"Yes, you do. You and Mr. Carpenter. You are the only ones who
really do believe in me. Even Ilse thinks that Perry has by far the better
chance of bringing home the bacon."

"But you are not going after bacon. You're going after rainbow gold."

"And if I fail to find it—and disappoint you—that will be worst of
all."

"You *won't* fail. Look at that star, Teddy—the one just over the
youngest Princess. It's Vega of the Lyre. I've always loved it. It's my
dearest among the stars. Do you remember how, years ago when you
and Ilse and I sat out in the orchard on the evenings when Cousin
Jimmy was boiling pigs' potatoes, you used to spin us wonderful tales
about that star—and of a life you had lived in it before you came to this
world. There was no three o'clock in the morning in that star."

"What happy, carefree little shavers we were those times," said
Teddy, in the reminiscent voice of a middle-aged, care-oppressed man
wistfully recalling youthful irresponsibility.

"I want you to promise me," said Emily, "that whenever you see that
star you'll remember that I am believing in you—*hard*."

"Will you promise *me* that whenever you look at that star you'll
think of me?" said Teddy. "Or rather, let us promise each other that
whenever we see that star we'll *always* think of each other—*always*.
Everywhere and as long as we live."

"I promise," said Emily, thrilled. She loved to have Teddy look at
her like that.

A romantic compact. Meaning what? Emily did not know. She only
knew that Teddy was going away—that life seemed suddenly very
blank and cold—that the wind from the gulf, sighing among the trees

in Lofty John's bush was very sorrowful—that summer had gone and autumn had come. And that the pot of gold at the rainbow's end was on some very far-distant hill.

Why had she said that thing about the star? Why did dusk and fir-scent and the afterglow of autumnal sunsets make people say absurd things?

CHAPTER II

I

"NEW MOON,

"NOVEMBER 18, 19—

"To-day the December number of *Marchwood's* came with my verses *Flying Gold* in it. I consider the occasion worthy of mention in my diary because they were given a whole page to themselves and illustrated—the first time ever any poem of mine was so honoured. It is trashy enough in itself, I suppose—Mr. Carpenter only sniffed when I read it to him and refused to make any comment whatever on it. Mr. Carpenter never 'damns with faint praise' but he can damn with silence in a most smashing manner. But my poem *looked* so dignified that a careless reader might fancy there was something in it. Blessings on the good editor who was inspired to have it illustrated. He has bolstered up my self-respect considerably.

"But I did not care overmuch for the illustration itself. The artist did not catch my meaning at all. Teddy would have done better.

"Teddy is doing splendidly at the School of Design. And Vega shines brilliantly every night. I wonder if he really does always think of me when he sees it. Or if he ever does see it. Perhaps the electric lights of Montreal blot it out. He seems to see a good bit of Ilse. It's awfully nice for them to know each other in that big city of strangers."

II

"NOVEMBER 26, 19—

"To-day was a glamorous November afternoon—summer-mild and autumn-sweet. I sat and read a long while in the pond burying-ground. Aunt Elizabeth thinks this a most gruesome place to sit in and tells Aunt Laura that she is afraid there's a morbid streak in me. I can't see anything morbid about it. It's a beautiful spot where wild, sweet odours are always coming across Blair Water on the wandering winds. And so quiet and peaceful, with the old graves all about me— little green hillocks with small frosted ferns sprinkled over them. Men and women of my house are lying there. Men and women who had been victorious—men and women who had been defeated—and their victory and defeat are now one. I never can feel either much exalted or much depressed there. The sting and the tang alike go out of things. I like the old, old red sandstone slabs, especially the one for Mary Murray with its 'Here I Stay'—the inscription into which her husband put all the concealed venom of a lifetime. His grave is right beside hers and I feel sure they have forgiven each other long ago. And perhaps they come back sometimes in the dark o' the moon and look at the inscription and laugh at it. It is growing a little dim with tiny lichens. Cousin Jimmy has given up scraping them away. Some day they will overgrow it so that it will be nothing but a green-and-red-and-silver smear on the old red stone."

"DEC. 20, 19—

"Something nice happened to-day. I feel pleasantly exhilarated. *Madison's* took my story, *A Flaw in the Indictment!!!!* Yes, it deserves some exclamation-points after it to a certainty. If it were not for Mr. Carpenter I would write it in italics. Italics! Nay, I'd use capitals. It is very hard to get in there. Don't I know! Haven't I tried repeatedly and gained nothing for my pains but a harvest of 'we-regrets?' And at last it has opened its doors to me. To be in *Madison's* is a clear and unmistakable sign that you're getting somewhere on the Alpine path. The dear editor was kind enough to say it was a charming story.

"Nice man!

"He sent me a cheque for fifty dollars. I'll soon be able to begin to repay Aunt Ruth and Uncle Wallace what they spent on me in Shrewsbury. Aunt Elizabeth as usual looked at the cheque suspiciously but for the first time forebore to wonder if the bank would really cash it. Aunt Laura's beautiful blue eyes beamed with pride. Aunt Laura's eyes really do beam. She is one of the Victorians. Edwardian eyes glitter and sparkle and allure but they never beam. And somehow I do like beaming eyes—especially when they beam over my success.

"Cousin Jimmy says that *Madison's* is worth all the other Yankee magazines put together in *his* opinion.

"I wonder if Dean Priest will like *A Flaw in the Indictment*. And if he will say so. He *never* praises anything I write nowadays. And I feel such a craving to *compel* him to. I feel that his is the only commendation, apart from Mr. Carpenter's, that is worth anything.

"It's odd about Dean. In some mysterious way he seems to be growing younger. A few years ago I thought of him as quite old. Now he seems only middle-aged. If this keeps up he'll soon be a mere youth. I suppose the truth is that my mind is beginning to mature a bit and I'm catching up with him. Aunt Elizabeth doesn't like my friendship with him any more than she ever did. Aunt Elizabeth has a well-marked antipathy to any Priest. But I don't know what I'd do without Dean's friendship. It's the very salt of life."

"JANUARY 15, 19—

"To-day was stormy. I had a white night last night after four rejections of MSS. I had thought especially good. As Miss Royal predicted, I felt that I had been an awful idiot not to have gone to New York with her when I had the chance. Oh, I don't wonder babies always cry when they wake up in the night. So often I want to do it, too. Everything presses on my soul then and no cloud has a silver lining. I was blue and disgruntled all the forenoon and looked forward to the coming of the mail as the one possible rescue from the doldrums. There is always such a fascinating expectancy and uncertainty about the mail. What would it bring me? A letter from Teddy—Teddy writes the most delightful letters. A nice thin envelope with a cheque? A fat one woefully eloquent of more rejected MSS.? One of Ilse's fascinating scrawls? Nothing of the sort. Merely an irate epistle from Second-cousin-once-removed Beulah Grant of Derry Pond, who is furious because she thinks I 'put her' into my story *Fools of Habit,* which has just been copied into a widely circulated Canadian farm paper. She wrote me a bitterly reproachful letter which I received to-day. She thinks I 'might have spared an old friend who has always wished me well.' She is 'not accustomed to being ridiculed in the newspapers' and will I, in future, be so kind as to refrain from making her the butt of my supposed wit in the public press. Second-cousin-once-removed Beulah wields a facile pen of her own, when it comes to that, and while certain things in her letter hurt me other parts infuriated me. I never once even *thought* of Cousin Beulah when I wrote that story. The character of *Aunt Kate* is purely imaginary. And if I *had* thought of Cousin Beulah I most certainly wouldn't have put *her* in a story. She is too stupid and commonplace. And she isn't a bit like *Aunt Kate,* who is, I flattered myself, a vivid, snappy, humorous old lady.

"But Cousin Beulah wrote to Aunt Elizabeth too, and we have had a family ruction. Aunt Elizabeth won't believe I am guiltless—she declares *Aunt Kate* is an exact picture of Cousin Beulah and she politely requests me—Aunt Elizabeth's polite requests are awesome things—*not* to caricature my relatives in my future productions.

"'It is not,' said Aunt Elizabeth in her stateliest manner, 'a thing *any* Murray should do—make money out of the peculiarities of her friends.'

"It was just another of Miss Royal's predictions fulfilled. Oh, was she as right about everything else? If she was—

"But the worst slam of all came from Cousin Jimmy, who had chuckled over *Fools of Habit.*

"'Never mind old Beulah, pussy,' he whispered. 'That was fine. You certainly did her up brown in *Aunt Kate.* I recognized her before I'd read a page. Knew her by her nose.' There you are! I unluckily happened to dower *Aunt Kate* with a 'long, drooping nose.' Nor can it be denied that Cousin Beulah's nose is long *and* drooping. People have been hanged on no clearer circumstantial evidence. It was of no use to wail despairingly that I had never even thought of Cousin Beulah. Cousin Jimmy just nodded and chuckled again.

"'Of course. Best to keep it quiet. Best to keep anything like that pretty quiet.'

"The worst sting in all this is, that if *Aunt Kate* is really like Cousin Beulah Grant then I failed egregiously in what I was trying to do.

"However, I feel much better now than when I began this entry. I've got quite a bit of resentment and rebellion and discouragement out of my system.

"That's the chief use of a diary, I believe."

557

III

"FEB. 3, 19—

"This was a 'big day.' I had three acceptances. And one editor asked me to send him some stories. To be sure, I hate having an editor ask me to send a story, somehow. It's far worse than sending them unasked. The humiliation of having them returned after all is far deeper than when one just sends off a MS. to some dim impersonality behind an editorial desk a thousand miles away.

"And I have decided that I can't write a story 'to order.' 'Tis a diabolical task. I tried to lately. The editor of *Young People* asked me to write a story along certain lines. I wrote it. He sent it back, pointing out some faults and asking me to rewrite it. I tried to. I wrote and rewrote and altered and interlined until my MS. looked like a crazy patchwork of black and blue and red inks. Finally I lifted one of the covers of the kitchen stove and dumped in the original yarn and all my variations thereof.

"After this I'm just going to write what I want to. And the editors can be—canonized!

"There are northern lights and a misty new moon to-night."

IV

"FEB. 16, 19—

"My story *What the Jest Was Worth* was in *The Home Monthly* to-day. But I was only one of 'others' on the cover. However, to balance that I have been listed by name as 'one of the well-known and popular contributors for the coming year' in *Girlhood Days*. Cousin Jimmy has read this editor's foreword over half a dozen times and I heard him murmuring '*well-known and popular*' as he split the kindlings. Then he went to the corner store and bought me a new Jimmy-book. Every time I pass a new milestone on the Alpine path Cousin Jimmy celebrates by giving me a new Jimmy-book. I never buy a notebook for myself. It would hurt his feelings. He always looks at the little pile of Jimmy-books on my writing-table with awe and reverence, firmly believing that all sorts of wonderful literature is locked up in the hodge-podge of description and characters and 'bits' they contain.

"I always give Dean my stories to read. I can't help doing it, although he always brings them back with no comment, or, worse than no comment—faint praise. It has become a sort of obsession with me to *make* Dean admit I *can* write something worth while in its line. *That* would be triumph. But unless and until he does, everything will be dust and ashes. Because—he *knows.*"

V

"April 2, 19—

"The spring has affected a certain youth of Shrewsbury who comes out to New Moon occasionally. He is not a suitor of whom the House of Murray approves. Nor, which is more important, one of whom E. B. Starr approves. Aunt Elizabeth was very grim because I went to a concert with him. She was sitting up when I came home.

"'You see I haven't eloped, Aunt Elizabeth,' I said. 'I promise you I won't. If I ever want to marry any one I'll tell you so and marry him in spite of your teeth.'

"I don't know whether Aunt Elizabeth went to bed with an easier mind or not. Mother eloped—thank goodness!—and Aunt Elizabeth is a firm believer in heredity."

VI

"April 15, 19—

"This evening I went away up the hill and prowled about the Disappointed House by moonlight. The Disappointed House was built thirty-seven years ago—partly built, at least—for a bride who never came to it. There it has been ever since, boarded up, unfinished, heart-broken, haunted by the timid, forsaken ghosts of things that should have happened but never did. I always feel so sorry for it. For its poor blind eyes that have never seen—that haven't even memories. No homelight ever shone out through them—only once, long ago, a gleam of firelight. It might have been such a nice little house, snuggled against that wooded hill, pulling little spruces all around it to cover it. A warm, friendly little house. And a good-natured little house. Not like the new one at the Corner that Tom Semple is putting up. *It* is a bad-tempered house. Vixenish, with little eyes and sharp elbows. It's odd how much personality a house can have even before it is ever lived in at all. Once long ago, when Teddy and I were children, we pried a board off the window and climbed in and made a fire in the fireplace. Then we sat there and planned out our lives. We meant to spend them together in that very house. I suppose Teddy has forgotten all about that childish nonsense. He writes often and his letters are full and jolly and Teddy-like. And he tells me all the little things I want to know about his life. But lately they have become rather impersonal, it seems to me. They might just as well have been written to Ilse as to me.

"Poor little Disappointed House. I suppose you will always be disappointed."

VII

"May 1, 19—

"Spring again! Young poplars with golden, ethereal leaves. Leagues of rippling gulf beyond the silver-and-lilac sand-dunes.

"The winter has gone with a swiftness incredible, in spite of some terrible, black three-o'clocks and lonely, discouraged twilights. Dean will soon be home from Florida. But neither Teddy nor Ilse is coming home this summer. This gave me a white night or two recently. Ilse is going to the coast to visit an aunt—a mother's sister who never took any notice of her before. And Teddy has got the chance of illustrating a series of North-west Mounted Police stories for a New York firm and must spend his holidays making sketches for it in the far North. Of course it's a splendid chance for him and I wouldn't be a bit sorry—if *he* seemed a bit sorry because he wasn't coming to Blair Water. But he didn't.

"Well, I suppose Blair Water and the old life here are to him as a tale that is told now.

"I didn't realize how much I had been building on Ilse and Teddy being here for the summer or how much the hope of it had helped me through a few bad times in the winter. When I let myself remember that not once this summer will I hear Teddy's signal whistle in Lofty John's bush—not once happen on him in our secret, beautiful haunts of lane and brookside—not once exchange a thrilling, significant glance in a crowd when something happened which had a special meaning for us, all the colour seems to die out of life, leaving it just a drab, faded thing of shreds and patches.

"Mrs. Kent met me at the post-office yesterday and stopped to speak—something she very rarely does. She hates me as much as ever.

"'I suppose you have heard that Teddy is not coming home this summer?'

"'Yes,' I said briefly.

"There was a certain odd, aching triumph in her eyes as she turned away—a triumph I understood. She is very unhappy because Teddy will not be home for *her* but she is exultant that he will not be home for *me*. This shows, she is almost sure, that he cares nothing about me.

"Well, I dare say she is right. Still one can't be altogether gloomy in spring.

"And Andrew is engaged! To a girl of whom Aunt Addie entirely approves. 'I could not be more pleased with Andrew's choice if I had chosen her myself,' she said this afternoon to Aunt Elizabeth. *To* Aunt Elizabeth and *at* me. Aunt Elizabeth was coldly glad—or said she was. Aunt Laura cried a little—Aunt Laura always cries a bit when any one she knows is born or dead or married or engaged or come or gone or polling his first vote. She couldn't help feeling a little disappointed. Andrew would have been such a *safe* husband for me. Certainly there is no dynamite in Andrew."

CHAPTER III

I

At first nobody thought Mr. Carpenter's illness serious. He had had a good many attacks of rheumatism in recent years, laying him up for a few days. Then he could hobble back to work, as grim and sarcastic as ever, with a new edge to his tongue. In Mr. Carpenter's opinion teaching in Blair Water School was not what it had been. Nothing there now, he said, but rollicking, soulless young nonentities. Not a soul in the school who could pronounce February or Wednesday.

"I'm tired trying to make soup in a sieve," he said gruffly.

Teddy and Ilse and Perry and Emily were gone—the four pupils who had leavened the school with a saving inspiration. Perhaps Mr. Carpenter was a little tired of—everything. He was not very old, as years go, but he had burned up most of his constitution in a wild youth. The little, timid, faded slip of a woman who had been his wife had died unobtrusively in the preceding autumn. She had never seemed to matter much to Mr. Carpenter; but he had "gone down" rapidly after her funeral. The school children went in awe of his biting tongue and his more frequent spurts of temper. The trustees began to shake their heads and talk of a new teacher when the school year ended.

Mr. Carpenter's illness began as usual with an attack of rheumatism. Then there was heart trouble. Dr. Burnley, who went to see him despite his obstinate refusal to have a doctor, looked grave and talked mysteriously of a lack of "the will to live." Aunt Louisa Drummond of Derry Pond came over to nurse him. Mr. Carpenter submitted to this with a resignation that was a bad omen—as if nothing mattered any more.

"Have your own way. She can potter round if it will ease your consciences. So long as she leaves me alone I don't care what she does. I *won't* be fed and I *won't* be coddled and I *won't* have the sheets changed. Can't bear her hair, though. Too straight and shiny. Tell her to do something to it. And why does her nose look as if it were always cold?"

Emily ran in every evening to sit awhile with him. She was the only person the old man cared to see. He did not talk a great deal, but he liked to open his eyes every few minutes and exchange a sly smile of understanding with her—as if the two of them were laughing together over some excellent joke of which only they could sample the flavour. Aunt Louisa did not know what to make of this commerce of grins and consequently disapproved of it. She was a kind-hearted creature, with much real motherliness in her thwarted maiden breast, but she was all at sea with these cheerful, Puckish, deathbed smiles of her patient. She thought he had much better be thinking of his immortal soul. He was not a member of the church, was he? He would not even let the minister come in to see him. But Emily Starr was welcomed whenever she came. Aunt Louisa had her own secret suspicion of the said Emily Starr. Didn't she write? Hadn't she put her own mother's second-cousin, body and bones, into one of her stories? Probably she was looking for "copy" in this old pagan's deathbed. *That* explained her interest in it, beyond a doubt. Aunt Louisa looked curiously at this ghoulish young creature. She hoped Emily wouldn't put *her* in a story.

For a long time Emily had refused to believe that it *was* Mr. Carpenter's deathbed. He *couldn't* be so ill as all that. He didn't suffer—he didn't complain. He would be all right as soon as warmer weather came. She told herself this so often that she made herself believe it. She could not let herself think of life in Blair Water without Mr. Carpenter.

One May evening Mr. Carpenter seemed much better. His eyes flashed with their old satiric fire, his voice rang with its old resonance; he joked poor Aunt Louisa—who never could understand his jokes but endured them with Christian patience. Sick people must be humoured. He told a funny story to Emily and laughed with her over it till the little low-raftered room rang. Aunt Louisa shook her head. There were some things she did not know, poor lady, but she did know her own humble, faithful little trade of unprofessional nursing; and she knew that this sudden rejuvenescence was no good sign. As the Scotch would say, he was "fey." Emily in her inexperience did not know this. She went home rejoicing that Mr. Carpenter had taken such a turn for the better. Soon he would be all right, back at school, thundering at his pupils, striding absently along the road reading some dog-eared classic, criticizing her manuscripts with all his old trenchant humour. Emily was glad. Mr. Carpenter was a friend she could not afford to lose.

II

Aunt Elizabeth wakened her at two. She had been sent for. Mr. Carpenter was asking for her.

"Is he—worse?" asked Emily, slipping out of her high, black bed with its carved posts.

"Dying," said Aunt Elizabeth briefly. "Dr. Burnley says he can't last till morning."

Something in Emily's face touched Aunt Elizabeth.

"Isn't it better for him, Emily," she said with an unusual gentleness. "He is old and tired. His wife has gone—they will not give him the school another year. His old age would be very lonely. Death is his best friend."

"I am thinking of myself," choked Emily.

She went down to Mr. Carpenter's house, through the dark,

beautiful spring night. Aunt Louisa was crying but Emily did not cry. Mr. Carpenter opened his eyes and smiled at her—the same old, sly smile.

"No tears," he murmured. "I forbid tears at my deathbed. Let Louisa Drummond do the crying out in the kitchen. She might as well earn her money that way as another. There's nothing more she can do for me."

"Is there anything *I* can do?" asked Emily.

"Just sit here where I can see you till I'm gone, that's all. One doesn't like to go out—alone. Never liked the thought of dying alone. How many old she-weasels are out in the kitchen waiting for me to die?"

"There are only Aunt Louisa and Aunt Elizabeth," said Emily, unable to repress a smile.

"Don't mind my not—talking much. I've been talking—all my life. Through now. No breath—left. But if I think of anything—like you to be here."

Mr. Carpenter closed his eyes and relapsed into silence. Emily sat quietly, her head a soft blur of darkness against the window that was beginning to whiten with dawn. The ghostly hands of a fitful wind played with her hair. The perfume of June lilies stole in from the bed under the open window—a haunting odour, sweeter than music, like all the lost perfumes of old, unutterably dear years. Far off, two beautiful, slender, black firs, of exactly the same height, came out against the silver dawn-lit sky like the twin spires of some Gothic cathedral rising out of a bank of silver mist. Just between them hung a dim old moon, as beautiful as the evening crescent. Their beauty was a comfort and stimulant to Emily under the stress of this strange vigil. Whatever passed—whatever came—beauty like this was eternal.

Now and then Aunt Louisa came in and looked at the old man. Mr. Carpenter seemed unconscious of these visitations but always when she went out he opened his eyes and winked at Emily. Emily found herself winking back, somewhat to her own horror—for she had sufficient Murray in her to be slightly scandalized over deathbed winks. Fancy what Aunt Elizabeth would say.

"Good little sport," muttered Mr. Carpenter after the second exchange of winks. "Glad—you're there."

At three o'clock he grew rather restless. Aunt Louisa came in again.

"He can't die till the tide goes out, you know," she explained to

Emily in a solemn whisper.

"Get out of this with your superstitious blather," said Mr. Carpenter loudly and clearly. "I'll die when I'm d—n well ready, tide or no tide."

Horrified Aunt Louisa excused him to Emily on the ground that he was wandering in his mind and slipped out.

"Excuse my common way, won't you?" said Mr. Carpenter. "I *had* to shock her out. Couldn't have that elderly female person—round watching me die. Given her—a good yarn to tell—the rest of her—life. Awful—warning. And yet—she's a good soul. So good—she bores me. No evil in her. Somehow—one needs—a spice—of evil—in every personality. It's the—pinch of—salt—that brings out—the flavour."

Another silence. Then he added gravely,

"Trouble is—the Cook—makes the pinch—too large—in most cases. Inexperienced Cook—wiser after—a few eternities."

Emily thought he really was "wandering" now but he smiled at her.

"Glad you're here—little pal. Don't mind being—here—do you?"

"No," said Emily.

"When a Murray says—no—she means it."

After another silence Mr. Carpenter began again, this time more to himself, as it seemed, than anyone else.

"Going out—out beyond the dawn. Past the morning star. Used to think I'd be frightened. Not frightened. Funny. Think how much I'm going to know—in just a few more minutes, Emily. Wiser than anybody else living. Always wanted to know—to *know*. Never liked guesses. Done with curiosity—about life. Just curious now—about death. I'll know the truth, Emily—just a few more minutes and I'll know the—truth. No more guessing. And if—it's as I think—I'll be—young again. You can't know what—it means. You—who *are* young—can't have—the least idea—what it means—to be young—*again*."

His voice sank into restless muttering for a time, then rose clearly,

"Emily, promise me—that you'll never write—to please anybody—but yourself."

Emily hesitated a moment. Just what did such a promise mean?

"Promise," whispered Mr. Carpenter insistently.

Emily promised.

"That's right," said Mr. Carpenter with a sigh of relief. "Keep that—and you'll be—all right. No use trying to please everybody. No use trying to please—critics. Live under your own hat. Don't be—led away—by those howls about realism. Remember—pine woods are just as real as—pigsties—and a darn sight pleasanter to be in. You'll get there—sometime—you have the root—of the matter—in you. And don't—tell the world—everything. That's what's the—matter—with our—literature. Lost the charm of mystery—and reserve. There's something else I wanted to say—some caution—I can't—seem to remember—"

"Don't try," said Emily gently. "Don't tire yourself."

"Not—tired. Feel quite through—with being tired. I'm dying—I'm a failure—poor as a rat. But after all, Emily—I've had a—darned interesting time."

Mr. Carpenter shut his eyes and looked so deathlike that Emily made an involuntary movement of alarm. He lifted a bleached hand.

"No—don't call her. Don't call that weeping lady back. Just yourself, little Emily of New Moon. Clever little girl, Emily. What was it—I wanted to say to her?"

A moment or two later he opened his eyes and said in a loud, clear voice, "Open the door—open the door. Death must not be kept waiting."

Emily ran to the little door and set it wide. A strong wind of the grey sea rushed in. Aunt Louisa ran in from the kitchen.

"The tide has turned—he's going out with it—he's gone."

Not quite. As Emily bent over him the keen, shaggy-brown eyes opened for the last time. Mr. Carpenter essayed a wink but could not compass it.

"I've—thought of it," he whispered. "Beware—of—italics."

Was there a little impish chuckle at the end of the words? Aunt Louisa always declared there was. Graceless old Mr. Carpenter had died laughing—saying something about Italians. Of course he was delirious. But Aunt Louisa always felt it had been a very unedifying deathbed. She was thankful that few such had come in her experience.

III

Emily went blindly home and wept for her old friend in the room of her dreams. What a gallant old soul he was—going out into the shadow—or into the sunlight?—with a laugh and a jest. Whatever his faults there had never been anything of the coward about old Mr.

Carpenter. Her world, she knew, would be a colder place now that he was gone. It seemed many years since she had left New Moon in the darkness. She felt some inward monition that told her she had come to a certain parting of the ways of life. Mr. Carpenter's death would not make any external difference for her. Nevertheless, it was as a milestone to which in after years she could look back and say,

"After I passed that point everything was different."

All her life she had grown, as it seemed, by these fits and starts. Going on quietly and changelessly for months and years; then all at once suddenly realizing that she had left some "low-vaulted past" and emerged into some "new temple" of the soul more spacious than all that had gone before. Though always, at first, with a chill of change and a sense of loss.

CHAPTER IV

I

The year after Mr. Carpenter's death passed quietly for Emily—quietly, pleasantly—perhaps, though she tried to stifle the thought, a little monotonously. No Ilse—no Teddy—no Mr. Carpenter. Perry only very occasionally. But of course in the summer there was Dean. No girl with Dean Priest for a friend could be altogether lonely. They had always been such good friends, ever since the day, long ago, when she had fallen over the rocky bank of Malvern Bay and been rescued by Dean.* It did not matter in the least that he limped slightly and had a crooked shoulder, or that the dreamy brilliance of his green eyes sometimes gave his face an uncanny look. On the whole, there was no one in all the world she *liked* quite so well as Dean. When she thought this she always italicized the "liked." There were some things Mr. Carpenter had not known.

*See *Emily of New Moon.*

Aunt Elizabeth never quite approved of Dean. But then Aunt Elizabeth had no great love for any Priest.

There seemed to be a temperamental incompatibility between the Murrays and the Priests that was never bridged over, even by the occasional marriages between the clans.

"Priests, indeed," Aunt Elizabeth was wont to say contemptuously, relegating the whole clan, root and branch, to limbo with one wave of her thin, unbeautiful Murray hand. "Priests, indeed!"

"Murray is Murray and Priest is Priest and never the twain shall meet," Emily shamelessly mischievously misquoted Kipling once when Dean had asked in pretended despair why none of her aunts liked him.

"Your old Great-aunt Nancy over there at Priest Pond detests me," he said, with the little whimsical smile that sometimes gave him the look of an amused gnome, "And the Ladies Laura and Elizabeth treat me with the frosty politeness reserved by the Murrays for their dearest foes. Oh, I think I know why."

Emily flushed. She, too, was beginning to have an unwelcome suspicion why Aunts Elizabeth and Laura were even more frostily polite to Dean than of yore. She did not want to have it; she thrust it fiercely out and locked the door of thought upon it whenever it intruded there. But the thing whined on her doorstep and would not be banished. Dean, like everything and everybody else, seemed to have changed overnight. And what did the change imply—hint? Emily refused to answer this question. The only answer that suggested itself was too absurd. And too unwelcome.

Was Dean Priest changing from friend to lover? Nonsense. Arrant nonsense. Disagreeable nonsense. For she did not want him as a lover and she did want him madly as a friend. She *couldn't* lose his friendship. It was too dear, delightful, stimulating, wonderful. Why did such devilish things ever happen? When Emily reached this point in her disconnected musings she always stopped and retraced her mental steps fiercely, terrified to realize that she was almost on the point of admitting that "the something devilish" had already happened or was in process of happening.

In one way it was almost a relief to her when Dean said casually one November evening:

"I suppose I must soon be thinking of my annual migration."

"Where are you going this year?" asked Emily.

"Japan. I've never been there. Don't want to go now particularly. But what's the use of staying? Would you want to talk to me in the sitting-room all winter with the aunts in hearing?"

"No," said Emily between a laugh and a shiver. She recalled one fiendish autumn evening of streaming rain and howling wind when they couldn't walk in the garden but had to sit in the room where Aunt Elizabeth was knitting and Aunt Laura crocheting by the table. It had been awful. And again why? Why couldn't they talk as freely and whimsically and intimately then as they did in the garden? The answer to this at least was not to be expressed in any terms of sex. Was it because they talked of so many things Aunt Elizabeth could not understand and so disapproved of? Perhaps. But whatever the cause Dean might as well have been at the other side of the world for all the real conversation that was possible.

"So I might as well go," said Dean, waiting for this exquisite, tall, white girl in an old garden to say she would miss him horribly. She had said it every one of his flitting autumns for many years. But she did not say it this time. She found she dared not.

Again, why?

Dean was looking at her with eyes that could be tender or sorrowful or passionate, as he willed, and which now seemed to be a mixture of all three expressions. He *must* hear her say she would miss him. His true reason for going away again this winter was to make her realize how much she missed him—make her feel that she could not live without him.

"Will you miss me, Emily?"

"That goes without saying," answered Emily lightly—too lightly. Other years she had been very frank and serious about it. Dean was not altogether regretful for the change. But he could guess nothing of the attitude of mind behind it. She must have changed because she felt something—suspected something, of what he had striven for years to hide and suppress as rank madness. What then? Did this new lightness indicate that she didn't want to make a too important thing of admitting she would miss him? Or was it only the instinctive defence of a woman against something that implied or evoked too much?

"It will be so dreadful here this winter without you and Teddy and Ilse that I will not let myself think of it at all," went on Emily. "Last winter was bad. And this—I know somehow—will be worse. But I'll have my work."

"Oh, yes, your work," agreed Dean with the little, tolerant, half-amused inflection in his voice that always came now when he spoke of her "work," as if it tickled him hugely that she should call her pretty scribblings "work." Well, one must humour the charming child. He could not have said so more plainly in words. His implications cut across Emily's sensitive soul like a whip-lash. And all at once her work and her ambitions became—momentarily at least—as childish and unimportant as he considered them. She could not hold her own conviction against him. He must know. He was so clever—so well-educated. He *must* know. That was the agony of it. She could not ignore his opinion. Emily knew deep down in her heart that she would never be able wholly to believe in herself until Dean Priest admitted that she could do something honestly worth while in its way. And if he never admitted it—

"I shall carry pictures of you wherever I go, Star," Dean was saying. Star was his old nickname for her—not as a pun on her name but because he said she reminded him of a star. "I shall see you sitting in your room by that old lookout window, spinning your pretty cobwebs—pacing up and down in this old garden—wandering in the Yesterday Road—looking out to sea. Whenever I shall recall a bit of Blair Water loveliness I shall see you in it. After all, all other beauty is only a background for a beautiful woman."

"Her pretty cobwebs—" ah, there it was. That was all Emily heard. She did not even realize that he was telling her he thought *her* a beautiful woman.

"Do you think what I write is nothing but cobwebs, Dean?" she asked chokingly.

Dean looked surprised, doing it very well.

"Star, what else is it? What do you think it is yourself? I'm glad you can amuse yourself by writing. It's a splendid thing to have a little hobby of the kind. And if you can pick up a few shekels by it—well, that's all very well too in this kind of a world. But I'd hate to have you dream of being a Brontë or an Austen—and wake to find you'd wasted your youth on a dream."

"I don't fancy myself a Brontë or an Austen," said Emily. "But you didn't talk like that long ago, Dean. You used to think then I *could* do something some day."

"We don't bruise the pretty visions of a child," said Dean. "But it's foolish to carry childish dreams over into maturity. Better face facts.

You write charming things of their kind, Emily. Be content with that and don't waste your best years yearning for the unattainable or striving to reach some height far beyond your grasp."

II

Dean was not looking at Emily. He was leaning on the old sundial and scowling down at it with the air of a man who was forcing himself to say a disagreeable thing because he felt it was his duty.

"I *won't* be just a mere scribbler of pretty stories," cried Emily rebelliously. He looked into her face. She was as tall as he was—a trifle taller, though he would not admit it.

"You do not need to be anything but what you are," he said in a low vibrant tone. "A woman such as this old New Moon has never seen before. You can do more with those eyes—that smile—than you can ever do with your pen."

"You sound like Great-aunt Nancy Priest," said Emily cruelly and contemptuously.

But had he not been cruel and contemptuous to her? Three o'clock that night found her wide-eyed and anguished. She had lain through sleepless hours face to face with two hateful convictions. One was that she could never do anything worth doing with her pen. The other was that she was going to lose Dean's friendship. For friendship was all she could give him and it would not satisfy him. She must hurt him. And oh, how could she hurt Dean whom life had used so cruelly? She had said "no" to Andrew Murray and laughed a refusal to Perry Miller without a qualm. But this was an utterly different thing.

Emily sat up in bed in the darkness and moaned in a despair that was none the less real and painful because of the indisputable fact that thirty years later she might be wondering what on earth she had been moaning about.

"I wish there were no such things as lovers and love-making in the world," she said with savage intensity, honestly believing she meant it.

III

Like everybody, in daylight Emily found things much less tragic and more endurable than in the darkness. A nice fat cheque and a kind letter of appreciation with it restored a good deal of her self-respect and ambition. Very likely, too, she had imagined implications into Dean's words and looks that he never meant. She was not going to be a silly goose, fancying that every man, young or old, who liked to talk to her, or even to pay her compliments in shadowy, moonlit gardens, was in love with her. Dean was old enough to be her father.

Dean's unsentimental parting when he went away confirmed her in this comforting assurance and left her free to miss him without any reservations. Miss him she did abominably. The rain in autumn fields that year was a very sorrowful thing and so were the grey ghost-fogs coming slowly in from the gulf. Emily was glad when snow and sparkle came. She was very busy, writing such long hours, often far into the night, that Aunt Laura began to worry over her health and Aunt Elizabeth once or twice remarked protestingly that the price of coal-oil had gone up. As Emily paid for her own coal-oil this hint had no effect on her. She was very keen about making enough money to repay Uncle Wallace and Aunt Ruth what they had spent on her high school years. Aunt Elizabeth thought this was a praiseworthy ambition. The Murrays were an independent folk. It was a clan by-word that the Murrays had a boat of their own at the Flood. No promiscuous Ark for *them*.

Of course there were still many rejections—which Cousin Jimmy carried home from the post-office speechless with indignation. But the percentage of acceptances rose steadily. Every new magazine conquered meant a step upward on her Alpine path. She knew she was steadily gaining the mastery over her art. Even the "love talk" that had bothered her so much in the old days came easily now. Had Teddy Kent's eyes taught her so much? If she had taken time to think she might have been very lonely. There were some bad hours. Especially after a letter had come from Ilse full of all her gay doings in Montreal, her triumphs in the School of Oratory and her pretty new gowns. In the long twilights when she looked shiveringly from the windows of the old farmhouse and thought how very white and cold and solitary were the snow fields on the hill, how darkly remote and tragic the Three Princesses, she lost confidence in her star. She wanted summer; fields of daisies; seas misty with moonrise or purple with sunset; companionship; Teddy. In such moments she always knew she wanted Teddy.

Teddy seemed far away. They still corresponded faithfully, but the correspondence was not what it was. Suddenly in the autumn Teddy's letters had grown slightly colder and more formal. At this first hint of frost the temperature of Emily's dropped noticeably.

IV

But she had hours of rapture and insight that shed a glory backward and forward. Hours when she felt the creative faculty within her, burning like a never-dying flame. Rare, sublime moments when she felt as a god, perfectly happy and undesirous. And there was always her dream-world into which she could escape from monotony and loneliness, and taste strange, sweet happiness unmarred by any cloud or shadow. Sometimes she slipped mentally back into childhood and had delightful adventures she would have been ashamed to tell her adult world.

She liked to prowl about a good deal by herself, especially in twilight or moonlight alone with the stars and the trees, rarest of companions.

"I can't be contented indoors on a moonlight night. I have to be up and away," she told Aunt Elizabeth, who did not approve of prowling. Aunt Elizabeth never lost her uneasy consciousness that Emily's mother had eloped. And anyhow, prowling was odd. None of the other Blair Water girls prowled.

There were walks over the hills in the owl's light when the stars rose—one after another, the great constellations of myth and legend. There were frosty moonrises that hurt her with their beauty; spires of pointed firs against fiery sunsets; spruce copses dim with mystery; pacings to and fro on the To-morrow Road. Not the To-morrow Road of June, blossom-misted, tender in young green. Nor yet the To-morrow Road of October, splendid in crimson and gold. But the To-morrow Road of a still, snowy winter twilight—a white, mysterious, silent place full of wizardry. Emily loved it better than all her other dear spots. The spirit delight of that dream-haunted solitude never cloyed—its remote charm never palled.

If only there had been a friend to talk things over with! One night she awakened and found herself in tears, with a late moon shining bluely and coldly on her through the frosted window-panes. She had dreamed that Teddy had whistled to her from Lofty John's bush—the old, dear, signal whistle of childhood days; and she had run so eagerly across the garden to the bush. But she could not find Teddy.

"Emily Byrd Starr, if I catch you crying again over a dream!" she said passionately.

CHAPTER V

I

Only three dynamic things happened that year to vary the noiseless tenor of Emily's way. In the autumn she had a love affair—as Aunt Laura Victorianly phrased it. Rev. James Wallace, the new, well-meaning, ladylike young minister at Derry Pond, began making excuses for visiting Blair Water Manse quite often and from there drifted over to New Moon. Soon everybody in Blair Water and Derry Pond knew that Emily Starr had a ministerial beau. Gossip was very rife. It was a foregone conclusion that Emily would jump at him. A minister! Heads were shaken over it. She would never make a suitable minister's wife. Never in the world. But wasn't it always the way? A minister picking on the very last girl he should have.

At New Moon opinion was divided. Aunt Laura, who owned to a Dr. Fell feeling about Mr. Wallace, hoped Emily wouldn't "take" him. Aunt Elizabeth, in her secret soul, was not overfond of him either, but she was dazzled by the idea of a minister. And such a safe lover. A minister would never think of eloping. She thought Emily would be a very lucky girl if she could "get" him.

When it became sadly evident that Mr. Wallace's calls at New Moon had ceased, Aunt Elizabeth gloomily asked Emily the reason and was horrified to hear that the ungrateful minx had told Mr. Wallace she could not marry him.

"Why?" demanded Aunt Elizabeth in icy disapproval.

"His ears, Aunt Elizabeth, his ears," said Emily flippantly. "I really couldn't risk having my children inherit ears like that."

The indelicacy of such a reply staggered Aunt Elizabeth—which was probably why Emily had made it. She knew Aunt Elizabeth would be afraid to refer to the subject again.

The Rev. James Wallace thought it was "his duty" to go West the next spring. And that was that.

II

Then there was the episode of the local theatricals in Shrewsbury which were written up with vitriolic abuse in one of the Charlottetown papers. Shrewsbury people blamed Emily Byrd Starr for doing it. Who else, they demanded, could or would have written with such diabolic cleverness and sarcasm? Every one knew that Emily Byrd Starr had never forgiven Shrewsbury people for believing those yarns about her in the old John House affair. This was her method of revenge. Wasn't that like the Murrays? Carrying a secret grudge for years, until a suitable chance for revenge presented itself. Emily protested her innocence in vain. It was never discovered who had written the report and as long as she lived it kept coming up against her.

But in one way it worked out to her advantage. She was invited to all the social doings in Shrewsbury after that. People were afraid to leave her out lest she "write them up." She could not get to everything— Shrewsbury was seven miles from Blair Water. But she got to Mrs. Tom Nickle's dinner dance and thought for six weeks that it had changed the current of her whole existence.

Emily-in-the-glass looked very well that night. She had got the dress she had longed for for years—spent the whole price of a story on it, to her Aunt's horror. Shot silk—blue in one light, silver in another, with mists of lace. She remembered that Teddy had said that when she got that dress he would paint her as an Ice-maiden in it.

Her right-hand neighbour was a man who kept making "funny speeches" all through the meal and kept her wondering for what good purpose God had ever fashioned him.

But her left-hand neighbour! He talked little but he looked! Emily decided that she liked a man whose eyes said more than his lips. But he told her she looked like "the moonbeam of a blue summer night" in that gown. I think it was that phrase that finished Emily—shot her clean through the heart—like the unfortunate little duck of the nursery rhyme. Emily was helpless before the charm of a well-turned phrase. Before the evening was over Emily, for the first time in her life, had fallen wildly and romantically into the wildest and most romantic kind of love—"the love the poets dreamed of," as she wrote in her diary. The young man—I believe his beautiful and romantic name was Aylmer Vincent—was quite as madly in love as she. He literally haunted New Moon. He wooed beautifully. His way of saying "dear lady" charmed her. When he told her that "a beautiful hand was one of the chief charms of a beautiful woman" and looked adoringly at hers Emily kissed her hands when she went to her room that night because *his* eyes had caressed them. When he called her raptly "a creature of mist and flame" she misted and flamed about dim old New Moon until Aunt Elizabeth unthinkingly quenched her by asking her to fry up a batch of doughnuts for Cousin Jimmy. When he told her she was like an opal—milk-white outside but with a heart of fire and crimson, she wondered if life would always be like this.

"And to think I once imagined I cared for Teddy Kent," she thought in amazement at herself.

She neglected her writing and asked Aunt Elizabeth if she could have the old blue box in the attic for a hope chest. Aunt Elizabeth graciously acceded. The record of the new suitor had been investigated and found impeccable. Good family—good social position—good business. All the omens were auspicious.

III

And then a truly terrible thing happened.

Emily fell out of love just as suddenly as she had fallen into it. One day she was, and the next she wasn't. That was all there was to it.

She was aghast. She couldn't believe it. She tried to pretend the old enchantment still existed. She tried to thrill and dream and blush. Nary thrill, nary blush. Her dark-eyed lover—*why* had it never struck her before that his eyes were exactly like a cow's?—bored her. Ay, bored her. She yawned one evening in the very midst of one of his fine speeches. Why, there was nothing to him but fine speeches. There was nothing to add to that.

She was so ashamed that she was almost ill over it. Blair people thought she had been jilted and pitied her. The aunts who knew better were disappointed and disapproving.

"Fickle—fickle—like all the Starrs," said Aunt Elizabeth bitterly.

Emily had no spunk to defend herself. She supposed she deserved it all. Perhaps she was fickle. She must be fickle. When such a glorious conflagration fizzled out so speedily and utterly into ashes. Not a spark of it left. Not even a romantic memory. Emily viciously inked out the passage in her diary about "the love the poets dreamed of."

She was really very unhappy about it for a long while. Had she no depth at all? Was she such a superficial creature that even love with her was like the seeds that fell into the shallow soil in the immortal parable? She knew other girls had these silly, tempestuous, ephemeral affairs but she would never have supposed she would have one—*could* have one. To be swept off her feet like that by a handsome face and mellifluous voice and great dark eyes and a trick of pretty speeches! In brief Emily felt that she had made an absolute fool of herself and the Murray pride could not stick it.

To make it worse the young man married a Shrewsbury girl in six months. Not that Emily cared whom he married or how soon. But it meant that *his* romantic ardours were but things of superficiality, too, and lent a deeper tinge of humiliation to the silly affair. Andrew had been so easily consoled also. Percy Miller was not wasting in despair. Teddy had forgotten her. Was she really incapable of inspiring a deep and lasting passion in a man? To be sure, there was Dean. But even Dean could go away winter after winter and leave her to be wooed and won by any chance-met suitor.

"Am I fundamentally superficial?" poor Emily demanded of herself with terrible intensity

She took up her pen again with a secret gladness. But for a considerable time the love-making in her stories was quite cynical and misanthropic in its flavour.

CHAPTER VI

I

Teddy Kent and Ilse Burnley came home in the summer for a brief vacation. Teddy had won an Art Scholarship which meant two years in Paris and was to sail for Europe in two weeks. He had written the news to Emily in an off-hand way and she had responded with the congratulations of a friend and sister. There was no reference in either letter to rainbow gold or Vega of the Lyre. Yet Emily looked forward to his coming with a wistful, ashamed hope that would not be denied. Perhaps—dared she hope it?—when they met again face to face, in their old haunted woods and trysts—this coldness that had grown up so inexplicably between them would vanish as a sea-fog vanishes when the sun rose over the gulf. No doubt Teddy had had his imitation love affairs as she had hers. But when he came—when they looked again into each other's eyes—when she heard his signal whistle in Lofty John's bush—

But she never heard it. On the evening of the day when she knew Teddy was expected home she walked in the garden among brocaded moths, wearing a new gown of "powder-blue" chiffon and listened for it. Every robin call brought the blood to her cheek and made her heart beat wildly. Then came Aunt Laura through the dew and dusk.

"Teddy and Ilse are here," she said.

Emily went in to the stately, stiff, dignified parlour of New Moon, pale, queenly, aloof. Ilse hurled herself upon her with all her old, tempestuous affection, but Teddy shook hands with a cool detachment that almost equalled her own. Teddy? Oh, dear, no. Frederick Kent, R.A.-to-be. What was there left of the old Teddy in this slim, elegant young man with his sophisticated air and cool, impersonal eyes, and general implication of having put off for ever all childish things— including foolish old visions and insignificant little country girls he had played with in his infancy?

578

In which conclusion Emily was horribly unjust to Teddy. But she was not in a mood to be just to anybody. Nobody is who has made a fool of herself. And Emily felt that that was just what she had done—again. Mooning romantically about in a twilight garden, specially wearing powder-blue, waiting for a lover's signal from a beau who had forgotten all about her—or only remembered her as an old schoolmate on whom he had very properly and kindly and conscientiously come to call. Well, thank heaven, Teddy did not know how absurd she had been. She would take excellent care that he should never suspect it. Who could be more friendly and remote than a Murray of New Moon? Emily's manner, she flattered herself, was admirable. As gracious and impersonal as to an entire stranger. Renewed congratulations on his wonderful success, coupled with an absolute lack of all real interest in it. Carefully phrased, polite questions about *his* work on her side; carefully phrased polite questions about *her* work on his side. She had seen some of *his* pictures in the magazines. He had read some of *her* stories. So it went, with a wider gulf opening between them at every moment. Never had Emily felt herself so far away from Teddy. She recognized with a feeling that was almost terror how completely he had changed in those two years of absence. It would in truth have been a ghastly interview had it not been for Ilse, who chattered with all her old breeziness and tang, planning out a two weeks of gay doings while she was home, asking hundreds of questions; the same lovable old madcap of laughter and jest and dressed with all her old gorgeous violations of accepted canons of taste. In an extraordinary dress—a thing of greenish-yellow. She had a big pink peony at her waist and another at her shoulder. She wore a bright green hat with a wreath of pink flowers on it. Great hoops of pearl swung in her ears. It was a weird costume. No one but Ilse could have worn it successfully. And she looked like the incarnation of a thousand tropic springs in it—exotic, provocative, beautiful. So beautiful! Emily realized her friend's beauty afresh with a pang not of envy, but of bitter humiliation. Beside Ilse's golden sheen of hair and brilliance of amber eyes and red-rose loveliness of cheeks she must look pale and dark and insignificant. Of course Teddy was in love with Ilse. He had gone to see her first—had been with her while Emily waited for him in the garden. Well, it made no real difference. Why should it? She would be just as friendly as ever. And was. Friendly with a vengeance. But when Teddy and Ilse had gone—together—laughing and teasing each other through the old To-morrow Road Emily went up to her room and locked the door. Nobody saw her again until the next morning.

II

The gay two weeks of Ilse's planning followed. Picnics, dances and jamborees galore. Shrewsbury society decided that a rising young artist was somebody to be taken notice of and took notice accordingly. It was a veritable whirl of gaiety and Emily whirled about in it with the others. No step lighter in the dance, no voice quicker in the jest, and all the time feeling like the miserable spirit in a ghost story she had once read who had a live coal in its breast instead of a heart. All the time, feeling, too, far down under surface pride and hidden pain, that sense of completion and fulfilment which always came to her when Teddy was near her. But she took good care never to be alone with Teddy, who certainly could not be accused of any attempt to inveigle her into twosomes. His name was freely coupled with Ilse's and they took so composedly the teasing they encountered, that the impression gained ground that "things were pretty well understood between them." Emily thought Ilse might have told her if it were so. But Ilse, though she told many a tale of lovers forlorn whose agonies seemed to lie very lightly on her conscience, never mentioned Teddy's name, which Emily thought had a torturing significance of its own. She inquired after Perry Miller, wanting to know if he were as big an oaf as ever and laughing over Emily's indignant defence.

"He will be Premier some day no doubt," agreed Ilse scornfully. "He'll work like the devil and never miss anything by lack of asking for it, but won't you always smell the herring-barrels of Stovepipe Town?"

Perry came to see Ilse, bragged a bit too much over his progress and got so snubbed and manhandled that he did not come again. Altogether the two weeks seemed a nightmare to Emily, who thought she was unreservedly thankful when the time came for Teddy to go. He was going on a sailing vessel to Halifax, wanting to make some nautical sketches for a magazine, and an hour before flood-tide, while the *Mira Lee* swung at anchor by the wharf at Stovepipe Town, he came to say good-bye. He did not bring Ilse with him—no doubt, thought Emily, because Ilse was visiting in Charlottetown; but Dean Priest was there, so there was no dreaded solitude *a deux*. Dean was creeping back into his own, after the two weeks' junketings from which he had been barred out. Dean would not go to dances and clam-bakes, but he was always hovering in the background, as everybody concerned felt. He stood with Emily in the garden and there was a certain air of victory and possession about him that did not escape Teddy's eye. Dean, who never made the mistake of thinking gaiety was happiness, had seen more than others of the little drama that had been played out in Blair Water during those two weeks and the dropping of the curtain left him a satisfied man. The old, shadowy, childish affair between Teddy Kent of the Tansy Patch and Emily of New Moon, was finally ended. Whatever its significance or lack of significance had been, Dean no longer counted Teddy among his rivals.

Emily and Teddy parted with the hearty handshake and mutual good wishes of old schoolmates who do indeed wish each other well but have no very vital interest in the matter.

"Prosper and be hanged to you," as some old Murray had been wont to say.

Teddy got himself away very gracefully. He had the gift of making an artistic exit, but he did not once look back. Emily turned immediately to Dean and resumed the discussion which Teddy's coming had interrupted. Her lashes hid her eyes very securely. Dean, with his uncanny ability to read her thoughts, should not—must not guess—what? What was there to guess? Nothing—absolutely nothing. Yet Emily kept her lashes down.

When Dean, who had some other engagement that evening, went away half an hour later she paced sedately up and down among the gold of primroses for a little while, the very incarnation, in all seeming, of maiden meditation fancy free.

"Spinning out a plot, no doubt," thought Cousin Jimmy proudly, as he glimpsed her from the kitchen window. "It beats me how she does it."

III

Perhaps Emily was spinning out a plot. But as the shadows deepened she slipped out of the garden, through the dreamy peace of the old columbine orchard—along the Yesterday Road—over the green pasture field—past the Blair Water—up the hill beyond—past the Disappointed House—through the thick fir wood. There, in a clump of silver birches, one had an unbroken view of the harbour, flaming in lilac and rose-colour. Emily reached it a little breathlessly—she had almost run at the last. Would she be to late? Oh, what if she should be too late?

The *Mira Lee* was sailing out of the harbour, a dream vessel in the glamour of sunset, past purple headlands and distant, fairylike, misty coasts. Emily stood and watched her till she had crossed the bar into the gulf beyond. Stood and watched her until she had faded from sight in the blue dimness of the falling night, conscious only of a terrible hunger to see Teddy once more—just once more. To say good-bye as it should have been said.

Teddy was gone. To another world. There was no rainbow in sight. And what was Vega of the Lyre but a whirling, flaming, incredibly distant sun?

She slipped down among the grasses at her feet and lay there sobbing in the cold moonshine that had suddenly taken the place of the friendly twilight.

Mingled with her sharp agony was incredulity. This thing could not have happened. Teddy could no have gone away with only that soulless, chilly, polite good-bye. After all their years of comradeship, if nothing else. Oh, how would she ever get herself past three o'clock this night?

"I am a hopeless fool," she whispered savagely. "He has forgotten. I am nothing to him. And I deserve it. Didn't I forget him in those crazy weeks when I was imagining myself in love with Aylmer Vincent? Of course somebody has told him all about that. I've lost my chance of real happiness through that absurd affair. Where is my pride? To cry like this over a man who has forgotten me. But—but—it's so nice to cry after having had to laugh for these hideous weeks."

IV

Emily flung herself into work feverishly after Teddy had gone. Through long summer days and nights she wrote, while the purple stains deepened under her eyes and the rose stains faded out of her cheeks. Aunt Elizabeth thought she was killing herself and for the first time was reconciled to her intimacy with Jarback Priest, since he dragged Emily away from her desk in the evenings at least for walks and talks in the fresh air. That summer Emily paid off the last of her indebtedness to Uncle Wallace and Aunt Ruth with her "pot-boilers."

But there was more than pot-boiling a-doing. In her first anguish of loneliness, as she lay awake at three o'clock, Emily had remembered a certain wild winter night when she and Ilse and Perry and Teddy had been "stormed in" in the old John House on the Derry Pond Road;* remembered all the scandal and suffering that had arisen there-from; and remembered also that night of rapt delight "thinking out" a story that had flashed into her mind at a certain gay, significant speech of Teddy's. At least, she had thought it significant then. Well, *that* was all over. But wasn't the story somewhere? She had written the outline of that alluring, fanciful tale in a Jimmy-book the next day. Emily sprang out of bed in the still summer moonlight, lighted one of the famous candles of New Moon, and rummaged through a pile of old Jimmy-books. Yes, here it was. *A Seller of Dreams.* Emily squatted down on her haunches and read it through. It was *good*. Again it seized hold of her imagination and called forth all her creative impulse. She would write it out—she would begin that very moment. Flinging a dressing-gown over her white shoulders to protect them from the keen gulf air she sat down before her open window and began to write. Everything else was forgotten—for a time at least—in the subtle, all-embracing joy of creation.

* See *Emily Climbs.*

Teddy was nothing but a dim memory—love was a blown-out candle. Nothing mattered but her story. The characters came to life under her hand and swarmed through her consciousness, vivid, alluring, compelling. Wit, tears, and laughter trickled from her pen. She lived and breathed in another world and came back to New Moon only at dawn to find her lamp burned out, and her table littered with manuscript—the first four chapters of her book. Her book! What magic and delight and awe and incredulity in the thought.

For weeks Emily seemed to live really only when she was writing it. Dean found her strangely rapt and remote, absent and impersonal. Her conversation was as dull as it was possible for Emily's conversation to be, and while her body sat or walked beside him her soul was—where? In some region where he could not follow, at all events. It had escaped him.

V

Emily finished her book in six weeks—finished it at dawn one morning. She flung down her pen and went to her window, lifting her pale, weary, triumphant little face to the skies of morning.

Music was dripping through the leafy silence in Lofty John's bush. Beyond were dawn-rosy meadows and the garden of New Moon living in an enchanted calm. The wind's dance over the hills seemed some dear response to the music and rhythm in her being. Hills, sea, shadows, all called to her with a thousand elfin voices of understanding and acclaim. The old gulf was singing. Exquisite tears were in her eyes. She had written it—oh, how happy she was! This moment atoned for everything.

Finished—complete! There it lay—*A Seller of Dreams*—her first book. Not a great book—oh, no, but *hers*—her very own. Something to which she had given birth, which would never have existed had she not brought it into being. And it was *good*. She knew it was—felt it was. A fiery, delicate tale, instinct with romance, pathos, humour. The rapture of creation still illuminated it. She turned the pages over, reading a bit here and there—wondering if she could really have written *that*. She was right under the rainbow's end. Could she not touch the magic, prismatic thing? Already her fingers were clasping the pot of gold.

Aunt Elizabeth walked in with her usual calm disregard of any useless formality such as knocking.

"Emily," she said severely, "have you been sitting up all night *again*?"

Emily came back to earth with that abominable mental jolt which can only be truly described as a thud—a "sickening thud" at that. Very sickening. She stood like a convicted schoolgirl. And *A Seller of Dreams* became instantly a mere heap of scribbled paper.

"I—I didn't realize how time was passing, Aunt Elizabeth," she stammered.

"You are old enough to have better sense," said Aunt Elizabeth. "I don't mind your writing—now. You seem to be able to earn a living by it in a very ladylike way. But you will wreck your health if you keep this sort of thing up. Have you forgotten that your mother died of consumption? At any rate, don't forget that you must pick those beans to-day. It's high time they were picked."

Emily gathered up her manuscript with all her careless rapture gone.

Creation was over; remained now the sordid business of getting her book published. Emily typewrote it on the little third-hand machine Perry had picked up for her at an auction sale—a machine that wrote only half of any capital letter and wouldn't print the "m's" at all. She put the capitals and the "m's" in afterwards with a pen and sent the MS. away to a publishing firm. The publishing firm sent it back with a typewritten screed stating that "their readers had found some merit in the story but not enough to warrant an acceptance."

This "damning with faint praise" flattened Emily out as not even a printed slip could have done. Talk about three o'clock that night! No, it is an act of mercy not to talk about it—or about many successive three o'clocks.

"Ambition!" wrote Emily bitterly in her diary. "I could laugh! Where is my ambition now? What is it like to be ambitious? To feel that life is before you, a fair, unwritten white page where you may inscribe your name in letters of success? To feel that you have the wish and power to win your crown? To feel that the coming years are crowding to meet you and lay their largess at your feet? I *once* knew what it was to feel so."

All of which goes to show how very young Emily still was. But agony is none the less real because in later years when we have learned that everything passes, we wonder what we agonized about. She had a bad three weeks of it. Then she recovered enough to send her story out again. This time the publisher wrote to her that he might consider the book if she would make certain changes in it. It was too "quiet." She must "pep it up." And the ending must be changed entirely. It would never do.

Emily tore his letter savagely into bits. Mutilate and degrade her story? Never! The very suggestion was an insult.

When a third publisher sent it back with a printed slip Emily's belief in it died. She tucked it away and took up her pen grimly.

"Well, I can write short stories at least. I must continue to do that."

Nevertheless, the book haunted her. After a few weeks she took it out and reread it—coolly, critically, free alike from the delusive glamour of her first rapture and from the equally delusive depression of rejection slips. And still it seemed to her good. Not quite the wonder-tale she had fancied it, perhaps; but still a good piece of work. What then? No writer, so she had been told, was ever capable of judging his own work correctly. If only Mr. Carpenter were alive! He would tell her the truth. Emily made a sudden terrible resolution. She would show it to Dean. She would ask for his calm unprejudiced opinion and abide by it. It would be hard. It was always hard to show her stories to any one, most of all to Dean, who knew so much and had read everything in the world. But she must *know*. And she knew Dean would tell her the truth, good or bad. He thought nothing of her stories. But *this* was different. Would he not see something worth while in this? If not—

VI

"Dean, I want your candid opinion about this story. Will you read it carefully, and tell me exactly what you think of it? I don't want flattery—or false encouragement—I want the truth—the naked truth."

"Are you so sure of that?" asked Dean dryly. "Very few people can endure seeing the naked truth. It has to have a rag or two to make it presentable."

"I *do* want the truth," said Emily stubbornly. "This book has been"—she choked a little over the confession, "refused three times. If you find any good in it I'll keep on trying to find a publisher for it. If you condemn it I'll burn it."

Dean looked inscrutably at the little packet she held out to him. So *this* was what had wrapped her away from him all summer—absorbed her—possessed her. The one black drop in his veins—that Priest jealousy of being first—suddenly made its poison felt.

He looked into her cold, sweet face and starry eyes, grey-purple as a lake at dawn, and hated whatever was in the packet, but he carried it home and brought it back three nights later. Emily met him in the garden, pale and tense.

"Well," she said.

Dean looked at her, guilty. How ivory white and exquisite she was in the chill dusk!

"'Faithful are the wounds of a friend.' I should be less than your friend if I told you falsehoods about this, Emily."

"So—it's no good."

"It's a pretty little story, Emily. Pretty and flimsy and ephemeral as a rose-tinted cloud. Cobwebs—only cobwebs. The whole conception is too far-fetched. Fairy tales are out of the fashion. And this one of yours makes overmuch of a demand on the credulity of the reader. And your

586

characters are only puppets. How could you write a real story? You've never *lived*."

Emily clenched her hands and bit her lips. She dared not trust her voice to say a single word. She had not felt like this since the night Ellen Greene had told her her father must die. Her heart, that had beaten so tumultuously a few minutes ago, was like lead, heavy and cold. She turned and walked away from him. He limped softly after her and touched her shoulder.

"Forgive me, Star. Isn't it better to know the truth? Stop reaching for the moon. You'll never get it. Why try to write, anyway? Everything has already been written."

"Some day," said Emily, compelling herself to speak steadily, "I may be able to thank you for this. To-night I hate you."

"Is that just?" asked Dean quietly.

"No, of course it isn't just," said Emily wildly. "Can you expect me to be just when you've just killed me? Oh, I know I asked for it—I know it's good for me. Horrible things always are good for you, I suppose. After you've been killed a few times you don't mind it. But the first time one does—squirm. Go away, Dean. Don't come back for a week at least. The funeral will be over then."

"Don't you believe I know what this means to you, Star?" asked Dean pityingly.

"You can't—altogether. Oh, I know you're sympathetic. I don't want sympathy. I only want time to bury myself decently."

Dean, knowing it would be better to go, went. Emily watched him out of sight. Then she took up the little dog-eared, discredited manuscript he had laid on the stone bench and went up to her room. She looked it over by her window in the fading light. Sentence after sentence leaped out at her—witty, poignant, beautiful. No, that was only her fond, foolish, maternal delusion. There was nothing of that sort in the book. Dean had said so. And her book people. How she loved them. How real they seemed to her. It was terrible to think of destroying them. But they were *not* real. Only "puppets." Puppets would not mind being burned. She glanced up at the starlit sky of the autumn night. Vega of the Lyre shone bluely down upon her. Oh, life was an ugly, cruel, wasteful thing!

Emily crossed over to her little fireplace and laid *A Seller of Dreams* in the grate. She struck a match, knelt down and held it to a corner with a hand that did not tremble. The flame seized on the loose sheets eagerly, murderously. Emily clasped her hands over her heart and watched it with dilated eyes, remembering the time she had burned her old "account book" rather than let Aunt Elizabeth see it. In a few moments the manuscript was a mass of writhing fires—in a few more seconds it was a heap of crinkled ashes, with here and there an accusing ghost-word coming out whitely on a blackened fragment, as if to reproach her.

Repentance seized upon her. Oh, why had she done it? Why had she burned her book? Suppose it was no good. Still, it was hers. It was wicked to have burned it. She had destroyed something incalculably precious to her. What did the mothers of old feel when their children had passed through the fire to Moloch—when the sacrificial impulse and excitement had gone? Emily thought she knew.

Nothing of her book, her dear book that had seemed so wonderful to her, but ashes—a little, pitiful heap of black ashes. Could it be so? Where had gone all the wit and laughter and charm that had seemed to glimmer in its pages—all the dear folks who had lived in them—all the secret delight she had woven into them as moonlight is woven among pines? Nothing left but ashes. Emily sprang up in such an anguish of regret that she could not endure it. She must get out—away—anywhere. Her little room, generally so dear and beloved and cosy, seemed like a prison. Out—somewhere—into the cold, free autumn night with its grey ghost-mists—away from walls and boundaries—away from that little heap of dark flakes in the grate—away from the reproachful ghosts of her murdered book folks. She flung open the door of the room and rushed blindly to the stair.

VII

Aunt Laura never to the day of her death forgave herself for leaving that mending-basket at the head of the stair. She had never done such a thing in her life before. She had been carrying it up to her room when Elizabeth called peremptorily from the kitchen asking where something was. Laura set her basket down on the top step and ran to get it. She was away only a moment. But that moment was enough for predestination and Emily. The tear-blinded girl stumbled over the basket and fell—headlong down the long steep staircase of New Moon.

588

There was a moment of fear—a moment of wonderment—she felt plunged into deadly cold—she felt plunged into burning heat—she felt a soaring upward—a falling into unseen depths—a fierce stab of agony in her foot—then nothing more. When Laura and Elizabeth came running in there was only a crumpled silken heap lying at the foot of the stairs with balls and stockings all around it and Aunt Laura's scissors bent and twisted under the foot they had so cruelly pierced.

CHAPTER VII

I

From October to April Emily Starr lay in bed or on the sitting-room lounge watching the interminable windy drift of clouds over the long white hills or the passionless beauty of winter trees around quiet fields of snow, and wondering if she would ever walk again—or walk only as a pitiable cripple. There was some obscure injury to her back upon which the doctors could not agree. One said it was negligible and would right itself in time. Two others shook their heads and were afraid. But all were agreed about the foot. The scissors had made two cruel wounds—one by the ankle, one on the sole of the foot. Blood-poisoning set in. For days Emily hovered between life and death, then between the scarcely less terrible alternative of death and amputation. Aunt Elizabeth prevented that. When all the doctors agreed that it was the only way to save Emily's life she said grimly that it was not the Lord's will, as understood by the Murrays, that people's limbs should be cut off. Nor could she be removed from this position. Laura's tears and Cousin Jimmy's pleadings and Dr. Burnley's execrations and Dean Priest's agreements budged her not a jot. Emily's foot should not be cut off. Nor was it. When she recovered unmaimed Aunt Elizabeth was triumphant and Dr. Burnley confounded.

The danger of amputation was over, but the danger of lasting and bad lameness remained. Emily faced that all winter.

"If I only *knew* one way or the other," she said to Dean. "If I *knew*,

I could make up my mind to bear it—perhaps. But to lie here—wondering—wondering if I'll ever be well."

"You will be well," said Dean savagely.

Emily did not know what she would have done without Dean that winter. He had given up his invariable winter trip and stayed in Blair Water that he might be near her. He spent the days with her, reading, talking, encouraging, sitting in the silence of perfect companionship. When he was with her Emily felt that she might even be able to face a lifetime of lameness. But in the long nights when everything was blotted out by pain she could not face it. Even when there was no pain her nights were often sleepless and very terrible when the wind wailed drearily about the old New Moon eaves or chased flying phantoms of snow over the hills. When she slept she dreamed, and in her dreams she was for ever climbing stairs and could never get to the top of them, lured upward by an odd little whistle—two higher notes and a low one—that ever retreated as she climbed. It was better to lie awake than have that terrible, recurrent dream. Oh, those bitter nights! Once Emily had not thought that the Bible verse declaring that there would be no night in heaven contained an attractive promise. No night? No soft twilight enkindled with stars? No white sacrament of moonlight? No mystery of velvet shadow and darkness? No ever-amazing miracle of dawn? Night was as beautiful as day and heaven would not be perfect without it.

But now in these dreary weeks of pain and dread she shared the hope of the Patmian seer. Night was a dreadful thing.

People said Emily Starr was very brave and patient and uncomplaining. But she did not seem so to herself. They did not know of the agonies of rebellion and despair and cowardice behind her outward calmness of Murray pride and reserve. Even Dean did not know—though perhaps he suspected.

She smiled gallantly when smiling was indicated, but she never laughed. Not even Dean could make her laugh, though he tried with all the powers of wit and humour at his command.

"My days of laughter are done," Emily said to herself. And her days of creation as well. She could never write again. The "flash" never came. No rainbow spanned the gloom of that terrible winter. People came to see her continuously. She wished they would stay away. Especially Uncle Wallace and Aunt Ruth, who were sure she would never walk again and said so every time they came. Yet they were not so bad as the callers who were cheerfully certain she would be all right in time and did not believe a word of it themselves. She had never had any intimate friends except Dean and Ilse and Teddy. Ilse wrote weekly letters in which she rather too obviously tried to cheer Emily up. Teddy wrote once when he heard of her accident. The letter was very kind and tactful and sincerely sympathetic. Emily thought it was the letter any indifferent friendly acquaintance might have written and she did not answer it though he had asked her to let him know how she was getting on. No more letters came. There was nobody but Dean. He had never failed her—never would fail her. More and more as the interminable days of storm and gloom passed she turned to him. In that winter of pain she seemed to herself to grow so old and wise that they met on equal ground at last. Without him life was a bleak, grey desert devoid of colour or music. When he came the desert would—for a time at least—blossom like the rose of joy and a thousand flowerets of fancy and hope and illusion would fling their garlands over it.

II

When spring came Emily got well—got well so suddenly and quickly that even the most optimistic of the three doctors was amazed. True, for a few weeks she had to limp about on a crutch, but the time came when she could do without it—could walk alone in the garden and look out on the beautiful world with eyes that could not be satisfied with seeing. Oh, how good life was again! How good the green sod felt beneath her feet! She had left pain and fear behind her like a cast-off garment and felt gladness—no, not gladness exactly, but the possibility of being glad once more sometime.

It was worth while to have been ill to realize the savour of returning health and well-being on a morning like this, when a sea-wind was blowing up over the long, green fields. There was nothing on earth like a sea-wind. Life might, in some ways, be a thing of shreds and tatters, everything might be changed or gone; but pansies and sunset clouds were still fair. She felt again her old joy in mere existence.

"'Truly the light is sweet and a pleasant thing it is for the eye to behold the sun,'" she quoted dreamily.

Old laughter came back. On the first day that Emily's laughter was

591

heard again in New Moon Laura Murray, whose hair had turned from ash to snow that winter, went to her room and knelt down by her bed to thank God. And while she knelt there Emily was talking about God to Dean in the garden on one of the most beautiful spring twilights imaginable, with a little, growing moon in the midst of it.

"There have been times this past winter when I felt God hated me. But now again I feel sure He loves me," she said softly.

"So sure?" questioned Dean dryly. "*I* think God is interested in us but He doesn't love us. He likes to watch us to see what we'll do. Perhaps it amuses Him to see us squirm."

"What a horrible conception of God!" said Emily with a shudder. "You don't really believe that about Him, Dean."

"Why not?"

"Because He would be worse than a devil then—a God who thought only about his own amusement, without even the devil's justification of hating us."

"Who tortured you all winter with bodily pain and mental anguish?" asked Dean.

"Not God. And He—sent me *you*," said Emily steadily. She did not look at him; she lifted her face to the Three Princesses in their Maytime beauty—a white-rose face now, pale from its winter's pain. Beside her the big spirea, which was the pride of Cousin Jimmy's heart, banked up in its June-time snow, making a beautiful background for her. "Dean, how can I ever thank you for what you've done for me—been to me—since last October? I can never put it in words. But I want you to know how I feel about it."

"I've done nothing except snatch at happiness. Do you know what happiness it was to me to do something for you Star—help you in some way—to see you turning to me in your pain for something that only I could give—something I had learned in my own years of loneliness? And to let myself dream something that couldn't come true—that I knew ought not to come true—"

Emily trembled and shivered slightly. Yet why hesitate—why put off that which she had fully made up her mind to do?

"Are you so sure, Dean," she said in a low tone, "that your dream—can't come true?"

CHAPTER VIII

I

There was a tremendous sensation in the Murray clan when Emily announced that she was going to marry Dean Priest. At New Moon the situation was very tense for a time. Aunt Laura cried and Cousin Jimmy went about shaking his head and Aunt Elizabeth was exceedingly grim. Yet in the end they made up their minds to accept it. What else could they do? By this time even Aunt Elizabeth realized that when Emily said she was going to do a thing she would do it

"You would have made a worse fuss if I had told you I was going to marry Perry of Stovepipe Town," said Emily when she had heard all Aunt Elizabeth had to say.

"Of course that is true enough," admitted Aunt Elizabeth when Emily had gone out. "And, after all, Dean is well-off—and the Priests are a good family."

"But so—so *Priesty*," sighed Laura. "And Dean is far, far too old for Emily. Besides, his great-great-grandfather went insane."

"Dean won't go insane."

"His children might."

"Laura," said Elizabeth rebukingly, and dropped the subject.

"Are you very sure you love him, Emily?" Aunt Laura asked that evening.

"Yes—in a way," said Emily.

Aunt Laura threw out her hands and spoke with a sudden passion utterly foreign to her.

"But there's only one way of loving."

"Oh no, dearest of Victorian aunties," answered Emily gaily. "There are a dozen different ways. *You* know I've tried one or two ways already. And they failed me. Don't worry about Dean and me. We understand each other perfectly."

"I only want you to be happy, dear."

"And I will be happy—I am happy. I'm not a romantic little dreamer any longer. Last winter took that all out of me. I'm going to marry a man whose companionship satisfies me absolutely and he's quite satisfied with what I can give him—real affection and comradeship. I am sure that is the best foundation for a happy marriage. Besides, Dean *needs* me. I can make him happy. He has never been happy. Oh, it is delightful to feel that you hold happiness in your hand and can hold it out, like a pearl beyond price, to one who longs for it."

"You're too young," reiterated Aunt Laura.

"It's only my body that's young. My soul is a hundred years old. Last winter made me feel so old and wise. *You* know."

"Yes, I know." But Laura also knew that this very feeling old and wise merely proved Emily's youth. People who *are* old and wise never feel either. And all this talk of aged souls didn't do away with the fact that Emily, slim, radiant, with eyes of mystery, was not yet twenty, while Dean Priest was forty-two. In fifteen years—but Laura would not think of it.

And, after all, Dean would not take her away. There *had* been happy marriages with just as much disparity of age.

II

Nobody, it must be admitted, seemed to regard the match with favour. Emily had a rather abominable time of it for a few weeks. Dr. Burnley raged about the affair and insulted Dean. Aunt Ruth came over and made a scene.

"He's an infidel, Emily."

"He isn't!" said Emily indignantly.

"Well, he doesn't believe what *we* believe," declared Aunt Ruth as if that ought to settle the matter for any true Murray.

Aunt Addie, who had never forgiven Emily for refusing her son, even though Andrew was now happily and suitably, *most* suitably, married, was very hard to bear. She contrived to make Emily feel a most condescending pity. She had lost Andrew, so must console herself with lame Jarback Priest. Of course Aunt Addie did not put it in so many blunt words but she might as well have. Emily understood her implications perfectly.

"Of course, he's richer than a *young* man could be," conceded Aunt

Addie.

"And interesting," said Emily. "Most young men are *such* bores. They haven't lived long enough to learn that they are not the wonders to the world they are to their mothers."

So honours were about even *there*.

The Priests did not like it any too well either. Perhaps because they did not care to see a rich uncle's possessions thus slipping through the fingers of hope. They said Emily Starr was just marrying Dean for his money, and the Murrays took care that she should hear they had said it. Emily felt that the Priests were continually and maliciously discussing her behind her back.

"I'll never feel at home in your clan," she told Dean rebelliously.

"Nobody will ask you to. You and I, Star, are going to live unto ourselves. We are not going to walk or talk or think or breathe according to any clan standard, be it Priest or Murray. If the Priests disapprove of you as a wife for me the Murrays still more emphatically disapprove of me as a husband for you. Never mind. Of course the Priests find it hard to believe that you are marrying me because you care anything for me. How could you? I find it hard to believe myself."

But you *do* believe it, Dean? Truly I care more for you than any one in the world. Of course—I told you—I don't love you like a silly, romantic girl."

"Do you love any one else?" asked Dean quietly. It was the first time he had ventured to ask the question.

"No. Of course—you know—I've had one or two broken-backed love affairs—silly schoolgirl fancies. That is all years behind me. Last winter seems like a lifetime—dividing me by centuries from those old follies. I'm all yours, Dean."

Dean lifted the hand he held and kissed it. He had never yet touched her lips.

"I can make you happy, Star. I know it. Old—lame as I am, I can make you happy. I've been waiting for you all my life, my star. That's what you've always seemed to me, Emily. An exquisite, unreachable star. Now I have you—hold you—wear you on my heart. And you will love me yet—some day you will give me more than affection."

The passion in his voice startled Emily a little. It seemed in some way to demand more of her than she had to give. And Ilse, who had graduated from the School of Oratory and had come home for a week before going on a summer concert tour, struck another note of warning that disturbed faintly for a time.

"In some ways, honey, Dean is just the man for you. He's clever and fascinating and not so horribly conscious of his own importance as most of the Priests. But you'll belong to him body and soul. Dean can't bear any one to have any interest outside of him. He must possess exclusively. If you don't mind that—"

"I don't think I do."

"Your writing—"

"Oh, I'm done with *that*. I seem to have no interest in it since my illness. I saw—then—how little it really mattered—how many more important things there were—"

"As long as you feel like that you'll be happy with Dean. Heigh-ho." Ilse sighed and pulled the blood-red rose that was pinned to her waist to pieces. "It makes me feel fearfully old and wise to be talking like this of your getting married, Emily. It seems so—absurd in some ways. Yesterday we were schoolgirls. To-day you're engaged. To-morrow—you'll be a grandmother."

"Aren't you—isn't there anybody in your own life, Ilse?"

"Listen to the fox that lost her tail. No, thank you. Besides—one might as well be frank. I feel an awful mood of honest confession on me. There's never been anybody for me but Perry Miller. And you've got your claws in him."

Perry Miller. Emily could not believe her ears.

"Ilse Burnley! You've always laughed at him—raged at him—"

"Of course I did. I liked him so much that it made me furious to see him making a fool of himself. I wanted to be proud of him and he always made me ashamed of him. Oh, there were times when he made me mad enough to bite the leg off a chair. If I hadn't cared, do you suppose it would have mattered what kind of a donkey he was? I can't get over it—the 'Burnley sotness,' I suppose. We never change. Oh, I'd have jumped at him—would yet—herring-barrels, Stovepipe Town and all. There you have it. But never mind. Life is very decent without him."

"Perhaps—some day—"

"Don't dream it. Emily, I won't have you setting about making matches for me. Perry never gave me two thoughts—never will. I'm not going to think of him. What's that old verse we laughed over once that last year in high school—thinking it was all nonsense?

Since ever the world was spinning

And till the world shall end

You've your man in the beginning

Or you have him in the end,

But to have him from start to finish

And neither to borrow nor lend

Is what all of the girls are wanting

And none of the gods can send.

"Well, next year I'll graduate. For years after that a career. Oh, I dare say I'll marry some day."

"Teddy?" said Emily, before she could prevent herself. She could have bitten her tongue off the moment the word escaped it.

Ilse gave her a long, keen look, which Emily parried successfully with all the Murray pride—too successfully, perhaps.

"No, not Teddy. Teddy never thought about me. I doubt if he thinks of any one but himself. Teddy's a duck but he's selfish, Emily, he really is."

"No, no," indignantly. She could not listen to this.

"Well, we won't quarrel over it. What difference does it make if he is? He's gone out of our lives anyway. The cat can have him. He's going to climb to the top—they thought him a wow in Montreal. He'll make a wonderful portrait painter—if he can only cure himself of his old trick of putting *you* into all the faces he paints."

"Nonsense. He doesn't—"

"He *does*. I've raged at him about it times without number. Of course he denies it. I really think he's quite unconscious of it himself. It's the hang-over from some old unconscious emotion, I suppose—to use the jargon of modern psychologists. Never mind. As I said, I mean to marry sometime. When I'm tired of a career. It's very jolly *now*— but some day. I'll make a sensible wedding o't, just as you're doing, with a heart of gold and a pocket of silver. Isn't it funny to be talking of marrying some man you've never even seen? What is he doing at this very moment? Shaving—swearing—breaking his heart over some other girl? Still, he's to marry *me*. Oh, we'll be happy enough, too. And we'll visit each other, you and I—and compare our children—call your first girl Ilse, won't you, friend of my heart—and—and what a devilish thing it is to be a woman, isn't it, Emily?"

Old Kelly, the tin peddler, who had been Emily's friend of many years, had to have his say about it, too. One could not suppress Old Kelly.

"Gurrl dear, is it true that ye do be after going to marry Jarback Praste?"

"Quite true." Emily knew it was of no use to expect Old Kelly to call Dean anything but Jarback. But she always winced.

Old Kelly crabbed his face.

"Ye're too young at the business of living to be marrying any one— laste of all a Praste."

"Haven't you been twitting me for years with my slowness in getting a beau?" asked Emily shyly.

"Gurrl dear, a joke is a joke. But this is beyond joking. Don't be pig-headed now, there's a jewel. Stop a bit and think it over. There do be some knots mighty aisy to tie but the untying is a cat of a different brade. I've always been warning ye against marrying a Praste. 'Twas a foolish thing—I might av known it. I should 've towld ye to marry one."

"Dean isn't like the other Priests, Mr. Kelly. I'm going to be very happy."

Old Kelly shook his bushy, reddish grey head incredulously.

"Then you'll be the first Praste woman that ever was, not aven laving out the ould Lady at the Grange. But *she* liked a fight every day. It'll be the death av you."

"Dean and I won't fight—at least not every day." Emily was having some fun to herself. Old Kelly's gloomy predictions did not worry her. She took rather an impish delight in egging him on.

"Not if ye give him his own way. He'll sulk if ye don't. All the Prastes sulk if they don't get it. And he'll be that jealous—ye'll never dare spake to another man. Oh, the Prastes rule their wives. Old Aaron Praste made his wife go down on her knees whenever she had a little favour to ask. Me feyther saw it wid his own eyes."

598

"Mr. Kelly, do you really suppose *any* man could make *me* do that?"

Old Kelly's eyes twinkled in spite of himself.

"The Murray knee jints do be a bit stiff for that," he acknowledged, "But there's other things. Do ye be after knowing that his Uncle Jim never spoke when he could grunt and always said 'Ye fool' to his wife when she conterdicted him."

"But perhaps she *was* a fool, Mr. Kelly."

"Mebbe. But was it polite? I lave it to ye. And his father threw the dinner dishes at his wife whin she made him mad. 'Tis a fact, I'm telling you. Though the old divil *was* amusing when he was pleased."

"That sort of thing always skips a generation," said Emily. "And if not—I can dodge."

"Gurrl dear, there do be worse things than having a dish or two flung at ye. Ye *kin* dodge them. But there's things ye can't dodge. Tell me now, do ye know"—Old Kelly lowered his voice ominously—"that 'tis said the Prastes do often get tired av bein' married to the wan woman."

Emily was guilty of giving Mr. Kelly one of the smiles Aunt Elizabeth had always disapproved of.

"Do you really think Dean will get tired of me? I'm not beautiful, dear Mr. Kelly, but I am very interesting."

Old Kelly gathered up his lines with the air of a man who surrenders at discretion.

"Well, gurrl dear, ye do be having a good mouth for kissing, anyway. I see ye're set on it. But I do be thinking the Lord intended ye for something different. Anyway, here's hoping we'll all make a good end. But he knows too much, that Jarback Praste, he's after knowing far too much."

Old Kelly drove off, waiting till he was decently out of earshot to mutter:

"Don't it bate hell? And him as odd-looking as a cross-eyed cat!"

Emily stood still for a few minutes looking after Old Kelly's retreating chariot. He had found the one joint in her armour and the thrust had struck home. A little chill crept over her as if a wind from the grave had blown across her spirit. All at once an old, old story whispered long ago by Great-aunt Nancy to Caroline Priest flashed into her recollection. Dean, so it was said, had seen the Black Mass celebrated.

Emily shook the recollection from her. *That* was all nonsense—silly, malicious, envious gossip of stay-at-homes. But Dean *did* know too much. He had eyes that had seen too much. In a way that had been part of the distinct fascination he had always had for Emily. But now it frightened her. Had she not always felt—did she not still feel—that he always seemed to be laughing at the world from some mysterious standpoint of inner knowledge—a knowledge she did not share— could not share—did not, to come down to the bare bones of it, want to share? He had lost some intangible, all-real zest of faith and idealism. It was there deep in her heart—an inescapable conviction, thrust it out of sight as she might. For a moment she felt with Ilse that it was a decidedly devilish thing to be a woman.

"It serves me right for bandying words with Old Jock Kelly on such a subject," she thought angrily.

Consent was never given in set terms to Emily's engagement. But the thing came to be tacitly accepted. Dean was well-to-do. The Priests had all the necessary traditions, including that of a grandmother who had danced with the Prince of Wales at the famous ball in Charlottetown. After all, there would be a certain relief in seeing Emily safely married.

"He won't take her far away from us," said Aunt Laura, who could have reconciled herself to almost anything for that. How could they lose the one bright, gay thing in that faded house?

"Tell Emily," wrote old Aunt Nancy, "that twins run in the Priest family."

But Aunt Elizabeth did not tell her.

Dr. Burnley, who had made the most fuss, gave in when he heard that Elizabeth Murray was overhauling the chests of quilts in the attic of New Moon and that Laura was hemstitching table linen.

"Those whom Elizabeth Murray has joined together let no man put asunder," he said resignedly.

Aunt Laura cupped Emily's face in her gentle hands and looked deep into her eyes. "God bless you, Emily, dear child."

"Very mid-Victorian," commented Emily to Dean. "But I liked it."

CHAPTER IX

I

On one point Aunt Elizabeth was adamant Emily should not be married until she was twenty. Dean, who had dreamed of an autumn wedding and a winter spent in a dreamy Japanese garden beyond the western sea, gave in with a bad grace. Emily, too, would have preferred an earlier bridal. In the back of her mind, where she would not even glance at it, was the feeling that the sooner it was over and made irrevocable, the better.

Yet she was happy, as she told herself very often and very sincerely. Perhaps there *were* dark moments when a disquieting thought stared her in the face—it was but a crippled, broken-winged happiness— not the wild, free-flying happiness she had dreamed of. But that, she reminded herself, was lost to her for ever.

One day Dean appeared before her with a flush of boyish excitement on his face.

"Emily, I've been and gone and done something. Will you approve? Oh, Lord, what will I do if you don't approve."

"What is it you've done?"

"I've bought me a house."

"A house!"

"A house! I, Dean Priest, am a landed proprietor—owning a house, a garden and a spruce lot five acres in extent. I, who this morning hadn't a square inch of earth to call my own. I, who all my life have been hungry to own a bit of land."

"*What* house have you bought, Dean?"

"Fred Clifford's house—at least the house he has always owned by a legal quibble. Really *our* house—appointed—foreordained for us since the foundation of the world."

"The Disappointed House?"

"Oh, yes, that was your old name for it. But it isn't going to be

Disappointed any longer. That is—if—Emily, *do* you approve of what I've done?"

"Approve? You're simply a darling, Dean. I've always loved that house. It's one of those houses you love the minute you see them. Some houses are like that, you know—full of magic. And others have nothing at all of it in them. I've always longed to see that house fulfilled. Oh— and somebody told me you were going to buy that big horrible house at Shrewsbury. I was afraid to ask if it were true."

"Emily, take back those words. You knew it wasn't true. You knew me better. Of course, all the Priests wanted me to buy that house. My dear sister was almost in tears because I wouldn't. It was to be had at a bargain—and it was *such* an elegant house."

"It *is* elegant—with all the word implies," agreed Emily. "But it's an impossible house—not because of its size or its elegance but just because of its impossibility."

"E-zackly. Any proper woman would feel the same. I'm so glad you're pleased, Emily. I had to buy Fred's house yesterday in Charlottetown— without waiting to consult you—another man was on the point of buying it, so I wired Fred instantly. Of course, if you hadn't liked it I'd have sold it again. But I *felt* you would. We'll make such a home of it, dear. I want a home. I've had many habitations but no homes. I'll have it finished and fixed up as beautifully as possible for you, Star—my Star who is fit to shine in the palaces of kings."

"Let's go right up and look at it," said Emily. "I want to tell it what is coming to it. I want to tell it it is going to *live* at last."

"We'll go up and look at it and *in* it. I've got the key. Got it from Fred's sister. Emily, I feel as if I'd reached up and plucked the moon."

"Oh, *I've* picked a lapful of stars," cried Emily gaily.

II

They went up to the Disappointed House—through the old orchard full of columbines and along the To-morrow Road, across a pasture field, up a little slope of golden fern, and over an old meandering fence with its longers bleached to a silvery grey, with clusters of wild everlastings and blue asters in its corners, then up the little winding, capricious path on the long fir hill, which was so narrow they had to walk singly and where the air always seemed so full of nice whispery

602

sounds.

When they came to its end there was a sloping field before them, dotted with little, pointed firs, windy, grassy, lovable. And on top of it, surrounded by hill glamour and upland wizardry, with great sunset clouds heaped up over it, the house—*their* house.

A house with the mystery of woods behind it and around it, except on the south side where the land fell away in a long hill looking down on the Blair Water, that was like a bowl of dull gold now, and across it to meadows of starry rest beyond and the Derry Pond Hills that were as blue and romantic as the famous Alsatian Mountains. Between the house and the view, but not hiding it, was a row of wonderful Lombardy poplars.

They climbed the hill to the gate of a little enclosed garden—a garden far older than the house which had been built on the site of a little log cabin of pioneer days.

"That's a view I can live with," said Dean exultingly. "Oh, 'tis a dear place this. The hill is haunted by squirrels, Emily. And there are rabbits about. Don't you love squirrels and rabbits? And there are any number of shy violets hereabouts in spring, too. There is a little mossy hollow behind those young firs that is full of violets in May—violets,

Sweeter than lids of Emily's eyes

Or Emily's breath.

Emily's a nicer name than Cytherea or Juno, *I* think. I want you to notice especially that little gate over yonder. It isn't really needed. It opens only into that froggy marsh beyond the wood. But isn't it a gate? I love a gate like that—a reasonless gate. It's full of promise. There *may* be something wonderful beyond. A gate is always a mystery, anyhow—it lures—it is a symbol. And listen to that bell ringing somewhere in the twilight across the harbour. A bell in twilight always has a magic sound—as if it came from somewhere 'far far in fairyland.' There are roses in that far corner—old-fashioned roses like sweet old songs set to flowering. Roses white enough to lie in your white bosom, my sweet, roses red enough to star that soft dark cloud of your hair. Emily, do you know I'm a little drunk to-night—on the wine of life. Don't wonder if I say crazy things."

Emily was very happy. The old, sweet garden seemed to be talking to her as a friend in the drowsy, winking light. She surrendered herself utterly to the charm of the place. She looked at the Disappointed House adoringly. Such a dear *thoughtful* little house. Not an old house—she liked it for that—an old house knew too much—was haunted by too many feet that had walked over its threshold—too many anguished or impassioned eyes that had looked out of its windows. This house was ignorant and innocent like herself. Longing for happiness. It should have it. She and Dean would drive out the ghosts of things that never happened. How sweet it would be to have a home of her very own.

"That house wants us as badly as we want it," she said.

"I love you when your tones soften and mute like that, Star," said Dean. "Don't ever talk so to any other man, Emily."

Emily threw him a glance of coquetry that very nearly made him kiss her. He had never kissed her yet. Some subtle prescience always told him she was not yet ready to be kissed. He might have dared it there and then, in that hour of glamour that had transmuted everything into terms of romance and charm—he might even have won her wholly then. But he hesitated—and the magic moment passed. From somewhere down the dim road behind the spruces came laughter. Harmless, innocent laughter of children. But it broke some faintly woven spell.

"Let us go in and see our house," said Dean. He led the way across the wild-grown grasses to the door that opened into the living-room. The key turned stiffly in the rusted lock. Dean took Emily's hand and drew her in.

"Over your own threshold, sweet—"

He lifted his flashlight and threw a circle of shifting light around the unfinished room, with its bare, staring, lathed walls, its sealed windows, its gaping doorways, its empty fireplace—no, not quite empty. Emily saw a little heap of white ashes in it—the ashes of the fire she and Teddy had kindled years ago that adventurous summer evening of childhood—the fire by which they had sat and planned out their lives together. She turned to the door with a little shiver.

"Dean, it looks too ghostly and forlorn. I think I'd rather explore it by daylight. The ghosts of things that never happened are worse than the ghosts of things that did."

III

It was Dean's suggestion that they spend the summer finishing and furnishing their house—doing everything possible themselves and fixing it up exactly as they wanted it.

"Then we can be married in the spring—spend the summer listening to temple bells tinkling over eastern sands—watch Philae by moonlight—hear the Nile moaning by Memphis—come back in the autumn, turn the key of our own door—be at home."

Emily thought the programme delightful. Her aunts were dubious about it—it didn't seem quite proper and respectable really—people would talk terribly. And Aunt Laura was worried over some old superstition that it wasn't lucky to furnish a house *before* a wedding. Dean and Emily didn't care whether it was respectable and lucky or not. They went ahead and did it.

Naturally they were overwhelmed with advice from every one in the Priest and Murray clans—and took none of it. For one thing, they wouldn't paint the Disappointed House—just shingled it and left the shingles to turn woodsy grey, much to Aunt Elizabeth's horror.

"It's only Stovepipe Town houses that aren't painted," she said.

They replaced the old, unused, temporary board steps, left by the carpenters thirty years before, with broad, red sandstones from the shore. Dean had casement windows put in with diamond shaped panes which Aunt Elizabeth warned Emily would be terrible things to keep clean. And he added a dear little window over the front door with a little roof over it like a shaggy eyebrow and in the living-room they had a French window from which you could step right out into the fir wood.

And Dean had jewels of closets and cupboards put in everywhere.

"I'm not such a fool as to imagine that a girl can keep on loving a man who doesn't provide her with proper cupboards," he declared.

Aunt Elizabeth approved of the cupboards but thought they were clean daft in regard to the wallpapers. Especially the living-room paper. They should have had something cheerful there—flowers or gold stripes; or even, as a vast concession to modernity, some of those "landscape papers" that were coming in. But Emily insisted on papering it with a shadowy grey paper with snowy pine branches over it. Aunt Elizabeth declared she would as soon live in the woods as in such a room. But Emily in this respect, as in all others concerning her own dear house, was "as pig-headed as ever," so exasperated Aunt Elizabeth averred, quite unconscious that a Murray was borrowing one of Old Kelly's expressions.

But Aunt Elizabeth was really very good. She dug up, out of long undisturbed boxes and chests, china and silver belonging to her stepmother—the things Juliet Murray would have had if she had married in orthodox fashion a husband approved of her clan—and gave them to Emily. There were some lovely things among them—especially a priceless pink lustre jug and a delightful old dinner-set of real willow-ware—Emily's grandmother's own wedding-set. Not a piece was missing. And it had shallow thin cups and deep saucers and scalloped plates and round, fat, pobby tureens. Emily filled the built-in cabinet in the living-room with it and gloated over it. There were other things she loved too; a little gilt-framed oval mirror with a black cat on top of it, a mirror that had so often reflected beautiful women that it lent a certain charm to every face; and an old clock with a pointed top and two tiny gilded spires on each side, a clock that gave warning ten minutes before it struck, a gentlemanly clock never taking people unawares. Dean wound it up but would not start it.

"When we come home—when I bring you in here as bride and queen, you shall start it going," he said.

It turned out, too, that the Chippendale sideboard and the claw-footed mahogany table at New Moon were Emily's. And Dean had no end of quaint delightful things picked up all over the world—a sofa covered with striped silk that had been in the Salon of a Marquise of the Old Regime, a lantern of wrought-iron lace from an old Venetian palace to hang in the living-room, a Shiraz rug, a prayer-rug from Damascus, brass andirons from Italy, jades and ivories from China, lacquer bowls from Japan, a delightful little green owl in Japanese china, a painted Chinese perfume-bottle of agate which he had found in some weird place in Mongolia, with the perfume of the east—which is never the perfume of the west—clinging to it, a Chinese teapot with dreadful golden dragons coiling over it—five-clawed dragons whereby the initiated knew that it was of the Imperial cabinets. It was part of the loot of the Summer Palace in the Boxer Rebellion, Dean told Emily, but he would not tell her how it had come into his possession.

"Not yet. Some day. There's a story about almost everything I've put in this house."

IV

They had a great day putting the furniture in the living-room. They tried it in a dozen different places and were not satisfied until they had found the absolutely right one. Sometimes they could not agree about it and then they would sit on the floor and argue it out. And if they couldn't settle it they got Daffy to pull straws with his teeth and decide it that way. Daffy was always around. Saucy Sal had died of old age and Daffy was getting stiff and a bit cranky and snored dreadfully when he was sleeping, but Emily adored him and would not go to the Disappointed House without him. He always slipped up the hill path beside her like a grey shadow dappled with dark.

"You love that old cat more than you do me, Emily," Dean once said—jestingly yet with an undernote of earnest.

"I *have* to love him," defended Emily. "He's growing old. *You* have all the years before us. And I must always have a cat about. A house isn't a home without the ineffable contentment of a cat with its tail folded about its feet. A cat gives mystery, charm, suggestion. And you must have a dog."

"I've never cared to have a dog since Tweed died. But perhaps I'll get one—an altogether different kind of a one. We'll need a dog to keep your cats in order. Oh, isn't it nice to feel that a place belongs to you?"

"It's far nicer to feel that you belong to a place," said Emily, looking about her affectionately.

"Our house and we are going to be good friends," agreed Dean.

V

They hung their pictures one day. Emily brought her favourites up, including the Lady Giovanna and Mona Lisa. These two were hung in the corner between the windows.

"Where your writing-desk will be," said Dean. "And Mona Lisa will whisper to you the ageless secret of her smile and you shall put it in a story."

"I thought you didn't want me to write any more stories," said Emily. "You've never seemed to like the fact of my writing."

"That was when I was afraid it would take you away from me. Now, it doesn't matter. I want you to do just as pleases you."

Emily felt indifferent. She had never cared to take up her pen since her illness. As the days passed she felt a growing distaste to the thought of ever taking it up. To think of it meant to think of the book she had burned; and *that* hurt beyond bearing. She had ceased to listen for her "random word"—she was an exile from her old starry kingdom.

"I'm going to hang old Elizabeth Bas by the fireplace," said Dean. "'Engraving from a portrait by Rembrandt.' Isn't she a delightful old woman, Star, in her white cap and tremendous white ruff collar? And did you ever see such a shrewd, humorous, complacent, slightly contemptuous old face?"

"I don't think I should want to have an argument with Elizabeth," reflected Emily. "One feels that she is keeping her hands folded under compulsion and might box your ears if you disagreed with her."

"She has been dust for over a century," said Dean dreamily. "Yet here she is living on this cheap reprint of Rembrandt's canvas. You are expecting her to speak to you. And I feel, as you do, that she wouldn't put up with any nonsense."

"But likely she has a sweetmeat stored away in some pocket of her gown for you. That fine, rosy, wholesome old woman. *She* ruled her family—not a doubt of it. Her husband did as she told him—but never knew it."

"*Had* she a husband?" said Dean doubtfully. "There's no wedding-ring on her finger."

"Then she must have been a most delightful old maid," averred Emily.

"What a difference between her smile and Mona Lisa's," said Dean, looking from one to the other. "Elizabeth is tolerating things—with just a hint of a sly, meditative cat about her. But Mona Lisa's face has that everlasting lure and provocation that drives men mad and writes scarlet pages on dim historical records. La Gioconda would be a more stimulating sweetheart. But Elizabeth would be nicer for an aunt."

Dean hung a little old miniature of his mother up over the mantelpiece. Emily had never seen it before. Dean Priest's mother had been a beautiful woman.

"But why does she look so sad?"

"Because she was married to a Priest," said Dean.

"Will I look sad?" teased Emily.

"Not if it rests with me," said Dean.

But did it? Sometimes that question forced itself on Emily, but she would not answer it. She was very happy two-thirds of that summer—which she told herself was a high average. But in the other third were hours of which she never spoke to any one—hours in which her soul felt caught in a trap—hours when the great, green emerald winking on her finger seemed like a fetter. And once she even took it off just to feel free for a little while—a temporary escape for which she was sorry and ashamed the next day, when she was quite sane and normal again, contented with her lot and more interested than ever in her little grey house, which meant so much to her—"more to me than Dean does," she said to herself once in a three-o'clock moment of stark, despairing honesty; and then refused to believe it next morning.

VI

Old Great-aunt Nancy of Priest Pond died that summer, very suddenly. "I'm tired of living. I think I'll stop," she said one day—and stopped. None of the Murrays benefited by her will; everything she had was left to Caroline Priest; but Emily got the gazing-ball and the brass chessy-cat knocker and the gold ear-rings—and the picture Teddy had done of her in water-colours years ago. Emily put the chessy-cat on the front porch door of the Disappointed House and hung the great silvery gazing-ball from the Venetian lantern and wore the quaint old ear-rings to many rather delightful pomps and vanities. But she put the picture away in a box in the New Moon attic—a box that held certain sweet, old, foolish letters full of dreams and plans.

VII

They had glorious minutes of fun when they stopped to rest occasionally. There was a robin's nest in the fir at the north corner which they watched and protected from Daffy.

"Think of the music penned in this fragile, pale blue wall," said Dean, touching an egg one day. "Not the music of the moon perhaps, but an earthlier, homelier music, full of wholesome sweetness and the joy of living. This egg will some day be a robin, Star, to whistle us blithely home in the afterlight."

They made friends with an old rabbit that often came hopping out of the woods into the garden. They had a game as to who could count the most squirrels in the daytime and the most bats in the evening. For they did not always go home as soon as it got too dark to work. Sometimes they sat out on their sandstone steps listening to the melancholy loveliness of night-wind on the sea and watching the twilight creep up from the old valley and the shadows waver and flicker under the fir-trees and the Blair Water turning to a great grey pool tremulous with early stars. Daff sat beside them, watching everything with his great moonlight eyes, and Emily pulled his ears now and then.

"One understands a cat a little better now. At all other times he is inscrutable, but in the time of dusk and dew we can catch a glimpse of the tantalizing secret of his personality."

"One catches a glimpse of all kinds of secrets now," said Dean. "On a night like this I always think of the 'hills where spices grow.' That line of the old hymn Mother used to sing has always intrigued me—though I can't 'fly like a youthful hart or roe.' Emily, I can see that you are getting your mouth in the proper shape to talk about the colour we'll paint the woodshed. Don't you do it. No one should talk paint when she's expecting a moonrise. There'll be a wonderful one presently—I've arranged for it. But if we *must* talk of furniture let's plan for a few things we haven't got yet and *must* have—a canoe for our boating trips along the Milky Way, for instance—a loom for the weaving of dreams and a jar of pixy-brew for festal hours. And can't we arrange to have the spring of Ponce de Leon over in that corner? Or would you prefer a fount of Castaly? As for your trousseau, have what you like in it but there *must* be a gown of grey twilight with an evening star for your hair. Also one trimmed with moonlight and a scarf of sunset cloud."

Oh, she liked Dean. *How* she liked him. If she could only love him!

One evening she slipped up alone to see her little house by moonlight. What a dear place it was. She saw herself there in the future—flitting through the little rooms—laughing under the firs—sitting hand in hand with Teddy at the fireplace—Emily came to herself with a shock. With Dean, of course, with Dean. A mere trick of the memory.

VIII

There came a September evening when everything was done—even to the horseshoe over the door to keep the witches out—even to the candles Emily had stuck all about the living-room—a little, jolly, yellow candle—a full, red, pugnacious candle—a dreamy, pale blue candle—a graceless candle with aces of hearts and diamonds all over it—a slim, dandyish candle.

And the result was good. There was a sense of harmony in the house. The things in it did not have to become acquainted but were good friends from the very start. They did not shriek at each other. There was not a noisy room in the house.

"There's absolutely nothing more we can do," sighed Emily. "We can't even *pretend* there's anything more to do."

"I suppose not," agreed Dean regretfully. Then he looked at the fireplace where kindlings and pinewood were laid.

"Yes, there is," he cried. "How could we have forgotten it? We've got to see if the chimney will draw properly. I'm going to light that fire."

Emily sat down on the settee in the corner and when the fire began to burn Dean came and sat beside her. Daffy lay stretched out at their feet, his little striped flanks moving peacefully up and down.

Up blazed the merry flames. They shimmered over the old piano—they played irreverent hide-and-seek with Elizabeth Bas' adorable old face—they danced on the glass doors of the cupboard where the willow-ware dishes were; they darted through the kitchen door and the row of brown and blue bowls Emily had ranged on the dresser winked back at them.

"This is home," said Dean softly. "It's lovelier than I've ever dreamed of its being. This is how we'll sit on autumn evenings all our lives, shutting out the cold misty nights that come in from the sea—just you and I alone with the firelight and the sweetness. But sometimes we'll let a friend come in and share it—sip of our joy and drink of our laughter. We'll just sit here and think about it all—till the fire burns out."

The fire crackled and snapped. Daffy purred. The moon shone down through the dance of the fir-boughs straight on them through the windows. And Emily was thinking—could not help thinking—of the time she and Teddy had sat there. The odd part was that she did not think of him longingly or lovingly. She just thought of him. Would she, she asked herself, in mingled exasperation and dread, find herself thinking of Teddy when she was standing up to be married to Dean?

When the fire had died down into white ashes Dean got up.

"It was worth while to have lived long dreary years for this—and to live them again, if need be, looking back to it," he said, holding out his hand. He drew her nearer. What ghost came between the lips that might have met? Emily turned away with a sigh.

"Our happy summer is over, Dean."

"Our *first* happy summer," corrected Dean. But his voice suddenly sounded a little tired.

CHAPTER X

I

They locked the door of the Disappointed House one November evening and Dean gave the key to Emily.

"Keep it till spring," he said, looking out over the quiet, cold, grey fields across which a chilly wind was blowing. "We won't come back here till then."

In the stormy winter that followed, the cross-lots path to the little house was so heaped with drifts that Emily never went near it. But she thought about it often and happily, waiting amid its snows for spring and life and fulfilment. That winter was, on the whole, a happy time. Dean did not go away and made himself so charming to the older ladies of New Moon that they almost forgave him for being Jarback Priest. To be sure, Aunt Elizabeth never could understand more than half of his remarks and Aunt Laura put down to his debit account the change in Emily. For she was changed. Cousin Jimmy and Aunt Laura knew that, though no one else seemed to notice it. Often there was an odd restlessness in her eyes. And something was missing from her laughter. It was not so quick—so spontaneous as of old. She was a woman before her time, thought Aunt Laura with a sigh. Was that dreadful fall down the New Moon stairs the only cause? *Was* Emily happy? Laura dared not ask. *Did* she love Dean Priest whom she was going to marry in June? Laura did not know; but she *did* know that love is something that cannot be generated by any intellectual rule o' thumb. Also that a girl who is as happy as an engaged girl should be does not spend so many hours when she should be sleeping, pacing up and down her room. This was not to be explained away on the ground that Emily was thinking out stories, Emily had given up writing. In vain Miss Royal wrote pleading and scolding letters from New York. In vain Cousin Jimmy slyly laid a new Jimmy-book at intervals on her desk. In vain Laura timidly hinted that it was a pity not to keep on when you had made such a good start. Even Aunt Elizabeth's contemptuous assertion that she had always known Emily would get tired of it—"the Starr fickleness, you see"—failed to sting Emily back to her pen. She could not write—she would never try to write again.

"I've paid my debts and I've enough in the bank to get what Dean calls my wedding doo-dabs. And you've crocheted two filet spreads for me," she told Aunt Laura a little wearily and bitterly. "So what does it matter?"

"Was it—your fall that took away your—your ambition?" faltered poor Aunt Laura, voicing what had been her haunting dread all winter.

Emily smiled and kissed her.

"No, darling. That had nothing to do with it. Why worry over a simple, natural thing? Here I am, going to be married, with a prospective house and husband to think about. Doesn't that explain why I've ceased to care about—other things?"

It should have, but that evening Emily went out of the house after sunset. Her soul was pining for freedom and she went out to slip its leash for a little while. It had been an April day, warm in the sun, cold in the shadow. You felt the coldness even amid the sunlight warmth. The evening was chill. The sky was overcast with wrinkled, grey clouds, save along the west where a strip of yellow sky gleamed palely and in it, sad and fair, a new moon setting behind a dark hill. No living creature but herself seemed abroad and the cold shadows settling down over the withered fields lent to the landscape of too-early spring an aspect inexpressibly dreary and mournful. It made Emily feel hopeless, as if the best of life already lay in the past. Externals always had a great influence upon her—too great perhaps. Yet she was glad it was a dour evening. Anything else would have insulted her mood. She heard the

sea shuddering beyond the dunes. An old verse from one of Roberts'
poems came into her head:

> Grey rocks and greyer sea.
>
> And surf along the shore,
>
> And in my heart a name
>
> My lips shall speak no more.

Nonsense! Weak, silly, sentimental nonsense. No more of it!

II

But that letter from Ilse that day. Teddy was coming home. He was
to sail on the *Flavian*. He was going to be home most of the summer.

"If it could only have been all over—before he came," muttered
Emily.

Always to be afraid of to-morrow? Content—even happy with to-
day—but always afraid of tomorrow. Was this to be her life? And *why*
that fear of to-morrow?

She had brought the key of the Disapppinted House with her. She
had not been in it since November and she wanted to see it—beautiful,
waiting, desirable. *Her* home. In its charm and sanity vague, horrible
fears and doubts would vanish. The soul of that happy last summer
would come back to her. She paused at the garden gate to look lovingly
at it—the dear little house nestled under the old trees that sighed softly
as they had sighed to her childhood visions. Below, Blair Water was
grey and sullen. She loved Blair Water in all its changes—its sparkle of
summer, its silver of dusk, its miracle of moonlight, its dimpled rings
of rain. And she loved it now, dark and brooding. There was somehow
a piercing sadness in that sullen, waiting landscape all around her—as
if—the odd fancy crossed her mind—as if it were *afraid* of spring. How
this idea of fear haunted her! She looked up beyond the spires of the
Lombardies on the hill. And in a sudden pale rift between the clouds a
star shone down on her—Vega of the Lyre.

With a shiver Emily hurriedly unlocked the door and stepped in.

The house seemed to be vacant—waiting for her. She fumbled through the darkness to the matches she knew were on the mantelpiece and lighted the tall, pale-green taper beside the clock. The beautiful room glimmered out at her in the flickering light—just as they had left it that last evening. There was Elizabeth Bas, who could never have known the meaning of fear—Mona Lisa, who mocked at it. But the Lady Giovanna, who never turned her saintly profile to look squarely at you. Had she ever known it—this subtle, secret fear that one could never put in words?—that would be so ridiculous if one could put it in words? Dean Priest's sad lovely mother. Yes, she had known fear; it looked out of her pictured eyes now in that dim, furtive light.

Emily shut the door and sat down in the armchair beneath Elizabeth Bas' picture. She could hear the dead, dry leaves of a dead summer rustling eerily on the beech just outside the window. And the wind—rising—rising—rising. But she liked it. "The wind is free—not a prisoner like me." She crushed the unbidden thought down sternly. She would *not* think such things. Her fetters were of her own forging. She had put them on willingly, even desirously. Nothing to do but wear them gracefully.

How the sea moaned down there below the fields! But here in the little house what a silence there was! Something strange and uncanny about the silence. It seemed to hold some profound meaning. She would not have dared to speak lest *something* should answer her. Yet fear suddenly left her. She felt dreamy—happy—far away from life and reality. The walls of the shadowy room seemed slowly to fade from her vision. The pictures withdrew themselves. There seemed to be nothing before her but Great-aunt-Nancy's gazing-ball hung from the old iron lantern—a big, silvery, gleaming globe. In it she saw the reflected room, like a shining doll's-house, with herself sitting in the old, low chair and the taper on the mantelpiece like a tiny, impish star. Emily looked at it as she leaned back in her chair—looked at it till she saw nothing but that tiny point of light in a great misty universe.

III

Did she sleep? Dream? Who knows? Emily herself never knew. Twice before in her life—once in delirium*—once in sleep** she had drawn aside the veil of sense and time and seen beyond. Emily never liked to remember those experiences. She forgot them deliberately. She had not recalled them for years. A dream—a fancy fever-bred. But this?

* See *Emily of New Moon*. ** See *Emily Climbs*.

A small cloud seemed to shape itself within the gazing-ball. It dispersed—faded. But the reflected doll's-house in the ball was gone. Emily saw an entirely different scene—a long lofty room filled with streams of hurrying people—and among them a face she knew.

The gazing-ball was gone—the room in the Disappointed House was gone. She was no longer sitting in her chair looking on. She was *in* that strange, great room—she was among those throngs of people—she was standing by the man who was waiting impatiently before a ticket-window. As he turned his face and their eyes met she saw that it was Teddy—she saw the amazed recognition in his eyes. And she knew, indisputably that he was in some terrible danger—and that *she* must save him.

"Teddy. *Come.*"

It seemed to her that she caught his hand and pulled him away from the window. Then she was drifting back from him—back—back—and he was following—running after her—heedless of the people he ran into—following—following—she was back on the chair—outside of the gazing-ball—in it she still saw the station-room shrunk again to play-size—and that one figure running—still running—the cloud again—filling the ball—whitening—wavering—thinning—clearing. Emily was lying back in her chair staring fixedly into Aunt Nancy's gazing-ball, where the living-room was reflected calmly and silverly, with a dead-white spot that was her face and one solitary taper-light twinkling like an impish star.

IV

Emily, feeling as if she had died and come back to life, got herself out of the Disappointed House somehow, and locked the door. The clouds had cleared away and the world was dim and unreal in starlight. Hardly realizing what she was doing she turned her face seaward through the spruce wood—down the long, windy, pasture-field—over the dunes to the sandshore—along it like a haunted, driven creature in a weird, uncanny half-lit kingdom. The sea afar out was like grey satin half hidden in a creeping fog but it washed against the sands as she passed in little swishing, mocking ripples. She was shut in between the misty sea and the high, dark sand-dunes. If she could only go on so forever—never have to turn back and confront the unanswerable question the night had put to her.

She *knew*, beyond any doubt or cavil or mockery that she had seen Teddy—had saved, or tried to save him, from some unknown peril. And she knew, just as simply and just as surely that she loved him— had always loved him, with a love that lay at the very foundation of her being.

And in two months' time she was to be married to Dean Priest.

What could she do? To marry him now was unthinkable. She could not live such a lie. But to break his heart—snatch from him all the happiness possible to his thwarted life—that, too, was unthinkable.

Yes, as Ilse had said, it *was* a very devilish thing to be a woman.

"Particularly," said Emily, filled with bitter self-contempt, "a woman who seemingly doesn't know her own mind for a month at a time. I was so sure last summer that Teddy no longer meant anything to me—so sure that I really cared enough for Dean to marry him. And now to-night—and that horrible power or gift or curse coming again when I thought I had outgrown it—left it behind forever."

Emily walked on that eerie sandshore half the night and slipped guiltily and stealthily into New Moon in the wee sma's to fling herself on her bed and fall at last into the absolute slumber of exhaustion.

V

A very ghastly time followed. Fortunately Dean was away, having gone to Montreal on business. It was during his absence that the world was horrified by the tragedy of the *Flavian's* fatal collision with an iceberg. The headlines struck Emily in the face like a blow, Teddy was to have sailed on the *Flavian*—Had he—had he? Who could tell her? Perhaps his mother—his queer, solitary mother who hated her with a hatred that Emily always felt like a tangible thing between them. Hitherto Emily would have shrunk unspeakably from seeking Mrs. Kent. Now nothing mattered except finding out if Teddy were on the *Flavian*. She hurried to the Tansy Patch. Mrs Kent came to the door—unaltered in all the years since Emily had first known her— frail, furtive, with her bitter mouth and that disfiguring red scar across her paleness. Her face changed as it always did when she saw Emily. Hostility and fear contended in her dark, melancholy eyes.

"Did Teddy sail on the *Flavian*?" demanded Emily without circumlocution.

Mrs. Kent smiled—an unfriendly little smile.

"Does it matter to you?" she said.

"Yes." Emily was very blunt. The "Murray" look was on her face— the look few people could encounter undefeatedly. "If you know—tell me."

Mrs. Kent told her, unwillingly, hating her, shaking like a little dead leaf quivering with a semblance of life in a cruel wind.

"He did not. I had a cable from him to-day. At the last moment he was prevented from sailing."

"Thank you." Emily turned away, but not before Mrs. Kent had seen the joy and triumph that had leaped into her shadowy eyes. She sprang forward and caught Emily's arm.

"It is nothing to you," she cried wildly. "Nothing to you whether he is safe or not. You are going to marry another man. How dare you come here—demanding to know of my son—as if you had a right?"

Emily looked down at her pityingly, understandingly. This poor creature whose jealousy, coiled in her soul like a snake, had made life a vale of torment for her.

"No right perhaps—except the right of loving him," she said.

Mrs. Kent struck her hands together wildly.

"You—you dare to say that—you who are to marry another man?"

"I am not going to marry another man," Emily found herself saying. It was quite true. For days she had not known what to do—now quite unmistakably she knew what she must do. Dreadful as it would be, still something that must be done. Everything was suddenly clear and bitter and inevitable before her.

"I cannot marry another man, Mrs. Kent, because I love Teddy. But he does not love me. I know that quite well. So you need not hate me any longer."

She turned and went swiftly away from the Tansy Patch. Where was her pride, she wondered the pride of "the proud Murrays"—that she could so calmly acknowledge an unsought, unwanted love. But pride just then had no place in her.

618

CHAPTER XI

I

When the letter came from Teddy—the first letter for so long—Emily's hand trembled so that she could hardly open it.

"I must tell you of a strange thing that has happened," he wrote. "Perhaps you know it already. And perhaps you know nothing and will think me quite mad. I don't know what to think of it myself. I know only what I saw—or thought I saw.

"I was waiting to buy my ticket for the boat-train to Liverpool—I was to sail on the *Flavian*. Suddenly I felt a touch on my arm—I turned and saw *you*. I swear it. You said, 'Teddy—come.' I was so amazed I could not think or speak. I could only follow you. You were running—no, *not* running. I don't know how you went—I only knew that you were retreating. How rotten this all sounds. *Was* I crazy? And all at once you weren't there—though we were by now away from the crowd in an open space where nothing could have prevented me from seeing you. Yet I looked everywhere—and came to my senses to realize that the boat-train had gone and I had lost my passage on the *Flavian*. I was furious—ashamed—until the news came. Then—I felt my scalp crinkle.

"Emily—you're not in England? It can't be possible you are in England. But then—what was it I saw in that station?

"Anyhow, I suppose it saved my life. If I had gone on the *Flavian*—well, I didn't. Thanks to—what?

"I'll be home soon. Will sail on the *Moravian*—if you don't prevent me again. Emily, I heard a queer story of you long ago—something about Ilse's mother. I've almost forgotten. Take care. They don't burn witches nowadays, of course—but still—"

No, they didn't burn witches. But still—Emily felt that she could have more easily faced the stake than what was before her.

II

Emily went up the hill path to keep tryst with Dean at the Disappointed House. She had had a note from him that day, written on his return from Montreal, asking her to meet him there at dusk. He was waiting for her on the doorstep—eagerly, happily. The robins were whistling softly in the fir copse and the evening was fragrant with the tang of balsam. But the air all about them was filled with the strangest, saddest, most unforgettable sound in nature—the soft, ceaseless wash on a distant shore on a still evening of the breakers of a spent storm. A sound rarely heard and always to be remembered. It is even more mournful than the rain-wind of night—the heart-break and despair of all creation is in it. Dean took a quick step forward to meet her—then stopped abruptly. Her face—her eyes—what had happened to Emily in his absence? *This* was not Emily—this strange, white, remote girl of the pale twilight.

"Emily—what is it?" asked Dean—knowing before she told him.

Emily looked at him. If you had to deal a mortal blow why try to lighten it?

"I can't marry you after all, Dean," she said. "I don't love you."

That was all she could say. No excuses—no self-defence. There was none she could make. But it was shocking to see all the happiness wiped out of a human face like that.

There was a little pause—a pause that seemed an eternity with that unbearable sorrow of the sea throbbing through it. Then Dean said still quietly:

"I knew you didn't love me. Yet you were—content to marry me—before this. What has made it impossible?"

It was his right to know. Emily stumbled through her silly, incredible tale.

"You see," she concluded miserably, "when—I can call like that to him across space—I belong to him. He doesn't love me—he never will—but I belong to him. . . . Oh, Dean, don't look so. I *had* to tell you this—but if you wish it—I *will* marry you—only I felt you must know the whole truth—when I knew it myself."

"Oh, a Murray of New Moon always keeps her word." Dean's face twisted mockingly. "You will marry me—if I want you to. But I don't want it—now. I see how impossible it is just as clearly as you do. I will not marry a woman whose heart is another man's."

"Can you ever forgive me, Dean?"

"What is there to forgive? I can't help loving you and you can't help loving him. We must let it go at that. Even the gods can't unscramble eggs. I should have known that only youth could call to youth—and I was never young. If I ever had been, even though I am old now, I might have held you."

He dropped his poor grey face in his hands. Emily found herself thinking what a nice, pleasant, friendly thing death would be.

But when Dean looked up again his face had changed. It had the old, mocking, cynical look.

"Don't look so tragic, Emily. A broken engagement is a very slight thing nowadays. And it's an ill wind that blows nobody good. Your aunts will thank whatever gods there be and my own clan will think that I have escaped as a bird out of the snare of the fowler. Still—I rather wish that old Highland Scotch grandmother who passed that dangerous chromosome down to you had taken her second sight to the grave with her."

Emily put her hands against the little porch column and laid her head against them. Dean's face changed again as he looked at her. His voice when he spoke was very gentle—though cold and pale. All the brilliance and colour and warmth had gone from it.

"Emily, I give your life back to you. It has been mine, remember, since I saved you that day on Malvern rocks. It's your own again. And we must say good-bye at last—in spite of our old compact. Say it briefly—'all farewells should be sudden when forever.'"

Emily turned and caught at his arm.

"Oh, not good-bye, Dean—not good-bye. Can't we be friends still? I can't live without your friendship."

Dean took her face in his hands—Emily's cold face that he had once dreamed might flush against his kiss—and looked gravely and tenderly into it.

"We can't be friends again, dear."

"Oh, you will forget—you will not always care—"

"A man must die to forget you, I think. No, Star, we cannot be friends. You will not have my love and it has driven everything else out. I am going away. When I am old—really old—I will come back and we will be friends again, perhaps."

"I can never forgive myself."

"Again I ask what for? I do not reproach you—I even thank you for this year. It has been a royal gift to me. Nothing can ever take it from me. After all, I would not give that last perfect summer of mine for a generation of other men's happiness. My Star—my Star!"

Emily looked at him, the kiss she had never given him in her eyes. What a lonely place the world would be when Dean was gone—the world that had all at once grown very old. And would she ever be able to forget his eyes with that terrible expression of pain in them?

If he had gone then she would never have been quite free—always fettered by those piteous eyes and the thought of the wrong she had done him. Perhaps Dean realized this, for there was a hint of some malign triumph in his parting smile as he turned away. He walked down the path—he paused with his hand on the gate—he turned and came back.

III

"Emily, I've something to confess, too. May as well get it off my conscience. A lie—an ugly thing. I won you by a lie, I think. Perhaps that is why I couldn't keep you."

"A lie?"

"You remember that book of yours? You asked me to tell you the truth about what I thought of it? I didn't. I lied. It is a good piece of work—very good. Oh, some faults in it of course—a bit emotional—a bit overstrained. You still need pruning—restraint. But it is good. It is out of the ordinary both in conception and development. It has charm and your characters *do* live. Natural, human, delightful. There, you know what I think of it now."

Emily stared at him, a hot flush suddenly staining the pallor of her tortured little face.

"Good? And I burned it," she said in a whisper.

Dean started.

"You—burned it!"

"Yes. And I can never write it again. Why—why did you lie to me? *You?*"

"Because I hated the book. You were more interested in it than in me. You *would* have found a publisher eventually—and it would have been successful. You would have been lost to me. How ugly some motives look when you put them into words. And you burned it? It seems very idle to say I'm bitterly sorry for all this. Idle to ask your forgiveness."

Emily pulled herself together. Something had happened—she was really free—free from remorse, shame, regret. Her own woman once more. The balance hung level between them.

"I must not hold a grudge against Dean for this—like old Hugh Murray," she thought confusedly. Aloud—"But I do—I do forgive it, Dean."

"Thank you." He looked up at the little grey house behind her. "So this is still to be the Disappointed House. Verily, there is a doom on it. Houses, like people, can't escape their doom, it seems."

Emily averted her gaze from the little house she had loved—still loved. It would never be hers now. It was still to be haunted by the ghosts of things that never happened.

"Dean—here is the key."

Dean shook his head. "Keep it till I ask for it. What use would it be to me? The house can be sold, I suppose—though that seems like sacrilege."

There was still something more. Emily held out her left hand with averted face. Dean must take off the emerald he had put on. She felt it drawn from her finger, leaving a little cold band where it had warmed against her flesh, like a spectral circlet. It had often seemed to her like a fetter, but she felt sick with regret when she realized it was gone—forever. For with it went something that had made life beautiful for years—Dean's wonderful friendship and companionship. To miss that—forever. She had not known how bitter a thing freedom could be.

When Dean had limped out of sight Emily went home. There was nothing else to do. With her mocking triumph that Dean had at last admitted she could write.

IV

If Emily's engagement to Dean had made a commotion in the clans the breaking of it brewed a still wilder teapot tempest. The Priests were exultant and indignant at one and the same time, but the inconsistent Murrays were furious. Aunt Elizabeth had steadily disapproved of the engagement, but she disapproved still more strongly of its breaking.

What would people think? And many things were said about "the Starr fickleness."

"Did you," demanded Uncle Wallace sarcastically, "expect that girl to remain in the same mind from one day to another?"

All the Murrays said things, according to their separate flavour, but for some reason Andrew's dictum rankled with the keenest venom in Emily's bruised spirit. Andrew had picked up a word somewhere— he said Emily was "temperamental." Half the Murrays did not know just what it meant but they pounced on it eagerly. Emily was "temperamental"—just that. It explained everything—henceforth it clung to her like a burr. If she wrote a poem—if she didn't like carrot pudding when everybody else in the clan did—if she wore her hair low when every one else was wearing it high—if she liked a solitary ramble over moonlit hills—if she looked some mornings as if she had not slept—if she took a notion to study the stars through a field-glass—if it was whispered that she had been seen dancing alone by moonlight among the coils of a New Moon hayfield—if tears came into her eyes at the mere glimpse of some beauty—if she loved a twilight tryst in the "old orchard" better than a dance in Shrewsbury—it was all because she was temperamental. Emily felt herself alone in a hostile world. Nobody, not even Aunt Laura, understood. Even Ilse wrote rather an odd letter, every sentence of which contradicted some other sentence and left Emily with a nasty, confused feeling that Ilse loved her as much as ever but thought her "temperamental" too. Could Ilse, by any chance, have suspected the fact that, as soon as Perry Miller heard that "everything was off" between Dean Priest and Emily Starr, he had come out to New Moon and again asked Emily to promise to marry him? Emily had made short work of him, after a fashion which made Perry vow disgustedly that he was done with the proud monkey. But then he had vowed that so many times before.

CHAPTER XII

I

"MAY 4, 19—

"One o'clock is a somewhat unearthly hour to be writing in a journal. The truth is, I've been undergoing a white night. I can't sleep and I'm tired of lying in the dark fancying things—unpleasant things—so I've lighted my candle and hunted up my old diary to 'write it out.'

"I've never written in this journal since the night I burned my book and fell downstairs—and died. Coming back to life to find everything changed and all things made new. And unfamiliar and dreadful. It seems a lifetime ago. As I turn over the pages and glance at those gay, light-hearted entries I wonder if they were really written by me, Emily Byrd Starr.

"Night is beautiful when you are happy—comforting when you are in grief—terrible when you are lonely and unhappy. And to-night I have been horribly lonely. Misery overwhelmed me. I seem never to be able to stop half-way in any emotion and when loneliness does seize hold on me it takes possession of me body and soul and wrings me in its blank pain until all strength and courage go out of me. To-night I am lonely—lonely. Love will not come to me—friendship is lost to me—most of all, as I verily feel, I cannot write. I have tried repeatedly and failed. The old creative fire seems to have burned out into ashes and I cannot rekindle it. All the evening I tried to write a story—a wooden thing in which wooden puppets moved when I jerked the strings. I finally tore it into a thousand pieces and felt that I did God service.

"These past weeks have been bitter ones. Dean has gone—where I know not. He has never written—never will, I suppose. Not to be getting letters from Dean when he is away seems strange and unnatural.

"And yet it is terribly sweet to be free once more.

"Ilse writes me that she is to be home for July and August. Also that Teddy will be, too. Perhaps this latter fact partly accounts for my white night. I want to run away before he comes.

"I have never answered the letter he wrote me after the sinking of the *Flavian*. I could not. I could not write of *that*. And if when he comes he speaks of it—I shall not be able to bear it. Will he guess that it is because I love him that I was able to set at naught the limitations of time and space to save him? I am ready to die of shame at thought of it. And at thought of what I said to Mrs. Kent. Yet somehow I have never been able to wish *that* unsaid. There was a strange relief in the stark honesty of it. I am not afraid she will ever tell him what I said. She would never have him know I cared if she could prevent it

"But I'd like to know how I am to get through the summer.

"There are times when I hate life. Other times again when I love it fiercely with an agonized realization of how beautiful it is—or might be—if—

"Before Dean went away he boarded up all the windows of the Disappointed House. I never go where I can see it. But I *do* see it for all that. Waiting there on its hill—waiting—dumb—blind. I have never taken my things out of it—which Aunt Elizabeth thinks a sure indication of insanity. And I don't think Dean did either. Nothing has been touched. Mona Lisa is still mocking in the gloom and Elizabeth Bas is tolerantly contemptuous of temperamental idiots and the Lady Giovanna understands it all. My dear little house! And it is never to be a home. I feel as I felt that evening years ago when I followed the rainbow—and lost it. 'There will be other rainbows' I said then. But will there be?"

II

"MAY 15, 19—

"This has been a lyric spring day—and a miracle has happened. It happened at dawn—when I was leaning out of my window, listening to a little, whispering, tricksy wind o' morning blowing out of Lofty John's bush. Suddenly—the flash came—again—after these long months of absence—my old, inexpressible glimpse of eternity. And all at once I knew I could write. I rushed to my desk and seized my pen. All the hours of early morning I wrote; and when I heard Cousin Jimmy going downstairs I flung down my pen and bowed my head over my desk in utter thankfulness that I could work again.

Get leave to work—

In this world 'tis the best you get at all,

For God in cursing gives us better gifts

Than men in benediction.

"So wrote Elizabeth Barrett Browning—and truly. It is hard to understand why work should be called a curse—until one remembers what bitterness forced or uncongenial labour is. But the work for which we are fitted—which we feel we are sent into the world to do—what a blessing it is and what fulness of joy it holds. I felt this to-day as the old fever burned in my finger-tips and my pen once more seemed a friend.

"'Leave to work'—one would think any one could obtain so much. But sometimes anguish and heartbreak forbid us the leave. And then we realize what we have lost and know that it is better to be cursed by God than forgotten by Him. If He had punished Adam and Eve by sending them out to *idleness,* then indeed they would have been outcast and accursed. Not all the dreams of Eden 'whence the four great rivers flow' could have been as sweet as those I am dreaming to-night, because the power to work has come back to me.

"Oh, God, as long as I live give me 'leave to work.' Thus pray I. Leave and courage."

III

"MAY 25, 19—

"Dear sunshine, what a potent medicine you are. All day I revelled in the loveliness of the wonderful white bridal world. And to-night I washed my soul free from dust in the aerial bath of a spring twilight. I chose the old hill road over the Delectable Mountain for its solitude and wandered happily along, pausing every few moments to think out fully some thought or fancy that came to me like a winged spirit. Then I prowled about the hill fields till long after dark, studying the stars with my field-glass. When I came in I felt as if I had been millions of miles away in the blue ether and all my old familiar surroundings seemed momentarily forgotten and strange.

"But there was one star at which I did not look. Vega of the Lyre."

IV

"MAY 30, 19—

"This evening, just when I was in the middle of a story Aunt Elizabeth said she wanted me to weed the onion-bed. So I had to lay down my pen and go out to the kitchen garden. But one can weed onions and think wonderful things at the same time, glory be. It is one of the blessings that we don't always have to put our souls into what our hands may be doing, praise the gods—for otherwise who would have any soul left? So I weeded the onion-bed and roamed the Milky Way in imagination."

V

"JUNE 10, 19—

"Cousin Jimmy and I felt like murderers last night. We were. Baby-killers at that!

"It is one of the springs when there is a crop of maple-trees. Every key that fell from a maple this year seems to have grown. All over the lawn and garden and old orchard tiny maple-trees have sprung up by the hundreds. And of course they have to be rooted out. It would never do to let them grow. So we pulled them up all day yesterday and felt so mean and guilty over it. The dear, tiny, baby things. They have a right to grow—a right to keep on growing into great, majestic, splendid trees. Who are we to deny it to them? I caught Cousin Jimmy in tears over the brutal necessity.

"'I sometimes think,' he whispered, 'that it's wrong to prevent anything from growing. *I* never grew up—not in my head.'

"And last night I had a horrible dream of being pursued by thousands of indignant young maple-tree ghosts. They crowded around me—tripped me up—thrashed me with their boughs—smothered me with their leaves. And I woke gasping for breath and nearly frightened to death, but with a splendid idea for a story in my head—*The Vengeance of the Tree*."

VI

"JUNE 15, 19—

"I picked strawberries on the banks of Blair Water this afternoon among the windy, sweet-smelling grasses. I love picking strawberries. The occupation has in it something of perpetual youth. The gods might have picked strawberries on high Olympus without injuring their dignity. A queen—or a poet—might stoop to it; a beggar has the privilege.

"And to-night I've been sitting here in my dear old room, with my dear books and dear pictures and dear little window of the kinky panes, dreaming in the soft, odorous summer twilight, while the robins are calling to each other in Lofty John's bush and the poplars are talking eerily of old, forgotten things.

"After all, it's not a bad old world—and the folks in it are not half bad either. Even Emily Byrd Star is decent in spots. Not altogether the false, fickle, ungrateful perversity she thinks she is in the wee sma's— not altogether the friendless, forgotten maiden she imagines she is on white nights—not altogether the failure she supposes bitterly when three MSS. are rejected in succession. And *not* altogether the coward she feels herself to be when she thinks of Frederick Kent's coming to Blair Water in July."

CHAPTER XIII

I

Emily was reading by the window of her room when she heard it—reading Alice Meynell's strange poem, "Letter From A Girl To Her Own Old Age," and thrilling mystically to its strange prophecies. Outside dusk was falling over the old New Moon garden; and clear through the dusk came the two high notes and the long low one of Teddy's old whistle in Lofty John's bush—the old, old call by which he had so often summoned her in the twilights of long ago.

629

Emily's book fell unheeded to the floor. She stood up, mist-pale, her eyes dilating into darkness. Was Teddy there? He had not been expected till the next week, though Ilse was coming that night. Could she have been mistaken? Could she have fancied it? Some chance robin call—

It came again. She knew as she had known at first that it was Teddy's whistle. There was no sound like it in the world. And it had been so long since she had heard it. He was there—waiting for her—calling for her. Should she go? She laughed under her breath. Go? She had no choice. She must go. Pride could not hold her back—bitter remembrance of the night she had waited for his call and it had not come could not halt her hurrying footsteps. Fear—shame—all were forgotten in the mad ecstasy of the moment. Without giving herself time to reflect that she was a Murray—only snatching a moment to look in the glass and assure herself that her ivory crepe dress was very becoming—how lucky it was that she had happened to put on that dress!—she flew down the stairs and through the garden. He was standing under the dark glamour of the old firs where the path ran through Lofty John's bush—bareheaded, smiling.

"Teddy."

"Emily."

Her hands were in his—her eyes were shining into his. Youth had come back—all that had once made magic made it again. Together once more after all those long weary years of alienation and separation. There was no longer any shyness—any stiffness—any sense or fear of change. They might have been children together again. But childhood had never known this wild, insurgent sweetness—this unconsidered surrender. Oh, she was his. By a word—a look—an intonation, he was still her master. What matter if, in some calmer mood, she might not quite like it—to be helpless—dominated like this? What matter if to-morrow she might wish she had not run so quickly, so eagerly, so unhesitatingly to meet him? To-night nothing mattered except that Teddy had come back.

Yet, outwardly, they did not meet as lovers—only as old, dear friends. There was so much to talk of—so much to be silent over as they paced up and down the garden walks, while the stars laughed through the dark at them—hinting—hinting—

Only one thing was not spoken of between them—the thing Emily

630

had dreaded. Teddy made no reference to the mystery of that vision in the London station. It was as if it had never been. Yet Emily felt that it had drawn them together again after long misunderstanding. It was well not to speak of it—it was one of those mystic things—one of the gods' secrets—that must not be spoken of. Best forgotten now that its work was done. And yet—so unreasonable are we mortals!—Emily felt a ridiculous disappointment that he didn't speak of it. She didn't want him to speak of it. But if it had meant anything to him must he not have spoken of it?

"It's good to be here again," Teddy was saying. "Nothing seems changed here. Time has stood still in this Garden of Eden. Look, Emily, how bright Vega of the Lyre is. Our star. Have you forgotten it?"

Forgotten? How she had wished she *could* forget.

"They wrote me you were going to marry Dean," said Teddy abruptly.

"I meant to—but I couldn't," said Emily.

"Why not?" asked Teddy as if he had a perfect right to ask it.

"Because I didn't love him," answered Emily, conceding his right.

Laughter—golden, delicious laughter that made you suddenly want to laugh too. Laughter was so *safe*—one could laugh without betraying anything. Ilse had come—Ilse was running down the walk. Ilse in a yellow silk gown the colour of her hair and a golden-brown hat the colour of her eyes, giving you the sensation that a gorgeous golden rose was at large in the garden.

Emily almost welcomed her. The moment had grown too vital. Some things were terrible if put into words. She drew away from Teddy almost primly—a Murray of New Moon once more.

"Darlings," said Ilse, throwing an arm around each of them. "Isn't it divine—all here together again? Oh, how much I love you! Let's forget we are old and grown-up and wise and unhappy and be mad, crazy, happy kids again for just one blissful summer."

II

A wonderful month followed. A month of indescribable roses, exquisite hazes, silver perfection of moonlight, unforgettable amethystine dusks, march of rains, bugle-call of winds, blossoms of purple and star-dust, mystery, music, magic. A month of laughter and dance and joy, of enchantment infinite. Yet a month of restrained, hidden realization. Nothing was ever said. She and Teddy were seldom ever alone together. But one felt—knew. Emily fairly sparkled with happiness. All the old restlessness that had worried Aunt Laura had gone from her eyes. Life was good. Friendship—love—joy of sense and joy of spirit—sorrow—loveliness—achievement—failure—longing— all were part of life and therefore interesting and desirable.

Every morning when she awakened the new day seemed to her like some good fairy who would bring her some beautiful gift of joy. Ambition was, for the time at least, forgotten. Success—power—fame. Let those who cared for them pay the price and take them. But love is not bought and sold. It is a gift.

Even the memory of her burned book ceased to ache. What did one book more or less matter in this great universe of life and passion? How pale and shadowy was any pictured life beside this throbbing, scintillant existence! Who cared for laurel, after all? Orange blossoms would make a sweeter coronet. And what star of destiny was ever brighter and more alluring than Vega of the Lyre. Which, being interpreted, simply meant that nothing mattered any more in this world or any other except Teddy Kent.

III

"If I had a tail I'd lash it," groaned Ilse, casting herself on Emily's bed and hurling one of Emily's treasured volumes—a little old copy of the *Rubaiyat* Teddy had given her in high school days—across the room. The back came off and the leaves flew every which way for a Sunday. Emily was annoyed.

"Were you ever in such a state that you could neither cry nor pray nor swear?" demanded Ilse.

"Sometimes," agreed Emily dryly. "But I don't take it out on books that never harmed me. I just go and bite off somebody's head."

"There wasn't anybody's head handy to bite off, but I did something that was just as effective," said Ilse, casting a malevolent glance at Perry Miller's photograph which was propped up on Emily's desk.

Emily glanced at it, too, and her face Murrayfied, as Ilse expressed it. The photograph was still there but where Perry's intent and unabashed eyes had gazed out at her were now only jagged, unsightly holes.

Emily was furious. Perry had been so proud of those photographs.

They were the first he had had taken in his life. "Never could afford any before," he had said frankly. He looked very handsome in them, though his pose was a bit truculent and aggressive with his wavy hair brushed back sleekly, and his firm mouth and chin showing to excellent advantage. Aunt Elizabeth had gazed at it, secretly wondering how she had ever dared make such a fine-looking young man as that eat in the kitchen. And Aunt Laura had wiped her eyes sentimentally and thought that perhaps—after all—Emily and Perry—a lawyer would be quite a thing to have in the family, coming in a good third to minister and doctor. Though, to be sure, Stovepipe Town—

Perry had rather spoiled the gift for Emily by proposing to her again. It was very hard for Perry Miller to get it into his head that anything he wanted he couldn't get. And he had always wanted Emily.

"I've got the world by the tail now," he said proudly. "Every year'll find me higher up. Why can't you make up your mind to have me, Emily?"

"Is it just a question of making up one's mind?" asked Emily satirically.

"Of course. What else?"

"Listen, Perry," said Emily decidedly. "You're a good old pal. I like you—I'll always like you. But I'm tired of this nonsense and I'm going to put a stop to it. If you ever again ask me to marry you I'll never never speak to you as long as I live. Since you are good at making up your mind make up yours which you want—my friendship or my non-existence."

"Oh, well." Perry shrugged his shoulders philosophically. He had about come to the conclusion anyhow that he might as well give up dangling after Emily Starr and getting nothing but snubs for his pains. Ten years was long enough to be a rejected but faithful swain. There were other girls, after all. Perhaps he had made a mistake. *Too* faithful and persistent. If he had wooed by fits and starts, blowing hot and cold like Teddy Kent, he might have had better luck. Girls were like that. But Perry did not say this. Stovepipe Town had learned a few things. All he said was:

"If you'd only stop looking at me in a certain way I might get over hankering for you. Anyhow, I'd never have got this far along if I hadn't been in love with you. I'd just have been a hired boy somewhere or a fisherman at the harbour. So I'm sorry. I haven't forgotten how you believed in me and helped me and stood up for me to your Aunt Elizabeth. It's been—been"—Perry's handsome face flushed suddenly and his voice shook a little—"it's been—sweet—to dream about you all these years. I guess I'll have to give it up now. No use, I see. But don't take your friendship from me too, Emily."

"Never," said Emily impulsively putting out her hands. "You're a brick, Perry dear. You've done wonders and I'm proud of you."

And now to find the picture he had given her ruined. She flashed on Ilse eyes like a stormy sea.

"Ilse Burnley, how dare you do such a thing!"

"No use squizzling your eyebrows up at me like that, beloved demon," retorted Ilse. "Hasn't no effect on me a-tall. Couldn't endure that picture no-how. And Stovepipe Town in the background."

"What you've done is on a level with Stovepipe Town."

"Well, he asked for it. Smirking there. 'Behold ME. I am a Person In The Public Eye.' Never had such satisfaction as boring your scissors through those conceited orbs gave me. Two seconds more of looking at them and I'd have flung up my head and howled. Oh, how I hate Perry Miller. Puffed up like a poisoned pup!"

"I thought you told me you loved him," said Emily rather rudely.

"It's the same thing," said Ilse morosely. "Emily, why can't I get that creature out of my mind! It's too Victorian to say heart. I haven't any heart. I don't love him—I *do* hate him. But I can't keep from thinking about him. *That's* just a state of mind. Oh, I could yell at the moon. But the real reason I dug his eyes out was his turning Grit after having been born and raised Conservative."

"You are Conservative yourself."

"True but unimportant. I hate turncoats. I've never forgiven Henry IV for turning Catholic. Not because he was a Protestant but just because he was a turncoat I would have been just as implacable if he had been Catholic and turned Protestant. Perry has changed his politics just for the sake of getting into partnership with Leonard Abel. There's Stovepipe Town for you. Oh, he'll be Judge Miller and rich as wedding-cake—but—! I wish he had had a hundred eyes so that I could have bored them all out! This is one of the times I feel it would be handy to have been a bosom friend of Lucrezia Borgia."

"Who was an excellent and rather stupid woman beloved for her good works."

"Oh, I know the modern whitewashers are determined to rob history of anything that is picturesque. No matter, I shall cling to my faith in Lucrezia and William Tell. Put that picture out of my sight. *Please,* Emily."

Emily put the maltreated picture away in a drawer of her desk. Her brief anger had gone. She understood. At least she understood why the eyes had been cut out. It was harder to understand just why Ilse could care so much and so incurably for Perry Miller. And there was just a hint of pity in her heart as well—condescending pity for Ilse who cared so much for a man who didn't care for her.

"I think this will cure me," said Ilse savagely. "I can't—I won't love a turncoat. Blind bat—congenital idiot that he is! Pah, I'm through with him. Emily, I wonder I don't hate you. Rejecting with scorn what I want so much. Ice-cold thing, did you ever really care for anything or any creature except that pen of yours?"

"Perry has never really loved me," evaded Emily. "He only imagines he does."

"Well, I'd be content if he would only just imagine he loved me. How brazen I am about it. You're the one person in the world I can have the relief of saying such things to. That's why I can't let myself hate you, after all. I daresay I'm not half as unhappy as I think myself. One never knows what may be around the next corner. After this I mean to bore Perry Miller out of my life and thoughts just as I bored his eyes out. Emily," with an abrupt change of tone and posture, "do you know I like Teddy Kent better this summer than I ever did before."

"Oh." The monosyllable was eloquent, but Ilse was deaf to all its implications.

"Yes. He's really charming. Those years in Europe have done something to him. Perhaps it's just that they've taught him to hide his selfishness better."

"Teddy Kent isn't selfish. Why do you call him selfish? Look at his devotion to his mother."

"Because she adores him. Teddy likes to be adored. That's why he's never fallen in love with any one, you know. That—and because the girls chased him so, perhaps. It was sickening in Montreal. They made such asses of themselves—waiting on him with their tongues hanging out—that I wanted to dress in male attire and swear I wasn't of their sex. No doubt it was the same in Europe. No man alive can stand six years of that without being spoiled—and contemptuous. Teddy is all right with *us*—he knows we're old pals who can see through him and will stand no nonsense. But I've see him accepting tribute—graciously bestowing a smile—a look—a touch as a reward. Saying to every one just what he thought she'd like to hear. When I saw it I always felt I'd love to say something to him that he'd think of for years whenever he woke up at three o'clock o'night."

The sun had dropped into a bank of purple cloud behind the Delectable Mountain and a chill and shadow swept down the hill and across the dewy clover-fields to New Moon. The little room darkened and the glimpse of Blair Water through the gap in Lofty John's bush changed all at once to livid grey.

Emily's evening was spoiled. But she felt—*knew*—that Ilse was mistaken about many things. There was one comfort, too—evidently she had kept her secret well. Not even Ilse suspected it. Which was agreeable to both the Murray and the Starr.

IV

But Emily sat long at her window looking into the black night that turned slowly to pale silver as the moon rose. So the girls had "chased" Teddy.

She wished she had not run quite so quickly when he had called from Lofty John's bush. "Oh, whistle, and I'll come to you, my lad" was all very well in song. But one was not living in a Scotch ballad. And that change in Ilse's voice—that almost confidential note. Did Ilse mean—? How pretty Ilse had looked to-night. In that smart, sleeveless dress of green sprinkled with tiny golden butterflies—with the green necklace that circled her throat and fell to her hips like a long green snake—with her green, gold-buckled shoes—Ilse always wore such ravishing shoes. *Did* Ilse mean—? And if she did—?

After breakfast Aunt Laura remarked to Cousin Jimmy that she felt sure something was on the dear child's mind.

CHAPTER XIV

I

"The early bird catches—the desire of his heart," said Teddy, slipping down beside Emily on the long, silken, pale-green grasses on the bank of Blair Water.

He had come so silently that Emily had not heard him until she saw him and she could not repress a start and blush—which she hoped wildly he did not see. She had wakened early and been seized with what her clan would doubtless have considered a temperamental desire to see the sun rise and make new acquaintances with Eden. So she had stolen down New Moon stairs and through the expectant garden and Lofty John's bush to the Blair Water to meet the mystery of the dawn. It had never occurred to her that Teddy would be prowling, too.

"I like to come down here at sunrise, now and then," he said. "It's about the only chance I have of being alone for a few minutes. Our evenings and afternoons are all given over the mad revelry—and Mother likes me to be with her every moment of the forenoons. She's had six such horribly lonely years."

"I'm sorry I've intruded on your precious solitude," said Emily stiffly, possessed of a horrible fear that he might think she knew of his habits and had come purposely to meet him.

Teddy laughed.

"Don't put on New Moon airs with me, Emily Byrd Starr. You know perfectly well that finding you here is the crown of the morning for me. I've always had a wild hope that it might happen. And now it has. Let's just sit here and dream together. God made this morning for us—just us two. Even talking would spoil it."

Emily agreed silently. How dear it was to sit here with Teddy on the banks of Blair Water, under the coral of the morning sky, and dream— just dream—wild, sweet, secret, unforgettable, foolish dreams. Alone with Teddy while all their world was sleeping. Oh, if this exquisite stolen moment could last! A line from some poem of Marjorie Pickthall quivered in her thought like a bar of music—

Oh, keep the world forever at the dawn.

She said it like a prayer under her breath.

Everything was so beautiful in this magical moment before sunrise. The wild blue irises around the pond, the violet shadows in the curves of the dunes, the white filmy mist hanging over the buttercup valley across the pond, the cloth of gold and silver that was called a field of daisies, the cool, delicious gulf breeze, the blue of far lands beyond the harbour, plumes of purple and mauve smoke going up on the still, golden air from the chimneys of Stovepipe Town where the fishermen rose early. And Teddy lying at her feet, his slim brown hands clasped behind his head. Again she felt inescapably the magnetic attraction of his personality. Felt it so strongly that she dared not meet his eyes. Yet she was admitting to herself with a secret candour which would have horrified Aunt Elizabeth that she wanted to run her fingers through his sleek black hair—feel his arms about her—press her face against his dark tender one—feel his lips on her lips—

Teddy took one of his hands from under his head and put it over hers.

For a moment of surrender she left it there. Then Ilse's words flashed into memory, searing her consciousness like a dagger of flame. "I've seen him accepting tribute"—"graciously bestowing a touch as a reward"—"saying to each one just what he thought she wanted to hear." Had Teddy guessed what she had been thinking? Her thoughts had seemed so vivid to her that she felt as if any one must *see* her thinking. Intolerable. She sprang up abruptly, shaking off his fingers.

"I must be going home."

So blunt. Somehow, she could not make it smoother. He must not—should not think—Teddy rose, too. A change in his voice and look. Their marvellous moment was over.

"So must I. Mother will be missing me. She's always up early. Poor little Mother. She hasn't changed. She isn't proud of my success—she hates it. She thinks it has taken me from her. The years have not made it any easier for her. I want her to come away with me, but she will not. I think that is partly because she cannot bear to leave the old Tansy Patch and partly because she can't endure seeing me shut up in my studio working—something that would bar her out. I wonder what made her so. I've never known her any other way, but I think she must have been different once. It's odd for a son to know as little of his mother's life as I do. I don't even know what made that scar on her face. I know next to nothing of my father—absolutely nothing of his people. She will never talk of anything in the years before we came to Blair Water."

"Something hurt her once—hurt her so terribly she has never got over it," said Emily.

"My father's death, perhaps?"

"No. At least, not if it were just death. There was something else—something poisonous. Well—bye-bye."

"Going to Mrs. Chidlaw's dinner-dance tomorrow night?"

"Yes. She is sending her car for me."

"Whew! No use after that asking you to go with me in a one-hoss buggy—borrowed at that. Well, I must take Ilse then. Perry to be there?"

"No. He wrote me he couldn't come—had to prepare for his first case. It's coming up next day."

"Perry is forging ahead, isn't he? That bulldog tenacity of his never lets go of an objective once he gets his teeth into it. He'll be rich when we're still as poor as church mice. But then, we're chasing rainbow gold, aren't we?"

She would not linger—he might think she wanted to linger—"waiting with her tongue hanging out"—she turned away almost ungraciously. He had been so unregretfully ready to "take Ilse then." As if it really didn't matter much. Yet she was still conscious of his touch on her hand—it burned there yet. In that fleeting moment, in that brief caress, he had made her wholly his, as years of wifehood could never have made her Dean's. She could think of nothing else all day. She lived over and over again that moment of surrender. It seemed to her so inadequate that everything should be the same at New Moon and that Cousin Jimmy should be worrying over red spiders on his asters.

II

A tack on the Shrewsbury road made Emily fifteen minutes late for Mrs. Chidlaw's dinner. She flung a hasty glance into the mirror before she went down and turned away satisfied. An arrow of rhinestones in her dark hair—she had hair that wore jewels well—lent the necessary note of brilliance to the new dress of silvery-green lace over a pale-blue slip that became her so well. Miss Royal had picked it for her in New York—and Aunts Elizabeth and Laura had looked askance at it. Green and blue was *such* an odd combination. And there was so little of it. But it did something to Emily when she put it on. Cousin Jimmy looked at the exquisite, shimmering young thing with stars in her eyes, in the old candle-lighted kitchen and said ruefully to Aunt Laura after she had gone, "She doesn't belong to *us* in that dress."

"It made her look like an *actress*," said Aunt Elizabeth freezingly.

Emily did not feel like an actress as she ran down Mrs. Chidlaw's stairs and across the sun-room to the wide verandah where Mrs. Chidlaw had elected to hold her dinner party. She felt real, vital, happy, expectant. Teddy would be there—their eyes would meet significantly across the table—there would be the furtive sweetness of watching him secretly when he talked to some one else—and thought of *her*—they would dance together afterwards. Perhaps he would tell her—what she was longing to hear—

She paused for a second in the open doorway, her eyes soft and dreamy as a purple mist, looking out on the scene before her—one of those scenes which are always remembered from some subtle charm of their own.

The table was spread in the big rounded alcove at the corner of the vine-hung verandah. Beyond it tall, dark firs and Lombardies stood out against the after-sunset sky of dull rose and fading yellow. Through their stems she caught glimpses of the bay, dark and sapphire. Great masses of shadow beyond the little island of light—the gleam of pearls on Ilse's white neck. There were other guests—Professor Robins of McGill with his long, melancholy face made still longer by his odd spade-shaped beard; Lisette Chidlaw's round, cream-coloured, kissable face with its dark hair heaped high over it and her round, dark eyes; Jack Glenlake, dreamy and handsome; Annette Shaw, a sleepy, gold-and-white thing, always affecting a Mona Lisa smile; stocky little Tom Hallam with his humorous Irish face; Aylmer Vincent. Quite fat. Beginning to be bald. Still making pretty speeches to the ladies. How absurd to recall that she had once thought him Prince Charming! Solemn-looking Gus Rankin, with a vacant chair beside him, evidently for her. Elsie Borland, young and chubby, showing off her lovely hands a little in the candlelight. But of all the party Emily only saw Teddy and Ilse. The rest were puppets.

They were sitting together just opposite her. Teddy sleek and well-groomed as usual, his black head close to Ilse's golden one. Ilse, a glorified shining creature in torquoise-blue taffeta, looking the queen with a foam of laces on her full bosom and rose-and-silver nosegays at her shoulder. Just as Emily looked at them Ilse lifted her eyes to Teddy's face and asked some question—some intimate, vital question, Emily felt sure, from the expression of her face. She did not recall ever having seen just that look on Ilse's face before. There was some sort of definite challenge in it. Teddy looked down and answered her. Emily knew or felt that the word "love" was in his answer. Those two looked long into each other's eyes—at least it seemed long to Emily, beholding that interchange of rapt glances. Then Ilse blushed and looked away. When had Ilse ever blushed before? And Teddy threw up his head and swept the table with eyes that seemed exultant and victorious.

Emily went out into the circle of radiance from that terrible moment of disillusion. Her heart, so gay and light a moment before, seemed cold and dead. In spite of the lights and laughter a dark, chill night seemed to be coming towards her. Everything in life seemed suddenly ugly. It was for her a dinner of bitter herbs and she never remembered anything Gus Rankin said to her. She never looked at Teddy, who seemed in wonderful spirits and was keeping up a stream of banter with Ilse, and she was chilly and unresponsive through the whole meal. Gus Rankin told all his favourite stories but like Queen Victoria of blessed memory, Emily was not amused. Mrs. Chidlaw was provoked and repented of having sent her car for so temperamental a guest. Annoyed probably over being paired with Gus Rankin, who had been asked at the last minute to fill Perry Miller's place. And looking like an outraged duchess over it. Yet you had to be civil to her. She might put you in a book if you weren't. Remember that time she wrote the review of our play! In reality, poor Emily was thanking whatever gods there be that she was beside Gus Rankin, who never wanted or expected any one to talk.

The dance was a ghastly affair for Emily. She felt like a ghost moving among revellers she had suddenly outgrown. She danced once with Teddy and Teddy, realizing that it was only her slim, silvery-green form he held, while her soul had retreated into some aloof impregnable citadel, did not ask her again. He danced several dances with Ilse and then sat out several more with her in the garden. His devotion to her was noticed and commented upon. Millicent Chidlaw asked Emily if the report that Ilse Burnley and Frederick Kent were engaged were true.

"He was always crazy about her, wasn't he?" Millicent wanted to know.

Emily, in a cool and impertinent voice, supposed so. Was Millicent watching her to see if she would flinch?

Of course he was in love with Ilse. What wonder? Ilse was so beautiful. What chance could her own moonlit charm of dark and silver have against that gold and ivory loveliness? Teddy liked *her* as a dear old pal and chum. That was all. She had been a fool *again.* Always deceiving herself. That morning by Blair Water—when she had almost let him see—perhaps he *had* seen—the thought was unbearable. Would she ever learn wisdom? Oh, yes, she had learned it to-night. No more folly. How wise and dignified and unapproachable she would be henceforth.

Wasn't there some wretched, vulgar old proverb anent locking a stable door after the horse was stolen?

And just how was she to get through the rest of the night?

CHAPTER XV

I

Emily, just home from an interminable week's visit at Uncle Oliver's, where a cousin had been getting married, heard at the post-office that Teddy Kent had gone.

"Left at an hour's notice," Mrs. Crosby told her. "'Got a wire asking if he would take the vice-principal-ship of the College of Art in Montreal and had to go at once to see about it. Isn't that splendid? Hasn't he got on? It's really quite wonderful. Blair Water should be very proud of him, shouldn't it? Isn't it a pity his mother is so odd?"

Fortunately Mrs. Crosby never took time to await any answer to her questions. Emily knew she was turning pale and hated herself for it. She clutched her mail and hastened out of the post-office. She passed several people on the way home and never realized it. As a consequence her reputation for pride went up dangerously. But when she reached New Moon Aunt Laura handed her a letter.

"Teddy left it. He was here last night to say good-bye."

The proud Miss Starr had a narrow escape from bursting into hysterical tears on the spot. A Murray in hysterics! Never had such a thing been heard of—never must be heard of. Emily gritted her teeth, took the letter silently and went to her room. The ice around her heart was melting rapidly. Oh, why had she been so cool and dignified with Teddy all that week after Mrs. Chidlaw's dance? But she had never dreamed he would be going away so soon. And now—

She opened her letter. There was nothing in it but a clipping of some ridiculous poetry Perry had written and published in a Charlottetown paper—a paper that was not taken at New Moon. She and Teddy had laughed over it—Ilse had been too angry to laugh—and Teddy had promised to get a copy for her.

Well, he had got it.

II

She was sitting there, looking whitely out into the soft, black, velvety night with its goblin-market of wind-tossed trees, when Ilse, who had also been away in Charlottetown, came in.

"So Teddy has gone. I see you have a letter from him, too."

Too!

"Yes," said Emily, wondering if it were a lie. Then concluded desperately she did not care whether it was a lie or not.

"He was terribly sorry to have to go so suddenly, but he had to decide at once and he couldn't decide without getting some more information about it. Teddy won't tie himself down too irrevocably to any position, no matter how tempting it is. And to be vice-principal of that college at his age is some little bouquet. Well, I'll soon have to go myself. It's been a gorgeous vacation but—Going to the dance at Derry Pond to-morrow night, Emily?"

Emily shook her head. Of what use was dancing now that Teddy

643

was gone?

"Do you know," said Ilse pensively, "I think this summer has been rather a failure, in spite of our fun. We thought we could be children again, but we haven't been. We've only been pretending."

Pretending? Oh, if this heartache were only a pretence! And this burning shame and deep, mute hurt. Teddy had not even cared enough to write her a line of farewell. She knew—she had known ever since the Chidlaw dance—he did not love her; but surely friendship demanded something. Even her friendship meant nothing to him. This summer had been only an interlude to him. Now he had gone back to his real life and the things that mattered. And he had written Ilse. Pretend? Oh, well, she would pretend with a vengeance. There were times when the Murray pride was certainly an asset.

"I think it's as well the summer is over," she said carelessly. "I simply *must* get down to work again. I have neglected my writing shamefully the past two months."

"After all, that's all you really care about, isn't it?" said Ilse curiously. "I love my work but it doesn't possess me as yours possesses you. I'd give it up in a twinkling for—well, we're all as we're made. But is it really comfortable, Emily, to care for only one thing in life?"

"Much more comfortable than caring for too many things."

"I suppose so. Well, you ought to succeed when you lay everything on the altar of your goddess. That's the difference between us. I'm of weaker clay. There are some things I couldn't give up—some things I *won't*. And as Old Kelly advises, if I can't get what I want—well, I'll want what I can get. Isn't that common sense?"

Emily, wishing she could fool herself as easily as she could other people, went over to the window and kissed Ilse's forehead.

"We aren't children any longer—and we can't go back to childhood, Ilse. We're women—and must make the best of it. I think you'll be happy yet. I *want* you to be."

Ilse squeezed Emily's hand. "Darn common-sense!" she said drearily.

If she had not been in New Moon she would probably have used the unexpurgated edition.

CHAPTER XVI

I

"NOV. 17, 19—

"There are two adjectives that are never separated in regard to a November day—'dull' and 'gloomy.' They were wedded together in the dawn of language and it is not for me to divorce them now. Accordingly, then, this day has been dull and gloomy, inside and outside, materially and spiritually.

"Yesterday wasn't so bad. There was a warm autumnal sun and Cousin Jimmy's big heap of pumpkins made a lovely pool of colour against the old grey barns, and the valley down by the brook was mellow with the late, leafless gold of juniper-trees. I walked in the afternoon through the uncanny enchantment of November woods, still haunted by loveliness, and again in the evening in the afterglow of an autumnal sunset. The evening was mild and wrapped in a great, grey, brooding stillness of windless fields and waiting hill—a stillness which was yet threaded through with many little eerie, beautiful sounds which I could hear if I listened as much with my soul as my ears. Later on there was a procession of stars and I got a message from them.

"But to-day *was* dreary. And to-night virtue has gone out of me. I wrote all day but I could not write this evening. I shut myself into my room and paced it like a caged creature. ''Tis the middle of the night by the castle clock,' but there is no use in thinking of sleep. I can't sleep. The rain against the window is very dismal and the winds are marching by like armies of the dead. All the little ghostly joys of the past are haunting me—all the ghostly fears of the future.

"I keep thinking—foolishly—of the Disappointed House to-night— up there on the hill with the roar of the rainy wind about it. Somehow this is what hurts me worst to-night. Other nights it is the fact that I don't even know where Dean is this winter—or that Teddy never writes a line to me—or just that there are hours when sheer loneliness wrings the stamina out of me. In such moments I come to this old journal for comforting. It's like talking it out to a faithful friend."

II

"NOV. 30, 19—

"I have two chrysanthemums and a rose out. The rose is a song and a dream and an enchantment all in one. The 'mums are very pretty, too, but it does not do to have them and the rose too near together. Seen by themselves they are handsome, bright blossoms, pink and yellow, and cheery, looking very well satisfied with themselves. But set the rose behind them and the change is actually amusing. They then seem like vulgar, frowsy kitchen maids beside a stately, white queen. It's not the fault of the poor 'mums that they weren't born roses, so to be fair to them I keep them by themselves and enjoy them that way.

"I wrote a *good* story to-day. I think even Mr. Carpenter would have been satisfied with it. I was happy while I was writing it. But when I finished it and came back to reality—

"Well, I'm not going to growl. Life has at least grown *livable* again. It was *not* livable through the autumn. I know Aunt Laura thought I was going into consumption. Not I. That would be too Victorian. I fought things out and conquered them and I'm a sane, *free* woman once more. Though the taste of my folly is still in my mouth at times and very bitter it is.

"Oh, I'm really getting on very well. I'm beginning to make a livable income for myself and Aunt Elizabeth reads my stories aloud o' evenings to Aunt Laura and Cousin Jimmy. I can always get through *to-day* very nicely. It's to-morrow I can't live through."

III

"JANUARY 15, 19—

"I've been out for a moonlit snowshoe tramp. There was a nice bite of frost in the air and the night was exquisite—a frosty, starry lyric of light. Some nights are like honey—and some like wine—and some like wormwood. To-night is like wine—white wine—some clear, sparkling, fairy brew that rather goes to one's head. I am tingling all over with hope and expectation and victory over certain principalities and powers that got a grip on me last night about three o'clock.

"I have just drawn aside the curtain of my window and looked out. The garden is white and still under the moon, all ebony of shadow and silver of frosted snow. Over it all the delicate traceries where trees stand up leafless in seeming death and sorrow. But only seeming. The life-blood is at their hearts and by and by it will stir and they will clothe themselves in bridal garments of young green leaves and pink blossoms. And over there where the biggest drift of all lies deep the Golden Ones will uplift their trumpets of the morning.

"And far beyond our garden field after field lies white and lonely in the moonlight. Lonely? I hadn't meant to write that word. It slipped in. I'm *not* lonely—I have my work and my books and the hope of spring—and I know that this calm, simple existence is a much better and happier one than the hectic life I led last summer.

"I believed that before I wrote it down. And now I don't believe it. It isn't true. This is stagnation!!

"Oh, I am—I *am* lonely—with the loneliness of unshared thought. What is the use of denying it? When I came in I *was* the victor—but now my banner is in the dust again."

IV

"FEB. 20, 19—

"Something has happened to sour February's temper. Such a peevish month. The weather for the past few weeks has certainly been living up to the Murray traditions.

"A dreary snowstorm is raging and the wind is pursuing tormented wraiths over the hills. I know that out beyond the trees Blair Water is a sad, black thing in a desert of whiteness. But the great, dark, wintry night outside makes my cosy little room with its crackling fire seem cosier, and I feel much more contented with the world than I did that beautiful night in January. To-night isn't so—so *insulting*.

"To-day in *Glassford's Magazine* there was a story illustration by Teddy. I saw my own face looking out at me in the heroine. It always gives me a very ghostly sensation. And to-day it angered me as well. My face has *no right* to mean anything to him when *I* don't.

"But for all that, I cut out his picture, which was in the 'Who's Who' column, and put it in a frame and set it on my desk. I have no picture of Teddy. And to-night I took it out of the frame and laid it on the coals in the fireplace and watched it shrivel up. Just before the fire went out of it a queer little shudder went over it and Teddy seemed to wink at me—an impish, derisive wink—as if he said:

"'You *think* you've forgotten—but if you had you wouldn't have burned me. You are mine—you will always be mine—and I don't want you.'

"If a good fairy were suddenly to appear before me and offer me a wish it would be this: to have Teddy Kent come and whistle again and again in Lofty John's bush. And I would not go—not one step.

"I *can't* endure this. *I* must put him out of my life."

CHAPTER XVII

I

The Murray clan had a really terrible time in the summer that followed Emily's twenty-second birthday. Neither Teddy nor Ilse came home that summer. Ilse was touring in the West and Teddy betook himself into some northern hinterland with an Indian treaty party to make illustrations for a serial. But Emily had so many beaus that Blair Water gossip was in as bad a plight as the centipede who couldn't tell which foot came after which. So many beaus and not one of them such as the connection could approve of.

There was handsome, dashing Jack Bannister, the Derry Pond Don Juan—"a picturesque scoundrel," as Dr. Burnley called him. Certainly Jack was untrammelled by any moral code. But who knew what effect his silver tongue and good looks might have on temperamental Emily? It worried the Murrays for three weeks and then it appeared that Emily had some sense, after all. Jack Bannister faded out of the picture.

"Emily should never have even *spoken* to him," said Uncle Oliver indignantly. "Why, they say he keeps a diary and writes down all his love affairs in it and what the girls said to him."

"Don't worry. He won't write down what *I* said to him," said Emily, when Aunt Laura reported this to her anxiously.

Harold Conway was another anxiety. A Shrewsbury man in his thirties, who looked like a poet gone to seed. With a shock of wavy dark auburn hair and brilliant brown eyes. Who "fiddled for a living."

Emily went to a concert and a play with him and the New Moon aunts had some sleepless nights. But when in Blair Water parlance Rod Dunbar "cut him out" things were even worse. The Dunbars were "nothing" when it came to religion. Rod's mother, to be sure, was a Presbyterian, but his father was a Methodist, his brother a Baptist and one sister a Christian Scientist. The other sister was a Theosophist, which was worse than all the rest because they had no idea *what* it was. In all this mixture what on earth was Rod? Certainly no match for an orthodox niece of New Moon.

"His great-uncle was a religious maniac," said Uncle Wallace gloomily. "He was kept chained in his bedroom for sixteen years. *What* has got into that girl? Is she idiot or demon?"

Yet the Dunbars were at least a respectable family; but what was to be said of Larry Dix—one of the "notorious Priest Pond Dixes"—whose father had once pastured his cows in the graveyard and whose uncle was more than suspected of having thrown a dead cat down a neighbour's well for spite? To be sure, Larry himself was doing well as a dentist and was such a deadly-serious, solemn-in-earnest young man that nothing much could be urged against him, if one could only swallow the fact that he was a Dix. Nevertheless, Aunt Elizabeth was much relieved when Emily turned him adrift.

"Such presumption," said Aunt Laura, meaning for a Dix to aspire to a Murray.

"It wasn't because of his presumption I packed him off," said Emily. "It was because of the way he made love. He made a thing ugly that should have been beautiful."

"I suppose you wouldn't have him because he didn't propose romantically," said Aunt Elizabeth contemptuously.

"No. I think my real reason was that I felt sure he was the kind of man who would give his wife a vacuum cleaner for a Christmas present," vowed Emily.

"She will not take anything seriously," said Aunt Elizabeth in despair.

"*I* think she is bewitched," said Uncle Wallace. "She hasn't had one decent beau this summer. She's so temperamental decent fellows are scared of her."

"She's getting a terrible reputation as a flirt," mourned Aunt Ruth. "It's no wonder nobody worth while will have anything to do with her."

"Always with some fantastic love-affair on hand," snapped Uncle Wallace. The clan felt that Uncle Wallace had, with unusual felicity, hit on the very word. Emily's "love-affairs" were never the conventional, decorous things Murray love-affairs should be. They were indeed fantastic.

II

But Emily always blessed her stars that none of the clan except Aunt Elizabeth ever knew anything about the most fantastic of them all. If they had they would have thought her temperamental with a vengeance.

It all came about in a simple, silly way. The editor of the Charlottetown *Argus,* a daily paper with some pretensions to literature, had selected from an old U. S. newspaper a certain uncopyrighted story of several chapters—*A Royal Betrothal,* by some unknown author, *Mark Greaves,* for reprinting in the special edition of *The Argus,* devoted to "boosting" the claims of Prince Edward Island as a summer resort. His staff was small and the compositors had been setting up the type for the special edition at odd moments for a month and had it all ready except the concluding chapter of *A Royal Betrothal.* This chapter had disappeared and could not be found. The editor was furious, but that did not help matters any. He could not at that late hour find another story which would exactly fill the space, nor was there time to set it up if he could. The special edition must go to press in an hour. What was to be done?

At this moment Emily wandered in. She and Mr. Wilson were good friends and she always called when in town.

"You're a godsend," said Mr. Wilson. "Will you do me a favour?" He tossed the torn and dirty chapters of *A Royal Betrothal* over to her. "For heaven's sake, get to work and write a concluding chapter to that yarn. I'll give you half an hour. They can set it up in another half-hour. And we'll have the darn thing out on time."

Emily glanced hastily over the story. As far as it went there was no hint of what "Mark Greaves" intended as a *denouement.*

"Have you any idea how it ended?" she asked.

"No, never read it," groaned Mr. Wilson. "Just picked it for its length."

"Well, I'll do my best, though I'm not accustomed to write with flippant levity of kings and queens," agreed Emily. "This Mark Greaves, whoever he is, seems to be very much at home with royalty."

"I'll bet he never even saw one," snorted Mr. Wilson.

In the half-hour allotted to her Emily produced a quite respectable concluding chapter with a solution of the mystery which was really ingenious. Mr. Wilson snatched it with an air of relief handed it to a compositor, and bowed Emily out with thanks.

"I wonder if any of the readers will notice where the seam comes in," reflected Emily amusedly. "And I wonder if Mark Greaves will ever see it and if so what he will think."

It did not seem in the least likely she would ever know and she dismissed the matter from her mind. Consequently when, one afternoon two weeks later, Cousin Jimmy ushered a stranger into the sitting-room where Emily was arranging roses in Aunt Elizabeth's rock-crystal goblet with its ruby base—a treasured heirloom of New Moon—Emily did not connect him with *A Royal Betrothal,* though she had a distinct impression that the caller was an exceedingly irate man.

Cousin Jimmy discreetly withdrew and Aunt Laura, who had come in to place a glass dish full of strawberry preserves on the table to cool, withdrew also, wondering a little who Emily's odd-looking caller could be. Emily herself wondered. She remained standing by the table, a slim, gracious thing in her pale-green gown, shining like a star in the shadowy, old-fashioned room.

"Won't you sit down?" she questioned with all the aloof courtesy of New Moon. But the newcomer did not move. He simply stood before her staring at her. And again Emily felt that, while he had been quite furious when he came in, he was not in the least angry now.

He must have been born, of course, because he was there—but it was incredible, she thought, he could ever have been a baby. He wore audacious clothes and a monocle, screwed into one of his eyes—eyes that seemed absurdly like little black currants with black eyebrows that made right-angled triangles above them. He had a mane of black hair reaching to his shoulders, an immensely long chin and a marble-white face. In a picture Emily thought he would have looked rather handsome and romantic. But here in the New Moon sitting-room he looked merely weird.

"Lyrical creature," he said, gazing at her.

Emily wondered if he were by any chance an escaped lunatic.

"You do not commit the crime of ugliness," he continued fervently. "This is a wonderful moment—very wonderful. 'Tis a pity we must spoil it by talking. Eyes of purple-grey, sprinkled with gold. Eyes that I have looked for all my life. Sweet eyes, in which I drowned myself eons ago."

"Who are you?" said Emily crisply, now entirely convinced that he was quite mad. He laid his hand on his heart and bowed.

"Mark Greaves—Mark D. Greaves—Mark Delage Greaves."

Mark Greaves! Emily had a confused idea that she ought to know the name. It sounded curiously familiar.

"Is it possible you do not recognize my name! Verily this is fame. Even in this remote corner of the world I should have supposed—"

"Oh," cried Emily, light suddenly breaking on her. "I—I remember now. You wrote *A Royal Betrothal.*"

"The story you so unfeelingly murdered—yes."

"Oh, I'm so sorry," Emily interrupted. "Of course you would think it unpardonable. It was this way—you see—"

He stopped her by a wave of a very long, very white hand.

"No matter. No matter. It does not interest me at all now. I admit I was very angry when I came here. I am stopping at the Derry Pond Hotel of The Dunes—ah, what a name—poetry—mystery—romance—and I saw the special edition of *The Argus* this morning. I was angry—had I not a right to be?—and yet more sad than angry. My story was barbarously mutilated. A happy ending. Horrible. *My* ending was sorrowful and artistic. A happy ending can never be artistic. I hastened to the den of *The Argus*. I dissembled my anger—I discovered who was responsible. I came here—to denounce—to upbraid. I remain to worship."

Emily simply did not know what to say. New Moon traditions held no precedent for this.

"You do not understand me. You are puzzled—your bewilderment becomes you. Again I say a wonderful moment. To come enraged—and behold divinity. To realize as soon as I saw you that you were meant for me and me alone."

Emily wished somebody would come in. This was getting nightmarish.

"It is absurd to talk so," she said shortly. "We are strangers—"

"We are *not* strangers," he interrupted. "We have loved in some other life, of course. And our love was a violent, gorgeous thing—a love of eternity. I recognized you as soon as I entered. As soon as you have recovered from your sweet surprise you will realize this, too. When can you marry me?"

To be asked by a man to marry him five minutes after the first moment you have laid eyes on him is an experience more stimulating than pleasant. Emily was annoyed.

"Don't talk nonsense, please," she said curtly. "I am not going to marry you at any time."

"Not marry me? But you must! I have never before asked a woman to marry me. I am the famous Mark Greaves. I am rich. I have the charm and romance of my French mother and the common-sense of my Scotch father. With the French side of me I feel and acknowledge your beauty and mystery. With the Scotch side of me I bow in homage to your reserve and dignity. You are ideal—adorable. Many women have loved me but I loved them not. I enter this room a free man. I go out a captive. Enchanting captivity! Adorable captor! I kneel before you in spirit."

Emily was horribly afraid he would kneel before her in the flesh. He looked quite capable of it. And suppose Aunt Elizabeth should come in.

"Please go away," she said desperately. "I'm—I'm very busy and I can't stop talking to you any longer. I'm sorry about the story—if you would let me explain—"

"I have said it does not matter about the story. Though you must learn never to write happy endings—never. I will teach you. I will teach you the beauty and artistry of sorrow and incompleteness. Ah, what a pupil you will be! What bliss to teach such a pupil! I kiss your hand."

He made a step nearer as if to seize upon it. Emily stepped backward in alarm.

"You *must* be crazy," she exclaimed.

"Do I look crazy?" demanded Mr. Greaves.

"You do," retorted Emily flatly and cruelly.

"Perhaps I do—probably I do. *Crazy*—intoxicated with wine of the rose. All lovers are mad. Divine madness! Oh, beautiful, unkissed lips!"

Emily drew herself up. This absurd interview must end. She was by now thoroughly angry.

"Mr. Greaves," she said—and such was the power of the Murray look that Mr. Greaves realized she meant exactly what she said. "I shan't listen to any more of this nonsense. Since you won't let me explain about the matter of the story I bid you good-afternoon."

Mr. Greaves looked gravely at her for a moment. Then he said solemnly:

"A kiss? Or a kick? Which?"

Was he speaking metaphorically? But whether or no—

"A kick," said Emily disdainfully.

Mr. Greaves suddenly seized the crystal goblet and dashed it violently against the stove.

Emily uttered a faint shriek—partly of real terror—partly of dismay. Aunt Elizabeth's treasured goblet.

"That was merely a defence reaction," said Mr. Greaves, glaring at her. "I had to do that—or kill you. Ice-maiden! Chill vestal! Cold as your northern snows! Farewell."

He did not slam the door as he went out. He merely shut it gently and irrevocably, so that Emily might realize what she had lost. When she saw that he was really out of the garden and marching indignantly down the lane as if he were crushing something beneath his feet, she permitted herself the relief of a long breath—the first she had dared to draw since his entrance.

"I suppose," she said, half hysterically, "that I ought to be thankful he did not throw the dish of strawberry preserves at me."

Aunt Elizabeth came in.

"Emily, the rock-crystal goblet! Your Grandmother Murray's goblet! And you have broken it!"

"No, really. Aunty dear, I didn't. Mr. Greaves—Mr. Mark Delage Greaves did it. He threw it at the stove."

"Threw it at the stove!" Aunt Elizabeth was staggered. "Why did he throw it at the stove?"

"Because I wouldn't marry him," said Emily.

"Marry him! Did you ever see him before?"

"Never."

Aunt Elizabeth gathered up the fragments of the crystal goblet

654

and went out quite speechless. There was—there must be—something wrong with a girl when a man proposed marriage to her at first meeting. And hurled heirloom goblets at inoffensive stoves.

III

But it was the affair of the Japanese prince which really gave the Murrays their bad summer.

Second-cousin Louise Murray, who had lived in Japan for twenty years, came home to Derry Pond for a visit and brought with her a young Japanese prince, the son of a friend of her husband's, who had been converted to Christianity by her efforts and wished to see something of Canada. His mere coming made a tremendous sensation in the clan and the community. But that was nothing to the next sensation when they realized that the prince had evidently and unmistakably fallen terrifically in love with Emily Byrd Starr of New Moon.

Emily liked him—was interested in him—was sorry for him in his bewildered reactions to the Presbyterian atmosphere of Derry Pond and Blair Water. Naturally a Japanese prince, even a converted one, couldn't feel exactly at home. So she talked a great deal to him—he could talk English excellently—and walked with him at moonrise in the garden—and almost every evening that slant-eyed, inscrutable face, with the black hair brushed straight back from it as smooth as satin, might be seen in the parlour of New Moon.

But it was not until he gave Emily a little frog beautifully cut out of moss agate that the Murrays took alarm. Cousin Louise sounded it first. Tearfully. *She* knew what that frog meant. Those agate frogs were heirlooms in the family of the prince. Never were they given away save as marriage and betrothal gifts. Was Emily engaged—to him? Aunt Ruth, looking as usual as if she thought everyone had gone mad, came over to New Moon and made quite a scene. It annoyed Emily so much that she refused to answer any questions. She was a bit edgy to begin with over the unnecessary way her clan had heckled her all summer over suitors that were not of her choosing and whom there was not the slightest danger of her taking seriously.

"There are some things not good for you to know," she told Aunt Ruth impertinently.

And the distracted Murrays despairingly concluded that she had decided to be a Japanese princess. And if she had—well, they knew what happened when Emily made up her mind. It was something inevitable—like a visitation of God; but it was a dreadful thing. His Princeship cast no halo about him in the Murray eyes. No Murray before her would ever have dreamed of marrying any foreigner, much less a Japanese. But then of course she was temperamental.

"Always with some disreputable creature in tow," said Aunt Ruth. "But this beats everything I ever feared. A pagan—a—"

"Oh, he isn't *that,* Ruth," mourned Aunt Laura. "He is converted—Cousin Louise says she is sure he is sincere, but—"

"I tell you he's a pagan!" reiterated Aunt Ruth. "Cousin Louise could never convert anybody. Why, she's none too sound herself. And her husband is a modernist if he's *anything.* Don't tell me! A yellow pagan! Him and his agate frogs!"

"She seems to have such an attraction for extraordinary men," said Aunt Elizabeth, thinking of the rock-crystal goblet.

Uncle Wallace said it was preposterous. Andrew said she might at least have picked on a white man. Cousin Louise, who felt that the clan blamed *her* for it all, pleaded tearfully that he had beautiful manners when you really knew him.

"And she might have had the Reverend James Wallace," said Aunt Elizabeth.

They lived through five weeks of this and then the prince went back to Japan. He had been summoned home by his family, Cousin Louise said—a marriage had been arranged for him with a princess of an old Samurai family. Of course he had obeyed; but he left the agate frog in Emily's possession and nobody ever knew just what he said to her one night at moonrise in the garden. Emily was a little white and strange and remote when she came in, but she smiled impishly at her aunts and Cousin Louise.

"So I'm not to be a Japanese princess after all," she said, wiping away some imaginary tears.

"Emily, I fear you've only been flirting with that poor boy," rebuked Cousin Louise. "You have made him very unhappy."

"I wasn't flirting. Our conversations were about literature and history—mostly. He will never think of me again."

"*I* know what he looked like when he read that letter," retorted Cousin Louise. "And I know the significance of agate frogs."

New Moon drew a breath of relief and thankfully settled down to routine again. Aunt Laura's old, tender eyes lost their troubled look, but Aunt Elizabeth thought sadly of the Rev. James Wallace. It had been a nerve-racking summer. Blair Water whispered about, that Emily Starr had been "disappointed," but predicted she would live to be thankful for it. You couldn't trust them foreigners. Not likely he was a prince at all.

CHAPTER XVIII

I

One day in the last week of October Cousin Jimmy began to plough the hill field, Emily found the lost legendary diamond of the Murrays,* and Aunt Elizabeth fell down the cellar steps and broke her leg.

*See *Emily of New Moon*.

Emily, in the warm amber of the afternoon, stood on the sandstone front steps of New Moon and looked about her with eyes avid for the mellow loveliness of the fading year. Most of the trees were leafless, but a little birch, still in golden array, peeped out of the young spruces—a birch *Danae* in their shadows—and the Lombardies down the lane were like a row of great golden candles. Beyond was the sere hill field scarfed with three bright red ribbons—the "ridges" Cousin Jimmy had ploughed. Emily had been writing all day and she was tired. She went down the garden to the little vine-hung summer house—she poked dreamily about; deciding where the new tulip bulbs should be planted. Here—in this moist rich soil where Cousin Jimmy had recently pried out the mouldering old side-steps. Next spring it should be a banquet board laden with stately chalices. Emily's heel sank deeply into the moist earth and came out laden. She sauntered over to the stone bench and daintily scraped off the earth with a twig. Something fell and glittered on the grass like a dewdrop. Emily picked it up with a little cry. There in her hand was the Lost Diamond—lost over sixty years before, when Great-aunt Miriam Murray had gone into the summer

657

house.

It had been one of her childish dreams to find the Lost Diamond—she and Ilse and Teddy had hunted for it scores of times. But of late years she had not thought about it. And here it was—as bright, as beautiful, as ever. It must have been hidden in some crevice of the old side-steps and fallen to the earth when they had been torn away. It made quite a sensation at New Moon. A few days later the Murrays had a conclave about Aunt Elizabeth's bed to decide what should be done with it. Cousin Jimmy said stoutly that finding was keeping in this case. Edward and Miriam Murray were long since dead. They had left no family. The diamond by rights was Emily's.

"We are all heirs to it," said Uncle Wallace judicially. "It cost, I've heard, a thousand dollars sixty years ago. It's a beautiful stone. The fair thing is to sell it and give Emily her mother's share."

"One shouldn't sell a family diamond," said Aunt Elizabeth firmly.

This seemed to be the general opinion at bottom. Even Uncle Wallace acknowledged the sway of *noblesse oblige.* Eventually they all agreed that the diamond should be Emily's.

"She can have it set as a little pendant for her neck," said Aunt Laura.

"It was meant for a ring," said Aunt Ruth, just for the sake of disagreeing. "And she shouldn't wear it, in any case, until she is married. A diamond as big as that is in bad taste for a young girl."

"Oh, married!" Aunt Addie gave a rather nasty little laugh. It conveyed her opinion that if Emily waited for that to wear the diamond it was just possible she might never wear it. Aunt Addie had never forgiven Emily for refusing Andrew. And here she was at twenty-three—well, nearly—with no eligible beau in sight.

"The Lost Diamond will bring you luck, Emily," said Cousin Jimmy. "I'm glad they've left it with you. It's rightly yours. But will you let me hold it sometimes, Emily,—just hold it and look into it. When I look into anything like that I—I—find myself. I'm not simple Jimmy Murray then—I'm what I would have been if I hadn't been pushed into a well. Don't say anything about it to Elizabeth, Emily, but just let me hold it and look at it once in awhile."

"My favourite gem is the diamond, when all is said and done," Emily wrote to Ilse that night. "But I love gems of all kinds—except turquoise. Them I loathe—the shallow, insipid, soulless things. The gloss of pearl, glow of ruby, tenderness of sapphire, melting violet of amethyst, moonlit glimmer of acquamarine, milk and fire of opal—I love them all."

"What about emeralds?" Ilse wrote back—a bit nastily, Emily thought, not knowing that a Shrewsbury correspondent of Ilse's wrote her now and then some unreliable gossip about Perry Miller's visits to New Moon. Perry did come to New Moon occasionally. But he had given up asking Emily to marry him and seemed wholly absorbed in his profession. Already he was regarded as a coming man and shrewd politicians were said to be biding their time until he should be old enough to "bring out" as a candidate for the Provincial House.

"Who knows? You may be 'my lady' yet," wrote Ilse, "Perry will be Sir Perry some day."

Which Emily thought was even nastier than the scratch about the emerald.

II

At first it did not seem that the Lost Diamond had brought luck to any one at New Moon. The very evening of its finding Aunt Elizabeth broke her leg. Shawled and bonnetted for a call on a sick neighbour—bonnets had long gone out of fashion even for elderly ladies, but Aunt Elizabeth wore them still—she had started down cellar to get a jar of black currant jam for the invalid, had tripped in some way and fallen. When she was taken up it was found that her leg was broken and Aunt Elizabeth faced the fact that for the first time in her life she was to spend weeks in bed.

Of course New Moon got on without her, though she believed it couldn't. But the problem of amusing her was a more serious one than the running of New Moon. Aunt Elizabeth fretted and pined over her enforced inactivity—could not read much herself—didn't like to be read to—was sure everything was going to the dogs—was sure she was going to be lame and useless all the rest of her life—was sure Dr. Burnley was an old fool—was sure Laura would never get the apples packed properly—was sure the hired boy would cheat Cousin Jimmy.

"Would you like to hear the little story I finished to-day, Aunt Elizabeth?" asked Emily one evening. "It might amuse you."

"Is there any silly love-making in it?" demanded Aunt Elizabeth ungraciously.

"No love-making of any kind. It's pure comedy."

"Well, let me hear it. It may pass the time."

Emily read the story. Aunt Elizabeth made no comment whatever. But the next afternoon she said, hesitatingly, "Is there—any more—of that story you read last night?"

"No."

"Well, if there was—I wouldn't mind hearing it. It kind of took my thoughts away from myself. The folks seemed—sort of—real to me. I suppose that is why I feel as if I want to know what happens to them," concluded Aunt Elizabeth as if apologizing for her weakness.

"I'll write another story about them for you," promised Emily.

When this was read Aunt Elizabeth remarked that she didn't care if she heard a third one.

"Those *Applegaths* are amusing," she said. "I've known people like them. And that little chap, *Jerry Stowe*. What happens to him when he grows up, poor child?"

III

Emily's idea came to her that evening as she sat idly by her window looking rather drearily out on cold meadows and hills of grey, over which a chilly, lonesome wind blew. She could hear the dry leaves blowing over the garden wall. A few great white flakes were beginning to come down.

She had had a letter from Ilse that day. Teddy's picture, *The Smiling Girl,* which had been exhibited in Montreal and had made a tremendous sensation, had been accepted by the Paris *Salon.*

"I just got back from the coast in time to see the last day of its exhibition here," wrote Ilse. "And it's you—Emily—it's you. Just that old sketch he made of you years ago completed and glorified—the one your Aunt Nancy made you so mad by keeping—remember? There you were smiling down from Teddy's canvas. The critics had a great deal to say about his colouring and technique and 'feeling' and all that sort of jargon. But one said, 'The smile on the girl's face will become as famous as Mona Lisa's.' I've seen that very smile on your face a hundred times, Emily—especially when you were seeing that unseeable thing you used to call your flash. Teddy has caught the very soul of it—not a mocking, challenging smile like Mona Lisa's—but a smile that seems to hint at some exquisitely wonderful secret you could tell if you liked—some whisper eternal—a secret that would make every one happy if they could only get you to tell it. It's only a trick, I suppose—*you* don't know that secret any more than the rest of us. But the smile suggests that you do—suggests it marvellously. Yes, your Teddy has genius—that smile proves it. What does it feel like, Emily, to realize yourself the inspiration of a genius? I'd give years of my life for such a compliment."

Emily didn't quite know what it felt like. But she did feel a certain small, futile anger with Teddy. What right had he who scorned her love and was indifferent to her friendship to paint her face—her soul—her secret vision—and hang it up for the world to gaze at? To be sure, he had told her in childhood that he meant to do it—and she had agreed then. But everything had changed since then. Everything.

Well, about this story, regarding which Aunt Elizabeth had such an Oliver Twist complex. Suppose she were to write another one—suddenly the idea came. Suppose she were to expand it into a book. Not like *A Seller of Dreams,* of course. That old glory could come back no more. But Emily had an instantaneous vision of the new book, as a whole—a witty, sparkling rill of human comedy. She ran down to Aunt Elizabeth.

"Aunty, how would you like me to write a book for you about those people in my story? Just for you—a chapter every day."

Aunt Elizabeth carefully hid the fact that she was interested.

"Oh, you can if you want to. I wouldn't mind hearing about them. But mind, you are not to put any of the neighbours in."

Emily didn't put any of the neighbours in—she didn't need to. Characters galore trooped into her consciousness, demanding a local habitation and a name. They laughed and scowled and wept and danced—and even made a little love. Aunt Elizabeth tolerated this, supposing you couldn't have a novel without some of it. Emily read a chapter every evening, and Aunt Laura and Cousin Jimmy were allowed to hear it along with Aunt Elizabeth. Cousin Jimmy was in raptures. He was sure it was the most wonderful story ever written.

"I feel young again when I'm listening to you," he said.

"Sometimes I want to laugh and sometimes I want to cry," confessed Aunt Laura. "I can't sleep for wondering what is going to happen to the *Applegaths* in the next chapter."

"It might be worse," conceded Aunt Elizabeth. "But I wish you'd cut out what you said about *Gloria Applegath's* greasy dish-towels. Mrs. Charlie Frost of Derry Pond, will think you mean her. Her towels are always greasy."

"Chips are bound to light somewhere," said Cousin Jimmy. *"Gloria* is funny in a book, but she'd be awful to live with. Too busy saving the world. Somebody ought to tell her to read her Bible."

"I don't like *Cissy Applegath,* though," said Aunt Laura apologetically. "She has such a supercilious way of speaking."

"A shallow-pated creature," said Aunt Elizabeth.

"It's old *Jesse Applegath* I can't tolerate," said Cousin Jimmy fiercely. "A man who would kick a cat just to relieve his feelings! I'd go twenty miles to slap the old he-devil's face. But"—hopefully—"maybe he'll die before long."

"Or reform," suggested Aunt Laura mercifully.

"No, no, don't let him reform," said Cousin Jimmy anxiously. "Kill him off, if necessary, but don't reform him. I wish, though, you'd change the colour of *Peg Applegath's* eyes. I don't like green eyes—never did."

"But I can't change them. They *are* green," protested Emily.

"Well, then, *Abraham Applegath's* whiskers," pleaded Cousin Jimmy. "I like *Abraham.* He's a gay dog. Can't he help his whiskers, Emily?"

"No"—firmly—"he can't."

Why couldn't they understand? Abraham *had* whiskers—*wanted* whiskers—was determined to have whiskers. *She* couldn't change him.

"It's time we remembered that these people have no real existence," rebuked Aunt Elizabeth.

But once—Emily counted it her greatest triumph—Aunt Elizabeth laughed. She was so ashamed of it she would not even smile all the rest of the reading.

"Elizabeth thinks God doesn't like to hear us laugh," Cousin Jimmy whispered behind his hand to Laura. If Elizabeth had not been lying there with a broken leg Laura would have smiled. But to smile under the circumstances seemed like taking an unfair advantage of her.

Cousin Jimmy went downstairs shaking his head and murmuring, *"How* does she do it? How *does* she do it! I can write poetry—but *this.* Those folks are alive!"

One of them was too much alive in Aunt Elizabeth's opinion.

"That *Nicholas Applegath* is too much like old Douglas Courcy, of

Shrewsbury," she said. "I told you not to put any people we knew in it."

"Why, I never saw Douglas Courcy."

"It's him to the life. Even Jimmy noticed it. You must cut him out, Emily."

But Emily obstinately refused to "cut him out." Old *Nicholas* was one of the best characters in her book. She was very much absorbed in it by this time. The composition of it was never the ecstatic rite the creation of *A Seller of Dreams* had been, but it was very fascinating. She forgot all vexing and haunting things while she was writing it. The last chapter was finished the very day the splints were taken off Aunt Elizabeth's leg and she was carried down to the kitchen lounge.

"Well, your story has helped," she admitted. "But I'm thankful to be where I can keep my eye on things once more. What are you going to do with your book? What are you going to call it?"

"The Moral of the Rose."

"I don't think that is a good title at all. I don't know what it means—nobody will know."

"No matter. That is the book's name."

Aunt Elizabeth sighed.

"I don't know where you get your stubbornness from, Emily. I'm sure I don't. You never would take advice. And I know the Courcys will never speak to us again, after the book is published."

"The book hasn't any chance of being published," said Emily gloomily. "They'll send it back, 'damned with faint praise.'"

Aunt Elizabeth had never heard this expression before and she thought Emily had originated it and was being profane.

"Emily," she said sternly, "don't let me ever hear such a word from your lips again. I've more than suspected Ilse of such language—that poor girl never got over her early bringing up—she's not to be judged by *our* standards. But Murrays of New Moon do *not* swear."

"It was only a quotation, Aunt Elizabeth," said Emily wearily.

She was tired—a little tired of everything. It was Christmas now and a long, dreary winter stretched before her—an empty, aimless winter. Nothing seemed worth while—not even finding a publisher for *The Moral of the Rose.*

IV

However, she typewrote it faithfully and sent it out. It came back. She sent it out again, three times. It came back. She retyped it—the MS. was getting dog-eared—and sent it out again. At intervals all that winter and summer she sent it out, working doggedly through a list of possible publishers. I forget how many times she retyped it. It became a sort of a joke—a bitter joke.

The worst of it was that the New Moon folk knew of all these rejections and their sympathy and indignation were hard to bear. Cousin Jimmy was so angry over every rejection of this masterpiece that he could not eat for a day afterwards and she gave up telling him of the journeys. Once she thought of sending it to Miss Royal and asking her if she had any influence to use. But the Murray pride would not brook the idea. Finally in the autumn when it returned from the last publisher on her list Emily did not even open the parcel. She cast it contemptuously into a compartment of her desk.

Too sick at heart to war

With failure any more.

"That's the end of it—and of all my dreams. I'll use it up for scribbling paper. And now I'll settle down to a tepid existence of pot-boiling."

As least magazine editors were more appreciative than book publishers—as Cousin Jimmy indignantly said, they appeared to have more sense. While her book was seeking vainly for its chance her magazine clientele grew daily. She spent long hours at her desk and enjoyed her work after a fashion. But there was a little consciousness of failure under it all. She could never get much higher on the Alpine path. The glorious city of fulfilment on its summit was not for her. Pot-boiling! That was all. Making a living in what Aunt Elizabeth thought was a shamefully easy way.

Miss Royal wrote her frankly that she was falling off.

"You're getting into a rut, Emily," she warned, "A self-satisfied rut. The admiration of Aunt Laura and Cousin Jimmy is a bad thing for you. You should be *here*—we would keep you up to the scratch."

Suppose she had gone to New York with Miss Royal when she had the chance six years ago. Would she not have been able to get her book published? Was it not the fatal Prince Edward Island postmark that condemned it—the little out-of-the-world province from which no good thing could ever come?

Perhaps! Perhaps Miss Royal had been right. But what did it matter?

No one came to Blair Water that summer. That is—Teddy Kent did not come. Ilse was in Europe again. Dean Priest seemed to have taken up his residence permanently at the Pacific Coast. Life at New Moon went on unchanged. Except that Aunt Elizabeth limped a little and Cousin Jimmy's hair turned white quite suddenly, overnight as it seemed. Now and then Emily had a quick, terrible vision that Cousin Jimmy was growing old. They were all growing old. Aunt Elizabeth was nearly seventy. And when she died New Moon went to Andrew. Already there were times when Andrew seemed to be putting on proprietary airs in his visits to New Moon. Not that he would ever live there himself, of course. But it ought to be kept in good shape against the day when it would be necessary to sell it.

"It's time those old Lombardies were cut down," said Andrew to Uncle Oliver one day. "They're getting frightfully ragged at the tops. Lombardies are so out of date now. And that field with the young spruces should be drained and ploughed."

"That old orchard should be cleared out," said Uncle Oliver. "It's more like a jungle than an orchard. The trees are too old for any good anyhow. They should all be chopped down. Jimmy and Elizabeth are too old-fashioned. They don't make half the money out of this farm they should."

Emily, overhearing this, clenched her fists. To see New Moon desecrated—her old, intimate, beloved trees cut down—the spruce field where wild strawberries grew improved out of existence—dreamy beauty of the old orchard destroyed—the little dells and slopes that kept all the ghostly joys of her past changed—altered. It was unbearable.

"If you had married Andrew New Moon would have been yours," said Aunt Elizabeth bitterly, when she found Emily crying over what they had said.

"But the changes would have come just the same," said Emily. "Andrew wouldn't have listened to me. He believes that the husband is the head of the wife."

"You will be twenty-four your next birthday," said Aunt Elizabeth.

Apropos of what?

CHAPTER XIX

I

"OCT. 1, 19—

"This afternoon I sat at my window and alternately wrote at my new serial and watched a couple of dear, amusing, youngish maple-trees at the foot of the garden. They whispered secrets to each other all the afternoon. They would bend together and talk earnestly for a few moments, then spring back and look at each other, throwing up their hands comically in horror and amazement over their mutual revelations. I wonder what new scandal is afoot in Treeland."

II

"OCT. 10, 19—

"This evening was lovely. I went up on the hill and walked about until twilight had deepened into an autumn night with a benediction of starry quietude over it. I was alone but not lonely. I was a queen in halls of fancy. I held a series of conversations with imaginary comrades and thought out so many epigrams that I was agreeably surprised at myself."

III

"OCT. 28, 19—

"To-night I was out for one of my long walks. In a weird, purple, shadowy world, with great, cold clouds piling up above a yellow sky, hills brooding in the silence of forsaken woods, ocean tumbling on a rocky shore. The whole landscape seemed

As those who wait

Till judgment speak the doom of fate.

"It made me feel—horribly *alone*.
"What a creature of moods I am!
"'Fickle,' as Aunt Elizabeth says? Temperamental,' as Andrew says?"

IV

"NOV. 5, 19—
"What a fit of bad temper the world has indulged in! Day before yesterday she was not unbeautiful—a dignified old dame in fitting garb of brown and ermine. Yesterday she tried to ape juvenility, putting on all the airs and graces of spring, with scarfs of blue hazes. And what a bedraggled and uncomely old hag she was, all tatters and wrinkles. She grew peevish then over her own ugliness and has raged all night and day. I awakened up in the wee sma's and heard the wind shrieking in the trees and tears of rage and spite sleeting against the pane."

V

"NOV. 23, 19—
"This is the second day of a heavy, ceaseless autumn rain. Really, it has rained almost every day this November. We had no mail to-day. The outside world is a dismal one, with drenched and dripping trees and sodden fields. And the damp and gloom have crept into my soul and spirit and sapped out all life and energy.
"I could not read, eat, sleep, write or do anything, unless I drove myself to do it and then I felt as if I were trying to do it with somebody else's hands or brain and couldn't work very well with them. I feel lustreless, dowdy and uninviting—I even bore myself.
"I shall grow mossy in this existence!
"There! I feel better for that little outburst of discontent. It has ejected something from my system. I know that into everybody's life must come some days of depression and discouragement when all things in life seem to lose savour. The sunniest day has its clouds; but one must not forget that the sun is there all the time.

"How easy it is to be a philosopher—on paper!

"(Item:—If you are out in a cold, pouring rain, does it keep you dry to remember that the sun is there just the same?)

"Well, thank heaven no two days are ever *exactly* alike!"

VI

"DEC. 3, 19—

"There was a stormy, unrestful sunset to-night, behind the pale, blanched hills, gleaming angrily through the Lombardies and the dark fir-boughs in Lofty John's bush, that were now and again tossed suddenly and distressfully in a fitful gust of wind. I sat at my window and watched it. Below in the garden it was quite dark and I could only see dimly the dead leaves that were whirling and dancing uncannily over the flowerless paths. The poor dead leaves—yet not quite dead, it seemed. There was still enough unquiet life left in them to make them restless and forlorn. They harkened yet to every call of the wind, which cared for them no longer but only played freakishly with them and broke their rest. I felt sorry for the leaves as I watched them in the dull, weird twilight, and angry—in a petulant fashion that almost made me laugh—with the wind that would not leave them in peace. Why should they—and I—be vexed with these transient, passionate breaths of desire for a life which has passed us by?

"I have not heard even from Ilse for a long time. She has forgotten me, too."

VII

"JAN. 10, 19—

"As I came home from the post-office this evening—with three acceptances—I revelled in the winter loveliness around me. It was so very calm and still; the low sun cast such pure, pale tints of pink and heliotrope over the snow; and the great, pale-silver moon peeping over the Delectable Mountain was such a friend of mine.

"How much difference in one's outlook three acceptances make!"

VIII

"JAN. 20, 19—

"The nights are so dreary now and there is such a brief space of grey, sunless day. I work and think all day and, when night comes down early, gloom settles on my soul. I can't describe the feeling. It is dreadful—worse than any actual pain. In so far as I can express it in words I feel a great and awful weariness—not of body or brain but of *feeling*, coupled with a haunting dread of the future—*any* future—even a happy one—nay, a happy one most of all, for in this strange mood it seems to me that to be happy would require more effort—more buoyancy than I shall possess. The fantastic shape my fear assumes is that it would be *too much trouble* to be happy—require too much energy.

"Let me be honest—in this journal if nowhere else. I know quite well what is the matter with me. This afternoon I was rummaging in my old trunk in the garret and found a packet of the letters Teddy wrote the first year he was in Montreal. I was foolish enough to sit down and read them all. It was a mad thing to do. I am paying for it now. Such letters have a terrible resurrective power. I am surrounded by bitter fancies and unbidden ghosts—the little spectral joys of the past."

IX

"FEB. 5, 19—

"Life never seems the same to me as it used to. Something is *gone*. I am not unhappy. But life seems a sort of negative affair. I enjoy it on the whole and have many beautiful moments. I have success—at least a sort of success—in growing measure and a keen appreciation of all the world and the times offer for delight and interest. But underneath it all is the haunting sense of emptiness. This is all because 'full knee-deep lies the winter snow' and I can't go a-prowling. Wait till a thaw comes, when I can get out to the balm of the fir-trees and the peace of the white places and the 'strength of the hills'—what a beautiful old Biblical phrase that is!—and I shall be made whole once more."

X

"FEB. 6, 19—

"Last night I simply could not endure any longer the vaseful of dyed grasses on my mantelpiece. What if they had been there for forty years! I seized them, opened the window and strewed them over the lawn. This soothed me so that I slept like an infant. But this morning Cousin Jimmy had gathered them all up and handed them secretly back to me with a gentle warning not to let them 'blow out' again. Elizabeth would be horrified.

"I put them back in the vase. One cannot escape one's kismet."

XI

"FEB. 22, 19—

"There was a creamy, misty sunset this evening and then moonlight. Such moonlight. It is such a night as one might fall asleep in and dream happy dreams of gardens and songs and companionship, feeling all the while through one's sleep the splendour and radiance of the white moon-world outside as one hears soft, far-away music sounding through the thoughts and words that are born of it.

"I slipped away for a solitary walk through that fairy world of glamour. I went through the orchard where the black shadows of the trees fell over the snow—I went up to the gleaming white hill with the stars over it, I lurked along fir copses dim with mystery and along still, wood aisles where the night hid from the moonshine, I loitered across a dreamland field of ebon and ivory. I had a tryst with my friend of old days, the Wind Woman. And every breath was a lyric and every thought an ecstasy and I've come back with a soul washed white and clean in the great crystal bath of the night.

"But Aunt Elizabeth said people would think me crazy if they saw me roaming around alone at this hour of the night. And Aunt Laura made me take a drink of hot black currant decoction lest I might have taken cold. Only Cousin Jimmy partly understood.

"'You went out to escape. *I* know,' he whispered.

'My soul has pastured with the stars

Upon the meadowlands of space.'

I whispered in return."

XII

"FEB. 26, 19—

"Jasper Frost has been coming out here from Shrewsbury of late. I don't think he will come any more—after our conversation of last night. He told me he loved me with a love 'that would last through eternity.' But I thought an eternity with Jasper would be rather long. Aunt Elizabeth will be a little disappointed, poor dear. She likes Jasper and the Frosts are 'a good family.' I like him, too, but he is too prim and bandboxy.

"'Would you like a slovenly beau?' demanded Aunt Elizabeth.

"This posed me. Because I wouldn't.

"'Surely there's a happy medium,' I protested.

"'A girl shouldn't be too particular when she is'—I feel sure Aunt Elizabeth was going to say 'nearly twenty-four.' But she changed it to 'not *entirely* perfect herself.'

"I wish Mr. Carpenter had been alive to hear Aunt Elizabeth's italics. They were killing."

XIII

"MARCH 1, 19—

"A wonderful music of night is coming to my window from Lofty John's bush. No, *not* Lofty John's bush any more.

"Emily Byrd Starr's bush!

"I bought it to-day, with the proceeds of my latest serial. And it is mine—mine—mine. All the lovely things in it are mine—its moonlit vistas—the grace of its one big elm against the starlight—its shadowy little dells—its June-bells and ferns—its crystalline spring—its wind music sweeter than an old Cremona. No one can ever cut it down or desecrate it in any way.

"I am so happy. The wind is my comrade and the evening star my friend."

XIV

"MARCH 23, 19—

"Is there any sound in the world sadder and weirder than the wail of the wind around the eaves and past the windows on a stormy night? It sounds as if the broken-hearted cries of fair, unhappy women who died and were forgotten ages ago were being re-echoed in the moaning wind of to-night. All my own past pain finds a voice in it as if it were moaning a plea for re-entrance into the soul that has cast it out. There are strange sounds in that night wind clamouring there at my little window. I hear the cries of old sorrows in it—and the moans of old despairs—and the phantom songs of dead hopes. The night wind is the wandering soul of the past. It has no share in the future—and so it is mournful."

XV

"APRIL 10, 19—

"This morning I felt more like myself than I have for a long time. I was out for a walk over the Delectable Mountain. It was a very mild, still, misty morning with lovely pearl-grey skies and smell of spring in the air. Every turn and twist on that hill-road was an old friend to me. And everything was so young. April couldn't be old. The young spruces were so green and companionable with pearl-like beads of moisture fringing their needles.

"'You are mine,' called the sea beyond Blair Water.

"'We have a share in her,' said the hills.

"'She is my sister,' said a jolly little fir-tree.

"Looking at them the flash came—my old supernal moment that has come so sadly seldom these past dreary months. Will I lose it altogether as I grow old? Will nothing but 'the light of common day' be mine then?

"But at least it came to me this morning and I felt my immortality. After all, freedom is a matter of the soul.

'Nature never did betray the heart that loved her.'

"She has always a gift of healing for us if we come humbly to her.

Corroding memories and discontents vanished. I felt suddenly that some old gladness was yet waiting for me, just around the curve of the hill.

"The frogs are singing to-night. Why is *frog* such a funny, dear, charming, absurd word?"

XVI

"MAY 15, 19—

"I know that when I am dead I shall sleep peaceably enough under the grasses through the summer and autumn and winter but when spring comes my heart will throb and stir in my sleep and call wistfully to all the voices calling far and wide in the world above me. Spring and morning were laughing to each other to-day and I went out to them and made a third.

"Ilse wrote to-day—a stingy little letter as far as news went—and spoke of coming home.

"'I'm homesick,' she wrote. 'Are the wild birds still singing in the Blair Water woods and are the waves still calling beyond the dunes? I want them. And oh, to see the moon rise over the harbour as we watched it do scores of times when we were children. And I want to see you. Letters are so unsatisfactory. There are so many things I'd like to talk over with you. Do you know I felt a little *old* to-day. It was a curious sensation.'

"She never mentioned Teddy's name. But she asked 'Is it true that Perry Miller is engaged to Judge Elmsley's daughter?'

"I don't think it is. But the mere report shows where Perry has climbed to already."

CHAPTER XX

I

On her twenty-fourth birthday Emily opened and read the letter she had written "from herself at fourteen to herself at twenty-four." It was not the amusing performance she had once expected it to be. She sat long at her window with the letter in her hand, watching the light of yellow, sinking stars over the bush that was still called Lofty John's oftener than not, from old habit. What would pop out when she opened that letter? A ghost of first youth? Of ambition? Of vanished love? Of lost friendship? Emily felt she would rather burn the letter than read it. But that would be cowardly. One must face things—even ghosts. With a sudden quick movement she cut open the envelope and took out the letter.

A whiff of old fragrance came with it. Folded in it were some dried rose-leaves—crisp brown things that crumbled to dust under her touch. Yes, she remembered that rose—Teddy had brought it to her one evening when they had been children together and he had been so proud of that first red rose that bloomed on a little house rose-bush Dr. Burnley had given him—the only rose that ever did bloom on it, for that matter. His mother had resented his love for the little plant. One night it was accidentally knocked off the window-sill and broken. If Teddy thought or knew there was any connection between the two facts he never said so. Emily had kept the rose as long as possible in a little vase on her study table; but the night she had written her letter she had taken the limp, faded thing and folded it—with a kiss—between the sheets of paper. She had forgotten that it was there; and now it fell in her hand, faded, unbeautiful, like the rose-hopes of long ago, yet with some faint bitter-sweetness still about it. The whole letter seemed full of it—whether of sense or spirit she could hardly tell.

This letter was, she sternly told herself, a foolish, romantic affair. Something to be laughed at. Emily carefully laughed at some parts of it. How crude—how silly—how sentimental—how amusing! Had she really ever been young and callow enough to write such flowery exultant nonsense? And one would have thought, too, that fourteen regarded twenty-four as verging on venerable.

"Have you written your great book?" airily asked Fourteen in conclusion. "Have you climbed to the very top of the Alpine Path? Oh, Twenty-four, I'm envying you. It must be splendid to be *you*. Are you looking back patronizingly and pityingly to *me*? You wouldn't swing on a gate now, would you? Are you a staid old married woman with several children, living in the Disappointed House with One-You-Know-Of? Only *don't* be stodgy, I implore you, dear Twenty-four. And do be dramatic. I love dramatic things and people. Are you Mrs. ———— ————? What name will fill those blanks? Oh, dear Twenty-four, I put into this letter for you a kiss—and a handful of moonshine—and the soul of a rose—and some of the green sweetness of the old hill field—and a whiff of wild violets. I hope you are happy and famous and lovely; and I hope you haven't quite forgotten

"Your foolish

"OLD SELF."

Emily locked the letter away.

"So much for that nonsense," she said scoffingly.

Then she sat down in her chair, and dropped her head on her desk. Little silly, dreamy, happy, ignorant Fourteen! Always thinking that something great and wonderful and beautiful lay in the years ahead. Quite sure that the "mountain purple" could be reached. Quite sure that dreams always came true. Foolish Fourteen, who yet had known how to be happy.

"I'm envying *you*," said Emily. "I wish I had never opened your letter, foolish little Fourteen. Go back to your shadowy past and don't come again—mocking me. I'm going to have a white night because of you. I'm going to lie awake all night and pity myself."

Yet already the footsteps of destiny were sound-on the stairs—though Emily thought they were only Cousin Jimmy's.

II

He had come to bring her a letter—a thin letter—and if Emily had not been too much absorbed in herself at fourteen she might have noticed that Cousin Jimmy's eyes were as bright as a cat's and that an air of ill-concealed excitement pervaded his whole being. Moreover that, when she had thanked him absently for the letter and gone back to her desk, he remained in the shadowy hall outside, watching her slyly through the half-open door. At first he thought she was not going to open the letter—she had flung it down indifferently and sat staring at it. Cousin Jimmy went nearly mad with impatience.

But after a few minutes more of absent musing Emily roused herself with a sigh and stretched out a hand for the letter.

"If I don't miss my guess, dear little Emily, you won't sigh when you read what's in that letter," thought Cousin Jimmy exultantly.

Emily looked at the return address in the upper corner, wondering what the Wareham Publishing Company were writing to her about. The big Warehams! The oldest and most important publishing house in America. A circular of some kind, probably. Then she found herself staring incredulously at the typewritten sheet—while Cousin Jimmy performed a noiseless dance on Aunt Elizabeth's braided rug out in the hall.

"I—don't—understand," gasped Emily.

DEAR MISS STARR:—

We take pleasure in advising you that our readers report favourably with regard to your story *The Moral of the Rose* and if mutually satisfactory arrangements can be made we shall be glad to add the book to our next season's lists. We shall also be interested in hearing of your plans with regard to future writing.

Very sincerely yours, etc.

"I don't understand—" said Emily again.

Cousin Jimmy could hold himself in no longer. He made a sound between a whoop and hurrah. Emily flew across the room and dragged him in.

"Cousin Jimmy, *what* does this mean? You must know something about it—how did the House of Wareham ever get my book?"

"Have they really accepted it?" demanded Cousin Jimmy.

"Yes. And *I* never sent it to them. I wouldn't have supposed it was the least use—the *Warehams*. *Am* I dreaming?"

"No. I'll tell you—don't be mad now, Emily. You mind Elizabeth asked me to tidy up the garret a month ago. I was moving that old cardboard box you keep a lot of stuff in and the bottom fell out.

676

Everything went—so—all over the garret. I gathered 'em up—and your book manuscript was among 'em. I happened to look at a page—and then I set down—and Elizabeth came up an hour later and found me still a-sitting there on my hams reading. I'd forgot everything. My, but she was mad! The garret not half done and dinner ready. But I didn't mind what she said—I was thinking, 'If that book made me forget everything like that there's *something* in it. *I'll* send it somewhere.' And I didn't know anywhere to send it but to the Warehams. I'd always heard of them. And I didn't know *how* to send it—but I just stuffed it in an old cracker box and mailed it to them offhand."

"Didn't you even send stamps for its return?" gasped Emily, horrified.

"No, never thought of it. Maybe that's why they took it. Maybe the other firms sent it back because you sent stamps."

"Hardly." Emily laughed and found herself crying.

"Emily, you ain't mad at me, are you?"

"No—no—darling—I'm only so flabbergasted, as you say yourself, that I don't know what to say or do. It's all so—the *Warehams!*"

"I've been watching the mails ever since," chuckled Cousin Jimmy. "Elizabeth has been thinking I've gone clear daft at last. If the story had come back I was going to smuggle it back to the garret—I wasn't going to let you know. But when I saw that thin envelope—I remembered you said once the thin envelopes always had good news—dear little Emily, don't cry!"

"I can't—help it—and oh, I'm sorry for what I called you, little Fourteen. You weren't silly—you were wise—you knew."

"It's gone to her head a little," said Cousin Jimmy to himself. "No wonder—after so many set-backs. But she'll soon be quite sensible again."

CHAPTER XXI

I

Teddy and Ilse were coming home for a brief ten days in July. How was it, wondered Emily, that they always came together? That couldn't be just a coincidence. She dreaded the visit and wished it were over. It would be good to see Ilse again—somehow she could never feel a stranger with Ilse. No matter how long she was away, the moment she came back you found the old Ilse. But she did not want to see Teddy. Teddy who had forgotten her. Who had never written since he went away last. Teddy who was already famous, as a painter of lovely women. So famous and so successful that—Ilse wrote—he was going to give up magazine work. Emily felt a certain relief when she read that. She would no longer dread to open a magazine lest she see her own face—or soul—looking at her out of some illustration—with "Frederick Kent" scrawled in the corner, as if to say "know all men by these presents that this girl is mine." Emily resented less the pictures which looked like her whole face than the ones in which only the eyes were hers. To be able to paint her eyes like that Teddy *must* know everything that was in her soul. The thought always filled her with fury and shame—and a sense of horrible helplessness. She would not—could not—tell Teddy to stop using her as a model. She had never stooped to acknowledge to him that she had noticed any resemblance to herself in his illustrations— she never *would* stoop.

And now he was coming home—might be home any time. If only she could go away—on any pretence—for a few weeks. Miss Royal was wanting her to go to New York for a visit. But it would never do to go away when Ilse was coming.

Well—Emily shook herself. What an idiot she was! Teddy was coming home, a dutiful son, to see his mother—and he would doubtless be glad enough to see old friends when their actual presence recalled them to his memory; and why should there be anything difficult about it? She must get rid of this absurd self-consciousness. She would.

She was sitting at her open window. The night outside was like a dark, heavy, perfumed flower. An expectant night—a night when things intended to happen. Very still. Only the loveliest of muted sounds—the faintest whisper of trees, the airiest sigh of wind, the half-heard, half-felt moan of the sea.

"Oh, beauty!" whispered Emily, passionately, lifting her hands to the stars. "What would I have done without you all these years?"

Beauty of night—and perfume—and mystery. Her soul was filled with it. There was, just then, room for nothing else. She bent out, lifting her face to the jewelled sky—rapt, ecstatic.

Then she heard it. A soft, silvery signal in Lofty John's bush—two higher notes and one long, low one—the old, old call that would once have sent her with flying feet to the shadows of the firs.

Emily sat as if turned to stone, her white face framed in the vines that clustered round her window. He was there—Teddy was there—in Lofty John's bush—waiting for her—calling to her as of old. Expecting her!

Almost she had sprung to her feet—almost she had run downstairs and out to the shadows—the beautiful, perfumed shadows where he was waiting for her. But—

Was he only trying to see if he still had the old power over her?

He had gone away two years ago without even a written word of farewell. Would the Murray pride condone that? Would the Murray pride run to meet the man who had held her of so little account? The Murray pride would not. Emily's young face took on lines of stubborn determination in the dim light. She would not go. Let him call as he might. "Whistle and I'll come to you, my lad," indeed! No more of that for Emily Byrd Starr. Teddy Kent need not imagine that he could come and go as went the years and find her meekly waiting to answer his lordly signal.

Again the call came—twice. He was there—so close to her. In a moment if she liked, she could be beside him—her hands in his—his eyes looking into hers—perhaps—

He had gone away without saying good-bye to her!

Emily rose deliberately and lighted her lamp. She sat down at her desk near the window, took up her pen and fell to writing—or a semblance of writing. Steadily she wrote—next day she found sheets covered with aimless repetitions of old poems learned in school-days—and as she wrote she listened. Would the call come again? Once more? It did not. When she was quite sure it was not coming again she put out her light and lay down on her bed with her face in the pillow. Pride was quite satisfied. She had shown him she was not to be whistled off and on. Oh, how thankful she felt that she had been firm enough not to go. For which reason, no doubt, her pillow was wet with savage tears.

II

He came next night—with Ilse—in his new car. And there was handshaking and gaiety and laughter—oh, a great deal of laughter. Ilse was looking radiant in a big yellow hat trimmed with crimson roses. One of those preposterous hats only Ilse could get away with. How unlike the neglected, almost ragged Ilse of olden days. Yet just as lovable as ever. Nobody could help loving Ilse. Teddy was charming, too—with just the right amount of mingled interest and detachment an old resident coming back to childhood's home would naturally feel. Interested in everything and everybody. Oh, yes, indeed, hugely! Ilse tells me you're bringing out a book. Capital. What's it about? Must get a copy. Blair Water quite unchanged. Delightful to come back to a place where time seems to stand still.

Emily almost thought she must have dreamed the whistle in Lofty John's bush.

But she went for a drive to Priest Pond with him and Ilse—and made quite a sensation, for cars were still great novelties thereabouts. And they had a merry, delightful time—then and for the few remaining days of their visit. Ilse had meant to stay three weeks but found she could stay only five days. And Teddy, who seemed to be master of his own time, decided to stay no longer, too. And they both came over to say good-bye to Emily and all went for a farewell moonlit spin—and laughed a great deal—and Ilse, with a hug, declared it was just like old times and Teddy agreed.

"If only Perry had been round," he amended. "I'm sorry not to have seen old Perry. They tell me he is getting on like a house afire."

Perry had gone to the Coast on business for his firm. Emily bragged a little about him and his success. Teddy Kent need not suppose he was the only one who was arriving.

"Are his manners any better than they used to be?" asked Ilse.

"His manners are good enough for us simple Prince Edward Islanders," said Emily, nastily.

"Oh, well, I admit I never saw him pick his teeth in public," conceded Ilse. "Do you know"—with a sly, sidelong glance at Teddy which Emily instantly noticed—"once I fancied myself quite in love with Perry Miller."

"Lucky Perry!" said Teddy with what seemed a quiet smile of satisfied understanding.

Ilse did not kiss Emily good-bye, but she shook hands very cordially as did Teddy. Emily was thanking her stars, in genuine earnest this time, that she had not gone to Teddy when he whistled—if he ever had whistled. They drove gaily off down the lane. But when a few moments later Emily turned into New Moon there were flying footsteps behind her and she was enveloped in a silken embrace.

"Emily darling, good-bye. I love you as much as ever—but everything is so horribly changed—and we can never find the Islands of Enchantment again. I wish I hadn't come home at all—but say you love me and always will. I couldn't bear it if you didn't."

"Of course I'll always love you, Ilse."

They kissed lingeringly—almost sadly—among the faint, cold, sweet perfumes of night. Ilse went down the lane to where Teddy was purring and scintillating for her—or his car was—and Emily went into New Moon where her two old aunts and Cousin Jimmy were waiting for her.

"I wonder if Ilse and Teddy will ever be married," said Aunt Laura.

"It's time Ilse was settling down," said Aunt Elizabeth.

"Poor Ilse," said Cousin Jimmy inexplainably.

III

One late, lovely autumn day in November Emily walked home from the Blair Water post-office with a letter from Ilse and a parcel. She was athrill with an intoxication of excitement that easily passed for happiness. The whole day had been a strangely, unreasonably delightful one of ripe sunshine on the sere hills, faint, grape-like bloom on the faraway woods and a soft, blue sky with little wisps of grey cloud like cast-off veils. Emily had wakened in the morning from a dream of Teddy—the dear, friendly Teddy of the old days—and all day she had been haunted by an odd sense of his nearness. It seemed as if his footstep sounded at her side and as if she might come upon him suddenly when she rounded a spruce-fringed curve in the red road or went down into some sunny hollow where the ferns were thick and golden—find him smiling at her with no shadow of change between them, the years of exile and alienation forgotten. She had not really thought much about him for a long while. The summer and autumn had been busy—she was hard at work on a new story—Ilse's letters had been few and scrappy. Why this sudden, irrational sense of his nearness? When she got Ilse's fat letter she was quite sure there was some news of Teddy in it.

But it was the little parcel that was responsible for her excitement. It was stamped with the sign manual of the House of Wareham and Emily knew what it must hold. Her book—her *Moral of the Rose*.

She hurried home by the cross-lots road—the little old road over which the vagabond wandered and the lover went to his lady and children to joy and tired men home—the road that linked up eventually with the pasture field by the Blair Water and the Yesterday Road. Once in the grey-boughed solitude of the Yesterday Road Emily sat down in a bay of brown bracken and opened her parcel.

There lay her book. *Her* book, spleet-new from the publishers. It was a proud, wonderful, thrilling moment. The crest of the Alpine Path at last? Emily lifted her shining eyes to the deep blue November sky and saw peak after peak of sunlit azure still towering beyond. Always new heights of aspiration. One could never reach the top really. But what a moment when one reached a plateau and outlook like this! What a reward for the long years of toil and endeavour and disappointment and discouragement.

But oh, for her unborn *Seller of Dreams!*

IV

The excitement at New Moon that afternoon almost equalled Emily's own. Cousin Jimmy gave up unblushingly his plan of finishing the ploughing of the hill field to sit at home and gloat over the book. Aunt Laura cried—of course—and Aunt Elizabeth looked indifferent, merely remarking in a tone of surprise that it was bound like a real book. Evidently Aunt Elizabeth had been expecting paper covers. But she made some rather foolish mistakes in her quilt patches that afternoon and she did not once ask Jimmy why he wasn't ploughing. And when some callers dropped in later on *The Moral of the Rose* was mysteriously on the parlour table, though it had been up on Emily's desk when Aunt Elizabeth saw the automobile drive into the yard. Aunt Elizabeth never mentioned it and neither of the callers noticed it. When they went away Aunt Elizabeth said witheringly that John Angus had less sense than ever he had and that for her part, if *she* were Cousin Margaret, she would *not* wear clothes twenty years too young for her.

"An old ewe tricked out like a lamb," said Aunt Elizabeth contemptuously.

If they had done what was expected of them in regard to *The Moral of the Rose* Aunt Elizabeth would probably have said that John Angus had always been a jovial, good-natured sort of creature and that it was really wonderful how Cousin Margaret had held her own.

V

In all the excitement Emily had—not exactly forgotten Ilse's letter, but wanted to wait until things had settled down a little before reading it. At twilight she went to her room and sat down in the fading light. The wind had changed at sunset and the evening was cold and edged. What Jimmy called a "skiff" of snow had fallen suddenly whitening the world and the withered, unlovely garden. But the storm-cloud had passed and the sky was clear and yellow over the white hills and dark firs. The odd perfume that Ilse always affected floated out of her letter when it was opened. Emily had always vaguely disliked it. But then her taste differed from Ilse's in the matter of perfumes as in so many others. Ilse liked the exotic, oriental, provocative odors. To the day of her death Emily will never catch a whiff of that perfume without turning cold and sick.

"Exactly one thousand times have I planned to write to you," wrote Ilse, "but when one is revolving rapidly on the wheel of things there doesn't seem to be an opportunity for anything one really wants to do. All these months I've been so rushed that I've felt precisely like a cat just one jump ahead of a dog. If I stopped for a breath it would catch me.

"But the spirit moves me to utter a few yowls to-night. I've something to tell you. And your darling letter came to-day—so I will write to-night, and let the dog eat me if he will.

"I'm glad you're keeping well and good-humoured. There are times I envy you fiercely, Emily—your New Moon quiet and peace and leisure—your intense absorption and satisfaction in your work—your singleness of purpose. 'If thine eye be single thy whole body shall be full of light.' That's either in the Bible or Shakespeare, but wherever it is, it is true. I remember you told me once you envied me my opportunities of travel. Emily, old dear, rushing about from one place to another isn't travelling. If you were like your foolish Ilse, chasing a score of butterfly projects and ambitions you wouldn't be so happy. You always remind me—always did remind me, even in our old chummy days—of somebody's line—'her soul was like a star and dwelt apart.'

"Well, when one can't get the thing one really wants, one can't help chasing after anything that *might* made a decent substitute. I know you've always thought me an unmitigated donkey because I cared so much about Perry Miller. I knew you never quite understood. You couldn't. You never really cared a hoot about any he-creature, did you, Emily? So you thought me an idiot. I daresay I was. But I'm going to be sensible in future, I'm going to marry Teddy Kent."

VI

"There—it's out!"

Emily laid down—or dropped—the letter for a moment. She did not feel either pain or surprise—one does not feel either, I am told, when a bullet strikes the heart. It seemed to her that she had always known this was coming—always. At least, since the night of Mrs. Chidlaw's dinner-dance. And yet, now that it had really happened, it seemed to her that she was suffering everything of death but its merciful dying. In the dim, twilit mirror before her she saw her own face. Had Emily-in-the-glass ever looked like that before? But her room was just the same. It seemed indecent that it should be the same. After a few moments—or years—Emily picked up the letter and read on.

"I'm not in love with Teddy, of course. But he's just got to be a habit with me. I can't do without him—and I either have to do without him or marry him. He won't stand my hesitation any longer. Besides, he's going to be very famous. I shall enjoy being the wife of a famous man. Also, he will have the simoleons, too. Not that I'm altogether mercenary, Emily. I said 'No' to a millionaire last week. A nice fellow, too—but with a face like a good-natured weasel's, if there can be such a thing. And he *cried* when I told him I wouldn't marry him. Oh, it was ghastly.

"Yes, it's mostly ambition, I grant you. And a certain odd kind of weariness and impatience with my life as it has been these last few years. Everything seems squeezed dry. But I'm really very fond of Teddy—always was. He's nice and companionable—and our taste in jokes is exactly the same. And he never bores me. I have no use for people who bore me. Of course he's too good-looking for a man—he'll always be a target for the head-hunters. But since I don't care *too* much for him I shan't be tortured by jealousy. In life's morning march when my bosom was young I could have fried in boiling oil anyone—except you—at whom Perry Miller cast a sheep's eye.

"I've thought for years and known for weeks that this was coming some day. But I've been staving Teddy off—I wouldn't let him say the words that would really bind us. I don't know whether I'd ever have scraped up the courage to let him say them, but destiny took a hand. We were out for a spin two weeks ago one evening and a most unseasonable and malignant thunder-storm came up. We had a dreadful time getting back—there was no place on that bare, lonely hill-road we could stop—the rain fell in torrents, the thunder crashed, the lightning flashed. It was unendurable and we didn't endure it. We just tore through it and cussed. Then it cleared off as suddenly as it had began—and my nerves went to pieces—fancy! I *have* nerves now—and I began to cry like a frightened, foolish baby. And Teddy's arms were about me and he was saying I *must* marry him—and let him take care of me. I suppose I said I would because it's quite clear he thinks we are engaged. He has given me a blue Chow pup and a sapphire ring—a sapphire he picked up in Europe somewhere—an historic jewel for which a murder was once committed, I believe.

"I think it will be rather nice to be taken care of. Properly. I never was, you know. Dad had no use for me until you found out the truth about Mother—what a witch you were! And after that he adored and spoiled me. But he didn't take any more real care of me than before.

"We are to be married next June. Dad will be pleased, I fancy. Teddy was always the white-haired boy with him. Besides, I think he was beginning to be a little scared I was never going to hook a husband. Dad plumes himself on being a radical but at heart he out-Victorians the Victorians.

"And of course you must be my bridesmaid. Oh, Emily dear, how I wish I could see you to-night—talk with you—one of our old-time spiels—walk with you over the Delectable Mountain and along the ferny, frosted woodside, hang about that old garden by the sea where red poppies blow—all our old familiar places. I wish—I think I really do wish—I was ragged, barefooted, wild Ilse Burnley again. Life is pleasant still—oh, I don't say it isn't. Very pleasant—in spots—like the curate's immortal egg. But the 'first fine careless rapture'—the thrush may recapture it but we never. Emily, old pal, would you turn the clock back if you could?"

VII

Emily read the letter over three times. Then she sat for a very long time at her window, looking blindly out on the blanched, dim world lying under the terrible mockery of a sky full of stars. The wind around the eaves was full of ghostly voices. Bits here and there in Ilse's letter turned and twisted and vanished in her consciousness like little venomous snakes, each with a mortal sting.

"Your singleness of purpose"—"you never cared for anyone"—"of course you must be my bridesmaid"—"I'm really very fond of Teddy"—"my hesitation."

Could any girl really "hesitate" over accepting Teddy Kent? Emily heard a little note of bitter laughter. Was it something in herself that laughed—or that vanishing spectre of Teddy that had haunted her all day—or an old smothered persistent hope that laughed before it died at last?

And at that very moment probably Ilse and Teddy were together.

"If I had gone—that night—last summer—when he called—would it have made any difference?" was the question that asked itself over and over again maddeningly.

"I wish I could hate Ilse. It would make it easier," she thought drearily. "If she loved Teddy I think I *could* hate her. Somehow, it isn't

686

so dreadful when she doesn't. It ought to be *more* dreadful. It's very strange that I can bear the thought of his loving her when I couldn't bear the thought of her loving him."

A great weariness suddenly possessed her. For the first time in her life death seemed a friend. It was very late when she finally went to bed. Towards morning she slept a little. But wakened stupidly at dawn. What was it she had heard?

She remembered.

She got up and dressed—as she must get up and dress every morning to come for endless years.

"Well," she said aloud to Emily-in-the-glass. "I've spilled my cup of life's wine on the ground—somehow. And she will give me no more. So I must go thirsty. Would—*would* it have been different if I had gone to him that night he called. If I only knew!" She thought she could see Dean's ironical, compassionate eyes.

Suddenly she laughed.

"In plain English—as Ilse would say—what a devilish mess I've made of things!"

CHAPTER XXII

I

Life, of course, went on in spite of its dreadfulness. The routine of existence doesn't stop because one is miserable. There were even some moments that were not altogether bad. Emily again measured her strength with pain and again conquered. With the Murray pride and the Starr reserve at her elbow she wrote Ilse a letter of good wishes with which nobody could have found fault. If that were only all she had to do! If only people wouldn't keep on talking to her about Ilse and Teddy.

The engagement was announced in the Montreal papers and then in the Island ones.

"Yes, they're engaged and heaven help every one concerned," said Dr. Burnley. But he could not hide his satisfaction in it.

"Thought at one time *you* and Teddy were going to make a match of it," he said jovially to Emily—who smiled gallantly and said something about the unexpected always happening.

"Anyhow we'll have a wedding that *is* a wedding," declared the doctor. "We haven't had a wedding in the clan for God knows how long. I thought they'd forgotten how. I'll show 'em. Ilse writes me you're to be bridesmaid. And I'll be wanting you to oversee things generally. Can't trust a wedding to a housekeeper."

"Anything I can do, of course," said Emily automatically. Nobody should suspect what she felt not if she died for it. She would even be bridesmaid.

If it had not been for that prospect ahead she thought she could have got through the winter not unhappily. For *The Moral of the Rose* was a success from the start. The first edition exhausted in ten days—three large editions in two weeks—five in eight weeks. Exaggerated reports of the pecuniary returns were circulated everywhere. For the first time Uncle Wallace looked at her with respect and Aunt Addie wished secretly that Andrew hadn't been consoled quite so soon. Old Cousin Charlotte, of Derry Pond, heard of the many editions and opined that Emily must be very busy if she had to put all the books together and sew them herself. The Shrewsbury people were furious because they imagined they were in the book. Every family believed *they* were the Applegaths.

"You were right not to come to New York," wrote Miss Royal. "You could never have written *The Moral of the Rose* here. Wild roses won't grow in city streets. And your story is like a wild rose, dear, all sweetness and unexpectedness with sly little thorns of wit and satire. It has power, delicacy, understanding. It's not just story-telling. There's some magicry in it. Emily Byrd Starr, where do you get your uncanny understanding of human nature—you infant?"

Dean wrote too—"good creative work, Emily. Your characters are natural and human and delightful. And I like the glowing spirit of youth that pervades the book."

II

"I had hoped to learn something from the reviews, but they are all too contradictory," said Emily. "What one reviewer pronounces the book's greatest merit another condemns as its worst fault. Listen to these—'Miss Starr never succeeds in making her characters convincing' and 'One fancies that some of the author's characters must have been copied from real life. They are so absolutely true to nature that they could hardly be the work of imagination.'"

"I told you people would recognize old Douglas Courcy," interjected Aunt Elizabeth.

"'A very tiresome book'—'a very delightful book'—'very undistinguished fiction' and 'on every page the work of the finished artist is apparent'—'a book of cheap and weak romanticism' and 'a classic quality in the book'—'a unique story of a rare order of literary workmanship' and 'a silly, worthless, colourless and desultory story'—'an ephemeral sort of affair' and a book destined to live.' What *is* one to believe?"

"I would just believe only the favourable ones," said Aunt Laura.

Emily sighed.

"My tendency is just the other way. I can't help believing the unfavourable ones are true and that the favourable ones were written by morons. But I don't really mind much what they say about the *book*. It's only when they criticize my heroine that I'm hurt and furious, I saw red over these reviews of darling *Peggy*. 'A girl of extraordinary stupidity'—'the heroine has too marked a self-consciousness of her mission.'"

"I *did* think she was a bit of a flirt," conceded Cousin Jimmy.

"'A thin, sweetish heroine'—'the heroine is something of a bore'—'queer but altogether too queer.'"

"I told you she shouldn't have had green eyes," groaned Cousin Jimmy. "A heroine should always have blue eyes.'"

"Oh, but listen to this," cried Emily gaily—"'*Peg Applegath* is simply irresistible'—'*Peg* is a remarkably vivid personality'—'a fascinating heroine'—'*Peg* is too delightful not to be credited while we are under her spell'—'one of the immortal girls of literature.' What about green eyes now, Cousin Jimmy?"

Cousin Jimmy shook his head. He was not convinced.

"Here's a review for you," twinkled Emily. "'A psychological problem with roots that stretch far into subliminal depths which would give the book weight and value if it were grappled with sincerely.'"

"I know the meaning of all those words by themselves except two, but put together they don't make any sense," protested Cousin Jimmy ruefully.

"'Beneath the elusiveness and atmospheric charm is a wonderful firmness of character delineation.'"

"I don't quite get that either," confessed Cousin Jimmy, "But it sounds kind of favourable."

"'A conventional and commonplace book.'"

"What does 'conventional' mean!" asked Aunt Elizabeth, who would not have been posed by transubstantiation or Gnosticism.

"'Beautifully written and full of sparkling humour. Miss Starr is a real artist in literature.'"

"Oh, now, *there's* a reviewer with some sense," purred Cousin Jimmy.

"'The general impression left by the book is that it might be much worse.'"

"*That* reviewer was trying to be smart, I suppose," said Aunt Elizabeth, apparently quite oblivious of the fact that she had said the very same thing herself.

"'This book lacks spontaneity. It is saccharine and melodramatic, mawkish and naive.'"

"I know I fell into the well," said Cousin Jimmy pitifully. "Is that why I can't make head or tail out of that?"

"Here's one you can understand—perhaps. 'Miss Starr must have invented the *Applegath* orchard as well as her green-eyed heroine. There are no orchards in Prince Edward Island. They are killed by the harsh, salt winds that blow across that narrow sandy strip.'"

"Read that again please, Emily."

Emily complied. Cousin Jimmy scratched his head, then shook it. "Do they let that kind run loose over there?"

"'The story is a charming one, charmingly told. The characters are skilfully depicted, the dialogue deftly handled, the descriptive passages surprisingly effective. The quiet humour is simply delightful.'"

"I hope this will not make you vain, Emily," said Aunt Elizabeth warningly.

"If it does, here's the antidote. 'This feeble, pretentious and sentimental story—if story it can be called—is full of banalities and trivialities. A mass of disconnected episodes and scraps of conversation, intermingled with long periods of reflection and self-examination.'"

"I wonder if the creature who wrote that knew the meaning of the words himself," said Aunt Laura.

"'The scene of this story is laid in Prince Edward Island, a detached portion of land off the coast of Newfoundland.'"

"Don't Yankees *ever* study geography?" snorted exasperated Cousin Jimmy.

"'A story that will not corrupt its readers.'"

"*There's* a real compliment now," said Aunt Elizabeth.

Cousin Jimmy looked doubtful. It sounded all right but—of course dear little Emily's book couldn't corrupt anyone but—

"'To review a book of this kind is like attempting to dissect a butterfly's wing or strip a rose of its petals to discover the secret of its fragrance.'"

"Too highfalutin," sniffed Aunt Elizabeth.

"'Honeyed sentimentality which the author evidently supposes is poetic fancy.'"

"Wouldn't I like to smack his gob," said Cousin Jimmy feelingly.

"'Harmless and easy reading.'"

"I don't know why, but I don't quite like the sound of that," commented Aunt Laura.

"'This story will keep a kindly smile upon your lips and in your heart as well.'"

"Come now, that's English. I can understand *that*," beamed Cousin Jimmy.

"'We began but found it impossible to finish this crude and tiresome book.'"

"Well, all *I* can say," said Cousin Jimmy indignantly, "is that the oftener I read *The Moral of the Rose* the better I like it. Why, I was reading it for the fourth time yesterday and I was so interested I clean forgot all about dinner."

Emily smiled. It was better to have won her standing with the New Moon folks than with the world. What mattered it what any reviewer said when Aunt Elizabeth remarked with an air of uttering the final judgment:

"Well, I never could have believed that a pack of lies could sound as much like the real truth as that book does."

CHAPTER XXIII

I

Emily, coming home one January night from an evening call, decided to use the cross-lots road that skirted the Tansy Patch. It had been a winter almost without snow and the ground under her feet was bare and hard. She seemed the only living creature abroad in the night and she walked slowly, savouring the fine, grim, eerie charm of flowerless meadows and silent woods, of the moon breaking suddenly out of black clouds over the lowlands of pointed firs; and trying, more or less successfully, not to think of the letter that had come from Ilse that day—one of Ilse's gay, incoherent letters, where one fact stood out barely. The wedding-day was set—the fifteenth of June.

"I want you to wear harebell blue gauze over ivory taffeta for your bridesmaid dress, darling. How your black silk hair will shine over it!

"My 'bridal robe' is going to be of ivory velvet and old Great-aunt Edith in Scotland is sending me out her veil of rose-point and Great-aunt Theresa in the same historic land is sending me a train of silver oriental embroidery that her husband once brought home from Constantinople. I'll veil it with tulle. Won't I be a dazzling creature? I don't think the dear old souls knew I existed till Dad wrote them about my 'forthcoming nuptials.' Dad is far more excited over everything than I am.

"Teddy and I are going to spend our honeymoon in old inns in out-of-the-way European corners—places where nobody else wants to go—Vallambroso and so on. That line of Milton's always intrigued me—'thick as autumnal leaves that strew the brooks in Vallambroso.' When you take it away from its horrible context it is a picture of sheer delight.

"I'll be home in May for my last preparations and Teddy will come the first of June to spend a little while with his mother. How *is* she taking it, Emily? Have you any idea? I can't get anything out of Teddy, so I suppose she doesn't like it. She always hated me, I know. But then she seemed to hate everyone—with a special venom for you. I won't be particularly fortunate in my mother-in-law. I'll always have an eerie feeling that she's secretly heaping maledictions on my head. However, Teddy is nice enough to make up for her. He really is. I'd no idea how nice he could be and I'm growing fonder of him every day. Honestly. When I look at him and realize how handsome and charming he is I can't understand why I'm not madly in love with him. But it's really much more comfortable not to be. If I were I'd be heartbroken every time we quarrelled. We're always quarrelling—you know me of old. We always will. We'll spoil every wonderful moment with a quarrel. But life won't be dull."

Emily shivered. Her own life was looking very bleak and starved just then. Oh, how—nice—it would be when the wedding was over— the wedding where *she* should be bride—yes, *should*—and was to be bridesmaid—and people done talking of it. "Harebell blue over ivory taffeta!" Sackcloth and ashes, rather.

II

"Emily. Emily Starr."

Emily almost jumped. She had not seen Mrs. Kent in the gloom until they were face to face—at the little side path that led up to the Tansy Patch. She was standing there, bareheaded in the chill night, with outstretched hand.

"Emily, I want to have a talk with you. I saw you go past here at sunset and I've been watching for you ever since. Come up to the house."

Emily would much rather have refused. Yet she turned and silently climbed the steep, root-ribbed path, with Mrs. Kent flitting before her like a little dead leaf borne along by the wind. Through the ragged old garden where nothing ever grew but tansy, and into the little house that was as shabby as it had always been. People said Teddy Kent might fix up his mother's house a bit if he were making all the money folks said he was. But Emily knew that Mrs. Kent would not let him—would not have anything changed.

She looked around the little place curiously. She had not been in it for many years—not since the long-ago days when she and Ilse and

Teddy had been children there. It seemed quite unchanged. As of yore, the house seemed to be afraid of laughter. Someone always seemed to be praying in it. It had an atmosphere of prayer. And the old willow to the west was still tap-tapping on the window with ghostly finger-tips. On the mantel was a recent photograph of Teddy—a good one. He seemed on the point of speaking—of saying something triumphant—exultant.

"Emily, I've found the rainbow gold. Fame—and love."

She turned her back on it and sat down. Mrs. Kent sat opposite—a faded, shrinking little figure with the long scar slanting palely across her bitter mouth and lined face—the face that must have been very pretty once. She was looking intently, searchingly at Emily; but, as Emily instantly realized, the old smouldering hatred had gone out of her eyes—her tired eyes that must once have been young and eager and laughter-lit. She leaned forward and touched Emily's arm with her slim, claw-like fingers.

"You know that Teddy is going to marry Ilse Burnley," she said.

"Yes."

"What do you feel about it?"

Emily moved impatiently.

"What do my feelings matter, Mrs. Kent? Teddy loves Ilse. She is a beautiful, brilliant, warmhearted girl. I am sure they will be very happy."

"Do *you* still love him?"

Emily wondered why she did not feel resentment. But Mrs. Kent was not to be judged by ordinary rules. And here was a fine chance to save her face by a cool little lie—just a few indifferent words. "Not any longer, Mrs. Kent. Oh, I know I once imagined I did—imagining things like that is one of my weaknesses unfortunately. But I find I don't care at all."

Why couldn't she say them? Well, she couldn't, that was all. She could never, in any words, deny her love for Teddy. It was so much a part of herself that it had a divine right to truth. And was there not, too, a secret relief in feeling that here at least was one person with whom she could be herself—before whom she need not pretend or hide?

"I don't think you have any right to ask that question, Mrs. Kent. But—I do."

Mrs. Kent laughed silently.

694

"I used to hate you. I don't hate you any longer. We are one now, you and I. We love him. And he has forgotten us—he cares nothing for us—he has gone to *her*."

"He does care for you, Mrs. Kent. He always did. Surely you can understand that there is more than one kind of love. And I hope—you are not going to hate Ilse because Teddy loves her."

"No, I don't hate her. She is more beautiful than you, but there is no mystery about her. She will never possess him wholly as you would have. It's quite different. But I want to know this—are you unhappy because of this?"

"No. Only for a few minutes now and then. Generally I am too much interested in my work to brood morbidly on what can't be mine."

Mrs. Kent had listened thirstily. "Yes—yes—exactly. I thought so. The Murrays are so sensible. Some day—some day—you'll be glad this has happened—glad that Teddy didn't care for you. Don't you think you will?"

"Perhaps."

"Oh, I am sure of it. It's so much better for you. Oh, you don't know the suffering and wretchedness you will be spared. It's madness to love anything too much. God *is* jealous. If you married Teddy he would break your heart—they always do. It is best—you will live to feel it was best."

Tap—tap—tap went the old willow.

"Need we talk of this any more, Mrs. Kent?"

"Do you remember that night I found you and Teddy in the graveyard?" asked Mrs. Kent, apparently deaf to Emily's question.

"Yes." Emily found herself remembering it very vividly—that strange wonderful night when Teddy had saved her from mad Mr. Morrison and said such sweet, unforgettable things to her.

"Oh, how I hated you that night!" exclaimed Mrs. Kent. "But I shouldn't have said those things to you. All my life I've been saying things I shouldn't. Once I said a terrible thing—such a terrible thing. I've never been able to get the echo of it out of my ears. And do you remember what *you* said to *me?* That was why I let Teddy go away from me. It was *your* doing. If he hadn't gone you mightn't have lost him. Are you sorry you spoke so?"

"No. If anything I said helped to clear the way for him I'm glad—glad."

695

"You would do it over again?"

"I would."

"And don't you hate Ilse bitterly? She has taken what you wanted. You *must* hate her."

"I do not. I love Ilse dearly as I always did. She has taken nothing from me that was ever mine."

"I don't understand it—I don't understand it," half whispered Mrs. Kent. *"My* love isn't like that. Perhaps that is why it has always made me so unhappy. No, I don't hate you any longer. But oh, I did hate you. I knew Teddy cared more for you than he did for me. Didn't you and he talk about me—criticize me?"

"Never."

"I thought you did. People were always doing that—always."

Suddenly Mrs. Kent struck her tiny hands together violently.

"Why didn't you tell me you didn't love him any longer? Why didn't you—even if it was a lie? That was what I wanted to hear. I could have believed you. The Murrays never lie."

"Oh, what does it matter?" cried tortured Emily again. "My love means nothing to him now. He is Ilse's. You need not be jealous of me any longer, Mrs. Kent."

"I'm not—I'm not—it isn't that." Mrs. Kent looked at her oddly. "Oh, if I only dared—but no—but no, it's too late. It would be no use now. I don't think I know what I'm saying. Only—Emily—will you come to see me sometimes? It's lonely here—very lonely—so much worse now when he belongs to Ilse. His picture came last Wednesday—no, Thursday. There is so little to distinguish the days here. I put it up there, but it makes things worse. He was thinking of her in it—can't you tell by his eyes he was thinking of the woman he loves? I am of no importance to him now. I am of no importance to anybody."

"If I come to see you—you mustn't talk of him—or of them," said Emily, pitingly.

"I won't. Oh, I won't. Though that won't prevent us from thinking of them, will it? You'll sit there—and I'll sit here—and we'll talk of the weather and think of *him.* How amusing! But—when you've really forgotten him—when you really don't care any more—you'll tell me, won't you?"

Emily nodded and rose to go. She could not endure this any longer. "And if there is ever anything I can do for you, Mrs. Kent—"

"I want rest—rest," said Mrs. Kent, laughing wildly. "Can you find that for me? Don't you know I'm a ghost, Emily? I died years ago. I walk in the dark."

As the door closed behind her Emily heard Mrs. Kent beginning to cry terribly. With a sigh of relief she turned to the crisp open spaces of the wind and the night, the shadows and the frosty moon. Ah, one could breathe here.

CHAPTER XXIV

I

Ilse came in May—a gay, laughing Ilse. Almost *too* gay and laughing, Emily thought. Ilse had always been a merry, irresponsible creature; but not quite so unceasingly so as now. She never had a serious mood, apparently. She made a jest of everything, even her marriage. Aunt Elizabeth and Aunt Laura were quite shocked at her. A girl who was so soon to assume the responsibilities of wedded life should be more thoughtful and sober. Ilse told Emily they were mid-Victorian screams. She chatted ceaselessly when she and Emily were together, but never *talked* to her, despite the desire expressed in her letters for old-time spiels. Perhaps she was not quite all to blame for this. Emily, in spite of her determination to be exactly the same as of yore, could not help a certain restraint and reserve, born of her secret pain and her fierce determination to hide it. Ilse felt the restraint, though wholly unsuspicious of the cause. Emily was just naturally growing a little bit New Moonish, that was all, living there alone with those dear old antediluvians.

"When Teddy and I come back and set up house in Montreal you must spend every winter with us, darling. New Moon is a dear place in summer, but in winter you must be absolutely buried alive."

Emily made no promises. She did not see herself as a guest in Teddy's home. Every night she told herself she could not possibly endure tomorrow. But when to-morrow came it was livable. It was even possible to talk dress and details calmly with Ilse. The harebell blue dress became a reality and Emily tried it on two nights before Teddy was expected home. The wedding was only two weeks away now.

"You look like a dream in it, Emily," said Ilse, stretched out on Emily's bed with the grace and abandon of a cat—Teddy's sapphire blotting her finger darkly. "You'll make all my velvet and lace gorgeousness look obvious and crude. Did I tell you Teddy is bringing Lorne Halsey with him for best man? I'm positively thrilled—the great Halsey. His mother has been so ill he didn't think he could come. But the obliging old lady has suddenly recovered and he's actually coming. His new book is a wow. Everybody in Montreal was raving over it and he's the most interesting and improbable creature. Wouldn't it be wonderful if you and he were to fall in love with each other, Emily?"

"Don't go matchmaking for me, Ilse," said Emily with a faint smile, as she took off the harebell dress. "I feel in my bones that I shall achieve old-maidenhood, which is an entirely different thing from having old-maidenhood thrust upon you."

"To be sure, he looks like a gargoyle," said Ilse meditatively. "If it hadn't been for that I think I might have married him myself. I'm almost sure I could have. His way of making love was to ask me my opinion about things. That was agreeable. But I had a hunch that if we were married he would stop asking for my opinion. That would *not* be agreeable. Besides, nobody could ever tell what he really thought. He might be looking as though he adored you and thinking he saw crow's-feet around your eyes. By the way, isn't Teddy the most beautiful thing?"

"He was always a nice-looking boy."

"'A nice-looking boy,'" mimicked Ilse. "Emily Starr, if you ever do marry I hope your husband will chain you in the dog-kennel. I'll be calling you Aunt Emily in a minute. Why, there's nobody in Montreal who can hold a candle to him. It's his looks I love really—not him. Sometimes he bores me—really. Although I was so sure he wouldn't. He never did before we were engaged. I have a premonition that some day I'll throw the teapot at him. Isn't it a pity we can't have two husbands? One to look at and one to talk to. But Teddy and I will be by way of being a stunning couple, won't we, honey? He so dark—I so fair. Ideal. I've always wished I was 'a dark ladye'—like you—but when I said so to Teddy he just laughed and quoted the old verse,

'If the bards of old the truth have told

The sirens have raven hair.

But over the earth since art had birth,

They paint the angels fair.'

That's the nearest Teddy will ever get to calling *me* an angel. Luckily. For when all's said and done, Emily, I'd rather—are you sure the door is shut so that Aunt Laura won't drop dead?—I'd *much* rather be a siren than an angel. Wouldn't you?"

"Let's check up the invitations now and make sure we haven't left anybody out," was Emily's response to this riot of words.

"Isn't it terrible to belong to a clan like ours?" said Ilse peevishly. "There's such a ghastly lot of old frumps and bores that have to be among those present. I hope some day I'll get where there are no relations. I wish the whole damn affair was over. You're sure you addressed a bid to Perry, aren't you?"

"Yes."

"I wonder if he'll come? I hope he will. What a goose I was ever to fancy I cared so much for him! I used to hope—all sorts of things, in spite of the fact I knew he was crazy about you. But I never hoped after Mrs. Chidlaw's dinner-dance. Do you remember it, Emily?"

Yes, Emily remembered *that*.

"Till then I'd always hoped a *little*—that some day when he realized he couldn't have you—I'd catch his heart on the rebound—wasn't that the Victorian phrase? I thought he'd be at the Chidlaws'—I knew he had been invited. And I asked Teddy if Perry were coming. Teddy looked right into my eyes meaningly and said, 'Perry will not be here. He's working on the case he has to appear in to-morrow. Perry's goal is ambition. He has no time for love.'

"I knew he was trying to warn me—and I knew it was no use to go on hoping—anything. So I gave up definitely. Well, it's turned out all right. Isn't it charming how things do turn out so beautifully? Makes one quite believe in an overruling Providence. Isn't it nice to be able to blame everything on God?"

Emily hardly heard Ilse as she mechanically hung up the blue dress in her closet and slipped into a little green sport suit. So *that* was what Teddy had said to Ilse that night years ago when she knew he had uttered the word "love." And she had been so chilly to him because of it. Well, not likely it mattered. No doubt he had only been warning Ilse because he wanted her to turn her maiden thoughts from Perry and concentrate them on himself. She felt relieved when Ilse finally went home. Ilse's light, continual chatter rather got on her nerves—though she was ashamed to admit it. But then her nerves were on edge under this long-drawn-out torture. Two weeks more of it—and then, thank God, at least peace.

II

She went up to the Tansy Patch in the dusk to take back a book Mrs. Kent had lent her the night before. The visit must be made before Teddy came home. She had been up to the Tansy Patch several times since that first evening and an odd sort of friendship had sprung up between her and Mrs. Kent. They lent each other books and talked of everything except the one thing that mattered most to them. The book Emily was returning was an old copy of *The South African Farm*. Emily had expressed a wish to read it and Mrs. Kent had gone upstairs and presently came down with it—her white face a little whiter and the scar burning redly across it as always when she was deeply moved.

"Here is the book you want," she said. "I had it in a box upstairs."

Emily finished reading the book before she went to sleep. She was not sleeping well now and the nights were long. The book had a musty, unaired odour—evidently the box Mrs. Kent spoke of had not been opened for a long time. And in it Emily found a thin letter, unstamped, addressed to Mrs. David Kent.

The curious thing about the letter was that it was, apparently, unopened. Well, letters often re-sealed themselves like that, if placed under pressure, when the flap had pulled open untorn in the first opening. Not likely it was of much significance. But of course she would mention it when she took the book back.

"Did you know there was a letter in this book, Mrs. Kent?"

"A letter. Did you say a letter?"

"Yes. Addressed to you."

Emily held the letter out to Mrs. Kent, whose face became ghastly as she looked at the handwriting.

"You found that—in that book?" she whispered. "In that book that hasn't been opened for over twenty-five years? Do you know—who wrote this letter? My—husband wrote it—and I have never read it— never known of it."

Emily felt herself in the presence of some tragedy—the secret torture of Mrs. Kent's life, perhaps.

"I will go away—so that you can read it alone," she said gently and went out, leaving Mrs. Kent standing in the shadowy little room, holding the letter in her hand—as one might hold a snake.

III

"I sent for you to-night because there is something I must tell you," said Mrs. Kent.

She was sitting, a tiny, erect, determined creature in the armchair by the window in the harsh light of a cold sunset. It was June but it was cold. The sky was hard and autumnal. Emily, walking up the cross-lots path had shivered and wished herself at home. But Mrs. Kent's note had been urgent—almost peremptory. Why in the world did she want her! Surely, it could not be anything in connection with Teddy. And yet what else could make Mrs. Kent send for her in this fashion?

The moment she saw Mrs. Kent she was conscious of a curious change in her—a change hard to define. She was as frail, as pitiful as ever. There seemed even a certain defiant light in her eyes. But for the first time since she had known Mrs. Kent Emily did not feel that she was in the presence of an unhappy woman. There was peace here—a strange, sorrowful, long-unknown peace. The tortured soul was—at last—off the rack.

"I have been dead—and in hell—but now I am alive again," said Mrs. Kent. "It's you who have done this—you found that letter. And so there is something I must tell you. It will make you hate me. And I shall be sorry for that now. But it must be told."

Emily felt a sudden distaste for hearing whatever it was Mrs. Kent had to tell. It had—must have—something to do with Teddy. And she did not want to hear anything—*anything*—about Teddy now—Teddy who would be Ilse's husband in two weeks.

"Don't you think—perhaps—it would be better not to tell me?"

"It must be told. I have committed a wrong and I must confess it. I cannot undo it—I suppose it is too late to undo it—but it must be told. But there are other things that must be told first. Things I've never spoken of—things that have been torturing me until I've screamed out loud at night sometimes with the anguish of them. Oh, you will never forgive me—but I think you will be a little sorry for me."

"I've always felt sorry for you, Mrs. Kent."

"I think you did—yes, I think you did. But you couldn't realize it all. Emily, I wasn't like this when I was a girl. I was—like other people then. And I was pretty—indeed I was. When David Kent came and made me love him I was pretty. And he loved me—*then*—and he always loved me. He says so in this letter."

She plucked it from the bosom of her dress and kissed it almost savagely.

"I can't let you see it, Emily. No eyes but mine must ever see it. But I'll tell you what is in it. Oh, you can't know—you can't understand how much I loved him, Emily. You think you love Teddy. But you don't—you *can't* love him as I loved his father."

Emily had a different opinion on this point, but she did not say so.

"He married me and took me home to Malton where his people lived. We were so happy at first—too happy. I told you God was jealous. And his people did not like me—not from the first. They thought David had married beneath him—that I wasn't good enough for him. They were always trying to come between us. Oh, I knew; I knew what they were after. His mother hated me. She never called me Aileen—only 'you' and 'David's wife.' I hated her because she was always watching me— never said anything—never did anything. Just *watched* me. I was never one of them. I never seemed able to understand their jokes. They were always laughing over something—me, half the time, I thought. They would write letters to David and never mention me. Some of them were always freezingly polite to me and some of them were always giving me digs. Once one of his sisters sent me a book on etiquette. Something was always hurting me—and I couldn't strike back—I couldn't hurt what was hurting me. David took their part—he had secrets with them he kept from me. But in spite of it all I was happy—till I dropped the lamp and my dress caught fire and scarred my face like this. After that I couldn't believe David could keep on loving me. I was so ugly. My nerves got raw and I couldn't help quarrelling with him over every trifle. But he was patient. He forgave me again and again. Only I was so afraid he couldn't love me with that scar. I knew I was going to have a baby, but I kept putting off telling him. I was afraid he would love it more than he did me. And then—I did a terrible thing. I hate to tell you of it. David had a dog—he loved it so much that I hated it I—I poisoned it. I don't know what possessed me. I never used to be like that—not till I was burned. Perhaps it was because the baby was coming."

Mrs. Kent stopped and changed suddenly from a woman quivering with unveiled feeling to a prim Victorian.

"I shouldn't talk about such matters to a young girl," she said anxiously.

"I have known for some years that babies do not come in Dr. Burnley's black bag," assured Emily gravely.

"Well"—Mrs. Kent underwent another transformation into passionate Aileen Kent again—"David found out what I had done. Oh—oh, his face! We had a dreadful quarrel. It was just before he went out to Winnipeg on a business trip. I—I was so furious over what he said that I screamed out—oh, Emily—that I hoped I would never see his face again. I never did. God took me at my word. He died of pneumonia in Winnipeg. I never knew he was ill till the word of his death came. And the nurse was a girl he had once thought something of and who loved him. *She* waited on him and tended him while I was at home hating him. That is what I have thought I could never forgive God for. She packed up his things and sent them home—that book among them. He must have bought it in Winnipeg. I never opened it—I never could bear to touch it. He must have written that letter when he was near death and put it in the book for me—and perhaps died before he could tell her it was there. Maybe she knew and wouldn't tell me. And it has been there all these years, Emily—all these years when I've been believing David died angry with me—unforgiving me. I've dreamed of him night after night—always with his face turned away from me. Oh, twenty-seven years of that, Emily—twenty-seven years. Think of it. Haven't I atoned! And last night I opened and read his letter, Emily—just a few lines scribbled with a pencil—his poor hand could hardly hold it. He called me Dear Little Wife and said I must forgive him—*I* forgive *him*—for being so harsh and angry that last day—and he forgave me for what I had done—and said I mustn't worry over it nor over what I had said about not seeing his face again—he knew I didn't mean it—

that he understood things better at the last—and he had always loved me dearly and always would—and—and—something more I can't tell anybody—too dear, too wonderful. Oh, Emily, can you imagine what this means to me—to know he didn't die angry with me—that he died loving me and thinking tenderly of me? But I didn't know it then. And I—I—don't think I've ever been quite right since. I know all his people thought me crazy. When Teddy was born I came up here away from them all. So that they couldn't lure him away from me. I wouldn't take a cent from them. I had David's insurance—we could just live on that. Teddy was all I had—and *you* came—and I knew you would take him from me. I knew he loved you—always. Oh, yes he did. When he went away I used to write him of all your flirtations. And two years ago— you remember he had to go to Montreal so suddenly—and you were away—he couldn't wait to say good-bye. But he wrote you a letter."

Emily gave a little choked cry of denial.

"Oh, he did. I saw it lying on his table when he had gone out. I steamed the flap open and read it. I burned the letter, Emily—but I can tell you what was in it. Could I ever forget! He told you he had meant to tell you how much he loved you before he went—and if you could care a little for him to write and tell him so. But if you couldn't not to write at all. Oh, how I hated you. I burned the letter and sealed up a copy of some poetry verses that were in it. And he mailed it never knowing the difference. I was never sorry—never, not even when he wrote me he was going to marry Ilse. But last night—when you brought me that letter—and forgiveness—and peace—oh, I felt I had done an awful thing. I've ruined your life—and perhaps Teddy's. Can you ever forgive me, Emily?"

IV

Emily, amid all the whirl of emotions roused by Mrs. Kent's tale, was keenly conscious of only one thing. Bitterness—humiliation—shame had vanished from her being. Teddy *had* loved her. The sweetness of the revelation blotted out, for the time at least, all other feelings. Anger—resentment—could find no place in her soul. She felt like a new creature. And there was sincerity in heart and tone as she said slowly:

"I do—I do. I understand."

Mrs. Kent suddenly wrung her hands.

"Emily—is it too late? Is it too late? They're not married yet—I know he doesn't love her as he loved you. If you told him—if I told him—"

"No, no, no," cried Emily passionately. "It *is* too late. He must never know—you must never tell him. He loves Ilse now. I am sure of that—and telling him this would do no good and much evil. Promise me—dear Mrs. Kent, if you feel you owe me anything promise me, you'll never tell him."

"But you—you will be unhappy—"

"I will not be unhappy—not now. You don't know what a difference this has made. The sting has gone out of everything. I am going to have a happy, busy, useful life and regret for old dreams will have no place in it. The wound will heal now."

"It was—a terrible thing for me to do," whispered Mrs. Kent. "I see that—at last."

"I suppose it was. But I'm not thinking of that. Only that I've got my self-respect back."

"The Murray pride," whispered Mrs. Kent, staring at her. "After all, Emily Starr, I believe pride is a stronger passion with you than love."

"Perhaps," said Emily smiling.

V

She was in such a tumult of feeling when she reached home that she did a thing she was always ashamed of. Perry Miller was waiting in the New Moon garden for her. She had not seen him for a long time and at any other hour would have been glad to see him. Perry's friendship, now that he had finally given up all hope of anything else, was a very pleasant part of her life. He had developed in the last few years—he was manly, humorous, much less boastful. He had even acquired certain fundamental rules of social etiquette and learned not to have too many hands and feet. He was too busy to come often to New Moon, but Emily always enjoyed his visits when he did come—except tonight. She wanted to be alone—to think things over—classify her emotions—revel in her restored sense of self-respect. To pace up and down among the silken poppy-ladies of the garden and talk with Perry was an almost impossible thing. She was in a frenzy of impatience to be rid of him. And Perry did not sense this at all. He had not seen her for a long while—and there were many things to talk over—Ilse's wedding in especial. He kept on asking questions about it until Emily really didn't know what she was saying. Perry was a bit squiffy over the fact that *he* had not been asked to be groomsman. He thought he had a right to be—the old chum of both.

"I never thought Teddy would turn me down cold like that," he growled. "I suppose he feels himself too big to have Stovepipe Town for groomsman."

Then Emily did her dreadful thing—before she realized what she was saying, in her impatient annoyance with Perry for casting such aspersions on Teddy the words leaped out quite involuntarily.

"You goose. It wasn't Teddy at all. Do you think Ilse would have *you* as groomsman—when she hoped for years you would be the groom?"

The moment she had spoken she stood aghast, sick with shame and remorse. What had she done? Betrayed friendship—violated confidence—a shameful, unpardonable thing. Could *she,* Emily Byrd Starr of New Moon, have done *this?*

Perry was standing by the dial staring at her dumbfounded.

"Emily, you don't mean that. Ilse never thought of me that way, did she?"

Emily miserably realized that the spoken word could not be recalled and that the mess she had made of things couldn't be mended by any fibs.

"She did—at one time. Of course she got over it long ago."

"*Me!* Why, Emily, she always seemed to despise me—always ragging me about something—I never could please her—you remember."

"Oh, I remember," said Emily wearily. "She thought so much of you, she hated to see you fall below her standard. If she hadn't—liked you—do you suppose she would have cared what grammar you used or what etiquette you smashed? I should never have told you this, Perry. I shall be ashamed of it all my life. You must never let her suspect you know."

"Of course not. Anyhow, she's forgotten it long ago."

"Oh—yes. But you can understand why it wouldn't be especially agreeable for her to have you as best man at her wedding. I hated to have you think Teddy such a snob. And now, you won't mind, will you, Perry, if I ask you to go? I'm very tired—and I've so much to do the next two weeks."

"You ought to be in bed, that's a fact," agreed Perry. "I'm a beast to be keeping you up. But when I come here it seems so much like old times I never want to go. What a set of shavers we were! And now Ilse and Teddy are going to be married. We're getting on a bit."

"Next thing you'll be a staid old married man yourself, Perry," said Emily, trying to smile. "I've been hearing things."

"Not on your life! I've given up that idea for good. Not that I'm pining after you yet in particular—only nobody has any flavour after you. I've tried. I'm doomed to die a bachelor. They tell me it's an easy death. But I've got a few ambitions by the tail and I'm not kicking about life. Bye-bye, dear. I'll see you at the wedding. It's in the afternoon, isn't it?"

"Yes." Emily wondered she could speak so calmly of it. "Three o'clock—then supper—and a motor drive to Shrewsbury to catch the evening boat. Perry, Perry, I wish I hadn't told you that about Ilse. It was mean—mean—as we used to say at school—I never thought I could do such a thing."

"Now, don't go worrying over that. I'm as tickled as a dog with two tails to think Ilse ever thought that much of me, at any time. Don't you think I've sense enough to know what a compliment it was? And don't you think I understand what bricks you two girls always were to me and how much I owe you for letting me be your friend? I've never had any illusions about Stovepipe Town or the real difference between us. I wasn't such a fool as not to understand *that*. I've climbed a bit—I mean to climb higher—but you and Ilse were *born* to it. And you never let me feel the difference as some girls did. I shan't forget Rhoda Stuart's dirty little slurs. So you don't think I'd be such a cur now as to go strutting because I've found out Ilse once had a bit of a fancy for me—or that I'd ever let her think I knew? I've left that much of Stovepipe Town behind, anyhow—even if I still have to think what fork I'll pick up first. Emily—*do* you remember the night your Aunt Ruth caught me kissing you?"*

*See *Emily Climbs*.

"I should think I do."

"The only time I ever did kiss you," said Perry non-sentimentally. "And *it* wasn't much of a shot, was it? When I think of the old lady standing there in her nightgown with the candle!"

Perry went off laughing and Emily went to her room.

"Emily-in-the-glass," she said almost gaily, "I can look you squarely in the eyes again. I'm not ashamed any longer. He *did* love me."

She stood there smiling for a little space. And then the smile faded. "Oh, if I had only got that letter!" she whispered piteously.

CHAPTER XXV

I

Only two weeks till the wedding. Emily found out how long two weeks can be, in spite of the fact that every waking moment was crowded with doings, domestic and social. The affair was much talked of everywhere. Emily set her teeth and went through with it. Ilse was here—there—everywhere. Doing nothing—saying much.

"About as composed as a flea," growled Dr. Burnley.

"Ilse has got to be such a restless creature," complained Aunt Elizabeth. "She seems to be frightened people wouldn't know she was alive if she sat still a moment."

"I've got forty-nine remedies for seasickness," said Ilse. "If Aunt Kate Mitchell gets here I'll have fifty. Isn't it delightful to have thoughtful relatives, Emily?"

They were alone in Ilse's room. It was the evening Teddy was expected. Ilse had tried on half a dozen different dresses and tossed them aside scornfully.

"Emily, *what* will I wear? Decide for me."

"Not I. Besides—what difference does it make what you put on?"

"True—too true. Teddy never notices what I have on. I like a man who *does* notice and tells me of it. I like a man who likes me better in silk than in gingham."

Emily looked out of the window into a tangled garden where the moonlight was an untroubled silver sea bearing softly on its breast a fleet of poppies. "I meant that Teddy—won't think of your dress—only of *you.*"

"Emily, why do you persist in talking as if you thought Teddy and I were madly in love with each other? Is it that Victorian complex of yours?"

"For heaven's sake, shut up about things Victorian!" Emily exclaimed with unusual, un-Murray-like violence. "I'm tired of it. You call every nice, simple, natural emotion Victorian. The whole world to-day seems to be steeped in a scorn for things Victorian. Do they know what they're talking of? But I like sane, decent things—if *that* is Victorian."

"Emily, Emily, do you suppose Aunt Elizabeth would think it either a sane or decent thing to be madly in love?"

Both girls laughed and the sudden tension relaxed.

"You're not off, Emily?"

"Of course I am. Do you think I'd play gooseberry at such a time as this?"

"There you go again. Do *you* think I want to be shut up alone a whole evening with undiluted Teddy. We'll have a scene every few minutes over something. Of course scenes are lovely. They brighten up life so. I've just got to have a scene once a week. You know I always did enjoy a good fight. Remember how you and I used to scrap? You haven't been a bit of good at a row lately. Even Teddy is only half-hearted in a set-to. Perry, now—*he* could fight. Think what gorgeous rows Perry and I would have had. Our quarrels would have been splendid. Nothing petty—or *quarrelsome*—about them. And how we would have loved each other between them! O-hone-a-rie!"

"Are you hankering after Perry Miller yet?" demanded Emily fiercely.

"No, dear infant. And neither am I crazy about Teddy. After all, ours is only second-hand love on both sides, you know. Cold soup warmed over. Don't worry. I'll be good for him. I'll keep him up to the notch in everything much better than if I thought him a little lower than the angels. It doesn't do to think a man is perfection because *he* naturally thinks so, too, and when he finds some one who agrees with him he is inclined to rest on his oars. It riles me up a bit when every one seems to think I'm so amazingly lucky to 'get' Teddy for a husband. Comes Aunt Ida Mitchell—'You are getting a perfectly wonderful husband, Ilse'—comes Bridget Mooney from Stovepipe Town scrubbing the floor—'Gosh but you're gettin' a swell man, Miss'—'Sisters under their skins,' you perceive. Teddy is well enough—especially since he found out he isn't the only man in the world. He has learned sense somewhere. I'd like to know what girl taught it to him. Oh, there was one. He told me

709

something about the affair—not much but enough. She used to snub him terribly—and then after she had led him on to think she cared she turned him down cold. Never even answered the letter in which he told her he loved her. I hate that girl, Emily—isn't it odd?"

"Don't hate her," said Emily, wearily. "Perhaps she didn't know what she was doing."

"I hate her for using Teddy like that. Though it did him heaps of good. Why do I hate her, Emily? Employ your renowned skill in psychological analysis and expound to me that mystery."

"You hate her—because—to borrow a certain crude expression we've often heard—you're 'taking her leavings.'"

"You demon! I suppose it's so. How ugly some things are when you ferret them out! I've been flattering myself that it was a noble hatred because she made Teddy suffer. After all, the Victorians were right in covering lots of things up. Ugly things should be hidden. Now, go home if go you must and I'll try to look like some one about to receive a blessing."

II

Lorne Halsey came with Teddy—the great Halsey whom Emily liked very much in spite of his gargoyleishness. A comical looking fellow with vital, mocking eyes, who seemed to look upon everything in general and Frederick Kent's wedding in particular as a huge joke. Somehow, this attitude made things a little easier for Emily. She was very brilliant and gay in the evenings they all spent together. She was terribly afraid of silence in Teddy's presence. "Never be silent with the person you love and distrust," Mr. Carpenter had said once. "Silence betrays."

Teddy was very friendly, but his gaze always omitted Emily. Once, when they all walked in the old, overgrown, willow-bordered lawn of the Burnley place, Ilse stumbled on the happy idea of pick-out your favourite star.

"Mine is Sirius. Lorne?"

"Antares of the Scorpion—the red star of the south," said Halsey.

"Bellatrix of Orion," said Emily quickly. She had never thought about Bellatrix before, but she dared not hesitate a moment before Teddy.

"I have no especial favourite—there is only one star I hate. Vega of the Lyre," said Teddy quietly. His voice was charged with a significance which instantly made every one uncomfortable though neither Halsey nor Ilse knew why. No more was said about stars. But Emily watched alone till they faded out one by one in the dawn.

III

Three nights before the wedding-day Blair Water and Derry Pond were much scandalized because Ilse Burnley had been seen driving with Perry Miller in his new run-about at some ungodly hour. Ilse coolly admitted it when Emily reproached her.

"Of course I did. I had had such a dull, bored evening with Teddy. We began it well with a quarrel over my blue Chow. Teddy said I cared more for it than I did for him. I said of course I did. It infuriated him, though he didn't believe it. Teddy, manlike, really believes I'm dying about him.

"'A dog that never chased a cat in its life,' he sneered.

"Then we both sulked the rest of the evening. He went home at eleven without kissing me. I resolved I'd do something foolish and beautiful for the last time, so I sneaked down the lane for a lovely, lonely walk down to the dunes. Perry came along in his car and I just changed my mind and went for a little moonlit spin with him. I wasn't married *yet*. Don't be after looking at me so. We only stayed out till one and we were really very good and proper. I only wondered once—just what would happen if I suddenly said, 'Perry, darling, *you're* the only man I've ever really cared a hang for. Why can't *we* get married?' I wonder if when I'm eighty I'll wish I'd said it."

"You told me you had quite got over caring for Perry."

"But did you believe me? Emily, thank God you're not a Burnley."

Emily reflected bitterly that it was not much better being a Murray. If it had not been for her Murray pride she would have gone to Teddy the night he called her—and she would have been tomorrow's bride—not Ilse.

To-morrow. It was to-morrow—the morrow when she would have to stand near Teddy and hear him vowing lifelong devotion to another woman. All was in readiness. A wedding-supper that pleased even Dr. Burnley, who had decreed that there should be "a good, old-fashioned wedding-supper—none of your modern dabs of this and that. The bride and groom mayn't want much maybe, but the rest of us still have stomachs. And this is the first wedding for years. We've been getting pretty much like heaven in one respect anyhow—neither marrying nor giving in marriage. I want a spread. And tell Laura for heaven's sake not to yowl at the wedding."

So Aunts Elizabeth and Laura saw to it that for the first time in twenty years the Burnley house had a thorough cleaning from top to bottom. Dr. Burnley thanked God forcibly several times that he would only have to go through this once, but nobody paid any attention to him. Elizabeth and Laura had new satin dresses made. It was such a long time since they had had any excuse for new satin dresses.

Aunt Elizabeth made the wedding-cakes and saw to the hams and chickens. Laura made creams and jellies and salads and Emily carried them over to the Burnley Place, wondering at times if she wouldn't soon wake up—before—before—

"I'll be glad when all this fuss is over," growled Cousin Jimmy. "Emily's working herself to death—look at the eyes of her!"

IV

"Stay with me to-night, Emily," entreated Ilse. "I swear I won't talk you to death and I won't cry either. Though I admit if I could just be snuffed out to-night like a candle I wouldn't mind. Jean Askew was Milly Hyslop's bridesmaid and she spent the night before her wedding with her and they both cried all night. Fancy such an orgy of tears. Milly cried because she was going to be married—and I suppose Jean must have been crying because she wasn't. Thank heaven, Emily, you and I were never the miauling kind. We'll be more likely to fight than cry, won't we? I wonder if Mrs. Kent will come to-morrow? I don't suppose so. Teddy says she never mentions his marriage. Though he says she seem oddly changed—gentler—calmer—more like other women. Emily, do you realize that by this time to-morrow I'll be Ilse Kent?"

Yes, Emily realized *that*.

They said nothing more. But two hours later when wakeful Emily had supposed the motionless Ilse was sound asleep Ilse suddenly sat up in bed and grabbed Emily's hand in the darkness.

"Emily—if one could only go to sleep unmarried—and wake up married—how nice it would be."

V

It was dawn—the dawn of Ilse's wedding-day. Ilse was sleeping when Emily slipped out of bed and went to the window. Dawn. A cluster of dark pines in a trance of calm down by the Blair Water. The air tremulous with elfin music; the wind winnowing the dunes; dancing amber waves on the harbour; the eastern sky abloom; the lighthouse at the harbour pearl-white against the ethereal sky; beyond all the blue field of the sea with its foam blossoms and behind that golden haze that swathed the hill of the Tansy Patch, Teddy—wakeful—waiting—welcoming the day that gave him his heart's desire. Emily's soul was washed empty of every wish or hope or desire except that the day were over.

"It is," she thought, "comforting when a thing becomes irrevocable."

"Emily—Emily."

Emily turned from the window.

"It's a lovely day, Ilse. The sun will shine on you. Ilse—what is the matter? Ilse—you're crying!"

"I can't—help it," sniffed Ilse. "It seems to be the proper, inescapable caper after all. I beg Milly's pardon. But—I'm so beastly afraid. It's an infernal sensation. Do you think it would do any good if I threw myself on the floor and screamed?"

"What are you afraid of?" said Emily, a little impatiently.

"Oh,"—Ilse sprang defiantly out of bed—"afraid I'll stick my tongue out at the minister. What else?"

VI

What a morning! It always seemed a sort of nightmare recollection to Emily. Guests of the clan came early—Emily welcomed them until she felt that the smile must be frozen on her face. There were endless wedding-gifts to unwrap and arrange. Ilse, before she dressed, came to look them over indifferently.

"Who sent in that afternoon tea-set?" she asked.

"Perry," said Emily. She had helped him choose it. A dainty service in a quaint old-fashioned rose design. A card with Perry's black forcible handwriting. "To Ilse with the best wishes of her old friend Perry."

Ilse deliberately picked up piece after piece and dashed it in fragments on the floor before the transfixed Emily could stop her.

"*Ilse!* Have you gone crazy?"

"There! What a glorious smash! Sweep up the fragments, Emily. That was just as good as screaming on the floor. Better. I can go through with it now."

Emily disposed of the fragments just in time—Mrs. Clarinda Mitchell came billowing in, in pale-blue muslin and cherry-hued scarf. A sonsy, smiling, good-hearted cousin-by-marriage. Interested in everything. Who gave this?—Who had sent that?

"She'll be *such* a sweet bride, I'm sure," gushed Mrs. Clarinda. "And Teddy Kent is *such* a splendid fellow. It's really an ideal marriage, isn't it? One of those you read about! I love weddings like this. I thank my stars I didn't lose my interest in youthful things when I lost my youth. I've lots of sentiment in me yet—and I'm not afraid to show it. And *did* Ilse's wedding stockings really cost fourteen dollars?"

Aunt Isabella Hyslop, *nee* Mitchell, was gloomy. Offended because her costly present of cut sherbet glasses had been placed beside Cousin Annabel's funny set of old-fashioned crocheted doilies. Inclined to take a dark view of things.

"I hope everything will go off well. But I've got an uneasy feeling that trouble is coming—a presentiment, so to speak. Do you believe in signs? A big black cat ran right across the road in front of us down in the hollow. And right on that tree as we turned in at the lane was the fragment of an old election poster, 'Blue Ruin,' in black letters three inches long staring us in the face."

"That might mean bad luck for you, but hardly for Ilse."

Aunt Isabella shook her head. She would *not* be comforted.

"They say the wedding dress is like nothing ever seen on Prince Edward Island. *Do* you think such extravagance proper, Miss Starr!"

"The expensive part of it was a present from Ilse's old great-aunts in Scotland, Mrs. Mitchell. And most of us are married only once."

Whereupon Emily remembered that Aunt Isabella had been married three times and wondered if there wasn't something in black cat magic.

Aunt Isabella swept coldly off, and later on was heard to say that "that Starr girl is really intolerable since she got a book published.

714

Thinks herself at liberty to insult any one."

Emily, before she had time to thank the Fates for her freedom, fell into the clutches of more Mitchell relatives. This aunt did not approve of another aunt's gift of a pair of ornate Bohemian glass vases.

"Bessie Jane never had much sense. A foolish choice. The children will be sure to unhook the prisms and lose them."

"What children?"

"Why, the children they will have, of course."

"Miss Starr will put that in a book, Matilda," warned her husband, chuckling. Then he chuckled again and whispered to Emily:

"Why aren't *you* the bride to-day? How come Ilse to cut you out, hey?"

Emily was thankful when she was summoned upstairs to help Ilse dress. Though even here aunts and cousins kept bobbing in and out, saying distracting things.

"Emily, do you remember the day of our first summer together when we fought over the honour of playing bride in one of our dramatic stunts? Well, I feel as if I were just playing bride. This isn't real."

Emily felt, too, as if it were not real. But soon—soon now—it would be all over and she could be blessedly alone. And Ilse when dressed was such an exquisite bride that she justified all the fuss of the wedding. How Teddy *must* love her!

"Doesn't she look just like a queen?" whispered Aunt Laura adoringly.

Emily having slipped into her own harebell blue kissed the flushed maiden face under the rose-point cap and pearls of its bridal veil.

"Ilse dear, don't think me hopelessly Victorian if I say I hope you'll be happy 'ever after.'"

Ilse squeezed her hand, but laughed a little too loudly.

"I hope it isn't Queen Victoria Aunt Laura thinks I resemble," she whispered. "And I have the most horrible suspicion that Aunt Janie Milburn is praying for me. Her face betrayed her when she came in to kiss me. It always makes me furious to suspect that people are praying for me. Now, Emily, do me one last favour. Herd everybody out of this room—everybody. I want to be alone, absolutely alone, for a few minutes."

Somehow Emily managed it. The aunts and cousins fluttered downstairs. Dr. Burnley was waiting impatiently in the hall.

"Won't you soon be ready? Teddy and Halsey are waiting for the signal to go into the drawing-room."

"Ilse wants a few minutes alone. Oh, Aunt Ida, I'm so glad you got here"—to a stout lady who was coming pantingly up the stairs. "We were afraid something had happened to prevent you."

"Something did," gasped Aunt Ida—who was really a second-cousin. In spite of her breathlessness Aunt Ida was happy. She always liked to be the first to tell a piece of news—especially unpleasant news. "And the doctor couldn't come at all—I had to get a taxi. That poor Perry Miller—you know him, don't you? Such a clever young chap—was killed in a motor collision about an hour ago."

Emily stifled a shriek, with a frantic glance at Ilse's door. It was slightly ajar. Dr. Burnley was saying:

"Perry Miller killed. Good God, how horrible!"

"Well, as good as killed. He must be dead by this time—he was unconscious when they dragged him out of the wreck. They took him to the Charlottetown hospital and 'phoned for Bill, who dashed right off, of course. It's a mercy Ilse isn't marrying a doctor. Have I time to take off my things before the ceremony?"

Emily, crushing her anguish over Perry, showed Aunt Ida to the spare room and returned to Dr. Burnley.

"Don't let Ilse know about this," he cautioned needlessly. "It would spoil her wedding—she and Perry were old cronies. And hadn't you better hurry her up a little? It's past the time."

Emily, with more of a nightmare feeling than ever, went down the hall and knocked on Ilse's door. There was no answer. She opened the door. On the floor in a forlorn heap lay the bridal veil and the priceless bouquet of orchids which must have cost Teddy more than any Murray or Burnley bride had ever paid before for her whole trousseau, but Ilse was nowhere to be seen. A window was open, the one over the kitchen stoop.

"What's the matter?" exclaimed Dr. Burnley impatiently, coming up behind Emily. "Where's Ilse?"

"She's—gone," said Emily stupidly

"Gone—gone where?"

"To Perry Miller." Emily knew it quite well. Ilse had heard Aunt Ida and—

"Damn!" said Dr. Burnley.

716

VIII

In a few moments the house was a scene of consternation and flabbergasted wedding guests, all exclaiming and asking questions. Dr. Burnley lost his head and turned himself loose, running through his whole repertoire of profanity, regardless of women-folks.

Even Aunt Elizabeth was paralysed. There was no precedent to go by. Juliet Murray, to be sure, had eloped. But she had got married. No clan bride had ever done anything like *this*. Emily alone retained some power of rational thought and action. It was she who found out from young Rob Mitchell how Ilse had gone. He had been parking his car in the barnyard when—

"I saw her spring out of that window with her train wrapped around her shoulders. She slid down the roof and jumped to the ground like a cat—tore out to the lane, jumped in Ken Mitchell's runabout and was off like the devil was after her. I thought she must have gone crazy."

"She has—in a way. Rob, you must go after her. Wait—I'll get Dr. Burnley to go with you. I must stay here to see to things. Oh, be as quick as you can. It's only fourteen miles to Charlottetown. You can go and come in an hour. You *must* bring her back—I'll tell the guests to wait—"

"You'll not make much out of this mess, Emily," prophesied Rob.

IX

Even an hour like that passed. But Dr. Burnley and Rob returned alone. Ilse would not come—that was all there was to it. Perry Miller was not killed—was not even seriously injured—but Ilse would not come. She told her father that she was going to marry Perry Miller and nobody else.

The doctor was the centre of a little group of dismayed and tearful women in the upper hall. Aunt Elizabeth, Aunt Laura, Aunt Ruth, Emily.

"I suppose if her mother had lived this wouldn't have happened," said the doctor dazedly. "I never dreamed she cared for Miller. I wish somebody had wrung Ida Mitchell's neck in time. Oh, cry—cry—yes, cry"—fiercely to poor Aunt Laura. "What good will yelping do? What a devil of a mess! Somebody's got to tell Kent—I suppose I must. And those distracted fools down there have to be fed. That's what half of them came for, anyway. Emily, you seem to be the only creature left in the world with a grain of sense. See to things, there's a good girl."

Emily was not of an hysterical temperament, but for the second time in her life she was feeling that the only thing she could do would be to scream as loud and long as possible. Things had got to the point where only screaming would clear the air. But she got the guests marshalled to the tables. Excitement calmed down somewhat when they found they were not to be cheated out of everything. But the wedding-feast was hardly a success.

Even those who were hungry had an uneasy feeling that it wasn't the thing to eat heartily under such circumstances. Nobody enjoyed it except old Uncle Tom Mitchell, who frankly went to weddings for the spread and didn't care whether there was a ceremony or not. Brides might come and brides might go but a square meal was a feed. So he ate steadily away, only pausing now and then to shake his head solemnly and ask, "What air the women coming to?"

Cousin Isabella was set up on presentiments for life, but nobody listened to her. Most of the guests were afraid to speak, for fear of saying the wrong thing. Uncle Oliver reflected that he had seen many funeral repasts that were more cheerful. The waitresses were hurried and flurried and made ludicrous mistakes. Mrs. Derwent, the young and pretty wife of the new minister, looked to be on the point of tears—nay, actually had tears in her eyes. Perhaps she had been building on the prospective wedding fee. Perhaps its loss meant no new hat for her. Emily, glancing at her as she passed a jelly, wanted to laugh—a desire as hysterical as her wish to scream. But no desire at all showed itself on her cold white face. Shrewsbury people said she was as disdainful and indifferent as always. Could *anything* really make that girl *feel*?

And under it all she was keenly conscious of only one question. "Where was Teddy? What was he feeling—thinking—doing?" She hated Ilse for hurting him—shaming him. She did not see how *anything* could go on after *this*. It was one of those events which *must* stop time.

X

"What a day!" sobbed Aunt Laura as they walked home in the dusk. "What a disgrace! What a scandal!"

"Allan Burnley has only himself to blame," said Aunt Elizabeth. "He has let Ilse do absolutely as she pleases all her life. She was never taught any self-control. All her life she had done exactly as she wanted to do whenever the whim took her. No sense of responsibility whatever."

"But if she loved Perry Miller," pleaded Laura.

"Why did she promise to marry Teddy Kent then? And treat him like this? No, you need make no excuses for Ilse. Fancy a Burnley going to Stovepipe Town for a husband.

"Some one will have to see about sending the presents back," moaned Laura. "I locked the door of the room where they were. One never knows—at such a time—"

Emily found herself alone in her room at last—too dazed, stricken, exhausted, to feel much of anything. A huge, round, striped ball unrolled itself on her bed and opened wide pink jaws.

"Daff," said Emily wearily, "you're the only thing in the world that stays put."

She had a nasty sleepless night with a brief dawn slumber. From which she wakened to a new world where everything had to be readjusted. And she felt too tired to care for readjustment.

CHAPTER XXVI

I

Ilse did not look as if she wanted excuses made for her when, two days later, she walked unannounced into Emily's room. She looked rosy, audacious, triumphant.

Emily stared at her.

"Well, I suppose the earthquake is over. What is left standing?"

"Ilse! How could you!"

Ilse pulled a notebook out of her handbag and pretended to consult it.

"I wrote down a list of the things you'd say. That was the first one. You've said it. The next is, 'Aren't you ashamed of yourself?' I'm not, you know,' added Ilse impudently.

"I know you're not. That's why I don't ask it."

"I'm not ashamed—and I'm not sorry. I'm only a little bit sorry that I'm *not* sorry. And I'm shamelessly happy. But I suppose I spoiled the party. No doubt the old meows are having the time of their lives. They've got their craws full for once."

"How do you suppose Teddy is feeling?" asked Emily sternly.

"Is he feeling any worse than Dean did? There's an old proverb about glass houses."

Emily crimsoned.

"I know—I used Dean badly—but I didn't—"

"Jilt him at the altar! True. But I didn't think about Teddy at all when I heard Aunt Ida say Perry was killed. I was quite mad. My one thought was to see Perry once before he died. I *had* to. And I found when I got there that, as Mark Twain said, the report of his death was greatly exaggerated. He wasn't even badly hurt—was sitting up in bed, his face all bruised and bandaged—looking like the devil. Want to hear what happened, Emily?"

Ilse dropped on the floor at Emily's feet—and looked coaxingly up into Emily's face.

"Honey, what's the use of disapproving a thing that was foreordained? That won't alter anything. I got a glimpse of Aunt Laura in the sitting-room as I sneaked upstairs. She was looking like something that had been left out overnight. But you have a streak in you that isn't Murray. *You* should understand. Don't waste your sympathy on Teddy. He doesn't love me—I've always known it. It's only his conceit that will suffer. Here—give him his sapphire for me, will you?" Ilse saw something in Emily's face she didn't like. "It can go to join Dean's emerald."

"Teddy left for Montreal the day after—after—"

"After the wedding that wasn't," finished Ilse. "Did you see him, Emily?"

"No."

"Well, if he'd go and shoot big game in Africa for awhile he'd get over it very quickly. Emily, I'm going to marry Perry—next year. It's all settled. I fell on his neck and kissed him as soon as I saw him. I let go my train and it streamed magnificently over the floor. I knew the nurse thought I had just got out of Dr. Percy's private asylum. But I turned her out of the room. And I told Perry I loved him and that I would never, never marry Teddy Kent no matter what happened—and then he asked me if I'd marry *him*—or I told him he must marry me—or neither of us asked—we just understood. I honestly don't remember which—and I don't care. Emily, if I were dead and Perry came and looked at me I'd live again. Of course I know he's always been after you—but he's going to love me as he never loved you. We were made for each other."

"Perry was never really in love with me," said Emily. "He liked me tremendously, that was all. He didn't know the difference—then." She looked down into Ilse's radiant face—and all her old, old love for this perverse, adorable friend rushed to eyes and lips.

"Dearest, I hope you'll be happy—always."

"How blessedly Victorian that sounds!" said Ilse contentedly. "Oh, I can be quiet now, Emily. For weeks I've been afraid that if I let myself be quiet for a moment I'd *bolt*. And I don't even mind if Aunt Janie is praying for me. I believe I rather hope she is."

"What does your father say?"

"Oh, Dad." Ilse shrugged her shoulders. "He's still in the clutches of his old ancestral temper. Won't speak to me. But he'll come round. He's really as much to blame as I am for what I've done. You know I've never asked anyone in my life if I could do a thing. I just did it. Father never prevented me. At first because he hated me—then because he wanted to make up for hating me."

"I think you'll have to ask Perry sometimes if you can do things."

"I won't mind *that*. You'll be surprised to see what a dutiful wife I'll make. Of course I'm going right away—back to work. And in a year's time people will have forgotten—and Perry and I will be married quietly somewhere. No more rose-point veils and Oriental trains and clan weddings for me. Lord, what an escape! Then minutes later I'd have been married to Teddy. Think what a scandal there'd have been then when Aunt Ida arrived. Because I'd have gone just the same, you know."

II

That summer was a hard time for Emily. The very anguish of her suffering had filled life and now that it was over she realized its emptiness. Then, too, to go anywhere meant martyrdom. Everyone talking about the wedding, asking, wondering, surmising. But at last the wild gossip and clatter over Ilse's kididoes had finally died away and people found something else to talk about. Emily was left alone.

Alone? Ay, that was it. Always alone. Love—friendship gone forever. Nothing left but ambition. Emily settled herself resolutely down to work. Life ran again in its old accustomed grooves. Year after year the seasons walked by her door. Violet-sprinkled valleys of spring— blossom-script of summer—minstrel-firs of autumn—pale fires of the Milky Way on winter nights—soft, new-mooned skies of April— gnomish beauty of dark Lombardies against a moonrise—deep of sea calling to deep of wind—lonely yellow leaves falling in October dusks—woven moonlight in the orchard. Oh, there was beauty in life still—always would be. Immortal, indestructible beauty beyond all the stain and blur of mortal passion. She had some very glorious hours of inspiration and achievement. But mere beauty which had once satisfied her soul could not wholly satisfy it now. New Moon was unchanged, undisturbed by the changes that came elsewhere. Mrs. Kent had gone to live with Teddy. The old Tansy Patch was sold to some Halifax man for a summer home. Perry went to Montreal one autumn and brought Ilse back with him. They were living happily in Charlottetown, where Emily often visited them, astutely evading the matrimonial traps Ilse was always setting for her. It was becoming an accepted thing in the clan that Emily would not marry.

"Another old maid at New Moon," as Uncle Wallace said gracefully.

"And to think of all the men she might have had," said Aunt Elizabeth bitterly. "Mr. Wallace—Aylmer Vincent—Andrew—"

"But if she didn't—love—them," faltered Aunt Laura.

"Laura, you need not be indelicate."

Old Kelly, who still went his rounds—"and will till the crack of doom," declared Ilse—had quite given up teasing Emily about getting married, though he occasionally made regretful, cryptic allusions to "toad ointment." There was none of his significant nods and winks. Instead, he always gravely asked her what book she did be working on now, and drove off shaking his spiky gray head. "What do the men be thinking of, anyway? Get up, my nag, get up."

Some men were still thinking of Emily, it appeared. Andrew, now a brisk young widower, would have come at the beck of a finger Emily

722

never lifted. Graham Mitchell, of Shrewsbury, unmistakably had intentions. Emily wouldn't have him because he had a slight cast in one eye. At least, that was what the Murrays supposed. They could think of no other reason for her refusal of so good a match. Shrewsbury people declared that he figured in her next novel and that she had only been "leading him on" to "get material." A reputed Klondike "millionaire" pursued her for a winter, but disappeared as briefly in the spring.

"Since she has published those books she thinks no one good enough for her," said Blair Water folks.

Aunt Elizabeth did not regret the Klondike man—he was only a Derry Pond Butterworth, to begin with, and what were the Butterworths? Aunt Elizabeth always contrived to give the impression that Butterworths did not exist. They might imagine they did, but the Murrays knew better. But she did not see why Emily could not take Mooresby, of the firm of Mooresby and Parker, Charlottetown. Emily's explanation that Mr. Mooresby could never live down the fact that he had once had his picture in the papers as a Perkins' Food Baby struck Aunt Elizabeth as very inadequate. But Aunt Elizabeth at last admitted that she could not understand the younger generation.

III

Of Teddy Emily never heard, save from occasional items in newspapers which represented him as advancing steadily in his career. He was beginning to have an international reputation as a portrait painter. The old days of magazine illustrations were gone and Emily was never now confronted with her own face—or her own smile—or her own eyes—looking out at her from some casual page.

One winter Mrs. Kent died. Before her death she sent Emily a brief note—the only word Emily had ever had from her.

"I am dying. When I am dead, Emily, tell Teddy about the letter. I've tried to tell him, but I couldn't. I couldn't tell my son I had done *that*. Tell him for me."

Emily smiled sadly as she put the letter away. It was too late to tell Teddy. He had long since ceased to care for her. And she—she would love him for ever. And even though he knew it not, surely such love would hover around him all his life like an invisible benediction, not understood but dimly felt, guarding him from ill and keeping from him all things of harm and evil.

IV

That same winter it was bruited abroad that Jim Butterworth, of Derry Pond, had bought or was about to buy the Disappointed House. He meant, so rumour said, to haul it away, rebuild and enlarge it; and doubtless when this was done he would install therein as mistress a certain buxom, thrifty damsel of Derry Pond known as "Geordie Bridge's Mabel." Emily heard the report with anguish. She slipped out that evening in the chill spring dusk and went up the dim overgrown path over the spruce hill to the front gate of the little house like an unquiet ghost. Surely it couldn't be true that Dean had sold it. The house belonged to the hill. One couldn't imagine the hill without it.

Once Emily had got Aunt Laura to see about bringing her own belongings from it—all but the gazing-ball. She could not bear to see that. It must be still hanging there, reflecting in its silver gloom by the dim light that fell through the slits of the shutters, the living-room just as it was when she and Dean had parted. Rumour said Dean had taken nothing from it. All he had put in it was still there.

The little house must be very cold. It was so long since there was a fire in it. How neglected—how lonely—how heartbroken it looked. No light in the window—grass growing thickly over the paths—rank weeds crowding around the long-unopened door.

Emily stretched out her arms as if she wanted to put them around the house. Daff rubbed against her ankles and purred pleadingly. He did not like damp, chilly prowls—the fireside at New Moon was better for a pussy not so young as he once was. Emily lifted the old cat and set him on the crumbling gatepost.

"Daff," she said, "there is an old fireplace in that house—with the ashes of a dead fire in it—a fireplace where pussies should bask and children dream. And that will never happen now, Daff, for Mabel Geordie doesn't like open fireplaces—dirty, dusty things—a Quebec heater is so much warmer and more economical. Don't you wish—or *do* you!—Daff, that you and I had been born sensible creatures, alive to the superior advantages of Quebec heaters!"

CHAPTER XXVII

I

It came clearly and suddenly on the air of a June evening. An old, old call—two higher notes and one long and soft and low. Emily Starr, dreaming at her window, heard it and stood up, her face suddenly gone white. Dreaming still—she must be! Teddy Kent was thousands of miles away, in the Orient—so much she knew from an item in a Montreal paper. Yes, she had dreamed it—imagined it.

It came again. And Emily *knew* that Teddy was there, waiting for her in Lofty John's bush—calling to her across the years. She went down slowly—out—across the garden. Of course Teddy was there—under the firs. It seemed the most natural thing in the world that he should come to her there, in that old-world garden where the three Lombardies still kept guard. Nothing was wanting to bridge the years. There was no gulf. He put out his hands and drew her to him, with no conventional greeting. And spoke as if there were no years—no memories—between them.

"Don't tell me you can't love me—you can—you must—why, Emily"—his eyes had met the moonlit brilliance of hers for a moment—"you *do.*"

II

"It's dreadful what little things lead people to misunderstand each other," said Emily some minutes—or hours—later.

"I've been trying all my life to tell you I loved you," said Teddy. "Do you remember that evening long ago in the To-morrow Road after we left high school? Just as I was trying to screw up my courage to ask you if you'd wait for me you said night air was bad for you and went in. I thought it was a poor excuse for getting rid of me—I knew you didn't care a hoot about night air. That set me back for years. When I heard

725

about you and Aylmer Vincent—Mother wrote you were engaged—it was a nasty shock. For the first time it occurred to me that you really didn't belong to me, after all. And that winter when you were ill—I was nearly wild. Away there in France where I couldn't see you. And people writing that Dean Priest was always with you and would probably marry you if you recovered. Then came the word that you *were* going to marry him. I won't talk of that. But when you—*you*—saved me from going to my death on the *Flavian* I knew you *did* belong to me, once and for all, whether *you* knew it or not. Then I tried again that morning by Blair Water—and again you snubbed me mercilessly. Shaking off my touch as if my hand were a snake. And you never answered my letter. Emily, *why* didn't you? You say you've always cared—"

"I never got the letter."

"Never got it? But I mailed it—"

"Yes, I know. I must tell you—she said I was to tell you—" She told him briefly.

"My *mother*? Did *that*?"

"You mustn't judge her harshly, Teddy. You know she wasn't like other women. Her quarrel with your father—did you know—"

"Yes, she told me all about that—when she came to me in Montreal. But *this*—Emily—"

"Let us just forget it—and forgive. She was so warped and unhappy she didn't know what she was doing. And I—I—was too proud—too proud to go when you called me that last time. I *wanted* to go—but I thought you were only amusing yourself—"

"I gave up hope then—finally. It had fooled me too often. I saw you at your window, shining, as it seemed to me, with an icy radiance like some cold wintry star—I knew you heard me—it was the first time you had failed to answer our old call. There seemed nothing to do but forget you—if I could. I never succeeded, but I thought I did—except when I looked at Vega of the Lyre. And I was lonely. Ilse was a good pal. Besides, I think I thought I could talk to her about you—keep a little corner in your life as the husband of some one you loved. I knew Ilse didn't care much for me—I was only the consolation prize. But I thought we could jog along very well together and help each other keep away the fearful lonesomeness of the world. And then"—Teddy laughed at himself—"when she 'left me at the altar' according to the very formula of Bertha M. Clay I was furious. She had made such a fool of me—me, who fancied I was beginning to cut quite a figure in the world. My word, how I hated women for awhile! And I was hurt, too. I had got very fond of Ilse—I really did love her—in a way."

"In a way." Emily felt no jealousy of that.

III

"I don't know as I'd take Ilse's leavings," remarked Aunt Elizabeth.

Emily flashed on Aunt Elizabeth one of her old starry looks.

"Ilse's leavings. Why, Teddy has always belonged to me and I to him. Heart, soul and body," said Emily.

Aunt Elizabeth shuddered. One ought to feel these things—perhaps—but it was indecent to say them.

"Always sly," was Aunt Ruth's comment.

"She'd better marry him right off before she changes her mind *again*," said Aunt Addie.

"I suppose she won't wipe *his* kisses off," said Uncle Wallace.

Yet, on the whole, the clan were pleased. Much pleased. After all their anxieties over Emily's love affairs, to see her "settled" so respectably with a "boy" well known to them, who had, so far as they knew at least, no bad habits and no disgraceful antecedents. And who was doing pretty well in the business of picture-painting. They would not exactly say so, but Old Kelly said it for them.

"Ah, now, that's something like," said Old Kelly approvingly.

IV

Dean wrote a little while before the quiet bridal at New Moon. A fat letter with an enclosure—a deed to the Disappointed House and all it contained.

"I want you to take this, Star, as my wedding-gift. That house must not be disappointed again. I want it to live at last. You and Teddy can make use of it as a summer home. And some day I will come to see you in it. I claim my old corner in your house of friendship now and then."

"How very—dear—of Dean. And I am so glad—he is not hurt any longer."

She was standing where the To-morrow Road opened out on the Blair Water valley. Behind her she heard Teddy's eager footsteps coming to *her.* Before her on the dark hill, against the sunset, was the little beloved grey house that was to be disappointed no longer.

THE END

OTHER BOOKS TO EXPLORE BY
L. M. MONTGOMERY

<u>THE ANNE OF GREEN GABLES SERIES</u>
Anne of Green Gables
Anne of Avonlea
Anne of the Island
Anne's House of Dreams
Rainbow Valley
Rilla of Ingleside
Anne of Windy Poplars
Anne of Ingleside
Chronicles of Avonlea
Further Chronicles of Avonlea
The Anne of Green Gables Poetry Book - Selected Poems from
    Anne and Her Friends

<u>THE STORY GIRL SERIES</u>
The Story Girl
The Golden Road

<u>THE EMILY STARR SERIES</u>
Emily of New Moon
Emily Climbs
Emily's Quest

<u>PAT OF SILVER BUSH SERIES</u>
Pat of Silver Bush
Mistress Pat

OTHER BOOKS TO EXPLORE BY
L. M. MONTGOMERY

NOVELS
Kilmeny of the Orchard
The Blue Castle
A Tangled Web
Magic for Marigold
Jane of Lantern Hill

POETRY
The Watchman & Other Poems

AUTOBIOGRAPHY
The Alpine Path: The Story of My Career

COLLECTIONS
The Anne of Green Gables Collection - Volumes 1-3
    (Anne of Green Gables, Anne of Avonlea and Anne of the Island)
The Emily Starr Series
    (Emily of New Moon, Emily Climbs and Emily's Quest)
The Story Girl & The Golden Road
Pat of Silver Bush & Mistress Pat
The Blue Castle & A Tangled Web
Magic for Marigold & Jane of Lantern Hill
Lucy Maud Montgomery Short Stories, 1896 to 1901
Lucy Maud Montgomery Short Stories, 1902 to 1903
Lucy Maud Montgomery Short Stories, 1904
Lucy Maud Montgomery Short Stories, 1905 to 1906
Lucy Maud Montgomery Short Stories, 1907 to 1908
Lucy Maud Montgomery Short Stories, 1909 to 1922

Lightning Source UK Ltd.
Milton Keynes UK
UKHW040712221222
414324UK00004B/430